MW00679805

Between March and May

Willard Cox

Dear Cindy and family,
You are very special to me. May the sunshine live at your doorsteps.
Love,
Willard Cox

Colonial

Press

2/8/98

Published by Colonial Press, Inc.
3325 Burning Tree Drive
Birmingham, Alabama 35226
1-800-264-7541

Printed in the United States of America
10 9 8 7 6 5 4 3 2 1

ISBN 1-56883-073-4

LIBRARY OF CONGRESS
Catalog Card No.
97-77476

Price $21.95

First Published 1997

This is a work of fiction and any resemblance between the characters in this book and real persons is coincidental.

COLONIAL PRESS PUBLISHER BIRMINGHAM

FOR

my wife and best friend, Mellie Rene. To my daughter Karen, her husband Joe and our grandchildren Thomas, Michael and Carson Hill.

To those who wish to read:

Lasciate ogni speranza voi ch'ent.
"Abandon hope, all you who enter here."

Inferno — Dante Alighieri

ACKNOWLEDGMENTS

Carl Murray, more than any other,
has made this publication possible.

These four "readers" played a significant role:

Linda Depew
Clayton Wilder
Tish Bryan Palmer
Dottie Brown

Pictures were contributed by friends:

Mildred McCarty
E. J. and Mae Ola Gibson
Fredrick and Janie Smallwood

Editing, typesetting, and page design were provided by:

3P - Papyrus & Pixel Productions

Susan Chandler Kelley

Typesetting ✶ Editing ✶ Desktop Publishing ✶ Graphics ✶ Web Pages
http://members.aol.com/sckelleyww/papyrus.htm *(Web Page)*
sckelleyww@aol.com *(Email)* 205-491-5057 *(Phone/Fax)*

Chapter 1

April landed on her front porch after a hop, skip and jump of the six steps. It was Friday. It was Spring. Who could ask for more?

As she dashed through the front door and turned toward the kitchen she saw her mother sitting in the den.

"Are you all right?" April asked with a sense of urgency in her voice. "I had expected to find you in the kitchen as usual."

"I thought I would rest and relax a few minutes. It's tobacco time again and the days only get longer. Meggie has just arrived to help. Sandra and Gena will be along in a few minutes." Her mother smiled and continued, "You have heard the story of too many cooks in the kitchen?"

"I was afraid something was wrong."

"No. Just a bit weary. How was your day? Your week? As I recall, the last six weeks of a school year are the most difficult and I suspect nothing has changed in the last twenty-three years."

April look at her mother more closely. She had seen this tired look before in late July or August but never before as early as the month of April.

"You are thirty-nine?"

"Yes, but today it is an old thirty-nine!

April smiled and said, "You do not look your age. I can only hope to look so well when I approach forty. When I think of you giving life to six children, keeping a house spotless, cooking three meals a day and keeping everyone in clean and ironed clothing, I am amazed. You could easily pass for thirty."

"Is there a reason why one applauds another so generously? I have a daughter who stretches the truth and her flattery has made her old mother feel young once again."

April responded, "I am repeating the words I hear everyone say. When I look at many of the wives of the local farmers, I see so many who have become old before their time. For some, at the age of thirty, youth has passed them by. Why, some farmers have worn out a second and third wife before they are fifty!"

Martha Randolph smiled. "There is one consolation. Your father has not given me the title of 'ole woman' yet."

"Your figure is perfect. You have no excess weight. I would guess you have not gained five pounds since you were a bride."

"Oh, I gained some extra pounds during and after my babies, but long hours, hard work and reasonable health habits have permitted me to stay about the same weight as when your father married me in 1936. And here it is 1959. Where has time gone?"

April again looked at her mother more closely. Her mother kept her brown hair rather short and it always appeared brushed in spite of the little time she had to give to her personal appearance. Her brown eyes, quite large, revealed the same gentleness, warmth and kindness as always. Her ample red lips and sparkling white teeth accentuated a soft expression of delight that always made everyone feel comfortable in her presence. It had never been her mother's nature to seek attention in the presence of others. She did not usually talk a great deal and seldom spoke of herself; she preferred to listen instead.

"What would you have done if you had been unable to have children?" April asked.

"That's a strange question, coming from you. To tell you the truth, I have never given much thought to such. I suppose I would have given more time to your father and I suspect that would have been unwise, because of his nature."

"How did you meet and marry Joseph?" April asked. "I do not recall you telling me any of the details."

"Just a few days after high school graduation in 1936 I married your father. I was sixteen. We completed only eleven years of school at that time. Georgia did not add a twelfth grade until the early Fifties.

"Your father was twenty-seven and there were those who said I was too young, or your father was too old, or both. But as far as I know, it has never created a problem or handicap for either of us.

"Your father had been an established farmer for many years. I think some in the community had wondered why he had waited until this time to marry since several girls, so I was told, would have jumped at the chance to marry this handsome farmer and become Mrs. Randolph. Yet it seemed that he always had some established goals, that he knew what he wanted and that he had a clearly defined timetable for every phase of his life."

April became more interested. "Do you recall when and how you met?"

"A bride always remembers when and where." Her mother smiled and gave a hasty chuckle. "I was in a local grocery store where I was shopping. As I turned into an aisle, there he stood. I had seen him at a distance but never so near before.

"He did not speak immediately but only stared at me. Finally he said, in a voice more softly than one would have expected from a man his size, 'I have never seen anyone half so beautiful and sweet. I can tell you are a gentle and unselfish lady. You could never be vicious or mean or deceitful. I see only softness and kindness in your eyes, your face.'

"These were not his exact words, because we know he does not always express himself in such a manner, but it means about the same, as near as I can remember."

"What did you say? What did you do? This sounds a great deal different from the Joseph I thought I knew!"

"I didn't say anything for a minute or more. I just stood there and stared back at him in utter dismay. I suppose I was in a state of shock.

"Then he asked, 'Is something wrong?' He looked down to check his clothing. Then he stared at me once again, his eyes glued to my face."

"Suddenly, he turned to me, moved a step closer and said, 'I think I'll just marry you when you grow up!'"

"What did you say? What did you do?"

"As far as I can remember, I don't think I said anything for several minutes. In fact, I'm not sure how much time elapsed. Then I said something silly like, 'It's nice to see you.'

"He looked me over from head to toe very carefully and deliberately, then moved into the next aisle, behind the large boxes of Kellogg's Corn Flakes, and continued his shopping."

April's eyes flashed as she hung on every word her mother had spoken. "And then what happened?"

"In a moment I found myself in another aisle, going in the opposite direction, but I never knew how I got there. My emotions were so strong, so profound and so naked that I felt it would be an insult to call upon common sense. Then suddenly I felt that common sense was something petty, unwanted, undesirable, and without any passion or imagination. Never had I felt like that before!"

"And then what?" April asked, shaking her head at what she had heard.

"I returned home with my bag of groceries, unsure of what I had come for or had purchased. I could not even remember paying the clerk until I looked in my purse. I was still in a deep state of shock. After the groceries were put away I sat down and reviewed every detail, every single word that had been said. I remember clearly his eyes as they surveyed me ever so carefully and completely. Then I thought, I could love this man. A few moments later I was even more sure of my feelings. I caught my breath; my emotions were much stronger than I had realized, perhaps stronger than I had wished. Then I said aloud, 'This thing is as crazy as can be!'

"A few days later my classmates spoke of this event; several persons had seen and heard what had taken place in the store. Some were kind but some were not. One said, 'I think he is in love with you but it has not been his intentions to marry any woman.' Another said, 'He is much too old for you.' Another turned it around and said, 'You are too young for this old man!' Still another asked, 'Why would you consider this man? He is uneducated. Why, he didn't even finish grammar school.' Still another said, 'He is a piney-woods man and will never rise above that status.' Someone even said, 'He is poor white trash, like his folks before him.' So you see, it was not a very good time for me."

"Then what?" April asked, more interested than ever.

"A few weeks later, after a rather brief and strange courtship, we became man and wife. I'll leave some things to your imagination. This is not to suggest something unseemly happened. Everything happened in proper order. We married, then all other things followed." She smiled.

Suddenly, Martha jumped from her seat and said, "Here I sit talking and I have forgotten all about dinner."

"Thank you for telling me this. It is all so strange. I am amazed," April said.

"Why don't you change your clothes and get out for a while," her mother responded. "It is a beautiful time of the year and I have as much help as I need. Don't be late for dinner and remember, your father has something to say to all of us after we have finished eating."

As April rushed toward her room she heard her mother say, "Don't you dare be late. Your father would not like that!"

Chapter 2

Charles Preston Randolph, the second child of Joseph and Martha, was nineteen years old and completing his freshman year at Florida State University in Tallahassee, as a commuting student.

With a height of six feet and two inches, he appeared even taller because his weight was slightly less than hundred and seventy pounds. His face was somewhat oval and his hair was thick and brown. His eyes, also brown, often expressed fun, excitement, and merriment, but on occasion they seemed to reflect a touch of sadness.

When girls saw him they could not turn their eyes away, nor did they want to. Charles learned this early in life and took full advantage of these characteristics.

He was quiet around most people. He, like his mother, had learned that much could be gained by being a good listener. Some, when first meeting him, interpreted this as shyness, even simple-mindedness. In time they discovered he was neither.

On this Friday afternoon Charles stood in the new gazebo his younger brother had recently constructed. As he walked leisurely around the inside of this eight-sided structure he noticed that its placement provided a spectacular view of the Randolph plantation in whatever direction one chose to look.

It was a soft spring day in early April. This was Charles' favorite time of day, almost twilight. He seated himself as comfortably as possible in a chair not designed to accommodate his lean, towering frame. He shifted his chair in an easterly direction to elude the rays of the warm afternoon sun. Only in early morning or late evening were the rays not deflected by the massive trees that surrounded and filled the area.

As he turned his head southward he saw a distant figure coming toward him. He easily recognized his only sister, who would be fourteen in a few days. She ran at an easy gait, her long black hair, as black as a raven, streaming behind. She ran as upright as an Indian maiden, her motion graceful and without effort.

As the distance closed between them he noticed how tall she was for her age. Her perfectly shaped head was set upon a long slender neck, which gave added emphasis to her height.

At this point April was too far away to make out other details but he knew each feature precisely. Below her nose was a deep and red mouth, neither too small nor too generous. When she smiled, which was often, slight dimples appeared in a most enchanting way. The perfect white teeth appeared whenever she smiled or laughed.

However, her eyes were her most astonishing feature. They were large, very large, and not very close together. Sometimes they appeared a deep purple but actually they were a vivid, flashing black. Most of the time they appeared soft, tender and compassionate. In moments of delight they twinkled and danced. Looking deep into those eyes, it was as if she knew one's most intimate thoughts and most guarded secrets; in moments she seemed to control one's very mind and soul.

The long, heavy eyelashes were as black as her hair. Her eyebrows covered the entire space above her eyes. Her skin was a shade lighter than one would expect with such dark features.

A big infectious smile filled her face as she stepped into the gazebo and placed both hands on Charles' broad shoulders. She was unaware that in this position Charles could clearly see her fully uplifted breasts. "Isn't this construction amazing? I had no inkling that Michael John had such talent! He is so proud. Have you offered him your congratulations?" She took one of the vacant seats so she could look directly into his eyes.

"Indeed I have. One could detect the undeniable pride as he described what he had done," Charles said.

"He made an A on the course," April said. "The thing that pleased him most, however, was the designation of his project by the teacher for a field trip. I suspect this is the first time he has been singled out in such a special way."

"Michael John gave you a lot of credit," Charles said. "What did he mean? What did you do?"

"Our brother was simply being kind and modest, as well as unselfish. I helped him with some mathematical computations. I also encouraged him. I did little else.

"I think he has a terror of people. His insecurity causes him to like harmless things like birds, trees and flowers. This is a precious quality but I want him to become more secure and self-reliant around people."

For a few moments neither spoke. Finally April said, "Part of our curriculum at school has little meaning for him. Finding unknowns in algebra and reading Shakespeare are two examples. But he never complains or laments, and he never speaks negatively about anyone except himself."

April stood and made a complete circle inside the gazebo. She seemed to drink deeply of the grandeur and spaciousness of the Randolph lands, whose soil lay deep and fertile. "It's such a beautiful day. It is nice to feel the warm sunshine and inhale the fresh air. Spring is here at last. We will not have another frost or freeze." She continued to move around.

Suddenly, in a demanding voice, Charles said, "Sit! You make me as nervous as a cat with your constant movement. You pace aimlessly about and don't know what you are doing or where you are going!"

April followed his instructions and eased into a chair once again, looking him directly in the eyes. With a suppressed smile she asked, "This makes you feel better?"

Charles ignored her question and asked, "How do you know that?"

"Know what? What do you mean, how do I know that?" April asked.

"How do you know the severe cold is over? Do you have occult powers? Some mystic source? I can remember it being cold — in fact, very cold — in April. Why, we have had cold weather in May."

"Charles, you spend too much time chasing girls or letting the girls chase you. Go look at the grape vines and the pecan trees. If you find green buds there, it's all over. I have looked. It's over.

"Now don't make the mistake of looking at the peach and pear trees. They send no true message and often show promise they cannot fulfill. Trees, like people, have to pay for their stupidity."

In a few moments Charles noticed April was looking up at the dogwood tree, where a mockingbird perched on a limb high above them. They listened as it emulated a dozen other birds. It seemed that this bird, like human beings, was cognizant of an audience; it performed with an extra bit of enthusiasm and vitality. Then it left the perch with a swiftness seemingly impossible and attacked a large black crow that had entered the mockingbird's domain. The mockingbird, one fifth the size of the crow, struck without warning. The crow gave a sharp cry and dashed for safety in the trees some distance away.

As the mockingbird returned it swooped down at the bird feeder, where two cardinals were enjoying a final meal for the day. The cardinals, seeing their enemy approaching, hurriedly departed for safety in the nearby azaleas. Then the mockingbird returned to its previous perch, glancing about with a look of pride and accomplishment. It picked at its ashy white feathers, then burst again into song.

During all this time Charles and April had not uttered a sound. Then, without warning and as if speaking to no one in particular,

April said, "The two of us were told of his virtues and taught that to kill one was bad luck. Even though he doesn't eat one bite from the feeder, he runs all others away. He isn't a nice bird. He has an undeserved reputation."

Charles said, "More than once you referred to the bird as a male. Can you tell the difference?"

"Not by appearance, but by their behavior. Males by nature are greedy. They want more than they need, more than they deserve. The male gloats over his possessions and lords over his kingdom. His domain is whatever he perceives it to be. Such perverse and abominable acts of behavior would be inconceivable in the female."

"Enough!" Charles said. "You don't need to use such words to impress me."

April responded, "You have insisted I improve my vocabulary. If I use it at home, some of the family members would not know what I was trying to convey. If I use such in my classroom at school, most of my peers would not understand. They would naturally believe I was a show-off or a smart-ass. If I don't use such words from time to time, this learning experience you insisted upon would disappear. As the old saying goes, 'You use it or lose it'."

Charles changed the subject, "What do you expect our father will tell us this evening? Care to guess?"

April paused a second, then replied, "I feel it is something big, something different."

"You do not believe it is another acquisition of land?"

"No," April said. "I have seen some strange vehicles around recently. I think it is something that will surprise us."

"I am not that sure, April. No one can love an acre of land as he does. Sometimes I think land is his first love. Yes, sometimes I believe it is his only love."

"I know he has been looking at an adjacent farm for years," April said, "but I don't believe it is land this time."

Charles said, "I thought last time it would be a new house, since Mother had spoken repeatedly about a house with ample bedrooms, more bathrooms and enough hot water to last forever. Since we had just finished three great farm years and the tobacco prices were quite inflated, the money was there. Yet it was not to be; he simply remodeled our current house and made an addition. I am sure that, after concealing her disappointment, Mother will not bring the subject up again and Father will be delighted that she won't."

April turned in her chair as if to go and Charles spoke hurriedly. "Please remain a few minutes longer. Darkness does not come early this time of the year. I know you are tired, since you have moved constantly since you arrived. You never stay still a minute."

"I know it, Charles. I cannot seem to be still, as you have remarked repeatedly. It would seem that you would know this after all these years!" Her eyes sparkled.

"I wish to discuss two things," Charles said.

April interrupted, "Perhaps you will change everyone for the best and you are to start with me. Perhaps in your own image? Certainly you have considered that God, in His wisdom, designates to each a proper station in life. You do know that it is impious impudence to attempt to overturn His wise design." April snickered.

"You sound like a predestined Presbyterian but I'll get right to the heart of the matter," Charles said. "It grieves me to find it necessary to do so and . . ."

"If you are so saddened," April said as she interrupted him again, "I would suggest we leave it until you are stronger and less depressed." April choked back another snicker and pretended to rise again.

"In the course of your conversation you used slang more than once and it should not be a part of your lifestyle. I know you have heard all the words. We need not review who or where.

"There are some acts, as undesirable as they are, that may have some justifications or rewards. For example, to steal may feed a hungry child. A fight, be it on the battlefield or in a tavern, may restore one to a position of honor. But unbecoming language is totally void of any merit or value. You do not win. You only lose.

"It is obvious you do not respond this way from lack of vocabulary. I am equally assured that it is not to impress another. Apparently you do so without thinking and from lack of patience with others."

April had not spoken a word. She seemed absorbed in her own thoughts. Then she asked, "You mentioned a second item?"

Charles looked again into her unrevealing eyes and continued. "You have reached a time in your life when your body is no longer that of a child. Changes occur at different ages. For some, sadly, it never occurs. In your case the change began at an age earlier than most." Charles let his eyes survey her from head to toe. Her body had rearranged itself into womanhood. The veering wind of adolescence had nearly completed its task and a woman rather than a child sat in his presence.

"Your present attire does not meet the minimum standards society has established for us. I believe it best you hear this from me than another. Others may look upon your grooming with less compassion and understanding."

April looked down at herself and saw what her brother had seen. Her high full breasts pressed and strained against a simple cotton blouse. The shape of the nipples could clearly be seen, round and protruding against the cloth. The cut of her blouse was more than a shade too low. The swells from each breast were visible from a normal eye level. April looked up and knew that she must respond. She wondered what she would say or where she should start. She owed an explanation to Charles. He expected it. He deserved it. Suddenly, she knew what she must do.

"Let's start with your first observation. I cannot tell you why I do it, other than because I do not think before I speak," April said.

Charles asked, "Have you thought about when and why it occurs?"

"Yes. It happens when I am angry, frustrated or impatient. My tolerance is quite limited with the lazy and indifferent. All I can promise you is that I will think more before I speak.

"As to the second item, I am a victim. It may sound silly but I wish to remain a child a little longer. Childhood is a special period when one can have a great deal of freedom without restraint or responsibility. It is a time to discover who you are through trial and error, through fantasy, through make-believe and illusion. Yes, and even through hoping, wishing and believing, even dreaming. I am not ready to leave childhood but I suppose I must. I hope you understand what I am trying to say.

"Sometimes I nearly laugh at some girls who are classmates. They work so hard to achieve an adult status. How strange mankind is. Everyone wishes to be something different than what they are. The young can't wait to get grown and those of old age would offer their very souls to be young again.

"But suppose we get back to me. I know I am really not a child any longer. There is no way to forget, since nature reminds me every twenty-eight days. I can also tell when I look in the mirror. It is not God's plan for us to remain in the same state very long.

"I am told that certain types of grooming excite the boys. I'm sure you know but I dare not ask."

Charles said in a serious manner, "I want you to become the best you can be. I have, at times, wished you were perfect because you have so much talent, understanding and beauty, but that would be unfair.

Perfection would grow disgustingly dull because there would never be any surprises. Yes, I prefer a shade of imperfection, even in you.

"In time you will ponder many hours as to what you will do with your life. Your decision will be difficult. You will curse this special gift because it will impose a burden upon you that others will never experience. In time it could become more of a burden than a blessing.

"I have given too much advice. It is a characteristic man does not give up readily. Now I want you to go home this very minute. Use the back door. It would require fewer explanations. Wear something special tonight. You will do this for me."

For a moment April did not move and it was well that Charles could not read her thoughts. Suddenly, she became conscious that, though not completely divorced from first youth, she was a woman, her flesh warm and firm. She looked again and was aware of the strong thrust of her breasts against the thin cotton blouse. She now knew of the bend of her thighs, the suppleness of her ankles. She felt a strong ecstasy snatch at her heart. She knew the days of January and February were gone and the days of spring were upon her.

Charles watched her every movement until she disappeared around the corner of the house where the new rooms had been added. After she was out of sight he once more shifted his body to find a more comfortable position in his chair. The gentle sky had turned lilac and silver. As if out of nowhere, the wind arose. All the flowers appeared to wave at him and at each other. His eyes turned skyward and he saw all the many dogwoods that provided a canopy of white as they swayed in the breeze. As April had said, it was an extraordinary day.

Once again his thoughts returned to his beautiful and unique sister. He remembered a Sunday morning some ten years ago when April had climbed into his lap as he sat in one of the rockers on the front porch. As he held the *Atlanta Constitution* he had been reading she asked him if he wished her to read the paper to him. He smiled and placed it so she could see it clearly. She had almost spoken a sentence before he realized that she was actually reading, not making something up in pretense. In a stunned silence he listened as she read one paragraph and then another, some of the words containing three and four syllables. After three or four minutes she jumped down from his lap as if by some special signal, then rushed to her tricycle and raced off across the front drive, leaving him in a state of amazement. There was no evidence that she felt she had done anything unusual.

Later he had asked each family member if they had taught her in some manner but all denied any such act. In disbelief they had demanded she repeat the performance in their presence. They sat in awe as she read again. Charles had heard of such a phenomenon but this was the first time he had been a witness. From that moment on, he had made April a very special part of his life. As the years passed they became inseparable. One surprise was to follow another.

In time he was to learn that when she went to bed she would be sound asleep in thirty seconds. As she grew older the pattern did not change. She seemed to close out all conscious thought and was immediately in a state of deep sleep.

In the fifth grade she was given her first mental maturity test. Her score exceeded the scale. The teacher was so stunned that she asked April to repeat the test. The results, however, were the same.

Charles studied all the books he could find relating to the gene puzzle. Several writers suggested that many of one's characteristics were developed before leaving the mother's womb. One author reported that it wasn't unusual for a small percentage, at an early age, to know what they would do in life. Among those he listed in his book were a minister, a doctor and a mechanic.

In Charles' own experience, he remembered the little call girl whom he had visited as a sophomore in high school. She had told him that she knew at age ten what her profession would be. She told him of the satisfaction she would receive and the pleasures she would give to others. "Think of the people," she said, "who get up each morning dreading what the day has to offer. Not me. I would do the same again and again." Charles smiled as he remembered the exchange, and how entertaining she had been.

When April started to school Charles had worried how she would get along with her peers and her teachers. Yet up until the present he had never heard of the first problem.

Perhaps the wise Socrates had best described April. "She was not only the most beautiful of women but a woman of mind and character, and charm and tenderness . . . ."

Yes, wherever April ventured he knew that life would never be dull or predictable. Excitement would abound for herself as well as all others who would be a part of her life. He smiled.

Chapter 3

Immediately following her marriage to Joseph Randolph, Martha made some changes she felt very strongly about. Joseph was a Methodist so she converted from the Baptist church to his. She believed a wife should follow her husband and she felt Joseph would be pleased. She also accepted a Sunday School class to teach. Never once was she to regret this decision.

A few days later she asked Joseph, "Do you think I have the time to be a choir member? I enjoy singing. Some have been complimentary who have heard me. Perhaps I should contribute something." She anticipated an immediate positive response.

"Let me think about it a day or two. I wonder if you ain't missed a part of the whole picture." Two days later Joseph said, "About that choir business you were talking about, I think it might be okay and the reason I say that is the choir practices after the prayer session they have every Wednesday night. Since you can get all this church stuff over in one going, we'll try it. A farmer's wife ain't got much business being away more than one night a week. In tobacco season you'd have to miss for a spell."

Martha had intended to talk about the tithe or gifts to the church. Had he tithed before they married? She was sure she knew the answer and knew this was not the time to discuss it. In the first twelve months of their marriage Joseph had attended two regular services and one funeral, of a tobacco farmer. Martha had become depressed for a time, until she accepted the fact that the activities which required him to leave his plantation would be very few.

After the birth of their first three sons Martha told Joseph, "I want one night each week that the entire family could have supper together. An hour together once a week is little to ask. The cost will be small and you have said a hundred times that you do not care to be away from the farm. It would cost much more to go out some place. I know that farm people never finish their work but simply stop a few hours to rest. I know that a good farmer works according to the sun and season and I know you are the best." She saw Joseph give a very slight and brief smile.

As time went by Martha added to her edict. "I want everyone to come bathed and dressed for supper in fresh clothes. I will not have you smelling like a pig pen or a mule lot. Besides," she continued, "we will talk only of the positive things, the good things. We have a hundred and sixty-seven hours left each week to talk business.

"I am going to see that each has something very special that they enjoy most. If we do not eat all the food, so be it. Nothing will go to waste. Yes, I have the right to spoil my very special family once a week."

It had been a measure of relief for everyone after the house had been expanded and remodeled. The dining area was now twice as large as it had been earlier. Now there was ample space for the beautiful table and chairs that could seat twelve. The large china cabinet and buffet, two of the items that had belonged to Martha's mother, blended in perfect harmony with the table.

It was here on this Friday night that they gathered once again. Joseph sat at his regular place at the head of the table and Martha at the opposite end, nearest the kitchen. On one side sat Joe, Stephen and David. On the other sat Charles, Michael John and April. Joe's wife usually attended but she had rushed to Virginia to see her mother, who was quite ill.

All of the family members clasped hands as Joseph gave his brief and standard blessing, giving thanks to God for family, health and food. The family ate quietly, as nearly all country people do. Occasionally one would find himself eating too rapidly and then remember that this was the night that no one had to hurry.

April and Charles looked from one side to another. Everyone seemed to wait on another to say something. They both knew that everyone was thinking about what their father would tell them after the meal. There seemed to be an atmosphere of solitude and uncertainty. April spoke, to break the silence. "You men are no different than I expected. I put on a new and special dress and no one has even noticed." She looked at Charles; his eyes darted downward and his face darkened.

Stephen spoke suddenly, with a sneer on his face. "No wonder we ain't got the money we want and need and oughta have. But maybe things will change for the better."

"Think of the good times, Stephen. We all have to have clothes to wear," their mother said. She attempted to get some conversation going but it was futile. All this time Joseph did not speak a word but turned his head toward whomever was speaking. This surprised no one because he usually spoke only when he felt it necessary.

After a while Martha said, "I see all of you have finished. Your father wishes all of us to join him in the den. Gena and Meggie are still here to take over, since I find it difficult to leave a dirty kitchen. These special young ladies do a better job than I do."

They seated themselves in the area Martha called the conversational zone, the quiet area. The television was on the other side of the den. All eyes turned to Joseph; all had seated themselves so they could easily see him. Martha remained to the side and rear. As they looked at Joseph they saw a kind of radiance light up in him. It was as if a man who had lived in darkness had suddenly seen a glory never before witnessed. It was as if some magical event had occurred and he had been released from a fear or a wretched darkness.

In a bass voice, which was firm but suppressed, Joseph began. "Tonight I wanta tell you some things I wanta do. I wanna tell you in my own way and I ain't one for fancy words. I have a plan to offer and you see what you think. If you take to it, a lotta changes are bound to happen, some soon, some later. This ain't some land addition like I told you about the last two times we met. This is something different and me and Martha are the only two that know about it." April and Charles eyed each other.

"I've had my place surveyed and according to the figures, I got fifteen thousand and six hundred acres. They oughta be right 'cause they charged enough for their work. Coulda bought me a hundred acres for what they charged. I . . ." A voice sounded and Joseph stopped. The expression on his face showed more than a slight displeasure.

"I didn't know we owned so much land! Bet it's worth a lotta money," Stephen blurted out.

Likely an interruption by anyone other than Stephen, his youngest son, would have merited some negative remarks, but Joseph only looked at him and gave a slight smile.

Joseph continued, "That's what the man said, Stephen, and we'll just have to take his word for it. Now I wanna finish what I have to say and don't stop me 'till I'm through. At the next meeting you can say what you please.

"Now let me see where I was. So, the surveyor said that's what we got, fifteen thousand and six hundred acres. He's made a plat, I believe he called it, and all of you can see it later. Anyway, my plan is to make it our land as Stephen said a moment ago. I want to change it from Joseph Randolph land to Randolph Place. It should belong to all of us. It's a family farm.

"You probably noticed some people coming and going in recent months. Been a lotta cars and trucks around that don't normally come our way. One of the groups was timbermen. There was a forester and some cruisers, they called themselves. They found out about my timber. They told me what I could do with it, now and later. I also have some maps and figures on that. You can look at them too.

"You mighta seen another bunch out here, a group hired to test for clay, fuller's earth. They told me where, how much and how good. There's some maps and figures on that too. I had the whole place tested while I was at it. Helps to know what you got. What they found is gonna make us all proud.

"Got three clay companies having a fit over my findings. I mean the two here and the one in Quincy, Florida. Two of 'em want the land. One wants just the clay. Gotta think about this for a spell. Hard to give up land.

"One other thing now and I'll soon be through with this part. Got more than one part. Back some time ago, maybe fifteen or twenty years, I bought a hundred acres of land down near Panama City in Florida. Most is on the water. Cost a lot more than farmland but I bought it anyway. Wasn't my bowl of soup to buy something away from me but I did. My friend who told me about it said in time to come I'd make a fortune. The time has come now when people can't seem to stay away from the water. The price has jumped so high it's time to let the people get on the water."

During the time Joseph had spoken you could have heard a pin drop. No one had missed a single word. From time to time they exchanged sidelong glances, yet everyone remained spellbound and wondered where it would all lead. The light of glory continued to glow about their father.

"I've been seeing a lawyer, my lawyer. He is a fellow named Slick Cannington. 'Spect some of you know him. I felt I needed his advice cause he knows a lot of things I don't and he's plenty smart. Oh, I don't put much trust, that is, real trust, in him 'cause he's a lawyer and we know about lawyers. But I had to have somebody.

"He says we oughta form a corporation, which would do some things and give a tax break, a big one. But I told him I also wanted to form some kind of grouping to take in all of us. I'm fifty now. I ain't what I was and never will be again. Any man oughta know that when he reaches fifty. So this is when I brought your ma in and we studied it and went over it time and time again, trying to come up with something that's good and fair for all. Joseph paused and looked into the faces of his children; he detected little from his brief observation other than that he had their undivided attention.

"This is the second part. What we have to offer is this and by the word 'we,' I mean me and your ma. She is a part of all of this. We could incorporate this place like a business. I wanta call it 'Randolph Place' 'cause that is what it is. We wouldn't sell no stock to no one. The Randolphs would own the stock, all the stock, always. It would be what Slick called a closed corporation. I want us to have a total of a hundred shares. Me and your ma discussed this was how we might divide things up. Gave a lotta thought but the answer was right there before us all the time.

"Of the hundred, I'll take twenty. The next twenty is for your ma. This would leave sixty shares and every child will get ten. You oughta know your ma didn't wanta take them twenty shares but I told her it was all off if she didn't."

Joseph held up his hand to indicate he wasn't finished. "Don't say nothing yet 'cause I got a little more. From the timber, some clear cut and some thinned, from the fuller's earth, and from the land on the water, we can put together about four million dollars."

All of the children looked at each other in stunned silence. Then they looked back to their father. Again, not one word was spoken.

"This figure," Joseph said, "is free and clear of debts and mortgages and taxes. It means the figure is clear even after the cost of Slick and the surveyor and the clay drillers. Yes sir, ain't a dime owed on nothing."

Joseph looked at the little book he held in his hands. Then he looked back at his family. "Just a little more and I'll stop. This figure of four million ain't a figure we just need to have hanging 'round. We will take two million and invest it in a lump sum. Get more interest that way than dividing it up. Of the two left we put one on short term. Will draw interest and we can get to it easy. The last million would go into the operating fund. We could get some interest on part of this, too. Could raise a couple of crops without borrowing money. But sometimes it's best to use another's money.

"Now back to the first two million. We can get six percent if we let 'em have it for five years. This would give twelve thousand each year to each of you. Me and your ma would get twenty-four apiece.

"Now I'm gonna work out some monthly income besides the interest. We'll work it out on age and what you do. Naturally you'll get more if you are married. Me and your ma will help April and Stephen till they are sixteen. They ain't ready to handle this kind of money yet.

"I'm nearly through now so hold on a little while longer. I know in the past little while you have asked yourself why Joseph Randolph is doing this. Why would he offer this deal? Why just now? I can read your eyes, your faces. You are saying there is something here we ain't seen yet! This don't sound like the man who drove all of us so hard and so long. Well, the answer is simple. We are family. You are all I got, your ma and me. Let it stand at that. Now for the third part.

"I'd like all of you to stay here but some of you in time are bound to go. Yep, I understand. I understand some things more'n you think I do. We'll make it worthwhile to stay but we ain't gonna hurt you if you decide to leave. I'll have a plan ready for you either way that ain't gonna disappoint you. I'll tell you my plan on Sunday. That's two days from now.

"You'll talk among yourselves if you like but not to your ma and me. And never, and I do mean never, will you discuss our business among others.

"After we finish our second meeting we'll vote on this thing. I figure it oughta take six of us to call it passed and get it going. We'll go now. Goodnight."

As they were walking out Joseph stuck his head back in the room and said, "Joe, if Mary gets home, leave her home." Joe, the oldest of the five sons, was the first to leave following the departure of their parents. His poker-faced expression did not give a clue as to how he felt about his father's remark.

As they were leaving the room David said, "Michael John, suppose we go into the library and look at the material Father spoke about." Michael John, without a word, followed his brother into the room they now called the library. Books lined three walls. There was a table with chairs, where one could read, or study or just get away to be alone and think. The walls had been heavily insulated so that outside noise couldn't disturb the serenity of the room.

"Well, I guess that leaves us," April said to Charles as she slipped into the chair beside him. "I tried to tell you it was something big and consequential, something different! But no, you wouldn't believe me. You thought it was another land deal or some little insignificant and diminutive matter. Not so. If I could only get you to listen to me, there is no telling how much you would learn!"

Suddenly, their father returned. "There is another side to what has been planned. This is gonna cause a lotta talk as we move on."

"I don't believe I understand," April said.

"Well, it's like this. Ain't no Randolph business been talked for four generations. No one really knows much about us. I planned it that way. No fancy cars or houses, no tell-tale signs. I'm gonna let 'em know one day, but not yet. Randolphs gonna be looked at in a different light than the poor white trash they called us. It will all come out in time and some are gonna be more'n surprised." He turned and was gone as quickly as he had arrived.

"Yes, I wore that new dress tonight and you didn't say a word, after you gave such specific instructions earlier. How can you observe some things so well at times and be so unperceptive about others?" April smiled openly, eyes sparkling.

"You know, April," Charles said, "I don't think this will change or modify anything except in two areas."

"It changes everything! How can you say it changes nothing? We are now an integral part of the operation. There are so many areas we can change for the better. I can hardly wait. We are Randolph Place!"

"Are we?"

"Certainly we are," April responded. "Don't you think he is going to do what he said?"

"Yes. For the first time we will know there is something for those that leave. I will be one of them. Certainly I have never left anyone with the impression that I wanted to farm. He did not give specifics but I suppose that is on the agenda for Sunday evening. Actually, you may not wish to stay either. If you married, your husband would not be a Randolph.

"The second item is a specific stipend on a regular basis. I have long felt I was too old to go and beg for a few dollars.

"One more thing," Charles continued. " Our mother has no option but to vote as our father does. Certainly one or more will vote the same way. You can be assured Stephen will. Oh, perhaps on some small insignificant item, they may challenge each other but not on anything that will change things. Only if and when Father changes will there be a modification that is meaningful. It all looks good on paper. It gives the appearance of a democratic operation but it is only an illusion. I am reminded of a man who ran a stable of horses over in England. I believe his name was Hobson. When you arrived to rent a horse you were informed you could always have your choice as long as you took the one nearest the door! Our situation is no different.

"What surprised you the most?" Charles asked abruptly.

"The stock division. In a way I'm not sure it is fair. Certainly not at the present. Joe does as much as all the rest. Let's wait, however, until we know all the facts."

Charles said, "There are other issues that could bring about a great deal of division. Some would call them moral issues. Some of our brothers feel growing tobacco is not good. Some of us are not happy about the way our minority race lives. It isn't much of a life for them.

"April, I suggest the two of us be very patient in the days and weeks to come.

"I repeat, the more things seem to change, the more they stay the same. It is an illusion. It is only make-believe."

"Joseph feels he has made a very special gift to the family," April said. "He continues to emphasize the term 'family'. Who can say he is a deceitful man? An evil man? He may, in time, even build Mother a new house."

"Never will he ever give it another thought. Never! There will always be another piece of land he can buy. No one can love an acre of land like our father."

"He could make a good case for himself," April said. "This dirt you speak about has given the two of us some new opportunities. I am not ready to condemn him. He didn't have to do any of this. You know, I don't believe we have seen the entire picture yet. There is something else we are missing."

"I think you are correct. Our father is not democratic by nature. He has never pretended to relinquish his authority. He hasn't now. But, as you say, we have missed something that is important. How long will it take to show up?"

CHAPTER 4

Martha Randolph and her six children would have understood Joseph much better had they had known about his early childhood and the three generations preceding him.

Little was known about Joseph's great-grandfather, who had been a settler before the Civil War. No one knew where he had lived earlier but it had not mattered. Seldom did one ask about the background of others during this era. Some had come for adventure, others for a fresh start and still others to escape the past.

Yet there were those who knew about Joseph's grandfather. He had settled on his father's place and become a backwoods farmer. Their land was some three or four miles from the hub of the little community called Attapulgus. He had been a very private person and had never felt secure around people because of his lack of education, his limited land holdings and his economic status.

The wife of Joseph's grandfather had been unschooled as well and was even more timid and insecure than her husband. Together they had worked hard and scratched out a living on the little farm. They had three children, two girls and a boy. The daughters had died as infants.

Joseph's grandparents would go into Attapulgus every three or four weeks to buy the items they could not produce. They went twice a year to Midway, the county seat, to pay their taxes and conduct affairs required of them. They were never more than a hundred miles away from home in their entire lives.

They attended a small church nearby that served a dozen families that lived in the vicinity. The little church had services every third and fifth Sundays and had only Sunday School on the first and fourth Sundays. On the second Sunday they rested.

The little group met, read some Scriptures, sang some songs, prayed unceasingly and heard the circuit rider deliver a hell-fire message. If the message was not delivered with the same intensity and vigor as D. L. Moody or Billy Sunday, they felt he had said nothing and expressed their unhappiness. Hard work was needed to find the deep-seated sins so carefully hidden. When the sermon was finished they returned to their little homes with a feeling of deep satisfaction. They had been cleansed once again.

In time the grandmother and grandfather passed on to their rewards and left the farm to Joseph's father. By that time the size had increased twofold.

It was here that Joseph's father would remain for his entire life. In his mid-thirties he married an old maid who lived on the adjacent farm. The two were a perfect contrast. He was a large man, six feet tall and weighing two hundred pounds, with not an ounce of fat. Joseph's mother was a tiny thing, weighing no more than a hundred at best, and she had to stretch to reach five feet in height. She was not a pretty woman and her figure would not have excited a drunk Indian.

What she did have, however, was a large farm of nearly three thousand acres. Her parents died after their nearly three-score years of hard work and left all the land to her, an only child.

After Joseph's father had married her this little woman's life was never the same again. A year to the day following their union Joseph was born. It had not been an easy birth and it was at this very moment that Joseph's mother knew her son would be an only child and that never again would she be a mother. She had done her duty.

From the beginning, the life of Joseph's father was changed. This tiny, frail woman, who worked harder than anyone else, took it upon herself to change her husband into the image she wished. Her dour Baptist mind and a code of ethics to match was to pin her husband down for the rest of his life. She beat the brains out of anything and everything he had once found pleasure in doing. She infrequently continued to do her duty as a wife in a physical way but she was careful, very careful, in their occasional lovemaking. There would be no other sons or daughters. In time she was to look upon such activities as tiresome, evil and vulgar. She thought of it as a painful duty.

It did not take long, once they were married, for her to develop a sense of sin. Idleness was among the greatest since it allowed time for other sins. She was suspicious of excessive laughter and dancing was never to be tolerated, because people would touch each other and this would lead to other sinful acts. A deck of cards, she believed, was invented by the devil and would surely lead to gambling, a sin she rated among her top ten.

Joseph and his father had many different emotions about Sunday. On Saturday all meals for Sunday were prepared. They were to be served cold on Sunday. She reminded them that you labor for six days but you were to rest and worship on the Sabbath. Joseph wondered about the difference between a fire in the wood stove to cook and a fire in a fireplace to keep warm, but he never got beyond the stage of wondering.

Throughout her entire life, she suffered bravely and uncomplainingly. She was convinced that this was the way God wanted everyone to live. Rewards would come later and would be in proportion to the amount of suffering. The more people suffered, the nearer they would be seated to their God as they passed into another Kingdom. She never seemed to reconcile what her duties would be when she reached the city paved with gold. Joseph's father once considered asking her about the duties and rewards, but thought better of the idea.

Most of her days here on earth began at a quarter to four. Labor was a word found often in her Bible and she felt this would solve most problems. In her few spare moments she read her Bible. The circuit rider had once recommended a book called *Pilgrim's Progress* but she decided against it. She had discovered ample passages to assure her family that she had discovered a path for all to follow that was clearly defined.

Joseph and his father always respected her because there always seemed a rightness in her face and a certainty in her voice. There would be few compromises because everything was right or wrong, good or bad, black or white. There were no shades of gray in her life and therefore none in others' lives.

Once, when Joseph's father had joined with some fellow farmers to celebrate a special occasion, a small bottle had appeared and they toasted the occasion. He soon learned it was not worth the wrath of this little woman. Only adultery was classified as a greater sin than drinking. It, too, led to the first and to other sins. Joseph's father never took another drink of alcohol.

When Joseph was fifteen he took a sip of some homemade brew upon a dare. He, too, learned for himself the foolishness of his ways. Upon his return home, his mother, with a nose like a beagle hound, detected that this second greatest sin had been committed. Joseph stood before her as she asked, "Would you go by Saint Peter at the Golden Gate in this manner? Would you approach the throne of God with alcohol on your breath? Get on your knees this very instant and ask for forgiveness and mercy!"

Never again did Joseph participate until after his mother's death and even then, he always had a guilty feeling on the rare occasion when he took a very small sip. Only after he discovered in his mother's Bible that Paul had suggested a little wine was good for the stomach was there a reconciliation of a sort.

Joseph had never spoken much about his early life. His family had asked from time to time about some early experiences but he said little. He had found no reason to review the past. However, from these early experiences Joseph had formulated a direction for himself and his family to follow and seldom did he veer from the pattern he had established. His family simply trusted him or remained silent.

Joseph sat in his favorite chair, where he had sat two nights earlier. He was a big man, with broad and powerful shoulders. There was not an ounce of surplus fat to be found. He seemed shorter than his six feet because of his size.

He had a large head with dark brown hair. It was thick and without a trace of gray. His face was large and squarish. He spoke with a bass voice that displayed confidence. He was a handsome man. He walked with a graceful movement. One would never guess that in his early years he had plowed hour after hour, day after day.

His pattern of dress was inflexible. Actually, it did not differ from most of the country farmers. Except for church and funerals, which required a coat and tie, he wore work clothes of cotton. Martha always insisted on clean clothes each morning.

Joseph had three suits of good quality. He had declared this was all he wanted or needed. He had explained that the weights were different and thus he could dress appropriately for all seasons. Little attention was given to style or color, in spite of Martha's efforts. Whenever the family suggested a more elaborate wardrobe, he refused to discuss the matter. "Why, I can buy five acres of good land for what you'd pay for a good suit!"

Because Joseph had been raised in a family where women were always respected, he never used profanity or vulgarity in their presence. It was no secret, however, that in his daily farm operation he did not follow this practice with the male employees or any of the black people.

Some of the family saw Joseph as two different people. When he was nice, he was very nice. When he was not nice, one wished for a place to hide. He demanded of all others as he demanded of himself. Work hard, get the job done, do it right the first time and do it with all deliberate speed. There was to be no other way, no shortcuts, no substitutes and few acceptable excuses. One worked first and played later, if there was any time later. That was the way he operated, all day, every day. He expected others to do the same. He reminded them that good things happened to you when this policy was followed.

This was the person who presided over the current family meeting. As if by compulsion, all the siblings sat in the same seats as two nights earlier. Their facial expressions gave little hint as to what they were thinking. Each seemed uncertain and apprehensive.

Joseph, sensing this mood, started by saying, "We wanna thank your ma for the nice meal." He hoped this would remove some of the tension. "And now it is necessary that we make some decisions about our future, about Randolph Place. I figure you have talked matters over among yourselves and done some thinking on your own.

"Now I want to tell you some other things. I'll make it plain. Always best to do it that way.

"At the last meeting I could tell we touched on some differences. I knew we would. Know all of you better than you think.

"Wouldn't doubt if you didn't question the stock division. Easiest question of all. You are all my children and every child, in this case, should be treated the same. Me and your ma plan to make up some differences in other ways.

"Now about leaving Randolph Place. Me and ma would like you to stay. My plan may encourage you to do that. But we ain't gonna hold you against your will. For one that's gotta go, whatever the reason, we'll do this: They'll get the two hundred thousand on deposit. Then we'll add a hundred thousand. Then we'll give you ten dollars an acre. So, we would be talking about near half a million. This ain't bad and might just encourage you to get gone but we hope not.

"If you stay, you will have some goodies too. The place, counting money, land, everything, may be worth fifteen million, give or take. Take ten percent of that and it'd be worth three times as much if you stay. Now we plan to go a step beyond. We'll build anyone a house when they get married. Would be yours as long as you live here.

"One thing we ain't figured out yet is what would happen if a married child dies and only Randolphs can own stock. We're working on this.

"Another thing, while I think of it, oughta be said for sure. I feel strongly about the reserve fund for three reasons. I believe we said a million. First, if someone left, the funds are gonna be there right then. No waiting. Wouldn't wanna sell no land. A man buys land, he don't sell it. Second, if a good deal comes along we can't let go by, we got the money. And last, if by chance we have some bad luck, we can overcome it.

"I've talked enough now. You'll all talk, starting with your ma."

Martha said, "For two years your father has worked and planned for this day. I believe it most fair and quite generous. I had preferred not to be a stockholder but he would have it no other way. This tells you something about your father.

"As he has said, you may have felt it was for some hidden reasons he has made this offer. There is only one reason. He loves all of us very much. Your father is not perfect. None of us are. But he has so many wonderful characteristics. That's why I married him.

"A generous offer awaits one who must go. Everyone does not choose to farm. We are all different. I would have you stay, but not against your will. So, as time passes, I will prepare myself for the day you choose to leave your nest. God has promised me the strength to let you go.

"Now I must touch on some matters that may be misunderstood. Let each find an area of work based on talent, interest and conscience. Secondly, our talents and our abilities are not the same. We should always expect the best efforts from everyone but never more than one is capable of. The last item along this line is responsibility. This must always be in proportion to authority, whatever the task. Mistakes will be made. All of us will make them. This will be true as long as man occupies this planet called earth. So when this occurs, and it will, we must not condemn each other, but offer support and encouragement during such crucial and trying times.

"The home is my domain. I am sure I can make it better. Give me your advice and your suggestions. Tell me what you don't like and we will make an effort to improve it."

Joseph said, "Now you can see why I married your ma. She helped to make all this possible." It was obvious that Joseph had been pleased with Martha's words. "Now we want to hear from everyone. We will hear first from Joe."

"I am impressed," Joe said. "Such a plan has required a great deal of effort. I had planned earlier to say many things and ask many questions. There is time for that later. So, at this time I will touch on only two items and trust I may speak freely about some other things later.

"First, we must be so organized that our father will continue as the chief coordinator. Brothers and sisters may not always work together as well as parents and children. A brother could ask another, Why are you telling me this? Who gave you the authority? I need not say more.

"Secondly, we need a compensation schedule. Everyone would wish to know what he has at a given time. Certainly age, experience and responsibility will have something to do with it."

Charles spoke, "I am very impressed. Our parents are quite generous. I hope we will keep our eyes glued to the mountains and not let the mole hills destroy us. I am not sure yet that I understand all the whys but that is not important.

"It is no secret, nor has it ever been, of my lack of interest in agriculture. I suppose people interest me more. This is not to say that farming is not essential, but I have few talents to offer in the operation. I would prefer to give such as I have in preparation for a profession. I want to be good at what I do but I do not even know what I wish to do at the present.

"I will not permit myself to be a stumbling block. I hope I will be the first to recognize it if I do and at that moment I will depart.

"I have some suggestions I will offer later but it has little to do with the proposal. I will defer such until another time."

Martha said, "Your contributions have not been limited to farming. Your efforts to help others in educational matters are most worthy. You have been generous with your time and talent."

Charles said, "There is one matter, however, I call to your attention, not for my sake, but for everyone's. By all standards, whatever measurements you wish to apply, you have been successful. The figures our father has given us are ample proof. You have worked hard. You have earned it. You deserve it.

"I have watched a number of individuals and families that have been equally successful set new goals and continue to work even longer and with more effort. They said, 'I'll slow down when I have enough.' But I ask you, what is enough? I don't know. I'm not sure you do either, though you may think so.

"Please take the time to reward yourself. Take a vacation. See some of our beautiful world. My dear family, you are very special to me. Don't wait. You have earned it, as I said. You don't have to prove anything ever again. Don't wait until something happens and miss it all, living a life of regrets. It is because I love you that I say these things."

David was next to speak. "Your plan is fair and generous, should one leave or stay.

"In a few weeks I will graduate. I do not wish, as things now stand, to go to college, though all of us should want to learn and know more. I want to remain here and work with row crops and cattle. I do not feel I would be comfortable in some other parts of the operation. I have always wanted to be a farmer. I love the land. I like to plant the seeds, watch them grow and see them harvested. There is nothing quite like it in the world. I am my father's son. I love the soil.

"I will mention one other item and you can move on." All looked at him, thinking the tobacco issue was about to surface. "Someday I may wish to leave, though I love each of you. I believe there is an innate feeling in all of us to have something of our own, our very own. I trust this is not a selfish attitude. Someday I will want my own place, a wife and children. Then I can do for them what our father has done and is doing for us."

Michael John saw his father's nod, offering to let him speak, but for several seconds Michael John remained silent. Finally he said, "I've tried to hear and understand all that has been said. I'm different from all of you. I know that. You know that. I have to work more with my hands. I like to fix things and build things. If there is a place for me in doing these things, I'll stay. I would not want to stay unless I can do my part. I will not be a burden." They knew he would say no more.

"What does a thirteen-year-old girl with five brothers do on Randolph Place?" April smiled and took some seconds to look at each. "You have not given me a clue. I do not have an answer either.

"I love to be with our mother but I have little interest in domestic responsibilities. I can drive a tractor better than any of my brothers but you insist this is a man's job.

"I have five more years in school. I have no idea what life holds for me. I suppose one day I'll marry if I can entrap some poor soul.

"In the meantime I will accept such duties as you think I can do. I can help Mother. I can assist Charles with the clerical duties.

"The proposal has much merit. I am in complete agreement that responsibility and authority cannot be equated differently than was explained. As Joe said, brothers and sisters do not always feel good about taking instructions from their siblings. A coordinator is essential. And yes, as Mother has said, we cannot ignore the dictates of our consciences.

"I am excited. I believe this will inject a better feeling for all. In time to come, I hope we can review some areas that distress me. The quarters may be a place we need to review more carefully. Yes, I believe the plan can serve the family in a number of special ways."

The lively eyes of Stephen sparkled as his father gave him a nod. He was a handsome young man with endless energy. He was also a fun loving person; yet no one worked harder at family tasks.

"The plan is great, just great! This is what I needed, what I wanted. I like farming. I will not be a college boy. I'm here to stay. I want to follow Father and Joe. And just think, I can soon have all the things I've ever wanted."

Joseph rose from his seat. He seldom sat so long in one place. In a minute he returned. No one had spoken while he was gone. "Anything else anybody wants to say? Now is the time." Everyone looked at Joseph without speaking. "Then I want us to vote on my plan. You will answer yes or no. We'll follow the order you spoke. I'll vote last."

"I also vote yes," Joseph said after he had received a positive response from each. "It's unanimous!"

He added, "I nearly forgot to mention it. As we vote our shares in the future, a tie vote will always go the way I go!" He laughed and all seemed to smile on cue. "Now tomorrow is a work day, a school day and a Monday. Let's get out of here and get some rest. I am pleased." He left the room immediately.

Charles and April moved into the small library. As they sat down April asked, "What do you think?"

"About what?"

"About everything, silly!"

"There will be few changes except in the compensation for individuals. Oh, I suppose there will be a more clearly defined job description for each. I am pleased with the plan should one leave. It was generous."

"Did David go too far?" April asked.

"No. He gave Father a pretty good shot, but Father likely expected such and prepared for it. Everything will be fine. There will be enough to do so he will not be involved in tobacco."

"And our mother, Charles, where will this new arrangement place her?"

"I don't know. There may be some surprises but I don't believe so in the near future. Other than the exceptions I mentioned, there will really be no changes. It will only seem so."

CHAPTER 5

Martha watched her children jump into David's car. "I guess it's Monday morning over half the world," she said aloud. "Why does Monday always have to be like this?"

"You talking to me?" Sandra asked as she entered the back door to the kitchen. "A happy good morning to you. It's such a fine April morning and a great day to be alive!"

Jack Jenkins and his wife Sandra had arrived twenty years ago. Jack was Joseph's foreman, his right hand man. Sandra had helped Martha soon after she and Jack arrived and had continued until the present. They were the only other white family on Randolph Place. Their one child, Gena, was the same age as April and in the same grade at school.

"Sandra, how can you always be so happy and cheerful all the time? It is Monday morning!"

"Why shouldn't I be happy? I have all the things that are important, everything that really matters. I have a good husband and he has a good job, thanks to the Randolphs. I have a beautiful daughter—but all mothers think their daughters are beautiful. She is happy. She smiles most of the time. Laughter seems to live on her doorstep. Charles helps her as he helps April. This is about the best thing that can happen to her.

"I have a good job thanks to you. I enjoy being with you.

"You have provided a nice home for us to live in. We have all we need. Can you think of one reason why I should not be happy on this beautiful April morning?"

"No. I cannot think of a reason. And I, as well as my family, are equally happy to have you and your family."

As Martha approached her car she remembered back to the time of Sandra's arrival. Sandra had said, "I need to work. I want to work for you. I know a lot about work. When I was a child we were very poor. There were eight children in my family. It would be my pleasure to help you. You are a family woman. I know you will do the right thing about pay." This had been the way it had started twenty years ago.

Martha closed the door on her '56 Chevy and guided the vehicle around the circular drive. The lane to the public highway had been paved a year or so ago. It extended nearly a mile and she knew it had not come cheap. She rode by and picked up the music, then went to the church.

"Come in," Mike Harper said. "I've been busy doing two things. There are always reports to file. Indeed we drown ourselves with paperwork and I suggest the church is no better because of it. Souls should be more valuable than paper."

"And your other chore?" Martha asked.

Mike laughed. He had a wonderful sense of humor. His wit was one of his trademarks. "I was hoping you would ask. I am preparing a sermon to preach to you on Sunday. I have to work hard to find some sin to pin on you! Can you help me?"

Martha smiled. "Any subject you choose will get the job done. Some days I need several sermons!"

She hurried to her car, then headed to the little house where Susan lived. Susan had been her best friend for so long. As Martha drove toward the small, modest frame house, she could not help wondering how Susan had managed. Lawrence, her husband, had died many years ago. Eric might have been ten and Jerome was about fourteen at that time.

Lawrence had run a little general store for a number of years and had tried his hand on a small farm. His farming, according to Joseph, had not been successful. Susan helped with the "clerking," as she referred to it, in the store. The store had not been much of a success either. Martha suspected that credit had been their downfall.

After Lawrence died Susan reduced the hours she kept the store open. She opened in the afternoons and on Saturday. In most of her remaining time, she sewed.

The town people referred to her as a seamstress but she always said she was simply "taking in sewing." Someone once asked Susan to get a dress ready by a certain time but she refused. "I'd have to sew on Sunday. That's God's day."

The door opened immediately when Martha knocked. "Oh, Martha, do come in! You are the very tonic I need today." They embraced each other tenderly. "You always pick me up!"

"Now Susan, I have some burdens to bear and you always help me. Why don't we just unload on each other!" Martha smiled.

Susan closed the door behind them and rushed to get Martha a cup of coffee. "Takes more than one cup on Monday." She placed the cup and saucer before Martha as they sat at the breakfast table.

Susan demanded an update on Martha's six children. Martha finished, then said, "Tell me about your boys. How is Jerome?"

"He works. He goes to school. He doesn't eat right. He doesn't get enough rest. It is enough to worry a mother to death."

Martha laughed. "They say the same about us. Slow down. Get more rest. Go get a physical examination. You may need a tonic. I guess it's nice to know someone cares!"

"Jerome will soon finish law school. He has to take a bar examination and then he can get a job."

"Where will he work?"

"Oh, he'll probably come back near here. Thinks I'm too old to be alone."

"And Eric? He is out west going to school?"

"Eric is in Oklahoma at Southeastern State College. He wants to be a teacher. He learned of the school by way of a professor from Georgia Teachers College who left and is now president there. Eric has a job, as does Jerome. They both have the same problems of work, study and rest."

"Susan, I have a special request. There is a program at our church to honor our seniors. I am on the dessert committee. Could you help me?"

"I'd be hurt if you didn't ask me. Do you have something in mind? A cake? Some pecan pies? What do you think?"

"Everyone loves your cakes but I like your pecan pies even better. Would two pies be too much to ask?"

"Mercy no! I'll bake a cake, too."

"No, I can't let you do that."

"Let's leave it like this. I'll do the pies. Then if you need something else, I'll fix a cake. You farm people are busy this time of the year."

Martha added, "Oh, I nearly forgot. I need some dresses for April and a couple for myself."

"Bring the material tomorrow and I'll get started. Gives me a chance to see you again!"

Martha eased her car toward the school. She must be on time. She would not wish Miss Knight to be kept waiting.

Martha knocked on the door of the principal's office. "Why come in, Mrs. Randolph. I know you. You are April's mother. I am Janice Smith, a student assistant. Mr. Baggs, who is usually teaching this period, is in Midway at a school meeting. It will be after lunch before he returns. Please come in and have a seat."

"Yes, I know you, as well as your people. Do you help Mr. Baggs daily at this period?"

"Yes. He teaches five classes each day. Some of us help when we can. I answer the telephone and do some typing, as well as filing. I enjoy meeting people. Is there some way I can help you?"

"Actually there is. Miss Knight is expecting me this period. Do you think you could let her know I am here?"

"Certainly. I'll ask you to play secretary a moment. Should the telephone ring, please ask them to hold a minute."

Two thoughts occurred as soon as Janice left. First, here was a school spirit with everyone making a contribution. How wonderful. But then she asked herself why a principal would be required to undertake such a teaching load. She would try to remember to ask Charles.

Janice and Miss Knight entered the office. "I do hope you have not been waiting long." Miss Knight extended her hand to Martha with a friendly smile. "You are kind to see me during your busy season. Charles told me that it starts in April and goes into August."

Martha smiled, "With five men and a daughter, it's always a busy time." She looked more closely at Miss Knight and noticed how beautiful she was. Her figure was as impressive as her face. She guessed her age near twenty-five. She wondered how one so beautiful and talented could be unmarried. Martha knew of no regular man in her life. Charles visited her often about assignments for April and Gena but Martha was unaware of any relationship between Miss Knight and Charles.

"Mrs. Randolph, suppose we slip into the office where the counselor works. She is busy teaching this period. This will give us some privacy and we can get out of Janice's way."

After they had taken chairs facing each other Miss Knight smiled again and said, "Thank you again for coming. Perhaps this will result in a better understanding. I hope we can assist each other. I think it is safe to say you have a talented and unique daughter. Of all the girls I have taught, your April is the most unusual, as well as the most talented. She is a delightful young lady."

"I suppose you see her in a different setting," Martha said. "I see her in the home in a mother-daughter relationship. You see her as a student."

Miss Knight continued, "There is really no way to describe her. She could breeze through the senior class curriculum. She can discuss any subject. She reads more than any other eight or ten students combined. She has no trouble with comprehension because of her superior vocabulary and can read at a great rate of speed. Call it speed reading if you like. On the other hand, she can take some time and can quote any part as she wishes."

"Are you saying she shows off or monopolizes her class? If so, you and the class must have a low opinion of her!"

"No. No, indeed. This is something difficult to explain. She may be the most popular student in class. They understand her and recognize her unusual characteristics. She speaks in a language they can understand, even though she can speak in one in which even I would be lost. She is extremely patient with the slower students. Often she will assist me in teaching them. She is likely more effective than I am. She never attempts to impress. She makes them feel comfortable.

"She is very considerate of me as well. There are few days she could not put me on the spot because of her questions. I usually say we may be able to get back to that later. Sometimes we do. Sometimes we don't. She never brings up the subject again unless I initiate it."

"I don't get a chance to see this side of her," Martha said. "Charles assists her with her school work."

"April likes competition. She makes a game of everything and insists learning is more fun this way. Some time ago she saw me after school and handed me some materials. There were eight hundred questions and answers divided into four groups according to difficulty. We played academic baseball for a week in history. The slower students could participate because of the manner she had prepared and grouped the questions. The students were elated. However, April had insisted that they never know of her involvement. I had suspected Charles had helped her or that it was his idea. Not so."

"She never tells me of such," Martha said.

"I think what I have said will assist you in seeing April from a different vantage point. Now I must tell you of some things I do not comprehend."

"I don't believe I understand."

"Sometimes she speaks in some unusual ways and expresses herself, shall we say, a bit differently from most of the others."

"I'm sorry. I hope you have and will deal with her in a firm manner."

Miss Knight laughed. "When she says these unusual things I take her aside and we talk about what she has said. When I do she is always cooperative."

"I would hope so."

"I think she attempts to correct the matter but it hasn't improved too much yet. Perhaps you have a suggestion." Miss Knight smiled generously.

"Would you think me terribly rude if I said I failed to see the humor? I am afraid you have lost me."

"What would you suggest, Mrs. Randolph? We can laugh or we can cry, so it seems. I'll explain myself further in a moment. What she says no longer shocks the students. They have come to expect it. I suspect they enjoy every second of it."

"Now you think and say this is awful and as a mother, learning this perhaps for the first time, I can understand. But what, may I ask, do I do? What can I do? Wash her mouth out with soap? Spank her? Send her home? Give her some extra work to do? Put her nose in a ring on the board? I am open to suggestions."

Martha paused and then said, "It isn't that easy, is it?"

"I'm sorry to bring up something such as this," Miss Knight said, "but I felt you had to know. I remember once when something similar occurred and some parents demanded to know why it had not been reviewed with them. I don't know that you would have felt that way but it's best you knew." Again Miss Knight smiled.

"Miss Knight, for a time I have been reluctant to ask what she says and when. I think I must ask this question."

"I have little explanation concerning such words that she uses. I believe she uses them when she becomes frustrated or impatient.

"Suppose we talk about the language first. Let me give you three recent examples."

Martha interrupted, "Three? Recent?" She could feel her face growing red.

Miss Knight laughed again. "In American History, as we discussed the Civil War, she referred to the stupidity and damn poor thinking and planning on the part of the South. She gave some statistics to justify her evaluation.

"Following the Civil War, she referred to Robert Toombs from Georgia who was very outspoken before and during the war. She said before the war he said the South could beat the North with corn stalks. When questioned about it following the war Toombs responded that the bastards wouldn't fight with cornstalks. She had a book about this quote.

"She continued to speak of Toombs. It seemed that after the war, he and a friend were walking down a street and Toombs tossed a silver dollar into the hat of a man begging on the street, who had lost both legs and one arm. He had on an old Union coat. When the friend asked Toombs if he realized the man was a former Union solder Toombs responded, 'He was the first son-of-a-bitch I have seen all day cut down to proper size'."

Martha could feel her face flushing, and getting more so by the minute.

"Two other examples I remember. She referred to Woodrow Wilson attempting to tell the Europeans how to conduct a peace treaty after World War I. She said, 'Hell, even our Lord didn't have but ten commandments. Wilson had insisted on fourteen.'

"She can often defend herself in that she can tell you where she found most of her information. She identified fifteen books that used the word 'damn.' She included *Gone with the Wind*. An equal number of sources used the word 'hell.' She said that 'shit' was something most people did nearly every day. She further stated that statistics indicated it the third most used word in the English language. I am sure she had the proof to support her statement. I was afraid to ask her the two words used more frequently!" Miss Knight smiled once more.

"As to the when, this usually takes place when she loses patience with capable but lazy and non-thinking people. I am not at all sure she does this to get attention. In fact, when I confront her, she becomes quite emotional and assures me she can't help it and that she is sure it can only get me in trouble for permitting a continuation of such abnormal behavior.

"I repeat, I have no solution. But let us not do something we will regret. I believe, as Charles does, that she will outgrow this problem. Let me beg you not to act in a manner which might destroy this wonderful person."

"I have no suggestion, Miss Knight. After thinking about it I also cannot find a solution at the moment.

"Again, I apologize for her poor behavior and misconduct. I am embarrassed for everyone. I suppose I am from the old school. I can never recall such in my day. Thank you for your kindness as well as your frankness. It is best I know. Please do as you feel best. I will show myself out."

After Mrs. Randolph departed Miss Knight reviewed all that had been said. She concluded she had learned nothing new. Instantly she decided that she would do nothing that would have a lasting negative effect upon this delightful person. Perhaps it would have served everyone best if a conference had never been suggested.

Martha could not remember leaving school. She wasn't even sure that she had thanked Miss Knight for her time and explanations. At the beginning Martha had been keenly disappointed. Miss Knight had been so graphic, so specific, and had laughed repeatedly. Yet now, as she thought about it, she knew that Miss Knight had April's welfare first and foremost in mind.

Then, like a bolt out of the blue, it struck her. The knowledge of April's demeanor and deportment was not limited to students in the class. Why, everyone in school knew about it. Everyone in the community knew. It was likely known throughout the county and beyond. A feeling of despondency and hopelessness descended upon her.

Upon returning home she saw a light on in the library, where Charles sat at a desk on which books and materials were scattered all about. She rushed in and closed the door. "We have to talk. We have to talk now!"

Charles immediately knew his mother was upset. He led her to a chair. "What has happened? You appear quite ill!"

After some moments Martha told her son all she had learned from Miss Knight. "Charles, you must help me. Something must be done! Something must be done now! I am sure everyone knows and wonders what kind of people we are. We can't let this continue. Some way, somehow, we must find a solution."

Charles listened carefully to all his mother said. Not once did he interrupt. Yet as she spoke, he could not help thinking of April's language the previous Friday afternoon.

Finally, after his mother seemed to gain partial control, Charles said, "Tell me what Mr. Baggs said."

"I didn't see him. He was away at a meeting. Why, I wouldn't dare talk with him about this. I would be so embarrassed I couldn't speak. I didn't even feel comfortable with Miss Knight."

"What did you think of Miss Knight?"

"In what way?"

"Oh, just in general, I suppose. Did you feel she should have dealt with the matter differently? Did she have suggestions?"

"No suggestions. The only consolation, the only hope I could find, was that she suggested April might outgrow the problem. But my God, Charles, will it be when she is sixteen? Twenty? That's not much to feel good about.

"At first I was disappointed. She laughed and smiled repeatedly, even as she told me what April had said."

"How did she say the class responded?"

"She said most of the students loved her to death. She helps with the slower students. Miss Knight mentioned some material April had provided. She feels the students are better because of her. After some thought, I guess Miss Knight has done all she or anyone could.

"And yes, she spoke of April's talents. She even said she could do senior work without effort. I find this hard to believe. Do you believe this is true?"

"Yes."

"Is she really that talented?"

"Yes."

"What will become of her?"

Charles paused, then spoke in a calm manner that he hoped soothe his mother. "Stop worrying about the language. It will go away in time, likely sooner than one would expect. People who know you will know this is not a way of life for you or the family."

"Do you think it will go away soon?"

"I do."

"Can you be sure? Absolutely sure?"

"No one can be completely sure of anything, Mother. But yes, it will go away and you will wonder why you worried and became so upset. This may be the smaller problem. I see a much larger one."

"Worse than this? Nothing, and I mean nothing, can be as bad. Nothing can be worse than this. I am not strong enough to deal with another problem, especially at this time."

"Her problem is not one of her own creation. We will say she was born with it. She is one of the most gifted people ever. She has managed to disguise this quite well, as she wishes to be like others and to be treated the same. She wants to be accepted. I think one can see why when we take a closer look. Someday, and perhaps already, she will recognize that being gifted is the loneliest state in the world.

"I've worked with Miss Knight more than anyone knows. We have developed plans and programs to challenge April. Some were successful but others only kept her busy. Never underestimate Miss Knight. She is perhaps the most talented and wonderful person I can ever hope to know. You will never know, you can never even guess, what she has done for your daughter.

"Now back to April. All tests given provided information which confirmed what we had already realized. I think the time has come when we must try something different to challenge April. She loves sports. She loves competition. School can provide some of this but I would suggest some facilities at home. We can discuss this later.

"At the moment, I would hesitate to discuss much of what we have said with other family members. I am not sure they would understand some things. Now you put this out of your mind. It is destroying you. In a short time you will look back and wonder why you were so concerned.

"I would like for you to consider doing something special for Miss Knight. You will never know the hours she has spent. I believe it should be something significant." Charles watched concernedly as his mother left, deep in thought, pondering their discussion.

In a moment Martha stuck her head back inside and said, "Charles you must run to town and get this grocery list filled. I got so excited I completely forgot."

CHAPTER 6

The first born son of Joseph and Martha was named Joseph Therin Randolph, Jr. Martha and Joseph were in complete agreement that he would be called Joe rather than Junior. Joseph had swelled with pride when Martha had insisted they name their son in Joseph's honor.

When Joe entered the first grade at Attapulgus as a six-year-old he was immediately accepted by his classmates and teacher. As the years passed the only criticism he ever received was that his capabilities exceeded his performance.

At the beginning of his junior year Joe discovered the world of girls, and even before then the girls had discovered him. At this time a girl named Alice Dixon staked her claim. The romance continued to grow and they became inseparable. After Joe got his own car he dropped Alice off at her home each afternoon, since her family lived on a large farm adjacent to Randolph Place.

Upon graduation from high school Joe enrolled in Abraham Baldwin Agricultural College (ABAC) in Tifton, less than a hundred miles from home. The reputation of the college was especially strong in the area of agriculture. No one knew if he actually desired college or if it was simply a case of expectations. Alice Dixon enrolled at ABAC at the same time.

In a few days Joe found himself in a quandary. He had anticipated courses that would expand his knowledge in agriculture, but he also found himself enrolled in the foundation courses of English, math, science and history. He remained the entire school year and easily passed all of his subjects. He returned home, however, and never went back to college another day. Upon returning he became a major participant on the plantation. His father entrusted him with any and all activities. Soon he was his chief lieutenant in tobacco.

Upon Joe's departure from ABAC, Alice Dixon had transferred to the University of Georgia. Joe saw her only during the summers, holidays and special weekends. They seemed to enjoy each other's company, but it was different now than previously. Some of the early flame had diminished.

When Joe reached the age of twenty-one he gave his family a surprise. He brought a beautiful girl home one evening and said, "Please meet Mary. She is now Mary Randolph. We were married today."

The family was speechless. Martha recovered first and said smilingly, "Welcome, Mary. I guess we were not expecting such an announcement. The cat seemed to have our tongues for a moment. We welcome you as the newest member of the Randolph family. We are pleased. I can see why Joe has married you. You are beautiful and I would guess you are as nice and good as you are pretty."

Mary and her family had once lived in Attapulgus but her father had been transferred to Virginia. When she had returned on a visit she and Joe had dated and she married him when he asked for her hand. In three months a new house stood next to the Randolph home. During the time it was being constructed they had stayed with Martha. In a matter of days, Mary and Martha became as close as mother and daughter. When the house was completed, Joe and Mary left the family home. These were happy times as they discovered each other, as only two young lovers can do.

On the same day that Martha and Miss Knight had met at school, another meeting took place. "We have to talk," Joe said to his father. "There is ample time. Our work is not pressing. We can go over to my house since Mary is still in Virginia. We can talk in privacy. It's best the two of us be alone."

Joseph spoke as they walked toward the house, "I hope this is important. Once the tobacco season starts, I don't wanna use up any time with something that ain't important. On little things we can wait. I hope you understand."

"It's very important," Joe said. "I think you can clear the air and make me feel better. I haven't cared much for the way things have gone lately but I have remained silent."

"Then suppose we hear what's on your mind. If you are talking about our meetings, I thought everything was settled except a few details. You ain't having family problems are you? Mary ought not be running off in our busy season. There is sickness in her family?"

"Yes, Father, there is sickness and no, we are not having any trouble. It might be called a Randolph problem. I have not understood this change-up. Maybe you can help me understand. I want you to hear me out. We are usually together on most things. Perhaps if I understand, I will feel better."

"I'm listening, Son. I've learned to listen a little better in recent years."

Joe asked, "How do you justify an equal stock division between the six of us? Think about this from where I sit. Stephen is a baby yet and April a girl. Michael John is limited in what he can do. David doesn't like tobacco and Charles doesn't like farming. Yet we have been treated the same. Without bragging, I probably have contributed more than all the others put together. Fair? I just don't understand."

Joseph was about to speak but Joe held up his hand and said, "Please let me finish. David is a good boy but who does he think he is, saying all those awful things about raising tobacco? You heard him say tobacco was sinful. If that be the case, I guess we are up to our asses in sin! This is the very thing that has allowed you to do all you have for him, for the others. It wasn't a few cows and a patch of peanuts that got us where we are. He accepts all the blessings, then calls it a weed and tries to make all of us feel guilty as hell.

"Charles talks about vacations. You can't take vacations and farm. He has been on a vacation all his life!

"April talks about life in the quarters! These people are not going to change. They always follow the same pattern. On Friday and Saturday nights they go out and get drunk. They throw all their money away. They end up in jail. You go to town and get them out on Sunday or Monday. They aren't worth a damn to anyone before Tuesday at best. Change? Never!

"And there was talk about making the place pretty and invite some people. I see no connection between farming and people using our time with their visits."

Joseph could tell Joe was feeling better, since he had left little doubt about his feelings. "Can tell you been thinking," he told Joe. "Glad to see you say what you think. This is the best way and it makes you feel better. Many of the things you have said are true. But there is a time to talk and a time to be quiet. It was good for everyone to say what they thought. Made 'em feel better, too. If more had been said, however, we could have had a split in the family and we don't want that.

"Now let me speak directly on what you said. Your ma made it clear about the stocks. But forget that. Your rewards will be coming as vice-president. I've got some other goodies for you. You will end up much better than the others.

"As to the tobacco, we'll grow it as long as we make a profit. David will have enough to do in other matters. He ain't gonna say no more.

"Now about our quarters people. You understand them. I understand them. As I've said before, you work 'em as long as you can and as hard as you can for as little as you can. That's business. If his pay is enough to make him self-sufficient, you done lost that bugger forever. But some changes are coming. Can't send the Sheriff after them no more. Government is going to get more into this. It's the popular thing, the political thing to do. Then we have these holier-than-thou groups getting involved. Got too much time on their damn hands. And now comes the churches and they will get all carried away. Gotta watch that church crowd. Put it all together and it ain't good. So what do we do? First, we'll jump up and do a couple of things to indicate our concern. You understand what I'm saying? You do, don't you?"

Joseph waited but Joe said nothing. He continued, "I know you can't take vacations in the tobacco season but it might just be nice to get away and see some things. Course ain't no way we both can be gone at the same time.

"To pretty up here some wouldn't be too bad. Our women like it and it is good to please them now and then. We got extra labor at times. We can put them buggers on welfare and get a little bonus. Wouldn't cost as much as you might think to pretty up some.

"I've got reasons, Son. I've always got reasons. They just ain't come out yet. The world is changing. We can't stand still. Joe, we have become somebody for the first time! Hear me, boy, hear me! Your great grandfather was a dirt farmer. They considered him nothing. Some called him 'poor white trash.' Wasn't educated and didn't own much. Then your grandfather made some advancement. He made a little more money, bought a little land and moved up. He married into a little land as well. And now here we are. We have made some money, bought some more land and worked our asses off, and now we are there. For the first time we are somebody. Never again can they look down on us because now we are on their level or above 'em. But I want to move up more. I will. I've got plans I ain't told nobody yet but you will all know soon!

"Now since we have interrupted our day, I think there is something I want to talk with you about. To tell the truth, everything would have been different if you had done as you oughta done."

"Father, I have no idea what you are talking about," Joe said.

"Some time ago you walked in and told us all, 'This is my wife, Mary!' I must admit I was one unhappy man, one unhappy father."

Joe interrupted, his face turning red. "And you got me to the side later and asked me where I got that whore! You had no right to say that. It wasn't true then. It isn't true now. I have always been disappointed. And in all this time you have never said you were sorry. I had hoped and expected you to admit your error."

Joseph said, "It ain't that important what she is or she ain't. The thing that is important is that you married the wrong woman!

"During all the time you were in high school I watched as a courtship got going between you and Alice Dixon. I would have bet anything that a marriage was in the making and I would have been one proud daddy. She was a pretty girl; maybe not beautiful, but right pretty. She had a hell of a figure, a great body. Was no trouble to tell that. She seemed smart enough. Oh, I've seen smarter, but smart enough. A wife doesn't have to be all that smart in the first place.

"The real important thing is, she was an only child. The parents were old when she got here and that wasn't all bad either. When she was seventeen her parents wanted to retire and travel some. They wanted some farmer, some son-in-law, to look after their daughter and take over. I thought that someone would be you.

"How much land did they own? You don't know, do you? I'll tell you! It was twelve thousand acres, twelve thousand beautiful acres! And what kind of land was it? The best. The very best. May well be the best land in the whole damn county. I got good land and some of his would have fertilized mine.

"Timber! Had between five and six thousand acres in virgin pine. Ain't the first saw or axe ever touched 'em. Ain't no way you coulda put a price tag on it! Besides that he had two thousand acres of pine ready to thin.

"One more thing, Son. Money! Yes, money! Just how much, I could only guess. They made money every year. He was a good farmer and he never had a bad crop! Why, they were up to their asses in money!

"And what did you do? You had the keys to the kingdom in your very hands and you threw them away. Alice was crazy about you. Her parents liked you. The whole bunch thought you hung the moon. And what did you do? You threw the best damn deal away that anyone coulda ever had, a deal that occurs once in five lifetimes. You pissed it all away! She was yours for the asking. Hell, you didn't even have to ask. It was a sure thing.

"Just think, Joe. Between the two of us, nearly thirty thousand acres. And to go with it, enough cash to buy another that size. You blew it, my boy, you pissed it all away. There ain't no way in hell you can explain it!

"Together we could have removed all the stigma from the past that hung over us. Such money and property shortens the memory. Never a back seat to a single soul. They say not to cry over spilled milk. For this I could've filled an ocean." Joseph said nothing more for a time.

Now Joe thought, so much is clear. He knew for the first time that in his father's eyes Mary was no more of a whore than if it had been Ida or Helen or Julia or Nadine. Anyone who had married his son would have been a whore except Alice. For a second he thought about which direction he should go. Should he stay or leave? What would happen in either case? He needed to buy some time to think.

"Let me tell you a little about Alice Dixon," Joe said. "This may shed some light. I've never discussed this before. I had believed it would not be necessary. I trust it will remain our secret.

"The first time we went out together we made love. She couldn't wait to get her dress up and her panties down. She could not know at this time that she loved me. Hell, she didn't even know me. I suspect no one will ever be found that loved sex more. But she, from the beginning, was a receiver. Yes, she was always a receiver, never a giver. I would think this is detailed enough. I guess for a while it was fun. There were never any denials and no surprises. Yes, I guess it was too good to turn down, but not exciting enough to make a lasting impression. It never improved.

"Then I was to learn that she was sleeping with two others; not just one, but two! It was obvious from the beginning that she would never be faithful to anyone. No, not to me, not to anyone. The more she got, the more she wanted." Joe thought there was a correlation between her sex and Joseph's desire for land but he dared not speak of such things. "But the only thing that counted, the only thing that really mattered, was that I didn't love her. That alone was all the reason I needed."

Joseph said, "I think you messed around too long. Girls don't wait forever when they get in heat. She saw you were not serious. I doubt if she would have looked at another if you had approached it the right way. Surely a Randolph should be able to keep one home!

"Now let me tell you about women. They were brought in the world to bring pleasure to men. Go read your Bible. It says so in the very first book. Goes all the way back to Eve dropping the fig leaves.

"Ain't you considered that many men, many married men, find pleasure away from home? This ain't unusual. May not be all bad either. Some women seem more bound to duty than pleasure. Find all kinds.

"If I had been you, I'd have closed my eyes and saw all that land and money. And you pissed it all away!"

Joe wondered if his father had been unfaithful to his mother, even though he didn't seem to be the kind of person who would do that. His thoughts, however, returned to the present. "Father, suppose we forget Alice as well as some other things. That's a part of the past. As Uncle Edd says, 'What is, is.' I think it is time for us to move on. If I erred, so be it. You said you had some new goals. I felt some principles and values were involved. It seems a man must have some standards and I believe I do."

Joseph, with impatience and disgust, looked at Joe and said, "As you grow older you gonna find such things as standards and values and honor a burden that can only get in your way. Only women and children let such tommy-rot fill their minds."

He continued, "I know our Good Book says that the meek is gonna inherit the earth but down here it ain't gonna happen. Ain't happened before now and I ain't seen no way it's gonna happen later. None of us ain't able to say what's gonna happen after death.

"To be poor and independent at the same time ain't possible. Some group said seek mediocrity, but this ain't gonna work either. Go below that thin line and they see you as a damn idiot. Get above the line and they believe you ain't done right.

"But it is well we talked. Ain't nothing like clearing the air. Now let's get back out there and make the best tobacco crop we ever had and we can leave our little talk between the two of us."

CHAPTER 7

"Thank goodness it is about over," David said. "In one way, it seems that going to school is all I have ever done. The old folks speak of these days as the best of our lives but this doesn't seem so. Perhaps we must grow old before we can know."

"Have you decided?" April asked.

"Decided what?"

"You know what I am talking about. Will you go to college? You are capable."

"Would all of you be greatly disappointed if I didn't? Sometimes it seems it is more pleasing to the parents than the individual. I'm sure they believe I would be better prepared for living."

"Does that mean you are not going?" April asked.

"This is where my heart is. This is where I belong. Oh, I suppose I could be a better farmer, perhaps, by going to college but I'd rather stay here."

"Later, if you discover differently, you can only blame yourself. You know this?" April asked.

"Yes. Maybe I should think about it some more."

They got up and started walking in the direction of the quarters. They heard a mourning dove in the distance. David said, "A year or so ago you hunted with some of our people here and killed a lot of doves. I didn't see you do that this last winter."

"No, I do not plan to hunt again. Life seems important. I'll leave that to others. It is especially disappointing to see one get under a tree rather than shooting at them on the wing. But I will not kill again."

As they walked along April spoke to each by name. He asked, "Do you know the names of all the people who live down here?"

"I think so. I think it means something to them to hear that one cares enough to learn and remember their names.

"I think I must leave, April. We have a meeting for tonight and I have to get home and clean up for supper. I think I have had all of this I can deal with for one day."

April asked, "Don't you have time to go see old Uncle Edgar a moment? He has been crippled most of his life. He never gets to leave the backyard behind the old shack where he lives with his daughter.

"Forgive me, April. I am so depressed that I feel I cannot stay another minute. Let me wait until I am stronger and surer. I'll return."

"I'll go by and see Uncle Edd a minute at the store. I wonder if something is wrong with them. They usually go to church on Sunday and I usually see them leave about the time we leave," April said.

"I'll see you at the meeting," David said as he turned toward their home. April moved in the direction of their little store that was run by Edd Winter. Everyone called him Uncle Edd.

Just who was Uncle Edd? April had asked but no one seemed to know. He had been here as long as she could remember. He was a Negro but had most of the characteristics of one of the white race. His skin was white. His language could compare with that of a college graduate. He could be anywhere from forty-five to sixty years old.

He had brought two people with him whom he identified as his grandchildren. The oldest, a young man, was attending college. The girl was the same age as April and was enrolled in the local black school. If anyone knew more of their history, they had not let it be known.

"Looks as if your customers are few," April said as she entered the door.

"Only a few were in. Tomorrow is pay day. Most have spent their money and used up their line of credit. They will all be here in the morning."

April looked at Meggie and asked, "Will you be as glad as I will be when school is out?"

The young girl, April's age, was as shy as she was beautiful. "I believe so. I will be happy to be out of school but I will miss my sessions with you and Gena and Charles."

"I have only a minute, Uncle Edd," April said. "Actually I was concerned because I haven't seen you and Meggie going to church for the last several Sundays." She saw Uncle Edd smile and Meggie blush a deep crimson.

"No, I believe we have missed the last three Sundays," Uncle Edd said.

"You've been naughty," April said, "and they have turned you out!" April noticed that Meggie's face became even darker as April and Uncle Edd smiled.

"You said that for a joke but that is exactly what has happened. I have been suspended," Uncle Edd said. "We had an unusual experience occur about a month ago." He continued to smile and Meggie moved over toward the two barred windows and looked out.

"I didn't know churches did this anymore. I believe it was a common practice a hundred years ago but this is new to me. Wish to tell me what happened?" April asked.

"I wish you wouldn't, Grandfather," Meggie said. "It isn't very nice." She had continued to look out the window as she spoke. She then turned and left the store.

April asked, "Will they withdraw your suspension?"

"Oh yes. Have no fear. I will be permitted to return for three reasons. First, I was right. Secondly, our old piano player has returned and thirdly, they will review the books and they will not punish themselves by removing a regular contributor. Money has a way of bouncing up in the most unusual places."

"Uncle Edd, I've never heard you say much about your religious beliefs. How strongly do you feel about such matters?"

Uncle Edd laughed. "I haven't completely decided yet. Sometimes I feel rather sure and then again I read some material in the Bible, especially the Old Testament, and I find some doubts. I really don't know if I believe in hell or not. I haven't decided. But if one is wise, he may wish to hedge his bets!"

After dinner the Randolph family assembled for the third time in the same room, yet this time something seemed different. There seemed to be a spirit of merriment. The inner turmoil, so poorly disguised at the first two meetings, was not present. Joseph had an infectious smile on his face.

"Let me bring you up to date," Joseph said. "Have signed a contract with the lumber people. Clay deal gonna be closed in three weeks. I took the deal to keep the land. Deeds signed on the water property and the money is in the bank.

"I want you, before the last week in August, to come up with some plans and figures. Ain't gonna have much meaning without figures.

"Your ma and April can do the beauty part. Me and Joe will work on the tobacco. Stephen can help us. Charles needs some figures on some office equipment. Government gonna make us make some more changes.

"David can work on row crops and the cattle. I want Michael John to have a plan for a new shop and equipment. April can work with her ma and Charles. Guess she should take a look at the quarters as well.

"Now I think I have a pay scale worked out. I'll leave it for you to study. If you ain't happy, we'll straighten it out in August.

“I want your ma to supervise April on her financial affairs and I’ll look after Stephen. Got to learn about money.

“Anyone wanna say anything?” Joseph asked.

April asked, “How will the six hundred acres be left after the clay is removed? Could it be left in some way so we can use the land? Pines? Fish ponds?”

“Great idea, April. Glad to see you use that pretty little head of yours. I’ll call Slick Cannington in the morning.

He smiled as he added, “I want the family to know there are other surprises on the way.”

After the group left Charles said to April, “Most democratic meeting on record. He never asked an opinion. We never voted on the first thing. Nothing has changed. I told you it would be the same!”

“Telephone, Charles,” his mother shouted. “You’re wanted on the telephone. It’s a lady, as I expected!”

Chapter 8

"Yes, this is Charles Randolph. May I ask who is calling?"

"Charles, this is Sara Knight. I hope I didn't catch you at a bad time. Perhaps you are studying?"

"No. There was a family meeting earlier. We have finished. Sometimes some of us chat following a meeting but this is not the case tonight. Please don't tell me April has jumped track again! I had guessed she was getting better."

"April is right on track as you say. She hasn't excited the class unduly in several days. I'm not sure it is all good, however, because most of us need a little excitement in our lives."

"Well, for God's sake, don't tell my mother that. To say that she stays uneasy is an understatement."

"I really called to ask you if you feel it is too late to come over to my apartment. I don't think it would take more than an hour or so. We need to talk. I am sure it is short notice and it's a little later than we sometimes get together. If you have work to do, please tell me."

"No problem, Miss Knight. I'm on my way."

"I am Sara Knight. We have reviewed this more than once. I insist on Sara. After all, I'm not much your senior!"

Sara Knight had rented an apartment from Mrs. Lacy, who had for many years boarded single teachers, as well as an individual who worked at the Clay Company. As Mrs. Lacy had grown older, and after women teachers were no longer required to remain single in order to teach, she had changed her house into two very nice apartments. Currently, one was occupied by Miss Knight and the other was vacant.

Charles knocked at her door at the side entrance and heard a voice say, "Please come in."

Charles thought this a bit unusual since she usually kept her door locked, opening it only after adequate identification. Her voice sounded somewhat different and he wondered if she was well.

As he entered the unlocked door and closed it behind him he saw Sara sitting on the sofa, where she usually sat when they worked and planned programs for April. On the coffee table before her were several Manila folders and two legal pads with some writing on them. Everything seemed exactly the same as usual, other than the unlocked door. Then he looked more closely and noted that she was dressed, so it seemed, in a housecoat. "I see you have had your bath already,"

Charles said. "I'm afraid you are ahead of me. I didn't even take time to shower." He laughed. "But after all, I haven't been plowing in the fields all day."

"I feel your mother has discussed April with you since the two of us talked." Charles was not sure if it was a question or a statement. She patted the sofa, indicating she wished him to sit by her.

"Mother was upset. Actually she was more than upset. Shattered would be a better description. We talked at great length. Not only was Mother greatly alarmed about April's language, but also it later dawned on her that others outside of class would know. With this realization, she was in a state of shock. As she said, 'It's all over the town, the county.'"

Sara laughed. "Oh yes, something like this is too good to keep. I'm sure it has made the rounds. But in the world in which we live today, this has become more commonplace. It doesn't excite others as it once did."

"I want to thank you once again, Miss — that is, Sara. I can never repay you for all you have done. You have worked so hard to help April and you have handled this delicate situation in a special way. I think Mother realizes this even more after thinking about it. I wish there was some way that I could repay you. When I mentioned this earlier you seemed to feel insulted. There must be something I can do for you." He looked intently into her beautiful face.

Sara smiled at him and said, "Politicians sometimes refer to a term, 'calling in my chips.' Perhaps it is time for me to do just that."

Charles looked inquiringly into her face. Her expression seemed different. There was a half smile. "I'm not sure I understand."

"Are you truly prepared to reward me for my hours and my best efforts?"

"Indeed I am. Thank goodness you have come to your senses after so long!"

Sara turned and looked away from Charles in a deliberate manner and asked, "What do you really think of me? We have known each other for months. We have worked closely together for many hours, many weeks. We have dined out a few times and gone to the movies on occasion but I can never recall you expressing yourself personally about me. What do you think of me? How do you feel about me?"

Charles was quick to respond. "I thought you knew. I think you are the most special lady I have ever known. You are a great teacher. You likely will be the best ever. You are so talented. I have never seen anyone so unselfish and interested in people, especially our youth. I know of no one I respect more." He looked at Sara to determine if she wished him to continue, because he knew of many other fine qualities. A look into her eyes did not provide a clue.

"I can go on and on. It would take hours for me to tell you all the good things. I have always enjoyed your company." Suddenly, Charles stopped and looked again into her face, her beautiful eyes. "Have I offended you in some way? Tell me I haven't! This would be the last thing I would wish to do."

"How do you see me as a woman? A woman likes to be thought of in those terms. I am not talking about citizenship or teaching skills. Never once have you told me that I was pretty or cute or desirable. Never once have you acted to show a personal interest in me. You have never kissed me or held me close or touched me in a manner that would suggest anything."

Charles blushed deeply, which was most unusual, and shifted his tall frame slightly in her direction. "You are a very beautiful lady." He surveyed her from head to toe in a very slow and deliberate manner. "Your figure is that of a Greek goddess and I suspect everything I have seen, and not seen, is real. But you must see this from my vantage point. I could never risk offending you. You are too meaningful, too precious. I could not take this risk. I have been tempted as often as I have seen you. I have longed for you more than you can ever know. But for me to take an initiative and offend you I could never do. I feel too strongly about you. I could not bear the loss. I do not know how to express it more clearly."

"Would you like to have a different type of relationship with me? A different kind of association, as you described it? If you should say yes, nothing would please me more. I know I have been much too bold, too forward, and most men, I am told, do not like aggressive women. I have waited until now because I, too, have not wished to offend. I do not wish to destroy our relationship, our feelings or our mutual respect. I don't think I can say anything more." She looked longingly into his eyes.

Charles said, "Sara, are we saying what I think we are saying? You know I want you. I've wanted you since the first time I saw you!"

Sara got up from the sofa and Charles did the same. Sara chuckled and smiled. "With the reputation you have as a lady's man, you may find me a major disappointment." She took a small step forward; he took her in his arms and sought her lips. They kissed long and passionately. Suddenly, she stepped back and Charles' expression was one of misunderstanding. He reached for her again but again she stepped back. She then untied the sash about her waist and opened her housecoat for him to see. This was all she wore. She stood naked in open shamelessness. Then she closed it quickly when he took a step in her direction.

"Wait, Charles, I have some things to say, some things I must say, and this is the time. Any relationship we may have will not obligate either of us. One may withdraw at any time without giving a reason, unless we wish. At this time I cannot evaluate your feelings. I am even unsure about my own. At this moment, you may withdraw if you have no interest in me. Time is not on your side. I wish an immediate decision. If you feel you must leave, do it now. Do it this very minute. Perhaps we could remain friends. We would have to see.

"I don't think we should talk anymore. I want you to go to the door and leave or I want you to go into the bedroom and take off what you have on. Everything! When you have done this, I will come to you."

When she had waited more than ample time she moved to the door and saw he was naked. She loosened her housecoat and let it drop to the floor where she stood. Each held out open arms and they pressed against each other. Again they kissed long and passionately. Once again Sara moved a step backward and said, "Oh, how I have waited for this moment. I have dreamed this dream night after night. Now I want to find out what kind of man you are." Again they joined together, kissed and touching, and they knew it would be a wonderful experience.

An hour later, as they clung to each other, Sara asked, "Are you sorry you came tonight? Are you sorry you did not leave when you had an option? Have I destroyed all the good things you thought about me?"

Charles said, "Let's not talk now. I have no words to describe my feelings. I feel so strongly. I think what each has given has told more than any words we could find at the moment."

Sara said, "If I live to be a hundred, this is the night to be remembered above all others. I hope I have pleased you half as much as you have pleased me."

"You must tell me, Sara, how I can repay you. This is the way it all started this evening. I think a life with you would be all I could ever want or wish."

"This is not the time for words, Charles; time may tell us something. It can be a friend or foe. One can never know for sure. Yet I believe we have time for one more curtain call. I want you to touch me again in all the right places and I want you to begin this very moment." She trembled.

As Charles dressed to leave a short time later he heard her say, "It could take several nights to determine if your reputation is true and valid, but at the moment, I don't believe you are overrated."

Charles turned his head toward her as he moved through the door to leave. "I suspect we will have to plan more often a way to keep April on track!"

CHAPTER 9

The small auditorium that seated three hundred and eighteen people had been filled long before the appointed hour on this third Thursday of May. Chairs were set up in the aisles and rear to accommodate the people who had come to see their children or their friends' children make their final appearance at the graduation exercises.

This was the night that seventeen seniors were to receive their diplomas. This was a night when many of the differences were forgotten as the saints sat next to the sinners, the wealthy merchant and tobacco farmer sat next to those on welfare and the Methodists and Baptists forgot, for an hour, their beliefs relating to baptism. Sprinkling or immersion seemed less important. All would be drenched in perspiration before the exercise was concluded in an auditorium without air conditioning. The temperature had registered ninety at five o'clock.

Within one hour and five minutes the Commencement Exercises had been completed. All parts of the program had been prepared and delivered by the students with three exceptions: A guest speaker, selected by the graduating seniors, spoke for fifteen minutes; the president of the Kiwanis Club gave awards to the honor students; Mr. Baggs, the principal, delivered the diplomas. All other parts of the program including the invocation, the introductions, the class history, a prayer, announcements and the benediction were delivered by the graduates.

When it was over, hundreds milled around in the halls. Some moved outside the building, telling each other how well a son or daughter had performed and comparing the occasion with theirs or their children's graduation in years gone by. As one said, "Nothing has changed except the faces."

The Randolphs tried to get Susan Lee to come home with them but she declined. She had quietly eased a gift into David's hands and left with the comment, "Old folks need to get home before dark and it is past that hour. Thank you for your invitation but tonight should belong only to the immediate family."

As soon as David and his family returned home they gathered in the den and discussed the evening. David was told how well he had delivered his prayer and how they were impressed with the contents.

After a while David spoke. "I hope you will not be too disappointed in me, but I have carefully reviewed the options and I do not wish to go to college. I want to stay here and farm. Farming is my life and I will have the added benefit of being with each of you.

"I owe so very much to all of you. You have provided me with the tools of life. You have helped me to see and know the difference between right and wrong. You have taught me the dignity of labor and the unlimited rewards that result from it. You have encouraged me when I was discouraged. You have endured my faults and weaknesses and helped me to correct some of them. You have never failed to love me when our opinions and beliefs differed. I could go on and on. Let's just say these are some of the many reasons I would like to remain home and farm. I know of few professions more honorable."

Only two persons would ever know that April had written the words David had just spoken.

"Now I will ask you to excuse me. I want some time to review yesterday, look at today and plan for tomorrow. It will be the first day of a new life. Again, I hope you will accept my decision. Good night to all of you."

When David had left the room, Charles said, "He has grown up. I wish I could be more like him. He is so good. I did not realize he could speak so clearly and eloquently. As much as I respect formal education, I believe he has made the right decision."

The last days of June passed swiftly. No one could remember a better season for the farmers. The gentle rains came intermittently, providing the moisture needed. The rapidly growing tobacco plants grew to lofty heights. The leaves on the tall stalks looked as large as elephant ears and the texture was nearly perfect. The workers filled one barn after another with the giant green leaves that would turn to a golden yellow in the days and weeks to come.

David was busy with his duties. The peanuts were plowed and sprayed. The hay was cut to feed the hungry herds in the winter. All seemed so right with the world.

Charles left early five days a week for F.S.U. He was accompanied by Sara Knight as she began her program to secure a six-year certificate. "I am not sure I am going to school to get an education or to be with you," she said. Charles insisted both reasons were valid.

There were community activities but the Randolphs did not involve themselves. A softball team was founded to compete in a newly formed league. Joseph Randolph supplied the uniforms. He had suggested the donor remain anonymous but it was discovered immediately and Joseph expressed no disappointment. The local Kiwanis Club had started a swimming pool and again Joseph contributed a tidy sum, with no attempt to keep it a secret. Life remained basically the same.

Prompted by time's passage, Charles reminded Martha, "Some months ago, Mother, you may remember that I suggested we do something appropriate for Miss Knight. Everyone has been so busy, we haven't talked about it," Charles said.

His mother said, "I must confess that it slipped my mind. But with the tobacco in the barns and in the packing house, we can do it soon." She studied her calendar, then turned to Charles, "Would the second Friday night in August be a good time? The two of you will have finished summer school. What do you think?"

"That would be a good time."

"What guests should we invite? Perhaps Mary and Joe?"

"I think it would be nice to have Mary and Joe. I was thinking about another. Why not invite Gena? April would be most pleased. Sara was Gena's teacher also and I would think Sandra and Jack would be most delighted to have their daughter included," Charles said.

"You will see Miss Knight and Gena?"

"I think," Charles said, "that you should invite them."

"You mentioned a gift earlier. Do you have something in mind? You are in her apartment from time to time."

"I know of something. I'll see to that. But would it not be appropriate for Gena to have some small gift?"

"Yes, indeed. I'll see to Gena and pay for it. She is saving her money for college."

"No. You can't buy her a gift. This would not be good. She would not let you. She has a great deal of pride. Suppose you give her a bonus of say, one hundred dollars, for the extra work she has done this summer. She couldn't refuse and in this way everyone can live with themselves."

The second Friday night arrived. Martha had planned a special meal of everyone's favorite foods. As the eleven gathered at the table Joseph blessed the food in his usual manner. He seemed in a very good mood and most guessed the outstanding tobacco crop had something to do with it.

Joseph was the first to express to Miss Knight his appreciation for the good year. Others joined in with praise and admiration. There could be no doubt that each spoke from the heart.

One look at Miss Knight told how pleased she was. "This is my first time to be with the whole family and with Gena. I would suspect that if all the Randolph children were like April, there would never be a dull moment."

The faces of Martha and April turned a bit darker, but then they realized that Miss Knight had no intention of elaborating.

Martha said, "Susan Lee has brought us something special for dessert. She makes the best pecan pie ever. I'll be back in a moment."

In less than a minute Martha reappeared and with her were Sandra and Meggie. "Hold on to your forks." In moments a more than modest piece of pie had been served to each.

After Sandra and Meggie had returned to the kitchen Miss Knight asked, "Who was the young girl with Mrs. Jenkins? Have I seen her before?"

Martha said, "She is Meggie Winter. She lives here."

"I suppose she has just moved in? I have never seen her in school. She is not old enough to have finished. I would guess she is about the age of April and Gena. You say she lives here?"

Charles saw that his mother seemed to be at a loss to respond, so he explained. "She is the granddaughter of Edd Winter. We call him Uncle Edd. He runs the little store here and is our lotman. And yes, she is the same age as Gena and April. You see, she goes to — to the other school here."

For several seconds no one spoke, then Charles continued, "Uncle Edd has two grandchildren who live with him. His oldest, a grandson, is in Harvard on a full scholarship. He has a superb mind and is a very fine person. Meggie is also a very fine young lady. She is a beautiful girl and also has a fine mind. I work with her, too, as I do with Gena and April."

"No one has better help than I do," Martha said. "Between Mrs. Jenkins and Gena, April and Meggie, I have an easy time."

One could see that Miss Knight felt she had mentioned something that was none of her affair. Gena, noting this, said, "I have a small gift for Miss Knight for all the many contributions she made last term. I'm sure nothing can repay you but, nevertheless, I wish to give this as a token of my feelings for you." She smiled and handed Miss Knight a small package. "Please open it."

Miss Knight took the package and shook it slightly. "You had no business doing such a thing. I want you to save your money for college."

"Without you and Charles and some other special people, there would be no college," Gena said.

After removing the wrapping paper Miss Knight produced a beautiful purse, obviously expensive. "Thank you, Gena. I am at a loss for words." No one had seen this emotional side of Sara Knight.

"Look inside the coin purse," Gena said.

Miss Knight produced a coin, then read the words found on it. "Two cents. I have never seen such a coin before."

"Suppose you let it represent what you wish. For me it is as special and unique as I find you."

"Gena, again I cannot think of words that could express my feelings at this time. May all your days be happy ones."

Martha spoke. "Miss Knight, the Randolph family appreciates you equally so. We often fail to really say the things we feel. Our family has asked that a small gift be sent to your apartment. Flowers are delicate and we did not wish them damaged. I am sorry we do not have a gift to present at this moment. We will always remember your many extra hours, your patience and certainly your wisdom in dealing with April. All of us thank you."

Miss Knight said, "Your dinner has been delightful. Being with all of you has been special. You are a wonderful family. You support your school and the school staff in such a special way. I am not going to say that I wish you had not invited me because I am delighted you did. I'm sure the flowers will be beautiful."

Joseph said, "Suppose we go to the den for a while." He let them into the spacious room that had been rearranged so that it now looked like one room rather than two.

After about fifteen minutes Charles said, "Our mother consented earlier to let Miss Knight tell our two girls about the program for next year and how it will differ from this year."

Martha said, "We reluctantly excuse you. It will be helpful to the girls. The men tell me they have one barn left in which the tobacco is being cured. We'll excuse them as well. Miss Knight, I'll see you a moment, before you leave."

As the four were about the enter the library Miss Knight said, "Since you work with the young lady I believe you called Meggie, would you object if she was asked to join us? I would like to know her better."

In moments Charles returned with this beautiful and shy young lady. She seemed to feel uncertain as to her presence or the role she was expected to play.

"Meggie, meet Miss Knight. She was the teacher who taught Gena and April this last school year."

Meggie extended her white and well shaped hand as if she was not sure what was expected of her.

"I am so glad you would join us, Meggie. Perhaps there is something here for everyone. I believe the same textbooks are used throughout the system." She had taken Meggie's hand firmly and placed her other hand over the two to give an added expression of pleasure.

Sara watched Meggie as the discussion continued. She was constantly alert, never missing a word. Then Sara Knight said, "Meggie, we haven't given you an opportunity to say a word. We are not very thoughtful. What can you tell us?"

"I have been so absorbed in what you and Charles have said. I would prefer the two of you continue, or perhaps April or Gena has a question or wishes to make some observations.

She then added, "I was just thinking how nice it would be if I had teachers like you to guide my thinking. To say more would be negative and there would be nothing to gain.

"I suspect there are many differences between our schools and perhaps the only thing in common would be the use of the same textbooks. But let us not dwell on this. As long as I have Charles, April, and Gena, I will survive. I consider myself very fortunate."

Thirty minutes later Sara expressed her thanks once again to Martha Randolph. As she was returning home she said to Charles, "I have never been more surprised, pleased or impressed with anyone than with Meggie. This girl is not a Negro. Charles, you must investigate this matter. It is not fair for Meggie to be the only white person among some three hundred and fifty blacks."

Charles said, "Uncle Edd has said that he is three-fourths white. I can only guess after that. But it seems that one drop of blood, regardless of all other things, would proclaim one a black, a Negro."

"You must do something," Sara insisted. "Promise me that you will do what must be done."

"What can I do?" Charles asked. "If they wanted me to know more, they would have told me. This is a private affair. I cannot interfere in the lives of others without being asked."

Sara handed the key to her apartment door to Charles. He turned the key, reached in and turned on the switch for the overhead light, then waited for Sara to enter.

"You must come in and see the flowers," Sara said. "I will insist that you convey my appreciation to your mother and April, to all of your family."

Suddenly Sara exclaimed, "I don't know if I like this or not." First she saw the beautiful roses, then she saw that a large, beautiful television had been placed where her old, small television had stood. She saw a card attached to the flowers. She withdrew it and read, "We love you!"

She turned back to Charles with a beautiful smile on her face and said, "It will require an hour for you to study the flowers so you may be well versed when you describe these lovely gifts."

CHAPTER 10

The family members assembled for the long delayed meeting on the last Thursday in August. As April looked into their faces, she could not remember seeing everyone in such a pleasant mood.

She saw the relief on the faces of Joseph and Joe. They had escaped the dangers of storm, hail and fire. Now all of the precious leaves were in the packing house, to be graded. Charles looked a bit tired. He had elected to go to summer school at F.S.U. and was excited that his academic expectations had been rewarded. Once David had made the decision not to go to college, he had flung himself into the row crop and cattle operation. No one could remember him being so happy. The long days seemed to add to his pleasure. Michael John was looking forward to his senior year. It would be his responsibility to get his sister and brother to school in his first automobile. Stephen had grown in stature but April saw little evidence of such growth in mental and emotional maturity. More than once he had expressed a fear to family members that Miss Knight would make demands upon him because of April's performance the previous year. Martha could not conceal her weary and fatigued look. The long days that usually started at four and ended at ten or eleven, some sixteen hours later, had left their mark.

"I call this meeting to order," Joseph said. "We are all here and I can tell you are in a good mood. I will want — "

Martha unexpectedly interrupted. "Excuse my interruption, but I would ask our family to pause one minute in silent prayer to give thanks to our God. We have been blessed in so many ways. We have had no serious illness, no accidents of significance and no deaths on Randolph Place. It appears we have had a bountiful harvest. Let us pause for one minute to express our thanks in our own way." A minute later they heard, "Amen."

Joseph said, "I want us to get ourselves a set of officers. I'm listening."

David offered, "I would make this suggestion: Our father, president; our mother, first vice-president; Joe, second vice-president; and Charles as secretary and treasurer."

Almost immediately Martha said, "I will not be an officer."

Before her echo had died Charles said, "I do not wish to be considered. As a part-time person and as one who will surely leave in time, I must insist my name be withdrawn. If David will withdraw his motion, I will suggest a slate." David nodded. "I offer a slate of our father as president, Joe as vice-president and David as our secretary-treasurer." In moments the motion was seconded and carried.

Joseph stated, "As I told you earlier, I wanted a report from all of you with some figures." He nodded for Joe to begin.

"Our best season ever," Joe said. "Quality good and weight about three hundred pounds per acre higher than usual. All adds up to a two and one-half million year. If our expenses are about the same as usual, our profits should be half that much. These figures verify that tobacco is our mainstay, our money crop." He glanced around furtively, to see if a negative reaction might surface. He saw nothing. "I would recommend three hundred acres again next year."

Joseph nodded to Charles, who responded, "I am waiting on some firm prices on two pieces of equipment that will be necessary to get and keep the records the government will require. The new equipment isn't cheap. A completed office to serve our needs appropriately will likely require ten thousand dollars. I suppose this would be tax deductible and thus give some relief."

David said, "Our nation seems to have been designated as the country to feed the world. Therefore, I suggest that we double our production in peanuts, corn, cattle and pasture. Land will not be a problem.

He went on, "We will net two or three hundred thousand this year, I would guess. I do not have the exact figures for our labor. Someday, in the next decade or so, Georgia and Florida will challenge Texas and Oklahoma in cattle production. It requires only an acre to graze a cow here. Twenty to forty acres are needed in parts of Texas. I believe my recommendations are realistic as well as safe. After all, as our father has said, there is no purpose in giving it all to the government in taxes."

"Tell us your plans, Michael John," his father said.

"I've had help from my teacher and the County Agent, as you suggested. I have a drawing and some figures on materials. I also have figures on needed equipment. It will cost about twenty-five thousand for the labor and materials for the building and another fifteen for equipment. But, after hearing Joe and David talk about future plans, we may need to enlarge. I based it on what we are doing now.

"We need to replace an old tractor that is worn out. We need an additional tractor. I can't give you a figure because I don't know the size tractors we need."

Joseph looked toward April. One could read his face and see his fears. April would discuss the quarters and he knew that all of her life she had said what she thought.

April looked about her. She saw the apprehension in Joseph's eyes. Joe also seemed to show an expression of uncertainty. "I am not ready to give a report on the quarters. Where does one start? It involves so much. They have so little. So at this time I suggest any effort for improvement be directed in the area of water and sanitation.

"Someday before long I will speak on this matter. When I do, there will be those who will not understand. But for now it is best to wait. If and when something is done, it will not be inexpensive."

"Stephen has worked with me and Joe," Joseph said, "so let's call on your mother at this time."

Martha gave a big, unusual smile. "Hold on to your hats, folks. As someone said, 'You ain't heard nothing yet.' I am about to suggest we spend some of this money that has been reported." Everyone looked at her. This was the last thing they would have expected her to say.

"I want us to start at the entrance to Randolph Place. We should have a sign for identification purposes. It should not be too large or too conspicuous, but one of quality and character.

"Along this road, nearly a mile in length, we would have boxwood, azaleas, spirea and crepe myrtles. The blending of colors will be a big factor. Then, behind these we will wish white dogwoods. Immediately behind these will come the peach and pear trees, for both beauty and fruit. And last, back of these will come the pecan trees. We must leave ample space for growth and maturity.

"I have selected the peach, pear and pecan trees for a purpose that I haven't mentioned. The peaches and pears will provide food. The pecan trees, in time, will produce an additional source of income and will be harvested at a time when much of the laboring force is idle. This should please your father," she added. Joseph smiled.

She continued, "Now I offer one last suggestion. We have been a family to stay at home more than most. This may not be all good or all bad. But since we are a home loving family I want us to add some facilities that will be meaningful to everyone. Joe likes golf. Perhaps a three hole golf course and a putting green. Then we should update our tennis court and place a basketball goal on one end. The swimming facilities should be updated for the blacks as well as ourselves.

"Cost? I have no idea. For the first time in my life I want to say, I don't really care about costs. Let's just do it!"

Joseph smiled more than anyone had anticipated. "Money ain't gonna stay with us long, based on what I've just heard. But you know, that's all right. We're family!

"Ain't no one complained about our pay schedule so we'll keep what we've got, 'less I hear something.

"I got one other thing to say. Over the years I've always felt we should do nothing to give a clue as to where we were or how we stood. We ain't needed big houses, big cars or a lot of fine clothes. These are usually tell-tale signs for rich people or fools. I had felt we should remain as we have; causes less attention. The poor feel more at ease around the poor, and if you look poor, the wealthy don't see a threat to themselves.

"But the time has come that people will see more of us and maybe they should. I don't know how they'll react. And when I tell you and others of my future plans, our business will no longer be a secret. Ain't gonna tell you all now but I'll tell you soon, maybe sooner than you all expected.

He closed the meeting. "We'll adjourn now."

Later Charles said to April, "Never have I seen our father so thrilled about spending money, unless he was buying land. There is more here, much more, than meets the eye. He is laying the groundwork for something down the road. None of this is without reason. It will become clearer, and soon."

The early days of September gave promise of an early autumn. The temperature and humidity had dropped noticeably. The leaves had lost some of their intense green color and a touch of brown and red had appeared.

Everyone seemed more relaxed. Joy seemed to be with all of them, except Stephen. In less than two weeks of school Martha had received a request from Miss Knight that a conference was needed, relating to her youngest son. Miss Knight had emphasized that if her husband could find some time, he should participate in the meeting.

"You go, Martha," Joseph had said. "You know my educational background. I would only be in the way. Besides, I am awfully busy in the packing house."

Thus, when Martha met with Sara, Joseph did not accompany her. She explained, "Joseph seems to think this the business of mothers and teachers."

Sara said, "I believe Stephen first suspected I would expect a performance much like April's but I believe he knows now that this is not so. Family members differ greatly. Yet I must tell you, I am uncertain as to what and how. He seems to have schooled himself against studying. His ideas of success are so strange and foreign that I suspect he is oblivious to reality. I must seek your help for some clue to open the door."

In less than a week, Stephen could not be found one morning at the time Michael John left to take them to school. Soon after Michael John departed Stephen walked into the room. "Guess I got left this morning. I'll go out and find Joe and help him."

"You will go to your room," his mother said. "You will find your books. I will check on you."

After their noon meal Martha sent Stephen back to his room. After he departed Martha said to her husband, "You have always said that people should do what they were supposed to do and get it right the first time; then good things would happen. I need your help with our son."

Joseph did not respond immediately. He seemed to hesitate, as if he was unsure. "Martha, ain't you a little hard on him? He's only a child. This is the only time in his life he will be truly happy. Let him be a real boy. I never had any such days and now feel I might have been cheated out of something. Ain't it right to give him a chance at happiness? He will grow up. Ain't this gonna be the only age he will be free of pain and suffering and all the evil things about us?" He did not smile as he picked up his hat and left, without waiting to see if Martha more to say.

All afternoon Martha found herself despondent and melancholy. A gloom seemed to settle over her. She had never been more sure that a major mistake had happened. She did not wish to think, in time to come, what might occur and she knew at this moment that she would regret this day and her silence.

Chapter 11

"Can you believe it was two years ago that we sat here in the gazebo and wondered what Joseph would tell us? How do you feel about what has occurred or, perhaps, what hasn't?" April asked.

"There are more changes than I expected. Things are better than I anticipated. I must say you were much more optimistic than yours truly," Charles said.

"What has pleased you the most?" April asked.

Charles laughed. "Leaving."

"Other than that?" April asked.

"Available income. It permits all of us a certain freedom.

"I think Mother is happier, more relaxed and confident. She is doing some things that she has enjoyed. If we get this open door policy working, it will be another blessing. She likes people. Long periods of isolation are not in our mother's best interest.

"Michael John is happier than most anyone. He will soon finish the shop and will have some much needed equipment."

"And Stephen?"

"April, I don't wish to discuss him. I see some things I don't like, nor do I understand."

"Where are you with Miss Knight? I understand she is returning for another year. Perhaps two and two add up to four? Single women teachers usually move on without some good prospects. Perhaps you are a good nominee."

"I do not know. There are times when I am optimistic that something may happen. Then, nothing seems to happen. How has your year been?"

"Great. Another thing, I don't excite my classmates as I once did."

"That's good news for Mother. Do you know how you managed to change?"

"I started to think before I started to speak. I recommend it for everyone!"

"Best thing I've ever done. The very best deal I've ever made. Been waiting for this for years and now it's like a dream come true."

April listened to see what Joseph was so excited about as she entered the room. "What is it, Joseph?" April asked.

"Just bought my three thousand acres. I suppose that will be my last purchase. I had hoped to buy it a little cheaper but I ain't gonna let the little difference get in the way. Somebody would have snatched it up right before my very eyes."

"Is this the tract you have looked at and talked about for years?" April asked.

"The very tract I've had my eyes on for years! Great land! Great timber! And Slick Cannington said there ain't no telling how much relief we'll get when it comes tax time. Don't wanna give the government all you make."

April changed the subject. "What do you know about the family of Robert White?"

"Good people. Fine family. They are honest and work hard. Rather poor, I suppose, but nevertheless, good folks. I guess Clint has been here over twenty years. His wife is dead. Got three children. Last two are twin girls. But you know that, since you are in school with them. Old settlers would say it would take more than three more generations to be one of them. Guess I'll ask why you are asking all these questions."

"Just curious. Robert and I have been classmates for a long time. He seems to be a nice young man. He will become a good athlete. He is big and strong. He does good work in school. We're right together as to grades."

"Yep. A good boy he is, and Clint is an honest man, but I doubt they will ever really amount to much. All he knows how to do is run a service station. A living of that sort is all he can ever expect.

"I'll check on my tobacco plants before supper." He picked up his hat and walked through the door. "Three thousand acres! I just knew I'd get it someday."

April moved to her room and closed the door. Tears filled her eyes. She went over and got a tissue. She asked herself, "Has he been like this always? Was it there and I refused to see it? Perhaps he has changed and a new Joseph has emerged. Where will it all lead?"

"Charles, I hope you and April will get us to Susan's house in one piece. Do you think we are safe?" Martha asked.

"She is fine," Charles said. "It takes some time to get the feel of a vehicle. She needs some practice so she can get her permanent license in April."

Susan opened the door as they approached the steps to the small porch. "Come in this second. It's chilly outside. I have some cake and coffee ready and my boys are dying to see all of you. Oh, they are not as handsome as Charles, but to an old lady with tired eyes, they look pretty special. I see them so seldom."

Jerome and Eric received a perfunctory kiss from Martha. The expression on their faces showed their pleasure in seeing the Randolphs again. Charles moved forward to shake hands with the boys and plant a kiss on Susan's cheek.

As April approached she said, "I don't know if I am expected to kiss you men or shake your hands. I think a kiss would bring more pleasure but maybe a handshake is more in order for the present." As she shook their hands she noticed a slight blush on Eric's face but Jerome's expression did not offer a clue of any sort. He continued to look into her face and into her eyes for several seconds.

Abruptly Jerome took both her hands, withdrew a half step and looked her over from head to toe. "And you are Mrs. Randolph's baby! I don't believe it!"

"That's me, Jerome," April said, smiling openly, her dark eyes flashing. "I am reminded of the story of the salesman who stopped at a farmhouse that provided bed and breakfast. He was told that they did not have another vacant room. They did not wish, however, to turn him away. 'You may sleep with the baby or in the barn,' he was told. He chose the barn. The next morning, as the salesman moved from the barn to the house to get breakfast, he saw a beautiful young girl approaching. The salesman asked, 'Who are you?' She responded, 'I'm the baby.' She asked, 'Who are you?' He responded, 'I am the fool who slept in the barn last night.'"

Eric blushed as Jerome and Charles exchanged sidelong glances and smiled. Jerome responded, "I'll not make such a mistake again and you are much too wise for your years!" Their eyes met for a second and a slight smile formed on their faces. Then Jerome chuckled, shook his head and said no more.

When they were seated and had been served April regarded Susan's two sons. Jerome looked a little thinner than she remembered and looked very tired, almost weary. Only his eyes and his hair looked the same. Those large brown eyes told her a little, but much remained a mystery. His skin seemed a little darker. He had looked rather short standing next to Charles, yet most people did when compared to his six-foot-two frame. She guessed Jerome at about five-ten.

April saw Jerome looking directly at her again as he said, "My mother could not do you justice with her description of you. You are a beautiful young lady."

Eric interjected, "Jerome seems to be staking his claim but I am not ready to concede. I must confess he has an eye like an eagle."

April looked at Eric. He was an inch or so taller than Jerome, his hair was much lighter and his blue eyes expressed openness and sincerity. She looked more closely at his eyes; they seemed to be filled with fun and laughter. Both men were handsome, but entirely different. She suspected Jerome to be more the serious type and Eric the more fun loving.

Susan said to everyone, "It is a joy to have my two sons with me again. And it is so good to know that soon they will finish their preparations. I wish Lawrence could have seen them. He would have been so proud."

April asked, "Jerome, where will you practice and will you specialize in a particular field of law? Certainly you know more than my useless brother here, since he doesn't know what he wants to do, nor where or when he wants to do it." She smiled at Charles.

"I plan to take the bar examination immediately following my graduation. I understand some good minds have taken the test a second and third time before passing it. As it now appears, I will come back to Decatur County and set up a practice or join some group. There is not a large firm in this area."

"Perhaps there is more money elsewhere," April said. "I would guess so."

"My priorities may not be the same as many of the others. There are some things that I would prefer not doing," Jerome said.

"And you, Eric?" April asked.

"My goal is simple. I have always wanted to teach. I may be interested in something nearby, as I would like to be near my family, and I would wish to be near a major university so I could continue my education on a graduate level."

"Will you bring a nice Indian maiden home with you when you return?" April smiled and her eyes sparkled.

"Not likely. Someday I will want a wife and family but that is far into the future. You will soon be sixteen. Perhaps I should wait on you?"

"My, my! This is my lucky day. Why hasn't Mrs. Lee brought her boys home earlier?"

"I'll use you as bait, April, to bring them back home!" Susan said as she smiled.

Charles asked Eric, "Do you like Oklahoma? Is it described realistically in the play and movie by the same name?"

"Perhaps to some degree. Certainly the wind comes sweeping over the plains most of the year. I haven't seen too many places where the corn is as high as the elephant's eye. Actually, I believe the weather and climate is much better here in south Georgia.

"The people are extremely friendly and yes, many wear cowboy boots. They say they are quite comfortable but I can't say through experience. It is the people who make Oklahoma what it is but I suppose that is true of any place, good or bad."

"And where is this college located?" Charles asked.

Before Eric could respond April asked, "Didn't you hear the name? Southeastern! Now where would Southeastern be but in the southeast? My, my, no wonder you don't know what you want to do!"

Eric smiled and responded, "In Durant, Oklahoma, and as April says, it's in the southeastern part of the state. Actually, we are only a few miles from the Texas border. We are about a hundred miles due north of Dallas. Durant is located near the Red River and a dam has formed a lake nearby that is called Texoma."

Martha asked, "Beautiful Indian maidens running around everywhere?"

"Not exactly. We have some in school but they don't all look like those you see in the movies. Years ago the Presbyterian Church had a school there, so I am told. The school closed and the students were sent to Southeastern. I understand they use some of the old facilities to house them."

Jerome said, "You have given your place a name — Randolph Place." This was part question, part statement.

"We have incorporated," Martha said. "I don't suppose it has changed very much, other than being given a new name. But it is beginning to look a little different since April and I have been selected as a committee of two to give it a new look. Please visit us."

Jerome said, "April, why not tell us how it is to live with five brothers. You have, no doubt, learned a great deal about men."

"It isn't easy being a lady!" April said and her black eyes flashed and sparkled. "You hear a lot of jokes and stories. But you see, I have the best of both worlds. Mother lets me escape the house work and the boys will not let me drive the tractor. It doesn't seem to matter that

I am more proficient than my tractor driving brothers. As mother said, come to see us, as I have ample time to entertain you."

"We have to go, folks," Martha said. "Hopefully we can all see each other again before the men leave. I can't call them boys anymore. Thank you for the refreshments and making our visit so delightful."

At dinner that evening Joseph said, "I want to ask you how you would feel about something." Everyone looked at him, but no one spoke; they waited for him to continue. Martha did not seem to know what he was about to say either.

"I want the Randolph family to give a new organ to our church. I wanta dedicate it in memory of my parents, as well as Martha's."

For a full minute, so it seemed, no one spoke. Then Martha said, "I am afraid you caught all of us by surprise. Oh, Joseph, that is such a wonderful gesture and it could not be more timely. The church needs have been known for some time. How nice and generous you are! I would be so pleased."

"It just seems the thing to do," Joseph said, pleased at Martha's response. "There is a need and we have been blessed in so many ways. I hope no one will think this is done because it is a tax deduction."

"Only one of evil and selfish thoughts could think in such a manner," Martha said. "Our entire church will get the benefits of such a generous gift."

"Have Mike Harper or someone get this in the works. I don't think we need to wait."

It was good that no one could read Charles' thoughts. He was reminded of the old saying that there is no springboard to philanthropy like a bad conscience or a new conquest! He wondered if it was the former, latter or both.

"Now I have another special surprise," Joseph said. "I know I ain't supposed to talk business at meal time but this should be told.

"You remember about that piece of property I spoke of over the years that I've had my eyes on. Well, it finally happened. It was put on the market. Seems some were interested in parts but the owner wanted to sell the whole thing and be done with it. As you know, it borders my — that is — our land. I had some checking done on the quiet side. It is all I believed and more. Had thought he would take two seventy-five but he wouldn't move off three hundred. So I traded with him. By doing this, we can avoid any taxes this year. Oh, God, how I hate to pay taxes!

"I've looked it over and over. As the man said, 'I love it like a bitch dog loves her runt puppy!' It's the best deal I've ever made, except for the water property in Florida.

"And our whole family deserves it. We have more than worked for it. We've done what the Bible says in that man was made for work and that is the way to grow and accumulate. The Randolphs are about to get there. Yes, sir, we are going to be somebody.

"But this doesn't mean we can let up. Ain't nothing less permanent than permanent prosperity! So we all got to buckle down for a few more years and give it all we got. Then the day will come when it will all be different. No longer will nobody look at us except in a right and proper manner.

"This is America, where a dream can come true. And it has. I've proved it. But the time ain't quite yet upon us. Three more years is all we need. Then we will have reached the Promised Land that Moses was not to see. But we'll see it. Just three more years.

"I guess I shouldn't think of it but years ago these old settlers, these old bluebloods, looked down their noses at me and others like me. I know how they spoke of my grandparents and my parents. Oh yes, I remember. But this only made me more determined. I knew that someday we would out-distance them all, if we just worked hard enough. No longer will they look at our old clothes and the houses we live in."

Martha said, "I'm not sure we should worry about not coming from the old blueblood families. In many cases these people came from those who cheated, robbed and took advantage of the uneducated. If they obtained their heritage in this manner, who would wish to be like them?"

Joseph broke into a big laugh that continued for several seconds. Everyone wondered what he was laughing about. "People today," he said, "hate you if you ain't got money. Now it seems that many hate you if you do. And if you have money and pretend you ain't got none, they hate you worse. It seems that people put you down either way."

Martha interrupted. "I am not sure how people feel. How can you know this is how people feel about us and others?"

"By the way they act," Joseph said. "They ain't gonna let you get your foot in the door on things they have been running for generations."

"I would hope," Martha said, "that we are becoming a nation of people who will be judged by a different criteria, perhaps character, honesty, kindness and generosity, such as the organ for the church. Those are some of the things by which we should be judged."

"I hope so, my dear Martha, but don't bank on it. You had better have some money. You can speak of love and kindness and honesty and all them good things and I ain't got nothing against them. But money and land are the fortress against all the rainy days and sudden storms and bad luck. Love is desirable but it's money that keeps the wheels turning."

Upon seeing her mother's face, April knew they needed to move to another subject. "I nearly forgot, Joseph. I wanted to chat with you about something I discovered. I have learned that there is a fifty-acre tract of land that borders your place, that is, Randolph Place. I . . ."

"Don't tell your father that, April. We just bought three thousand acres a few minutes ago." Martha laughed.

Joseph abruptly glanced at Martha, as though trying to interpret any hidden meaning in her remark.

April said, "Oh, I wasn't talking about Joseph buying it. I was speaking of myself. One of true Randolph blood can always sniff out a piece of land. How could I be the daughter of Joseph Randolph and not want an acre or two for my own?

"I have walked over the land on numerous occasions. It is exactly what I want. It can be bought for a hundred dollars an acre. It is not farm land or pasture land. If so, it would be more expensive. On the other hand, I expect its timber would nearly pay for it, but I wouldn't wish to cut a tree."

"Can't be much at a hundred an acre," Joseph said.

"How do you know about this?" Martha asked April.

"It is owned by the parents of one of my classmates. She told me. I have enough money. I know I can't do it legally until I'm sixteen, unless I have permission, but if I don't buy it, someone else will."

"I know the land," Joseph said. "Water flows through it. It has an old mill site. You know, I think April oughta be a land owner. As she says, it's in the blood of the Randolphs and she's a chip off the old block. Yes, I'm for it. I'll get the legal work done."

April smiled. She could not believe her good fortune.

Charles looked at his mother, then at the other family members. He wondered if anyone remembered that Joseph had given Martha the responsibility and authority to govern all monetary decisions until April reached sixteen. Charles was convinced more than ever that his father had not changed. Nor would he.

CHAPTER 12

April sat in their small library with a book in front of her but her thoughts were elsewhere. She heard the door open and her mother stuck her head into the room.

"Sorry, I did not know you were here."

"Come on in," April said. "I have reached a point where I cannot seem to concentrate. It is good you are here. I have been concerned about you in recent weeks."

"Oh, I'm fine, April, but I am concerned about you. Is there something wrong? You stay much too busy. I think the time has come that will necessitate you making some decisions. You never have a free minute. You apparently inherited some of your father's characteristics. The two of you are not patient. Do it right. Do it now. Don't stop until you have finished and on and on. Patience has many rewards. There will be many times in life it will serve you well."

"I lost in the American Legion Oratorical Contest. I should have done something differently," April said.

"Charles told me you did an outstanding job. You were the only sophomore competing against juniors and seniors. The girl that placed first had participated last year. You have two more years."

April spoke as if she had not heard her mother. "Our basketball team could have performed better."

Martha responded, "All people do not compete the same way. When you play as a team you will find those who, for whatever reasons, do not always give their best. It's a game with them. I believe it goes beyond that for you. Yes, I'm sure it goes a lot deeper. You may influence others but you don't control them. This is the way people are and have always been. I suggest you give your best, keep your head high and let that be it. If you really think about it, you can learn or gain more by losing than winning. I don't need to give you the reasons. You already know."

A few nights later Joseph dropped his *Atlanta Constitution* on the floor beside his chair, then looked at April, who asked, "Can I buy a car soon? I'm nearly sixteen. I'm ready to get a permanent license. Mother and Charles have been helpful."

"What kind of car?" Joseph asked.

"Nothing new or expensive. I do want one that is reliable and safe. A car, as far as I am concerned, gets you from point A to point B. I want a vehicle to serve me, not the reverse. I don't have time to pamper an automobile. As I look about, I believe half the people driving are confused as to who is the slave and who is the master."

"Your mother feels you are ready?" Joseph asked.

Martha was brief. "She is ready. I feel more secure when she drives than when I drive."

"Let me look around," Joseph said.

April said, "There is something else. I have not heard about the status of my fifty acres. It should be put in my name."

"As you wish," Joseph said. "You sure ain't timid about some things." He smiled. It was obvious that he liked what he saw in April. She had never made an effort for him to pay for the land or the car.

A week later April saw a "like new" 1956 Chevy in front of the house. "I had it checked by Clint White. He thinks it is as good as new.

Joseph added, "I also have your deed. It is in the library. Write me a check for both. As you said, your car, your land, and your money. You know, April, you gotta be a little cold-blooded in business. You could have got the land a little cheaper."

April said, "The land is worth the price. Actually the timber would pay for the it."

She added, "I prefer a philosophy of live and let live. That family will have some difficult times very soon. The mother has cancer. She will not live. It will be long and drawn out. They will need every cent and more, as well as the prayers of all of us. I have done the right thing."

CHAPTER 13

Surprises and changes were becoming a way of life for the Randolphs. Less than a week after April had become a land and car owner another surprise was revealed.

"I'm going to get married this summer," David said as the family gathered on Friday evening. "A date has not been set, but likely between June and August. For some, twenty years old may seem a bit too young but I'm ready. The important thing is, I've found the perfect girl." No one said anything and waited for him to continue.

"I'm going to marry Kathleen Lane. Everyone calls her Kathy. She has accepted my proposal and has agreed to marry me as soon as she finishes high school this year.

"You will love her. She is near perfect. She is pretty, nearly beautiful. She is kind and thoughtful and unselfish. She is smart. She will be an honor graduate.

"We have a lot in common. She is a farm girl and thus understands life on a farm. She doesn't talk a great deal but sometimes she talks more than I do. She is an outdoors girl and she has more energy than anyone." It was obvious to everyone that David loved her deeply.

"She is a good girl and maybe that is the most important thing about her. She is active in her church and sings in the choir. I know all of you will learn to love her nearly as much as I do."

"Congratulations!" April said. "The cat doesn't have your tongue when it comes to Kathy. She seems so very special." They smiled at each other.

"I'm happy for you," his mother said. "It's about time we started getting some more girls on this place."

Joseph asked, "Lane? I ain't sure I know the family. You said a farm girl. Is her father a farmer? I thought I knew all the farmers in the county. If he is from Decatur County, he ain't no big or important farmer. I suppose he is from a neighboring county."

David looked at his father, unable to camouflage his emotion. "Yes, they are a farm family. I don't recall saying they were big farmers. They live in the southern part of the Smithville area, about twenty or so miles from here."

"Lanes? Lanes? I should know them but I don't. They must be new to the area. I suppose they bought some farm recently."

"No. They have farmed here for years. Some of their family farmed their land before them as I recall."

"They own their land? I don't suppose they rent or share-crop? But maybe they do."

"Oh, I believe they own their farm. A half section someone said. Let's see, a section is six hundred and forty acres. They must own between three and four hundred acres. Mr. Lane does most of the work except in the harvest season. It seems that some five farmers pool their resources at that time."

"When did you say you planned to marry?" Joseph asked.

"We had thought about June but we can't get our house ready by that time. Let's just say sometime this summer."

David turned toward his mother. "Do you suppose we could have her here for lunch some Sunday? I think she would enjoy coming to our church. She would feel comfortable, since some of her classmates are in the church. Though she seems timid and shy until she knows you, she isn't as much that way as first appears."

"How would a week from Sunday do?" Martha asked. "This would give everyone time to make arrangements. It would be a delight to have her in our church as well as our home."

"Thank you, Mother. Thank you. I'll tell her immediately."

"Does she have brothers or sisters?" April asked. "Perhaps some older. If they were younger, I would know them in school."

"Kathy had a brother that died suddenly as a small child. She has no living brothers or sisters."

Michael John smiled at David and asked, "Have you forgot something?"

"You are talking about a house plan! It is nearly completed. It will be ready by Sunday week. I want us to look at the house sites at that time. I'm sure Father can tell us which lot we can have."

"Do you plan a church wedding?" Charles asked.

"No. We want our families to come to the parsonage of her minister. I hope no one is disappointed. This is what she wants and I am equally satisfied."

Ten days later Kathleen Lane entered the Randolph home for the first time. She was a small person, several inches shorter than David, who was two or so inches less than six feet. She had a slender body. She had a voice that was clear, but not loud. She wore a big smile and her eyes were large and blue, direct and clear. There was an openness that suggested kindness and gentleness. Her hair was blond and seemed to shine as she tossed her head or when the wind ruffled it. Her skin and complexion were clear in spite of the time she spent outdoors.

Though small, she had an excellent bone structure that was much more durable than the delicate impression one gathered at first glance. She even looked younger than her eighteen years.

The Randolphs were quick to discover that David and Kathy seemed quite comfortable with each other. One would have guessed they had been closely associated for years. They exchanged sidelong gazes, smiled and held hands, obviously possessing deep feelings for one another.

In thirty minutes Kathy had won the hearts of everyone, with the possible exception of Joseph, who said little and did not reveal his feelings.

After lunch the entire family proceeded to join them as they looked at some lots below the house where Joe and Mary lived. "What do you think?" David whispered in a low voice.

"They are all so beautiful. Perhaps Joe and Mary would consider us as next door neighbors, since I understand that Charles does not plan to build here."

David nodded and smiled. "This would be great. I would be pleased."

Moments later Martha said to Kathy, David and the others, "I have never witnessed a love that is as pure and deep. You have my full blessings; I can see I am to become the most fortunate mother ever."

The following Friday evening the family assembled in their corporation meeting. "I have made all the arrangements to close the deal for my three thousand acres." Joseph's smile was broad and deep. "It is the best business deal I have ever made, other than the land I bought on the water. It will bring our acreage to eighteen thousand and six hundred. Why, the timber alone, if I wished to cut it, would practically pay for the place. But I ain't . . . that is, I am not planning to do that.

"The cost is three hundred dollars an acre, which figures out to nine hundred thousand. I'll pay no less than a third down and borrow the rest from our friend Bruce McPherson at The People's Bank. I'll leave ample funds in the reserve and operating funds."

"Tell us about the land, Father. I don't recall seeing you so excited," Stephen said.

"This is fine land, my boy, fine land! Two thousand acres are in timber that is more than ready to cut. The other thousand is ready for row crops or pastures. We have several options. We can row crop, place in pasture or plant pines under the new government program. There is water available. This land joins mine on the east.

"I've waited for years for this chance and now it's mine. Your old man ain't, that is, hasn't lost it all yet. We have now reached a point that you can stand in our yard and as far as you can see in any direction, you will know you are looking at Randolph land." He looked about him and he could see the many smiles.

Martha spoke. "Your father has something else to tell us, something you could never guess." Then to Joseph she directed, "Tell your children what you wish to do."

Everyone could see that Joseph was filled with excitement. His face glowed in the same manner as when he had described his plan. "You may be looking at the next county commissioner from this district. I am about ready to declare myself a candidate. I know it sounds crazy and it just don't sound like me at all. But I believe it is time to come out of the dark and get involved."

The group looked at Joseph, then at each other. Each seemed to wait for someone else to react. Abruptly Joseph said, "I thought you would be pleased, would be proud."

Charles said, "Father, at the moment it doesn't seem to be a case of being pleased or displeased. It is a surprise. It is perhaps the most unexpected ever. It is the last thing some of us would ever expect to hear you say. You must give us time to let it all sink in.

"This is not to suggest you would not make a good commissioner. On the contrary, your record as a person and as a successful businessman is well known, well established. But for a person who has kept himself and his family isolated, to some degree, for so long, for a person that has deliberately removed himself from any spotlight or attention, it is more than a surprise."

Suddenly, the picture became clearer for Charles: Joseph's effort to improve his speech, his approval for more of an open door policy, his gift to the softball team and the organ given to the church were all part of a well conceived plan now suddenly revealed before their very eyes. Now Charles realized why Joseph had done these things.

"I'm sure I've surprised everyone. I've even surprised myself a little. I had hinted more than once, even years ago, that I had some special plans that would affect all of us. I hope you will approve of my plan, my desire, and give me all the support possible. Actually it is for you and others that I find myself doing this. Someday it will all come together and be clearer. I am a little disappointed in your reactions. If I had known you would not wish this, I would have hesitated."

April's black eyes flashed and a half smile encompassed her face. "I would not wish to remove any wind from the sail. I see you as a great Father, an excellent farmer, a proven businessman, a good leader and the hardest worker ever, but I find it difficult to bring into focus your role as a politician!"

Joseph seemed more than a little hurt. He could not disguise his feelings. "What I had planned to do was really for all of you. This is our final step into the sunshine. This is the time we will learn our role and position in life. I would not look upon myself as a politician, as April mentioned, but as a worker for the people, a public servant. I can help make wise decisions and make sure our money ain't, that is, isn't spent in a foolish manner or stolen. I know how to do this."

A voice sounded from the rear. "Papa, sometimes people get hurt in this business. Everyone may not know you are honest or a good businessman. Folks don't always vote for the one that can do the best job. I wouldn't want to see you hurt," Michael John said.

Joseph seemed to feel that these remarks had a dual meaning. On the one hand it expressed concern and compassion. On the other hand it suggested more than a little doubt.

"How will our present commissioner react? Will he support you," Charles asked, "or perhaps another?"

"I don't think he will get involved openly. I hope, maybe expect, him to help me in a quiet sort of way. It is hard for a good farmer to vote against another good farmer. My greatest concern would be outside our district. You see, the whole county votes on all the commissioners. But I have some friends out of my district and this is a farming county."

April said, "I know so little about politics, about running for an office. I think our father would make a great county commissioner but so few know how fine he really is. As Charles said, he hasn't been in the spotlight. This is the first time in my life that I have this unusual feeling."

"I ain't, that is, I haven't made a final decision yet. That's the reason I'm talking with you all. I'd need to know, have to know, that I had the whole support of all of you, all the way. People ask for votes in this county. They go door to door and make personal contact. They want to look me or my family in the eye. Ain't, that is, isn't, it good I got such a big family?"

"Who else will seek the position?" April asked.

"I don't know. I was just thinking. If I could get enough support quick-like, I might just discourage someone else."

"I think it is time for all of us to say we're behind you all the way," Martha said. "You are a good man and would represent our people in a special way."

Stephen spoke, "You are a winner. We'll help you win. I believe it would be nice to be a son of a commissioner." They all smiled in a sense of relief.

"What other business do we have?" Joseph asked. No one spoke.

"I'll leave you then. I wanna think about this matter a little more before I say for sure." He left abruptly and everyone knew he had already decided.

It was April who spoke first after he left. "Let's get our heads together. I have no doubt as to his decision. Who has an idea as to how we can help?"

"Sis, I don't know about this political business," Michael John said. "Strange things happen. He would not take a whipping lightly!"

"Then let's make sure he doesn't have to," April said. "Who has an idea?"

"We could start by having a big birthday barbecue party for him," Joe said. "We could start the open door policy with a bang!"

"A birthday party for a fifty-three-year-old man?" Charles asked. "That is usually for the very young or the very old!"

"I think Joe is right," April said. "We could invite some two hundred people, feed them some special barbecue and let Joseph announce his intentions at that time. We could plan to use the packing house, since they have finished with the tobacco. Should it rain, we would be safe."

"Women would not feel comfortable," Martha said. "It would not be appropriate for them."

"Why not all men?" David asked. Men love barbecue and usually this type food is too heavy for the girls." He smiled.

"I like that idea," April said. "Someday women will play a more significant role in politics but that day is not here yet."

"I think our father would like this," Joe said. "Suppose we gather, say two nights from now, and work out the details."

Two nights later they gathered once more. They insisted Joseph not be present but he had learned something from Stephen of what was happening.

"Let's start with the basics," Martha said. "Date, hour and menu first."

"His birthday is on Friday. This seems appropriate," April said.

"Give the men a chance to clean up after work," Mary said. "Five-thirty? Let them gather and talk and perhaps eat at six?"

"And our menu?" Martha asked.

"Barbecue, Brunswick stew, baked potato, salad, tea and coffee," David said. "Men like this. Perhaps a dessert would be appropriate. Oh yes, hot rolls."

"These items can be prepared in large quantities." Joe said. "We have people on the place who are good at this very thing."

Martha spoke again. "We have the date, hour and menu. How many do we invite?"

"Three hundred," April said. "Make sure they are all old enough and registered to vote. We can seat that number comfortably."

Joe said, "We can get tables and chairs from the school lunchroom."

"Yes," April said. "We could send a gift to the school. This would be appropriate. They would have to accept it. I also checked on tablecloths and napkins. We can rent according to our needs."

"We can use the silverware from the school also," Michael John said. "Got 'till Monday to return it. Let's not use some flimsy plastic. Men hate that. But I expect we would need plastic cups and glasses and the school does not have such."

Charles said, "Yes, a gift of say five hundred dollars to the P.T.A. or Athletic Association would be appropriate. I understand such things are done and accepted, in a proper spirit, of course." He smiled more than was necessary.

"There are some other minor details," Martha said, "such as serving and parking and seating arrangements but these will not be difficult. However, we have left off the most important and perhaps most dangerous aspect of the entire event. Who shall be invited? More harm can be done, more lost than gained, if we are not careful." They looked at each other and nodded.

"I hadn't thought of such," David said. "It shows I am not politically smart."

"Mother is right," Charles said. "Where do you start and where do you stop? Anyone have an idea?"

There was total silence. Each looked at the other waiting for a suggestion, a solution. The silence continued.

"This can make you or break you, so to speak," Charles said. "As I think about it, I can see where this must be resolved in a most careful manner." More silence.

Suddenly, April seemed to explode. "I've got it! I've got it! It was there all the time and I couldn't see it. It is as simple as ABC." She laughed.

"Well, if you have it, tell us," David said excitedly. "I see no solution whatsoever."

April said smiling, "We are not going to invite anyone. We are going to let a committee do so and we can have an input. We can also make sure the committee is formed of those who know who should be here. If someone is offended later, we can say we are sorry but the committee sent out the invitations. We should be most vague as to who the committee members may be! For example, how could Bruce McPherson refuse to serve on such a committee? He knows where the butter comes from that butters his bread!"

"And our role will be to provide the food, drink and facilities?" Martha asked.

"Exactly." April beamed.

"Let us hope that April stays out of politics," Charles said. "She could be our first woman president.

"Now one other thing. Some kind of brief program will be needed. Our family must be introduced and we would need two or three key people to 'demand' that Joseph place his hat in the ring."

"I've been wanting to clean up the packing house for years," Martha said. "Now I have reason to do so in spite of my men! I'll look into this."

"Before we leave," Charles said, "I bring what I would consider good news and bad news. Of course you want the bad news first. Miss Knight is leaving at the end of this school year."

"Why didn't I know this?" April asked. "We have been close."

"She has just made a final decision and she must communicate with others such as the principal, superintendent and local trustees first."

"I can't believe this," April said. "I thought perhaps we would learn of your intentions to marry her. I think she loves you and you, her!"

"She will make someone a perfect wife. I had hoped it might be me, but she told me over and over we could never be more than the best of friends. When I mentioned a deeper and lasting relationship, she simply closed the door. I suppose her reasons were her own. She said she had stayed twice as long as she had intended."

"But why, Charles? I don't understand. I know beyond any doubt she loves you!"

"I don't know. Perhaps she will discuss the 'why' before she leaves."

"Who will take her place?" Martha asked.

"That is the good news, or I believe it to be. I think Mr. Baggs and others are interested in Eric Lee. His teaching certificate will cover grades seven through twelve. It would be great for him and the school. A good place and level for him to start."

"It would be great for Susan as well," Martha said.

"You will say nothing beyond this room until it all becomes a part of public record," Charles said.

Chapter 14

"You have waited more than two years! You are a big coward! I cannot understand how a person like you could ignore this matter as you have. We must know the truth. The truth sets one free! Have you forgotten?" Sara had not smiled as she spoke.

The next day Charles entered the little store to discover Uncle Edd reading and chuckling. Charles commented, "You must have found something quite entertaining, but after all, you usually do."

"I have indeed. I try to make a habit of it if possible. At my age, you do not delay any pleasures that may come your way."

"Uncle Edd, I want to talk about a delicate matter and I hardly know where to begin. It is a very sensitive matter and you could feel unkind toward me, something I would go to great lengths to avoid. There are few I respect or admire more than you. If I discuss this matter as promised, I may lose a meaningful relationship, one that I treasure very much."

"Charles, there is nothing you could ever say to me that would make me feel differently about you. Next to my two grandchildren, you, your mother and April mean more than all others. Why don't you speak freely?"

"More than two years ago a very close friend and special person told me that she was certain that Meggie was not a Negro, that she had no Negro blood in her. This person seemed very certain. It was a person I respect very much." Charles paused.

"Go on, Charles. I'm listening."

"Two years have passed since this was said. To please this person I promised I would pursue her observation. But as time passed, I became a coward and felt it none of my business." Again Charles paused, waiting to see if Uncle Edd was ready to respond. Again Uncle Edd said nothing and the look in his eyes gave Charles no hint of his thoughts or feelings.

"You are not making this easy for me," Charles said, but there was still no response. "I know little or nothing of your history or the history of Craig or Meggie. You arrived many years ago. My father gave you a job and a house in which to live. You became the lotman and the store keeper. You have said little about your past and I have asked nothing. I felt that had you wanted me to know, you would have told me. I respect your privacy and trust you. I always have, completely. You seem to be one that feels it is well to live the present and look to the future. I . . ."

"Charles, I want to interrupt you and hopefully for good reasons. You obviously feel unsafe, unsure, and I would not wish you to feel uncomfortable. I am going to tell you a little of my past. Remember, I said a little. But I believe it will be enough to deal with your concerns and my concerns.

"Let's start with the bloodline. As you can see, I have some white blood in me. I am one-fourth black and three-fourths white. That makes me as black as the ace of spades." He laughed. "I was married to a white woman and we lived in the North. We had one child, a son. He is seven-eighths white. He looked as if he was pure white. Then he married a white woman. My son and this white woman are the parents of Craig.

"My son had wanted several children and when Craig was two, they attempted to have a second child. After some months, in which they were not successful, my son conferred with a doctor and was told that a child at the moment was impossible but that conditions might reverse themselves in a matter of months or years. He kept his problem a secret, perhaps out of shame, perhaps out of hope.

"When Craig was about five, she became pregnant again. That child was Meggie, my beautiful Meggie. I do not have to describe her. After Meggie arrived he, for some reason, began to have doubts and returned to the doctor. The doctor confirmed that his status had not changed nor would it change. He was still not sure, so he went to a second specialist. Again, the diagnosis was the same. And so he knew. He told me, but no other. For my son, life was over.

"I shall omit much of what occurred later. It would not change anything. Soon I was given legal custody of Craig and Meggie. I worked two jobs for a while to make ends meet. It is not important for anyone to know how I ended up in the South or here at Randolph Place. The fact is that I am here. Craig is at Harvard, thanks to you, and, as you know, Meggie is here.

"I am a selfish old man. For years I have continued to tell myself I would let Meggie go, go to her own people, her own race. You spoke of being a coward moments ago. I was one, even more so. I loved her. I didn't think I could let her go. This feeling became even stronger after Craig left. She was all I had. There are usually two sides to a coin. I hope you understand.

"So the years passed and I remained a selfish old coward, until recently. It is strange that you come at this time because I have been working with an attorney for some months. I have proof, beyond any and all doubts, that her father was white. The courts will rule shortly that she is white, a member of the Caucasian race.

"However, this is only one phase of the matter. I cannot release her, except to your family. A home with the Jenkins family could be considered but I would prefer the Randolphs. There are many delicate matters. Let's start with Meggie. What will this do to her? How will she react?

"I am selfish enough to think about myself. I can let her go if your mother would take her. I would be close so I could still see her and love her. I think she would still love me in spite of my inaction and deceit. I don't think your father would be too happy but I feel that, in the final analysis, he would agree.

"How would your school, the white school, react? *Nigger, nigger?* How would the community react? And of all places, the church? You would really find out about some of our Christians!

"In the Book of Matthew in the Bible it says, 'Suffer little children, and forbid them not, to come unto me, for of such is the kingdom of heaven'. Yet isn't it likely that some of your church people would wish to amend the words of Jesus? I believe many would add, 'As long as they are not black or once believed black'."

Charles responded, "Yes."

"Now put yourself in Meggie's place for a moment. How would she look at me for not acting sooner? Charles, I need some help.

"One more word and I stop. Let me reiterate, I cannot go into the details of the past. This very fact has influenced my previous decisions. Many people would get hurt. The past must remain a secret." Charles could see that Uncle Edd did not intend to continue.

"As you say, Uncle Edd, what is, is. Now we must go from this point. I must ask once more. You can get proof, beyond even the slightest doubt, that she is completely white?"

"Yes. Be assured."

"And you are prepared to have this discussed in every household in Attapulgus, in Decatur County and even in other places?" Charles asked.

Uncle Edd said, "I have no control over this. I am not sure I am prepared, if Meggie becomes a part of your home, to see the Randolphs suffer as they may. No, as they will. People will be unfair. You know this."

"Let me sleep on this, Uncle Edd. I am not ready for what I have learned. Mistakes, as much as possible, must be avoided."

As Charles was about to leave Uncle Edd said, "The sun will come up tomorrow and likely right on schedule. Let us look at the bright side."

Chapter 15

As Victor McPherson walked across the street in his hometown of Midway he looked up at the building and noted the new sign that read, "The People's Bank." He had suggested to his father that the old sign was no longer appropriate. Maybe, just maybe, his old man would learn to think differently in this new age. He had suggested that his father get out and see what the more progressive banking institutions were doing. The new sign, however, was the only indication that he had listened or heard the first word Victor had said. Victor had just returned from Athens where he was a sophomore at the University of Georgia. It would be a short visit since the spring break would last less than a week.

As he entered the bank he was greeted by two of the nearby tellers, as well as the customer loan officer. Most of the personnel he knew, since he had worked in the bank the summer before. It was about that time he had begun to long for a leisure trip to Europe. "Can't learn about banking and local customers while dragging your ass around Europe," his father had said. "If you are going to take over this bank, you must start now."

As he turned the corner where his father's office was located he saw that the sign on the door looked the same as it had a dozen years ago. It read, "Bruce B. McPherson, President." Victor knew that the title below his father's name did not really tell the story. Actually, his father was more than president. He owned sixty percent of the stock and had once owned it all. There had been four businessmen who wanted a piece of the action, so he had sold each of them five percent. They had needed each other. Then, for the bank to live up to its name, he had sold two percent to each of ten men of influence and property. The Board of Directors was composed of seven men, but his father made all the operational decisions.

Victor opened the door to his father's office and was greeted by a smiling Alice Adams, who had been his father's secretary for a number of years. "Why, it's Victor himself." She smiled. "College is agreeing with you. You look better than ever, but how can one improve on perfection?"

"You are still the same beautiful, flattering and delightful lady that always says the very things I love to hear. Tell me, Miss Alice, how have you escaped all the handsome men who would give their very fortunes to have you look at them twice? I expect they would give their souls to go a step or so beyond!" Victor smiled and Alice Adams blushed, as she was expected to do.

"Now you are the one who can make a girl feel good. I'll bet there isn't a girl that is safe with you around. I just hope you meet a girl someday that will take the air out of your sails. I'd like to be present when it happens, and it will. You won't know what hit you!

She added, "Your father is expecting you. He is in the accounting department. I expect he is checking on your balance, if you have one. I'll just bet you are one expensive boy and worth every penny of it."

Victor sat down, then studied his father's secretary, a very attractive woman. She had a fine figure and always made a nice appearance. All of her dresses looked as if they had been tailored. Her voice was soft and pleasing and she had learned to smile on cue. Victor was not sure if it was natural or if she had simply acquired this technique for better business relations.

He looked more closely. No, she could not have reached thirty-five. She had never been married. As far as he knew, she had not dated in the last few years. She lived with her mother in a house only a few blocks from the bank. Everyone that knew her spoke of her devotion to her mother and to her job.

Most called her Miss Alice, which seemed to please her, but Victor sometimes called her Double A. After being told why, she seemed even more pleased. "You're just double everything in every way and in every place I look." Victor had then looked her up and down from head to toe, letting his eyes zero in on her lovely breasts. Alice had blushed slightly but it didn't take a great deal of intelligence to know she had enjoyed every second of his inspection.

Her voice brought him back to the present. "I'll run up and get your father. He will be pleased to learn you are here."

"Oh no. I'll see enough of that harsh taskmaster while I'm here. I'd rather just sit here and look at you. You look so much better than my father ever looked."

Again, Alice blushed and smiled, with many thoughts of which she could not speak. Alice had never been quite sure how to take Bruce McPherson's son. He was a handsome devil and when he looked at her, it brought a sensational feeling for which she had no explanation. She knew, for obvious reasons, he could not say and do all the things she believed he might enjoy. Yet on the other hand, she knew she must play such a game with equal care. There was much at stake and she was no fool.

"You haven't changed," she said. "I can read you like a book." She smiled. "I can't understand why your father can't do the same. If I was twenty, I'd be afraid to get in the car with you. And at my age, I may very well feel the same way!"

"Would that be because you didn't trust me or didn't trust yourself?" Victor asked smiling.

"Both!"

"You're the best, the very best. He couldn't operate a week without you." His eyes moved once more over her body. "And with your looks he should double your salary, to have such a beautiful girl at his fingertips!"

This time Alice blushed deeply. "God help the girl that listens to you. The poor child wouldn't have a chance, not a small chance, a dog's chance, if you please." Alice changed the conversation once more. "When do you return?"

"I'll go back after lunch Sunday. Unfortunately, the roads are not good and it requires patience, a characteristic often absent."

"Your father may have some plans for you and you may wish to confer with him before you proceed too far. But you didn't hear me say that!"

"He will get no work from me. I've got plans, big plans." He switched subjects as well. "Say, Alice, what is in all those files he has in his office? This is somewhat unusual for a bank president."

"Those files are unique. If you want to know about them, I'd rather you ask Bru — that is, Mr. McPherson."

"Don't go upstairs, Alice, but do give Bookkeeping a call and let him know I'm here. I'll go in his office and look around. I've been sitting too much today anyway." He left, entered his father's office and closed the door. He strolled about, noting that the office was no different. The desk was covered with files and applications.

The furniture was also the same; however, the old carpet seemed more worn than he remembered. When he mentioned a replacement his father had responded, "If you look too prosperous, your people will think you are getting wealthy at their expense. Bankers and lawyers are often looked upon with suspicion." When Victor had mentioned the old uncomfortable chairs Bruce had said, "If they get their loan they won't remember. If they get too comfortable, they will want to stay and talk all day!"

Victor looked out the window at the muddy waters of the Flint River, making its way to Lake Seminole where it would join the

Chattahoochee River and form the Apalachicola, to weave its way to the Gulf of Mexico.

Victor opened the bottom drawer of his father's desk and pulled out an old pair of binoculars. He saw a Negro couple fishing at the same spot from which he had fished ten years ago. They had six poles and operated with a philosophy that the more poles, the more chances, and thus, more fish. He wondered if their catch would influence their evening meal.

Victor put the binoculars back, then looked more closely at his father's office. He counted twelve four-drawer legal files against one wall. Why? Alice wouldn't tell. He placed his hand on the handle to investigate but withdrew it, not because of ethics, but because he heard the door open.

"Good to see you." His father shook his hand and pulled him forward in a fatherly embrace.

"Sit down, Son," Bruce said. "You must be worn out from the long trip home. It's a damn shame south Georgia can't get a road. They have so many new circles going around Atlanta you could get drunk on them. And we get nothing. Tell me about yourself. I count the days until you can join me. Have you seen your mother and sister?"

"I'm doing fine in school. I'll make the Dean's list again. The school still has a few parties and I try to keep a proper balance between my social and academic responsibilities. Yes, I've seen Mother and Lesa. Your daughter has grown up and is very pretty. I hope she is using her time wisely."

"Your sister is going to have to make it on her looks and some other qualities. She is not a scholar, nor will she become one. But this is not as important for girls as for men. Women have other attributes.

He added, "Your mother always gets excited when you come home and nearly always seems disappointed when you do not spend much time around the house. I hope you will think about this."

Victor responded, "I can't spend too much time around the house. Bless her heart, but one can get caught up in a hurry. But you know that."

"You do as you think best. You have tonight, Thursday night and Saturday night. I have plans for us Friday afternoon and evening."

"But, Dad, this isn't going to work out. I have some definite plans for Friday evening. I am to be in Tallahassee with some very special people. This was arranged days ago. It's too late to change. I think a special lady would be disappointed."

"Change your plans," Bruce said. There was no smile on his face. "You have Thursday and Saturday. Friday belongs to me."

"This will upset some people. I can't do it," Victor said.

"You have already upset your father. I will hear no more."

"I was to have dinner with someone special," Victor said.

"You are *going* to have dinner with someone special. I promised a dear friend and business acquaintance we would be present at a special event. We are going to Attapulgus, my old hometown, to help celebrate Joseph Randolph's fifty-third birthday. It will be a barbecue dinner. Three hundred guests are expected. Many of them are my customers. I have accepted invitations for the two of us."

"You mean you are dragging me to this old man's birthday party?! What is so special about Joseph Randolph? What is so special about Attapulgus? You don't live there anymore. It's a hick town!"

"Don't call it a hick town, Son. It does have a nickname of Hack but hick and Hack are seven letters apart. As a future leader of The People's Bank, I suggest you never identify any town as a hick town. You still have some growing up to do. It seems our dear old university has not completed its endeavor to educate you."

Bruce walked over to one of the twelve filing cabinets, opened a drawer and pulled out a file. "Sit down. You're fixing to get another lesson in banking. You wanted to know something about this man! I'm going to tell you some things about 'this old man,' as you call him.

"Joseph Randolph is fifty-three. His wife is forty-two. They have six children and eighteen thousand acres of land. He grows three hundred acres of shade tobacco. He just borrowed nearly a million dollars from me. This is no nickel and dime man. He is big business.

"When you are invited and asked to take a part in the program, you go. You don't ask questions, you go. He will announce he is running for a seat on the county commission. He will get elected. It's good to have a good friend and customer on the commission.

"His children range in ages from over twenty-four years to about fourteen. All are boys except one. The girl's name is April. I know her very well.

"On Friday afternoon, shortly after lunch, we will ride to Attapulgus and learn something of the community. You must have knowledge of people. I want you to start now. Attapulgus is where we will start."

Victor asked, "Do you have such a file on all your customers?" He pointed toward the files.

"I have a complete file on all my customers. They are detailed and updated. I also have a file on those I would like to have as customers. I even have a special file on those who cannot and must not become customers. Banking involves a lot, if you are to be successful. Banking involves going to birthday parties for fifty-three-year-old men. You may rest assured we will be there."

"I didn't know all this!" Victor said. "You never told me."

"There was no reason to do so before now. You have had a lot on your mind. All your thoughts have not been on school and banking. I can look at your checking account and tell. Now why don't you go and spend a few moments with your mother. She does not know or understand some of the things we know."

CHAPTER 16

"Suppose I drive," Bruce said to his son. "I want you to have a good look at this very special place. I'll point out some things as we go along."

"Mother doesn't seem to care much for Attapulgus," Victor said. He glanced at his father to see his reaction.

"No. She judges everything in terms of money and show. Attapulgus has never majored in either. It is the people that really make a place. I am not sure she has ever understood this. Suppose we talk about other things." Bruce turned the Buick onto U.S. 27, where a sign read: Attapulgus — 13 miles. Just below it said: Tallahassee — 40 miles.

"Since there is little to see for some miles, suppose we talk about the Randolphs. There are many details I did not mention earlier. Joseph Randolph was a native of Attapulgus, as were his father and grandfather. Mrs. Randolph and her family were not old settlers; they arrived during the Depression. Her parents were later killed in a car accident.

"Joseph quit school before he entered high school. He married Martha Whigham the year she finished high school. As I recall, it was 1936. Soon after they married they started putting together a plantation and family, both of considerable size. There was a report that his wife received a sum of money from her parents' death that added considerably to their holdings, but of this I cannot be certain.

"The family, as it grew, kept much to themselves in what was called the backwoods. They participated in the church and the school and Martha visited the sick. Aside from this, they were seldom seen except when they were in Midway on business. There is no family that works so diligently as this family of successful farmers.

"As I mentioned the other day, there are six children. Joe, their oldest son, works chiefly in tobacco. The second son, Charles, is enrolled at F.S.U.; he keeps the records and makes the payroll for the employees. He has made it no secret that he is not to be a farmer. The third son's interest involves the row crops and cattle operation. Neither are small and they keep getting larger. The next son, Michael John, is a little odd, so they say. He looks somewhat different from the other family members. His interest is in the mechanical part of the operation and they say he has special talent in construction as well.

The youngest is Stephen. He used to come to the bank with his father. He is a handsome and fun loving chap. I understand no one works as hard or long as he does in their operation."

"What about the girl?" Victor asked, smiling. "You seemed to have jumped over her. Is there some reason? I'll bet the five brothers have spoiled her rotten!"

When Bruce laughed heartily for several seconds, Victor became uncertain. Had he said or asked something he shouldn't?

"She is something else," his father said. "Pretty as a damn picture and more. You'll just have to see for yourself because I doubt anyone can describe her adequately. When she was small, Joseph brought her to the bank with him. Some said it was to call attention to her, but some of us thought it was to call attention to himself. She always called him Joseph and this seemed a bit unusual to refer to her father by his given name.

"She was so fresh and pretty! People walking by turned and looked back at her when she had passed. She seemed to leave a scent of sweetness behind her, but some few of us know that is not always so.

"This little girl, who is no longer a little girl, is named April and justifiably so. She is, indeed, like springtime. She smiles and laughs a great deal, but don't sell her short. She never misses the first damn trick. I believe she is about sixteen now and is a beautiful woman — all woman!" Again Bruce burst out into laughter, causing Victor to glance toward him as he continued. "She pulled two stunts on me over a period of a year or so, when she was about five or six, I suppose. I will always remember."

"What do you mean?" Victor asked. "How can a mere tot of five or six do such?"

Bruce said, "Let me give you a scenario. Joseph had brought April in to set up a checking account and a savings account. I knew of many small children whose father had established a savings account, but none that had a checking account. Seemed a bit unusual.

"April asked, 'Do you get interest from a savings account? A checking account?'

"I responded, 'A small sum from savings. One must be a senior citizen to receive interest from a checking account.'

"April asked, 'What rate of interest do you pay?'

"'Three and one-half percent'," I responded.

"April asked, 'Is it compounded quarterly? A hundred dollars at three and one-half percent annually would be three dollars and fifty cents but if it compounded quarterly, it would be greater.'

"I just stood there with my mouth open!"

Victor asked incredulously, "She understood compound interest?"

"Indeed she did," Bruce responded.

"What did you do? What did you say?"

"I told her we would do so just for her. When she finished her transaction and turned to leave, she looked at me once more and asked with a serious expression on her face, 'Are you an M and M Banker?'

"'I don't understand,' I responded.

"She smiled and said, 'It is one without malice or mercy.'

"I asked her, 'Do you know what malice means?'

"April said smilingly, 'Oh you must know that, Mr. McPherson. It means ill will or animosity. But I really don't believe you have such characteristics. It was the mercy I was most concerned about!'"

"This is hard to believe!" Victor said.

"She sure as hell did. I thought about asking her if she understood the word animosity but I thought better of it. I could see Joseph was amazed as well as embarrassed. I suppose she read all this somewhere."

"You mean a five-year-old reading such?" Victor asked.

"She was reading at three and no one ever took credit for teaching her. Strange child, this girl," Bruce said.

"You said a second time. What else did she pull? I'm half afraid to ask."

Again Bruce chuckled. "About six months later I suppose, she came in again with her father. I had arranged an operational loan for Joseph. He had gone to sign some papers and April had remained with me. Suddenly, she got up from her chair and came over to my desk. She moved forward and looked very carefully at my face, looking directly into my eyes. She did this for perhaps some five or ten seconds. She then returned to her chair without smiling, shaking her head sadly. I had no explanation for the unusual behavior, so I asked her if there was something wrong. I even felt to see if my fly was open, although I knew she could not see behind my desk. I looked to see if I had spilled coffee or food on my shirt or tie. I asked, 'April, what's wrong?'

"'Just looking at your eyes,' she said and again shook her head in a remorseful manner. 'Just looking at your eyes,' she repeated.

"In a moment April continued. 'I am reminded of a story of the great Depression. A good man, a very good man, had fallen on hard times. His family was hungry and one of his children was sick. He went to one of the three banks in the community and asked the banker for a two hundred dollar loan. The banker, learning of his lack of collateral, turned him away. This same process was repeated at a second bank. He proceeded to the third and last bank. He insisted it was a life and death matter, but for the third time he was rejected. As the defeated man got up from his chair and thanked the banker he turned and said, 'You have a glass eye, don't you?'

'The banker responded, 'How can you tell? You are the first person to know of my glass eye. It has been a secret over the many years.'

'The banker, acting in frustration, continued. 'I'll loan you the two hundred dollars if you can tell me which is the glass eye!'

'The man responded, 'The left eye. It has to be the left eye. I am certain.'

'The banker said, 'You are correct but how could you know? You must have certainly guessed.'

'Oh no,' the borrower said. 'Today I have looked carefully into the eyes of three bankers and your left eye was the only one that showed any sympathy!'"

"My God, Dad, does she have such a vocabulary? Such a sense of humor? Certainly you have expressed it in your words, not hers!"

"Her very words, Son. Her very words. I remember as if it happened yesterday. Before she left she said, 'It seems that there is nothing that offends a banker more than to find a man both poor and righteous. If he has a conscience, he finds himself in an awful position. I may need to look into your eyes often. I am not sure about your conscience.'"

Victor said, "She must be vicious, with little compassion for others."

"No. I believe not. I understand she is kind and gentle and understanding. She used some unbecoming language a few years ago in the school, which became well known, but I've heard nothing as she has grown older. It seems she is a very smart and near perfect lady."

"I'm anxious to see this April. She must be some girl. And you say she is good looking?"

"She has beauty and a figure to go with it. Old Joseph has one hell of a girl on his hands."

"What else can you tell me about them?" Victor asked.

"They formed a corporation about three years ago. From fuller's earth, timber and some beach property they had on the Gulf of Mexico, they put together a large sum. I believe the total then was about four million. Joseph has over eighteen thousand acres of land. He knows how to make money. Someone once said the talent for making money was unpredictable. Those in the real world of making money know better. Yes, he has a nose for money. I doubt many know of his real wealth. They have kept their business to themselves. They could be compared to an island standing alone.

"They are a strange lot. Such people were called piney-woods people or backwoods people generations ago. Over the years, they have stayed to themselves. They go to church, so I am told, and support it well. I am in a position to know this. They support their school, which is an excellent one. They visit some close neighbors when they are sick and go to funerals. That's it.

"They work from daylight till after dark. They have their Negro families, their quarters people, as they call them. I would suppose they get the quarters people in debt, as is done by other tobacco farmers. Then these people are there for life, in a kind of agricultural serfdom, somewhat similar to the old Southern slave days. I suppose some of the tobacco boys sometimes think of kindness, but it does not serve their purpose. This is a cruel necessity. It has been so for ages and most give little thought to it anymore.

"Joseph has a white foreman named Jenkins. I believe him to be a fine man, as well as his family. He has a lotman that looks nearly white but has some Negro blood in him. They call him Uncle Edd. He's been there a long time. No one knows of his past. He is single and supports two grandchildren. It seems the children are nearly white also. His oldest grandson is in Harvard."

"Harvard as in Boston?" Victor asked.

"Yes. Got a full scholarship. Was something about it in our county paper. Seems he made the highest score ever recorded on the college entrance exam in Georgia.

"Enough about the Randolphs for now. Let's look over my old home town, Attapulgus. The sign back there showed the current population at 714."

CHAPTER 17

"Where did Attapulgus get its name?" Victor asked his father. "I suppose you know this place better than most."

"The town was founded in 1817. The name of Attapulgus comes from an Indian word, Atap'halgi, which means dogwood grove. At first it was named Pleasant Grove but it was changed to Attapulgus when a post office was established in 1838. It seemed that another town in Georgia had already acquired the name of Pleasant Grove and two towns could not share the same and have a post office. In 1839 the Pleasant Grove Academy here became the Attapulgus Academy. Attapulgus also has a nickname, Hack. It dates back to the early Twenties. Some said it was a time when people hacked each other up but I doubt it.

"It may be the most unique little town I've ever known, and it has nothing to do with it being my birthplace. The town really revolves around the churches and the school. Many small towns do. There will be great changes in a few years and it will all disappear as we have known it."

"Why?" Victor asked.

"I'll explain as we look over the community. There is the school. The main building was constructed in 1923; other additions followed. The large wooden building is the gymnasium; we called it 'the shell' because it was never sealed, until recently. Local funds and WPA labor produced this in 1934.

"The school, as we know it now, will disappear in ten years or less. If consolidation doesn't do it, integration will. When the school goes, so will many other valuable areas of community life.

"Over there you see the athletic field. The school played football here in 1941 and 1942. They won the State Championship in their classification the first year. Some say they stopped because the football coach went to war. Others said that football and academics didn't mix. Whatever the reason, that was the beginning as well as the end.

"The other institutions that hold the town together are the churches. Here you see both churches, within a block or so of each other, and the school nearby. For the most part, the Baptists and Methodists dwell in peace. The Presbyterian Church burned and they did not replace it."

They rode in silence for a minute. In the distance a sea of white appeared. Bruce explained, "This is a typical tobacco shade, where they grow cigar wrapper tobacco, quite different from cigarette tobacco. It is expensive to grow and sells for a good price. Strange as it may seem, this is one of the two places in our country where it grows. The other place is in Connecticut. I cannot tell you why."

"How do cigar and cigarette tobacco differ?" Victor asked.

"They're different types of tobacco. The cigar tobacco must be protected from the sun under the shade of the white cheesecloth you see ahead. A great deal of hand labor is required in cigar tobacco. It costs about five times as much to produce it as cigarette tobacco and it brings about five to seven times as much per pound. Suppose I get Joseph to give you a tour this summer. He is the biggest independent grower — perhaps the best."

As they continued Victor noticed some flags flying beyond a fence. "What is that?" he asked. "It appears to be a golf course."

"It is. One of the best nine-hole courses ever. People from all over come to play here. The Clay Company owns it. It was once very exclusive, only for their executives' use, but things have changed. It may be the only club in the country where you come, place your dollar green fee in a box and play. It's on the honor system. Costs twenty-five dollars to join as a member and dues are two dollars monthly. On top of that, they serve you and your family four delightful dinners per year. There is a large, well stocked lake below in which the members can fish as often as they wish.

"The second industry that makes the community so unique is fuller's earth. Of the entire world, only in this area is this special clay found."

"Tell me about it," Victor said.

"If we start at the beginning, we go back to our Bible. It seems that Saint Mark described the garments of Jesus as He stood on the Mount of Transfiguration. It said something like this: 'And He was transfigured before them and His garments became glistening, intensively white, as no fuller on earth could bleach them.' In those times such a craftsman was called a fuller; it was his task to draw the oils from garments made from the skins of animals. I will not go into all the details because it would take hours. However, this fuller's earth clay is used today in some three hundred products. Their best product is Attapulgite; there is a great demand for it.

"The first fuller's earth plant was built in 1918 but it later burned. The Atlantic Refining Company purchased what was left of it and built a large new plant in the Twenties. It is located on the same site today.

"Many changes have occurred since the beginning. At one time the Clay Company, as it was always called, owned some seventy houses for their workers. Then they got out of the housing business, so the remaining houses occupied by whites were owned by individuals. In 1955 a catalyst plant was added. This division now makes the larger part of the profits."

"What kind of products do they make?" Victor asked.

"They make an oil and grease absorbent which is used in the oil industry as a floor cleaner. It's also used as pet litter; as a carrier for insecticides, herbicides and soil fumigants; and in waxes, vitamins and brewery products." Bruce laughed. "I've only begun. They will probably have you eating it next.

"In 1933 the Clay Company contracted with Hall Construction Company to dig and transport the clay to their plant. It was first done by rail, then by truck. They purchased a dragline in 1933 to dig the clay and take overburden off the clay. Took thirty-three rail cars to bring it in. The machine had no wheels or tracks. It sat on feet and could walk. It was run by electricity and a line had to be constructed at the site. That may have originated the name 'dragline.'

He continued. "There is so much history. One would have had to live here to know and understand."

"How many people did the Clay Company employ? How many are employed now?"

Bruce answered, "Perhaps six hundred at one time. Maybe a hundred or so less today, since machines do the work that some laborers did earlier. Oh, I nearly forgot. The Clay Company is the largest taxpayer in the county. Money, my son, money. That seems to be where everything starts or ends, perhaps both!

"As I said earlier, the town, as we older people know it, will disappear. The big lumber industry is gone. Tobacco will go in less than ten years. They no longer have a doctor. The drug store will go next. Oh yes, the picture show burned down.

"Victor, you asked me earlier what made Attapulgus so different from other small towns and I mentioned tobacco and clay. However, the big difference is its people. It is always the people that determine the status of any place. This is an educated community. There are more college graduates here, both men and women, than one would ever guess. Those who are not themselves educated insist on sending their kids to college. It's a way of life. Their percentages, based on school population, are much greater than Midway, and Midway is well above the state's average. A teacher has never been in trouble here for demanding high academic standards. Academics and citizenship come first. Everything else is secondary.

"There are some educators, now, who spend all their time talking about new facilities. I have nothing against this but that doesn't make a school. It is the teachers, the pupils and the parents. And the home life.

"High moral standards are a way of life here. There has been one pregnancy in high school of an unmarried girl in thirteen years. No student or graduate has been charged with a violation of the law beyond speeding or improper parking.

"Occasionally the people here squabble among themselves but it is usually not serious. However, if an outside force creates a problem, they all join together. Then you have a battle on your hands.

"There is no way to name all the doctors and engineers and teachers and ministers and nurses this community has produced. They are short on lawyers but this may not be all bad!"

"Dad, I'm really glad I spent the afternoon with you. I have learned a great deal, not only about your community, but about you. I don't believe I can separate you and your home community. I am lucky to be your son.

"Now why don't you take me to Randolph Place and let me enjoy some good food and get a look at that girl named April. Are you sure she is all you said?"

"Suppose you judge for yourself. Then you can tell me what you think."

CHAPTER 18

About three miles from the center of town Bruce and Victor left the public road and entered the world of Joseph Randolph. On the left was a small sign that read, "Private Road." On the other side was a sign that read, "Randolph Place," and which had a special design. Not unduly large, it possessed distinction and quality.

"The sign is very nice," Victor said.

"Take a look at this road," Bruce said. "It was paved a short time ago."

On each side of the road, as far as one could see, stretched a flower wonderland: a pattern of azaleas in assorted colors, and pink and white spirea, with crepe myrtles blended among them all.

Behind the flowers rose a row of dogwood trees, not yet old enough to bloom. To the rear of these bloomed pear and peach trees, providing a dazzling array of blue, pink and white. Beyond these stood a row of pecan trees, still six or eight years shy of production maturity.

"I find this combination unusual," Victor said. "Very unusual. Is there an explanation?"

"Yes. This represents the Randolphs perfectly. Martha Randolph's love of beauty is apparent, as is Joseph's feeling that one should produce a product one can eat, or sell, or both. Thus you have the combination you see. It is different. I would not attempt to guess the number of plants involved. It must have required a great deal of labor, of which they have a surplus, except in tobacco season."

"Look at the cloth waving softly in the background. I believe you said it was cheesecloth?" Victor asked.

"That's right. They have three hundred acres this year. This is an unheard of number of acres for an independent farmer without a contract. I am not sure he has the personnel needed to cultivate and harvest such an amount. He will likely have to cure out some barns in order to have ample room."

"Cure out?" Victor asked.

"Yes. There are many things to learn. You have been a good student today. This is enough for one time. Let's leave some things for April to show you. I suspect she knows the entire process as well as Joseph or Joe. After all, she can tell if you have any sympathy in your eyes!"

They entered a grove of trees where they saw two houses and the foundation of another being constructed.

"The old rambling house is where Joseph lives," Bruce said. "The one next to it is where his oldest son, Joe, lives. The one under construction is for David. I understand he is getting married this summer."

As they drove to the right they saw a Negro boy pointing to an area where fifty or more cars were already parked. Bruce pulled his Buick alongside another car. The little boy held up his hand to indicate Bruce was in a proper position. The boy then gave a big smile; it looked as if half his face was made up entirely of beautiful white teeth.

As they opened the doors and got out they were approached by another youthful Negro boy, perhaps ten years old. He was dressed in a white shirt and wore a red tie. "Welcome," he said. "My name is Roosevelt." He also gave a big open smile, when he closed the door of their car. "Mr. Joseph said to ask you to come on over and join them in front of the packing house. He said it was fitting for one to get refreshed on a hot spring day like this." They followed the boy toward the building up ahead.

They walked from the parking area toward the building, where many men were standing. They spotted two peacocks whose long, erectile, oscillating tails flashed brilliant patterns of green, blue and gold, illustrating the term "strutting like a peacock." Some thirty or forty yards distant three turkeys distanced themselves from the crowd, moving with a springy walk and little bending of the knees, which produced an odd swinging motion.

A few seconds later Bruce jumped in alarm as two squirrels burst out of nowhere, racing toward a tall long-leaf pine. They chased each other up the long slender trunk, bark flying as they circled. Seconds later the squirrels froze in their tracks, looked down upon the crowd and barked their protest at having their play interrupted. Their tails rolled up, then straightened, indicating their dismay.

A mockingbird looked down from its perch to survey the entire area. It seemed to realize this was not a normal day in the life of the Randolphs.

Joe Randolph rushed to greet them as they approached. "Mr. McPherson, it's so nice to have you with us. We are equally delighted your son could come." He shook their hands warmly.

"My father will be happy that you were able to come," he continued. "He will be with you in a moment. Come this way and let me get you some refreshments."

Joseph saw the McPhersons and excused himself from some county officials with whom he had been talking. "Welcome," he said as he approached and extended his hand to each of them. "I see you have some refreshments. I suppose Victor is enjoying his holidays."

"Indeed I am, sir. My father has just spent some time showing me your lovely community and bragging about it every inch of the way."

"It was a shame Attapulgus lost Bruce McPherson," Joseph said. "He is a true native son, the very best."

Victor said, "Often a man is not respected in his home town. It is good to know that people here speak kindly of him."

"Bruce," Joseph said, "Why don't you introduce your son around. I expect you know them all and he will be doing business with most of them in two or three years. I'll be back with you as soon as I can greet some other guests."

Bruce studied a cluster of guests before him. Their speech was casual, quick and witty and they possessed a worldly attitude, shocked by few things. They believed themselves to be an honored group. Most had not stolen, except legally, and they all had a great deal in common. He and Victor then maneuvered among these men, most of whom Bruce already knew. They chatted about the warm weather, the planting of crops, the stock market, the good rain and the new government regulations being formulated in Washington. He and Victor then moved on to mingle with others.

As Bruce spoke with an old farmer friend, Victor noticed a stranger approaching him. By the man's dress, it was obvious he was not from one of the best families. When Clint White extended his hand, Victor hesitated for a moment before taking it. As he did so, he glanced beseechingly at his father, seeming to ask a form of forgiveness in advance. Victor knew Clint was not truly one of his own and wondered why he must intermingle with such inferiors. Later he discovered his father had witnessed every detail.

With drinks freshened, the two continued to mix with the different groups. As Bruce led Victor from one to another he remarked, "Is it not surprising that each person eventually ends up in a group where he feels most comfortable or with which he has the most in common? It never fails. Water seeks its own level.

"Oh, I nearly forgot. I will sit separately from you. I am a small part of the program."

They heard Joe's voice in the distance. "We have set up five buffet tables just inside. This will allow each of you to get your barbecue more rapidly and find a seat. We trust you can all be served before your food gets cold. Consider the side tables, if you do not like barbecue; there is a collection of ham, turkey and beef awaiting you."

Within minutes each guest had his plate of food and was seated at a table where iced tea and tossed salad had been placed in advance. A basket of hot steaming rolls sat centered on each table.

The Randolph family came in last, approaching the three tables that had been placed together in an area toward the front. Joseph entered first, followed in sequence by Martha, Joe and Joe's wife, Mary. Next came Charles, David, Michael John, April and Stephen. Martha, Mary and April were the only women present.

Joe stood at his table and the room once again became quiet. "Mike Harper will give our blessing. After the blessing there will be more tea and coffee on the way, as well as some additional hot food."

Afterward six Negro girls, all dressed in white dresses with red aprons, appeared and served the needs of everyone. They continued to circulate, keeping the glasses and cups filled and the hot rolls and barbecue before the guests.

It was then that Victor turned his attention to the tables occupied by the Randolphs. His eyes shifted from Joseph, who sat at the end and moved to the others. Suddenly, his eyes rested on the girl named April, whom his father had said he could not describe. Now Victor understood.

For some reason he had expected to find a spunky, smiling little girl who had teased his father more than once. Instead, he saw a girl with hair so black it gleamed. Her complexion was lighter than he had envisioned with such dark features. Her eyes looked as black as her hair and the white around the irises made them appear even larger. Vivid and dancing, they sparkled as she looked upon the groups. The eyes usually mirrored the soul. Intelligence? Kindness? Passion? Yes. There was also a look of softness and compassion.

Victor studied her other features. Her nose was perfect in size and shape. Her mouth was moist, red and full. Her face could turn from seriousness to delight in a moment. She seemed to be amused about something. He wondered what she was thinking.

Then for a moment she seemed restless, as if she might prefer to be elsewhere, yet she showed little concern with so many strangers and adults present.

He noticed her upper body. The breasts were high and full, pressing against her dress. She could easily pass for twenty-five or fifteen. Yet another look also revealed the face of a very mischievous child.

Victor felt someone touch his arm and turned, as the person sitting next to him whispered, "I gather you do not care for barbecue. You have hardly touched your food. You should eat it while it is warm."

Victor looked at the man more closely and responded, "You are correct. It is much better when it is hot. I guess I let my mind stray for a moment." They both smiled, seeming to understand each other perfectly.

Victor looked down and commanded himself to eat. He found he really was hungry and ate much faster than he should. After he had wolfed down much of the food he eyed April closely again. Her carriage seemed so regal. She held her shoulders back and her long neck guided her head as she gazed upon those gathered. Her movements were as natural as breathing, indicating she had spent little time developing such gestures. Were her breasts real? There was no doubt whatsoever. He had inspected enough to know.

It was at this moment that Victor made a decision and a promise: I shall have this girl! I may have to lie; I may have to cheat; I may have to marry her — I may want to marry her. But by God, I'll have her, one way or another!

Then reason seemed to take over: I've seen hundreds of beautiful women and had more than my share. Why should I feel this way about a young farm girl in a rural community who still has two years before she finishes high school?

He had no answer. He felt himself tremble as he looked once more. At that moment a voice from his other side said, "Drink deeply, because there will be few such as this lovely lady in a lifetime. If I were single and twenty, rather than sixty and married, I'd just steal her and take her home with me!"

Feeling like he had been caught with his hand in the cookie jar, Victor asked his father, "Was it that obvious?"

Bruce smiled. "Your eyes have never left her for the last twenty minutes, except for the few seconds required to gulp down your food. You wouldn't have me believe you were looking at our next county commissioner? But I do not blame you. I understand she has even more talent than beauty, though I would have to question such a statement. No one can be that damned smart! Indeed you have good taste, Son. I wouldn't let that one out of my sight." He laughed again and turned away.

While Victor studied April in detail, Joseph found himself considering the people before him. Then his thoughts drifted back to a time in his childhood. An visiting older cousin had given Joseph a quarter to go see the wild animals in the circus that had stopped in town, on its way to the winter quarters in south Florida.

There, with fascinated eyes, Joseph had watched the man with the little flimsy whip enter the cage where tigers seemed to be everywhere. Soon the man had them on their stools; yet their eyes told him that if he made one mistake, they would attack.

Now Joseph abruptly felt as if he were the tamer and all these people present, or at least most of them, were the tigers; he too knew that one mistake would be his last. He would never be able, even for a moment, to relax. He felt he detected the same distrust in the eyes of those before him now as he had seen in the tigers. For a moment, he understood, and was afraid.

Joseph looked to his left, where a group had seated themselves together. He knew, beyond all doubt, that this small group was the power behind the throne. They seldom placed themselves on display, but let others do their will for them. He thought, Yes, I know them for what they are, and they are as eminent a set of sons of bitches as ever gathered together.

Then his son Joe arose from his seat to speak. "The Randolphs are pleased to have you as our guests. I hope you found the barbecue to your liking. I suspect that all of you should enjoy it while you can, because you have taken away the family night from your wives. Please ask them to forgive us.

"This day, fifty-three years ago, our father was born here in this small community of Attapulgus. He happened to have the good fortune of marrying a girl whom six of us call Mother, those six you see before you. First, know my mother, Martha. I am Joe. The remaining, in order, are Charles, David, Michael John, April and Stephen. To my left is my wife, Mary.

"We are a quiet, home loving family of farmers. We love the soil and in turn, it has been good to us. My father wishes to say a few words and I understand some special friends also wish to speak."

Joseph stood. He looked somewhat uncomfortable but in a few moments seemed in full command. He spoke in a quiet, calm voice which immediately removed any feeling of doubt as to his honesty or seriousness of purpose.

"I thank you, as Joe has done. You have met my family and that is what life is all about. In the past we have stayed at home and worked. We have worked hard. We have tried to be good citizens and take care of our business, and let others do the same. I recommend this formula for all of us. May God bless each of you."

As he returned to his seat he again looked upon the hundreds that had gathered. Some of these had despised him in his youth. Yet here they were now, supposedly bestowing upon him an honor. However, many doubts remained. They were really here, most of them, to look after their own needs, protect their way of life and, above all, protect their money.

Abruptly he asked himself if his reasons were not the same. For possession? For power? Yet he felt his true motive was different. He wanted to be seen as 'somebody,' to remove the history and stigma of the backwoods boy of the past.

He sat upright and attempted to look comfortable. He was on display. They were the evaluators, the judge as well as the jury. They would always control things. And they were here to decide if he was their boy! Would they stay with him if he was elected? If so, why? They didn't love him. No, they expected a dividend.

I am to do their will. This is the price they will demand. They will insist on their pound of flesh!

Joseph's reverie ended when Bruce McPherson moved front and center. He took a second to look around at the group assembled. "Gentlemen, and our three charming ladies, we are really here for two purposes this evening. We have accepted the kind invitations and eaten this delightful meal.

"But there is something more important, more lasting, something that will benefit all of us for years to come. We have learned our present county commissioner from this district will not seek another term. Thus, our second purpose today is to request Joseph Randolph to become a candidate for this important position. I . . ." There was a round of applause as the group rose from their seats as one. Then they sat down.

"Gentlemen, I have known this man as a person, a friend, a businessman, a farmer and yes, as a customer for a quarter of a century. He is honest and honorable. He is a proud family man and tonight we can see why. He has the knowledge and insight to make us a great leader. You will always know where he stands. He is straightforward. He has courage to do the right thing. He will work for us as hard as he has worked for his family. He is a school, church and community man.

"You would know, if you know me at all, that I usually do not endorse, outright, political candidates. I'm sure you understand why. But tonight I make the exception. I request that Joseph Randolph seek the position on our county commission and it will be my pleasure to work to ensure his success."

This was followed by two other strong endorsements, first from Lynn Edge, Chairman of the County Commissioners, followed by one from Curtis Mathews, Chairman of the Board of Education and Chairman of the First National Midway Bank. Mr. Mathews spoke of the many occasions Joseph had stepped forward to support the youth. He mentioned Joseph's support to minorities, such as Craig Winter, now attending Harvard. "Come out of the shadows," Mr. Mathews said, "and together we can make Decatur County the best ever."

Joseph stood. "What can I say? How can I thank you? For too many years we should have been doing more. We thought we were doing right by staying at home but now we know we must join with others to make this an even better place to live, to work and to play.

"I take this opportunity to tell you that I will offer my services and seek the post of county commissioner from my district. I pledge the same kind of work and leadership for others as I have given my family over the years. At this moment I officially declare myself a candidate." April had written these words, which Joseph had memorized and delivered.

Mike Harper stood. "Dear God, bless each of us and give guidance to our friend and neighbor, Joseph Randolph. Amen."

Abruptly Joseph found himself depressed and could not understand why. Wasn't this what he had always wanted? Was not this what he had prayed for a thousand times because it could be the final step in becoming the person of his dreams?

Something was missing but he could not identify it. It was like a desperate thirst that could not be quenched. He felt himself lifting a cup to his lips, only to discover that it was empty.

CHAPTER 19

Bruce walked over to where his son sat. "Suppose we wait here for a few minutes. Most will not linger long. They will thank the Randolphs and move out."

Victor whispered to his father, "You did a great job and expressed yourself well. But I must ask, are there not dangers in what you have done? Certainly it can be disastrous for bank presidents to go around endorsing political candidates. You left no doubt as to your advocacy and support. Is there not a hazard in such practices?"

Bruce smiled. "I do not make a practice of endorsing candidates, but Joseph will win. It is good to have a commissioner in your corner, if not in your pocket. One weighs such matters carefully. A large majority present will support him. Most farmers do not eat another farmer's barbecue, then support another candidate. Actually, I believe he will run unopposed. For every account I lose, I will gain three. Remember too, there are not many who borrow a million dollars from my bank.

"We have all the farmers and all the fools that do not think for themselves on our side. In Decatur County they always form a majority.

"There are no morals in politics. We trust that his wishes and ours are the same. If we find this untrue, we will create and buy us another boy.

"My dear son, I do a great deal of thinking about such matters. Should I have erred, however, a significant cash contribution to an opponent provides an insurance policy."

When the last of the guests had gone Bruce and Victor made their way toward the area where the Randolphs had gathered. Joseph moved forward and again shook hands with father and son. "You made all the difference, my friends. I am most grateful."

Bruce nodded in acknowledgment, as if he had done nothing, then said, "Let Victor and me meet your family once more. It has been years since I've seen everyone. They are all so grown."

Victor shook hands with each, making sure that April would be the last. He looked at her closely as his hand closed on hers. She was more beautiful and enchanting, and yes, more desirable than he had envisioned earlier.

As April shook his hand she could immediately see he was a charmer. He was tall and lean, with an outdoors tan. She suspected it was limited to the tennis courts, the swimming pools and perhaps a golf course. She noticed his clothing was impeccably tailored, obviously not from the local stores in Midway. He wore a diamond ring, at least two carats too large, in a conspicuous manner.

"You've grown up, April," Victor said smiling.

"Girls usually do if given enough time." She gave a half smile that could be interpreted in more ways than one.

Suddenly, he felt the most urgent desire to touch her; however, he was certain this was not the time or place. As he stood facing her he felt the most powerful sexual urge he could ever remember.

"I hope you like what you see." April smiled, as it was obvious Victor was staring at her. She chuckled slightly and he was fascinated by the sound of her voice, warm, deep and rich.

She turned abruptly toward Bruce. "I haven't looked into your eyes lately," she said with a grin. "Perhaps you have discovered a conscience over the years? You do have one?" She smiled intensely and looked at his excellently cut suit of deep 'banker's blue.' She noticed that his shoes shined like mirrors.

"You never know when you will encounter a conscience," Bruce said. "Sometimes you find them in unlikely places. Sometimes they can only get in the way. However, you would tell me this talk leads to money and certainly we do not wish to talk of money." He gave his best smile.

She returned the big smile and replied, "Most often when a man says he does not wish to speak of something, he usually means he can think of nothing else! Tonight has brought together a relationship that consists of friendship, success and bank accounts. How could one dare think or speak of one without thinking of the other two?"

She turned back quickly to Victor. "Am I to understand that you will soon be working in the bank with your father?"

"My father feels I should learn more about the county and its people. I could think of no better way than for you to invite me to see your tobacco operation this summer. You would make a wonderful guide."

"Perhaps Joseph or Joe can arrange a time to show you. They run the tobacco operation."

"I was told you would be excellent. Likely the men would be busy," Victor said. "I might show you the banking operation for a swap-off."

"We will see. Your father would tell you I need a better understanding of banks and bankers!"

Abruptly Victor changed the subject. "I have an idea. Why don't you enroll in our Midway High School your last two years. You have a car now and a driver's license. I'm sure a broader curriculum could provide you with more opportunities. I'm sure a diploma from Midway would be accepted more readily by a major college or university. I am told you are an excellent student. I think Midway would admit you as a transfer student."

"No thank you. I would not consider changing schools."

"I don't understand," Victor said. "Perhaps you have not thought of the many additional opportunities."

"My friends are here. I am involved in many activities. We have a fine staff with an outstanding academic record. There are other advantages by remaining here. For example, I would lose three hours or so weekly in transportation time and time is always valuable. There are other reasons but those should be ample."

Bruce attempted to catch his son's eye when he realized the direction things were going; however, it was obvious his son was caught up in himself and had no intentions of being denied.

Suddenly Victor laughed. "Just think, you wouldn't have to explain to everyone where you graduated. They would say, 'Atta-what?' or 'Where is this place? Never heard of it.' It would likely save a lot of embarrassment. Midway is so much more prestigious!"

Charles attempted to get April's attention but was unsuccessful. Finally he eased over and whispered so that others would not hear, "Don't do it. They are our guests."

April took several moments to regain control. Then she said in a soft and kind voice, "We offer all the academic courses you offer. I can think of only three areas which are not found here. First, I'm not a football player. Second, I have no desire to toot a horn. Third, I already have a license to drive.

"Our school is accredited. No one has trouble being accepted in good schools. We send fifty percent to college. I believe your school is at thirty-seven percent and that's not bad, as that's seven percent over the State average.

"There is one other thing that obviously you did not understand. Unless my family moved to Midway, I could not compete in any sports program or literary event.

"Your father knows about the Attapulgus School. Perhaps he can fill you in on the details. After all, they accepted him in college and I would guess he was very proficient. He would certainly know about the values and standards in our school and community."

Victor, having caught his father's warning glance, decided a change of subject would be in order, perhaps something positive and uplifting. "By the way, April, I was thinking as we were driving down today about the name Randolph. This name has carried a great deal of prestige throughout our nation's history, especially in the beginning years. Have you, by any chance, traced your background? Perhaps you are a direct descendant of some of our nation's early leaders."

"We can claim no fame as to our past," April said. "I believe there was William, one of the founders of William and Mary College. And yes, Sir John, his son, who was in the Virginia House of Burgesses. Then there was Edmund, the governor of Virginia, as well as a Constitutional Convention member and author of the famous Virginia Plan. I believe he served as the first Attorney General under President George Washington. There were others of distinction but I must confess we can give no claim to any of them."

Bruce laughed and said, "Nor can my family give claim to the leaders and builders of our country. There was an Aimee Semple McPherson who lived in the early nineteen-hundreds and founded a Bible College where she stressed salvation, divine healing and baptism by the Holy Spirit. But April would know that Aimee would never have admitted a relationship to one in the banking business." There were laughs all around.

Victor said, "My mother has spent a great deal of effort and money to establish that she is a direct descendant of William the First."

"Are you speaking of William the Conqueror, the first Norman king of England?" April asked.

"The same," Victor said, smiling.

"I must confess, I know little of your mother. I only know her when I see her. I had no idea she was interested in genealogy. Indeed, her family does go back a long way. I believe William was born in 1027 and conquered England in 1066.

"Yes, that's right," Victor replied.

"Perhaps your mother feels that she has accomplished her purpose. I would think she would be satisfied having determined some ancestor so prominent. Tracing one's background beyond nine hundred years would likely prove difficult, I would think."

"Oh, you don't know Mother. She will continue her search. She is a very determined person."

"Perhaps she would consider this a good point to stop. I think she would find it difficult to surpass such a prestigious and renowned relative," April said.

"I believe you are likely correct as to finding another so prominent and prestigious, but one can never tell what one may find," Victor said.

"Yes," April said. "It is true that one never knows what is lurking around the next corner. I still think, however, that this an ideal point to stop. You see, William the Conqueror was an illegitimate child, a confirmed bastard! It is just possible that your mother may discover some unexpected skeletons in the closet.

She then said, "Goodnight. Thank you for your presence and your support in Joseph's political endeavors." She smiled and moved through the door.

Bruce said to the remaining Randolphs, "We came as honored guests and acted like clowns. I'm sorry. I'll work even more diligently in your behalf. You may be assured that one young man who will know more about Attapulgus before we reach Midway. Goodnight, everyone. Joseph will make a fine commissioner!"

Bruce and Victor had reached the public road before Bruce spoke. "I do not believe I have ever seen anyone get his ass kicked more deservingly. I hope you have learned at least some small item from this experience. You apparently heard little of what I said this afternoon. Actually, I don't believe you heard the first damn thing!

"The real tragedy in life is making a total fool of yourself when it isn't necessary. That is difficult to bear. This is what you did this evening. I suspect the time will come when you will pay dearly.

"All afternoon I tried to tell you about Attapulgus and its people, as well as its institutions. There are times when I think too much of your mother comes out in you. She has always resented my hometown. I suppose the reasons are her own. They are not important.

"April was kind, very kind to you. She didn't give you a third of the statistics that I would have thrown at you. It is incomprehensible that my son can get himself entrapped in such an indefensible position. No, you didn't hear the first damn word!

"You tried to impress April. Well, you certainly did. How can you insult your hosts in such a damning and ridiculous manner is beyond me! Oh, I saw you earlier at the table when you acted like a lovesick school boy. I even saw you earlier when you hesitated to shake hands with Clint White. And you are about to take over a creditable banking institution? You sat there in a trance and your neighbor had to remind you of your purpose in being at the Randolphs. But let that be enough of that for now."

Victor, in an effort to sidetrack his father, asked, "Why is Joseph Randolph going into politics? He has ample money and land. There seems little to gain. It all seems so foreign to him. He must have a reason or motive that has not surfaced."

"He has a reason. In a way, it is personal. Their background is the basic reason. For three generations these people have stayed out of circulation and worked. Three generations ago they were characterized as piney-woods people, at best. The first group, perhaps the second generation, was referred to as poor white trash by some. Now seventy-five years later, the backwoods people have come out of the woods and are something different from what most believed. They are quite wealthy, as I said this afternoon. Now they wish, or at least Joseph wishes, for himself and his family to be looked upon differently. This is what he would call the final step into a new and different world. You have no idea what this means to him."

"And you have been his banker over all these years?"

"Oh yes. In fact, I have indirectly helped him to put his empire together. I have helped discreetly with many of his land acquisitions."

"You knew much more about tonight than you let on?" Victor asked.

"We plan ahead," Bruce said. "Joseph would be one of us. In the end, our wishes are basically the same. I am not sure he has admitted this to himself. It's possible he hasn't realized the full implications.

"We created their guest list for this occasion. If someone is offended, Joseph will not be responsible. For your information, this was April's idea. We never really gave out the names of those serving on the invitation committee. There was only one disagreement and I still believe Joseph was unwise. Sheriff Henderson was not present. Their differences, I believed, were smaller than he realized. But that is behind us."

"I was impressed with Mrs. Randolph. She is a quiet person that stays in the background," Victor said.

"She is a fine lady. She is the best acquisition Joseph ever made. I don't know how he got her. She keeps a good relationship for them in church, school and community."

"Michael John did not say anything," Victor said. "He looks a little different from the others."

"I understand he is outstanding in construction. He is the man that maintains all their equipment," Bruce said.

"Some of them will not wish to go to college," Bruce continued, "but I suspect all their children will go. Each generation seems to move up one step." Then, "What surprised you the most, Victor?"

After a minute he responded, "Two things stand out. I had expected to see a large and beautiful colonial home. Secondly, I would have guessed their cars would have been large and new. Not so in either case."

"Yes, you are right. They have sent out few messages. It has always been this way, until now. I don't know if they realize it or not but it will never be the same again."

"Their clothing was adequate but not expensive," Victor mentioned.

"I didn't know you took your eyes off April long enough to make such observations."

When Bruce eased the Buick into their driveway, he noticed lights on in the living room and a few other rooms. As he and Victor entered the house Bruce commented, "I see it is much earlier than I had realized. We just ate a bit early."

His daughter, Lesa, asked, "Who did you see? What did they have for dinner? I suppose you men enjoyed the occasion, while the women had to stay at home. We had come to expect Friday evening as one for our entire family."

Bruce said, "Just slow down. I would say that we had a good time. The barbecue dinner was good, perhaps a little heavy for some. We saw about three hundred men and three ladies of the Randolph family. It was the usual crowd you would expect. There were farmers, businessmen, some from every walk of life. It was the usual political crowd. It would not have been a very appropriate place for women, since it was in the packing house. Oh yes, Victor couldn't keep his eyes off Joseph's daughter."

"Oh, Bruce," moaned Agnes, his wife, "how could you have your son around that Randolph girl? Who is she? Actually, who are the Randolphs? I'll tell you who they are. They are nobodies. Why would our son be interested in a Randolph girl? To be seen with her would leave a bad impression. There are some who would like to grab our son to better themselves in name and wealth. I just wonder if you have reminded him of this, as you were once among the same crowd. You have always been blinded when it comes to Attapulgus. Nothing good has come from that place except you and on occasions some of my friends still wonder about even that. I guess you will always be an Attapulgite in your heart."

"I don't understand either," Lesa said. "I hear that Randolph girl is no lady. Word is she uses all kinds of uncommon and crude language. I've been told some of the words are more than crude. I would not even feel comfortable quoting her. No, no, we don't need to let such into our circle."

Bruce said, "I suppose I cannot control your thoughts, but such remarks would do a great deal of damage to our business and our relationship with many customers. These comments could do us a great deal of harm."

"Why Bruce," Agnes said, "you actually spoke more than once of me living in that dump of a town. You gave no thought as to my leaving my real friends and living among those country bumpkins. You knew my real and true friends were here and only here could I find a few that would be my equal. I hope you have learned some of the truly important things of life."

Bruce said, "I hear that the Randolph girl spoke in an uninhibited manner for a short time but that was years ago. Many of us, hopefully, will outgrow early childhood mistakes. I suppose all of us, in one way or another, did some things as children that we do not feel good about. I will remind you once more that Joseph Randolph has been a very valuable customer for a quarter of a century."

"Why didn't they select an appropriate place and invite the women? They know that Friday evening is usually an evening that families spend together. But I guess these country people would not know that," Agnes said.

Lesa said, "Maybe Father felt he had to go. I guess money is money. But he should have never exposed Victor to such inferior people! Intermingling with your inferiors can only create problems. Victor could have taken his mother and sister to some decent place to dine."

"But Lesa, don't you see? Your father had to show your brother his precious Attapulgus! The only good thing I know about that place was Bruce leaving it."

Bruce looked about him. "I have had a long day. I have some early appointments at the bank. I'm sure Victor can fill you in on such details as you may require."

As he was leaving the room he heard Agnes say, "He can sit and talk with his old cronies all evening but he can't take fifteen minutes to be with his wife and daughter."

When Bruce had left, Lesa asked, "How were the women dressed?"

"I'm not sure I looked closely at any of the women," Victor lied. "I suppose you could say they were groomed nicely. They were dressed in what one might describe as Sunday clothes. They were definitely not in evening wear."

"I suppose Joseph's wife is an old woman by now," his mother said. "After a yard full of children and farmer's hours, she must really look old and worn out."

"I expect she looks like any woman in her early forties. I believe she is several years younger than her husband. She seems as you might expect of someone who is very proud of her family. Actually she does not say much, or at least, she didn't tonight."

Agnes said, "I hope they appreciate the McPhersons. We have been letting them have money for years. I don't know how they could have made it without us."

"We have been helped too. You would wish to remember that they have paid a lot of interest over the years as well," Victor said.

Lesa interrupted. "What did Joe's wife look like? What about that girl they call April?"

"Joe's wife looked nice. You could call her pretty, I think. She was as quiet as Mrs. Randolph. She smiles a lot and seems to be an alert observer.

"I am not sure how one would describe the young girl, April. I really didn't pay too much attention. By the time you eat and talk with those around you there isn't too much time. I believe she had black hair. Sophomores in college don't get too excited about children that have more than two years to go in high school." Victor knew another lie would serve his purpose best.

"She plays a game called basketball," Lesa said. "I had always thought such as that should be left to the boys. I recall someone saying they beat our teams. They must have had special officials or cheated in some manner. Why, we must have six times as many students to choose from."

"I'll turn in too," Victor said. "Father mentioned that I was expected in the bank in the morning. Then I've got to go to Tallahassee tomorrow evening."

His mother said, "Since you were out tonight, I had expected to see more of you later. Lesa and I would like to hear of your college life. You don't tell us much."

"There really isn't much to tell," Victor said. "You try and eat three times a day if you have time. You go to your classes. You go to the library. You study every spare minute. That just about says it all.

I know you and Father would be disappointed if I let my grades slip. I don't seem to have a spare minute."

Victor thought about Saint Peter. Had not this disciple denied Christ three times? And it was upon this man Christ built His church. Surely, he too, could be forgiven for his few white lies in the last ten minutes.

"Well, Lesa," her mother said, "it seems we are all alone again. I hope you will choose wisely when it is time for you to marry. I would also think it wise for you to be the one to hold the purse strings. That could have been my first and biggest mistake."

When Victor entered his father's office the next morning Bruce smiled and said, "She really did you in last evening. You were as lost as Little Bo Peep's sheep."

Victor smiled, "I seem to recall that this happened to you more than once. You know, I believe her to be the most unusual person I've ever known. She seems to see and know your inner thoughts. Yet she makes sure you never see very much of her."

"I told you," Bruce said. "Now as father to son, I believe I'd go see a florist this morning. A dozen roses can say a great deal. But before you do that, I want to talk to you about a delicate matter. I speak of your mother. As I have grown older, many things have become more apparent.

"You know the early history, my son. Your grandfather owned The People's Bank. Your mother was an only child and a bit spoiled. I worked for her father after finishing college. I worked hard and learned from him and others. We liked and respected each other. As his age increased and his health declined, it became more and more obvious that I would serve him in two roles. He wanted me as a son-in-law, as well as the person to take over his bank. There was not another at this time that he felt would qualify for both roles.

"I learned the science of banking from her father and also learned some things that he did not know. But most of all, I learned to make money, lots of money. This pleased her father. After all, why should one be a banker for any other reason than to make money?

"The second thing I did was to leave Attapulgus. This was not easy for me. You could see as much yesterday afternoon. As time went by, I thought of words of wisdom from two sources. The Bible says that a man's wealth is a strong city. In simple words, money is the answer.

But Stevenson disagreed. He said that an aim in life is the only fortune worth finding.

"Do not make the mistake I made. I believed the latter, but followed the former. While I want you to have a fortress, I also want you to have other things in life that matter. What is wrong with holding both hands?

"After your mother and I married there were some of Agnes' friends who told her that perhaps she could change this country boy for the better, even though he is deeply scarred. One told her I had a degree but was not educated. Another said I was unable to recognize or identify the 'real people' but perhaps she could change me.

"I am reminded of the words of Mark Twain. 'Are we going to continue to impose our alleged superior ways of living on those who dwell in darkness, or are we going to give the poor things a rest?' I suppose she feels she has started a process but it is obvious that she feels her task incomplete.

"In a way, I am really sorry for your mother. She never got anything of real value out of life except you and your sister and she has all but destroyed your sister already. Your mother has denied real living, a real romp in the hay.

"Sex, except to reproduce, was dirty, as well as time consuming. She was always more interested in her community position and how the bank was doing. Her values were wrong but this she has never discovered. I do not believe it possible for her to know the real meaning of life.

"Don't let this happen to you. An evil person can destroy bodies. But one like her can destroy your soul. The real tragedy is that they go through life and never know the agony and pain they cause others. Her father knew, but didn't tell her. Your own father knows and isn't going to tell her either. Neither of us had the courage.

"A friend of mine told me that some of her friends had said I didn't seem like a very happy person and they could not understand why. 'He has a beautiful wife who is devoted to him and two lovely children. And she has given him a position in the social world and more money than he can deal with properly. The old country boy is not appreciative. Perhaps he is much too greedy. It's a case of too much, too soon!'

"You are my hope. I want you, should you decide to marry, to find someone with real values and someone who loves you rather than worldly things of little value."

"But Father, I had thought you would have me be more like you. I cannot believe that money has less meaning to you than some others I know."

"As one becomes older, one has a clearer eye for real values. It is unfortunate that some will never know and most will wait until it is too late to change.

"I'll be watching you. There is an old saying that if you have no money, your children don't care about you; get money and they wish you were dead. Children think they know more about everything. I am not certain just yet as to how you feel!" Bruce left his office without another word.

Victor remained in his seat for ten minutes. Then he felt a hand on his shoulder.

"Are you waiting for your father? He has a number of people he has to see."

Victor got up from his chair and turned to face Alice. Again he looked at her beautiful face, her daring eyes and the breasts that seemed to want to fight their way to freedom. "Look after him, Alice. Serve him well. He is surrounded by loneliness." He held both her hands for a moment, but said no more. In a second he was gone.

CHAPTER 20

Joseph Randolph a commissioner? You live with a man for twenty-five years and you suddenly discover you didn't know him.

Martha could not sleep. There were so many things to ponder. Why had he insisted on taking such a step? Why was it so important to him? Was this his final step to assure an escape from the image that he believed others had of his people?

Joseph slept as soundly as a baby. She could see her husband's face in the faint light of the room. She turned and made another effort to sleep but continued to lie awake.

What if he wins? How would his life and the lives of her family change? She was sure he would work hard to be a good commissioner. But would those about him force him to become a tool for their benefits? She suspected that the very people who had honored him and said nice things would demand their pound of flesh.

More importantly, what would happen if he lost? Knowing her husband, he would take it as a personal rejection. It would destroy him completely. He would lose his dream, seclude himself more than ever before and try to lose himself in work. It took little imagination to know what this would do to his family.

He knew so little about politics. He knew how to work, to organize, to manage, to be a successful farmer and yes, to make money. All his previous experience and knowledge would be of little value in a political endeavor, however.

She thought about April's encounter with Victor. Joseph had expressed his unhappiness when they had returned to the house but she had defended April. No guest has a right to insult a host or say unkind things about one's home community. She smiled as she thought about William the Conqueror.

In the early hours of the morning Martha drifted into an uneasy sleep. Suddenly, she was wide awake again. Her hand reached out to reassure her that Joseph was there. She could tell it was still dark outside. Had she heard something? Someone? Could she have been dreaming?

"Mr. Joseph, Mr. Joseph, wake up. Do you hear me, Mr. Joseph? Martha recognized the voice of their foreman, Jack Jenkins.

"What is it, Martha," Joseph asked as she punched him for a second time. "It ain't time to get up."

"Jack is calling you. Are you awake?"

Again they heard Jack's voice. "Wake up, Mr. Joseph. There are some problems in the quarters."

Joseph shouted so Jack could hear. "There are always problems in the quarters. What can be so bad at this time in the morning?"

"I believe this is serious," Jack said.

"Jack," Joseph said, "go on down. I'll be there as soon as I can get some clothes on."

Jack left saying, "It could be someone has been killed. I'm on my way down there."

"Certainly no one has killed someone," Martha said. "Certainly this has not happened!"

"Just a crazy bunch of drunk blacks," Joseph said. "Someone has worked another over. Ain't they always fighting when they get to drinking? Better they do it here than in town. This way you ain't gotta pay to get them out of jail. I'll go see."

"I'll go with you. I'll get my first aid kit," Martha said.

"Go back to sleep."

"I can't do that. I'm wide awake now."

"Then put on some coffee. I'm sure I'll be back in a few minutes. Me and Jack can handle this." Joseph took a flashlight from a drawer, opened the door and was gone.

As Martha put on her housecoat she heard a voice and a rap on the door. April and Michael John hurried in.

"We heard Jack," April said. "Do you think there is serious trouble?"

"Your father didn't seem to think so. What are you two doing? Go back to bed." She saw they were already dressed.

"Papa may need help," Michael John said. "I'll go see if I can do anything."

"I'll go too," April said.

"You shouldn't go, April. I don't think this wise," Martha said.

"I'll see after her," Michael John said. "I'll keep her out of the way."

"I don't feel good about this. Don't get too close. I'll have some breakfast ready when you two get back."

Joseph's truck bounced down the washboard roads that had not been scraped in several months. The county had done this for him until recently, then said they would be required to stop because others had complained about them working on private roads. Would he approve of such as a commissioner? He would give it some thought.

As Joseph rounded the last curve he saw lights and activity ahead. A dozen or more quarters people seemed to be milling around in the road. As he drew closer he noticed they had gathered at the house where Maybe Jones lived. A single electric light burned, casting a faint shadow over the porch and yard. As he opened the door to the truck he had a feeling this was more than the usual quarrels that were part of their way of life on Friday and Saturday nights. He took his flashlight and approached the group.

Jack Jenkins made his way to Joseph. "I think we have a bad situation on our hands. That's Maybe sitting on the porch, leaning against the wall. I can't tell what he's saying."

As they walked to the porch they heard Maybe say in a mournful voice, "I done done it. I didn't mean to but I had to do it and now it's too late. I hadn't ought to."

"What have you done?" Joseph demanded, shaking him by the shoulders.

"It's too late and I'se done it, Mr. Joseph. I didn't want to hurt 'em so." There were tears in his eyes and he shook as if with a chill.

"What have you done, Maybe? For God's sake, shut up that damn crying and tell me what the hell is going on!" Joseph shouted.

"I done killed 'em; done killed 'em both. Wat'n meanin' to do it but dey comes at me wid dat 'nife, one just back of de other. I swings de axe and it bust dey heads wide open. Din't mean to do it but ain't had no other way. Now I ain't got myself thinking right." Maybe hung his head and broke into a deeper sobbing as he continued to tremble. His lips continued to move, but he did not utter another audible sound.

At that moment Joseph turned and saw the lights of another vehicle approaching. He could see Michael John and April about to get out of the truck.

"What are you two doing here?" Joseph's voice was loud and angry. "Ain't I got enough problems on my hands?"

April said, "We are here if you need us."

"Get back in the truck this second! Wait until me and Jack can find out what's going on. I don't want you out until I know what's what."

Jack followed Joseph into the small wooden house. The number of quarters people had now doubled and a dozen conversations were taking place. Joseph focused his flashlight around the two front rooms and saw nothing unusual.

They moved into a back room and saw two old double beds with some tangled, dingy sheets on each. An old spread and dirty blanket lay on the floor.

They moved to the door which led to the room referred to as the shedroom, a room that had been added after the original structure had been finished. The beam of light came to rest on two forms on the floor before them. Joseph moved one step forward to get a better look. He saw two bodies, one resting partly on the other. They could see that one was a man, the other a woman. There was blood everywhere.

As they looked closer they saw the head of the man had been split from the top of his forehead to his chin, leaving a wide gap down the middle of his face. One of his eyes seemed to dangle from the socket.

Joseph moved the beam to the other form and saw it was a woman who appeared to be dressed in a gown. Her head was open from the eyebrow to the lower part of her mouth. Two or three loose teeth seemed to be caught between her lips.

Jack said, "They are both dead. There can be no doubt."

"Yep," Joseph said, "Dead as a door nail, dead as hell."

They walked back into the front room and Joseph said, "We had better get things moving. We don't need any doctors. We need the undertaker."

"Better call the sheriff," Jack said. "It's not like it once was. There was a time you took matters into your own hands but we can't do that this day and time."

Joseph walked back to the room once more and looked through the door; his beam from his flashlight verified what they had seen the first time. "This is one hell of a mess, Jack, and we will have to make some changes with our labor force. It would have to happen just when the tobacco season was starting." His light focused on an axe with blood all over it. It was not difficult to know this was the instrument of death.

"Let's get out of here, Jack. I thought I could take most anything but this is about to make me sick."

As soon as they returned to the porch Joseph made a number of observations. Maybe was shaking uncontrollably. The number of quarters people continued to increase and had moved several steps closer to the house. They seemed to be waiting for some word. There was some daylight now so he could make out Michael John and April in the truck.

Joseph moved down the two steps into the grassless yard. He held up his hand for silence and the people stopped to listen. "Hear me now," Joseph said. "Lila Jones and Posey Green are in the back room. Both are dead. Ain't no doubt about that. There ain't nothing, at this point, that can be done. I want all of you to stay in the road. Better still, go home if you will. There ain't one thing you can do. I'm going to send Jack to tell Posey's wife and children. Some of you may need to keep a check on her. She has no business up here. Now where are Maybe's children?"

A voice in the background said, "Dey wid deir cousin. Dey stayed wid her last night."

Joseph turned toward the truck and saw Michael John and April getting out to meet him. He looked back and saw that few had moved toward their own houses.

"I suppose you heard me?" Michael John and April nodded their heads. "It's bad. It's real bad. I don't want you to see them.

"Now listen carefully. I have several things I want you to do. Are you listening?" They nodded.

"I want you to go back home and tell your mother what has happened. Then tell her to make two telephone calls. Have her call Sheriff Henderson. She can tell him two people are dead and it ain't from natural causes.

"Then have her call Lottie Layton. She does all my dead work, my funerals. She will need to come prepared to pick up two bodies. Got that now?" He didn't wait for them to respond.

"Then one of you go tell Joe. He will come. Then see that Sandra gets the word and tell her Jack will come later."

"Are you going to need to call the coroner?" April asked. "Isn't he usually called when something like this happens?"

"Sheriff Henderson can do as he wishes. That's his business. Since Maybe has said he did it, they may not need him."

Joseph turned and walked back over to the quarters people. They stopped their conversations as he approached. "The sheriff will be here shortly. He may have some questions for you. Can any of you tell me what happened? What did you see? What brought this on? Some of you say something! You sure as hell gotta know something about this." They looked at Joseph, turned and looked at each other, then looked down at their feet, but no one spoke.

"If you ain't seen nothing, maybe you heard something. Was there a cry for help?" Joseph asked. "If you didn't hear nothing and you ain't seen nothing, how in the hell did you happen to be here? Someone knows a damn sight more than they're saying!"

It was then that Fail Patterson stepped forward and spoke. "Mr. Joseph, us woke up hearing a yelling and a carr'in' on. I come over and some others did likewise. Us found Maybe yelling and taking on lak a wild man. What he said didn't make no sense a-tall. He seemed to be saying, 'I didn't wanna do it.' He said it over and over. He was on de porch. He stepped off de porch, then jumped back lak he was shot. He sat down and started mumbling again. He was plumb crazy!

"Now Mr. Joseph, ain't nobody down dis way but knows what's been doing. Some time a while back Maybe and Posey swapped women. In fact, dey swapped dey whole families. Some say it was bad fur Maybe, as he took on three mo' mouths. Posey got six, Maybe three. Anyways, some three-four weeks back dey undid what dey had done and both went back lak dey shoulda and dey had de right ones again. Seemed to make de whole quarters feel good dey had. And wid dat last switch, things settled down.

"Us got some of de stuff left from you'alls party and we had a hopping good time. But I ain't got no idea 'bout what did take place. Dey was a lots of singing and laffing as us got likkered up. Now dat's all I knows. Dat's all I speck anyone knows and dat's de truth."

In moments Joe arrived. Joseph gave him the details he had learned. They walked back over to the edge of the porch.

Maybe moaned, "Lila, I didn't wanna hurt you but you ain't done right. You coulda not caused me to do dat. You say dat Posey outta yo' mind. But he comes at me wid dat 'nife. Oh, God, help dis po' nigger's soul!" Maybe quieted when he saw Joseph and his son.

Joseph ordered, "Now Maybe, get yourself settled down and tell me and Joe exactly what happened."

"I'se gonna try as best I 'member but it ain't all so clear. Us done all you said fur de meal. We ate some of de food. Wus fit fur a king. Us drank de stuff you'all left. I remember us stopping and talking 'bout ole times. I falls asleep. When I wakes, I goes into de room to get me some real sleep on a bed. Den I seed that nigger Posey on de side of my bed wid his hand on my Lila. When he sees me, he runs his hand in dat pocket and out comes dat big 'nife. I runs in de back room to run out but de door was locked. I seed him coming, 'nife and all. I grabs de axe and swings hard as I can do. I knowed I hit solid. Knowed I'd hurt 'im bad. I turns to put de axe down and here comes Lila wid de same 'nife. I moves to get de axe so to knock de 'nife away. Somebody slips in Posey's blood and I hits her dead in de head instead. Why dat Lila wanted to kill me I don' know. Dat's it. Dat's all of it. Next thing I knows, I'm here on de porch and a bunch of people in de road. Next I know, you and Mr. Jack is wid me. What dey gonna do wid me, Mr. Joseph? Dey gonna take me to de jail?"

"Let's wait and see, Maybe. Lean back and try to rest. The sheriff and Lottie Layton will be here any moment. You have any insurance, Maybe?"

"No, suh, I ain't never had no money left for such wid all dem mouths to feed. I ain't got the first dime's worth."

Moments later they saw another vehicle approaching as the sun was peeping up in the east. As the vehicle drew nearer, they saw it was a black hearse, with Lottie and two other people. She explained, "Got here as soon as I could. Had to round up my men. What you got for me this time, Mr. Joseph?"

"Two bodies are in the back room." Joseph pointed to the house. "The man is Posey Green. The woman is Lila Jones. Can't move them until the sheriff comes." Lottie wrote the names in her little notebook.

Joseph added, "Maybe Jones, Lila's husband, is on the porch. He said he killed them. May have to go to the jail to get the information on Lila. Posey's wife lives a few doors down."

"Mr. Randolph, Lottie been looking after you for twenty years. We'll go about things as usual. They didn't say if they got no insurance?"

"Maybe said he ain't. I would guess Posey is in the same boat. They don't look after their business."

"Ain't it so, Mr. Randolph. Looks like my folks ain't gonna learn much about living, or dying either, for that matter. But don't you worry none, not the first minute. We know just what to do. You just leave it to Lottie."

"Now Lottie, I don't expect anything too big. I don't want you to get carried away and get me a hell of a big bill."

"You know I won't do that. We been treating each other like we should for a long time. Ain't nothing gonna change that, Mr. Randolph. Now don't you worry. I'll look after all the details. I might ask this. You want a double funeral? Comes some cheaper. Don't know how all these folks gonna feel about it though."

"Lottie, I think that would be the very thing to heal all the differences. They both belonged to the same church. This could be the very thing."

"Gonna give this matter some thought. Naturally it's gonna call for two programs and two sets of nearly everything."

"Do you suppose we could have this in a day or two, Lottie? You know damn well these people ain't gonna do no work until these bodies are put in the ground."

"Mr. Randolph, there ain't no way. Now you think about it. I can't get these people ready by tomorrow, which is Sunday. They won't have a funeral 'cept on Sunday. There's no way we are going to change the days of the week."

"God, Lottie, I'm right in the middle of the biggest crop ever. I lose two of my best people because of this and the whole damn bunch will sit around the whole week and all the work goes to hell!"

"Can't help it. You know I would if I could. Say, what kinda shape them buggers in? I bet they all messed up!"

"I doubt you can do much, Lottie. You'll have to keep the caskets closed."

"Folks ain't gonna like it but you're right. That's what we gonna need to do."

Lottie turned toward her two men. "Roosevelt, you and Detroit be getting the things out you gonna need. There's two of 'em. Just put your equipment over to the side by the porch so we can be ready when the sheriff's done."

Lottie turned back to Joseph. "You ain't gonna keep a bunch of sorry niggers straight on Friday and Saturday nights. It just ain't in them. Never has been and never will be. It's their nature to tomcat on the weekend. Most white people don't understand. You got to be one to know one. You take that bunch at Midway. You ain't lived till you been a nigger on Saturday night with two dollars in your pocket.

Then she asked, "You see any reason, Mr. Joseph, why I couldn't peep in? Could get some idea as to what's before us."

"I believe I'd wait, Lottie. The sheriff's been a little strange recently. I'd like to tell him that me and Jack are the only ones to go inside."

Joseph looked at his watch. He wondered about the sheriff. In the past he had always been 'Johnny on the spot.' Before when Joseph's hands had left, even out of the State, the sheriff had them back in no time. Six months ago it began to change.

Joe called Joseph to the side. "Think it wise to use Lottie all the time?"

"Why not? Ain't we had a good relationship with the woman?"

"If you're going into politics you may wish to spread it around. I don't need to tell you what a few bucks will do. You know, they are beginning to vote pretty good now."

"I'll get more if I stay with Lottie."

Joe laughed. "Heard about her when they had the wreck? She picked it up on the police scanner, I understand. Seems she grabbed her assistants and took off. Who gets there first usually gets the funeral. When she got there bodies were scattered all around. She started packing them in the hearse like cord wood. They had four and pulled out. In their hurry they ran over another body. Someone said he wasn't dead. They stopped and threw him in also. When they got to town all were dead. Some said she told them the last was going to die anyway. You certainly have to admire the service."

They looked down the road and saw another vehicle approaching. As it got closer they could see a light on top of the car. Two deputies got out, one white and the other black. They walked up to Mr. Randolph. "I'm Deputy Smith. This is my associate, Deputy Rains." Joe and Joseph shook hands with deputy Smith but ignored the other man. "Sheriff Henderson will be here shortly. It was a busy evening. Every Friday evening is busy. Suppose you give us the information you have."

Joseph told them all he had seen and learned.

"While we're waiting on Sheriff Henderson," Smith said, "we will see what else we can learn. Deputy Rains will check with the group in the road. I'll chat with the fellow on the porch."

"You need us?" Joe asked.

"Best I do this. I'm trained to know what to do." He approached the figure on the porch.

"I'm Deputy Smith. I'm going to ask you a few questions while we are waiting on the sheriff." Maybe raised his head slightly. Deputy Smith had taken out his notebook.

"Do you want to tell me your name?"

He heard a mumbled sound. "Maybe."

"I'm not sure that I heard you," Deputy Smith said, "or that you heard me. Let's start again. Do you wish to tell me your name?"

There was a mumbled sound again, "Maybe."

"Maybe, my ass. No damn maybe about it." His hand went to his billy stick, but then remembered this was not like the old days. "Let's try once more. The law requires you give me your name. You want to try once more and tell me your name?"

There was another mumble. "Maybe So."

Deputy Smith placed his hand under Maybe's chin, then slammed his head against the wooden wall. "You smart son-of-a-bitch, I'm fixing to bust your ass!"

Maybe mumbled, "Maybe So Jones be my name."

"I don't want some nickname. I want your real name. Don't try pulling that shit on me."

"Dat's it. Dat be my name. Only name I got. Daddy gave it to me. Said later he weren't too sure."

"All right, Maybe So Jones, suppose we move on. This your house?"

"I lives here. Belongs to Mr. Joseph. All de houses you see belongs to him."

"How long you been living here?"

"Long time. Been a long time for sho'. Don't rightly 'member no date."

"Mr. Randolph has told me there are two dead bodies in your house."

"Yes suh."

"You know who they are?"

"Yes suh."

"Then who the hell are they?"

"Dey be Lila and Posey."

"Lila and Posey who? I think you are trying to make it difficult for me!"

"Lila Jones. She be my wife. Posey is Posey Green."

"Lila is or was your wife?"

"Yes suh."

"How long have you been married?"

"Can't say. Been a long time; time and memory sorta gets away from you."

"You have a marriage license?"

"No suh. Us just hitched up on our own."

"How old is or was your Lila?"

"Don't rightly know. Said she be uncertain 'bout it."

"What was Lila's name before you married her?"

"She didn't know who her papa was. No way to be certain, she say."

"I see," Deputy Smith said. "Where was she from? Where was she born? Where was her home?"

"Don't know, suh. She was wid a bunch of cotton pickers in Alabama when us joined up. Said she sho' didn't like no cotton pickin'!"

"Now this Posey — Posey Green. What can you tell me about him?"

"He worked here. Us work together. Been doing for Mr. Joseph for a long time. Posey been my friend." He added confusedly, "You know, Mr. Sheriff, I'se sorta mixed up just now. Ain't everthing all clear."

"You kill those people in there?"

"Didn't mean to. Didn't wanna do it."

"According to Mr. Randolph, they are both chopped up pretty bad. In fact, he said real bad. And you say you didn't want to do it? Maybe So Jones, they are going to burn your black ass!"

"Couldn't hep it, sur. Dey comes at me wid this 'nife."

"Half their heads gone and you call it an accident or self defense. You must take me for a fool!

"What do you do here," the deputy continued.

"I works."

"Well I'll be damned! You works!"

"Ever one works on dis place. When Mr. Joseph say work, us works. Ever-body."

Deputy Smith took another look at his little notebook. "Let me go over this with you. Tell me if I made a mistake. You say you are Maybe So Jones but your pappy wasn't so sure he was your pappy. You have or had a wife named Lila but you don't really know if you had a wife because you just hitched up. You don't know her maiden name because she didn't know who was her pappy. You don't know how old she was or where she came from but you know she picked cotton in Alabama and didn't like to pick cotton.

"You tell me you work but you never told me the nature of your work. You have been living here a long time but you don't know how long.

"You got a dead friend in there named Posey, Posey Green. He is or was a friend and was for a long time but you split your friend's head open with an axe and you couldn't help it.

"In a few minutes Sheriff Henderson will be here and he will ask for my report. Do you expect me to give our own Sheriff Henderson such a report when he comes? Just how big a damn fool do you take me for?"

Deputy Smith felt a hand touch his shoulder, then turned his head to see the girl standing behind him. He had no idea how long she had been there or how much she had heard.

"Sorry, Miss, I'm afraid I didn't see you. Guess my language wasn't so good. Do you want to tell me who you are?"

She asked, "Who are you?"

"I'm Deputy Smith, ma'am. I'm from the Sheriff's Department. I'm the chief deputy for your sheriff. He will be here soon and will expect a report."

"Do you have another name other than Smith? I expect there are over four hundred Smiths in our county."

"I'm Deputy Harman Smith, ma'am."

"I am April Randolph, Chief Deputy Harman Smith. I believe I heard you ask this man how big a damn fool he thought you were. I wondered if he responded?" She gave more than a slight smile.

"Just doing my duty, Miss April Randolph." His face was a deep shade of red.

"Do you always use such language? It suggests strongly of a poor vocabulary. It is said that some resort to such language to impress others. Certainly the color of his skin was no factor!"

"Sorry, Miss. This fellow is either crazy or he takes me for a fool!"

"He isn't crazy," April said with a naughty smile. She continued, "Have you read him his rights? Did you think to mention that he was entitled to counsel?"

"Miss, I wish you would let the law deal with this. This man is a murderer!"

"Has he been tried in a court of law? This man is an employee here. His name is Maybe So Jones. His address is Route 1, Box 55, Randolph Place, Attapulgus, Georgia." April moved away and found her father talking to Lottie.

Another vehicle drove up. Sheriff Henderson opened his car door as Joseph approached him saying, "I had expected you earlier. Is there something wrong?" His voice did not sound cordial, nor did he smile.

Sheriff Henderson responded, "You asked me what is wrong, sir. You should know that something is always wrong in my business. That is why they have a sheriff."

The sheriff went over and talked to his deputies for several minutes, then returned to Joseph. "Please tell me what you have learned."

Joseph gave him most of his information, but decided he would let the sheriff dig a little for himself.

The sheriff said, "You have been inside? Do you know if others have?"

"Me and Jack looked in from the door to where the bodies are. We did not enter. I have seen no other enter. I have told you what I saw."

The sheriff went to his car, then returned with a camera and a flashlight. He motioned for his two deputies to join him. Those outside could see several flashes.

When they returned to the porch he told Deputy Smith, "Get the suspect. Put the cuffs on him. Based on what I saw, I believe it would be the only safe thing to do."

He turned to Joseph. "Our coroner is out of town. From all I have learned, I do not believe it is necessary to attempt to locate him. I am taking the axe with me as evidence. Would you like a receipt?" He turned quickly, without waiting for a response. "You may tell your undertaker she can get the bodies now."

He then abruptly added, "Oh, I nearly forgot. Happy birthday! A little delayed, I suppose. Sorry I missed the party. I guess someone forgot to send me an invitation or it got lost in the mail. From what I've seen this morning, it appears that someone went to great lengths to make it exciting."

Suddenly, Sheriff Henderson turned back toward Joseph. "Did you tell me if you saw weapons? Something other than the axe?"

"I didn't go inside. I believe this was said to you earlier. Therefore, I saw none nor did I look for one. I would think that is part of your job." Joseph turned and walked the other way, over to the undertaker. "Get the bodies, Lottie. Has been a long morning."

"You want me to do the usual?"

"Yes. As you have always done."

"All right, Roosevelt, you and Detroit, let's go!" In ten seconds Lottie returned. "It's a mess, Mr. Joseph. Gonna take a little more than I expected. No way to tell till I saw them. Gonna take a lot of work." She turned back and shouted, "What you boys doing? Let's get 'em and go."

When they were gone Jack said, "Sheriff didn't seem too friendly. In fact, he didn't seem friendly at all."

"A man can stay on a job too long, Jack. Evidence all around you. Happens to most government men. Looks as if it has trickled down from Washington, to Atlanta, and on down to Decatur County." He continued, "Can we make it, Jack? Good thing we had not started gathering."

"Yes sir. It will not be real easy but we can make it."

Joe asked, "No insurance?"

"That's right. Ain't no insurance."

"This is rough," Joe said. "Two dead. Might as well be three. Maybe will not return soon."

Joseph nodded. "Owed a lot of money. Always do. Now two funerals and a bunch of kids to keep up. No work for a week. This is a bad day." He sighed. "Let's go get a cup of coffee. Martha will have some breakfast but I don't think I can eat a bite."

Chapter 21

When Joseph entered the breakfast room, Martha saw a haggard, frightening figure. His beard was more than a day old and it framed a face as pale and ashen as the winter sky. He seemed to collapse into a chair at the table in exhausted relief. As he dropped his hat by the chair she noted his hair had not been combed. He was wearing the dirty work clothes he had worn the day before. Martha could not believe this exhausted and weary man was the same person who, twelve hours earlier, looking so dignified and courtly, had served as host for more than three hundred people of Decatur County. She placed a steaming cup of coffee before him.

"It's hot as blue blazes."

She thought the statement unwarranted since no one had ever made coffee hot enough for her husband. "Sit right there and try to relax. I'll have some food for you in a moment." The aroma of the frying bacon had drifted into the breakfast room.

She retreated to the kitchen and returned with a plate of eggs, bacon and toast. In moments she had refilled his cup, as well as hers, and joined him at the table. "Your morning has not been a good one. I can see you are upset. What's done is done and we cannot do anything to change it. As Uncle Edd says, 'What is, is.' It is so ironic that something like this could happen on your birthday. Everything had seemed so perfect. All of the kind gentlemen had so many nice things to say about you."

Joseph raised his cup and drank deeply of the hot coffee. "It would have been near perfect, if April had not stuck her foot in her mouth again. Ain't she gonna ever learn?"

"I hope you don't hold that against her. She defended those ideals that are near and dear to her. She only told the truth. I think a guest should not come into another community and speak so unkindly. Victor has some things to learn."

"But ain't Victor got a right to think and speak kindly of his hometown? I would be disappointed in him if he didn't," Joseph said.

"That is all April did. I believe it was Victor that initiated the subject that triggered the exchange."

"We don't live in Attapulgus. I keep telling you this," Joseph said, not willing to let the subject drop.

In an attempt to change the subject Martha asked, "What did you think of the comments in the meeting?" Yet her mind was still on the problem in the quarters.

"I was pleased. They said what is usually said. You eat a man's food and it is expected that something nice be said. But you know, Martha, you can't help but wonder what would happen if you don't act in the manner they expect. I got some bad feelings inside."

"You will get elected. You will make a very fine commissioner. You always stand for the right."

"Some of those present ain't too interested in what is right. They want their interests protected at all costs."

"You have many friends. You have made few enemies, if any. I do not know of anyone that feels unkindly toward you." She dared not think of Joseph not winning. "I hope you will be patient with your family during this time. We know so little about politics. We will need direction during the campaign. We have stayed at home. We do not know many people. This frightens me."

"We will work out a plan. We will work together."

"I am not sure," Martha said, "how I would react should there be those who would say unkind and untruthful things about you. You know and I know that there are such people who seem to enjoy hurting others. This is what bothers me most."

"There is another matter," Joseph said. "I guess it would have more significance than you think."

"I don't understand."

"Until now few people knew or could guess our worth. Now our secret won't be a secret no more. There will be those who will ask how the Randolphs moved up so quickly. They ain't gonna remember the work of three previous generations of Randolphs. They ain't gonna remember the nearly thirty years we have given. Those that have or own little don't always have a high opinion of those that have accumulated. How we got what we got will mean little to many. Times are changing in a hurry."

Martha said, "I am sure they will not leave any stones unturned. That's the price one must pay to enter politics. This was one of many fears your family had when you told us your plans to run for the commissioner's seat. I think you questioned our interest, loyalty and concern at the beginning. We just did not wish to see you hurt. It was not a lack of support. It was our concern and love for you that mattered.

Then she said, "Allow me to change the subject. I want to talk about the nine children in the quarters who no longer have either a mother or a father. I am not sure what impact this devastating event will have on them. Perhaps . . ." There was a knock on the back door. Martha opened it and said, "Why, it's Uncle Edd. Come in. Have a seat and I'll get you a cup of coffee." She motioned toward a chair.

Uncle Edd quietly shook his head. He would only take a seat upon Joseph's insistence. Joseph remained silent. Placing his hand on the back of a chair, Uncle Edd spoke, "Fail Patterson has worked out something for the children. They are with relatives and friends. Posey's wife, Nellie, has not accepted the fact that her husband is dead. She believes he is out tomcatting." He looked at Martha. "My apologies to you, Mrs. Randolph."

He continued. "Perhaps someone will check on their needs? Food? Clothing? Something appropriate to wear to the funerals? As you know, the blacks place a great deal of emphasis on funerals. You may also wish to consider that once the bodies are in the ground, the neighbors will consider their responsibilities completed. I hope you do not feel that I am attempting to manage your affairs.

"You know that I find myself in a difficult position. They will not communicate with me freely, as they would one another. They look upon me as a 'white man's nigger,' not only because of my role here, but also because of the light color of my skin. They are equally aware that I cannot accept many of their ways of life and have little patience with those with certain characteristics." He added, "Should you wish an extension of credit or changes in your current policies, please let me know how much and to whom."

"I'll have to think about this. It has come about so suddenly," Joseph said.

When Uncle Edd left Martha looked at her husband. "I hope you will be generous at this time. It would seem the right thing to do."

"As I review Maybe's story, I become concerned," Joseph said. "He spoke of the attacks by Posey and by Lila with a knife. But there ain't no knife. You knew they had swapped families?"

"Yes. There are few secrets on Randolph Place. I am not sure if such knowledge is good or bad." She gave her husband a rather unusual, forced smile. "You don't think, then, that Maybe was telling the truth?"

"I ain't seen one yet that wouldn't lie like a dog, even without a reason. Seems to be in their blood. Always has. Of course Uncle Edd and his folks may be an exception. After all, they are more white than black. Considering the circumstances, however, Maybe had to tell 'em something!"

"Will you get Mr. Cannington to defend him?"

"Hadn't had no time to think yet on that matter. Lawyers cost money. Slick costs a lot of money. This could be sending good money after bad."

"Will they release Maybe on bond?"

"I don't think so. He would likely skip the country. I would if I was in his place."

"I'll clean up the kitchen while you instruct Uncle Edd. We all have a great deal to do."

CHAPTER 22

"The meeting will come to order!" The tone of his voice and the expression on Joseph's face told everyone that all was not well. "We are gonna take stock 'bout where we are and where we'll need to go.

"By now everyone knows all they need to know about Friday night and Saturday morning. I cannot remember us being in a bigger mess in a long time. We have just lost two of our people and I suspect the third ain't gonna be with us for a spell.

"We got nine children to look after and no more than half are big enough to work. Maybe was into us for about five thousand. Posey's debt was nearly as much. Neither one had a dime's worth of insurance. We have two funerals to pay for.

"We have our biggest tobacco crop ever on the way and we won't be able to get the first day's work out of anyone this week. Most will sit and mourn the whole blessed week, since they think the ground will accept them only on Sunday. My God, even our Lord didn't require a week and they buried Him on Friday!

"Posey was one of my three best men, and Lila could out-string 'em all by a hundred sticks a day. Maybe, a good tobacco man wherever you put him, will be out of pocket for God knows how long.

"Maybe is gonna need a lawyer. They don't come cheap. But I don't think a lawyer will help him. It's just sending good money after bad.

"Anybody got any ideas?" he asked.

"Once they are buried, won't this go away?" David asked. "Once they get back to work and get busy, that should end any ill will among them."

"Lottie is gonna bury both at the same time. A double funeral may ease some pain. Lottie said this way would be cheaper too. If she is right about getting them united again, it will be better."

"Bury both at the same time?" Charles asked. "I am not sure I understand. Just doesn't seem right. I've heard of husband and wife, or two children of the same family, but not something like this."

"Lottie oughta know," Joseph said. "She's been doing this work all her life." Charles shook his head and said nothing more.

"Naturally there will be some differences. She said we should have separate programs and pallbearers but the preacher can get two through at the same time."

"Programs? This is new to me," April said.

Martha spoke. "Programs are an important part of their burial services. But let's get back to what your father is concerned about. I think it will be important that we all attend as a family and show our support. This may unify and help to bring our people together again."

"Lottie called," Joseph said. "Funeral will be at two a week from today. I have agreed to say a few words, as have some others."

"Sometimes they have five or more give a minute or two minute testimonial," Martha said. "Your father can do a great deal to start a healing process."

Joe asked, "Will Sheriff Henderson release Maybe in your custody for the funeral?"

"He will allow him to attend under guard. They have become very regulation conscious. We can expect no favors from Henderson. I thought Judge Whitehead might help but he is gonna follow the sheriff's recommendations. Seems like the good Lord isn't very good to us just now."

Silence prevailed for a minute before a voice was heard. "Has it not been a policy over the years to secure a lawyer when one of our people has a problem? Should Maybe be an exception? Wouldn't our people expect to see this policy continued? What is done or not done will send a message," April said.

Joseph's face showed some anger, as if he had been challenged. "How so? What message? He's a goner. No purpose in adding to the cost."

"Wouldn't our people expect it?" Martha asked. "Perhaps it *would* send a message. Is it not possible that they would feel unprotected?"

Joseph whirled around and stared at Martha in a very strange manner. "It seems my wife sees some things I ain't seen. I try and make it a habit to think on these things." Joseph's face color deepened. Everyone looked down at their feet rather than at each other. This was a first for all of them. Never once had the children heard Joseph challenge their mother in such a manner.

April was stunned. "Has our policy changed?" she asked. "When we reorganized years ago it was said that an opinion from one and all would always be welcomed." She looked straight at her father. Then she decided to go a step beyond. "A court appointed attorney sends an automatic signal of guilt to everyone. Should not a jury make such a decision?

"Secondly, our people have had a deep respect for Joseph and all the Randolphs, as he has never forsaken them in times of sickness, death or trouble. Has such a policy been abandoned?

"Lastly, what kind of reaction would be normal to wake up and find another man in the bed with your wife? When an uninvited guest attacks a man in his own home with a weapon such as a long knife, one may expect something to occur out of the ordinary."

"Maybe is guilty as hell," Joe shouted. "April doesn't understand how this crazy bunch lives. Maybe has caused us enough trouble already. He owes us over five thousand dollars. He's killed two of our best people. We got to bury the dead and feed all those children. Many of them cannot work at all. And now April wants to tell us how to look after a bunch of damn blacks!"

"Shut up Joe," Joseph yelled. "We can have opinions but we don't talk that way around our women. I ain't gonna have it!"

Joe looked at his mother. Her expression was one he had never witnessed before. He was uncertain as to what to say. Then he turned toward her and said, "I'm sorry. I'll try and remember. But as far as April is concerned, I have no apology to make. From what I have learned, she has said all of this and more. The entire family was embarrassed, perhaps disgraced."

"Give me a few minutes," he continued. "I was told we could all speak freely. I want to tell you about these buggers in the quarters. I don't think some have ever really looked at them. They are ignorant. They are lazy. They can't understand instructions nor can they follow them. You have to tell them in detail, over and over, everything to do. If you turn your back for a minute, it's to do all over again.

"They have no character. They steal. It's as natural as breathing for them. They will not pay their debts. They drink like fish. They get in jail and you have to buy them out. They don't look after their families. They have from one to three babies, all bastards, before they learn anything. They don't marry. They take up with others like a pack of animals. They switch wives like it was a game. That was part of the problem here.

"They are dirty. They don't keep their bodies or clothes clean. They get themselves an old car, the bigger the better, put a fox tail on the thing and here they go. They don't know how to drive. They won't maintain a car. They load them up a crowd, roll the windows down, wave to everyone they see, blow the horn if it will blow and drive it until they have used up the two dollars worth of gas they probably bought on credit.

"They get sick and you take them to the doctor and buy their medicine. They die and have no insurance so you put them away. You feed all their children so they will not starve. Yes, and as soon as they grow up the girls start all over with their bastards and the men head to jail once again. It's an endless cycle.

"I could go on and on. I really have not gone below the surface. And now our sister wants to tell everyone how to deal with this crowd! I've about had all of this I want to hear!"

April, in a quiet voice, said, "I agree with nearly all you have said. You have identified them correctly. We are not apart in that our observations are basically the same. But there is still another side of this picture. I would not dare do so now but the time will come when I will wish to present another picture, as real and true as Joe has described. For now, however, I continue to believe Maybe should have a lawyer that is not appointed by the court."

Then Martha spoke in a low voice. "We will not be destroyed by enemies from a distance. If destruction comes, it will come from within. Do you have any idea what we are doing to our own family, to each other?"

Unexpectedly, April spoke again. "I want to tell you a brief story. I believe it is unknown to all of you. I believe this will help you to understand my feelings. A part of it is very personal.

"Eight years ago I disobeyed the rules that we were to follow with no exceptions. I went swimming alone. As a good swimmer, I could see no danger. Yes, it was a violation of our policies. I did so deliberately. I have no excuse. It nearly cost me my life. I developed a cramp and was going down for the second time. I screamed for help and I was heard.

"A person passing by plunged into the water and pulled me to safety. By now you have guessed it was Maybe Jones. I learned later that he could not swim, but he never hesitated for a second. We made a pact between us to never let anyone know. He accepted my thanks and remained silent. He never asked for anything more. As far as I know, this is the first time it has ever been told.

"Now, unless I am forbidden, I plan to attempt to save him for two reasons. First and foremost, I believe he has told the truth. I believe it self defense. Secondly, I must take this opportunity to repay a long standing debt.

"I would like to secure and be responsible for an attorney for him. It will not cost any individual anything, nor will it cost the corporation. I accept the responsibility.

"I believe Joe said that Maybe should get what he deserved. I agree completely. He deserves a fair trial. He should be judged by his peers. He should have legal representation. I must see that this is done. I can do no less for a friend who saved my life."

Thirty minutes later, Martha found a secluded place. Tears filled her eyes as she thought of the many differences that had developed between the members of her family. This would signify the end of the family circle. She knew it would never be as before again. She wondered where it would all end.

CHAPTER 23

April was awake at five thirty the next morning. Thank goodness today was a teacher planning day and there was no school for the students. She picked up a legal pad and began to write. It was nearly seven when she finished. She then dressed and walked toward the kitchen.

"Good morning, April," her mother said. "I suppose you will have a day of rest since you have no school today."

"I have a great deal to do. I hope I can get all of my little tasks and errands done. Where is everyone?"

"Stephen is still sleeping. The rest are working. All have finished eating except Stephen and your father. He was the first to leave. It seems our day will not be normal and he felt he needed to be out and doing. He said he would be back about seven. Wait and the three of us can eat together. I believe I hear him now."

"Good morning, Joseph. You seem to be quite busy this morning," April said.

"Busy? The only ones busy are the Randolphs, the Jenkins and the Winters. Me and Jack went to the quarters to get things going but that was not to be. What a joke! I should have done some fanny kicking right on the spot. There must have been a dozen reasons why they couldn't work. Let me see if I can remember." His look at April said, 'Joe is right. They just won't do.'

"Naturally three or four were sick. One couldn't walk with a bad leg. Another was down in the back. Still another could not leave his sick wife. Then one needed to take his child to the doctor and had no way to get there so naturally a neighbor had to get him to town. Thus, the neighbor was out of pocket.

"There was a group that had to go to town to see about some clothes for the funeral. Fail Patterson was needed to take Nellie Green to the funeral home. I'm sure I have left out some others.

"You know, I had really wanted three more good years but I believe I would settle for two. Then I think I'll send the whole bunch packing. Yes, I'd agree on two good years and then I'd say to the Lord and our Washington, D.C. crowd, 'You can have these buggers!'"

Suddenly, he turned directly to April and said, "I think old Maybe is guilty as sin but to please you, after he saved my disobedient child, I'll get a lawyer. I suppose this is a man's job."

"Joseph," April said, "we agreed last night about this matter. I want to repay this man for saving my life. I also believe him innocent in that he had no choice but to defend himself. With all you have facing you on the farm and in the political arena, I'd prefer to do as it was resolved last evening." She finished eating and excused herself.

Back in her room, she made a telephone call. "Jerome, this is April Randolph. I want to get an appointment with you today. Our teachers are having a planning day and we are not in school."

"Good to hear you again," Jerome said. "It would even be nicer to see you. Bet you are more beautiful than before. And yes, beginning lawyers always have a flexible schedule."

"I can't evaluate you as a lawyer yet but you have picked up some pointers in knowing how to make a poor country farm girl feel good. I am not sure how you would use this recently obtained knowledge in a court of law but you could win a lot of cases elsewhere."

Jerome laughed. "You haven't changed. How can I help you?"

"I want to talk with you. I have to be in Midway. I'll work into your schedule."

"I'll finish my few chores this morning. Shall we say twelve o'clock?"

"I'll be there. Thank you for seeing me on such short notice." She hung up the telephone and smiled. Every time she heard his voice something seemed to happen to her. Then she thought of the ten year age difference and gloom settled in. Until she considered the age difference between her mother and father and smiled again.

Once April got to Midway her first stop was at the sheriff's office. She entered and was confronted by a middle aged woman that she assumed was a secretary. "I am April Randolph from Attapulgus. I would like to see Sheriff Henderson."

Without looking at April and continuing to look at the book before her the woman asked, "What may I tell him is the nature of your visit?" The way she asked the question made April flinch.

"Business," April said, not smiling.

"I am afraid that is not sufficient, young lady. The sheriff is . . ."

"I am April Randolph. You may call me April if you like. I don't believe I got your name. Perhaps I was not alert." Then it dawned on April that she should not hurt this person, who was as faceless in a world of people as a grain of sand on Joseph's eighteen thousand acres. This little authority, this one brief moment, was all she had or could ever expect in life, all that would separate her from the masses. April studied her face, her dress, her figure. Yes, it was obvious that this pitiable arrogance was all there would ever be in a lifetime. She must be kind.

The secretary ignored April, struggled to her feet, opened a door marked 'Sheriff Henderson' and disappeared.

In a few moments the secretary returned, took her chair and remained silent. The door which she had entered opened and Sheriff Henderson approached April. "Why hello, young lady," he said. "I believe that last time I saw you was in the quarters where two dead people were found. I believe you spoke at length with Deputy Smith, Deputy Harman Smith." He smiled to let her know he was aware of what had taken place. "What can I do for you?"

April looked at Sheriff Henderson and decided she liked him less than the secretary, and liked the secretary even less than she had two minutes earlier. She said, "May we go into your office? Surely we wouldn't want to interfere with your secretary."

Sheriff Henderson said nothing but walked over to his office door and held it open while she entered. "Please have a chair." He pointed to a chair nearby. "I had not expected to see you. Most of my business is usually conducted with adults."

"My family is quite busy. I believe you know something about the life of a farmer. I guess we may say I am the official representative of the Randolphs today. I have some questions to ask you."

"Certainly," he said, without any emotion and with what she interpreted as total indifference. "What do you wish to ask me?"

"Am I to understand that Maybe So Jones, who is in your custody, cannot be released on bond?"

"Correct. Your father has been advised of his status. Judge Whitehead makes such decisions. The judge and I are not in disagreement. Based on his recent behavior, he would be considered dangerous. It is thought that he might flee to avoid prosecution."

"What procedures are necessary," April asked, "for an attorney and myself to talk with your prisoner?"

"I am not sure I understand. Perhaps I did not hear you clearly. I was led to believe there was to be a court appointed attorney and a guilty plea. Why is your father not here?"

"My father is busy making a living. Certainly you have not forgotten that my father is a farmer." She knew the moment she said it that she had once again spoken sarcastically; Charles had warned her repeatedly about this. "I am responsible for this man. If you have doubts you may call 465-3 . . ."

"Just what is your request, young lady?" The sheriff interrupted her before she could finish.

"Please call me April, Sheriff Henderson. People always feel more comfortable when they are addressed properly by their name. It is spelled and pronounced like the fourth month of the year." She knew immediately that once again she had spoken in a manner that would not be overlooked.

Sheriff Henderson found himself in a position different from any he could ever recall. If ever a person needed a good lesson, this girl did. But he also remembered that he was an elected official and for it to be said he was impolite to a well established farmer's daughter could do a great deal of damage.

"Miss April Randolph, just what can I do for you?" His tone mimicked April's.

"I wish to establish a time that my attorney and I can see Maybe So Jones. Secondly, I wish to confirm that he may attend the funeral of his wife this coming Sunday at 2 p.m. in Attapulgus. Thirdly, I would like to get some measurements for some clothing, as I assume he will be permitted to attend the funeral in clothes other than a prisoner's uniform."

"Anything else?" The sheriff did not smile.

"I think that covers it, at least for the moment."

"I had told your father that it would save Decatur County some money not to go to trial. I understand he wants to be a commissioner and this would demonstrate to the public his concern for the financial status of the ones he wishes to represent."

"I believe the Pecos River flows from New Mexico southeast through west Texas to the Rio Grande. It is only west of this river that they seem to hang before they try. As a fine outstanding arm of the law, I am sure you would not wish to damn and sentence a man before he can be tried before a jury of his peers. We don't take them out and lynch them anymore, east of the Pecos. I guess we will just have to spend a little of the taxpayers' money. Now if you will give me a time, I will not hinder your busy schedule."

"You may come with an attorney at two o'clock today. Good day, Miss April Randolph." He rose, moved to the door and held it open, indicating the conference had been concluded.

As April was leaving she noted the expression had not changed on the secretary's face. She was tempted to thank her for the many acts of kindness but remembered Charles' warning.

She pulled her Chevy into the parking space of a converted residence that now housed the Lottie Layton Funeral Home. The location gave a vivid picture of some of the changes occurring. It was an area where the blacks had entered but all the poor whites had not made an exit. This pattern, she knew, was not unusual in many of the towns and cities.

As April entered she saw a nice looking young and well dressed Negro girl, who appeared to be in her twenties, sitting behind a desk, typing. She smiled as April approached, immediately stopped typing and stood up. April realized this three century old practice had not changed. "I am Ethel Smith. How can I help you?" The girl smiled pleasantly, revealing beautiful white teeth.

"I am April Randolph. I have an appointment. Please remain seated. I hope I have arrived on time."

Ethel Smith smiled as she sat back down. "Miss Layton will be with you in a few moments. Please sit down. So you are Miss April Randolph from Attapulgus. For some reason I had expected one a mite older. Let me get you a cup of coffee or a soft drink."

"No thank you. I believe not." Two observations flashed through her mind. First, she could not help comparing the two secretaries she had encountered in the last hour. The second observation was a rather large sign on one wall: 'If you drive, don't drink; if you drink, don't drive. But if you get confused, call Lottie.' April assured the girl, "Please continue your work. It seems you are quite busy." At that moment a door opened and April saw Lottie Layton for the second time in less than a week. Lottie's wearing apparel was obviously quite different.

"Why, Miss April, Lottie is so glad to see you. You look good, but a trifle thin. I hope you don't act like some of these girls that get so thin they'll blow away." April had been around Negroes all her life and knew that if you were not a little plump, they felt you were unhealthy.

"You were kind to see me on such short notice," April said. "Is it Miss or Mrs. Layton? Please excuse me for asking. I would not wish to be rude."

"You ain't rude, Miss April. At the moment I am between husbands. I don't think you should call me either. Just call me Lottie. Now come into my office and we'll take this matter into hand. You met Ethel?"

"Yes, she is very nice."

Lottie held the door open for April to enter. April noted the nice furniture and the new desk, behind which were some framed certificates. She noticed that one was a county license to operate and another was a license from the State of Georgia.

"Now you sit down and rest yourself while we talk. I find it difficult to keep my mind off the happenings at your father's place. It was a sad morning in the lives of so many. But don't you worry. Old Lottie is going to have everything ready and in place before Sunday. You know, we do this over and over but we never get used to the jolts that come upon us."

"Miss Layton, I am here to review with you what you have done thus far, what you still need to do and what we can do to get everything in place."

"By working night and day and leaving no stone unturned, we now know where we are and where we're going. I ain't so organized this morning but we'll see as best we can.

"We have the bodies prepared. Ain't a pretty sight to see and we shore won't be opening no caskets. I'll let you peep 'fore you leave, if you wish.

"I've selected the caskets. They ain't the most expensive, since I remember the words of your daddy, but they ain't cheap either. One would be proud to be buried in them caskets.

"Now I ain't put these people in expensive clothes. Good Lord gonna redress 'em for the streets of gold and nobody will see them again here.

"To sum it up so far, we got the bodies already dressed and in place in the caskets.

"The funerals are set for Sunday at two o'clock at their church. Makes a special day for the church. Brings out a heap of people. Rev. D. C. Handmaker is ready to preside. Been their preacher for years. Deacon Smith, first deacon, will assist. Don't know exactly how much time it will take to get safely home, since they didn't come to church too much. Can't put a time on the length and we gotta remember we got two to pull through.

"We're ready to get the programs now. I have all the officials who will be helping. I got the pictures for the programs. Them programs are gonna be on nice slick paper, not none of that cheap stuff like some use. You gonna be pleased, child!"

April took out a little notebook. "Let me run over what I have and if I am not correct, you tell me. The bodies are prepared, dressed and in caskets. The time, place and officials have been determined. The programs are nearly complete and on slick paper." April nearly smiled too much.

"I don't know how you remember all of this 'cause you don't work with such regularly. Again, you must remember we can't be sure of an ending time 'cause we don't know how long it will take for the preacher to pull two through."

"Let me ask about some items I have listed," April said. "I'll just jump from one to another. The graves?"

"All set, planned and ready. Will bury them right back of the church. Got the sites picked out."

"Someone to transport the families to the church?"

"All ready. Church officials will have them there and on time."

"Proper clothing for the families of the deceased?"

"Oh, Miss April, thank God you brought this up. Had forgot about Maybe. All the rest are all set. Gonna cost a few dollars. Some of dem people ain't got the first thing to wear."

"I'll look after Maybe. I have it down on my list. I'll get sizes this afternoon. Now how about food for the families?"

"We got most of it set for this week. Your mother has got herself into this. But next week, once they are in the ground, it's gonna be a different story."

"Let's get this week concluded," April said, "and we'll worry about next week when next week comes. Let's get back to the church again. Are places reserved for family and special guests? I am not experienced in these matters."

"All worked out, Miss April. Been a busy time and will cost a little here and there but we got it all fixed up."

"Death certificates?"

"All finished. Ain't gonna need a lot 'cause they ain't got no insurance. Shame all this gotta fall on your poor daddy."

"Only a few more questions. I hope it is not too painful. Did you see the bodies yourself when they were being moved from Maybe's house? Exactly what did you observe?"

"I sho' did and it was not good for the eyes. Blood everywhere, Miss April. Part of Posey's face just hanging on. It was awful, just plain awful!"

"You went in with your two men? I believe you called them Roosevelt and Detroit?"

"I went in and looked pretty close. I gave my boys the word, then we got them into the hearse and into town. I'm sure you saw us then. The sheriff took poor Maybe with him and we got the bodies on out."

"Did you see a knife?"

"Ain't seen the first sign of no knife."

"Did anyone help Roosevelt or Detroit?" April asked. "I don't recall seeing anyone assist."

"No sir, not one of them sorry field hands offered to lift a finger. We did it all by ourselves. But that's our job. Does seem that someone might have offered to help but they don't feel good around dead folks, especially some of their own."

"Did your assistants see or mention a knife?"

"Not one word. I see what you getting at now. With a knife, maybe Maybe's got a chance."

"Perhaps you could get Ethel to write the address and telephone numbers of Roosevelt and Detroit on a piece of paper. They may remember something that would be helpful. Of the two, do you have one more in charge or responsible than the other?"

"Ethel, get in here." When the girl entered, Lottie gave her instructions. "Ethel will get this down but they ain't got no phones.

"I ain't put neither of these boys in charge of the other but Detroit tells Roosevelt every single thing to do, just like he ain't got no sense. Detroit likes to Lord over everyone if they will let him."

"I'm ashamed to take so much of your time," April said. "I believe I will not look at the bodies at this time."

"You tell that daddy of yours that Lottie will look after his people as always and for him not to worry his head none about it."

April picked up the information from Ethel on her way out. She glanced at her watch. She had time to get to Jerome's office and take him out to lunch. She smiled; the best part of the day was yet to come.

A brass plate on the door identified Jerome's office, located on a side street, not too far from the courthouse. April opened the door and found herself in a small office. A beautiful woman sat behind a desk, reviewing some material in a folder. "Come in," she said. "You must be April Randolph. Mr. Lee said I would know you immediately, as you were the most beautiful girl in the world. Now I understand. I am Barbie Adamson, his secretary. I am also his receptionist, typist and anything else he can get me to do." At that moment she realized what she had said and turned a shade of pink.

"Thank you. Jerome did not tell me he had a beautiful secretary. It's a wonder he ever gets anything done." April laughed. "That's the way of lawyers. Would you tell Mr. Lee that I am here and if he is not busy, I'll take him out to lunch."

Jerome opened his office door and entered. "I see you two have met. April, this is the best secretary and nicest person you will ever meet."

Miss Adamson gave a big smile. "I keep thinking I'll catch him in a falsehood but he continues to come up with the truth every time." She laughed. "Better watch these lawyers, Miss Randolph."

"I suppose each of us should warn the other. He always says the right thing. He knows how to make a poor farm girl feel good!" April said.

"Miss Adamson, I have warned you in advance. This lady is far beyond her years. I have yet to find her a corruptible woman with a doubtful reputation, but I dare not look the other way!" Jerome said.

Miss Adamson smiled. "If I were you, I wouldn't look away, but my reasons would be different. I wish some handsome man would come by and offer to take me to lunch. April, you are as delightful as he has described you. I'll bet the boys in Attapulgus have a difficult time keeping their minds on math and science." She turned to Jerome. "Mr. Lee, I will be leaving for lunch. You have no appointments on your calendar for the rest of the day."

A few minutes later Jerome and April were eating in a restaurant across town. "Miss Adamson is correct, April. You are the most beautiful girl ever!"

"I'm going to buy your lunch, Jerome. Don't worry or fret. You are my guest. I'll get you obligated to me. Why didn't you tell me about that beautiful secretary of yours? She suggested you tried to get her to do many things!"

Jerome's face darkened. "Well, a man has to do something with his time. A beginning lawyer doesn't have all that much to do!" He changed the subject. "What have you been doing?"

"You wouldn't believe the first word and I'm not sure I would believe it either. We have an appointment at two o'clock to see Maybe Jones. I want you to hear his story. I may be your first client since you hung your shingle."

The waitress brought their lunches. It tasted as good as it looked and smelled. When they had finished Jerome said, "You want me to defend a Negro man who has taken an axe and chopped up his wife and best friend. I am a beginning lawyer, not a miracle worker."

"Oh, we'll win! I have great confidence in you. If you do well in this case, I have another problem I'll let you help me solve. I am not pleased with the way that women are treated."

"Oh! I didn't know you were one of those. You seem to have forgotten your role. When we consider the progress the fair sex has made, it is remarkable. Some years ago a woman's role was to reproduce and to serve the many needs of man. She was trained, if brought up properly, to be respectful and sympathetic. She was to speak little. She was to be seen as needed. A woman was to be decorative in dress so as to arouse a gentleman's interest. She was trained to take care of a home or manage the servants that did. Good food and clean clothing were a part of her responsibility.

"Now we have given you additional opportunities, such as the right to vote and to hold certain offices. I am not sure how wise we have been or if you are ready for a next step!"

April smiled. She had not seen this side of Jerome. "But you have not enumerated all of the changes. Now we are expected to enter the market place to supplement, or in some cases, support the male because of his inability or his unwise use of time. We are to continue to remain silent most of the time and be good listeners. And yes, we are to produce your babies and be back in harness within two weeks. Indeed, we have come a long way!"

"You are not supposed to know these things, much less talk about them," Jerome said.

April switched gears. "You knew I was getting a new sister. No, mother is not pregnant. David is marrying a girl named Kathy Lane. She will make a wonderful wife. They are very much in love."

"Perhaps some day I can find one," Jerome said. "I'm not sure I could support one just yet, but perhaps, in time, I can. I think I would want someone just like you!"

"Tell me your detailed qualifications so I can get started with my training period." She smiled and her black eyes sparkled.

Jerome reached over to pick up the check. "Oh no you don't," April said. "You don't know the first thing about me. I asked you out to lunch. This is the first of many steps I must take to get you obligated to me!"

They returned to his office and reviewed every detail of Maybe's case. When the time came, they left to go to the sheriff's office. As they entered, the same lady April had previously encountered said, "So it's you again!" while rolling her eyes skyward.

"Would you please tell your sheriff that the girl following March is here — again. He will understand."

Sheriff Henderson opened his office door and approached. "I am having the prisoner brought to the conference room." He led them through a series of three doors, until they reached a little room equipped with a small table and four straight chairs. There were no windows. The walls were blank. A bare light bulb hung above.

Jerome asked, "Mr. Henderson, are these the regular facilities to be used as a conference room?"

"This is what your taxes are paying for. When a person is being held after the death of others, we must take precautions." With that he turned and left the room.

A few seconds later the door opened again. The first person to enter was a guard in uniform, a pistol on his hip. He was a huge man. Behind him was Maybe, walking in steps no longer than twelve inches. His shackles clinked as he walked. He was in handcuffs. He wore blue denim clothes with the words "Prisoner" stenciled on each garment. They were baggy and ill fitting. Behind him was another guard armed in the same manner as the first. They motioned for Maybe to have a seat. The guards looked at each other, at Maybe, and then in the direction of Jerome and April. They moved back from the table, but made no effort to move toward the door.

"You may leave," April said. "We will knock on the door when we have finished our conference."

"You better be careful," one guard said. "If he will kill his wife and best friend, no one can feel safe."

As soon as they heard the door click Maybe said, "Lordy, Miss April, I'se glad to see a friend. Things ain't been good. I don't rightly feel so good."

"Have they struck you or beaten you?" April asked.

"No ma'am, not 'xactly. They pushes me around, jerks me here and there, but they ain't hit me."

"Do you know Mr. Lee, Maybe? This is the son of Susan Lee, our best friend. He is a lawyer, an attorney. He wants to talk to you. Perhaps he can help you."

"I'se glad to make your 'quaintance, Mr. Lee. You be lak your ma and you is special sho 'nuff."

"Maybe, I must ask you to go over once again every detail, from the start of the birthday party until the time the sheriff took you away. I expect you have repeated it already more than once but I must hear it in your own words."

Jerome listened patiently as Maybe told his story. More than once, he became emotional. When he had finished Jerome said, "I will ask you two or three questions. When you returned home, did you go to bed?"

"Yes suh and no suh. I went to sleep in the chair in the room where we cook and eat. Didn't take no clothes off, just slipped out of my shoes."

"And you were awakened by noise in another room?"

"Yes suh. I did hear some people talking. I walks to de door and looks in. I could see it be Posey sitting on the bed wid his hand on my Lila. I seed him reach in his pocket and bring out dat 'nife. I runs to de back room but de door don't open. I spied de axe as he comes at me wid de 'nife. I swings dat axe wid all my might and could tell I stopped 'im dead in his tracks. I drops de axe and den I spots my Lila. She done found dat 'nife and here she comes. As she brings dat 'nife down she slips in de blood and where I didn't mean to hurt her, I hits her in de head and she falls on Posey. I drops de axe and went on de porch. You knows the rest."

"Did you pick up the knife, Maybe? What happened to it?"

"I ain't touched de 'nife. I ain't seen it again."

"Describe the knife."

"Dat 'nife was knowed over de whole place. Posey bragged about it; had it for years. Big 'nife wid one long blade. De handle's like pure pearl. Had P.G. on de side."

Jerome got a description of how the two were dressed, as Maybe remembered. Suddenly, Jerome turned to April. "Maybe is tired. I have most of the information I need."

He turned to Maybe once again. "Your wife and Posey were not having sex when you saw them?"

"No suh. They just be touching."

April turned to Jerome and handed him a tape measure. "Get his waist, inseam and chest measurements. I'll write them down."

When Jerome had finished April asked, "What size shoes?"

"'Bout 'levens."

"Maybe, someone will bring you some nice clothes to wear to the funerals. I want you to look real nice. Now if Mr. Lee will take your case, would you like him for a lawyer?"

"Ain't got no money, Miss April. I'd be highly pleased, but ain't no lawyer work for nothing. I knows that."

April rapped on the door and it opened instantly. "We have finished," April said, and they moved to the next room.

As they reached the hall April saw Sheriff Henderson. "Hope you had a nice visit," he said and grinned slightly.

April did not respond to his remark. "He will be at the funeral?"

"Yes. We'll have to follow regulations but he will be there."

"I'll have some clothing and shoes sent." April said.

"We will check the regulations," the sheriff said.

When they returned to Jerome's office April asked, "Will you take the case?"

"Let me review my notes and get my thoughts together. Perhaps I can have an answer by tomorrow.

"I don't believe I have ever seen one so unusual as you. I wonder what you will be like when you grow up?" he asked.

"One can never tell, Jerome. One can never tell. I'll hear from you tomorrow. Oh, I nearly forgot to tell you. I will be personally responsible for all fees involved. This is not Joseph Randolph business or Randolph Place business. This is between the two of us."

When she returned home she went directly to their little store. When Uncle Edd saw her he smiled. "Had a couple of good stories to tell you but they will keep. You've been a busy young lady."

"Uncle Edd, I need your help. I have Maybe's sizes and measurements. Men would know about such things. I want you to go and get Maybe a nice suit, shirt, shoes, belt, underwear and socks. Get him a tie as well. Get it to the jail in time so Maybe will have it for the funeral. Here is a signed check. Fill it in and bring me a bill so I can keep my account balanced."

A few moments later April told her mother much of what she had done.

"We may have some more problems," her mother said. "The Maybe event has created some strong feelings in the quarters. I am afraid we will have discord long after the funerals are over."

"Jerome is supposed to let me know if he will take the case tomorrow. I am not sure about how he feels. He is an unusual person, as well as a lawyer. I suspect his values are different from most."

CHAPTER 24

April was disappointed to learn that Jerome had called to postpone his visit a day longer than he had originally planned. "Did he say why?" she asked her mother.

"No. He simply said it would be Wednesday evening. I suppose it could have been any number of reasons."

On Tuesday evening Joseph called in his family once again to complete plans for the week and for the funerals. Since this was not a stockholder's meeting, Mary had been invited.

"Sorry we have been of little help," Joseph said. "It seems that the whites work while the blacks mourn." The sarcasm could be detected in his voice.

"Mary has really been a trouper the last three days," Martha said. "I don't believe we could have made it without her."

Joe spoke. "I'd just as soon she not play nursemaid to those buggers. They accept this as weakness rather than kindness." It was not difficult to know that he still felt very strongly about the quarters people.

"Children are involved, Joe. When this happens, we must be concerned. They have no control over certain matters," his mother said.

"Lottie Layton was by the house," Martha continued. "She believes she has everything planned and ready. She said April had been most helpful in the preparation."

"April?" Joe asked.

"Yes. We were busy and I asked April to check on some things when she was in Midway."

Mary said, "I have been happy to be a small part of this unusual time. I have learned some things that I did not know. I'm glad Mrs. Randolph asked me to assist."

"How many are going to the funeral?" Joseph asked. "Might be good for all of us to attend but I ain't gonna make anyone go."

Joe and Stephen did not raise their hands and no one asked why.

"We will take two cars then," Joseph decided.

"April can update us about her conference at the funeral home," Martha said.

"I met with Miss Layton yesterday and . . ."

"Miss Layton? Miss Layton? My God, when did we start addressing those people with such titles? My, my! We have, indeed, reached a new low. I can't believe what I am hearing!" Joe said sarcastically.

"Sorry, Joe. Let me start again," April said in a quiet voice. "I had a conference with Lottie Layton at her funeral home. We reviewed all aspects as best we could. Everything is in place, or will be in ample time. Cars and drivers are secured. The church is ready. Areas are reserved for special guests. The programs are ready to be printed. Their minister, D. C. Handmaker, will preside. Naturally the caskets will not be opened. Grave sites are being prepared."

"What about Maybe?" David asked.

"I visited Maybe at the jail and . . ."

"You what?" Joe asked. "You have spent your time at the jail with this crazy bum who has caused all the trouble? You do get around. Seems you are now running Randolph Place!"

Martha spoke more sharply than usual. "I had hoped we had learned some lessons recently. It seems my hopes and dreams are about to vanish."

"That's all right, Mother. Everyone has a perfect right to his opinion. Maybe will be allowed to attend the funeral. Sheriff Henderson seems a trifle upset with the Randolphs at this time but we can review this later," April said.

"What about some clothing for Maybe?" David asked. "I guess no one has thought about that."

"The problem is resolved," April said.

"You done dressed that bugger up, on top of everything else?" Joe asked as he continued to fret over the course of events.

"It will not cost you a dime, Joe. Neither will it cost the corporation," April said. "Suppose we move on and . . ."

"Dad, am I hearing right?" Joe asked. "Food, clothing, supplies, extended credit and God only knows what else. And legal help on top of it all. I think I've heard enough." With a hard look of anger in his cold eyes, Joe got up and left the room.

The group looked at Mary with an expression of pain. They knew she had no choice. "Would you excuse me? I think it would be best this way," Mary said, and slowly left the room.

"Has Jerome accepted the case?" Charles asked.

April said, "He will make a decision tomorrow evening."

"Slick Cannington would serve you better but it's your money. I don't think Slick or anyone else can help him though," Joseph said.

Martha said, "I have asked April to help us during this time. She has done what I have asked of her. If there is blame, I will accept the responsibility. She has responded in the best possible way."

Joseph said, "We'll get through this week some way. Next week will be a new beginning. But we ain't gonna fill our dreams, the way we're going."

At seven o'clock the next evening April went to her room and locked the door. She went to her closet and selected a flared skirt that had been an inch or so too short a year ago. She found a blouse that fit much too snugly and noted the low cut. She smiled and thought about what Charles had said three years ago in the gazebo.

She took off her shoes and clothes and walked naked over to the full length mirror on the back of the closet door. She stood erect, shoulders back and her head high. She was unable to see as she wished and switched on an additional light. She looked at herself full face, then profile. She then moved into the shower and let the water trickle down her body. She placed her hands under her breasts and pushed up slightly, although it was obvious they needed little support. She thought of Jerome and wondered if he would think she was a child if he could see her now. She smiled as she toweled her body.

An hour later Martha answered the door. "Please come in, Jerome. I'm sure April will be here in a few moments. We are all so fortunate to have you home again." It was a guess as to who was the most surprised when April moved into the room.

Jerome smiled. "Mrs. Randolph, it is amazing how quickly one reaches womanhood." April smiled broadly but her mother simply stood and stared, with a stern expression.

Jerome took both of April's hands in his and said, "A great deal has happened since you visited us three years ago." April's eyes sparkled as she continued to hold Jerome's hands. Abruptly, she dropped them, realizing what was happening.

He turned to Mrs. Randolph. "I am sure this has not been a good week."

"We will survive," Martha said. "April's father is restless, as always, during tobacco season. His schedule has been altered but we will make it. He is also anxious about the commissioner business. He knows so little about politics. I do know, however, that he would work hard to make a good commissioner."

"Mother will excuse us, Jerome. I have school tomorrow so we need to get about our business. Suppose we go into the library."

When they were seated Jerome said, "I like this room very much. Do you spend a lot of time here?"

"Yes. I like it in many ways. Other family members enjoy it as well. One has room to spread out. It is quiet and private.

She asked, "Why did you go into law? Many of the characteristics you have are not very compatible with those usually associated with a lawyer. Many lawyers do not enjoy a good reputation. We have already spoken years ago as to how Shakespeare and our Lord felt." She smiled.

"Lawyers seem to be condemned here and hereafter. Most people don't even make two sentences as to how they feel about the profession, but when trouble comes along, everyone seems to look for one. I cannot tell you in a few words why I am what I am. I'm not sure I could in a great number of words. Few people would understand, or believe, if I tried."

"Try me."

"Justice, throughout history, has not always prevailed, nor has it been administered fairly. There will always be the strong and the weak, the intelligent and the foolish, the rich and the poor. There will be the good as well as the evil. These things I cannot change.

"However, I feel that I can make a contribution in the lives of people. I am not a knight in shining armor but I feel an urge to assist the poor and helpless, as so many seem to prey on these unfortunates.

"I think many young men, and women, feel this way when they finish law school and enter the real world. But in time, often only a short time, many of the lawyers get caught up in the business of making money, a great deal of money, and establishing a special reputation for themselves. The hopes and dreams one acquires in law school are soon forgotten for many, perhaps most. Temptations are always present.

"I do not plan to operate like most. I knew this from the beginning. Most have or will call me a fool. I cannot accept compromise when something is right rather than wrong, when something is good rather than bad. Though it is said that our very Constitution was a bundle of compromises, there are some things I cannot do. Someday, I want to believe, man will rise above and find what is good. I know there are some things that are not always easily known, and that brings us to my purpose in being here. For forty-eight hours I have wrestled in this area, this shade of gray. I am convinced you believe Maybe acted to defend himself. I think you believe this with all your heart. At first I was convinced that your action was only to repay an old debt."

"Jerome, tell me you will take the case!"

"All of the evidence tells me one thing and you tell me another. As the matter now stands, Maybe cannot be exonerated of the charges against him. Without a knife, there is no possible way. There are few things going for him."

"You must take the case," she insisted.

"Perhaps an experienced attorney can serve you much better."

"Jerome, I want you. Had I wanted another, I would not have come to you."

"April, please don't do this to me. If we lose, and it is most likely, our relationship would never be the same. Maybe has nothing going for him. Everything is against him. You can't name one thing in his favor."

"Are you saying he is guilty? You don't believe him?"

"Maybe is not a saint. His character leaves much to be desired. He will be looked upon as guilty from the start. They won't have to prove him guilty and I don't know how to prove him innocent. This is not the way the law is supposed to work but it will be as I have described. Have you examined all the evidence? The axe, the bodies, the pictures and goodness knows what else. Character went out the window the moment they swapped families. He can't win. Without the knife, there is no way to substantiate his story, and, if there is no knife, he deserves to be punished severely. As I said moments ago, I delayed making this decision because I must feel that a client is innocent."

"He did it in self defense. I know Maybe more than most. He would not have done this out of anger, out of disappointment or because he felt betrayed. No, it was self defense."

"I came tonight to tell you I would not take the case. Now you are about to convince me that he acted to protect himself. But suppose he did? We still can't win."

"We will find a way, Jerome. You are telling me you will take the case. This is what you are saying, isn't it?"

"All of my few faculties, my little judgement, all of my instincts say no. But I'm going to take the case. I don't think we can win. I can't walk on the water. Neither can I change water into wine. I'm going to regret this the rest of my life."

Abruptly Jerome stood up to leave. April approached him and threw her arms around him. She pulled his head down and kissed him passionately. Then she realized he had not responded in a like manner. She drew back, smiled and asked, "Are you afraid?"

Again she moved her body against his and she knew he could see her breasts clearly and feel them against his chest. She kissed him again with all the passion she could muster. She felt his arms surround her for a few moments, but then he drew back.

"Do you believe I am a child?" she asked.

"No. I don't think you were ever a child in any way but there are some things you must learn in time. Goodnight, April. I think we have a great deal to consider."

April was not sure if it was Maybe or her actions that required consideration. Perhaps both.

CHAPTER 25

As April left the cemetery to return to the car an unexplained depression seemed to engulf her. She could not remember feeling such a despondency. After arriving home she answered all questions with a yes, no or I don't know response. In a matter of minutes she had spoken sharply to Charles twice. She remembered hearing someone say that sometimes you hurt those whom you love the most.

When April had retired to the library to be alone it was Charles who intruded. "I have not seen you like this before. You want to talk about it?"

"I do not know the nature of my problem."

Charles said, "I believe we all get like that from time to time. Let me suggest three things. First, give all the aid and support you can to our mother. She has had some difficult times recently. Secondly, it would be good for both you and our mother to continue with your beautification project. Lastly, why not give more time and attention to the place you have purchased? I think that is where your heart is.

April changed the subject completely. "Will Eric Lee get the job in the seventh grade?"

"Probably."

"Will this be good? One is often not accepted adequately in one's home community."

"It will be good to start at the seventh grade level. He can move to the higher grades in a year or two."

"What do you think about Jerome?"

"In a professional or personal way?"

"Both."

Charles said, "He will be a very fine lawyer but it will not be easy for him if he remains here. I can think of two reasons immediately. First, he is a country boy. Secondly, he marches to a different drummer."

"I don't understand."

"His standards and values are different. This could make other lawyers feel uncomfortable. He would not be one of them. As such, he will not be accepted by them. It will not be easy to start a successful practice here."

"And as a person?"

"Why are you so concerned about Jerome? He is more than twenty-six years old. Men his age do not get very excited about girls your age. Please don't dream yourself into a land of make-believe. I do not wish to see you hurt."

"I will be working with Jerome, since he has agreed to take Maybe's case. The better I know him and understand him, the more I can assist him."

"I am not sure this is all about Maybe but I will not linger on that matter. Jerome does not let his life become an open book. It isn't that he has something to hide or that there is something about him undesirable. He is a private person. He is good. He is smart. He is a family oriented person. Perhaps that is the reason he is working here. Only his mother would know the real Jerome. Mothers always know more about their children than their children realize. Eric is different. One can know Eric in a month or so. Not so Jerome.

"I trust Jerome as much as anyone I know. There are few like him. There will be few like him.

"You like this man, don't you? You really like this man!" Charles said.

"I like most people. There is usually something good to be found in most. You need to know the bad but you build and grow from the good. Also, as you said earlier, there are many differences."

April spotted Michael John. "I need to see you."

"I'm very busy. What is on your mind?"

"Housing."

"It's on my mind as well," Michael John said. "I added two men yesterday. I want David's house to be ready when he and Kathy marry."

"We talked about needing a helper to assist at my place."

"I've done nothing. I haven't had a free moment."

"What would a helper be required to do?"

After Michael John had provided such facts as he felt necessary he asked, "Do you have someone in mind?"

"Perhaps. What would you think of Robert White?"

"He helps his father."

"He could help here and his father could find a part time person."

"Then see him. I think he would be fine."

April said, "I prefer you see him. You could give a job description and answer his questions."

"I'll see him in a day or so."

"You know, Michael John, since David is getting married, you should be next." She saw his face turn red.

"Charles is next," he said.

"But Charles has himself a girl all staked out. Miss Knight could be our new sister."

Michael John shook his head but said nothing.

"You don't think so?" April asked.

"I don't think so in either case. I would bet Charles and Sara Knight never get married. And who would want me, April? I'm no prize. We both know that. I'll just watch the others for a while."

"I think some real nice, smart, pretty girl is going to come along and grab you. You won't know what hit you. You have so much to offer some young lucky lady."

"Not yet. Perhaps someday, but not soon."

"You could give some special girl everything. There would be a new house, new furniture, a car and whatever her heart desired. And yes, all the pretty clothes a girl likes to have."

Michael John became very serious. "I wouldn't want someone to want me because I could give her these things. I want someone to want me because she loves me. I suppose that just about rules out everyone. April, why don't we just stick to houses?"

"You have grossly underestimated everything about yourself. No one has grown in so many ways in the last four years. Please don't be so hard on yourself. Someday soon it will happen. You see, Michael John, a woman just knows about these things."

CHAPTER 26

"When can Charles and I have an hour to discuss a matter with you?" Martha looked at her husband.

"Martha, what can be so important? Ain't it possible that we can talk at another time? This is tobacco time!"

The expression on Martha's face could not be concealed. "I don't believe you have to remind me of that!" Her voice was on edge. "My first reminder is when the clock goes off at a quarter to four." Joseph turned his head in disbelief, as he had never been confronted by Martha in this manner before.

"I suggest we meet in the library after supper." She turned and walked toward the laundry room, where the two washing machines had just completed their cycles. Joseph, stunned for a moment, turned and moved toward the door.

After supper had been completed Joseph went into the den and picked up the *Atlanta Constitution*. As he did he glanced toward Martha to see her reaction. It was as if he wanted or expected her to remind him of her request. She said nothing. Then, like a small child pouting, he got up without saying a word and went to the little library.

Charles and April watched their mother; she had asked them to join her. She waited a few seconds, got up and nodded to the two. All three of them then joined Joseph. He sat at the table as if bored to death. He seemed to be saying, "Why are you doing this to me?"

When they were seated he looked from one to another sullenly. This was unlike the Joseph they knew. "What is this important matter that can't wait?" No one could recall such a mood.

Martha said in a quiet, normal voice, "It has been determined that Meggie Winter, who is really not a Winter, is not a Negro girl. She is a white girl."

"I ain't sure I heard you right," Joseph said. "What did you say?" He had gotten up out of his chair, but then sat back down.

"An investigation has been completed. It has been substantiated that both of her parents were white. Actually, she is not the granddaughter of Uncle Edd."

Joseph sat stunned for a moment, both confused and perplexed. Finally he said, "Let me see if I understand all this. You are telling me that this black girl ain't a black girl no longer? And if she ain't a black girl, she must be a white girl? She has been living with a man, believed to be her grandfather, who is black, and a brother, that is not a brother, who is black. She has been going to a black school with a bunch of quarters people and has been going to a black church that is full of black people. But she is white! What in the hell is going on here? Somebody better have some real good explanations, real good proof. And where, if this is true, does it leave me? What will the voters say when they hear about all this?

"Here I am at the beginning of my best farming efforts, discord running rampant in the quarters, operating without three of my best people, and you tell me we now have a girl that was, for sixteen years, a Negro girl and is now about to become a full fledged white person!" Joseph, his face flushed, pounded on the table and shouted, "Somebody had better have some good reasons for not telling me about this!"

He turned suddenly when Charles spoke. "Suppose I start. Many . . ."

"How are you involved in all this," he interrupted. "Are you the one that made this black into a white? Ain't it right for me to be in on this from the beginning?"

Charles started again. He spoke quietly in an effort to bring about a more relaxed climate. "As I started to say, a person in the community, a most respected person, approached me expressing a great deal of doubt about Meggie's race. This person was positive that the child was white. For the most part, I dismissed it from my mind. There were many reasons. We'll get to that later if you wish detailed explanations.

"Recently this same person approached me again. It was obvious that if I did not make some effort, someone else would. I believed it better that I do something discreetly, without a lot of fanfare. My first step was a conference with Uncle Edd. There were many things I did and did not learn. One thing I did learn, however, was that he had already started an investigation himself. It was nearly completed.

"As we talked, he insisted we find such facts as were needed but leave all other areas of his life and the life of some others a part of the past. I cannot tell you all the reasons why Uncle Edd initiated this investigation, other than that he felt it essential. I joined, upon his request, in an effort to learn the truth.

"In time we learned, verified and substantiated that she was, indeed, a white child. Both of her parents were white. I am sure an explanation is in order.

"Uncle Edd is three-fourths white. He married a white woman early in life and they had a son. Thus the son was seven-eighths white. He in turn, that is, Uncle Edd's son, married a white woman. They had a child. We all know this person. He is Craig Winter. He is one-sixteenth black.

"Some few years later Craig's wife delivered another child, Meggie. It is a long story and I will provide such details that I know later if you insist. But Meggie's father was not Uncle Edd's son. Her father was a white man. Thus, we find Meggie a white person. She is not actually related to Uncle Edd, if you think through it, but she is a half sister to Craig, as they had the same mother. As far as I am concerned, this is all one really needs to know. All of this is now a part of the legal record elsewhere. There is absolutely no doubt.

"Now Father asked, 'Why did I not know about it?' Uncle Edd insisted that no one know until the total truth was learned. I only knew a few hours ago. With the many problems confronting our father, I felt he would be best served by waiting until the investigation was complete. I also waited until Uncle Edd agreed that others should know the facts, the truth. If I have failed, I accept the blame. Mother and April were not aware until a very short time ago."

There was a momentary hush among them, as if they were putting all these unusual events together.

Martha asked, "Why was Uncle Edd silent all these years? Why did he take steps to correct what may be termed an injustice at this particular time?"

"I can only guess," Charles said. "Perhaps it was to protect some of the parties involved. Perhaps something else. If he wants others to know, he will tell them. I believe he acted in a manner he felt best. I am sure it was difficult for him to learn that his son's wife was not faithful. Why bring up the unpleasant past if it wasn't necessary?"

April spoke for the first time. "I am sure there will be some painful events to occur in the immediate future."

"Uncle Edd said it was time the three of you knew. That is why Mother asked that we meet."

"I ain't feeling good about being left out of this all important matter," Joseph said. "Ain't it strange that the legal head of the family and the president of the corporation ain't been told nothing from the beginning?"

"Father, I am not sure when Uncle Edd began his investigation. If all of us had known, what would have been different? Now you know the facts that were only confirmed hours ago. It is not like someone did not want you to know. If ever a man has been confronted with problems, it has been you. No one wanted to add more."

After Martha opened the discussion she remained entirely in the background, except for two questions. "It was today that Uncle Edd and Meggie were over to talk with me. Naturally they were very emotional. Think with me a moment. It would be like all of us learning that April or Stephen would have a new life and some form of separation would be forthcoming.

"I have some strong feelings about the matter," Martha said, "but I am reluctant to express them now. I know that Uncle Edd wants the best for Meggie, regardless of the pain he must endure."

"The decision of the court is final? There ain't gonna be no changes, no reversal?" Joseph asked.

"It is final," Charles said.

"What options are there for Meggie? Will the court place her up for adoption? Will they permit her to make a decision on her own? She ain't of legal age. What's gonna be done with the child? Surely ain't none of us thinking of her living with us. What an impact on everybody! What would it do to everyone? Can you see the headlines of our local paper? 'Randolphs take Negro who is not a Negro for their very own!'"

Martha looked at her husband with disbelief. "Are we saying that it was fine for a Negro girl to be in our home as a maid or cook, but as a white girl she should not?"

"This will kill me politically. I might as well withdraw. With integration on the minds of everyone, it will be too much!"

April said, "It could be a big advantage to you. This would be looked upon as an act of segregation. I would think such an act could give you an advantage. Also, I hope this is not the major criteria to be considered in making a decision that will determine Meggie's future."

"I want each of us to think about this for an hour," Martha said. "Then we can return and make some decisions." She got up and walked through the door.

An hour later Joseph said, "There ain't no perfect solution, but me and Martha feel it would be best for her to become a part of this household. We can take such steps in the courts, if necessary. I must say, she is a fine child. Also, it could help more than harm my political career. April was quick to point this out. I am also aware we can ill afford to lose Uncle Edd."

Each spoke of their acceptance of this decision.

"I gather then that this is all settled?" Charles asked. He looked at the other three.

"We will wait to move on this until after the qualifying date has come and gone," Joseph said. "It ain't but a few days. Will take some planning anyway."

Martha asked, "Will Charles be the one to tell Uncle Edd and Meggie what has been decided?"

They all nodded. Then Charles said, "It would be well that many things be determined. Our mother can give her some responsibilities. It would be helpful for all household members to know and understand."

Martha stood and said, "The right thing has been done." She moved toward the door.

Chapter 27

Charles looked at his desk, cluttered with account and payroll sheets, as well as invoices. Were there enough hours left to complete his work? He did not wish to seek excuses, since his father had been most difficult recently. He then heard a knock on his closed door and wondered who could be interrupting at this time. "Come in," he said. The tone of his voice did not reflect the same meaning as his words.

His "three girls" filled the door. "I heard all the enthusiasm in your voice," April said. "One look at your desk is worth a thousand words. Charles, how can you make such a mess?" The other two girls looked at Charles, then at April, and smiled.

"I was about to look you girls up. I'll need some help before Saturday morning. We have a large number of extra people working now."

Gena said, "We will make a trade with you. We'll pull your marbles out of the fire for an invitation for Thursday evening. You really don't have a choice!"

"You are right but isn't it a little unusual for girls, even in this new liberated age in which we live, to be so brazen? It seems three minors are attempting to force their company upon one lone male."

"What time should we be ready, Charles, and what shall we wear?" Meggie asked, her eyes sparkling. No longer, Charles noted, was she the frightened, insecure girl Miss Knight had seen when she had been a guest in their home.

"Six o'clock. The traffic will be heavy. I would suggest you wear about what you would wear to church."

"Wait a minute, girls!" Meggie nearly shouted. "We have not been thinking and we are more than selfish. Certainly April must go, but Gena and I should not. Look at all of Charles' family. I am sure that each graduate gets a limited number of seats. No, we can't even think about going." Gena nodded in agreement.

"Yes, girls, all three of you can go. Mother and I have talked. She can't go. We do not need to discuss why. In fact, Mother suggested that the three of you go as my guests."

"We will be ready," Gena said, "and so will your payroll on Saturday. I really wonder how you ever made it without us!"

On Thursday evening they left for Tallahassee, after being warned by Joseph that the payroll must be ready. April had taken a back seat with Meggie, while Gena sat with Charles.

"Gena is thrilled," April said. "You cannot help but be aware that she is desperately in love with you."

Charles turned his head slightly toward the back as Gena blushed. "All young girls are in love with someone. I am honored that Gena feels kindly toward me. Even you two will find something good about me in time."

"I hope so," April said. "Do we look all right? We have never been to a college graduation."

"Nor have I," Charles said laughing. "It is a first for all of us."

"I am so proud of Charles," Meggie said. "Are you the first in your family to graduate? Will you be the first to walk across the stage and receive your college diploma?"

"I could well be the first. April will assure me I will not be the last. However, you are wrong about one thing."

"You did graduate?" Meggie asked in a pretended alarm.

"Oh, I will graduate and get a diploma but I will not walk across a stage. Those graduating with a Bachelor's degree sit and watch the others. Only those receiving a Master's degree or a Doctor's degree will go on the stage. You may accompany me to the library to pick up the diploma after the commencement program is completed. Oh, I nearly forgot. Your reserve seats will be a great distance from the stage."

"Doesn't seem fair. You should get to cross the stage in our little school," Gena said.

"Perhaps a year from now we can do it all over again and I will cross the stage. I start a graduate program next week. Miss Knight will continue also. She will finish her six-year program."

"She is leaving, Charles. Why? Where will she go?" Gena asked.

"She hasn't told me."

"She hasn't told you?" Meggie asked.

"No."

"You think a lot of her?" Meggie continued.

"Yes."

"Why don't you marry her?" Gena asked.

"She probably wouldn't have me."

"I would have you," Gena said.

"Who will replace her?" Meggie asked.

"Let's wait for an announcement from the superintendent, the principal or the trustees. I would guess you know the replacement but I can say no more at this time."

Charles moved the car into the parking lot. "You have a long walk. The school has grown so rapidly that they can't get enough roads and parking lots where they are needed."

The girls made their way to their seats. They were a great distance from the stage. They were amazed at the academic regalia. "I have never seen so many colors and designs," Gena said. "I suppose it all stands for something."

In less time than they had guessed, the program ended. Charles met them and they made their way to the library. As they moved toward the building Meggie said, "There would be no limit as to what a person could do with their life. There is so much for one to learn. I hope someday all of us can be a part of this or some other good institution."

"You will. My mother made that promise years ago. However, you must make some choices at some point. I am told it would take twenty-five hundred years to take all the courses offered at this institution. Think of all the great universities. This one is not one of the largest yet but in time it will be."

"We are just a group of ignorant girls," April said. "We can't hope to become truly educated!"

As Charles was handed his diploma he handed it to the girls to see. "Seems very small to represent four years of work. Attapulgus has a larger diploma than this!" Gena said.

When they were back in the car Charles said, "In a way, scholars are like actors and entertainers in that they give each other awards. This requires an audience and thus they all promote each other." He laughed and continued, "Without such we might disappear."

"Now tell us what you plan to do with the rest of your life?" April asked. "You have gained a degree and lost a potential wife. You are a mystery!"

Charles said, "So many roads and so little time. I wish I knew. Oh, how I wish I knew. My goals seem so different from most. You may not believe it, but I have no desire to make a lot of money. You have been a witness to this already. I am not interested in making a big name for myself, even if I could.

"At the risk of sounding noble, I must find something in which I can accomplish two things. I must find a profession in which I feel something worthwhile can be accomplished each new day. It must be exciting — a challenge. Secondly, it must be something in which I can serve others as well as myself." He hoped the girls could not read his thoughts as he thought of the little call girl he had encountered as a sophomore, who had been so honest and delightful.

"Medicine?" April asked.

"No."

"Law?" Gena followed.

"No. It could be exciting, but no. Most of them will surely go to hell."

"Jerome will not," April nearly shouted.

"Teaching?" Meggie asked. "You seem to enjoy your work with us. From what I can learn about teachers' salaries, making money could be dismissed from your mind."

"April, a moment ago you responded regarding law. Were you defending lawyers or only Jerome?"

"I only know one. I am in no position to judge others. I also have an opinion about bankers but let's not touch on that."

"I know what you will do, Charles, and I may wish to join you if you will let me," Meggie said.

"Tell me so we can both know what we are to do, Meggie."

"We will go into educational research. We need to know so many things we have not learned. I can think of a hundred areas we could research. There are so many unanswered questions. I want you to do this, Charles, and I want to help you."

Gena said, "Changing the subject, but how will we pay this gentleman back for all the hours he has given us over the many years?"

April laughed. "Your question has merit but you spoke of Charles as a gentleman. I would suspect many would challenge this description."

Charles laughed. "I am reminded of a saying. I don't know who said it first, but it goes like this: 'An old man is fond of giving good advice to console himself because he is no longer in a position to give a bad example.' I believe this describes me best. I am a true gentleman because of my age.

"I am delighted you have honored me with your presence. You say I have influenced your lives but perhaps you have influenced my life even more. I suspect that without the three of you, I would have departed long ago. You have made me pleased with my decision to stay.

"We must all prepare ourselves for many changes in the near future. All of our lives will change more than we realize; but such talk is for another day."

As Gena got out of the car at her home she reached over and patted Charles on the cheek. "We congratulate you again. Thank you for letting us be a part of this occasion. And yes, we will come over and do your work for you. Goodnight." Charles waited until she had unlocked her front door and entered.

Charles then parked the car between Meggie's house and his own. April opened the car door and moved toward her house. "Goodnight. See you tomorrow." She disappeared.

"Can you spare a few more minutes?" Meggie asked. Charles could see her fine and delicately carved head as she opened the door to the front seat and slid in. In the soft light she appeared a little haughty but he then realized it was a cover for insecurity. "My life will be completely different very soon. I will need your continued assistance and your guidance. My life will change and I must know you and others are there to help in my transition. I can't make it without you."

"You will be fine, Meggie. You are a strong person. Yes, your life will change, perhaps more than you realize, but I suspect you have explored these areas already. Someday you may wish to thank Sara Knight. She had more insight than all of us. Suppose we take it a day at the time."

Meggie reached in her purse and pulled out a small package. "This is for you. Please do not say I should not have done it. It is a gift of the heart."

Charles removed the paper and opened the box. There was a card and he switched on the inside light to read, "Congratulations." She moved over and kissed him on the cheek in a brother-sister manner. Then she pulled him toward her and kissed him firmly on the lips. Charles remained rather rigid and offered no response. She withdrew her lips and said, "The inscription on the back tells my real feelings." Once again her lips sought his and she pushed her body against him. She felt his body change from the rigid manner she had encountered; he put his arms around her and responded warmly and passionately. In a moment he pushed her gently from him and looked in her eyes as the moonlight struck her face. They sparkled as never before.

"I have reacted in a manner that was improper," Charles said. "I have done you a dishonor. I had not planned to do that or let such happen. What can I say?"

"You need not speak. I have learned what I need to know. I hope you think of me as often as you look at your watch. Now peck me on the cheek in a brotherly manner and I will say goodnight." He waited until he saw her enter and close the door to her home.

When Charles went to his room he looked closely at the new watch. It was both beautiful and expensive. He turned and looked at the back. Inscribed were the words, "I love you."

CHAPTER 28

As April was about to leave the house she was intercepted by her father. "You gonna be helping me this afternoon. Tell your mother, in case she needs some help."

"I don't understand. I have several obligations today. There are materials to order for both houses and . . ."

"David can get married anytime. Your play house can wait. We gonna put first things first."

"And first things are?" April asked.

"I guess you had planned to see that crazy Maybe again?"

"Yes, I was going to stop by. What are 'first things'?" she asked again.

"We both promised Bruce McPherson you would review the operation with his son. I believe we usually live up to our promises."

"I would do it, though I must confess it would bring no pleasure. I would help if I had some notice or was able to choose a time." She continued, "I don't think you understand my feelings about this person. He represents some things I detest." She repeated, "I don't believe you understand."

"He represents what you detest? And I thought you to be the bright one! You detest what he represents! His family represents money and power. They will make me a county commissioner. There ain't no one that detests money and power. They are usually one and the same.

"I want him to see it all and you can answer such questions as he might wanta know."

"You and Joe know so much more. Wouldn't you serve his needs better?"

"You will conduct the tour. I am beginning to wonder about your fairness. He is young and the young get carried away at times. We all did. This is a nice looking man. He is intelligent. He has a good college record. He was at the top of his class in high school and . . ."

"You seem to have researched him carefully in some ways. He is a gentleman? Stories abound to the contrary! Can a man that thinks such of Attapulgus, that would be so unkind, be a special friend?"

"We ain't living in Attapulgus. I have said this a hundred times. The people of this community ain't always been kind to me and my people. But we're wasting time. Be ready. He will be here at one-thirty."

On the exact half-hour the door chimes rang, announcing his arrival. April could hear her mother's voice. "Come in, Victor. It's nice to see you again. You don't look like the weary school boy. I'll tell April you are here."

"It is nice for Mr. Randolph and April to arrange this for me. I'm sure it will be an exciting time."

April entered the den. "How are you, Victor? You don't look the worse for wear. Perhaps the University of Georgia and Midway operate somewhat the same!" There was a twinkle in her eyes but she did not smile.

"I hope you will allow me to make some amends. My father did not speak kindly about my behavior."

He turned to Mrs. Randolph. "You have a very spirited and beautiful daughter. One without spirit is not a complete person."

"Would you stay for dinner?" Martha asked. "It will take some time to see the operation. You will be tired and hungry."

"He probably couldn't eat such as we poor country farmers serve," April said. Again she didn't smile.

"Thank you, Mrs. Randolph. I must decline. It is not because of what may be served." He looked at April. "I have an engagement. Please remember me again."

April announced, "Perhaps we should start. We wouldn't wish you to miss your engagement. It will take longer than a few minutes. We will ride in the truck. Leave your coat and tie in your car. Please let me open and close my own door to the truck, as we will be in and out often. Shall we start?"

They started first at what had once been the plant bed. "This is where it all starts. Chemicals are used to purify the soil. The seeds, as small as mustard seeds, are planted. The seeds spring into plants and they are transferred to the shades. Oh yes, a mustard seed is very small." She laughed. They got back into the pick-up.

As they rode April explained. "The fields have been prepared with a heavy concentration of fertilizers, commercial as well as barnyard. We call it cow manure. President Truman used another term to identify such in his earlier years." She never smiled.

"Once the shade cloth is attached, mules must be used from that point on. The cloth comes in large sheets and is sewed together and attached to the wires above. Any questions?"

"Two fertilizers?"

"Yes. One is for the plant in the beginning. The other sustains the growth much longer. Once the tobacco starts growing, it grows rapidly."

"How are the plants set out?"

"By hand, one at a time. They are each watered separately and immediately. All of this is done by hand, one dipper at the time."

"And the tobacco grows rapidly?"

"Yes, once it starts. Sometimes on a hot day and night as much as seven or eight inches."

"When do you start taking the leaves off?"

"Suppose we wait until we get to the shade. You will see the process. You will not wish to stay long there. The temperature can easily reach a hundred and twenty degrees and there is no breeze."

In two minutes they were in the shade. "It *is* hot!" Victor said. "How do they work under these conditions?"

"Not like they work in an air conditioned bank!" She smiled, but said no more.

Victor looked at the plants growing skyward. "Why the string on each plant?"

"The plant grows so rapidly the root system cannot sustain it without support. The process is called wrapping and must be done several times. Again you see the need for manual labor."

They watched as the leaves were pruned from the stalk. "The men remove the leaves from the stalk. They call this priming. They take two, three or four leaves. It allows the others to grow larger. Over a period of time we take from sixteen to twenty, sometimes twenty-two, from a stalk."

They saw some young children take the leaves to a central place for transfer to the barns. Sweat dripped from each. The young girls were not wearing any bras. The outline of their breasts could be clearly seen as the blouses stuck to their bodies. They did not seem to notice.

It was as if April had a personal relationship with each. She spoke and called each by name. "You know all of them?" Victor asked. "Their names, that is?"

"I think so. This creates a better relationship for everyone.

She continued. "The leaves being removed now are probably the third priming. They will be larger and more valuable. The first leaves are called sand leaves because of the position next to the ground. Sometimes the sand will damage them."

At that moment they heard a shout nearby. "Damn it, be careful with those leaves!"

April smiled. "That is Stephen. He can use such language as well as the grown-ups. He feels it will improve his status. Come and meet him."

As they moved in his direction Stephen moved forward to meet them. "Hello, Victor. I heard you were to visit today."

"Growing tobacco involves much more than I realized."

Stephen smiled and said, "I'll just be a banker! Keeping these blacks on track isn't the easiest job in the world."

"We'll not delay you," April said. "We are on our way to the barn."

April parked to avoid blocking the vehicles bringing the tobacco into the barns. "This is a standard sized barn. The windows, all of wood, open from the bottom and are on hinges. The barns are usually close to the shades for obvious reasons. The center aisle is filled with tobacco on tables. It is distributed to the stringers as needed. Each person has a role to play. As the sticks are strung and tied they are removed from the racks by those called 'luggers,' who carry them to the point of the 'puncher,' who moves them upward to the hangers to be hung for drying or curing."

"How many leaves on a stick?"

"Twenty-eight to thirty-two. It depends on size."

"How many sticks, as you called them, can a stringer string in a day?"

"It varies with the individual. Perhaps an average of four hundred."

"Are the stringers paid by the stick or the hour?"

"By the stick. They are brought to them in units of fifty by the person called the stick boy. He punches their card when he delivers the sticks. He also delivers the string with the sticks."

They looked up and saw Joe approaching. "Welcome," he said as he shook Victor's hand. "I hope you are being served adequately?"

"Indeed I am. She is a wonderful host and guide. I know so little. I can understand now some of the tensions felt by you farmers in this season. We are not here to interrupt your work. April is about finished. I can take in only so much. I wish to find an excuse to return." April made sure she was looking elsewhere.

"I'll run," Joe said. "Supervision is required and we have lost some good people since last year."

She led Victor over to an elderly black woman was stringing. "Aunt Jenny, this is Mr. McPherson, Victor McPherson. He is a city boy and has come to see a tobacco operation. I want him to watch you string a stick. Go a little slower and explain what you do." She smiled and watched Victor closely.

"You can show him, Miss April." Jenny looked at Victor. "She can string a hundred more sticks a day than us."

"You?" Victor looked at April.

"I strung some one summer. Aunt Jenny likes to make me feel good. Watch her."

"You ties de string on one end, get your needle threaded and here you go. Goes like dis. You runs the needle through the middle part of the stem and you grabs wid care de next leaf. You do the same but you turns de leaf so you got back to back and belly to belly."

April laughed. "Go ahead, Aunt Jenny. This city boy doesn't understand such things!"

Victor watched, amazed at her speed and accuracy. "Did I hear you say something?"

"I'se counting. Us gets twenty-eight on this priming. Leaves lot bigger." She moved her fingers quickly and looped and tied the string on the other end. She looked at Victor and smiled as she placed it on her rack.

April said, "Your turn!"

It took Victor more than ten minutes to string one stick. "It isn't all that easy, is it?" He smiled.

April called, "Wallace?" A young white lad of sixteen or so approached. "Wallace Baldwin, meet Mr. McPherson. Mr. McPherson is a guest from Midway. He runs the bank where we get our money. He charges more interest than he should but we understand." She laughed, then instructed Wallace. "Please give Aunt Jenny another punch on her card. We have delayed her."

"We are happy that you would visit us. Your father runs The Peoples's Bank?" Wallace asked.

"Yes. I go to school. It's a great deal more fun."

Wallace raced back as another stringer called for sticks.

"Bless you, child," Aunt Jenny said as they moved toward the other end of the barn.

April said, "This is the part I am most displeased about. We could call this the nursery." Several old quilts had been spread on the ground and several Negro babies crawled about. Their ages ranged from a few days to several months. A girl that appeared to be about fourteen was nursing a small child. Her breasts were fully exposed. She smiled at them and said, "Have to take us some time wid our babies. Seems like dey always be hungry. We love to see our babies but us loses a lot of sticks."

"How old are you Nellie?" April asked.

"I'se fifteen last week."

"What is your baby's name?" April asked.

"Lincoln, ma'am."

"I believe you named your older child Mary?"

"I did that. Yes'm. She's at granny's house. She ain't got to be fed like this youngun. Two be enough, Miss April. Men tell you dis and dat but it ain't always dis and dat!"

April looked at Victor and smiled. "Yes, men are like that. It is best to always be careful, watch closely and believe little they say!"

Victor smiled but said nothing. He was ready to move on. The pails holding the soiled diapers left an unpleasant odor.

"Why not set up a nursery elsewhere?"

"It would cause them a longer loss of time, so they say. I suggested that strongly. But I'll not get into that."

"Let me tell you the rest now, Victor, as we move to the packing house. The leaves are cured in the barn and moved to the packing house. It is done by a special process whereby they get the tobacco in what is called 'case.' In the tobacco warehouse it is inspected and graded one leaf at a time. It is placed into a form called a 'book'.

"Then the buyers come. We do not work under contract. Joseph tried this one year and said never again. Then the seed bed is prepared once again and we go through the same process."

"Welcome to the land of the golden leaf," Charles said as they entered the office where he was working. "You are working with your father this summer?"

"Yes. I would rather be in Europe but again I was refused.

"How do you see tobacco in the future?" Victor asked. "We hear some talk." April and Charles looked at each other as to who would respond.

Finally Charles said, "I doubt it will be grown in this area for another five years. The process of homogenization will have a great deal to do with it. The government will change a lot of laws and make some new ones. When the profit is gone, so is tobacco."

"As time goes by, you will hear stronger protests about the harmful effects of tobacco and in time I suspect there will be evidence," April said.

As they walked toward Victor's car she heard him say, "I hope we can be friends. Perhaps we can get together again?"

"Victor, I am sixteen. I have two years of high school left. I have a life that is completely different from yours. Suppose we let some years pass and then we can look again."

Joseph approached. "Nearly missed you. Glad you are here. Did you get a good look? Was April doing her job?"

"Indeed she has. She was perfect. She knows tobacco like my father hopes I can learn banking."

"Come back as you wish. You are always welcome. Maybe I will not be as busy next time."

Joseph and April watched as Victor's car moved down the lane. "That boy will go a long way. It would be well to keep an eye on him. He certainly has an eye on you. I suspect we ain't seen the last of that lad."

April wanted to say that country and city don't mix any more than oil and water, but she remained silent.

"I hope you were nice to him. It was very important."

"I was nice, Joseph. I would not wish to disappoint you."

"We'll see what the future holds! Who knows? Yes, that boy could go a long way!" Joseph said as he rushed back to the barns.

Chapter 29

As the days moved deeper into June April found herself more involved with house building than she had anticipated. She moved from one construction site to another, since Michael John had insisted she keep him informed and that she place orders for needed materials. She watched the step-by-step process and was reminded of the similarity of a house and person. A great deal of time and attention must be given to the foundation. Michael John joined her and they looked at what had been done. She felt good about what she saw. She could envision how it would all look later.

"How do you feel about everything?" he asked. "Patience is not your best characteristic." He laughed.

"I am pleased. It takes longer when old material is not used. The carpenters are very skilled in what they do. They give a good day's work. No one can ask more."

"What do you think about the decision to employ Robert? Do you believe it wise?" Michael John asked.

"At the beginning he stood back because of his youth and inexperience. However, once he understood what was needed, he moved forward to accomplish the tasks. We had thought of someone, as you suggested, to hold, pass and clean up, but he does much more. In a few days it may be difficult to determine the helper by observation. Perhaps an increase in salary would be appropriate."

Michael John talked with the carpenter he had selected to be in charge. He made some notes and returned to April. He seemed to hesitate before he spoke. "I may have some news for you that may not be pleasing."

"Try me," April said. "I am never displeased with you."

"I wish you had not said that because you will be disappointed. I may need to take the crew here and place them on David's house. I believe it is important that his house be finished before he gets married."

"Indeed so. Don't give it another thought. We must finish his house so he can have a place to take Kathy. I have a lifetime to finish mine."

"I hoped you would say that. However, we will not stop on yours until it is totally protected from the weather. I know I can count on you to see that adequate material is delivered on time. I'll run. This is tobacco season!"

After Michael John had left April turned to look toward the house once again. She could not be more pleased. Suddenly, she looked at Robert. Perspiration was running down his face but he didn't seem to mind. He looked so big, so strong. Why, he was nearly as tall as Charles and there was not an ounce of fat on his body. He was a handsome young man and his posture was as straight as a gate post, his head held high on his ample shoulders.

April wondered why she had never looked closely before. His hair was a very light brown and it was not long upon his neck. His eyes were large and blue, with a twinkle displaying spirit and enthusiasm. Perhaps mischief? No. She had never seen such. Most of the time he was thoughtful and serious. His face expressed character and determination. His ready smile easily drew people to him and his concern for others retained them.

Why haven't I noticed Robert White before? He has been here all this time. We have been in the same class in school for ten years.

She looked closely once more and returned to her car. She closed her eyes and in minutes she seemed to see two images very clearly. There was Robert, as she had seen moments ago. Then there was another who recently discovered she wasn't a little girl anymore. She felt so unsure.

April soon learned the best time to visit her construction site. If she came before twelve, they were working. If she came at twelve, they were eating. But if she came at twelve fifteen, she would not interrupt. It was to be the time when she would learn the real Robert, the Robert so few knew.

She knew that he lived in a small frame house only a few blocks from the school. She also knew, as did everyone, that his father ran a small service station near the center of town. She knew that Robert had twin sisters, Michelle and Mimi. They were a grade behind Robert. She knew that Robert's mother had died a few years ago and that Clint White had never remarried. He spent all of his time working and looking after his three children.

What else did she know about this recently discovered young man? He was smart. He had a high average and was the top male student in their class. He was quiet. He seemed to always think before he spoke. He was a fine athlete and would probably, before he graduated, be remembered as one of the best, if not the best. He had a good relationship with his teachers as well as his classmates. Why had she not recognized all these characteristics before now? She had no answer.

As they talked one day Robert said, "I wish I was quick like you. You always seem ready for what comes and you always respond immediately. You are miles ahead of all of us. How wonderful this must be."

"Your way is better," April said smiling. Then she laughed. "Certainly you haven't forgotten our experiences in the seventh grade with Miss Knight?" Both seemed to blush.

She said, "Your way is best. You think and then speak. You have a great deal less to explain later when you do it that way. I place myself in a most compromising position all too often. I find it amusing that each of us seems to admire the approach the other uses."

A few days later her mother asked, "Why do you always go to see your new house at lunch time?"

"Have I created a problem? It was not my intention. I can rearrange my schedule. I had gone at this time so that I would not stop them from their work or their lunch."

"Do you use some of the time to talk with Robert? I hope so. He is so nice."

"How can mothers always know?" April's eyes sparkled. "Can a daughter have no secrets?"

"All girls your age have secrets. I did, as I recall."

"How is it that I just now seem to have discovered him after having been with him more than a thousand hours each year for ten years?"

"There comes a time in everyone's life in which they discover or seem to discover something that has been there all the time. You see it only when it is time to see it. I am happy that you enjoy your new association with him."

The next day April asked Robert, "Do you play golf?"

"No. I have worked as a caddie. It was a way to pick up a few dollars. I like to walk. I like the outdoors. I like people. And yes, I learn a great deal about the people who play golf." Robert smiled. "I putted a few times when I got to the course early. I couldn't keep my head down. I always wanted to see where the ball was going. It seems to require a great deal of discipline and concentration. I come up short on both."

"You would make a great golfer!"

"Why do you say that? There is no way for you to know this."

"You have the basic requirements. You are strong and coordinated. But most important, you have the temperament. You would be calm and you would think before you acted."

"You are wrong for two reasons," Robert said. "When you go out and do the same thing the same way twice and nothing comes out the same as you did it the first time, it would cause too much pain and frustration."

"And the second reason?" April asked.

"It is a game for the affluent. It is for those who have a great deal of leisure time. I do not possess these attributes nor is it likely that I will for years to come. Perhaps never."

"I don't like this kind of talk. You are what you are and may become what you wish."

"There is much distinction between the affluent and the poor. It has always been so. You know that," Robert said.

"This does not sound like you. What do you do on your Sundays? Your father closes his business."

"No, Dad doesn't open on Sunday. He feels that twelve to fifteen hours six days a week is enough. He likely feels more strongly than most as to how this day is used. For us it is family day and church day. We seldom miss Sunday School and morning service. Sometimes we do not go in the evening. This is the day the four of us can sit down and be a family. We can talk, speak freely, ask questions and offer opinions. We try, as Dad says, to speak kindly of others. Sometimes we study in the afternoon. Others times we play. On occasions we have company. It's that kind of day for us. Most would consider it dull."

April responded, "We are similar. Oh, there are some differences. Farmers can't close down. The cows and mules and chickens cannot understand a day without food. Sunday has the same meaning as Monday for them." Then she asked, "Tell me about your mother, if you will. If it is difficult, we will talk about other things."

"Mother died in 1955. I was nine, the twins eight. My mother was a good person. She was like your mother in many ways. I never saw her do an unkind thing in her life. She dearly loved my father. She loved her children. Truthfulness, sincerity, honesty, kindness and compassion were her trademarks. We may wish to include work. This was evidenced in many ways — meals, cleaning house, clean clothing and on and on. For her, cleanliness was next to godliness. Her values would meet the test of time. Keep your head up, work hard, behave yourself and be somebody were her constant reminders. No two people could have loved each other more than my mother and father.

"Mother was sick some months before she died. After visits to several doctors it was determined she had cancer. There was nothing to be done. I don't suppose I heard her complain once until about a week before she died. Medicine would no longer ease the pain. It nearly killed all of us to see her die a little more each day.

"I suppose children see things differently. We asked our father how God, whom we love very much and who has loved us, could do this to her. Our father helped us to understand some things we had not thought about. No one will ever really know his strength and courage.

"After her death we lived to ourselves for a period. We worked hard, saved every dime we could and paid all the doctor and medicine bills. They were patient with my father because the bills had multiplied over the months. Finally, they were all paid and we felt better.

"Just before Mother died I remember coming to the door of her room. She was talking with my father in a weak voice. 'Find someone after I am gone,' she said. 'You will need someone to look after you and the children. I will be gone in a few days and you will need another.' Father never promised that he would. He continued to tell her that he knew she would soon be better but we all knew this was not to be. It was the only lie I ever heard my father tell.

"After her death we worked out a plan as to our individual duties and responsibilities. Dad said he would likely never marry again because he could not find one that would meet the standards of our mother. Even if he thought he might find another, it would not be fair, as he would be comparing her and this would not be right. I have not known of anyone in whom he has been interested.

"I have one concern, April. It is a deep concern. One day he will be older and we children will have a life of our own. He would insist on this. What will he do? He would consider himself a burden for the three of us. It is not good to grow old alone."

She did not respond to his question. "Thank you for sharing these intimate thoughts with me about your family."

CHAPTER 30

Robert White arrived in his father's old pick-up truck. April saw he had changed his Sunday clothes and was wearing a sport shirt and slacks. He approached the house in an uncertain manner.

"Come in, Robert." April met him on the porch. "You're the best looking man I've seen today. I wonder what would happen if you were ever late?"

"You will help me? I feel unsure of myself. This is a new experience," Robert said.

"Be yourself. That is why everyone loves you so." April smiled.

As Robert shook hands with everyone he said, "This may not be a good time for a visit. All of you are very busy."

Joseph said, "Most of our Sundays do not require the same efforts. Have a seat. Martha is in the kitchen. April tells me many good things about you. She says you always do your best and your best is more than ample."

"I am grateful for an opportunity to work this summer. Building houses seems similar to the building of one's life. You need a good foundation and you do it right, one step at the time. I hope I have not abused a lengthy friendship."

Michael John said, "I have never seen one work so hard or learn more quickly. I hope he is as pleased as we are."

At that moment Martha rushed out and Robert rose from his seat. "We are so glad you are here. You will excuse us for being a little late. The preacher kept us a little longer. It is likely he felt the Randolphs required a little extra." She took Robert's arm as she moved them toward the dining room. April could see that some of Robert's tension and uncertainty had vanished.

When they were seated Joseph gave once again his standard blessing. "I hope you can find something you like, Robert. As you can see, farmers live off the land."

"I am not accustomed to such a feast. At home when we eat our lunch on Sunday, we usually review our previous week and plan our next one. I feel like I am intruding."

Joseph laughed. "Martha will not let us speak unkindly at meal time. She insists we speak of the good things. We have all learned to listen to this lady!" Martha blushed.

Robert said, "We are Baptist. I really see little difference between some of the faiths. Sometimes our preacher keeps us later than you Methodists. I suppose it is the number of sins that we have committed. Takes more for some of us than others." He laughed. "I suppose most people follow the religion of their parents."

"I believe you had a revival not too long ago," Charles said. "Some of us were in attendance a night or so. Your guest minister was very good. I was impressed."

"Yes, I was there for most of the services," Robert said.

"I will soon have a new daughter. You knew that David was getting married?" Joseph asked.

"So I have learned. There is little that escapes the ears of a service station attendant. Some of what you hear you would not care to take home with you. But I want to congratulate David. There is not a finer girl or one so pretty in all our high school." He looked at April. "Perhaps there is one exception."

David smiled. "I am very fortunate. How well I know this. And Michael John says he will have a house for us."

"Thank you for a delightful lunch," Robert said a few minutes later. "This has been most special for me. I believe April promised to show me a part of Randolph Place."

As April and Robert moved from one area to another April said, "My family loved you. I could tell. A girl knows these things."

After riding for some time April said, "This area is Joseph's latest addition. He is quite excited. I have not had an opportunity to really see for myself but it has a fine stand of timber on two thousand acres."

"Two thousand?"

"Yes. The parcel contains three thousand."

"How many acres go to form Randolph Place?" Robert asked. "Is it a secret?"

"It was, but not anymore. People learn a great deal about political aspirants. I believe the figure is something over eighteen thousand acres."

"I would have never guessed. Your business is not known as well as others'. It seems you have chosen to remain in the background."

They approached April's place, where Robert worked. She said, "I guess you see enough of this place but I never seem to get my fill." They climbed the steps to the deck overlooking the upper lake. They stood looking; for several minutes not a word was spoken. There was a strange, quiet beauty that seemed beyond description. The water wheel that had been installed made its never-ending rotation as the cups filled on one side and emptied on the other.

April turned to Robert and asked, "Can you envision some miller and his family living here a century ago? I suspect they enjoyed the setting but likely the circumstances were different. For them it was a way to make a living and provide for a family. For me it is like ice cream on cake. In a way it seems a little unfair."

Suddenly, April turned without warning, placed her hands on his shoulders, pulled his head down and kissed him on the mouth. Then she drew back and said, "You must get used to the unexpected if you stay around me! I just seem to do what seems right at a given moment. Hey, you haven't said a word! Cat got your tongue?"

Robert blushed deeply. "That was my first kiss. I guess you could tell that."

April turned, as if nothing had occurred, and walked inside. "I am so excited." She looked up at the cathedral ceiling and said, "I am so glad you suggested this. Now it will not have that crushed feeling. You were also wise to suggest the half bath so one would not need to go into a bedroom. You have been most helpful." She continued to take everything in as she moved around. Then they returned to the deck once more.

"Why this fifty acres, when you had eighteen thousand?"

"Have you ever wanted something that was yours and yours alone? All of the eighteen thousand acres belongs to all the Randolphs. This is mine. Am I selfish? Perhaps I am."

"No. I suppose we all want something of our very own. It doesn't always have to be big or valuable. It is something that belongs to you."

"Oh, Robert, I can envision so many things. A place for wildlife where they can be safe; a place to fish, to paddle a boat; a place to come and think and dream and read; a place to be alone or with others; a place to hear the music one wishes to hear; a place for laughter and a place where one can be serious and quiet."

"I understand," Robert said. "Yes, I understand."

"Perhaps I have not mentioned something that may be the most important characteristic of all. It will never be totally completed. It will always remain unfinished. There will always be something to be done to make it different or better, perhaps both. Then one day, when I am no more, maybe someone else would wish to continue. It will be like an unfinished song. Oh, Robert, am I selfish? Tell me I am not. I wouldn't want to be."

"No. I believe I understand all you have said. Sometimes I must confess, I do not completely understand you, but this is good. No one should ever be completely understood by another. There are many reasons. For example, why did you kiss me? I have watched you say and do the unusual but this seemed out of character."

"Why does the sun shine or the wind blow? It seemed the thing I wanted to do. It was a way of expressing some of my inner feelings. You are very special. I enjoy your company. You are the best person I have ever known. That's enough for now."

Robert went by April's home and again expressed his thanks to Mrs. Randolph, then moved swiftly to his father's truck.

"You are extremely fortunate to have such a classmate and friend, April. I do not recall enjoying the company of anyone more than Robert," Martha said.

CHAPTER 31

"Telephone," Martha said as Joseph ate the last bite and was leaving the table. In a moment he returned, grinning from ear to ear.

"Good news? I haven't seen you smile like that in days."

"It is. It is just that. I wanna call a quick meeting tonight so I can tell everyone. It will have to be late, as late as nine o'clock." With that Joseph practically ran from the house on his way to the shades and barns. Martha had not the slightest hint of what he had just learned.

April said to her mother as she entered the kitchen, "You cannot continue at the pace you are going. Working from four in the mornings until ten or eleven at night is tearing you apart. I had thought Joseph would recognize this. The two of us must talk."

"You will do nothing of the kind. His schedule is much more hectic than anyone's. He never complains, nor should we. The busy season will soon be over. You will not say the first word to your father."

"It is the same as always with one exception," April said.

"What do you mean? What exception?"

"More!"

"What does that mean?" her mother asked.

"More of everything! More acres of tobacco, more work, more strain, more of everything and it results in more money, more land and more farms. And yes, I would guess he would include more acceptability. And for what? If you never go anywhere, never do anything different, never have friends to come see you, never make a better life for anyone, you ask why."

"Don't talk like that, April. It would break your father's heart! He is doing all of this for you, for me, for all our children. He wants us to be secure from all fears. These were fears he had as a child. You must try to understand."

"I may understand much more than many think. We are getting closer to a time when changes must occur."

"It is you I worry about. You do much of my work. You keep two construction jobs going. You are learning the duties Charles is responsible for. You haven't relaxed this summer. You have little time to read. On top of that, you have accepted the responsibility for Maybe. You will hate me, as well as yourself, when you suddenly recognize what has happened to the carefree days of childhood. Youth passes all too quickly."

"I still must insist on a different schedule for you," April said. "I want you to sleep later. I can get the men off to work."

"You know I can't do that, my dear daughter. I'll call on Sandra and Gena more. I suspect Meggie will soon be with us."

Martha switched subjects. "When you were a child you and your father were close, so very close. There was never a closer association. The two of you seemed to understand each other. I no longer see that relationship. What has happened? Sooner or later we must talk about this."

"We all change, Mother. Our values change. Even our dreams change. As one matures, she no longer sees things as a child. Perhaps we should leave this for another time."

"Tell me about Maybe. I can't seem to find time to go see him. I'm sure, except for you, that he feels abandoned. Have you and Jerome found a way? Found some defense?"

"It doesn't look good. The trial comes up in a few days. I do hope, however, that Joseph will not interfere in this matter. I must confess my disappointment. If this man had saved *his* life, I believe Joseph would feel differently. On the other hand, I'm not sure."

Martha looked at her in an expression of disbelief. "This is not the best of times for your father, April. He must do as he feels best. And yes, he is your father."

"I'll try to remember, Mother. I will try. I will try for your sake."

"Good news! Good news on every front. I wanted to tell all of you," Joseph said. Everyone was present including Mary. They sensed from his face and voice that he felt ecstatic jubilation.

"A call came today from Slick Cannington. I will have no opposition! No one else wished to qualify. Certainly we have no Republican strength in the county for November. I'm home free." He looked into their eyes and he could tell they were pleased, but some did not reflect his elation; this left an empty feeling.

Then he continued. "It means so many things. The people want me! They trust me! It means I can think of my tobacco crop rather than trying to visit the voters day and night. It means you ain't gonna have to ride and walk the hot and dusty roads seeking votes. It means I can save money on campaigning.

"But the most important thing is that the people have said I am somebody! That we are all somebody! Ain't it great? Don't you understand? Certainly I have made it clear!"

Stephen spoke first. "It is good news. I ain't had any doubts."

"I know you are relieved. We are all relieved and thankful and proud," Martha said. "I am sure we all feel this way. You will not just make a good commissioner, but a great one. Now your many talents can serve everyone and Decatur County can only benefit. We had a few fears of the unknown, but we have never doubted you as a husband and father and provider."

"Our tobacco is beautiful." Joe said. "Only this morning we agreed that this is the best crop ever."

"Yes, our day is near. No longer will there be doubts about the Randolphs!" Joseph said.

Martha said, "April is going to be busy in the next few days. Maybe is to have his trial. Let us hope everything goes well."

"Just as everything had settled down a bit and this comes up. My people will get all excited again. I may wanna get this thing delayed!" Joseph said.

"Some of us could possibly be in court with April. It could make Maybe feel better," Michael John said.

"Yes, I could go for a day," David said.

"Wait! Wait!" Joseph's voice was nearly a shout. "You will do no such. How can you think about being away at this time? Some of us will be called as witnesses but that's as far as it will go. Some seem to have lost their senses. No, I ain't gonna have it. I've tried to understand April's feelings, since she said he saved her life. But if she had listened and followed instructions, she wouldn't be obligated."

April was about to rise to leave when she saw Charles shake his head. "Then it's all settled," Charles said. "April will do as best she can and we will fill her responsibilities while she is gone. I have made arrangements to miss classes for a couple of days. I'll look after April's responsibilities."

"I can help as well," Mary said.

"I hope it is for my mother rather than that sorry black," Joe said. "By the time we feed them, dress them, buy them a car, put them in a new house, look after the sick and bury the dead, they will have it made. What we don't do now, the government will." Joe got up and left the room. Again Mary felt she should follow as before.

"Then it's all settled," Martha said. "Let's think of the good. We will not have to campaign this summer." Martha had intended to discuss the change for Meggie but she knew this was not the moment.

April made an appointment with Jerome and went to his office to discuss the case a last time before the trial.

"You see nothing different?" April asked, answering the question she had asked by her tone of voice.

"No. We have reviewed the matter. I have talked several times with Maybe. There is nothing new. Self-defense will be difficult without a knife. It's that simple."

"There has to be a knife," April said. "Maybe did not dream all of this."

"How does one know what another dreams?" Jerome asked.

"Would Sheriff Henderson do something such as remove evidence because he is not happy with my father?"

"I don't believe he would."

April left moments later. She had many fears. She knew the chances of success were not good.

When she returned home Joseph called April into their library. "Let's not get up there and make a fool out of yourself and the Randolphs. You must remember the position I am soon to hold. You have made a grave error. He is guilty beyond all doubt."

"I thought this would be determined by a judge and jury. I will never question your right or the right of anyone to have an opinion or feel as they wish. I can only hope you will give me the same consideration. Let us not do this to each other."

As Joseph opened the door to leave he looked back at April and said, "Dream on. You have so much to learn."

CHAPTER 32

The deputy sheriff called, "All rise and come to order. The July term of the Superior Court of Decatur County of the State of Georgia is now in session. The Honorable Hollis C. Whitehead presiding." There was a sudden hush in the courtroom as all eyes turned to the door back of the bench from which the judge would enter.

Judge Whitehead, wearing a fresh black robe, entered in a stately manner, took his seat on the bench and said, "Please be seated." For a full minute he surveyed the courtroom. He was on familiar ground. This was and had been his kingdom for years. The quietness continued as they waited for his instructions.

To his right were a hundred or more that had received their summons for jury duty. To his left was a section that had been reserved because these people would move from one side to another as they heard their name called. Back of this section were perhaps two hundred Negroes of all ages, both men and women. Half of them seemed quite young and he wondered why they were not at work.

Back of the people who had received a summons were perhaps a hundred white men, most of them senior citizens. These men would fill another empty day. It would offer something different.

Judge Whitehead looked at the center. There were at least three hundred in this section. The front half of the area was occupied by whites and the area to the rear was occupied by blacks. In years past, the Negroes had been required to go to the balcony; however, with the restoration of the courtroom, the balcony had been eliminated. Yet the races continued to segregate themselves as before. The judge heard a baby cry in the rear and a mother making an attempt to silence the child. One further outburst would terminate their day in court.

Travis Johnson, the very efficient Clerk of the Court, was in place and the court recorder had her machine ready and waiting. To his right, where twelve chairs were in place, were the customary persons that were always present. There were seven lawyers the judge recognized, two county deputies, a juvenile official, a city policeman and a local newspaper reporter.

Judge Whitehead, as he reviewed these twelve, thought about the joke he had heard recently about a man who took his parrot with him everywhere. One Saturday night they had gone to the Red Dog Saloon and the parrot had asked, "Where are we? Where are we?" The owner of the parrot replied, "Red Dog Saloon."

The next morning the man and parrot went to the church they attended. During a period of silent prayer the parrot called out in a loud voice, "Red Dog Saloon, Red Dog Saloon."

In a state of embarrassment the man whispered to his parrot, "Be quiet, be quiet. This is the church. This is our church."

The parrot responded, "Same crowd, same crowd!"

Judge Whitehead looked more closely at these twelve and thought, Same crowd, same crowd. He wondered about their duties.

He then looked at the long table before him. In the chair to his right was Herman Wilson, the District Attorney, dressed in a custom blue suit. To his left was the young attorney, Jerome Lee, and the defendant he represented. To the other side of the defendant was a beautiful young girl whom the judge did not immediately recognize.

This day would be another day in the life of the legal system and he supposed he should get started. Once again he looked in disbelief at the large crowd that had gathered. "I will ask the Clerk to call the names of the jurors who have received a summons. When your name is called, answer and please speak loudly."

The Clerk called a name and the deputy repeated it in a loud voice. When all the names were called, the Clerk indicated that all were present. "A good way to start," Judge Whitehead said. "I usually have to send for one or more."

He continued. "The first case on docket will be the State of Georgia versus Maybe So Jones. There is an indictment against the defendant resulting from the death of two persons. Everyone seems to be in place; so suppose we commence. Mr. Lee, suppose you introduce or present the young lady seated with you. I am sure the Court would like to have her presented."

Jerome Lee rose and indicated for April to do the same. "Your Honor, if it pleases the Court, I am happy to present Miss April Randolph. It is the wish of the defendant and his attorney to have Miss Randolph assist on behalf of the Defense." They sat down.

The judge turned to Travis Johnson and said, "Call the first sixty names on your list." To those summoned he said, "As your name is called, please respond and come over to the reserve seats opposite of where you are now."

After the sixty people had responded and moved to their new seats the judge spoke again. "Is the State ready to proceed?"

"We are, Your Honor."

"Mr. Lee," the judge asked, "Are you ready to proceed?

"We are, Your Honor."

"Mr. Lee, ask the defendant to rise," the judge ordered. "How does the defendant wish to plead?"

"Your Honor, I'se not guilty."

"You may be seated," the judge stated.

"Now ladies and gentlemen," Judge Whitehead stated, "the defendant is being tried in a capital case. In simple terms, this means that should the defendant be found guilty, he can receive the maximum sentence, which as you know, is a death sentence. Now in light of this, I ask if any of you . . ."

The baby in the rear started crying again. The judge said, "This court will not be interrupted in such a manner. We will excuse the woman with the crying baby."

After the two left the courtroom he spoke again. "As I was saying, if any of you sixty people whose names were just called are opposed to serving on a case, a capital case, please stand." Seven of the group rose.

"Please give your name, starting on the first row and then return to the other side of the courtroom." When this had been completed the judge ordered the Clerk to call the next seven names on his list, to replace the seven that had been excused.

Again the judge spoke. "I will dismiss the remaining jurors until Wednesday morning at nine o'clock. You may be excused." About half of those who had been dismissed remained in the courtroom.

"Now," Judge Whitehead said, "I will ask a second question. Are there any of you who feel you cannot serve on this jury and render a verdict based on the evidence you hear? Another way of expressing this is, have you, for any reason, pre-judged the defendant prior to hearing the evidence? If so, please stand." No one moved.

"My last question is this. Are any of you related, by blood or marriage, to the defendant, Maybe So Jones, the families of the deceased, Posey P. Green or Lila Jones, or to Mr. Wilson, Mr. Lee or Miss Randolph?" Again no one stood.

"I shall declare a ten minute recess. I do not expect anyone to be tardy when that time has been concluded." The judge left at a rapid pace.

"Do you need to be excused, April?" Jerome asked. "This will likely be the only opportunity until lunch." As he asked he looked into her face, her eyes sparkled. He looked at the suit she was wearing, noticing how well it seemed to fit and how it blended with her dark features.

April saw he was inspecting her and said, "Your wonderful mother made this suit. She always provides a perfect fit. I do hope it does not portray me as a child. And no, I do not need to go to the restroom."

Jerome said, "Suppose we think a minute about the jury selection. I believe we will need to lean toward youthful persons. They may not take their marriage vows as seriously as the older people."

"I would take a marriage vow seriously. Do you not believe this?" April asked.

"I think you would always take any vow you made seriously, but there is much difference between you and some of our youthful people of today." He continued, "I have researched all of the members who have been selected. As we go along, I may slow the process because I must refer to my notes."

"You did this in advance?"

"Yes, that's part of my job. I must study to show myself approved!" He smiled. "It's important to know as much as possible."

"I see three black people among the sixty," April said.

"Yes. We would excuse the woman immediately. At the moment, I would be inclined to accept the two men. One of these is quite a rounder. The other is not lily white. He seems to have crossed the line."

"Yes, I agree. One or more black women would be fatal to this case. By the way, do you consider yourself a rounder? I believe you used that term a moment ago. I believe I can see certain advantages. I am told variety is the spice of life. It may not be all bad."

Jerome smiled and leaned over and whispered, "Don't suggest such in the presence of Maybe. We are here today because of such practices."

April became serious. "We have an edge in one way. We have twenty strikes and the State only ten. Besides, the State must act first in the selection."

"Who told you this?" Jerome asked. "I don't recall saying this to you."

"I have been reading. I try to study now and then." Again she smiled.

Jerome said, "One other thing. Try to keep Maybe as cheerful as possible. You would be better than me at this."

April reached over and patted Maybe's back lightly and he turned. "Try and keep a pleasant face, Maybe. It's important. Can you do that for me?"

"I'll try, Miss April. I'll sho' try!"

She turned back once again to Jerome. "If you ever decide to have a girl friend in the years to come, for God's sake, don't select someone without brains, regardless of how she looks. After all, I doubt any man can stay in bed most of the time!" Jerome could feel his face turning red. He hoped the judge would soon return and his wish was quickly granted.

"Is the State ready? Mr. Lee, are you ready?" Judge Whitehead asked. Both responded positively.

"As your name is called, please give your address and occupation. If retired, give your last area of employment," the judge said.

Mr. Wilson and Mr. Lee would not be hurried. Most of the first questions were similar: "Are you married? Have you been married previously? Do you have children? Have you heard about this case? If so, how did you hear? Have you formed an opinion prior to this trial? Do you feel you can listen to the evidence and make a decision based on the evidence?"

After nearly two hours four persons had been selected. There were three rather young men and one middle-aged man. Jerome had used five strikes, the State four. Jerome had struck the Negro woman, but not until he had asked her all the questions. April would try to remember to ask Jerome why he spent all the time asking her questions when he had already concluded he would strike her.

At five minutes to twelve Judge Whitehead said, "We will adjourn until one-thirty." As soon as the judge disappeared the people hurried from the courtroom.

"Where do we eat?" April asked. "Everything will be crowded."

"I have some reservations," Jerome said. "In fact, I have them for each of the first three days."

"It will take three days?"

"I think so. By the way, the café has a booth with a curtain for a little privacy. Perhaps we can discuss the case. I don't think I care to share you with anyone!"

"Why so many people, Jerome? I had not thought a case involving Negroes would draw so much interest, so much attention."

"Perhaps it is the nature of the case. I'm sure most know what it is all about, including the sixty selected for jury duty. After all, if you were my wife and I caught you in the bedroom with another man, well . . . enough said." Jerome's face showed a slight pink.

Jerome and April took their seats and placed their orders. As they waited they were about to review the earlier proceedings when they heard some rather loud and raucous voices from the next booth. The occupants could not be seen but could be heard without difficulty. April nodded her head in such a way as to suggest to Jerome that they listen.

"Don, they got that boy all dressed up! Bet that suit cost a hundred dollars."

"Nathan, you can whitewash and dress 'em up but you can't change 'em. They're all cut out of the same cloth. Ain't gonna make nothing else out of them! What you think, Harry?"

"Done wasted all the day and ain't got a third of the jury selected. No wonder our county doesn't have any damned money. The courts and lawyers get it all. What you think, Howell?"

"I've been watching that good looking girl, fellows. I don't know what the hell she is doing there, because she can't help the boy's case, but she is one hell of a looker."

"Howell, I hear her old man has as sorry a bunch of damn blacks as there is in the whole county. Word come down that there isn't a decent white man or black gonna work for him if they can help it!"

"Yep. You right, Nathan, but it doesn't seem to matter, since he is gonna be the next commissioner, and that all goes to prove that we don't have any commissioners we can trust. Why hell, they spend it all on welfare; mostly on the darkees. I bet that boy being tried gets money and stamps."

"Don, you're probably right. But my road by my house ain't seen a road scraper in six months."

"I hear that damn black split the heads of his wife and friend wide open with an axe. He must have caught them in bed together. What you think, Howell?"

Jerome was about to lean over and stop the conversation when he felt April's hand on his. She shook her head and whispered, "We can learn some things we may need to know."

They listened again. "Hear this young Lee is gonna base his case on self-defense."

"I heard no weapon was found."

"Ain't got a chance in hell without a weapon. Time the jury sees that axe and some pictures that they have taken, it will all be over."

"Harry, it's just a bunch of blacks acting like a bunch of blacks. Don't get excited and all fired up. That boy is gonna work our roads for a long, long time."

They looked up as the waitress brought the food. "Hope it's not cold," she said. "Got a big courthouse crowd today."

"I'm sorry you insisted on hearing that, April. It was my mistake, bringing you here. I'll cancel my reservations."

"Oh no you don't. One of them has a good eye. You heard his description of me. It isn't every day I hear such nice things. You never tell me such nice things!"

It was fifteen after five when the twelve members of the jury and the alternate had been selected. Both sides had used up their strikes. Jerome felt he had to take one juror that would hurt his case, as he had used all of his strikes. He would have preferred more black males, but it was not to be.

"You will not discuss this case," Judge Whitehead said. "If I hear a hint, I will lock you up overnight. You will be in place at nine in the morning."

Twenty minutes later April arrived home and went directly to her room to change into something more comfortable. Upon changing she went to the kitchen, where her mother asked, "What kind of day did you have? I will want to hear about it after dinner."

"Tell me what I can do," April said.

"Everything is ready. I've had help." She didn't say who or the nature of the help.

At dinner the different family members looked at April from time to time; she caught their glances out of the corner of her eye. Finally Stephen asked, "What did you do today while we worked in the fields and barns?"

It took several seconds for April to get control. "A jury was selected. I will ask to be excused. I had a big lunch and I do not feel hungry. I want to go to my room. I'll return later and help Mother." She quietly left the dining room.

Later when she returned, the dining room and kitchen had been restored to order. "I meant to help you. I had no idea you would be finished."

"Charles and David were a big help. Each will make some lucky girl a good husband." Her mother smiled.

When April approached the den she was confronted by her father, who said, "Did you know I stayed in the witness room all day? So did Michael John. This bothers me more than a little!"

"I have no control over the events," April said. "I suppose court is like education in that it is a slow process."

"I hope you will tell Jerome I don't wish to be kept longer than is necessary. I'm disappointed in him!"

April looked straight into her father's face and asked, "Who called you as a witness? Was it the State or Jerome?"

Joseph's face colored as he said, "The State, but Jerome would have if the State didn't. You tell him to hurry and get me back where I belong. No one, including you, especially you, will ever know how much time and trouble and money I've spent on that black boy. You never discussed the lawyer's fee with me. Bet it ain't a small sum!"

"No. I don't recall I did. I saw no necessity, as it did not involve the corporation. I had said I would be responsible." She continued, "I'm sure Jerome will do what he believes best for his client. That's his job. As I recall, it is the judge who excuses a witness. I'm sure Judge Whitehead will do as he feels best. Now I'll ask you to excuse me."

She turned to go to her room, then turned back. "I guess Meggie will be moving in, since you have no opposition. I'm sure she can assist Mother more efficiently once she gets here." Then she turned and left.

Joseph looked at April as she left and thought that there had been too much, too soon.

CHAPTER 33

At nine o'clock the following morning Judge Whitehead looked over his domain once again to determine if everyone was in place. Again the courtroom was packed to capacity. There seemed to be a great number more than yesterday and there was a greater number of white people. Why? Just some more of the same. Oh, a little different twist perhaps, but nevertheless, more of the same.

"Mr. Wilson, Mr. Lee, you will approach the bench." They stood before him in their blue suits and white shirts.

"We spent a long day yesterday. I am not sure it was entirely necessary. I want to keep this court on schedule. I hope we can keep it to the essentials. Therefore, I shall review your opening statements carefully. Some lawyers wish to do the same thing three times. Some want to try a case in both the opening and the closing statements. I have served in many different capacities prior to a judgeship. I hope you will remember this."

He then stated, "Mr. Wilson, we are ready for your opening statement to the jury."

"Thank you, Your Honor." He moved over in front of the thirteen people on the jury. It was obvious his new suit had not come from the racks of the local clothing stores. Many believed that Mr. Wilson was on the way to bigger and better things. All who knew him were aware that he was an ambitious person but most were unsure of his goals. Some said a judgeship on the state level. Some said a district judge in the federal courts. Others suspected he had an eye on the governor's mansion. It did not hurt to come from a wealthy family; his father had been most successful. His wife had also come from a wealthy, prominent family and would be an heiress to a large fortune.

Herman Wilson, in an erect and stately manner, said smilingly, "Ladies and gentlemen, I am Herman Wilson, representing the State as your District Attorney. We should know each other, as we will see a great deal of the other in the next two days. I thank you for giving your time and talents so that we may be assured that our precious judicial system will function properly in our democratic society." He glanced toward the judge and thought he saw him looking at his wrist watch. He looked back at the jury and gave them his best smile, speculating to himself that they were not present because they wished to serve. Also, he must remember to use a vocabulary they would understand.

"A grave responsibility rests upon each of you. I know you will listen carefully to all the evidence in order to make a decision. It will be you who will render a guilty or not guilty verdict."

He turned and pointed a finger at Maybe, who quickly averted his gaze downward. "This person sitting before you is a man named Maybe So Jones. He has been charged with the murder of his wife and a man he has referred to as his best friend, a man who worked side by side with him for decades. I don't think your task will be difficult, as the evidence is complete and conclusive, in fact, overwhelming. I do not believe there will be a shadow of doubt when you have heard all the evidence. It is your duty to listen, to be alert, and then deliver your honest opinion on the basis of the evidence you hear.

"Our procedure will take you to the scene of this hideous crime, this brutal slaughter. It will take you from the sad beginning to the atrocious and despicable conclusion.

"This Maybe So Jones," again Herman Wilson turned slowly and pointed his finger at the defendant, "has taken a brutal weapon, an axe, ladies and gentlemen, and willfully and deliberately smashed it into the heads of his wife and friend, instantly taking the lives of these two, a loving wife, a long standing friend. In the process, he left behind nine half orphaned children. We know it was deliberate. It is possible it was premeditated. We will show you the weapon that he used to commit this ghastly and gruesome crime. We will bring before you witnesses who were told by the defendant that he did such an act. We will show you pictures of the victims and the repulsive manner in which he left them. It is indeed appalling.

"The case is so obvious, so clear, so uncomplicated that I find it difficult to understand why someone should insist that you give of your time and the County's money to go through this process. But I am sure in the end that your task will be easy and simple. It is not a case in which one must ponder and wonder who did it. He did it!" Again he pointed at Maybe, and again Maybe dropped his head. "He said he did it. However, let us wait so that you may hear the evidence and judge for yourselves."

Mr. Wilson moved two steps back toward his seat, then turned suddenly once more in the direction of the jury box. "I suspect you will hear it was self-defense or some other impractical justification. From whom was he defending himself? A frail loving wife and an unarmed friend?

"I will not elaborate anymore. The evidence will be forthcoming, step by step." Herman Wilson returned to his seat in a calm and dignified manner, knowing that he had accomplished his purpose. He did not wish more details now. Don't tell them everything or there will be no fun.

The people had filled the courthouse beyond capacity but they had remained quiet, eager to catch every word the dynamic Mr. Wilson had spoken. The judge seemed to sense a need for the crowd to move and whisper for a few seconds. He let this continue for thirty seconds before he said, "The Court will come to order." He rapped his gavel to give added emphasis. In ten seconds the courtroom was in total silence.

"Mr. Lee, you may make your opening statement."

Jerome made his way before the jury, thanking the judge as he moved forward. He had decided to move quickly, in contrast to Mr. Wilson. "Ladies and gentlemen, I am Jerome Lee, attorney for the defendant, Maybe Jones, that you see before you. I am not a court appointed attorney but have been retained by the defendant." He looked at Herman Wilson, to leave an impression that he felt some of the circus atmosphere could have been omitted.

"I know you will listen to each word spoken, to all the testimony given by the witnesses. It is obvious you are a fair and alert group.

"Some would wish you to believe this is an unusual case; however, when you examine it closely you will find little unusual about it. It is a story of a man defending himself, which we all have a right to do; defending his home, which is a man's castle, however poor the facility may be; and defending his honor, which every man has a right to do.

"As the case proceeds I will expect each of you to place yourself in the position of the defendant. This is the only way you can truly understand what he did and why he did it. As you do this, it will become sufficiently clear why the defendant acted as he did. I believe you would have done the same. There was no choice.

"My honorable opponent has more than suggested it was premeditated. Nothing could be further from the truth.

"I hope, in fact, I'm sure you will remember at all times that it is the responsibility of the State to prove, without reasonable doubt, that he is guilty. Yes, the burden of proof is always on the State to prove one guilty beyond a reasonable doubt. The fate of this man will rest in your hands. His life and welfare are as important to him as yours is to you.

"When you have heard all the evidence I am sure you will find Maybe Jones not guilty as charged." He returned to his seat. He looked at the members of the jury. There was little he could determine.

Judge Whitehead said, "Mr. Wilson, please call your first witness. I believe all of them have been sworn in."

"I call Mr. Joseph Randolph to the stand."

When he had taken his place in the witness stand, Mr. Wilson said, "So that the Court may know you, please give your name, address and occupation."

"I am Joseph T. Randolph, Sr. I live in Attapulgus; that is, I have an Attapulgus address, though I am out of the city limits. I am a farmer by trade."

"Mr. Randolph, suppose you tell the Court what kind of relationship has existed between you and the accused."

"Maybe Jones moved to my farm as a green boy many years ago. He has remained with me as an employee over the years. He lived in one of my houses with his wife, that is, his deceased wife, and their three children."

"Now Mr. Randolph, did you have an opportunity to see the accused on Saturday morning, April the third of this year? And if so, please describe what you saw."

"I was awakened by Jack Jenkins, my foreman, about daylight or a little before. He reported that a person from the quarters, that is, the area where most of the workers live, had come to his house and said there was trouble in the quarters. He said he believed it was big trouble. I went immediately. I saw that a large number of workers and some of their families had gathered in the road and were milling around. A light was burning on the porches of several of the houses. As I got out of my truck a worker pointed toward the house where Maybe Jones and his family lived."

"What did you see? What did you do?"

"I went over to the porch and saw the form of a man huddled against the wall on the front porch. He was crying and taking on. I could recognize him as Maybe, Maybe Jones."

"What did he say? What happened? Tell us in your own words."

"He was taking on so you could hardly tell what he was saying. Finally, between Jack and myself, we determined that he was saying that he had killed Lila, but that he had not wanted to. He said he thought he had killed Posey Green as well."

"Please identify Lila and Posey Green for us."

"Lila is or was his wife. Posey is another worker who lives or did live down from him in the quarters, in another house."

"Then what happened?"

"I had my flashlight so me and Jack went into the house."

"And what did you find? What did you see?"

"There in the back room, a room called the shed room, as it had been added after the original house was built, were the bodies of Lila Jones, his wife, and Posey Green, a fellow worker. Lila was stretched over part of Posey's body. Both were obviously dead, as they had been struck in the head with some instrument. A great deal of damage had been done to each. It was not pleasant to look at."

"And then what did you do?"

"I returned with Jack to the porch where Maybe remained, crying and muttering, but I was not able to piece it all together for a moment. After I got him calmed down he told me what happened or what he said happened."

"What did he tell you?"

"He repeated that he had just killed Posey Green, as well as his wife. He said that he had not meant to but they had attacked him with a knife, one following the other."

"Did you see such a knife, Mr. Randolph? Did you or Mr. Jenkins see a knife?"

"No. We really didn't look for one because at that time we knew nothing of a knife. We learned this from Maybe after we got back on the porch. We simply looked in at the door to see what had happened. They were both dead."

"But you saw no knife!"

"No. I did not see one. I was not looking for any weapon. We simply determined if they were dead."

"Maybe told you he struck and killed the two?"

"Yes. He said he struck them with an axe. He said he went to the room to escape but the door to the outside would not open. He said he used an axe to protect himself."

"But he said he struck them and killed them with an axe?"

"Yes. I believe I said that earlier. The sheriff found the axe and took it at the same time he took the defendant to jail."

"A few more questions, Mr. Randolph. Were the bodies of the deceased dressed? Do you recall what you saw?"

"Posey Green had a shirt and pants on. Lila Jones was dressed in what appeared to be a gown. I must confess I gave little attention to their dress."

"Shoes?"

"Lila Jones was without shoes. I can't say about Posey Green."

"Let's go back to the defendant. When you talked with him, did he seem normal, that is, that he knew what he had done?"

"Yes. He knew he had struck them. He was somewhat incoherent at times when we attempted to learn all that had happened."

"Did the defendant give you the details of what he said happened?"

"He said he had been asleep, was awakened by some noise, moved into a bedroom and saw Posey Green with a hand touching his wife. He said he shouted at Posey Green and that Posey Green reached in his pocket, produced a knife and attacked him. He said he could not get the door open to escape, so he took the axe and struck Posey Green before Posey could use the knife. Then he said moments later that he looked again and saw Lila Jones approaching. She had apparently picked up the knife that Posey Green had attempted to use. He said he struck her but had not intended to hurt her. He guessed she had slipped on something, perhaps the blood on the floor."

"So there is no doubt in your mind that he struck and killed them both?"

"That's what he said he did."

"When was the sheriff contacted?"

"I sent my daughter back to the house and asked her to ask my wife to call the sheriff and the undertaker. They were contacted."

"Did Sheriff Henderson come?"

"He sent two deputies first. He arrived later."

"What did the deputies do?"

"One talked with some of the people who had gathered. Deputy Smith talked with the defendant."

"What happened when Sheriff Henderson arrived?"

"He talked first with his deputies, then with me briefly. Then he went into the house, returned outside and told me the undertaker could get the bodies."

"Did the sheriff say that a weapon had been found?"

"He brought out a bloody axe. He asked me had I seen other weapons as he started to leave and I said no, that I had not looked for any. In fact, I believe I suggested that was his job. I did not ask and he did not say what he had discovered except the axe."

"And the defendant did tell you himself that he killed these two people?"

"Yes. I believe I have testified to that more than once already."

"I have no more questions Your Honor," Herman Wilson said.

"Your witness, Mr. Lee," Judge Whitehead said.

"Thank you, Your Honor."

"Only a few questions. I know this is your busy season." An uncertain expression appeared on Joseph Randolph's face.

"I believe you said you worked with the defendant since he was a young man?"

"That is so."

"What kind of person have you yourself found this man to be over the many years?"

"He has been one of my better workers. He has been among the most dependable. He has been cooperative. He has created few problems, compared with most of the others."

"I am not sure what that is supposed to mean," Jerome said.

"I don't have to get him out of jail on Monday morning!"

"Have you found him honest?"

"He has been with me. He owes a lot of money but he tries to pay his debts."

"Have you seen him violent or out of control or attacking others?"

"No. Some of the men act up and talk bad to each other but I have never seen him involved in anything serious."

"So what you have described as to what you discovered on that April morning is completely different from any previous experience?"

"Yes."

"I have no further questions."

Judge Whitehead asked, "Redirect, Mr. Wilson?"

"One question, Mr. Randolph. You don't really know nor can you say what the defendant does when he is not under your direct supervision? You cannot really speak of his home life or social life or what he does away from the job?"

"I think I would have heard . . ."

"Wait, Mr. Randolph. The court is concerned about what you know, not what you think or what you believe or what you have heard. So you really have no way of knowing for certain what the accused does or doesn't do except under your direct supervision? Please just answer yes or no."

"No. I don't believe anyone can account for anyone except himself all of the time."

"Your Honor, I do not plan to recall this witness."

"I do not plan to recall, Your Honor," Jerome said.

"Mr. Randolph," Judge Whitehead said, "you are excused."

"Your next witness, Mr. Wilson."

"I call Sheriff Ralph Henderson."

When the sheriff had been seated Mr. Wilson said, "I think we all know you but for the record, state your name and occupation."

"I am Ralph Henderson. I am sheriff of Decatur County where I have served in this position for fourteen years."

"Were you called to go to Randolph Place on April third of this year?"

"I was."

"Did you go?"

"I did. I sent two deputies, Smith and Rain, immediately. I was tied up in some other business. I got there an hour or so later."

"What did you see, what did you learn and who did you talk with?"

"I talked immediately with my deputies when I arrived to determine what they had done and what they had learned.

"We searched the defendant's house and discovered the bodies of Lila Jones and Posey Green. We inspected carefully, made some pictures and removed a weapon. There was an axe that the defendant said he used as a weapon.

"Deputy Smith said he had talked with the suspect and he had admitted murdering the . . ."

"I object Your Honor," Jerome shouted. "He refers to the defendant as one who has committed murder. At this point no one can say a murder has been committed."

"Objection sustained. I would suggest you rephrase your question," the judge said.

"Sheriff Henderson, do you see a person here today that said he killed Lila Jones and Posey Green? If so, would you identify this person."

Sheriff Henderson said, "That is the man. The defendant said he killed them."

"Now Mr. Henderson, did you see another weapon, other than the axe, and did you look?"

"We found no other weapon. We looked carefully."

"Did you arrest the suspect?"

"We did. He was brought to Midway and placed in jail. He was indicted by the grand jury and charged with murder."

"Were the deceased dressed? If so, how. Please describe what you saw."

"The woman, determined to be Lila Jones, was dressed in a garment I would call a gown. She had on panties. The male, Posey Green, was dressed in pants and shirt. He did not have on any shoes."

"Sheriff Henderson, is this the axe you found on the scene?"

"Yes. We found it in the room with the deceased. The defendant said he used it to take the lives of the two."

"Did the defendant actually tell you why he killed the two?"

"He said he was attacked by them with a weapon, a long knife."

"I believe you stated only an axe was found as a weapon."

"That's correct."

"One last question. I show you these pictures. Do you recognize them?"

"Yes. These are the pictures I took of the deceased." He handed them back to Mr. Wilson.

"Your Honor, unless there are objections, I submit this as evidence taken at the scene by Sheriff Henderson."

Jerome walked up, looked at the pictures and placed them back on the table.

Mr. Wilson took them over so they could be passed among the members of the jury. Their expressions told all that was needed. "They speak for themselves," Mr. Wilson said.

"You may cross-examine, Mr. Lee," Judge Whitehead said.

Jerome moved toward the witness box, then paused a few seconds. The courtroom became as quiet as a graveyard. It seemed that everyone was waiting for something to happen.

"Sounds as if you have been busy, Mr. Henderson." They looked closely at each other.

"There are some things that are not clear, Sheriff Henderson. We might say they seem a little fuzzy, so to speak." He paused and the quietness remained. Everyone seemed to look at one another. Judge Whitehead saw the two glare at each other.

"How many doors are there to the house where the defendant resided, where the bodies were found?"

"Three."

"And where are these three doors located? Speak up, sir, if you will, so the jury can learn more about the scene of the accident." Sheriff Henderson was obviously not pleased. To suggest he speak louder had been unnecessary and to use the term accident was nearly unforgivable.

"There are two doors on the front porch, leading into the house into separate rooms. There is one on the back that is found in what has been referred to as the shed room. This is the room that contained the mutilated bodies of Posey Green and Lila Jones." It was obvious he would retaliate at every opportunity.

"Three doors, Sheriff Henderson? Are you sure? Surely you have paid careful attention to the scene where you discovered the two mutilated bodies you described?"

Jerome turned back to the table where April and Maybe sat and picked up a picture. He moved over to the sheriff and handed it to him. "Do you recognize the house?"

Sheriff Henderson's face turned a deep red.

"It doesn't . . ."

"Please, Sheriff Henderson, you haven't answered the question. Let me repeat it. Do you recognize the house?"

"Yes."

"Tell us what house this is."

Sheriff Henderson could feel his face turning a deeper color. "This is the house where the bodies were found."

Jerome was about to ask him if it was the house where the mutilated bodies were found but refrained. "How many doors do you see on the back?"

"Two, but it has nothing to do with this case." Jerome handed the picture to the judge and then passed it to the jury. He deliberately moved in a slow manner.

"Now about the windows, Mr. Henderson. How would you describe them? I'll not ask about the number." It became obvious the sheriff was quite frustrated. Judge Whitehead looked down at Jerome to suggest they were about to reach a point at which he might intervene.

"Some were of glass panes or lights, whichever term you prefer. Two of them were wooden windows that looked more like doors, but they served as windows."

"Can they be secured, that is, fastened or locked? And were they secured?"

"The wooden windows were closed and fastened from within. The windows with panes or some panes were open. They could not be secured unless one placed a stick above the lower window as is done at times. They were not secured."

"Screens?"

"None."

"Now Sheriff Henderson, isn't it entirely possible, with four doors, one you had not discovered, and a number of windows that were not secured, that someone could have entered through these unsecured places without being seen?"

"No one was seen entering or leaving. I checked with everyone. There were no tracks or evidence of entry."

"Now Sheriff Henderson, your response leaves a little something to be desired. First, you didn't answer my question. Secondly, how do you know that you talked with everyone? Thirdly, it would seem possible that one entering would not necessarily have left tracks. At this time, however, let us return to the first and perhaps most important question. Let me repeat it once more. Isn't it possible that someone could have entered through the doors or unsecured windows without being seen? A simple yes or no will suffice for a response."

"Yes." The sheriff looked pale, as if he might be ill.

"One more question and we will stop. I feel it most important in that the law is rather specific and detailed about the matter. Did you call the Decatur County Coroner, Mr. Ronald Boxer? And, if he was not available, did you call a person he had designated in his absence? Am I not correct that when one or more unnatural deaths occur, this is the normal procedure? Are you to say this was not done? On the other hand, I don't believe you have said anything." Jerome saw the sheriff take a big swallow but his dry mouth had produced no saliva.

Sheriff Henderson's face turned crimson, then again turned white and pale. When he spoke, his voice was not fully under control. "If we had not identified the deceased, or determined how they died or who was responsible for their deaths, Mr. Boxer or an assistant would have been called. Since all of these facts, and they were and are facts, had been validated, they were not called. It has long been a practice in Decatur County to let the coroner go to the funeral home if he or we feel it necessary. I believe this practice was followed. This procedure has been followed for many years before I was elected sheriff."

"But a practice and a law can differ. Should one follow a practice or the law?" There was a grave silence, then Jerome hurriedly said, "I withdraw the question. The answer is obvious to all."

Judge Whitehead looked down on these two. This wasn't a battle; this was outright war. He wondered what had been said or done earlier to trigger such a confrontation.

"Now just a little more," Jerome said. "I know time is money and we need to save all we can in our county, but I feel I must go a step beyond. Do you consider this practice acceptable?"

"Yes."

"Is this practice followed the same as to people of all races?"

"As far as I know," the sheriff said. "The law is for all people."

"Once again, is it not possible that someone could have entered and removed a knife or other valuable evidence?"

"I believe I have responded to the question previously."

"That's all, Your Honor." Jerome returned to his seat. Mr. Wilson gestured to the judge that there would not be further questions at this time.

"I ask that Sheriff Henderson remain for recall," Jerome said.

"So noted. We will have a fifteen minute recess." He rushed toward his chambers.

"Restroom?" Jerome asked.

"No." April said.

Jerome said, "Without a knife, we are in trouble. I have tried to create some doubt, but I suspect this is not enough."

"How did the pictures look?" April asked.

"Awful. Maybe really pounded them. Their faces didn't even look like faces. A picture is worth a thousand words and the jury will remember."

"Why did you hammer the sheriff so? As much as I dislike the man, I nearly felt sorry for him. Remember I said nearly!"

"Two reasons, really. I first wanted to create some doubt about several things. And, it will be hard for a Negro to vote to find another Negro guilty, if he feels that the black is not being treated as the whites. You turn over all the stones.

"Actually, there is another reason. The sheriff, as you well know, has not been very congenial over the weeks. I suppose I should not have been so unkind at times."

As court reconvened Mr. Wilson called Lottie Layton. She was dressed in her finest. He asked that she identify herself.

"I am Lottie Layton. I live here in this beautiful city of Oaks, the city where I operate the Lottie Layton Funeral Home. That is my profession. I serve throughout the county and beyond at times." Judge Whitehead's eyes rolled upward.

"Tell us what occurred on that tragic Saturday morning when you were called to go to Randolph Place. Tell us only what you saw or heard yourself."

"I got to the place just as the sun was about to break. My assistants, Mr. Roosevelt Boyd and Mr. Detroit McHenry, were with me. When I pulled up, a lotta people had gathered. Lot of people milling 'round. Some were talking and some were crying. Mr. Randolph was there and he told me what he had seen.

"We waited. Mr. Joseph told us not to go in till the sheriff said go in. Finally the sheriff said, 'You can get dem whenever you like.' He had two deputies helping him, one black and one white.

"I goes in and Mr. Joseph ain't wrong. Was no sight to see. One eye's hanging on Posey. I was afraid it would drop off and get lost. Lord, there was blood all over. We got 'em loaded; I told Mr. Joseph I'd look after them as usual and we were gone."

"Lottie," Mr. Wilson asked, "were the two victims dressed and if so, how?"

"So much blood it was hard to tell about colors. Posey was dressed 'cept for his shoes. Lila, poor thing, had a gown on. She had on panties but no bra. Ain't needed no bra."

"Did you see any weapons?"

"I saw that axe they brought out. It was dripping in blood. That what you mean?"

"I was thinking of other weapons. Did you see a knife or other weapons?"

"No sur, ain't no knife to be found."

"No further questions." Mr. Wilson returned to his seat with a smile.

"Mr. Lee, you may cross-examine."

"Miss Layton, did you see or talk with anyone that saw a knife?"

"No sur. Ain't no black going into a house full of dead folks. It just ain't done. I done been around enough dead folks to know."

"One last question, Miss Layton. Were you actually present when your men did their work, that is, removing the bodies?"

"Mr. Lee, you knows Lottie looks after her business. I went in and got Roosevelt and Detroit going and I was in and out till they finished. After they started I had to go out for a minute but I was in and out all along."

"No more questions, Your Honor."

"We will recess until two o'clock. We are running a little late," Judge Whitehead said.

CHAPTER 34

As Jerome and April approached the booth Jerome had reserved they heard the voices of the same men in the next booth that were there the previous day. Jerome pointed to an empty table nearby, but April pointed to the booth and proceeded to take the same seat as the day before.

"Why, April, why?" Jerome asked in a whisper. "Certainly you heard enough of these idiots yesterday!" It was obvious he was not in his best mood.

"Jerome, they are just like listening to the jury talk. You asked me what I thought earlier. These are the people from whom we can learn. Listen." She motioned him to silence when one man spoke.

"How do you see it, Nathan?"

"That black boy is long gone, man. There was never any knife. No one saw it at any time."

"They kept asking if they had on their clothes. Wilson is saying nothing much was going on."

"What you think Lee has in mind, Don?"

"I don't know, but he better expect few favors from the sheriff! He kept asking about doors and windows."

"How about him making an issue about the coroner? Hell, they ain't used a coroner on a bunch of blacks in twenty years, to my knowledge."

"Wouldn't you like to see those pictures, Harry? Talking about an eye about to drop off and a mouth full of loose teeth."

"Hush, man! You keep talking like that and I can't eat a bite."

"Don, if they don't come up with a knife, that bad boy is 'up shit creek without a paddle'."

"You're right. I think it's cut and dried now. I think the jury has already made up their minds. You been watching their faces? It tells you all you need to know."

"Howell, did you see the two members of the jury that nearly passed out when they saw the pictures? They turned as white as a sheet."

"Wonder who Lee is going to call as a witness? I don't expect we will have to wait long. Wilson knows he has the case won. He may not call many more."

"I see that young chick, the Randolph girl, is still there. She's been quiet today. Seems she's trying to keep that black boy's spirits up, but he spends most of his time looking down at the table top."

"You look at that girl's black eyes, Harry? You ever seen anyone like her? That is some woman!"

"Eyes? You did say eyes? How in the world can you talk about eyes when all I can see is a beautiful set of tits! Never seen any higher or that stood out and up as they do. No doubt in my mind about them being real. Hell, man, I can tell the real thing when I see it."

Again Jerome's face turned a deep red and once again, he was about to get to his feet, when April indicated for him to remain still and quiet.

April smiled and whispered, "I'm sorry you are confused. The term he used is a synonym for breasts. I thought you knew about those things. I suppose you hadn't even noticed. How do you think that makes a girl feel? For some reason, I thought you had!"

They listened. "If I was one of those young rich boys, I'd be there every time they threw out dishwater. It ain't all just above the waist. It's everywhere. I've never seen a better figure!"

"What in the hell is she doing up there in the first place? Where is her old man? And why should she be so concerned about saving that black boy?"

"Her old man is making money. There's money in that tobacco. Ought to be, 'cause they don't pay their labor enough to live on. Maybe she's up there to distract the judge and jury. Be hard as hell, if I was sitting up there, to keep my mind on the business at hand."

"Here's our food, fellows. Eat up and let's get back. I wanta see a lot of things!"

April smiled at Jerome but he did not smile back in return. "You found out what you needed to know — about the case, that is. It's possible that you learned something else. I had guessed, and yes, hoped, that you might have noticed." She nearly laughed but Jerome did not change his expression. "Jerome, I want to suggest you keep this case going for several more days. It's amazing what one can learn. It's all so exciting."

Jerome moved his food around on his plate but said nothing. "Oh, come on Jerome. Eat up! You need your strength."

They finished eating in silence. When they had finished April asked, "Let's talk about your witnesses and the schedule you have in mind. Give me your ideas."

"I expect there will be three hours or so this afternoon. Wilson will call some more witnesses to reinforce what has been said. I believe he feels he has finished for all practical purposes. This will simply be a little added feature to show off his talents."

"How many will you call? Who do you plan to call and for what purpose?"

"I'll call several to confirm that Maybe has previously been a fine citizen and it's not his nature to be bad. We will try again to suggest others could have been in the house and removed the knife.

"I cannot put Maybe on the stand. Mr. Wilson would have him so confused, he would say anything.

"After this there are only the closing arguments. I can create doubt. I can insist the burden of proof is on the State.

She mused, "Going back a minute, I suppose you would simply have to base the case on the missing knife, and thus self-defense and the honor of protecting one's home. Yet when people switch wives and yes, even families, there isn't much to build upon."

She continued, "Can you keep things going until eleven o'clock tomorrow? I have some ideas. I will need that much time."

The she added, "And Jerome, you are too serious. There should be a little fun in your life. And you should definitely be honored to have a girl with eyes like mine sitting with you and holding your hand. Look, Jerome. Tell me what you see! You don't just need to confine it to the eyes. Didn't you hear what Harry said? Don't tell me you were not listening. Yes, I definitely believe Harry to be the bright one, the brightest of them all.

She encouraged him, "We are going to win Jerome. Just be calm and concentrate on the things that really matter, the real things! I see right now, my work is cut out where you are concerned!"

When they returned to court Herman Wilson did as Jerome had suspected. He spent an hour and a half reinforcing the fact that no one was seen entering or leaving the house through any door or window.

Then he called on Magnolia Love, a woman who lived in the quarters. She had a reputation of not having a good reputation. It seemed she had been a girlfriend to all the men at one time or another. After she had been properly identified as to where she lived and worked Mr. Wilson asked, "Do you know, beyond a doubt, that a strange and unique relationship existed between the Jones and Green families?"

"I guess you white people would call it so. Some of us don't exactly get excited about such things. Some two or three months ago Maybe and Posey swapped families and . . ."

"Wait, Magnolia. Please stop at this point," Mr. Wilson said. "Just what do you mean when you refer to the term family swapping?"

"These men folks had a long git-a-long with the wife of the other. It was generally known by the quarters folks. About two and a half months before this mess started, they just up and swapped. Maybe went to Posey's house and Posey to Maybe's house. The children stayed put. I knowed it wasn't a fair swap. Six younguns for three is not a fair trade. Swap was just too one-sided. It didn't last. Some three weeks before this killing time they switched back — just like that." She snapped her fingers. "No one had given any more thought to the matter until this mess occurred."

Judge Whitehead pounded his gavel because the noise had gone far beyond a desirable level.

"What else can you say about Maybe Jones that you can speak about firsthand?"

"Well, sir, he's good at more things than just plowing a mule." She gave a big smile and again, the judge pounded his gavel.

"He's not bad. He feeds his family, be it four or eight." The judge raised his hand but the group quieted quickly.

"Magnolia, will a good man take the life of his wife? Will a good man take the life of a friend who is so close he turns his wife and children over to him?"

"You people, sir, don't understand us. We find it necessary to find some joy whenever and wherever and however we can. We have so little and we don't let too much slip away if we can help it."

"One last question, Magnolia. Do you feel in danger or threatened having a murderer living so . . ."

"Your Honor!" Jerome stared. "This kind of thing has gone on much too long."

"Mr. Wilson, suppose you and Mr. Lee approach the bench."

"Mr. Wilson," Judge Whitehead said, "You have crossed the line. You are much too experienced to make such errors. One could almost think it was deliberate. Actually, if Mr. Lee pushed the matter, he could likely find just cause to demand a new trial. I don't believe this would make many of your people feel kindly should this occur. If you come close to this again, I will find you in contempt and provide an opportunity for the Defense to make such motions as they wish."

"I'm sorry, Your Honor. I guess I became careless. My apologies to Mr. Lee." Mr. Wilson said.

When they returned Mr. Wilson said, "No more questions, Your Honor."

Fail Patterson took the stand next. Mr. Wilson said, "Fail, much has been said about the families of Jones and Green. In fact, the two of us talked of such earlier. Tell us what you know."

"Sir, you be wrong. Us ain't been talking about such. You be de one doing de talking." There was a stir in the courtroom.

Judge Whitehead was losing patience. After there was quietness he said, "I can't believe this is happening in my court!" Again he glared toward Mr. Wilson and also at Fail Patterson. "Mr. Wilson, suppose you restate your question in a different manner."

"To your knowledge, not hearsay, but to your knowledge, did Maybe Jones and Posey Green swap families?"

"Yes sur."

"Do you know if a divorce was involved?"

"Not to my knowledge. Us don't usually do things that way. Sometimes we gets a preacher to marry us up but we don't go beyond. Some don't always use a preacher."

One last question. "Do you know of your own knowledge if any animosity existed between Maybe and Posey?"

Don't know 'xactly what the animosity means but if I understand, everything seemed fine 'till Saturday morning."

Herman Wilson said, "No further questions."

Jerome got up and moved toward the witness box. "It seems you are saying that Maybe Jones is a pretty good fellow, a pretty decent fellow, and could have been provoked into such action."

Mr. Wilson jumped up. "This calls for an opinion, Your Honor. He cannot know nor can anyone know what is in the mind and heart of another."

Before anyone could stop him Fail said,"A good man spite what dey say!"

Judge Whitehead said, "Have that last statement struck from the records."

"One last question. Do you know if Posey usually carried a knife with him? And if so, describe it."

"Posey had the best 'nife in the quarters. If he had his pants on, he had dat 'nife wid him. Had one long blade. Kept it sharp as a razor. 'Nife handle was pearl white wid an eagle on de side wid P.G. on it."

Mr. Wilson rose quickly. "Your Honor, there has not been a knife placed in evidence. An axe is the only weapon that has been produced."

"I'm going to overrule your objection," Judge Whitehead said. "Based on previous testimony, a knife of such design has existed though it has not been placed in evidence."

"I have no further questions, Your Honor." Jerome returned to his seat.

"Your Honor," Mr. Wilson said, "I believe I have substantiated all the facts, all the evidence needed. I will not waste the court's time and the county's money by calling further witnesses. The State rests."

Judge Whitehead looked at Mr. Lee. "Can you give me an idea as to the time you will require with your witnesses? The hour is late."

"I can only estimate, Your Honor. I can only guess as to the time Mr. Wilson may need to cross-examine. But, to respond as best I can, I would guess two or three hours."

"I'm going to adjourn until nine tomorrow morning. Again, the jurors are cautioned not to discuss this case." He got up and walked slowly toward his chambers. The deputy removed Maybe through the rear door.

"I want a promise that you will keep things going until eleven," April said. "I must run. I don't have much time. I'll see you at nine in the morning. And Jerome, when you have a moment, think on what Harry said to his three friends."

After a brief stop at his office Jerome went directly home. He was tired. He was not in a good mood. Tomorrow this ordeal would be over. From the beginning he had never felt good about accepting the case.

"I have supper ready. Get your hands washed so we can eat while it's still warm. I had anticipated you would eat before you finished your plans," his mother said. "You look tired."

After Susan had said the blessing they seemed to seek each other emotionally. Jerome thought he saw a mist in his mother's eyes.

"Why the feast?" Jerome asked. There was a roast, creamed potatoes and gravy, small lima beans, squash, a tossed salad, homemade biscuits and iced tea. He had no doubt that a dessert awaited them.

"I knew you would be tired. I know you are discouraged. I guess you have asked yourself why you became involved in this case. You know, a mother can just sense these things."

"I thought about all those very things on the way home. I'm not sure I will ever get involved in such again. I was never totally convinced that Maybe was innocent. Certainly you know I accepted the case because of April. She believed in his innocence, or she said she did. Yes, I suppose she really did but for a long time I felt her actions resulted only because Maybe had saved her life."

"She has helped you?" his mother asked.

"Yes. She has assisted in many ways. She helped pick a jury. She has attempted to keep Maybe in good spirits but he tends to be despondent. She has attempted to give me encouragement. You know, I have never seen one so bright and serious at times and yet at other times she reminds you of one even younger with her jokes and good humor. You never know exactly what to expect. I cannot attempt to describe her."

The telephone rang. Jerome got up, went to the other room and answered after the third ring. "Hello," he said. "Sorry to take so long." He had recognized Joseph's voice. "I was having dinner." Jerome could sense Joseph's ill mood.

"Is April with you? She usually tells someone if she is going to be late."

"No. She left ahead of me. She said she had an errand to run. I am sure her car is not broken down unless it is between Attapulgus and your place."

"Jerome, I think this crazy trial has gone on about long enough. I missed a day and a half. Others have lost time. Some are still there. Yes, there was four or five of my people locked in that damn witness room. Some of those who are not there might as well be. Their mind ain't on their work. And I'm not too happy about April's role. I saw her when I was on the stand in front of all those people, just like she was on display. I hope this damn spectacle is about to end. When do you feel it will be over?"

"It will be in the hands of the jury tomorrow. The witnesses that have been retained should be free by lunch time. None of your people are involved on the jury."

"Well, I sure as hell hope so. I hope someone is getting something from this because it ain't Joseph Randolph." The telephone went dead.

"Your food is nearly cold. I could tell them you are in the bathroom or not here if it rings again; but I suppose that would be a lie and we'll not do that." She smiled.

"Is a lie ever good? Is it ever right?"

"It's never right," Susan said, "but I believe there are a few times it could come close."

They enjoyed the rest of their meal and were finishing their dessert when the telephone rang once more. "I'll not let you lie." He smiled as he once again moved to the telephone. This time he had let it ring four times.

"April ain't home yet! Has she come by your place? Do you know the nature of the errand she told you about?"

Jerome paused, then decided he would not be so nice this time. "The answers are no and no. She is not here. Neither do I know the nature of her errand. I'm sure she will be home soon or call. Would you please have her call me when she comes in, as I am concerned about her safety also." Again, the telephone went dead.

"Is April all right? I could tell that was Joseph from your responses. Tell me nothing has happened!"

"She is not at home. Mr. Randolph was concerned. I want to think she is fine. She's a big girl. She reminds me from time to time." He wondered how his mother would interpret his last remark. He went on, "You know, I have never realized how impatient and direct Mr. Randolph can be. I am not sure some of his habits and attitudes will serve him well as a commissioner."

"This is his season to be impatient, Jerome. It's always been like that. Joseph Randolph has a great number of fine characteristics and no one can be more concerned about his family. Would this not be the reason he has called twice?"

Jerome finished his dessert. Suddenly, he said, "You know, I am not sure of my reasons but I don't think I trust Joseph Randolph. I know he has been good to you. I know how you feel about Martha and the family."

"Joseph Randolph has been influenced by his background. Let us leave Joseph at this time. He has had a long way to travel," his mother said.

Jerome was really not ready to leave the subject of Joseph Randolph but he knew it best to do so. He felt, however, he had one thing he must say. "He would still be back where his family originated had it not been for his wife. She is a very special person. I suspect few people really know how special she is. She is the stabilizer, the balance wheel."

"Don't you want some more dessert? You never realized you ate with the telephone ringing. You're as skinny as a rail."

"No. This is enough."

"You go to your study. I'll clean up tonight and I don't need your help. You need to get some rest as well. Finish and go to bed early."

"Thank you for preparing my favorite dinner. You will be God's top angel when you leave about forty years from now."

"Don't wish that on me, Jerome. You know how I feel about old age. We have discussed that before. God will answer my prayers. He has promised me He will take me to Him when I can no longer look after myself. Now enough of that. You get to work!"

"I would like to hear from April. I'll work some. I'm going to set my clock to get up early, very early. I will eat breakfast in town and finish my work at the office while I am fresh. Under no circumstances are you to get up early."

As he moved to go to his room the telephone rang again. His mother answered it. He waited in the hall.

In some moments his mother turned and said, "That was April. She said she was home safely and for you to go to bed and get some rest. She said everything was going to be fine. What is that supposed to mean?"

"I don't know. I wish I did. I wish I was that optimistic." He closed the door.

CHAPTER 35

Jerome sat in the same booth, eating breakfast, at a little after six. He was not sure why he had gone to the same booth but it had felt right. He looked at the next booth. It was occupied, but not by the same four. He offered a silent prayer.

Once again, he reviewed his plans he had made the previous evening. He must go with the self-defense theory even without the knife, and with the right to protect one's own home, as well as oneself. There was nothing else. The family swapping had destroyed any hope based on character. His closing arguments would have to center on reasonable doubt. Someone could have entered. It could have been self defense. But this offered little hope.

He remembered the pictures of the smashed faces, the hanging eye. He knew the jury would remember the pictures in detail.

He drank his coffee and stared into space. He was about to ask himself once more why he had taken the case. He knew. The reason had been sitting by him and it wasn't Maybe Jones.

He also felt his mother had done nothing to discourage him in making a decision. Few were closer than the Randolphs and the Lees. Yet he couldn't place any blame on either, since he had not been forced to take the case.

Two women. The two most important people in his life. He knew he loved one. He was becoming more sure he loved the other. He thought about the differences — age, education and economics. Yet he continued to dream.

Jerome was in his place at court earlier than usual. Maybe had been brought in as well. He was in his funeral suit, but it looked unclean and wrinkled. "It will come to an end today, Maybe. We will know something soon."

"How you see this now?" Maybe asked. "Far as I can tell, don't look none too good, do it?"

Jerome thought for a few seconds. He was reminded of a doctor conferring with a patient with a terminal disease. Do you tell them the truth and destroy all hope? Do you keep one ever hopeful? He wasn't sure.

As he was about to answer, still seeking for some words of both reality and hope, he heard a voice behind him. "Now don't you and Maybe look good this morning? Nothing like a good night's rest and naturally I sleep as a child!" She looked at Jerome for a reaction, black eyes twinkling, a smile on her face.

Jerome looked closely at her and thought, that fellow was right. They are high and they leap out at you and they even seem to move upward! Then his other consciousness took over and he thought, My God, I have no right or business thinking of such things!

April looked at him closely, as if she had read his very thoughts. "Joseph seemed overly concerned about my whereabouts last evening. I suspect he was not pleasant when he called you. He wasn't in the best of moods when he talked to me. He talked and I listened!"

She reached over and patted Maybe on the arm. "Don't you worry. We are going to make it fine."

She turned to Jerome. "Keep this thing going until eleven or until I give you the word." They were interrupted by the "All rise please. . . ."

When Judge Whitehead had taken his seat he called the two attorneys before him. "We are a full day behind schedule and as I review matters, I can note why! I do hope you gentlemen will be considerate of the court's responsibilities. Mr. Lee, call your first witness."

"Your Honor, I call the Reverend D. C. Handmaker." The minister, dressed in his finest, took his seat in the witness stand.

"Reverend Handmaker, please state your name, address and occupation. Speak loudly, as we have a capacity crowd this morning and they are still settling in. Speak as if you were trying to keep your congregation awake in your church!"

Judge Whitehead seemed more than a little concerned; his face darkened. He was not sure whether this was a criticism addressed toward him.

"I am D. C. Handmaker. I live and preach in Attapulgus, though my duties may carry me to many places, as the world is really my parish. I am the minister of the Fourth Morning Star Missionary Baptist Church, where I have served for twelve years."

Judge Whitehead looked at the witness, his watch, at Herman Wilson and at Jerome Lee. He rolled his eyes toward the ceiling to indicate the day had not started as he had expected.

"What is your relationship with the defendant?" Jerome asked.

"He is a member of my church, the Fourth Morning Star Missionary Baptist Church. He has served as deacon, though it was some years ago."

"What kind of person have you found Maybe Jones to be?"

"He is a good member, a good brother. He gives to the church from time to time. But we know he has a big family and we are reminded of the widow's mite. He says and thinks kind things about his brothers and sisters in God."

Mr. Wilson raised his hand as if to the heavens and let his eyes roll upward.

"Have you ever known, of your own knowledge, or even by hearsay, of this man committing a crime?"

"No. Other than his recent incarceration, I have never known Brother Jones to spend a minute in jail."

April thought, He is either ignorant of his membership, has a poor memory or lies.

"And Reverend Handmaker, as you have firsthand knowledge of this man, probably knowing more about him than most others, do you believe Maybe So Jones could have killed Lila Jones and Posey Green without just cause?"

Herman Wilson shot out of his seat like a rocket. "Your Honor, Your Honor, the defense counselor knows better than to ask for such an opinion! This man cannot testify about such. He must speak only of the facts or what he has heard firsthand."

Judge Whitehead said, "Mr. Lee, I must warn you. Though you have not had years of experience in the courts, this is one of the first things one is supposed to learn in law school." Judge Whitehead nearly smiled, since he knew Jerome had made his point. He suspected that lawyers would always do this as long as there were courts, crime and lawyers.

"Let me ask another question. Have you ever known the accused to hurt anyone?"

"Not in my twenty years."

"You are saying that you were surprised to learn that this occurred and charges had been filed?"

Mr. Wilson rose again. "Your Honor, the defense is attempting to ask questions in a manner so he answers them for the witness."

"Go ahead," Judge Whitehead said. "Answer the question."

"I was stunned. It was completely out of character for this gentle and caring man, this man who has befriended so many, to be accused of such."

"I have no further questions, Your Honor." Jerome returned to his seat.

Herman Wilson practically bounced to the floor. "Mr. — that is, Reverend Handmaker, what do you consider the qualities that go to make up a good man, a gentle man, a kind man and a caring man?"

"Why sir, one who displays such characteristics," the preacher responded. Jerome smiled.

"How would you evaluate a man, sir, who, by his own admission, struck down his wife and best friend with this very axe and has admitted doing so?" He walked over and picked up the axe.

"I believe, at the time he made the confession, and according to my understanding, he was defending himself against armed people whose intent was to do him harm. I also recall that he said he didn't want to do it."

"Reverend Handmaker, I must ask you if Mr. Lee has schooled you in these responses?"

Jerome jumped up. "Your Honor, I can't believe I heard the last remark!"

Judge Whitehead said, "Mr. Wilson, in the future you will leave out such personal suggestions. I am about to become a little more than concerned. I hope we will remember. This morning has not started as well as I had hoped or expected."

Mr. Wilson continued, "The two deceased are gone — gone for all time. I'm sure you would know, as you presided at the funerals if I have my information correct. You will recall the caskets were not open. Could you tell us why?"

"Because it was requested."

"Your Honor," Jerome said as he rose again, "I do not believe much of what has been said is in the form of a question. It would appear more like a closing statement." He sat back down.

Before the judge could speak Mr. Wilson said, "I have no further questions."

There was movement in the courtroom but as Judge Whitehead looked out, it became quiet again.

Jerome looked at April. She seemed to be glancing over her shoulder periodically.

"Call your next witness, Mr. Lee."

"Your Honor, I call Nellie Green."

Nellie Green took the stand. Her dress was simple, clean and obviously quite old. Her hair was not well groomed.

"Give your name, address and occupation."

"I'se Nellie Green. I lives in de quarters of Mr. Joseph's place in Attapulgus. I mostly string 'bacco and sews on shade cloth."

"Now Nellie, I know my calling you is highly irregular, so I will be most careful. Before this tragic Saturday morning, had you ever seen Maybe Jones, this man that sits at the table, do anything unkind to your husband or anyone else?"

"No suh. He be kind to me and my chilluns, though my own boys ain't been kind to him always."

"One other question and I will be through." Suddenly, Jerome glanced back at the table and saw April motion for him to come to the table. When he approached, April smiled, her black eyes dancing. "When you finish, ask for a ten minute recess. You are to ask her about the knife?"

"Yes."

"Retain her for further questioning and ask for a recess of ten minutes like someone who has to go to the restroom."

Jerome turned back to Nellie Green. "Did Posey have a knife, a sort of special knife?"

"Yes sur. It be his pride and joy."

"Would you describe it?"

"It be white. One big blade and always sharp. Had P.G. on de side. I'd know it anywhere, anytime."

"Have you seen it since he passed away?"

"No suh. Sho ain't. Ain't no place to be found."

Jerome ended with, "Your Honor, as soon as Mr. Wilson finishes with this witness I would request a ten minute recess."

Mr. Wilson got up. "I'm sure it is painful for you to testify. In fact, I'm surprised to see you here." He turned and looked at Jerome.

"Did you hear this man sitting at the table say he killed your husband and his wife?"

"No sur. I din't hear him say dat, but he did tell Mr. Joseph."

"No further questions."

"We will recess for fifteen minutes." The judge moved toward his chambers.

As soon as the judge had departed April jumped up and fought her way through the crowd to the back of the courtroom. After she talked several minutes with Carson Blair she returned to the table where Jerome had remained. There was a smile on her face.

She handed a small package to Jerome. "I knew I was right. I just knew it." She patted him on the shoulder, then turned and patted Maybe. "You'll sleep in your own bed tonight, Maybe."

Immediately she turned back to Jerome. "Listen carefully. We don't have a lot of time. This is the knife. Now let me tell you what happened, because we must play a little game. I sent our policeman, Carson Blair, to see Lottie's helpers. I knew it had to be them. Mr. Blair is a deputy so he has done nothing illegal. He went to the home of Detroit McHenry and demanded the knife. He told him he had seen Roosevelt earlier. He told Detroit that if they gave him the knife, he would work toward a charge of simple theft. If not, it could mean ten to twenty years for tampering with evidence. He said that a man's life was at stake.

"We must leave an impression that they were returning the knife when they learned what was at stake. A promise was made to attempt to keep the charge down to simple theft. Carson Blair, Detroit McHenry and Roosevelt Boyd are in the lobby. They will remain until they are called. Now what do you do?"

"I could take the knife to Judge Whitehead and explain."

"Must it be done this way?" April asked, her eyes sparkling. "Let's sock it to old Herman Wilson. I want to see his face when he sees the knife! The old rascal has it coming. You can ask the judge when he returns to let you call the three new witnesses. I don't think he can refuse. Well, what do you say? Say something!"

Jerome smiled. "We will try it your way."

"We could really work on Sheriff Henderson as well. What do you think?" April asked.

"I'm tempted but let us not burn any bridges. You may want to cross them again some other day."

The judge returned and said, "Mr. Lee, your next witness."

"Your Honor, I request permission for Mr. Wilson and me to approach the bench." The judge nodded.

"Your Honor, so that we may get as many facts as possible, I would like to add three witnesses to my list. By doing so, I will not call all of those on my list. I think it would save the county time and, as it was said, time is money."

"Three?" the judge asked. "Who are these three? Why were they not placed on the original list?"

"Two of them are Lottie Layton's helpers. I had thought Lottie would be adequate but I believe these two could add to the evidence."

"And the other?"

"Carson Blair. He is the policeman in Attapulgus and serves as a sheriff's deputy from time to time."

"It may take hours to locate these people, Your Honor." Mr. Wilson said. "Mr. Lee has just reminded us that time is money." He smiled.

"These three are in the lobby, Your Honor. It would only take a minute."

"These three are in the courthouse now?" Judge Whitehead asked.

"Yes sir."

Mr. Wilson said, "Since they are present, I have no objections. May I suggest we recess early for lunch. They can be sworn in, and we can move out immediately after lunch."

"You are very considerate," Jerome said. "I think this would work out very well."

"Since it is a bit early, I'll call a recess for lunch. We will report back a half hour early. I'll keep this court on schedule."

In moments April and Jerome were on their way to lunch. He said, "We could go somewhere else. I guess our friends, your friends, I should say, are back again."

"This will be our last chance," April said with a smile. "I wouldn't miss it for anything. Perhaps they have made some additional observations." In moments they were seated once again in the booth.

One said, "You know anything about the girl?"

"I do," another answered. "My brother's boy was in her class for a spell about three or four years ago. He was there only a part of the year because they moved, but he learned a lot while he was there. Hell, he says she is as damn smart as she is pretty. Said the teacher couldn't even answer her questions but he learned the teacher's trick. When she couldn't answer the teacher would say this ain't a part of the lesson and we'll take it up when we can. I guess she would go study up and sometimes she'd come back and talk about it but sometimes she never did. He said at times the girl would get excited or disgusted and say some right naughty words. But I'll tell you one thing. She ain't missed the first damn thing since this case started."

"What words, Harry, did she say?"

"Said most all of them so my nephew said."

"Well, that bugger has had his day. It's all over."

Another voice said, "You fellows slept through the whole thing. That boy will never serve a day!"

"The hell you say, Nathan. He can't win."

"You missed it. You were looking at that girl's tits when you oughta been looking where you oughta been looking. That girl rushed to the back and got a small package during the recess. She smiled like hell, boys. She's got the knife!"

"I saw 'em," another said.

"The knife or the tits?" another said, laughing.

"Both. Howell's right. I ran out to get ahead of the crowd. My bladder don't work like it used to. Saw her talking with a fellow in a uniform. He handed her something and she broke out in one hell of a smile. I thought she would kiss him!"

"That Lee ain't no dumb fellow. Ain't had much to work with. Had a bad horse to ride."

"When that knife shows, the D.A. and the sheriff better run for cover. You boys hold on, 'cause you ain't seen nothing yet."

April pushed her knee against Jerome's leg to get his attention and whispered, "They think you are a nice and smart man. I could have told them that."

As the men got up to leave one was saying, "Better get back. Gonna be a big crowd this afternoon."

As they started to move away one saw April and Jerome through the half drawn curtain. He stopped and his face turned red. Then he smiled. "How long you been in there?"

April smiled back, black eyes dancing. "Three days! Indeed, we have learned a great deal." The others stopped to look and listen.

"You mean you been there all of these three days?" His face turned as red as an Indian.

"Never missed the first word," April said. "I believe your names are Howell, Nathan, Don and Harry, though I am not sure I can tie together your names with your faces.

"But Howell, you are right about Jerome Lee. He is smart. You are to be commended for your observations.

"I would also commend Harry for his vivid and accurate description of me. It is obvious he sees a great deal more than Mr. Lee. Perhaps when you have a few spare moments, you can help him!" She smiled as they continued to look and listen in stunned silence. "Why don't you gentlemen go back and get you a good seat because, as one of you remarked only a few minutes ago, you ain't seen nothing yet! Again, I commend Harry and Howell!"

As the men left one said, "Well, I'll be damned."

CHAPTER 36

"Mr. Lee, call your next witness," Judge Whitehead said.

"I call Carson Blair to the stand."

"Mr. Blair, should I call you Chief Blair, as you are the Police Chief at Attapulgus, or Deputy Blair, as you are a member of the emergency group that assists the sheriff when needed?"

"Whatever you feel most comfortable with, Mr. Lee. I expect most law officers have been called many things." He smiled and Jerome smiled back.

"You live in Attapulgus?"

"Yes sir."

"How long have you served in each capacity?"

"Eleven years as police chief and I believe eight years on the sheriff's emergency squad."

"Now Mr. Blair, I want to show you a knife. Do you recognize this knife?" You could hear a pin drop in the courtroom.

"Yes sir, it is the knife I gave to your assistant, April Randolph, an hour or so ago."

"Where did you get this knife? This is the knife you gave April Randolph?"

"Yes, this is the knife I gave her. I was in contact with a Detroit McHenry, an assistant to Lottie Layton, of the Layton Funeral Home. He said he had just learned that the knife was of some importance as to evidence in this trial and . . ."

"Your Honor! What's going on here?" Mr. Wilson shouted. "Something is not right!"

"Please remain seated, Mr. Wilson. You will have ample opportunity to question this witness in a moment." Mr. Wilson, his face as white as a sheet, sat down and slumped in his chair. "Continue with your questions," Judge Whitehead said.

"As I said, Detroit McHenry said he had learned of the importance of the knife in the trial and wanted to right a wrong as quickly as possible. I was likely contacted because the two of us have known each other for some time and he knew I was an officer of the law. As I said, we had occasions in the past to know of each other."

Mr. Wilson stood once more. "Your Honor, in light of this unexpected development, I wish to request a recess. Perhaps we could adjourn until tomorrow morning."

"Mr. Wilson your request is denied. As you said earlier, we need to expedite such matters and be as resourceful as possible with the monies of Decatur County. Please continue, Mr. Lee, but before you do so, let me tell the people of this courtroom that I will have order and I will do what is necessary to get it."

"I really don't believe there are further questions, Your Honor. I do wish to place the knife in evidence."

Mr. Wilson, if he had questions, asked none.

Jerome said, "I call Roosevelt Boyd." When the witness was seated Jerome asked, "Please give your name, address and occupation, Mr. Boyd."

"I'se Roosevelt Boyd. I lives here in the projects in Midway. My job is to assist Miss Layton at her funeral home."

"And how long have you worked with her?" Jerome asked.

"I'se been in Miss Layton's employ close to nine years; in fact, come December, it will be nine years."

"Do you remember going to Attapulgus on a Saturday morning, April 3rd of this year?"

"Yes suh. We picked up two bodies on de Randolph Place in de quarters."

"And those people were Posey Green and Lila Jones?"

"Yes sir."

"Do you remember any details? Tell us what you recall."

"We come out some time just before light on that Saturday morning. We picked up the bodies soon as the sheriff said we could. It was sorta messy. Lots of blood. Was no place for someone wid a light stomach."

"Tell us about the knife. Where was this knife?" Jerome went over and picked it up.

"Well suh, it's lak this. Us was getting de body on de stretcher we used to carry 'em on and as we rolled over the woman dis knife rolled out of de bottom of de gown that was all matted wid blood. It was messy."

"Was the knife open? Was the blade out?"

"Yes sur, it was out."

"And what happened to the knife?"

"Well suh, us, that's Detroit and me, talked about who oughta have it. It sho' seemed Posey weren't gonna need a knife no more. I told Detroit we flip a coin, wid the winner getting the knife and de other pay the loser two dollars. Detroit said no. He just kept the knife and gave me two dollars."

"Did you tell anyone about the knife?" Jerome asked.

"No suh, didn't think no more 'bout it till today, when all this here come to light. Glad to have it off my mind."

"Your witness," Jerome said.

For a moment the district attorney seemed to rise, then dropped back to his seat. "No questions."

"Please call your next witness, Mr. Lee."

"I call Detroit McHenry to the stand."

"Please give your name, address and occupation," Jerome said.

"I'm Detroit McHenry. I lives in de projects. I helps Miss Layton in her funeral business. I been with her 'bout seven years."

"Did you and Mr. Boyd assist Miss Layton in getting the bodies from Randolph Place on Saturday, April third?"

"Don't know as to date. It was a Saturday morning and we picked up two bodies, a man and a woman."

"I will not ask a lot of details, Mr. McHenry. I will get to a specific point. Do you recognize this knife?" He held the knife up for the witness to see.

"Yes sir, dat's de knife I gave to Mr. Blair dis very morning. I heard about the trial and de importance of dis knife, so I contacts Mr. Blair and gives the knife to him to bring to you all."

"Where was the knife found?"

"In de folds of de bloody gown on the dead woman. It was rolled up in de folds. It fell out as we loaded her on de stretcher."

Jerome smiled and asked, "How was it determined if you or Mr. Boyd was to receive the knife?"

Detroit smiled and said, "We talked about matching for it. Den he insisted I gives him two dollars for his part."

"Mr. McHenry, it seems obvious to me that it was not a case of obstructing justice because you did not know of the significance of the weapon until now. And once you learned, you stepped forward to right a wrong. Am I correct?"

"Dat's so, dat's so. Us ain't meant no harm to no one. Dat black boy ain't gonna use that knife in dis ole world no more."

"But you took a knife that didn't belong to you. How do you explain that?"

"Didn't seem to b'long to nobody at that point. It was sorta 'finders-keepers' as de ole saying goes."

"No further questions, Your Honor."

Herman Wilson moved his head slightly and looked into the distance, seeing nothing.

Jerome quickly recalled three witnesses to identify the knife, then said, "Your Honor, it had been my intention to call Maybe Jones, the defendant, to the stand but I see no real purpose."

Judge Whitehead said, "After a ten minute recess we will have the closing statements to the jury." He left the room hurriedly.

Maybe Jones smiled into the face of April and said, "I told 'em dat the first time but you two de only ones to believe. And I thanks you. I'll have a chance to pay you back, to get even for saving my life."

"We're already even, Maybe. Hopefully we have saved each other. It isn't all over yet."

Jerome said, "Maybe, April was really the only one who believed you. She was sure. I wasn't. Don't give me credit. She deserves it all."

"Mr. Lee, proceed with your closing arguments." Judge Whitehead looked tired and weary.

Jerome moved over in front of the jury box. He looked into the faces of a panel of men and women who seemed alert, but tired.

"Ladies and gentlemen, for three days you have listened to dozens of people and thousands of words. I know you are tired. I commend you for giving your attention to the matters at hand because what was at stake was the life of a man; a man who had defended himself as best he knew how. He had no choice. He did what was natural to protect himself from bodily harm. You and I would have done the same.

"I confess to you that I do not understand the way of life of many people, people like Maybe Jones and Posey Green and many others. They have some strange ways, strange customs. They live together without a license to do so, they part without a legal separation. So many seem to have families without husbands and often they do not learn a lesson the first or even a second time. I can't explain what I do not know, what I do not understand.

"I can't tell you why Maybe and Posey swapped families nor can I tell you why they decided to swap back. You and I, however, are not here for the purpose of trying to understand this. We are here to determine if this man, Maybe Jones, did or did not kill these people defending himself. No one living except the defendant can tell you firsthand what happened. He has repeatedly said from the beginning that he struck these two unfortunate people to save his own life.

"I think there would have been much doubt if the weapon, the knife, had not surfaced. Let us be grateful that it did so justice may prevail. I do not believe you can any longer have doubts as to what occurred. And, yes, we weep that two lives have been lost, a father and mother of children, many children, but there is nothing we can do to bring them back.

"In a few minutes Judge Whitehead will charge you to review the evidence and give a verdict as to the innocence or guilt of this man. I don't see how there can be doubt when you evaluate all the evidence. But even in case of doubt, you must remember that a person must be found guilty beyond *reasonable* doubt.

"I could stand here and review the testimony of each witness and take hours of your time to tell you once again what you have already heard from the many witnesses. But I have enough confidence in you that you will do the right thing, that you will find this man innocent of these deaths by reason of self defense.

"Again, I thank you for the responsibilities you have accepted in helping to keep our system of government, our precious Constitution and our Bill of Rights alive and working."

Herman Wilson had intelligence enough to know that his case had likely gone up in smoke. He wasn't even sure the grand jury would have indicted this man had the knife been present from the beginning. He also knew that it was not worth destroying his relationship with the sheriff and coroner because he would need their support a hundred times again. Yet, as a district attorney, he was expected to make the best case he could for the State. He seemed torn between his belief and his duty. It was obvious they were not the same.

"Members of the jury, there sits a man at this table who in two strokes of this axe removed from this world, forever, a father of six and a mother of three. Nine children have a loss beyond comprehension. This is the man that did it. Perhaps it was jealousy, vengeance, revenge or just meanness but whatever the reason or reasons, these people are gone. They will not return. That man over there made it a certainty. I suppose the only good thing one can say is that it was not a lingering death for either. They did not suffer long if one can find any comfort in that. We do not need to say more. He did it. He said he did it.

"Let's get to the very heart of the matter — the knife. This seems a big mystery in that for days and weeks and even months, no one seemed to know the first thing about a knife. Then, suddenly, it appears at the last moment, in a fashion difficult to understand. It reminds me of an old cowboy movie where the hero rushes in at the last minute and rescues the damsel from the railroad tracks just before the train arrives. I find the time of the discovery of the knife amazing.

"Yes, we have a knife and it seems to be the knife belonging to the deceased, Posey Green. But do you know for sure that this knife was found in the gown of the deceased? No one else, according to the testimony of those who saw these people, saw a knife. Isn't it just a little strange that Mr. Randolph didn't see it, Mr. Jenkins didn't see it, Sheriff Henderson and his deputies didn't see it, Lottie Layton didn't see it and the pictures don't show it? Indeed, this is strange.

"You think about this. You don't have to doubt the deaths. He said he did it. He didn't say he tried to disarm Posey, but he struck him a profound death blow. You will remember the pictures.

"And the knife. I find it something beyond comprehension. As you deliberate, think about placing this man back on the streets to perhaps strike again and again. Can society afford such? Would you care to be in his presence? All of these things you must ask yourself.

"I thank you for being a good jury. I am sure these three days have not been easy for you." Herman Wilson returned to his seat with mixed emotions.

Judge Whitehead charged the jury. "There are two charges made against the defendant. He is charged with said crimes resulting in the deaths of Lila Jones and Posey Green. These are capital crimes and the penalty, if found guilty, can include the death penalty. You will remember that for one to be found guilty, he must be found guilty beyond a reasonable doubt. You will retire, select a foreman and begin your deliberations. You will advise the door keeper when you have reached a decision." Judge Whitehead left for his chambers.

Jerome took April by the arm. "I have it understood that the court will notify me when a decision is reached. Suppose we go to my office and relax a moment."

April took Jerome's arm as they worked their way through the throngs of people. Jerome had been astonished at the number who had attended the trial. Was it because of the nature of the case? Probably. Was it because the District Attorney always drew a crowd because of his spirited manner, enthusiasm and zeal? Probably. Was it because they wanted to see if a young country lawyer could hold his own when the odds were stacked so heavily against him? Probably not. Was it because of April's presence? Who could say. Something got them to court. Something held their attention. April would likely suggest they ask the four in the booth.

Yes, the public loves a good contest. It loves a winner more. Nothing had changed much in the hearts of men since the Christians were pushed into the arena with the lions.

As Jerome and April walked along several stared and looked back over their shoulders. When had they ever seen a girl so beautiful?

When Jerome unlocked the door to his office he saw his secretary had written: 'Call Joseph Randolph.' He decided he could do it later, if he did so at all. He didn't have enough energy left to do battle with anyone. Nothing else on his desk required immediate attention.

He and April sat in the two chairs in front of his desk. Both remained silent, as if silence was the most precious thing in the world at the moment.

Finally he said, "Care to talk about this afternoon?"

"The witnesses said what needed to be said as to the knife. I'm not sure all accepted the story of Detroit rushing out to save the day but it was adequate. It really didn't matter how it came about.

She added, "I'm glad you did not review the case in your closing remarks beyond what you did. The jury was weary. They had heard enough. I'm sure you recognized this."

"What about Herman Wilson's closing?" Jerome asked.

"Don't underestimate this man, ever! He is smart. There were times when others could have lost control. He didn't. He apparently is very talented and he has learned a great deal from experience.

"I'm sure he had to change his plan completely, but most never would have known. When the knife appeared, he had to regroup. Anyone else would have given up. Not so Herman Wilson. He was filled with emotion. He was convincing. He had them smelling blood again. This man makes me shake all over. He takes what he has and gets the most from it.

"Jerome, your performance was near perfect. Once you had the knife, you were flawless. I think you have saved Maybe. I cannot believe the charge will be reduced to manslaughter. It will be all of one or the other.

"Sometimes I questioned myself. Did I do this because of a past debt or because I believed him innocent? My thoughts varied from time to time.

"How long would you guess it will take the jury to reach a decision?"

Jerome responded, "My professors in law school cautioned us about this kind of guessing. Most feel there is not a guide or pattern to follow." He changed the subject. "You will get a new sister soon? I guess David is excited."

"Jerome, you wouldn't guess how sweet Kathy is. She is nearly perfect!"

"Like you?"

"Oh my, Jerome. You don't know the first thing about me. Don't you recall the four gentlemen talking about my experiences in the seventh grade?

She continued, "Kathy and I look quite different in that she is a blond. She is such a good person. You must meet her. David is several years older than she is. My father is eleven years older than my mother. And yes, you are ten years older than I am." Jerome looked at her and shook his head in dismay.

The telephone rang and Jerome answered. "I'll be right over. April and I will be there in minutes." He turned to her. "The jury is about to return. We must leave immediately."

"What does it mean, Jerome, when they stay out such a short time? Is it in our favor?"

"Why don't we go and see? After what you said about Wilson's closing, I'm not nearly as sure as I thought I was."

When they arrived Maybe was already in his place. The courtroom had filled once more and there was considerable noise. April looked at Maybe. His face looked ten years older than three days ago. There was no spark left in his eyes.

April looked to her left and saw Herman Wilson. He showed a poker face, his thoughts completely concealed. He sat very erect, as one would expect of a warrior sitting at a council table. He looked unruffled, as if he had just arrived at a party.

Judge Whitehead looked out upon his courtroom, his own private kingdom. Again, it was filled to capacity.

He said to the clerk, "Please have the sheriff escort the jury back into the courtroom."

As they marched in and took their seats April looked closely into the face of each. She saw little to indicate what to expect. She whispered to Jerome, "Can you read them?" He shook his head and did not speak.

As soon as they sat down, April, still watching each move, saw slight smiles for just a split moment on the faces of two as they looked at her. She punched Jerome and whispered, "We have won. I'm sure of it!"

Judge Whitehead looked at Maybe and said, "The defendant will please rise." Jerome rose immediately and practically pulled Maybe from his seat, who seemed not to hear the first word. Jerome then took April's arm to tell her to rise also, though she had no idea why.

"Has the jury reached a decision?" Judge Whitehead asked.

The foreman spoke. "We have, Your Honor." The deputy walked over, took the slip and carried it back to Judge Whitehead. The judge looked at it for a few seconds, then handed it to the clerk sitting below. "In a moment I will ask the clerk to read the verdict. Before he does, however, I want to say that every person will remain seated until the jury has cleared the building." He nodded to the clerk.

"We, the jury, find the defendant, Maybe So Jones, not guilty!"

As the jury was leaving another deputy came over and said, "I am instructed to take the defendant by the jail to pick up his belongings, then return him to his home."

Maybe rose, a big smile on his face and tears of joy running down his cheeks. "I will remember, Miss April. I will remember." He took the hand Jerome offered and shook it firmly, then left with the deputy.

As the last member of the jury left the room Herman Wilson came over and took Jerome's hand in a firm clasp. "Mr. Lee, you have a more than promising future. Congratulations. It was a great performance, especially for one so young. But naturally you had the best help ever." As he took April's hand he said, "It was nice to have you in court, Miss Randolph. I hope you will study law. We need a great mind and a pretty face; it is obvious that you have both." With that he turned and left.

"Thank you again, Jerome. I hope we can sit and talk soon. Charles has expressed a desire to have you visit. I will always want you near!" April smiled, stood on her tiptoes and kissed his cheek. "I can do better next time," she said, then made her way out of the courtroom.

Chapter 37

"Congratulations!" Susan Lee met Jerome at the door of their home.

"How did you know?" Jerome asked.

"April stopped and told me five minutes ago. She said so many nice things about you. I believe she said you were letter perfect. I am so proud of you."

Jerome said, "It is good to know that justice has prevailed. Actually, I had little to do with the results. It was April's insight that determined the outcome."

"April also spoke about the many opportunities to learn. She said that all the experiences were not in the courtroom. I didn't know what she meant. She mentioned the lunch hour and said you could explain."

"As I said, April won the case. I didn't. She snatched victory out of certain defeat. I'll explain it all later. I am speaking of the court case. She can tell you about the lunch hour.

"Is it possible that you have a piece of pie left?" he asked.

Susan smiled and moved hurriedly toward the refrigerator. "How can you know so much about me?"

When he had finished his pie his mother asked, "You are glad this is over?"

"Yes indeed."

"You didn't feel good about this case?"

"No."

"Why did you feel so?"

Jerome thought for a few seconds. "I had not believed it self defense. I wasn't even sure April believed it herself at the beginning. I felt that she was simply paying a debt because he saved her life."

"Then you took the case to please April?"

"I guess we could say that."

"You know she is only sixteen?"

"Yes. I think about it all too often."

Susan said, "I'll change the subject. How did Herman Wilson react and what do you think of him?"

"He is a fine district attorney. He is smart. We are fortunate to have such a person in this position."

"What did he say?"

"He congratulated me. He also encouraged April to be a lawyer. I think he felt there was some sensationalism involved when the knife surfaced at the last moment. He compared the ending with that of an old western movie."

He added, "April figured out who had the knife. Then she devised a plan and it worked. She is as smart as she is pretty."

"What will she do with her life? She can become anything she wishes."

Jerome smiled again. "I believe only God knows."

When April arrived home her mother met her with a big smile on her face. "Oh, April, I'm so glad. I'm so happy for you and Jerome, and for Maybe as well. Sit down and eat. I know you are starved to death."

"How did you know the outcome?"

"Susan called as soon as you told her. She couldn't keep it another minute. Then I saw the sheriff's vehicle as he turned taking Maybe home. Maybe had a smile on his face as big as a watermelon."

A voice sounded; April turned to see her father. "Well, I see you got back. Glad that thing is finished. Your mother has not had the help she has needed."

"Oh, April, your father frets so about me. I guess in a way I'm glad because it shows he cares. Though I have missed you, we have managed to keep our heads above water. And I am equally glad this is behind us."

"Now that you got that bugger out and back here, have you considered that he may create one heck of a problem? Our folks are still divided, still upset."

April felt herself shudder inside but was immediately aware of the position in which she found herself. "I am glad that justice and fair play has prevailed. Certainly we are all happy that an innocent man has been vindicated. I am sure, as I have watched with pride over the years, that your sense of justice and reason always stands unchallenged. Perhaps a call to Jerome would be in order. He has worked diligently to see that an innocent man was not destroyed."

"I am sure Jerome was paid or will be paid for what he did. You have been so busy with what you call law and order that many important matters have been forgotten."

"What important matters? You have lost me. What can be more important than the reign of justice and decency?" April asked.

"April, this is a land of reality. It is not one of make-believe or daydreams. Lila is gone. Posey is gone. Their debts can never be recovered. We have nine children to see about. But even so, if this ended at this point, it would be one thing. There ain't gonna be no peace among these people again. Life will be disrupted for all of us. Actually, we would have been served better if the jury had found him guilty. These folks will never forgive or forget.

"I have tried one of the two approaches that I knew. I tried to trade him to another tobacco grower where he could make a fresh start. They wanted no part of him."

"What was the other?" April asked.

"I could run him off and take my losses. In the long run, this would probably be best. I think it would save money."

"Joseph, do you have any idea how long it will be before we can broaden our horizons and do some of the things that everyone was so excited about some months ago? It seems that everything eventually still leads to one of three things. We make money, we buy land and we become somebody. Perhaps the three cannot be separated.

"I thought with the progress of the beautification program, the opportunity to serve as one of our county leaders and the joy and satisfaction of your gift to the church would have opened the door to other things. I saw Mother's eyes sparkle when a lengthy vacation or trip was mentioned. I saw your son, perhaps the first of the Randolphs to graduate from college with highest honors. I saw the people of the county sing praises of you because of your achievements. I had thought this might be a new day, a new beginning. I said to myself, at last, at last.

"But nothing has really changed about the things that are important. It was just too good to be true.

"Every family member had been so happy. They worked and planned to assure your success.

"For three days I have served to see that an innocent man was not destroyed. When I returned I had hoped to hear someone say something kind, such as 'Justice still reigns supreme.'"

Suddenly, Joseph let out a sigh and said, "I have worked all my life for my family. Ain't no one coulda worked harder. All I have done has meant little or nothing to most of you. You talk about money, about land. It is my land that I gave to all of you. It is really my money you are spending. It is through my work and efforts that we have been accepted among the people.

"I now see it was all a mistake. I ain't never been appreciated by my own family. My kindness was looked upon as weakness by my own children, my own family. My children tell me where they will work and where they won't. They tell me how bad I am because I raise tobacco. I even tried to learn to speak correctly but what is the use?" Joseph got up as if he carried a heavy load upon his shoulders and walked slowly from the room.

April looked at the pale face of her silent mother who had sat and heard and suffered. "I'm sorry, Mother. I guess I had expected some of my family other than you to say thank you for helping an innocent man who was in no position to help himself.

"Charles is wrong. He told me that nothing that was important had really changed. Yes, I repeat, he was wrong. It has changed, but not for the better. Our problems are greater than ever before. Our division has become so great that I wonder if we will ever be the same again." April went to her room. She took her clothes off and got into the shower. She was about to look at her breasts to see if they were as Harry had described, then she looked elsewhere. It all seemed to be meaningless and without value.

She tried to sleep but sleep did not come. She thought to herself, I don't want to think of Maybe or court cases or Jerome or Robert or anyone. Suddenly, it became apparent that she must change her role. She decided to work, smile and say little, speaking only of things that had no meaning or value.

Then she thought of her mother, caught in the middle, whose loyalty must always be first and foremost to her husband. God had commanded it so.

For the first night ever, April did not close her eyes.

CHAPTER 38

"I hope you will not be angry if we stay here this evening," Sara said. "I want to be alone with you. I don't care to share you with anyone, not even for a minute. I hope you don't mind." She smiled.

"No, of course I don't mind. I don't care to share you with anyone either. I keep thinking about our association. Sara, I have begged you, though not recently, to let me become a permanent part of your life. I continue to feel as I have felt for years. You would know that. Women can sense such things. The last time we discussed it you said you would respond in time. I have detected you preferred not to reopen the dialogue. I love you now. I have loved you for a long time. I cannot understand. You said you loved me. You said there was not another in your life. You have never given me an ample reason why you would not be my wife."

"I remember," Sara said, "some years ago that you became angry when we discussed this matter. You even said some harsh things, but we both knew you did not mean what you said. You were gone several weeks before you returned.

"Once you returned, however, our reunion brought about joy and rediscovery. All things were good again, perhaps more meaningful than ever before. We reconstructed our lives once again with all the beauty and intensity we had known earlier. You gave me a near perfect happiness and life has never been so good."

Charles smiled. "You are, indeed, a very special Eve. You use all of the feminine traits and tricks to make me love you more. It makes me wonder what you are up to this evening."

"I am up to nothing," Sara said, smiling. "Do you think girls always want something?"

"Always." Charles patted her hand, then her cheek. They looked at each other in the same special way they had for many months. The passion of each seemed as evident as ever. "You are like a woman in heat in that you can make a man do your will and he really doesn't know when or how it happens. I am like putty in your hands."

Sara smiled and took his hand, letting it rest on her leg well above the knee. "There is nothing quite so refined as a girl who knows what she wants. One should enjoy their activities and accept such associations and benefits with the utmost enthusiasm. After all, when I arrived in Attapulgus no one told me that my heart should be pure."

She smiled and stuck out her tongue; Charles watched with amazement.

Suddenly, Sara's face became serious. "Tonight I am going to tell you why I cannot be your wife. It is a long and rather strange story. This is why I suggested we not go out. I have long debated the wisdom of telling you and I am still uncertain. However, I finally concluded you were deserving and entitled to know."

Charles said, "There are no acceptable reasons you can possibly provide. I have long since considered every aspect. There is nothing, absolutely nothing, you can tell me to justify your refusal unless you do not love me as I love you."

"I love you more than you can ever know, dear Charles. Perhaps it is because of my deep and intense love that I made such a decision.

"When I arrived in this special little community of Attapulgus I planned to stay a year, no more than two. I came here for three reasons. First, a teacher must have employment in order to eat and pay the bills. Secondly, I had heard Attapulgus was special in every way and I wanted to be a part of such a community and work in a very special school. Lastly, I had given some thought as to finding someone special to share a life with and to marry."

"I may not be special but you have a very firm offer." Charles did not smile.

"Let me go on while I have the strength and courage to tell my story. It was during my year with April that I found you and fell deeply in love with you. Then, after a period of time, I realized I could not marry you. Oh, I gave you some reasons and perhaps one or more was meaningful, but I believe we both knew they were not the real reasons. But at that time I was selfish and felt I could not let you go. You are the only reason I remained as long as I have. You are so good in so many ways."

"There was a time I felt you deserved a virgin. Many men feel their mates should be spotless, regardless of their own status, but I couldn't give you something I no longer had. It would have been delightful to know you were the one and only but that was no longer possible. I think you understand all of this. As important as some consider virginity, this was not the real reason.

"You will recall that I have seldom talked of my past, even in a limited manner. It seemed that once you practically demanded to know more but you knew I had no desire for the past to be more than it was — the past. After some weeks you quit asking. You did not push anymore. You were thoughtful and kind. For all this I loved you even more, if that were possible.

"As you can see, I have put off my story as long as I can. It really can be divided into two parts. The first is short and simple. I cannot be a mother. I could not have your children. I . . ."

Charles interrupted, "It doesn't . . ."

"Wait Charles, I have not finished. As I said, there will never be any of my own children. Knowing you as I do, you would respond twofold. First you would say it doesn't matter, and secondly you would say we could adopt. So don't bother to say these things. In some ways, I know as much about you as you know about yourself.

"Now I will give you more to think about. My mother was a prostitute, a professional whore. As far as I know, this was her only profession. I don't believe she was ever ashamed of her work. She was only concerned that she would be discovered by her daughter. She took great steps for this to remain cloaked in secrecy.

"I do not know who my father is or was. I am not sure my mother knew, but it is possible that she did. Women are quite perceptive about such things. If she knew, it remained a secret.

"I can go into greater detail if you wish and perhaps you would have a better understanding. It is a long story. I will leave it up to you. As I said, I have nothing else to do."

Charles nodded, indicating he would like for her to continue.

"Some time ago, when my mother was young, she became a whore in a rather prominent and exclusive whorehouse. I suppose it was like country clubs in that some are more exclusive than others. Here she learned and mastered her trade. Some might describe it from the bottom up!" She smiled and continued. "Apparently she was quite successful, from what she told me later. It was here she learned many things. Because of her beauty, enthusiasm, personality and charm she found herself being sought and singled out far more than any other. It does not require a great deal of imagination to see this would lead to jealousy and envy.

"Realizing this, she decided to leave and establish her own house. She had a partner in the beginning, but then decided to go it alone.

"As a madam, it was not long before she learned some things she had not considered earlier. Looking after oneself is one thing, but looking after a dozen girls is another. There was always a health problem. The law was there to get its share of the rewards, mostly in cash. Then there was a need to employ a big bruiser to keep down trouble, as someone always wanted to be contemptible.

"Soon the disadvantages seemed to outweigh the benefits, though she made money, lots of money. I suppose the economy affects many businesses but a good house will more than survive in bad times. Next to a funeral home, it may be the most sound and sure business ever.

"Sometimes, either in her first or second role, Mother was to make contacts with some very special people. She became very close to three distinguished gentlemen. They were all wealthy; in fact, quite rich and affluent. Each of the three asked her to share her life with him, not as a 'kept woman,' but as a wife. Each was ready to leave his family, regardless of the costs or consequences. My mother was not a home breaker, however. Actually, upon a close examination, she was a home saver.

"Within a short time she sold her business for a huge sum. She decided to journey into a new adventure. She took some of the money and bought a fine home in a nice neighborhood. Here she set up a schedule to please each of the three gentlemen. Naturally it was a little delicate but my mother was not a stupid person. In the months to come she continued to be besieged by each of the three to become a wife. Again, she adamantly refused. I would guess that Mother was more content at this time in her life than ever before.

"Then something occurred that she had not planned. She became pregnant with me. At first she was filled with doubt and remorse. The one thing she had not planned to happen — happened. For weeks she was at a loss as to what move she should make. She then told each of her three gentlemen she was pregnant. Each was elated and naturally believed it his own. Again, each was ready to abandon his family and become a new husband and father.

"Finally, one of the three suggested he buy her a new home and visit as opportunities availed themselves. When she mentioned a new home to the other two, they were more than happy to do the same. Naturally, each had no idea of the others.

"After I was born each continued to believe he was the father. Funds were provided. Trusts were established. There was more money than we would ever need or use. During this time, however, she never had one visit in the house where I grew up. She never let them see me. She only shared some pictures from time to time. She lived in three separate worlds, in two different houses, and spent a great deal of time with her daughter. Naturally, at this time I knew nothing of her real life. I had guessed she was in real estate or insurance. She never talked of her work.

"The years passed. I went to the very best private school. I went to one of the three leading churches. I could have dressed like a queen. Yes, I could have my cake and eat it too.

"Then it happened! When I was a junior in high school I learned what had been the big secret that had existed for some seventeen years. When I found out about my mother, when it became evident that the most beautiful and perfect person in the world was not perfect, the whole world came tumbling down about me. The beautiful and perfect halo had gone and could never return. There was nothing left. I was left in desolation, my world in disarray.

"It took many, many weeks to even get over the initial shock. Then I began to pick up the pieces and start over. Yet when such a crash occurs, it seems that all the pieces cannot be found, nor will they ever fit again. Mother and I, for a period, pretended it was something like a bad dream, but it was never the same.

"The school year was about to end. It was at this time she discussed openly most of the things with me. It seemed, after a time, to make her feel better, like removing a heavy burden. Later, I remembered much of what she told me.

"But I am getting ahead of my story. She said some changes should be made for the sake of everyone. One night after dinner she told me what I should do. She informed me, attempting to hold back her tears, that she would be leaving soon. The house was deeded to me, bank accounts opened and trust funds established. They were quite sizable. I was instructed to finish my senior year and go to college for four or more years. We went over these plans with great care. I had enough money to go to college for ten years. However, I am getting ahead of my story again.

"I left one morning to do some shopping; when I returned home several hours later she was gone. Her clothing and personal effects had been removed. Then I found a letter telling me of her love. She also gave instructions that I was not to make any attempt to locate her. She said she had acted in my behalf. It was a bad time."

"Have you seen her since?" Charles asked.

"No. I kept my eyes open and visited many of the places we had been together in the past, but I never found her. There was no trail to follow."

"What do you think happened?" Charles asked.

"I can only guess, but I am not sure it is even an educated guess. It is possible that something happened to the wife of one of the three gentlemen. Perhaps a death occurred. Mother would have never gone with one unless something of this sort happened. Strangely, in spite of her profession, my mother had a strong code of ethics.

"And now the last stage. You would guess most of it. I went to college, got a degree and graduated with highest honors. You knew I was no dumb Dora!" She laughed. "I got a second degree. I wanted to be the best I could be. There are few things more important than a good education." She laughed again. "Remember, I said few things!

"And that is my story. It is not important as to where I lived, went to school or where I taught earlier.

"I do not know if I have a living mother. I do not know who my father is or if he is living or dead. Perhaps it is best.

"Before my mother left she told me interesting stories that I mentioned earlier." Again she laughed. "I thought some were very unique, even humorous."

"Stories?" Charles asked.

"I call them stories. I will share them, if you wish, but I suspect some would be familiar." She smiled generously.

"I would love to hear your stories." Charles smiled broadly. "I have an idea there is something here for me to learn."

"My mother participated regularly in church. She . . ."

"Wait. Something doesn't add up! Did she feel a constant need for forgiveness?"

"No. I'm not sure she had any feeling of guilt or sin. I'll explain that in a minute. She always gave ten percent to the church — off the top. She figured her ten percent even before she paid the law. She said it was all very clear in the Scriptures! In fact, she often spoke of the church and the brothel as having some similarities."

"Similarities?"

"Yes. Let's look at the role of each. Suppose we look at the church first. Oh, they marry and bury and baptize. That's standard. But what is the real role of the church? What should be the real role? It is a place for one's needs to be met. It is a place to quench a thirst. It is a place where one can seek relief and feel refreshed and clean inside.

"And how does it happen? He hears the word, sings songs of praise, prays for forgiveness and is extended a helping hand by his brothers and sisters. He finds relief from the things that bothered him most. His sins have been forgiven and his troubles seem to be reduced, if not totally removed. A preacher lays a hand on him and says, 'Brother, you are healed'. He accepts the hand of brotherhood and feels good, feels clean.

"Now if one is as he should be, he leaves a few dollars as a token for the benefits that were bestowed upon him. Though he leaves with a purse a little lighter, there is a broad smile on his face. If such a feeling occurs again, he will know a place for healing.

"Now let us take a look at the brothel. It, too, is a place for one's needs to be met. As in the church, one can quench his thirst. The sisters are there for you with outstretched hands to cure the ills of the mind and body.

"Sometimes, when the duties of the home are not supplied, man seems to have little choice but to seek relief. It is then that the ministers of the brothel can give that little extra boost that is needed and when he is finished he can return to his normal place with the lights of glory all about him. Yes, the brothel can give that little shot from the blue and all can be made whole again.

"The brothel and the church set a man free. The lights of Heaven shine and his troubles and pains disappear.

"And just as the church must bring in a special person, an evangelist, to deal with some who have deep seated problems, so does the brothel provide something extra for those in greatest need."

Sara smiled and asked, "Shall I continue?"

"Oh yes. This is all so refreshing."

"I am told of one difference in which the dangers of the church are much greater than the brothels."

"Dangers?"

"Yes. When a man enters a brothel he does so with caution and suspicion. He goes in with one hand on his pocketbook and with a feeling of uncertainty. Before he proceeds, he wishes to learn something about costs, length of services, and health and sanitary conditions. He is equally concerned about safety, as well as confidentiality. He must know he will not be caught with his britches down or his pocket picked. He is constantly alert to dangers.

"Not so in church. He walks in totally confident that this is God's house and the preacher God's man. Most seem to believe the preacher can do no wrong. However, they are not gods, but humans, and there can be significant and lasting damage. The cost in labor and currency is never spelled out completely. Before one cause or project is complete, three more are started. Projects and souls often differ greatly. Some of the preachers are 'on the way up' and often the evaluation is based on receipts and causes. His promotion is hanging in the balance. All of God's men may not be in touch with God. The church goer can become so deeply involved so quickly that there is not always a safety net for him should he wish to retreat or escape."

Sara laughed again. "The women, the wives, should be more appreciative. Many marriages have been saved and many attitudes changed because of events that did not take place at home."

"Why do the preachers not close the brothels? Certainly everyone knows of their existence. It is a poorly kept secret. I would think they would dispatch them will all deliberate speed," Charles said.

"The preachers will not do this. Oh, one serving his last charge before retirement may touch on it from time to time but even this one will go slowly."

"I don't understand," Charles said.

"Who are the patrons of the brothels? It is most often the church people. The preachers know who pays the church better than the banker knows who pays the interest on time. Certainly you would know that Bruce McPherson knows all of these things!"

Charles laughed. "I have some more questions, as I seem to know so little about such things." They smiled at each other but neither made a comment. "Where do the whores come from? Who trains them? There is so little known about the source of supply."

Sara smiled again. "Where does the wind come from? You know, I am reminded of people telling jokes. There is always a ready supply but no one has ever confessed as to where they originated. A whore seems to burst forth in full bloom, very much like a flower. They are usually not noticed until they start blooming.

"Mother said that once the first petal of the flower is plucked there is no stopping. It's like a clock, always ticking, always going forward. She said that at times a house will lose a girl. A patron will fall in love with one, convince himself she is there through no fault of her own. He keeps telling himself that a place like this is not for her and suddenly, in his mind, she is honest and pure and true. They marry and find a safety net by going to another town. It is said that most will become great wives and mates."

"Since we don't know where they come from, where do they go?" Charles asked.

"Most are like professional athletes. They don't know when to stop their careers and they just hang on as long as they can. Often, in later years, they become bitter. Mother said the saddest of all sad events is when a whore finally realizes that her services are no longer desired or needed. They seem to fade away, as a certain general described himself."

"What is the greatest service a brothel can perform?" Charles asked.

"I suppose there are many. As someone said, 'There is something for everyone'. However, the greatest contribution is for the shy and timid man. The whore recognizes that this person needs knowledge and experience. It may be a first time. It may be that he feels he does not have ample equipment. Yet if he feels he is buying time and services, he will not feel rejected. It is a great safety net. There will be no condemnation because one seldom cuts off the supply of wealth. Usually through the combined efforts of two working together, he can gain confidence and experience."

"Your mother was very special. I can tell." Charles said.

"She had it all. Seems so unfair for some to be given so much and some so little. She was beautiful. She had the perfect figure. She had intelligence. She had wit, humor and charm. When men saw her, they turned and stared and wanted to take her home with them. When women saw her, they felt trapped in an ocean of envy and jealousy.

"Men couldn't keep their hands off her and at the very same moment seemed fearful that a touch would damage the merchandise. She was the model who was used to evaluate all others.

"There are some sad experiences also. One such experience had a great deal to do with my mother changing her role. A beautiful young girl expressed a desire to work for her and professed some experience. She used a drunken step-father as the excuse for leaving home.

"The first time she took a man to her room, Mother noted a terror in her eyes. There was a look of lost innocence. This had been the first time for the girl. This was a major reason that Mother made some changes in her life.

"One last thing I'll mention. Just as a church takes on certain characteristics of the preacher, so will the houses take on the characteristics of the madam.

"Mother said one type house was much like a business in which the men knew what they wanted and the girls knew how to provide it. You place your order, you receive your merchandise, you pay for the services and you are on your way.

"The second house is less formal. Here one would experience a little more joy, fun and laughter. The environment was more friendly and you left with a better feeling of warmth and understanding.

"The third differed a great deal from the first and more than a significant difference from the second. Here you found those that were eager to listen if one wished to discuss any problems. One could always find sympathy or understanding or both. The schedule was less rigid and one did not feel cramped or restricted. Usually, in this type establishment, the girls had a greater knowledge of how to deal with certain type men. One man may have a frigid wife. Another a wife who is a pretender. Also, there were always those wives who performed as if they considered it a duty. The girls always seemed to know.

"Actually the three type houses were not in competition. The men knew their needs and quickly learned who supplied them in accordance to their wishes. The cost was usually about the same. Your chances of getting a disease were about the same. Each house gave considerable attention to one's health because if the word got out that dangers existed, it could damage the volume of business within a few days.

"My tale is finished. I suspect you have not learned much, except the personal aspects. In fact, the grapevine has much to say about you over the years, beginning at an early age.

"I am impatient when I hear people speak harshly about sex. They want to make it something unclean. Actually it is the vital force that rules the world. We would have a people-less world without it and the Bible tells us constantly that we should multiply. I know of no other way. How can one truly speak of it as vile or indecent or corrupt?

"Dear Charles, I have not permitted you to speak. I have spoken much more than I had planned, but seldom does one find such an attentive listener. I was equally afraid that you might have said something to change my plans.

"In the morning I will leave very much like my mother did. I have never told you or anyone from whence I came nor shall you know where I will go. I will not return here again, not ever. I know that never is a long time, but it must be this way.

"You have made my stay very special, as you are special. I do not find adequate words to describe the pleasures you have given me. Yet when you leave this house tonight, it will be for the last time. We will not look back again at yesterday. There is only tonight left. There will be no tomorrow.

"I love you very much and because of this, I want to make love with you one last time. It will tell of my love for you. It is the most profound and heartfelt meaning of love. I wish to love you so deeply, so freely, that there will be no words to describe its goodness. Tonight you will get a glimpse of my very soul. You will never forget me, as this will be a constant reminder.

"We have an hour left in our lives together. Love is worth ten thousand words. It is the only pure truth left to mankind. We will not need words, only love."

An hour later Charles walked out of her room, out of her house and out of her life. As she had asked, he walked through the door and never looked back.

They were never to see each other again throughout life, though a day never passed that they did not remember each other.

CHAPTER 39

Martha looked forward to the day when all of the tobacco would be in the packing house. Only a small amount was left in the barns and the shades were being stripped of their cheesecloth. The last weeks had been demanding, mentally as well as physically.

Her thoughts were interrupted as she heard her husband. "Ain't it wonderful to know this is all behind us once more. I would think just two more years. Just think Martha, only two more years!"

"I am glad you are happy. I was thinking of the quarter century and more we have had with each other. I hope I have not disappointed you."

"How could you think, much less say, something like that? We have had a few difficult times but we've come through it."

"I suppose I will make things more difficult, but it is time to bring Meggie home. Though I know you are not overly fond of the idea, school will soon be starting and it is time." She saw a cloud on his face he could not conceal.

"I ain't sure of the wisdom of this arrangement but I have agreed earlier and I ain't found no adequate reason to break my promise. I'll let you tend to this as you wish and when you feel the time is right. I'll expect her to pick up her share of the load. I hope you will have such an understanding.

"I'll check the last barn. The tobacco should be ready to remove in two or three days." He moved away without further comment. He could not disguise his unhappiness about the arrangements.

As Martha turned to go she heard another voice. "Glad to see you resting and taking a few minutes away from your routine. When have you scheduled your check-up? Children are concerned about their mother's health.

"Soon, Charles, very soon, but I suspect my problems are more mental than physical, though we are told they cannot really be separated. What of you, Charles? You seem like a fish out of water. I would guess you loved Sara Knight deeply."

Charles took a deep swallow. "No one will know how much she meant to me. No one will know the real Sara Knight. Yes, I miss her. I miss her so very much. She was a happy person; she laughed often, as you know, and helped help others do the same. But people get over disappointments. I'll be fine. I'll find some new lady friends. I'll get lost in graduate school. And yes, I have my three girls here that will help me forget."

"Oh, I told your father it is time to bring Meggie home. I . . ."

"He isn't thrilled, is he? I suspect this is another of your concerns."

"No, he isn't thrilled and yes, it concerns me."

"Meggie will experience many changes in all phases of her life. She knows this, I'm sure. I'm positive she has reviewed all aspects."

"What will be her most acute problems? I'm sure you have reviewed all of this as much as she has."

"Everywhere, my dear mother. There will not be any part of her life that will ever be the same again: home, school and church, for starters. Then, you must remember her relationship with Uncle Edd."

"Where will the greatest dangers lie?"

"Not where you would guess!"

"What do you mean?"

"You would place the home and school first, perhaps the school. I would say the church. Yes, of all places, the church! Suffer little children, come unto me, as long as you are not black or once believed to be black. Oh, don't get me wrong. I'm not for our churches to come together. We are not ready. We may never be ready.

"Some of the people you have had in your Sunday School classes, some you sing with in the choir, will look upon you differently. And if they look at you this way, how will they look at Meggie?"

"Charles, I can't believe these good Christian people would respond that way!"

"Be prepared for many hurts and disappointments."

Martha shook her head in disbelief. "Well, what of the school?"

"Young people adjust more readily than those not so young if the adults will give them a chance. I have some plans here. I can help and will."

"And in our home?"

"Stephen will be the most difficult. Out of respect for you, Father will take what he will consider the bitter cup. Between you, April and myself, we can manage. David will be in his own home, but he will be a friend. It is good that Joe has his own home. Mary will be as nice as Joe will let her. Before many weeks pass you will know more about many people than you have ever known."

"Thank you for sharing your thoughts. I can prepare myself better because of our discussion." She got up and walked slowly toward her home. The burdens were quite apparent. Charles wondered if he had helped or only added to her heavy load.

Charles waited until Uncle Edd had finished his responsibilities as a lotman, then walked over to the little house where Uncle Edd and Meggie lived.

"Come in," Uncle Edd said. "I have been expecting you. The time has come, hasn't it?"

Charles nodded. "Perhaps it would be helpful if we talked." Uncle Edd motioned for him to enter and guided him to a seat in the small modest living room.

"We are alone. Meggie is with your mother. I feel better when she is with her than any human in the world, including the two of us. I am a prejudiced man, Charles. I am prejudiced against injustices and fools, both black and white. It seems the world is full of them, or perhaps I have just seen people for the first time. I have reached a point where I cannot commit my Meggie to such people. I must see that she is in a good school and around people who are capable and responsible. I feel that this move will provide the opportunities to which she is entitled."

"This is not going to be easy for you or for Meggie either," Charles said. "Often, however, youth have a built-in mechanism that helps them through the changes in their lives."

"Don't look at me like that, Charles." His face was both amused and melancholy at the same time. "We must remember what our Bible tells us. 'The days of our years are three score and ten and if by reason of strength, they may be four score years, yet in their strength, labor and sorrow. For it is soon cut off and we fly away.' Yes, this is so. How well I know. In youth the days are short and the years are long. In old age the years are short and the days are long. Youth is the time to prepare for later years and old age. I have experienced some of this. I have wonderful memories. I am, to a large degree, happy and content. It is for Meggie I am concerned."

"Thank you for your confidence in me as well as in April and my mother. Meggie will have the best as long as I am sane and have breath in my body. I make you that promise."

"Before we get back to Meggie, my dear Meggie, I think of you. I had once believed that Sara Knight would be your crown and glory. Apparently this was not to be, for reasons I do not wish to know. Now I suspect that you will cast your eyes about you. I hope you do not necessarily get too excited with the first thing you see. You need to find a real woman and that will require some looking. You'll have to look hard and long to find another Sara Knight. I'm sure you will not rush off with the first pretty face or fanny you see. Look into a woman's soul. Some of them may still have one." He smiled gently and continued. "I can remember that as a young boy I dreaded the hectic, rainy and uncomfortable weekends. In those days, on Sunday everything was closed tighter than a virgin. Yet I always managed to find a place of delight and on such days they did a splendid business. In fact, two shifts were often needed. Oh, God, why does one's youth go so quickly? A real man will never betray himself unless he is a saint or a fool and there is little difference. I don't think I ever wished to be either."

"I do not have to tell you that seventeen ends the age of innocence. For the people I know and have known, for so many of my people, the time is much earlier. This is an age that would be declared the age of danger. The four of us must preserve our Meggie during this stage. After that, she must assume the responsibility for herself."

As he was about to continue the door opened and Meggie entered with a big smile. When she saw Charles, her face turned somber. The two men rose for her to take a seat. She spoke, "I see the time is near." She attempted to smile but it seemed to elude her. "I have spent the last weeks in a grayness. The wheels of reason seem to stand still, as if waiting for the appointed hour. It seems as if sounds of reason approach and then recede like a meaningless and slow moving tide under a false moon. I have tried to prepare myself for this day, this hour, but I find myself weak as from some unknown disease." There was moisture in her beautiful black eyes.

Uncle Edd spoke in a soft voice, "I have always told you the truth on the subjects we have discussed. I was not brave or strong enough to enter into certain areas or subjects. I was weak and selfish. I know that now. We must talk of many things and yet we must let some of the past remain the past."

"You are not happy, Grandfather. I can tell. It grieves me so," Meggie said, unable to look directly into his eyes. "What will you do?" She looked bewildered.

"I am not sure you have ever asked me that before. I have prepared somewhat for this day, though one puts off such preparation. I can get by as I wish to get by. I have more clothes than I need and a car to go. I have ample food, actually more than is good for one my age and condition. Some would say my life is different from the life others live. I hope so because there are many who I feel know nothing of living. If it wasn't what I wanted, I would change it. There is little hustle or bustle in my work. I do not have to spend endless hours over bank accounts, investments and the stock market. I live this life by choice and I make no apologies. My only regret is that you lived this life so long.

"I do not let people think for me. The opinions of others sometimes form a jail for you. It's like being in a locked room of their beliefs, not yours. This is the first step that others will use to control your soul. If this happens, you are gone forever. I selected much of the life I wanted to live and will continue to do so. Do not ask, what will I do, but ask what will you do with your own life? You must live it as your own.

"One other thing, dear Meggie. As you get older, keep a little childhood in your soul. If you find good fortune, so be it. Yet it is more blessed to have good sense, and common sense, if you have a choice. Sometimes they do not go hand in hand, but hopefully, you will find a great deal of both."

"But will you be happy?" Meggie asked as she displayed deep emotion.

"As much as I wish to be or have a right to be. It takes different forms and different amounts for different people. Strangely, too much happiness can have some disadvantages. There is no evidence that it enhances one to paint great pictures of art or write a great book. Sometimes it is discontent or unhappiness that causes one to excel.

"Let us not dwell on this. You will practically be with me as we will be near. Craig will soon have another life of his own. It is as it should be."

"Do you feel you can adjust?" Meggie asked, still not satisfied.

"I repeat, you are not a little child any longer to be put off with fairy tales. Lies are always wrong. Oh, I suppose they have their uses, but they are wrong.

"I did not tell you adjustment would be easy. How could it be? How can two people spend more than a dozen years together and not feel some ties? But adjust I will. Though age has removed some of the early years when I was reckless, rollicking and sometimes hell-raising, there are many ways I can entertain myself to avoid hopelessness and monotony. I feel no guilt when I look at myself and ask, Where did it all go? A sadness, yes, but no guilt. Only a fool will not realize that those early years will not return.

"But for you, it is all before you. Some say that youth is wasted on young people. Not so, unless you permit it.

"I will speak of only one other thing at this moment. I think church is important. You should, in my opinion, change churches. The reasons are obvious. However, I don't feel the Randolphs would demand you go to their church, though I have no objections. Some churches offer some choices. Some go strongly for the heavy hell fire and damnation sermons needed to pull them through. Some go for music. Perhaps others go for prayer. In some churches, not found here, they go to light candles.

"There are different reasons to go to church. You may find yourself among the best company but I suspect this is not always true. Some go to show off clothes and grooming and put on airs. Some go because the churches are handy or they can make some contacts for other reasons. Some may think they are going to become God's pet but I suspect He looks at His children equally.

Uncle Edd spoke to them both. "Now I have had my say. For a period, I was talking to keep from crying. Meggie has spoken of some adjustments on my part, but she may find her adjustment greater.

"I've got to go to the store. I want the two of you to remain, if you will. Charles can point out some things and you can ask questions. I always love great listeners!" He closed the door quietly.

For several minutes the two looked at each other and said nothing, perhaps thinking of the many words they had heard.

Charles looked at Meggie as if he had never seen her before. She was so young, so innocent. She was really more beautiful than he had realized. It seemed she had many of April's characteristics. Certainly he could now see the reasoning of Sara Knight. Her brow, her fine nose and white chin showed no evidence of what had been proclaimed earlier. Her black hair tumbled on her long neck and her rigid shoulders showed evidence of good training. She had remarkably sweet and ample breasts, high and firm. Her waist was very small and from it her hips swelled in accordance, with grace and smoothness. The glint of those fierce black eyes could be seen under the black lashes. She seemed watchful and a bit insecure with the recent change and rearrangement of her body toward womanhood.

Charles asked, "You have thought about the changes that will be forthcoming?"

"I have thought of nothing else. Not only have I thought of myself, but others as well. At my previous school I was content to be a nobody because nobodies did not attract undue attention. It had to be that way. I could not have survived had I not. I don't believe you would understand. The white people worry because they fear being caught in a position where knowledge cannot be obtained. These people, where I have been, are already in captivity because many, perhaps most, have always been where it has never existed. For many it will never change. Some would say this, in time, will cease to be a problem but I don't believe it. Not soon.

"The Negroes at my previous school will be like the rejection of Cain. They have been doomed to ignorance and shame. When and how does one go about changing Cain to Abel?

"A human being is not a real human without an education. Yes, the slave has been set free; however, he will remain a slave if he remains uneducated. Students do not wish to think. They will not permit silence or solitude because these allow time for thinking.

"Perhaps my thoughts should be on a school that has not been a part of my life. What will my peers, who may not acknowledge me as a white, think and say? How will the teachers react? What will this do to April and Gena? If they offer support, will this not cast them in a less favorable position? Tell me what you see, what you believe, what you think and more importantly, what you would do."

"April and I have given this some thought. I think for a few days I would play a game similar to the one you did at your previous school. I would be seen more than heard for a time. I would respond in such a way as to let all parties know of your knowledge and capabilities but I would refrain from the spotlight. When others, who do not know, see the real you, it will make all the difference." Charles did not tell her that he had gone into detail with Mr. Baggs about her future. Mr. Baggs had assured him he would do those things required to serve her needs and assure her safety.

"Once the students and teachers determine that you can participate on or above grade level I believe much rejection or resentment will disappear. Students respect superior students. But you must be careful not to make others feel inferior. This could do a great deal of harm. No one, regardless of their inabilities, wishes to feel inferior."

"I believe I understand what you have said. It is always good to know where one is going and that there are guidelines and safety nets," Meggie said.

"I believe that some members of your class will be surprised, perhaps shocked, in that they would have expected to find someone entirely different," Charles said. "It may be much like Craig's experiences at Harvard."

"And a place of worship?"

"You are a church person. I am sure Mike Harper will give you a warm invitation. You should go to a place where two things prevail.

First, you should feel comfortable. Secondly, you should go where the beliefs of the church do not conflict severely with your own. I think you will be accepted in school more quickly than in church, though it should be the opposite. Young people, your peers, can adjust better than some adults. Why don't you discuss this with my other girls? My mother can probably give you more insight. Kathy and Mary can be helpful."

"And in your home? I have some real concerns. I am not blinded to the fact that the levels of acceptance can and will vary among individuals. I think the two of us understand."

"Lean on my mother, April and me. Be nice to everyone. Go out of your way to do so, yet not to a degree that is not realistic. Michael John will be supportive.

"I don't have to tell you this, but go the extra mile in the responsibilities that you are to share. Deeds, more than words, send a message."

"How will they feel as I continue a close relationship with my grandfather? It must always be so."

"I think most everyone can and will understand."

"And you will be there to catch me if I fail? If I fall?

"Always."

Meggie smiled, jumped up and pecked him on the cheek. "There is no way I can fail. I am the most fortunate girl alive. Someday perhaps I can repay you, at least in part, for giving me a life to live, a new world to explore. I'll never let you down."

Charles got up and went to the door. As he opened it to leave he turned and said, "I never doubted it for a moment."

When Meggie spent her first night in the Randolph home, to her surprise, she slept with complete abandon. Long after Meggie was asleep Martha Randolph quietly opened the door to her room. She saw the black hair spilling over the white pillow. The sheets were not twisted or tossed. Martha knew that a new beginning had occurred. She left the room with a smile on her face.

CHAPTER 40

For days April continued to busy herself in such chores as helping her mother and keeping materials on hand for the constructions. She smiled and was friendly with everyone, but said little to initiate conversations. When some aspect of Maybe's trial was mentioned she usually said, "It's over. Let's turn the page and go to a new chapter."

After discussing the finishing of David's house's interior Michael John said, "You seem so different in recent days. You have no suggestions. You offer no opinions. It is so unlike you. Are you all right?"

"I'm fine. I am busy. There is Meggie's adjustment. I attempt to help Mother as much as possible. We continue to work on our beautification plan. Also, I am busy with my fifty acres."

David and Kathy asked her to accompany them to shop for some furniture. She went with them but she offered few suggestions.

She went to see Maybe when his work day was completed because she felt it her duty. What she had learned had not made her feel better. Maybe had explained in the best way he could how Joseph and Joe had seemed so unconcerned, so unfriendly and indifferent. He spoke of Posey's two older children acting hostilely and fanning the flames of hate. He even hinted of his disappointment that April had not visited earlier.

"You needed some time to adjust and readjust with your children," April had said.

Finally the Saturday arrived for David and Kathy's wedding. In a little chapel, next to the church Kathy had attended all of her life, the two families met with the minister. Charles served as best man. Joseph was unable to conceal his disappointment completely. April served as maid of honor.

It was a rather awkward arrangement in that Joseph had spoken little as they gathered. Martha, recognizing that Joseph had not been very friendly, made an all-out effort to disguise her husband's indifference.

David was as nervous and fidgety as a cat. He seemed somewhat uncomfortable in his new suit and accessories. He walked with a bit of uncertainty, in his new shoes. But he was, indeed, a good-looking groom.

It was Kathy who brought a flood of sunshine upon the occasion. She smiled. She laughed. She worked at making the two families who knew so little of each other more comfortable.

April looked closely at Kathy. She was a picture of beauty. She was so daintily dressed. She seemed even smaller than April remembered. She guessed Kathy was about five-two. In addition to her beautiful face, the eyes seemed to tell everything. They were large and blue, direct and clear, with an openness that expressed kindness and compassion. She had a full mouth with well formed lips. Her nose blended with her other features. Her hair was so light that it looked more blond than light brown. Her voice was soft and clear, her complexion a little darker than one might expect with her hair and eyes. She moved in such a manner as to display boundless energy. She could have been fifteen or twenty-five or anywhere in between. No one could remember seeing her out of control. She was always present to hold the hand of the discouraged or despondent.

On this Saturday evening Kathy and David stood before the minister and made their promises and pledges to each other, as the Lanes and Randolphs looked on. It was a lovely wedding, uniting two people whose adamant love for each other radiated for everyone to see. They accepted the best wishes and congratulations, then quietly disappeared.

David picked up his bride and carried her across the threshold. "Aren't you glad you didn't get a big woman!" Kathy said, laughing.

"Welcome to our new house," David said. "It will be up to us to make it a home." He lowered her to her feet.

Kathy moved into his arms and raised her face to his. They kissed passionately. As they did Kathy sensed a feeling of insecurity about David. "I must have done something special in my life to find one like you," Kathy said, then re-entered his arms to be held and kissed again. Once more Kathy could sense that David felt insecure.

As they looked at each other he said, "I am the lucky one, the most fortunate person ever. Just think, I get to share the rest of my life with you. Not only are you most beautiful, but you have so many other wonderful qualities that make you what you are. It will take a lifetime for me to tell you all of them."

"But you really don't know me yet, David. And there are some things I don't know about you but I am anxious to learn." David blushed as she pulled him to her and held him tight, then turned her face upward to look into his eyes.

Suddenly, David looked into her beautiful blue eyes and said, "I think we must always be honest with each other and it has to start now. I suppose most men my age have experienced many women. It has not been my lot to do so. My male friends would likely declare me a fool, but I have always felt that I would have no right to an untouched virgin and bride unless I could offer the same. I hope you are not disappointed."

"Oh, David, thank you. I suspect few brides are so lucky, so fortunate. No greater gift can a couple give to each other. Please don't be ashamed because I am so very pleased. Neither of us should feel embarrassed. God has given each to the other in this form. Let us accept this gift with joy."

Kathy kissed David again and said, "I want to know all about my husband. I suspect each of us would feel more comfortable if we rid ourselves of all these new clothes. I remember our minister saying something like 'joining together'." Again she smiled. "I am going into the bedroom next to the master bedroom. I want you to go where we will sleep and prepare yourself. I want you to do this now. I'll go to the other bedroom. When we are ready I will come to you." She kissed him once again and she could feel that some of his timidity had disappeared.

In minutes Kathy had removed her shoes and clothing. She looked at herself in the mirror and wondered how David would react. She wondered how she would react as well.

In a few more moments she spoke, "David, it's like hide-and-go-seek. I'm coming to you, ready or not." She walked down the hall and entered their room. She could see that David had left a light on in the bathroom and the door open perhaps an inch, which left the room in shadows.

As she came to the bed she could see his smile but could still detect an uncertainty. She knew that she would need to proceed in a manner in which he would feel comfortable. She laid down beside him and kissed him deeply. "Touch me, David. I want you to touch me." She guided his hand to her breasts, then to her soft but firm legs. Again she could tell that he was unsure. Once again she guided his hands, then suddenly felt him shudder. Then she said, "I think the time has come to follow our preacher's instructions."

Two hours later, as they lay in each other's arms, Kathy asked, "Do you think you can spend the rest of your life with me? I can only hope you are half as happy as you have made me!"

"I was so unsure, Kathy. I am not sure it was as you expected. We said we would always be honest with each other."

"David, I am the most fortunate person alive. I want to have your children in time but not too soon. For now, I don't wish to share you with anyone." She moved over on top of him and said, "Now I am the hunter and you are the hunted."

Just as the sun was peeping over the horizon in the east David felt a hand upon him. In moments they once again enjoyed the gifts of life.

"Get your robe on," Kathy said. "Don't you smell the coffee?"

After breakfast they showered together. This time they could see each other; they touched and kissed. "I had hoped to have you in the shower earlier," Kathy said. "It's time that I saw all of you, as I have the rest of my life to be a part of you."

An hour later they left for Mexico Beach, about a two-hour drive away, where David had made reservations. They put on their bathing suits and walked out into the salty water as the tide moved them out together in an uncertain manner. "You have to hold me, David. If the tide sweeps me away, you must go with me."

They looked out into the Gulf of Mexico and saw the fishing boats several miles out, trolling to and fro. They felt the waves rise upon their bodies. They moved to a point where the water was at Kathy's shoulders. She took David's hand and placed it in the right places.

"You're a sexpot. You never gave me a hint."

She held her face to him and they could taste the salt water as their lips met.

In the next four days they explored the beach in each direction for miles. They rode in each direction a hundred miles and ate seafood when they got hungry. As they passed through Port St. Joe they stopped for some gas. The aroma from the local paper mill left something to be desired. "How do you stand this?" David asked the service station operator.

He laughed. "We sorta get used to it after so long. It's when we don't smell it that we become worried. That means our people are not working. I suspect I hear your question at least a dozen times a day." He smiled.

As they strolled along the beach on their last day Kathy said, "You must tell me your thoughts this second. We have both promised to always speak as we wish."

"All of my life I have dreamed that I would find someone to love and love deeply. That is the only real love two should have for each other. I wanted someone to be there always to share my deepest thoughts, thoughts one would never say to another. Regardless of how much love may exist though, the two of us would never agree all of the time completely, but if sufficient love is always present, all differences can be resolved and the relationship can remain as before. This is the kind of love, real love, that we can share."

The four wonderful days ended. The two would think often of all the joys they had discovered and shared. It was the beginning of a love story like few had ever had the opportunity to know.

CHAPTER 41

Meggie Winter arrived on the first day of school with her head held high, though she was not certain she had disguised her inner fears. She was flanked by April and Gena as she entered the front door. There they were met by Robert White and proceeded to their homeroom.

Meggie was aware that she was the target of many stares, some not very well disguised. She could see the lips of students move in the distance but she could not hear their words. She took the second seat on an outside row of desks, with Gena sitting ahead of her and April to her rear. Adjacent to her was Robert White, who attempted to adjust himself in a desk a size or more too small for his large frame.

After the bell rang the teacher stood and said, "I am Coach Willis Daniels. I will be your homeroom teacher this year. Our principal, Mr. Baggs, will be here in a moment. He has, for years, greeted each class personally on opening day. As soon as he leaves we will discuss what shall take place here each morning during this brief fifteen-minute period. Here is Principal Baggs now."

"Welcome," Mr. Baggs said smiling. "It is nice to see all of you again. I hope you enjoyed your summer break.

"We have one new student in our junior class this year. I wish to offer a special word of welcome to Meggie Winter, a transfer from another county school. She lives with the Randolphs on their farm.

"We are delighted to have her as a new student. Please be patient as she learns the many names of those about her.

"We are prepared to have our best year ever. The students, parents and faculty, I am sure, will work together to ensure our success. I hope each of you will take every opportunity to be the best you can be.

"I will visit you again and see you later in my class. There are some others to welcome on our first day of school." He smiled and quickly departed.

Coach Daniels said, "I, too, welcome you. For those who have been here for some time, I need not remind you that you are attending an institution that can and will help each of you. However, you must also attempt to help yourselves. You just witnessed a very special man. Only a few would have any idea how much he has meant to the individuals, the school and the community."

A week passed before Meggie began to feel somewhat secure. There were students' names to learn and new teachers with different methods of instruction. She was able to respond in each class when called upon, but she never volunteered, nor did she ask the first question. She remembered the suggestions Charles had outlined.

As the days passed she was able to pick up segments of conversations in the halls, the restroom, the gymnasium and even in the lunchroom: 'She doesn't look like a black.' 'She is an attractive person.' 'She must study a great deal, as she always knows the answers.' 'She doesn't talk like the Negroes on our plantation.' 'Why do you suppose the Randolphs took her into their home?' 'How did they find out she was white?'

Meggie had expected something much more crude. She was sure, had their positions been reversed, she would have asked some of the same questions or made some of the same statements.

In days to come Meggie gained the admiration of all the faculty members and a large majority of the students. She knew that April, Gena and Robert had played no small role in her rapid acceptance. She had quietly thanked them but they had simply suggested that they had done nothing. She was told that she alone had won her way into the hearts of nearly everyone.

Two new people were to become part of the faculty as the 1962-63 school year opened in Attapulgus. April knew one quite well and was anxious to know the other.

Eric Lee had returned to his hometown and alma mater to replace Miss Knight. His responsibilities, in addition to the seventh grade, included some literary programs and the many exercises that occur at the conclusion of each school year. A supplement of three hundred dollars had been added to his salary, not by the county officials, but by the local trustees.

Eric Lee introduced April to the other new faculty member. "This is Miss Robin Wells," he said. "Please meet April Randolph. She is a junior this year."

"Welcome to our school, as well as to our community," April said. "We believe each to be very special."

"This is one of the reasons I applied here," Miss Wells said. "The reputation of your school and people is not limited to the local area. I am most fortunate. I hope I can contribute. I hope everyone will be patient with a beginner."

Eric said, "It took Miss Wells only three years to secure her degree. This tells all of us something about her." Sometime later April told Eric how impressed she had been with Miss Wells.

Robin Wells was not really pretty but was attractive. She had brown hair, an open face, large brown eyes, a mouth neither too large nor too small and a good figure. She was three inches or so shorter than April, who had reached five-seven. She was not skinny, yet neither was she fat.

When Miss Wells told April that she had already learned a great deal about her, April could feel her face grow red. Your sins follow you, she thought, as she remembered her experiences in the seventh grade.

Miss Wells hurried to say, "I am told your academic record is unsurpassed. It has also been said that you seem to be involved in many activities."

April breathed a sigh of relief. "Where are you living," she asked.

"I have the apartment where Miss Knight lived. It is very nice."

A day later Eric saw April and asked, "What are people saying about me?"

"Everyone is excited about you being here. Many feel a male teacher in grade seven is a good idea. I look forward to my association with you, later, in some of the activities. But I find myself on pins and needles when I am around you!"

"I don't believe this," Eric said. "You must explain."

"I am afraid I will forget and call you Eric rather than Mr. Lee. That would be an injustice to you."

"I suppose you must address me in that manner. I will need to adjust as well."

CHAPTER 42

"Basketball practice will start next week," Coach Daniels said to his team. "It is best that we have a good understanding before we start. I am going to tell you what I expect of you. I will tell you what you can expect of me. I think we can have good teams if we pay the price.

"Academics come first. We will pass all courses. The Georgia High School Association states a number of courses required. I require all of them." Fifteen minutes later the meeting had been concluded. No one could doubt the role he would play.

Upon arriving home, April learned that her two married brothers and their wives would join them in what Martha called a country supper. "I have wanted to get all of you together and this is the first time someone didn't have a conflict," Martha said smiling. "This can be called our official welcome for Kathy. As I look at all of you, I don't know what I have done to deserve such a family."

Once seated at the table, everyone looked toward the smiling face of Kathy as she said, "First, I want to thank you for this 'official welcome.' I have felt welcome since I arrived. I am the fortunate one. Next, what should I call everyone, especially Mr. and Mrs. Randolph?"

"Why not Martha and Joseph?" April asked.

"No, I can't do that. It just doesn't seem right for me. Would there be objections if I address you as Miss Martha and Mr. Joseph?"

"That will be fine," Martha said.

"Very well, Miss Martha, Mr. Joseph, my dear husband, Mary and my new brothers and sister. No one can ever know, even guess, my supreme happiness. You have accepted me graciously as a part of your family. Truly, I have been made to feel welcome. I hope I can always live and act in such a manner to deserve your love and kindness."

A few minutes later Michael John said, "April, why don't you tell us about the two new teachers in your school?"

Out of character and still remaining much more silent than in previous times, April said, "Stephen is at school and has seen them, I'm sure. Perhaps he has an impression of the two."

Stephen was at a loss for words for once in his life. "I think April could do it better. I saw her talking with both of them. They are not teaching me so I've had no reason to meet them."

"I welcomed them to Attapulgus and assured them they could expect full support from everyone. It seemed a little odd, I suppose, for a student to make such a remark. They seemed, however, to appreciate the welcome."

Unexpectedly Joseph asked, "How do you feel about them? What do you hear others say?" No one could remember this kind of interest on his part. He usually left all of that to Martha.

"We all know Mr. Lee. I am told he is well liked and off to a good start. I believe some are born to teach. He is one of those."

"And the girl?" Joseph asked. "I believe her name is Wells."

"I also met Miss Wells. Catch that, Charles? She is rather young, as Mr. Lee said. She finished college in three years. She seems enthusiastic about the school and her work. She said she was renting Miss Knight's old apartment. I believe she will make a fine addition. Mr. Baggs usually helps until the new teachers feel secure.

"Speaking of teachers, Charles, I would be interested in learning something about Miss Knight. I shall always be indebted to her for her extra efforts and especially her understanding."

Everyone looked at Charles but he remained silent.

"You do know, don't you?" April asked.

"No," he said.

"You don't know and you practically lived there for four years? I don't understand. Why would you not want us to know? You didn't have a fight and cause her to leave?"

"No, we parted as friends, close friends. About the last thing we discussed was you. She thought a great deal of you."

"And you don't know where she has gone? I don't understand," April repeated again.

"My very thoughts, April. I'm not sure I understand. She felt she needed to leave. Enough about Miss Knight."

Mary turned toward Kathy. "The word is out that the two of you have agreed to teach a class at Sunday School. I believe I heard it would be the students aged fourteen to eighteen."

David nodded at Kathy. "Tell them, Kathy, of our plans."

"We will try it jointly for a year. It was thought that perhaps some younger teachers may relate to this age student. We were honored to be asked. I suspect, as teachers, that David and I will learn more than our students."

David said, "Kathy and I have done some soul searching. God has been so very good. We need to do what we can in return. We have set a few goals. We will tithe. We have agreed not to speak unkindly of another. We have promised to look for the good in all and build on that. This is not to suggest how others should live, but it is the way we want to live."

"Miss Martha, Mr. Joseph and everyone, thank you for the kind welcome," Kathy said. "Thank you for accepting me as a part of your family."

Robert parked his father's pick-up beside April's car. As he entered April's house he found her preparing a salad and baking potatoes. "May I kiss the cook?"

April smiled. "Work comes first and rewards later. You surprised me. I didn't know you had caught on so quickly! Why don't you get the grill ready for lighting? The others will be here shortly."

At five-thirty Eric Lee and Robin Wells arrived in Susan Lee's car. They got out, looked about them and nearly stumbled over each other as they looked about in awe. Robin said, "I believe one shall not see a place so beautiful, so unusual and so perfect."

As they reached the deck Eric said, "We can't wait to see inside." Before entering they stopped for several minutes, looking in all directions.

April showed them the inside. "Do you like it?" she asked.

"Perfect. It is perfect. I wouldn't change a thing," Robin said.

As they returned to the deck they saw Charles, Michael John, Gena and Meggie coming. Introductions were made. Charles said, "If these were high school teachers, I would be suspicious of April's motives."

In less than an hour they were sitting around the table. "Why didn't Jerome come?" April asked. "He was invited."

Eric said, "He had an earlier commitment. Now excuse me a moment." He rushed outside.

Moments later he returned with two of the pies his mother had fixed. "Mother said she wanted all of us to have some of her specialties."

After dinner they all sat around to see what would happen next.

April said, "At this time we all give a special welcome to Miss Wells and Mr. Lee. We are happy that you are a part of our school and community. We will be all the better because of you two. Good reports are cascading around already."

Charles said, "Nearly every new teacher, single teacher, that is, usually finds a mate in two years or less. We do not expect you to be different. This assures us of a great faculty. We plan it this way!"

April looked toward Michael John and said, "This young man is our builder and we haven't given him a chance to speak."

"Good teachers give us good students. Good students give us the kind of community we seek. Welcome. The two of you will make it better," Michael John said.

Robert said, "Michael John is an excellent builder. I have worked with him. He does things right." Michael John blushed.

April said, "I had thought of some things we might do. First, however, we want to know a little about our new faculty members. Some of us know a little of Mr. Lee, but he has been gone for years."

"Ladies first," Eric said, laughing. "I am afraid you know me all too well already." Everyone looked toward Robin.

With what appeared to be a slight feeling of insecurity Robin said, "I wonder how many new beginning teachers get such a warm and beautiful welcome as this? I am honored to be a part of your community and your school. I commit myself to become the best teacher I can be.

"Beginning teachers do not usually eat so well in such a delightful setting. I congratulate April on her new place, her new home away from home. It is perfect. Why don't we hear from Mr. Lee?"

"Robin has said it all. No one could have expressed it better. Let's go back to Miss Wells. I am sure everyone wishes to know a little more about you."

Robin spoke briefly of her preparations and her teaching goals. "Learning can and should be fun most of the time. This makes all the difference. I see evidence of this throughout your school. These four beautiful juniors prove that day after day." Robin had a way of turning the attention from herself to others.

Minutes later Robin said, "I think April needs a policy whereby all clean up what they mess up. We can all chip in and it will only take minutes."

"Not yet," April said. "All of you have a price to pay for your dinner." April smiled as everyone looked at her.

"Your help is needed in a very special way. I want to give this place a name. No one is to speak for three minutes while they think. Now think!"

Then each in turn offered a suggestion. "April's Place." "April Fool." "April's Pond." "Forever April." "Just April."

"Your direction is wrong. The name should have more meaning than just to recognize an individual. Let us forget the names of April and Randolph. Now think again."

"The Nest." "The Rainbow." "Hidden Waters." "Whispering Wind." "Twilight."

Suddenly, Michael John said, "I have it! I believe I've got it. It's different from all others suggested."

"Tell us," Meggie said. "Don't keep us in suspense."

Charles interrupted. "The House That Michael Built." He laughed.

"That's not funny, Charles, but I do have the name," said Michael John. How about Somewhere Else? It is and will be different from all other places. It's like you are in another world; yes, like you are Somewhere Else."

Everyone seemed to speak at once. "That's perfect." "I love it." "Nothing else will ever be like it."

"Perfect. Just perfect," April said. "It will be like a land of make-believe where one hopefully can come and find answers, joy, and whatever one seeks at a given time. Thank you, Michael John. Now that we have named my home, we need to clean up, as Robin — that is Miss Wells — has suggested."

When April and Charles arrived back at the Randolph home Charles asked April, "What did you think of the occasion? Did you notice anything unusual?"

"Yes. I was so proud of Michael John. He has found a place for himself. He is about to come out of the shadows into the sunlight. And you? What did you notice?"

"Robin. Robin Wells. She is very special but I found it strange that she did not speak once as to her family or background. She always guided us into a different direction. Was it intentional or accidental? For me, I believe it was intentional."

"She really didn't say much, did she? Actually, she said nothing along that line. Perhaps it is a private matter; or she could have believed that it was not a point of interest. She seems like a very private person."

Charles said, "I don't believe it was an accident. Time will tell."

CHAPTER 43

"What are you doing here?" Uncle Edd asked. "You are supposed to be in Boston."

"We have some very dear friends, Grandfather. There were those who felt I should return home. Charles sent me a ticket," Craig said. "There is nothing like being home at Christmas time." He continued, "That was a brave thing you did. I am not sure how you found the courage. Tell me about Meggie."

"It was the right thing to do. I hope that I have not done a grave injustice by being so selfish for so long. We continue to be very close and I believe we always will be. Some of the Randolph family have continued to encourage a close relationship. I suspect we could say there is some indifference. Likely one or more were in opposition to the present status. The important thing is that she does have ample support and she seems very happy. Her greatest apprehension and anxiety seem to center around me. She is happy, however, and that is all that matters."

"Then she has adjusted?" Craig asked.

"Oh yes. Charles, April and Mrs. Randolph have contributed more than anyone will ever know. They have gone the second mile. The school personnel, especially the principal, have also assisted. She has learned so many things in the last four months."

"Would you do the same again?" Craig asked.

"I would. I believe both of us understood my hesitation." He continued, "I am sure you realize that not everyone has accepted her completely. It is possible that a few never will. I believe the youth have accepted her more than some adults. Hard to change the thinking in old people like me. Craig, she is smart. She is good. With those qualities, she will be fine. She will go a long way."

"If you and Meggie are doing all right and are happy, then I will be fine too.

"Don't you see?" Uncle Edd said, smiling. "I'm not dead yet. As in Saint Augustine's prayer, 'Make me chaste, O Lord, but not yet.'" There was a twinkle in his eye. "I have less responsibility and more free time now. I manage to fill some of the hours. There is a social club that I attend from time to time in another community. Man doesn't need to drop his waste too near home. One can become careless and step in it. But, we meet, play some cards and talk of old days and young years. This helps us forget some of the ills of our age. This, on occasion, leads to sex. Nothing like a visit to the club to stimulate your health and sanity. You know, if I get a chance to talk with God one day, I'll suggest He let the mind and the body age in the same manner and at the same rate.

"I have a close friend that works at the Department of Human Services. I suppose to some her reputation could be slightly questionable. Not long ago the two of us went to a dance and we whirled across the floor. She wasn't dressed to whirl but she did. I suspected that she had other activities on her mind aside from dancing. She noted I had not lost my sense of observation so she took me by the hand and led me to the porch. As we left the porch I turned quickly and told her I believed someone was following, as I had distinctly heard footsteps behind us. I insisted we were being followed.

"She responded, 'It is only your conscience, my dear. He is always a poor companion, an unnecessary party, and can be easily lost.'

"So you see, my days and especially my nights are filled with delightful opportunities. Life can be what you wish to make of it.

"I don't dwell on my own sins too much. Once they are behind you, you can feel better. Sometimes something good will come of a few sins. Didn't David, our King David, kill Uriah the Hittite for the sake of stealing his wife? Did not King Solomon, the wise one, result from his sinful ways? Give a little time and some things may go well. One must learn patience. One must learn to be silent. In this there may be a message for you.

"Someday," Uncle Edd continued, "you'll need a companion. You'll need someone to keep house and supply your physical needs. Don't let your first encounters blur your eyesight and senses. This is a way of saying don't let the urges of your genitals cause you to lose your perspective and common sense, as it has for so many. I want you to find a pure woman. There must be a few left. But make sure she is not overbearing and, of all things, stupid. Find one you can love deeply and respect at all times. She, in turn, must feel as you do. The greatest sin in life is living or trying to live where love is missing.

"I am concerned about the younger generation, your generation. They speak of saving the world for their children and themselves. That's the same thing my generation said or thought. Children have a way of becoming older men and women and they don't save the world. For most, hope becomes a lie. Strangely, the process is repeated, one generation after another.

"As you formulate your life, of all things, be kind. True kindness is very rare. Look carefully because many acts that seem to be in the name of kindness are really designed for the benefit of the giver or someone else.

"Some of us know what men are like. If you are wise to their ways, you must only rarely let them know that you know. If you let them know that you really know, and they know you know, they will destroy you. You will have an enemy for life. You will have left no room for them to escape with some honor.

"I have been sitting here giving you one word of advice after another. It is obvious that you should be giving advice to this old man."

"You're not that old," Craig said, laughing. "I've learned that today."

"My life is spent to a large degree. Think not of me. I am concerned that you and our Meggie find a rightful place in the world. I have one final thing to say to you. I once could have said it to Meggie as well, but it no longer applies to her. We know that you have exceptional ability and talent. Yes, and character, as well. We also both know that black is black and white is white. In time, a black man of your sort must choose a path to follow. Many, such as you, have selected to follow in the path of the successful white man and your contact with the Negro is no more than is forced upon you. The other path that many follow is to return to their own people. It usually is not for the right reason. As you return, the Negroes trust you because of your superior education and training and because of the color of your skin. More often than not, this kind of black man will fleece them as the white man has never fleeced them before. I am reminded of an old saying: 'There is nothing like a black out-blacking a bunch of blacks.' I don't believe this is in your heart or that it will ever be.

"Most men, Craig, are not good; they are unkind; they are not compassionate or tender or just. It simply isn't man's nature. We are the most evil of the species. I hope you will be better. At this point I am optimistic. But you and you alone must decide what to do with your life. It belongs to you. Use it wisely."

And so Craig returned after his visit with his grandfather and Meggie. He would have many hours to think about what this wise one had said.

The next day Joseph entered the store where Uncle Edd was serving some of the people. It was the last of the customers and time to close.

"Close the door, Uncle Edd. I need to talk with you. I need your advice." Uncle Edd was fearful his look would reveal his thoughts because he knew that Joseph Randolph seldom sought advice. He gave it.

Joseph began, "For a year or more, maybe longer, there has been unrest among my people, or maybe I should say, your people. It first appeared just before Maybe pulled his stunt. Now it seems to be worse. Maybe's return has brought anything but peace and harmony. Now with the government raising more hell from time to time, that will only add to the problems. Kennedy and these marching preachers are working hand in hand."

Uncle Edd said nothing. He suspected, no, he knew, that Joseph Randolph was working up to something.

"You haven't said nothing," Joseph said.

"No sir. I am not sure what I would say or what you would wish me to say. I don't think you have finished." He smiled and Joseph knew that Edd knew, the very thing Uncle Edd had warned Craig against.

"I have been thinking about bringing a new family, a black family, to my place."

Uncle Edd remained silent. He didn't ask who because he was sure he would learn that in a moment.

"I have learned through another farmer that Big John Jackson and his family are not happy. He has been a black foreman for years and he knows how to get things done. He is a black and he knows how to talk their language so they can understand. He has a wife and daughter. The woman could help my Martha, as she is beginning to feel her age a bit."

Uncle Edd still did not speak. "Well, what the hell you think?" Joseph asked. "It seems like an opportunity at the right time. I am told he can quickly get the attention of some of my indifferent people."

Uncle Edd moved his head slowly in disapproval. "At this age and stage one might catch more flies with some sugar than vinegar. This man is not liked or respected by his people."

"I wouldn't bring him here to be liked. I would bring him here to use a strong arm. This is something that seems to be missing and he could quiet this unrest."

"Do you know Big John Jackson and his family?" Uncle Edd asked in a soft, quiet voice.

"Been knowing him for years. He has a way of getting things done. That's exactly what I need. It is exactly what this place needs."

Uncle Edd said nothing.

"Ain't you gonna tell me what you think? That's why I am here!"

Uncle Edd recognized it was not advice Mr. Randolph sought, but approval. "Would it be all the same if I said nothing? No one can really know much of anything about another."

"I demand to know what you think. I have watched you over the years. Few things surprise you. Few things escape you. You seem to have a way of knowing. That's why I'm here!"

Uncle Edd thought for a few moments, seeking the right words. Then he asked, "Isn't it possible that it would increase your problems? I don't believe these people here would like him or accept him. His reputation is not a good one."

"What we need is discipline, keeping these people in line. It would be better for a nig — that is, a black to do this rather than a white in the day we now live," Joseph said.

"Mr. Randolph, do you know his people, that is, his family, very well? His wife and daughter?"

"The report is that they are fairly good at house work. It seems that there is some white blood in them. Why, they are only a step behind you."

Uncle Edd smiled. "As the old saying goes, been a lot of blacks in the woodpile! Might have been some white ones as well. If one can believe in street talk, they have a questionable reputation."

"Oh?"

"Yes sir. It is a rather unusual situation. I would guess Big John is about sixty, give or take a year or two. His wife is less than half that age — say thirty. The girl is sixteen, in fact, just turned sixteen and was a drop-out from school a short time ago.

"Now a man his age may require some domestic help in some of his tasks." Uncle Edd smiled broadly but Joseph remained silent. "I hear the young thing is somewhat like her mother. I guess we could say, 'Like mother, like daughter.' However, let me hurry to say I cannot offer any firsthand information about either.

"There is a saying that I have heard that may apply here. 'A man gets frustrated when he discovers for the first time he can't do it the second time, but he really gets alarmed when he discovers the second time he can't do it the first time.' I am told the latter best describes Big John Jackson. One in such a position would be alarmed.

"It would seem to me that if Big John is alarmed, some of his friends and neighbors may wish to assist him. I think this will happen. In fact, I more than suspect it will. Then you are going to have some situations like Posey and Maybe."

"You seem to know a lot about this," Joseph said.

"All street talk and secondhand information."

"And the daughter is a chip off the old block?"

"Street talk, Mr. Joseph. Secondhand information." Uncle Edd smiled.

"Could be like two bitch dogs in heat?" Joseph asked.

"My very thoughts!" He then added, "Mr. Joseph, I've been thinking about two things for a long time. Neither one is really my business. I wonder if I may speak on these subjects and you feel that I am not running your business?"

"Go ahead."

"I think that some of the better people you have and the other black tobacco people feel that they should not continue to go traipsing down the street of want and unhappiness in that there is no way to make ends meet. I suspect, through government interference, that many changes will occur. I don't know if it will help my people. Actually, I think not. It will, however, catch the white man off guard and the present, as we know it, will become the past. Tomorrow is nearly today. Please think on this."

Joseph thought for a few seconds and then said, "You said two things."

"There are many men who pass up today for tomorrow. They give up their whole lives for the future. They give it up all the way back to youth. They deny themselves and others joy and laughter and pleasure with the idea it will come later — tomorrow. Our Lord said not to take heed for tomorrow. For so many men the time ends before the joy of tomorrow arrives.

"'Remember thy Creator,' we are told, 'in the days of thy youth before the evil days come when thou shall say, 'I have no joy in them.' It's all in the Good Book.

"Today is all you have. Oh, I'm for some planning and saving, but live today. Don't pass up this very minute. Someday you and many others may look back and take a good look at your goals that seemed so important for the moment and they were much less important than you had believed.

"A preacher friend of mine once said that Satan was the most intelligent of all the angels. Do you suppose this is why God loved him so, as reported? Is it not possible that God feels we still need some entertainment, someone to entertain us when life becomes so harsh and demanding and boring? You know, if Satan didn't do something for us from time to time, it would seem that God would have rid us of that character.

"You are still under fifty-five. It is possible that you have been selected for the three score and ten or even more. But you don't know this. Don't wait, Mr. Joseph, don't wait.

"About Big John Jackson, I cannot say with certainty. But about living, I can recommend you start this very day."

Joseph insisted, "Uncle Edd, you don't understand. I have a plan, a timetable. Two more years and we can reach the Promised Land. Two more years!

"Now back to our original subject. Suppose we establish a line of credit for Big John. He will be moving tomorrow. We'll settle him in the big house on the new place I just bought."

CHAPTER 44

On the first day of January, 1963, Joseph Randolph was sworn in as a County Commissioner. He was joined by his family, Susan Lee, her two sons, Jerome and Eric, Jack Jenkins and some businessmen and politicians from throughout Decatur County.

When asked his intentions, Joseph said, "I'll work for you as I have worked for myself and my family, always trying to do the right and fair thing."

On Friday afternoon of the same week Charles, while working on a payroll in his office, answered the telephone. "Yes, this is Charles Randolph. Who is calling please?"

A voice said, "This is Jake Barber, Mr. Randolph. I live in the northern part of the county. At the very moment, however, I am in Midway serving as chairman of the Grand Jury during this session.

"Your name has been presented to us for consideration to serve as a member of the Board of Education. As you know, there are five members. One is appointed or reappointed each year to serve a five-year term.

"The current member of your district has asked that he not be considered again. After giving consideration to several names submitted to us the committee believes that you are the most qualified. As such, it has become my responsibility to contact you for a reaction. Consider this an official request from our group. We know you are enrolled in school out of state, but your residence is here.

"Some of us feel very strongly that you should be our new member." He laughed, then continued, "I must tell you that one's compensation is all of twenty dollars per month. There are up to fifteen meetings each year. It is really a position of service." He laughed again.

"The board's duties relate primarily to policy making for our schools, teachers and children. Naturally, the elected superintendent is the chief administrator.

"This is the most critical time ever in education that I can remember in my lifetime. We need people who can help make wise decisions during this time. We believe that person is you. We can give you some time to study and review this before you make a decision. The new appointee does not take office for two months."

Charles said, "I'm not sure what I should say. I am honored to be considered when so many are qualified. As you know, I am single. Some would likely prefer married men with children to serve on the Board. I once thought that a child in school should be a prerequisite."

"We are satisfied with your record and qualifications. We are aware that you are single," Mr. Barber said.

"My father has just started serving as a County Commissioner. Would there be some legal or moral objections? After all, two in the same family may be much too much." Charles laughed.

"There are no legal aspects. One is appointed, the other elected. As to the moral issues, we have reviewed this as well. From your place is a black student enrolled in Harvard. From your place and in your home is one who once attended a black school. You gave your time and talents, we are told, and continue to help this individual and others.

"Our committee does not have its head in the sand. There will be integration during your term of office. We need some realistic people who are interested in children to be there to make workable policies. The coming years will not be easy."

"If it is the wish of the Grand Jury, I will give it consideration. But in doing so, I commit myself to what is best for children first, teachers second and to all others last. If I cannot operate in that manner and if there are those who would object to that approach, my name should be withdrawn immediately from consideration."

"This is the reason we want you, Mr. Randolph. I shall express your very words to our group."

"Again, I thank you and the group for their consideration," Charles said.

Back at home, Charles assembled his mother, Meggie and Gena to tell them the news. "I have been asked to be a member of the Board of Education."

"What length term?" Meggie asked.

"Five years. They appoint or reappoint one each year."

Joseph entered and listened to the conversation.

"You will make a great member and your contributions will not be small ones," his mother said.

Gena spoke. "I know of no one more concerned with our youth. I am a living example."

"I feel sorry for you," Meggie said, "though the last thing you usually seek is sympathy."

"Sorry for me? I don't understand."

"Charles, I know some things no other person present would know. I have been down both roads so to speak. You cannot envision some of the problems that will occur. It will be as if the educational world has been turned upside down. You are a very brave man or a total fool. I haven't decided." She did not smile.

Joseph spoke. "It may not come, Meggie. It has been nearly ten years since this Brown thing was brought up. Time moves slowly in the deep South."

"I am surprised they considered you," April said. "You are young, single and not a father, as far as I know." Several looked at April and some faces turned red. "You are in college and the college is outside of Georgia. Also, I can never recall one family having two members on two important boards at the same time. I feel as strongly as Meggie, but for different reasons."

"These were all mentioned when I was called. Every single item was reviewed."

"And their reaction?" his mother asked.

"Mr. Barber, the chairman who called, suggested that I was practically insulting the committee, as if they had not done their homework."

"I am happier for education than for you," Meggie said.

Joseph cleared his throat and all heads turned in his direction. "I believe this a poor decision, a very bad decision, if you accept. Think about it. Any debatable decision, any unfavorable act, will bounce back my way. If integration comes, this will reflect on me, on all the Randolphs. And yes, there is another problem. For years we have tried to keep our taxes down. The property owners get hurt, not the riff-raff, and I suspect that Charles will want to change our county as April would change our quarters! No, I don't care for what I see." He rose immediately and left the room.

A cloud seemed to form over the group. For a few minutes everything had looked so bright. Now they looked at each other and no one spoke.

"Charles, you are right," April said. "I should have never doubted. Nothing has changed. But let's not lose faith. Someday there will be a new beginning."

Each kept his or her thoughts and emotions inside as they retreated.

CHAPTER 45

"The unrest in the quarters continues," Joe said. "I believe it's more intense than ever before. With our liberal President and the marching preachers, it will get worse. The Maybe Jones affair still causes dissension. Some are still concerned about the disappearance of Posey's boys."

Joseph responded, "Give us two more years, Joe, and we will give the buggers to Uncle Sam. If we can keep our shoulders to the wheel just a little longer, we gonna change many things."

Charles was tempted to ask what changes but decided it unwise. Certainly there would be few significant changes as long as big money could be made growing tobacco. To do this, cheap labor would be required. This profit would buy more land. Yet why should he ask or question. He would be gone in less than three years.

The business was concluded in a matter of minutes. Unexpectedly, Joe asked, "Would this not be a good time for April to report on the quarters? It is quite early. Nothing is pressing. As I recall, she said that she would respond in time. I must confess, however, that I'm somewhat confused. She has acknowledged her acceptance of my description of these crude people. Perhaps there is nothing else to say." Everyone looked in her direction.

April glanced quickly at the family members. After a lapse of several seconds she spoke. "I've been prepared for some time, Joe, but I have said nothing for a very special reason. We have witnessed a division among the family in recent times. We need something to reunite us. Serious division is a dangerous state. Our mother has spoken of this more than once. Joseph has acknowledged this as well. I would not wish to say or do anything that would cause further division."

"If we are in agreement," Joe asked, "how can this divide us? I do not feel that we see the quarters in the same manner. I think this would be a great time. If we are together, perhaps this would unite rather than divide us."

April looked briefly at each family member. She had many apprehensions. There was a look of fear and doubt in her mother's face. Joseph and Stephen nodded their heads in agreement with Joe. The expressions of Charles and Michael John gave no hint as to their feelings.

April began, "When the corporation was established, Joseph told us he did it because he loved us. Since that moment our lives have been changed in many aspects. We were assured by him that we could speak our thoughts freely. I believe his words were, 'Tell me what you like and don't like so we can make it better. If we agree on all major matters, we will find happiness, as well as success.'"

"That's what I said, April. I believed it then and I believe it now," Joseph responded.

"Mother also told us at that time," April continued, "that mistakes would be made by all of us as long as man occupied this place called earth. She further stated that when disagreements appeared, we should not condemn each other but offer suggestions, encouragement and support. She also said that the right to speak should never be denied." April looked at her mother and saw her nod her head in agreement.

"It is with such promises that I feel I can speak my thoughts freely. Joe appears to think we see things differently in the areas he has described and discussed. This is not so. We are completely together in our observations. I do feel, however, that he stopped short of the total picture. You will note, we have only one difference. Actually, in some areas, I will go beyond his scope and sphere." A look at Joe showed a half-smile, but also a look of uncertainty.

"I would guess we have a hundred Negroes living at Randolph Place. This includes everyone, of all ages, except Uncle Edd, who doesn't live in the quarters. Some are second and third generation families. Some have come over the years through migration.

"All of us have walked through the quarters a hundred times, yes, even a thousand times. It has not changed much in my lifetime. Everyone and everything is simply older. I am not sure, however, that we have always seen the same things.

"I will attempt to describe what I observed on a recent visit. Then we can determine if we are seeing the same.

"As I approached the quarters I saw the many tenant houses. Some would describe them as shacks. One can immediately see they are basically of the same design. They are all made of wood. All of them are quite old. Some have wooden windows like the tobacco barns. A few have windows with glass. Some have both. In many, where window lights or panes are missing, something has been nailed over them.

"There is no evidence that any of the houses have ever been painted. All have porches on the front, of which many have boards missing. All the roofs are covered with sheets of tin that are now rusted and leaking. Some of the sheets are only partially attached, as the wind has taken its toll. All of the houses have a fireplace and chimney.

"The houses seem very close together. I do not understand the reason. There is little privacy. There is always a danger of fire. Should this occur, it is likely several would be destroyed. We all know there is not a scarcity of land.

"As I entered one of the houses I first noticed the unsealed walls where old yellow newspapers had been nailed in an attempt to keep out a bit of the cold winter wind. The overhead was unsealed and a single light was hanging from above. Half or more of the houses have no electricity, thus they depend on a kerosene lamp as a source of light.

"I looked at the worn floors and saw a child feeding some chickens under the house by dropping some corn through the cracks of the floor.

"I looked for some appliance that would provide heat but there was only a single fireplace. In some of the houses the fireplace serves a dual purpose, as all homes do not have stoves.

"I walked into a room we will refer to as a bedroom. I saw an old discolored mattress on a shaky frame and another worn mattress on the floor. There was a broken mirror attached to the wall. To the side was an old dilapidated chest of drawers with one drawer missing. Two drawers, half open, contained old, tattered clothing. There were two old trunks on the floor, one with a broken lid and another without any lid. A disintegrating cardboard suitcase was nearby.

"I moved into another room and saw an old bed on one side and a table a few feet away where they ate their meals. The legs of the table were uneven and were held together by a series of braces. Five old straight chairs, bottoms out, surrounded the table, along with two wooden apple crates standing on end.

"Outside on the shaky front porch were two old stuffed chairs that had been rescued from the city dump. At the end of the porch was an old swing. One end rested on the floor as the rusty chain had broken.

"Before we leave that house I want to tell you about the family who lived there. I saw a pregnant woman stooping over the fireplace in an attempt to cook an evening meal composed of collard greens seasoned with a small piece of fatback.

"I saw the clothes of another woman. They were old and worn as well as dirty and ill-fitting. She said she had paid three dollars down and a dollar a week for sixteen weeks to one of the dishonorable salesmen who prey upon our people and others. His cost had been two dollars.

"I saw another young girl that was pregnant. She had never had a husband. She had already delivered two bastards previously. One of her two children was teetering around, the diaper filled and leaking. I could not determine if the moisture on the floor had resulted from the diaper, the leaking roof or both.

"I looked into their faces and their eyes. I saw old age upon them, though they have not left the teen years. There was no sparkle in their eyes. They smiled little. They moved as if there was little energy remaining. They said little or nothing.

"As I moved off the porch I saw six children playing in the grassless yard. They were playing stealing sticks, a game most of us played as small children. For them they must play something that does not require equipment. The children's clothes were ragged and they had no shoes on their feet.

"As I moved across the yard a rooster was chasing a hen. The mother on the porch was likely debating the possibility of a chicken for lunch on Sunday or an egg for breakfast tomorrow. A mangy dog of skin and bones nearly raised his head but decided he did not have the energy to investigate. He managed a mournful bark.

"I saw the woodpile where an old rusty axe had been left sticking in a block of wood. A piece of wire had been wrapped around the handle to keep it together where it had been broken. Nearby I saw the old rusty clothesline with some dingy and torn sheets blowing in the gentle breeze. The rusty streaks could be seen, as the wire, no longer galvanized, had left its ugly marks.

"Around the corner of the house I saw two old cars. One had been there for years on wooden blocks. The old windshield was cracked, the tires and wheels missing. The other car, nearly ten years old, had a flat tire. On the back of the vehicle were three antennas, an animal tail attached to one. The body of the car had been more than dented in several places. There were two pillows on top of the back seat near the rear window. Two items on strings dangled from the rear-view mirror. These people seem to operate on a theory that bigger is better. Obviously they have not associated the size and weight with gas consumption. I am sure some slick car salesman still smiles when he remembers how he fleeced another of our people.

"As I continued beyond the cars I saw an old man walking slowly from an old outdoor toilet. The parts of the old rusty hinges still remained on the door but it was pieces of leather from an old shoe that now served as hinges. I could see an old Sears Roebuck catalog through the open door. As the breeze blew you could smell the odor as it drifted toward the houses.

"There were three old men sitting on the edge of the porch, their feet dangling below. Two were smoking roll-your-own Prince Albert cigarettes. The other puffed on his pipe. One whittled with a pocket knife. They spoke little and seemed to stare out into space. The expressions on their faces told a story. They were simply sitting there, waiting out their time in the warm sunshine. One could only guess their thoughts. It could have been about what life might have been if things had been different.

"I saw some middle-aged men and women returning from the tobacco barns and shades. After the thirteen-hour workday they slowly made their way homeward to be rewarded with their collards, turnips and a hoecake of bread. If they were lucky, there would be a small piece of fatback.

"Only the young had a sparkle in their eyes and a little spring in their walk. Will it be five or ten years before they join the ranks of the older ones, the ones condemned to exist as I described? Perhaps it was best they didn't know or couldn't see what was before them.

"Now before I continue, let me add to Joe's observations. As they proceed with their poor English they add a half-dozen 'you knows' as they attempt to communicate.

"So many of the young girls do not learn the tragedy of having babies without husbands. Some do not learn after the first and second times. I am told that in one all black high school more than sixty percent of the students have no idea of the identity of their fathers.

"I concur that they get into their old traps of big worn-out cars, roll down the windows, blow the horn, yell and wave at those walking or riding in other similar vehicles. They ride until the two gallons of gas, likely purchased on credit, are exhausted.

"I am in full agreement that most are unclean, untruthful and unreliable. I believe, however, we let ourselves forget that they are not totally unwanted. It seems they serve a purpose, in spite of all the negative observations."

April looked about her. She had expected to see some of the listeners no longer attentive, but they continued to hang on each word, not knowing what was to come. Joe continued to nod his head in complete agreement.

"So you see, Joe, in a large sense, we both saw the same things you described. They own nothing of value. They have no money, certainly no savings. They are hopelessly in debt and will be unable to pay their debts in a lifetime and more. Even in the busy tobacco season when everyone is working, they cannot make an ample amount to live. I speak of the best of times. In other seasons of the year they even have less. If one cannot pay his debts or get ahead, he ceases to care about the things that are important, the things we could call good. If I found myself in a similar position, I wouldn't either. I'd likely get my few dollars at the end of each week, buy myself a bottle and for a few minutes or a few hours, I would live in a dream world and pretend it wasn't so. Most of them do exactly that. I now have a better understanding of their world. It becomes a period of gray timelessness.

"So, dear family, I am about to finish my story. You have been kind and considerate to let me have my say. As of this moment Joe and I are basically in agreement but now I must go a step beyond; this is where we will differ greatly. It seems that Joe is saying that this will always be so and one can never expect anything different or better.

"I believe changes are possible but it will come slowly, very slowly. It will not come overnight. It will take much more time and effort than I had believed earlier. Yes, and it will come to only a few in the beginning.

"The key word is HOPE. Presently, except for the young, they have, at best, a deluded hope or, at worst, are without HOPE. I am reminded of a quotation from Dante Alighieri. He said, 'Lasciate ogni speranza voi chéntraté. Translated, this means 'Abandon hope, all ye who enter here'. Is this the way it is here? Could this be a description of Randolph Place? If so, will it always be? If not, when will it change? When can one expect it to be different? I believe most of the people here have already abandoned all HOPE. For the old, it is too late. For most in middle age, the cycle will continue. It is only with the youth, the young, that we can build, should such a direction be chosen. They have not yet reached the point of no return. Only educational concern, trust and love can bring HOPE!

"Our problems and their problems are as far apart as east and west, as the north and south poles. Food for the body and clothes to cover their nakedness are priorities for them. For us it is a selection of what we would choose to eat and what suit or dress is appropriate for the occasion. Our problem is the best utilization of our time and talents on eighteen thousand acres. Their concern is a half-acre garden and from what source shall they secure the necessary seeds to plant!

"Again I refer to Joe's descriptions. Lazy? Yes! Why would they not be? If one owes more this week than last week after working thirteen hours a day, why be concerned? Uneducated and ignorant? Yes, indeed. Without any doubt and few exceptions this is what one will find. How can it be otherwise when the parents and the homes are as I have described? How can they be educated when their parents are uneducated; when many of their teachers are poorly trained? Some of their teachers received degrees on the basis of attendance. How can the students learn when they do not attend school for weeks at a time in order to work and put food in their bellies? Unclean? Again, yes. Where are they to take a bath? How will they heat ample water when it is cold? How can they wear clean clothes when many do not own enough to change? You know the questions as well as the answers.

"At the moment they know only hurting and hating, greed and cruelty. Yes, this is all they know. This is all they have ever known! That is what their parents did and what their grandparents did before them. They believe no one cares, that nothing matters. Tell the truth or tell a lie, what is the difference as long as it accomplishes one's purpose? Take what you can, right or wrong, at the first opportunity.

"Yes, as Joe described them, there will always be some drawers of water and some choppers of wood. This has always been so. For some, it will always remain so. Some will never seek anything other than his pay, a place to lay his head and a woman with whom to sleep. But I believe there are some who wish more. It is upon these we must direct our efforts; with these we can make a beginning.

"Let us not teach by voice or example that only money and property are sacred and that one's soul is buried under the dirt and stones of materialism. We must teach them something good, something noble, something worthwhile is available for them. Let us let them know that someone cares. Man cannot function on bread alone. If, however, one must choose between bread and HOPE, let it be HOPE.

"It is so easy for us to ease our consciences by saying, 'Lord, you had them before we did. I don't know how to change them. I'll give them back to you.'

"But these people have played a significant role in building Randolph Place. Without these people, as unacceptable as we have described them, much of what we see and call our own would have been impossible. Yes, we drive them, we explain and instruct over and over and we become so frustrated and impatient that we want to shout and curse. But when we really take an honest evaluation, we know that it is upon their shoulders we have stood to reach the sky and at the same time they have been pushed beneath the soil of the earth!

"We must examine and acknowledge the evidence of hurt we have caused these people. We must examine our hearts and see with our own eyes the true status of these people. In a sense, they are our brothers and sisters, though we are prone to ignore the words of our Lord. Why must we look? Why must we seek? Because we cannot continue to pretend they are not God's children. We cannot continue to lie, be it by word or deed. We share the same air they breathe, we are warmed by the same sun and see by the same light. If we refuse to look and see, we, in turn, may be damned forever.

"I wonder if you ever realized that the essence of slavery is taking the product of another's labor by force or coercion? Once, this force, a hundred years ago, was based on ownership of another person. Now it can be done by economics, through monies and a thirteen hour work day in the fields or the manufacturing plants. They have no choice if they are to exist. Actually, money, in a sense, has replaced ownership. It seems we can be more comfortable with this method because it can be done indirectly and thus becomes less personal. It makes us less conscious of the evil.

"Uncle Edd," April continued, "has pointed out to me and others some dangers if we should wish to resurrect these people, his people, in a sense. 'Help them,' he said, 'to become self-sustained and it must not be with long-term charity. Seldom does one forgive a giver. This is the nature of man. They will, at the first opportunity, bite the hand that feeds them.'

"He also said, 'Do not attempt to confer happiness but opportunity. From opportunity they can secure happiness. Then and only then will they know the real meaning of life. Charity will destroy a receiver, except in rare emergencies. My people have not had an opportunity to know these things.'

"'Lastly,' he said, 'there is a danger that the government will become unduly and improperly involved for all the wrong reasons. If this occurs, your efforts will be multiplied manyfold.'

"As I told you, I walked through the quarters a thousand times. I was about to reach a point where I did not see what I was seeing. It is a point where the emotions and conscience are dimmed or dismissed. As the story goes, we no longer see the trees, only the forest. One can, in time, temper himself or herself to see only what one wishes to see.

"So again I will ask, is there to be a start? Shall we give these downtrodden people a glimpse of HOPE? Shall we show a love for our neighbors and brothers rather than simply speak of it?

"If you do, however, I must call to your attention a danger as it relates to our fellow tobacco farmers, and perhaps all the other farmers in this area. To pay them a little more, to reduce their working hours or to house them decently would cause other farmers to look upon us with unkindness and betrayal. Certainly we know that wages have been fixed for years for all the farmers. There are some other aspects that would be unpleasant as well.

"You once asked me for an evaluation and my recommendations. I suspect they were not really wanted by everyone. You will recall only once did I mention in times past that a better source and supply of water would be a start. I said no more. There was not an ample foundation upon which to build. There was really no place to start. A new beginning would be necessary. But, whatever we do, if we choose to do anything, let us help them in such a way so they may find HOPE.

"I do not plan, as things are presently, to bring this matter up again. In time, should I not be able to accept what we see now, I would have no other choice but to leave. I wish I could believe I have not brought more division among us. It was not division I was seeking. Perhaps I said something I didn't mean to say but I had no choice. To say less would have required the matter be discussed later, perhaps again and again. I do not have sufficient strength to approach the subject ever again. Thank you for letting me tell my story."

All eyes immediately turned toward Joe and his father. It was obvious that some reaction would be forthcoming.

It was Joe who spoke first. Perhaps it was because it was upon his insistence that April approached the subject. "You are living in a dream world. Realty has passed you by. I would not have thought the extreme radical liberals would have captured you so completely. You have been very dramatic, very graphic and at times sensational. As for me, however, I continue to feel as I described earlier. Yes, I want to be fair and in order to do so, I must say you have told the truth as you have seen it. I have no doubt you have seen even more bad than you described.

"April, you simply don't understand these people. They have a philosophy of 'let me be happy and not be concerned about anything. Let me live outside my means even if I have to borrow the money or simply steal it.' It never ends. They haven't changed. They will always remain as we now find them.

"Earlier I had described what I saw and believed these people to be. As you said, our observations have been basically the same. But I believe, as strongly as ever, that these people can never be helped. For them kindness is still weakness. They hold out their hands and ask, 'What you brung me today? What else you got for us?'

"They feel we owe them for what occurred over the last few hundred years. I didn't run them buggers down in Africa. Their own tribal chiefs and members did! I didn't sell them to the Yankee and English ship-owners. Their own chiefs did. They did it to each other. I refuse to share any blame.

"Now our glorious politicians we have sent to Washington are about to put them on Easy Street. They will put them in the best of housing and provide for many of their needs which will, in time, cover their wants. But in time, as you reported on what Uncle Edd said, it will destroy them. It will not be long before they feel someone owes them a living. The more you give them, the more they will expect. When all of them get registered to vote, they will get more and more and do less and less. They will be a determining factor for the politicians. These politicians will never cut off the voice that elects them. In time this will destroy the middle class, which is the major source of revenue for our nation. The rich will find loopholes and methods to avoid participation. The poor have never paid. Yes, in time we will destroy our nation.

"How do you help a group that has advanced so little, if any at all, in four hundred years?

"You also referred to them as our brothers and sisters. I claim no relationship with these people. Actually, they are not totally removed from eating grasshoppers and each other. If one closes his eyes and listens carefully, he is apt to hear in the distance the a beat of their tom-toms!

"There are some things people do not choose to talk about anymore. You once said that we should not kill all our heroes. Take ole Honest Abe. He suggested the United States pay the slave owners and ship them all back where they started. In this he was not successful. There were likely a combination of reasons.

"Go a step beyond and a careful examination brings out the fact he did not attempt, in his Emancipation Proclamation, to free all slaves but only those held in the states that withdrew from the Union. He knew more about them than many thought. It wasn't all about slavery, but politics.

"One last word," Joe said. "I cannot support a program that is a one-way street. Again, I refer to your Bible. It speaks clearly of their talents and ability."

Joe got up slowly and moved toward the door. All watched him as he withdrew. Never once did he turn or look back.

All eyes turned to Joseph. No one could guess what he would say. He just seemed to sit there, looking into space. He seemed so unsure. Abruptly he changed, as if he had decided on what course he would follow. Some expected that he would lash out, but this was not the case.

"All of us have been told how bad we are and how bad we have been. Shame has been heaped on this family. Yet, there ain't one of us that ain't accepted the fruits. New houses, new cars and a lot more have been accepted by all my family. April has shamed all of us and when we look and compare, she has likely been given more than any other. She had time to play while we worked from before daylight to after dark. As my old daddy said, 'Too much, too soon!'

"She said tonight that never again would she talk about such. This is the only good thing I can see we got out of this. Yep, my only girl, my own child."

With a sad face, Joseph left the room. As he got to the door he turned back once more and repeated, "She has heaped shame as well as guilt, disgrace and pain on all of us."

Those remaining looked at each other. Stephen looked at the group, then moved rapidly into the hall, following his father. He turned and said, "All the time, she played while we worked."

Suddenly, everyone turned toward their mother, as she spoke for the first time.

"Old habits will be slow to change, but I do not think I could live with myself and do nothing. I must try. Trust and HOPE must be the first steps. Life without HOPE is no life at all."

April returned to her room. This would be the most difficult night of her life. She was sure of one thing she had promised. She would never open the subject again, as long as Joseph lived.

Chapter 46

February of 1963 did not seem the best of times for the Randolphs or for the Attapulgus school.

The girls' basketball team felt the sting of defeat in the tournament after a successful season. They had won eighteen games and lost four.

The boys played their way into the State Tournament only to feel the agony of defeat in their first game. They lost by two points, in the final seconds.

April wrote a new speech for the oratorical contest. She gave it the title of "The People's Constitution." As the days passed she continued to advance toward the State Finals. However, since she competed against the best talent in the state, she was selected second best. Her only consolation was knowing she had one last chance, in her senior year.

Eric had served as her coach; she learned some of his good qualities and talents. "We will win it all next year," she told him. He seemed to take defeat in a more negative manner than she had guessed.

Charles called Superintendent Broom and identified himself.

"Congratulations, Mr. Randolph. We will be most fortunate to have you as a member of the Board of Education."

"Thank you, Mr. Broom, but I have not accepted the appointment. The Grand Jury has given me some time before I make a decision. I really called to ask a favor, actually three favors."

"I don't believe I understand," Mr. Broom responded. "If you have some questions I can answer, you're welcome to come by and we can confer."

Charles said, "It could be highly irregular but I need to know more than I know now. I wish to attend your next board meeting as a guest. I . . ."

Mr. Broom interrupted, "We have open meetings for one and all. You are welcome anytime."

"Thank you," Charles said. "I would also like your permission to visit the schools. I know so little. Naturally, I would make an appointment with the principal of each school."

"I believe you said three," Mr. Broom said. He had not responded to the second request.

Charles continued, "My third request would be to review some materials in your office so that I would have more knowledge about the system and my responsibilities should I accept the appointment."

"I see no problem," Mr. Broom said. "A well informed person can always make better decisions. Our next board meeting is the third Tuesday of this month. We would be delighted for you to attend."

Charles climbed the narrow steps to the second floor of the old Midway Post Office, which now housed the Decatur County Board of Education. Charles seated himself in a chair behind the long table where the group sat. He immediately recognized Mr. Mathews, who had spoken at his father's birthday barbecue.

Superintendent Broom said, "Gentlemen, this is Mr. Charles Randolph, recently appointed to the board, though he has not yet accepted. He is the son of our newest County Commissioner, Mr. Joseph Randolph.

"Mr. Randolph is a graduate of our local school system, a graduate of F.S.U. and is currently enrolled in their graduate school. I believe he is majoring in Education."

Charles rose and shook the hands of each, then sat back down.

"You know our Chairman, Mr. Mathews. Perhaps you know of Mr. Solomon, a local manufacturer; Mr. Jackson, who is involved in several businesses; Mr. Marker, a successful farmer. You know that Mr. Mathews is also a farmer. I know this fine group will be helpful and cooperative as you enter into the affairs of education.

"Also present is our curriculum director, Mrs. Helen Bronson. Last, but not least, is our very efficient bookkeeper, Mrs. Blue. She can help me explain how we spend the taxpayers' money."

Charles said, "It is my pleasure to be among so many fine and talented men and women. I trust all of you will be patient with one so inexperienced. As Mr. Broom told you, I have not yet accepted the appointment. I still need to know more before making a decision."

In a matter of moments the minutes of the last meeting were read and approved. The four sentences gave little evidence of what had occurred.

Superintendent Broom said, "I believe I should be the one to point out that we keep our minutes to a minimum. From a technical standpoint, I am the official secretary. It has been a practice for many years not to detail our minutes. When people give their time, talents and service with little or no compensation, it seems rather foolish to ask these busy people to repeat again the details of what they already know.

"I'm sure, Mr. Randolph, that in time you can understand and appreciate our methods. There is always a reason." Charles could see the approval in the eyes of the members.

"What do you have on your agenda for us today?" Chairman Mathews asked. "I do not believe I see guests present other than Mr. Randolph."

"First, Mr. Cannington, our legal advisor for our board, has reviewed some communications from the Office of Civil Rights and the Justice Department. It seems they continue to press for a short and long range plan as to integration. We have responded that we wish to approach this cautiously, as so much is at stake for our youth. We emphasized that the period since Brown versus the Board of Education has been less than a decade. We advised them that a team from our staff would continue their work on this matter and that the interest of the child would always be our first consideration."

Charles watched as each seemed to take a turn to nod in approval.

"Our report reminded them of our present building program. This will greatly enhance the educational opportunities upon completion. Blacks will soon be housed better than whites."

"You are moving wisely and with care and caution," Mr. Solomon said. "Anything more drastic could cause much pain and suffering."

"You are to be commended," Mr. Marker said. "I hope our people know and understand the superior job you are doing."

"Our world here is different," Mr. Jackson said. "The people in Washington do not understand our way of life. Our people are behind your noble efforts."

"What else do you have for us?" Mr. Mathews asked. "We want to remain until we have disposed of all policy matters. We know that you are the one to deal with administrative matters."

"I have passed our receipt and disbursement material around," Mr. Broom said. "Do you have questions? I do not recall any unusual expenditures."

"The Tax Commissioner has delivered all county disbursements?" Mr. Jackson asked.

"Yes, and all receipts are deposited in the appropriate accounts.

"In the March or April meeting I will submit a budget for the next school year for your consideration. As you recall, the law requires a special meeting for this purpose and the budget must be published in the local newspaper."

"What do you hear, Superintendent Broom, about our most recent budget? Would you care to react as to our taxpayers?" Mr. Marker asked.

"They have been reasonably quiet, as their attention is equally focused on racial matters. However, I believe they would not be receptive to a tax increase at this time," Mr. Broom said.

Mr. Solomon said. "I agree with Mr. Broom. He is most perceptive."

"At the next meeting we will need to review and approve a school calendar for next year," Mr. Broom said. "A committee is busy at this very moment on this matter. The peanut farmers wish different starting and closing times than do the tobacco people because of their harvest seasons. The committee will have something ready for us.

"Gentlemen, this is all I have for you today. Our meeting has run a little longer than usual. I'm hopeful you will forgive me."

Charles spoke quickly before someone moved to dismiss. "I can understand matters a great deal more if I am familiar with your structure, your organization. Therefore, I request approval to visit each plant, naturally, with an appointment."

The members of the Board first looked at each other, then at Superintendent Broom.

"I find the request reasonable," Mr. Broom said. "I am sure he will choose a convenient time in each case."

Charles continued, "Next, I would like to review some items here in the office. A look at the policies and a recent budget would be helpful. All of this is so strange to me."

"I have no objection," Mr. Broom said. "An informed person is always in a position to contribute more. I would simply remind you that the role of the board is one of policy making. Policy making and administration are two different things."

Mr. Jackson said, "I had not planned to mention this but some of us may not completely understand Mr. Randolph. There has been talk of one believed to be black moved into an all-white school. This has raised eyebrows. I am not sure we know what Mr. Randolph is for and what he is against."

Charles could feel his face turning a different color. He knew he must be very careful in his response. "All of you gentlemen have a right to know what I am for and what I am against. I am for a country, state and county of law and order. I do not believe any individual or group has a right to do otherwise.

"Now, Mr. Jackson, in response to your statement, there was a child attending an all-black school. She has been proven, beyond all reasonable doubt, a person of the white race. This has been done in a court of law. It was felt she should be placed among her own people. Certainly you would not propose, knowing this, that she remain where she was. If so, you would be the first to insist on integration and I do not believe this would be your feelings, your wishes."

Mr. Mathews, his face more than a slight pink, said, "I believe there is a motion and second that we adjourn." Probably no group ever dispersed more quickly.

As Charles was leaving Mr. Broom said, "I'll so advise the schools of your visits in the near future."

Charles was halfway home before he realized it. He knew that there would be many new experiences in the immediate future should he accept the appointment.

Chapter 47

Ten days after attending his first board meeting Charles began his systematic review of the schools in the county. He decided his alma mater would be the best starting point.

"Seems like old times," Mr. Baggs said. "We are delighted you have received this appointment, though many of us who really care do not understand you placing yourself in such a position."

Charles asked, "I'm not causing you to miss a class, am I? I don't want to interrupt."

"No, this is my free period."

"How many classes do you teach?"

"Five. Little has changed since you left."

"Other duties?"

"The same. I keep a study hall."

"Seven periods a day? I don't know why I ask. I work with my girls."

"Seven. We cannot offer the courses needed any other way."

"Your faculty?"

"The best. The very best. There are thirteen of us on the staff."

"Your beginning teachers?"

"Two. They will be superior with a little more experience. I am lucky. The students are fortunate, as well as the community.

Then Mr. Baggs interjected, "I should not ask, but I will. Do you hear from Miss Knight, Charles?"

"No." This was all he said, then he returned to the questioning. "Do you have a secretary? Again, why do I ask, except for the record."

"No." Mr. Baggs smiled.

"Who keeps the school records?"

"We all do. All of the faculty contribute. I check their work, but they are very accurate."

"Where are they kept?"

"We have two sets. One is kept in the office for immediate reference. The other is locked in the lunchroom. That building is not made of wood, thus there is less chance of fire."

"Who does the lunch reports?"

"The lunchroom manager. I finish the final report after she does it and I check her work."

"How do you get paid?"

"By the county office, twelve times each year. It is a matter of public record. My salary is seventy-eight hundred annually with a six-year certificate. This includes my supplement."

"Who receives supplements?"

"Aside from myself, the coach. He gets a thousand dollar supplement annually. I think the real tragedy is that pay is based on years of college and years of experience. This does not reflect the contribution or lack of such. But this is the way it is done. I can think of several reasons why they refuse to do it differently, but a public business could not exist if they pursued such a course."

"You have custodial help?"

"Yes, but he can't do it all. The teachers are responsible for their rooms. I wish it wasn't so."

"School buses?"

"Three. One makes two short runs. We have to come earlier because of this."

"Percentage transported?"

"Well over fifty percent. I will check my records for specifics."

"Oh no, don't bother. What time is your first student picked up?

"Seven o'clock. Some ride an hour and a half each way daily."

"Where do the buses get their fuel? Where are they repaired?"

"All are serviced and repaired in Attapulgus. One gets fuel in Faceville, where the bus route originates."

"I hear your bell ringing. With your permission, I'll look around. I wish a quick look at the rest rooms, the library, the science lab and the gymnasium."

"It's still a shell," Mr. Baggs said, laughing. "Would you look in on our classes? They would be pleased and honored."

"Thank you, no. Give me a rain check. I want to visit four schools today."

Charles visited each place and was about to leave when he saw the lunchroom manager motion for him to come over.

"You had better come see us, Charles Randolph," she said. "We are happy about your new role."

"I'm not sure I can say the same should I accept the appointment." Charles grinned at his friends.

She continued, "I will not hold you up, but I had to tell you of a recent event. Mr. Baggs knows. We have received a directive that no one eating free in the lunchroom can be allowed to do anything in the way of services. We have never required such but now we have a problem. One man, a poor man, has seven children in our school. Two of them asked to do a chore for a meal. It was working beautifully. Now the government will not permit it. The students will not be able to eat free. Mr. Baggs says Superintendent Broom cannot make an exception. How tragic it is when we forbid people to earn their keep! Do you think Superintendent Broom can change this?"

"I doubt that he can. Our boys in Washington have lost their way. I'll check but I expect it will remain. Thank you for telling me. How sad our world has become."

The Attapulgus Elementary School was housed in an old wooden building. It was at the edge of the city limits. He entered the building and was met by an attractive and well groomed Negro woman. "I am Evelyn Barton. I was told to expect you. I received your letter. Please tell me how I can help you."

"Thank you for seeing me. I want to learn as much as possible about the school system. Perhaps they left your telephone out of the directory by mistake," Charles said. "This is the reason I contacted you by mail. Perhaps you should notify the telephone company."

Mrs. Barton smiled. "We have no telephone. It was not an error." She shook her head slightly and continued, "How may I help you?"

"Perhaps a quick look at your plant and a few questions."

"Which would you like to do first?"

"A quick look, perhaps." Charles looked but did not believe what he saw. He continued to walk with the principal in silence. "I see you have a clean building," he finally managed to say. She smiled.

"We can try to be clean."

Charles saw a coal heater in each room. A single light hung from the ceiling, casting a shadow. The students were overcrowded. There were a thousand chipped spots on the blackboard, which was no longer black.

Less than three hundred books were on the shelves in the small room used for a classroom and library. The lunchroom was too small and poorly equipped. The school would be hard pressed to pass a fire safety inspection.

In a few minutes they went to her office. She motioned for him to have a seat. He waited until she was seated. Again, she smiled. His clothes closet at home could have housed her office two or three times.

"How long have you served as a school principal here?"

"This is my third year."

"How would you rate your school?"

"There are many areas to be rated — the building, the program, the equipment and so on. I would not care to use a figure. It would not be in the best interest of everyone. Perhaps you can do so for us. I am not trying to be difficult.

"You see, as we talk, I may not wish to answer certain questions. It seems that this would provide an answer. It is likely that there are those who will ask about my responses." She smiled again.

"You are a smart lady. How long will you remain here?"

"I will leave at the end of this year. I am enrolled in a graduate program at the same school you attend. I must have a one-year residency to complete my Doctor's degree."

"You did not wish to be considered at the new school being constructed?"

"I understand the position has been filled."

"Do you have a good faculty?"

"There are some bright spots, some dedicated people."

"Do you interview and recommend your staff?" There was silence.

"How many students are transported?"

"Nearly all of them. Six percent walk."

"Do your buses run on time?"

"Sometimes."

"Are new buses serving your school?"

"No."

"How often do you have a fire drill?"

"Weekly. The legal requirements are monthly. I cannot let my students get trapped."

"What will a new school do for your students?"

"They would be safer. They would be warmer in the winter. They will have better lights and a painted room. They would be much better from a materialistic standpoint. The secret of a school, any school, however, is the faculty. You know something about this. The school you attended has the best faculty in the system and this influences everything.

"Mr. Randolph, what I am about to say cannot benefit me but I must say it. They get little here and return to the quarters where they may find less. What can be expected in a situation like this? I ask God to give me strength to endure what I cannot change. What is to happen to my people?"

Charles got up to leave. "Thank you for the visit. I don't believe you can change much either here at school or in the quarters, but I hope so." Charles left and refused to look back.

He went across to the other side of town. He had called Mr. Hugo earlier and set up a time. As he looked at his watch, he knew he was exactly on schedule.

Charles looked at the school as he approached. It had been constructed in 1954, at the same time four classes had been added to his school. As he rode onto the campus he saw students everywhere. Again, he looked at his watch. It couldn't be lunch. Perhaps it was recess.

Charles walked down the hall and found a door that said "Principal." He knocked and heard a voice say, "Come in."

He opened the door and saw a man behind a desk. To his side, very close by, was a young girl of perhaps twenty-three.

"Excuse me," Charles said. "I did not know you were in conference. I'll wait until you have finished."

He was about to close the door when the man spoke, "Come on in." He did not get up or offer his hand. The girl who had been seated beside him retreated rapidly from the office.

"I would be happy to wait. I am not here to create problems."

"The lady is on my staff," he said. "I am Roosevelt Hugo. I don't believe I know you."

"I am Charles Randolph. I called earlier about an appointment. Perhaps it slipped your mind or you didn't put it on your calendar."

"I do remember now. Thought you were another salesman. They are always coming by for some deal. Now tell me, what is your business? I don't seem to recall. You said you were Charles Randolph?"

"Yes. I may be the new board member. I believe Superintendent Broom was to tell the personnel, the principals, of my visit." Roosevelt made no effort to respond.

Charles heard a shout. "Where has my class gone?" He could see it was the lady that had been with Mr. Hugo.

"I would like to ask some questions and look around your school," Charles said.

"What can I tell you?"

"How many students are enrolled?"

"Three hundred and fifty-three."

"Attendance?"

"Excellent."

"Staff? How many teachers do you have?"

"Twelve including myself."

"Are you a teaching principal?"

"No. The administrative load is too heavy for that."

"How do you arrange to get in all your classes with eleven teachers? You have one teaching home economics? Agriculture?"

"We plan and organize carefully."

"You have grades eight through twelve?"

"That's so."

"Let's see. You have English, science, mathematics, social studies, typing, bookkeeping and physical education, I believe?"

"Exactly. We also have agriculture and homemaking."

"How many are transported?"

"About ninety percent."

"Do you have good buses? Good drivers?"

"We have no problems. Superintendent Broom speaks highly of us."

"You have adequate furniture, desks and equipment?"

"Some of our desks have a little age."

"Do most of your students eat in the lunchroom?"

"All eat in the lunchroom but some bring their own food."

"You have a gymnasium?"

"No."

"Where do you play your athletic events?"

"We usually play two games at the other school's gym."

"Mr. Hugo, I want to thank you. With your busy schedule of administrative duties, I will not detain you. I'll take a peep here and there as I leave. Please don't get up." Charles had seen no evidence of such a gesture.

As Charles left he saw one teacher attempting to teach about eighty students in the lunchroom. It was an impossible task.

As he walked outside he saw large groups playing and even larger groups observing, all yelling and jumping into the air. As he approached an outdoor basketball court he asked an observer, "Are you taking physical education? I don't see your instructor."

"Ain't got no instructor. We're the walking class. We ain't got enough desks or enough teachers. We brings a dime to join the walking class. We gets one period off every day; some days we gets two."

"Oh, so that's the way it works," Charles said. "Where does your ten cents go?"

"Mr. Hugo, he got to raise money for de audit, whatever that be. Don't really understand!"

As Charles approached his car he saw Mr. Hugo coming his way. "Glad you could come. Makes us proud to have special visitors. I bet you can report to Superintendent Broom and the board the improvements we've made since they got us a new building."

Charles moved swiftly to get to the last school. It was about ten miles away in a very secluded area. He pulled in just as two buses were leaving. He remained in his car until they had cleared the school area.

Charles was not sure the little wooden building had ever been painted. The wooden steps bent severely under his weight as he entered. He heard a voice, "Come in, Mr. Randolph. Welcome to Mount Olive Elementary."

He then saw the person who had spoken. She was a short lady. She carried more than a few extra pounds and she was of a very dark skin.

"I'm Mary Swift. You can just call me Mary. We don't have visitors often. I got your mail. We do not have a telephone. We look forward each year to our Superintendent's visit. He tries to get here yearly. He has missed only twice in the last eight years. I believe he came twice one year, but I can't be sure. Come on in so we can talk and you can see what we got. Gonna have a new school soon and Mr. Broom done told me I'm it. Yes sir, gonna be the new principal of that new consolidated school!"

"Mrs. Swift, I know you are tired from your long day. I will ask only a few questions and look about a minute." He asked, "How long have you served as principal here?"

"This will be nine years."

"Where did you attend college?"

"Fort Valley State. It's up in the peach country. It's a fine institution and it turns out a lot of good teachers."

"How many teachers on your staff, not including you?"

"Four."

"Were all present today?"

"No sir."

"I saw only three leave. Perhaps one left earlier?"

"No. Only three today. Couldn't get a substitute."

"You have no telephone?"

"No. Mr. Broom said with the new school and all, we could just continue as we are."

"How many pupils do you have on roll?"

"Right at two hundred."

"What time do you and your staff arrive in the morning each day?"

"Seven-fifteen."

"Why so early?"

"Buses come early."

"It's dark, totally dark in the winter at that time," Charles said.

"Yes sir."

"What time do the teachers leave in the afternoon?"

"Soon as the buses run. I got a special schedule from Mr. Broom."

"What time is the first child picked up each day in the morning?"

"Six-thirty."

"You have grades one through . . . ?"

"Seven."

"So when all the teachers are present, including yourself, each of you have about forty?"

"Yes sir."

"A rather heavy load?"

"They are not all here everyday."

"Five teachers, seven grades and two hundred pupils? Are my numbers correct?"

"Mr. Broom may get us another teacher. His heart is really in our school."

"Yes, I can see that very thing!" Charles knew the instant he spoke that he should have remained quiet.

"Seems to me you would earn more teachers from the State."

"You don't understand. Allotments are based on attendance, not enrollment. These farmers keep the students out to work." Suddenly, she looked down, remembering that he lived on a big tobacco farm.

"Do you report these as unexcused absences? Isn't there what we once called a visiting teacher?" Mrs. Swift did not respond.

"Let's walk about," Charles said as he stood up.

They looked briefly in the classrooms. Charles had never been so discouraged. One light hung from above, one stove in each room that burned coal and the walls were not sealed. He would get a fair picture of the outside from where he stood. The blackboards all had a thousand points of light.

"Where are your rest rooms?"

"We have outdoor toilets. Naturally, we have two for the boys, two for the girls. One each is designed for the small children. Sometimes we have a few problems if we run a little short of lime."

"You are working under some difficult conditions, Mrs. Swift."

"Yes sir, this is right. But one more year after this and we'll have that new building. We are so excited."

"I'll bet you are."

"Mr. Broom said on his last visit that it was a shame to leave such a beautiful and ideal setting. It's quiet so the kids can learn and we don't have to worry about the dangers of traffic. As Mr. Broom said, we'll be leaving an ideal setting!"

"Do you have a custodian? I nearly forgot."

"No. But we get a lot of large and strong boys. Some of them are seventeen. They are strong and they can help us a lot."

"I have kept you longer than I expected. Please do all you can to help your students. They are our future."

"That's so, Mr. Randolph. That's so."

Charles returned to Attapulgus immediately. He wanted to get by himself and shout, curse and yes, he even thought of hurting someone. Now he knew why some had expressed their sympathy on his consideration of a position on the board.

CHAPTER 48

"I would like to talk with you about a graduate study, Dr. King. I have been astonished at what I have learned while visiting some of the schools in Decatur County."

Doctor King had migrated from Texas and was well respected in educational research. "Yes, I believe I saw in a newspaper that you had been appointed to the Board of Education in your county. I will say congratulations with tongue in cheek. This may not be the best of times." He smiled and they both were aware of the crucial days ahead for the public schools in the South.

"Thank you," Charles said. "I have not accepted the appointment, as of now. Already, I have seen so many discouraging areas that I am beginning to feel I made a mistake by considering the appointment." He laughed, then continued. "Perhaps I should move my residency to this campus and I would have a legitimate excuse for being a coward."

"Is it your desire to pursue some specific problem that has gained your attention? Just what do you have in mind?"

"I have been greatly disappointed, perhaps I should say shocked, about the school bus program in our county. It is not a pretty picture. Actually, as far as I can see, it is dismal. I can't really believe what I have discovered."

"Tell me what you believe is so dismal."

"In three of the schools I visited children ride school buses three hours or more each day. Some actually ride four hours in the other school. In certain seasons they must wait and board a bus in the dark and be returned home in the dark. I am sure it has many negative effects on all, but I can't even imagine a six-year-old confronted with such a problem. In some cases the first grade student must start before six in the morning to get ready. When you consider an ineffective heater and the door being constantly opened and closed as others board the bus, it should also have an effect on their health, as well as the learning process.

"Let me," Charles said, "be critical for a moment. Many of our leaders, parents and politicians tell you they will do anything for their most precious possessions, their children. They say they will make any sacrifice to assure a good educational environment. This isn't so."

Doctor King laughed and said, "As long as it doesn't require money or time! It's the same everywhere. You really have had an experience recently, haven't you? I can tell. In a way, I am glad this has happened. I have been wanting some capable and sincere student to do one or more studies in this area. Few studies have been made in this particular area.

"I suggest you do a small study in this area of interest in seeking your first graduate degree. I believe that such a study could be enlarged in several areas and your samples increased ten fold; this would likely be accepted as your major research in a doctoral program. Care to take me up on this? I see you have a deep interest and grave concern."

"Do you mean this?" Charles asked.

"Certainly. The results could assist school administrators all over. But before you start, let me make you aware of two things you need to know. First, it will be a slow process. There are few shortcuts. Secondly, your present beliefs are not always right. That is the purpose of your study. Do a pilot study, a pilot program. I'll help you and guide you along. Speaking of a pilot study, a hundred or two hundred samples would be ample. This first effort will help you design your larger study."

A week later Charles returned to visit with Dr. King and review what he had learned. After he gave a brief review of what he had found Dr. King said, "I didn't discover much research some years ago. It is an area in which we should have something we can believe and know. Check with your school people for permission to use their records and test results. I think there would be enough in your own school in Attapulgus. Then you can tell me what you plan to do and how.

"Changing the subject, you may not know, or perhaps you have forgotten, that should you accept the position as a member of the Board of Education, you are required to keep your residency in Decatur County. At the same time we require your residency here at the school. You would be able to serve less than half your term if you accepted."

Charles knew at this very moment he could not accept this position. His decision had been made for him. He thought of his father and knew he would be most pleased.

CHAPTER 49

It was the fourth week in May. A slow, gentle rain was falling from the clouds above. The farmers and their families looked skyward and expressed their heartfelt thanks to God.

The corn farmer who planted early could be assured that this would provide the ample moisture needed at the most critical point. They looked at the many ears that seemed to fill the stalks and knew that the kernels would mature and ripen fully.

The peanut farmer looked down the long, straight rows of the leguminous plants and knew they had successfully passed the initial critical period. In a little more than two months they would spread so that it would look like a sea of green. This was his bread and butter crop. A smile filled his face, as he could envision monies with which to pay the bills and have a little left.

The cattle farmer looked at his wide and open pastures. He knew that the slight tinge of brown would be replaced by a sea of green grass immediately. Here his cows with their new calves would stand in grass knee deep and eat until their bodies were large and slick. There would also be ample hay for the herds in the winter.

No one would smile more than the shade tobacco farmers. This rain would assure them of one of the best crops ever. The leaves were large and of good texture. In less than two weeks they would begin their harvest that would last into August. This was the rain needed to finish a near perfect crop.

The men in the fuller's earth pits were pleased that the rain did not come until mid-afternoon. This allowed them to fill their bins and warehouses with the special clay so essential in the gasoline refineries.

The crews with their logs loaded would get out before the ground became too soft. The same was true for the pulpwood crews. They would have ample time to get to the railroads for unloading.

Coach Willis Daniels looked up at the rain drops falling. He did not tell his baseball team, already seven runs behind, that he too was pleased. It had been a long season and if the game was rained out, it would assure the boys of a winning season.

At six o'clock the Thomasville-Tallahassee television station reported that a light rain would probably continue through the evening and early morning hours, but would likely stop by Saturday noon or before.

At seven-thirty the Randolphs gathered for family night. Never could Martha remember her family in such a good mood. They talked of the good things. Joseph was in high spirits. A week from now he would begin his last few steps to the Promised Land. School was out, and this seemed to delight everyone, especially Stephen.

When the meal had been completed Joseph said, "I have some calls to make. I want to see who will start gathering and when. I may need a little extra labor from time to time."

An hour later Joseph announced, "I believe we will all start gathering in the next ten days. They all seemed optimistic. Then all of us can watch the green leaf turn to gold."

At the break of day Martha heard Joseph come into their bedroom. "Where have you been? I didn't know you were up and out. Why didn't you wake me up?"

"It's still raining just like the weather boy predicted. This is Saturday. You will be up all too early starting next week. Best you rest while you can."

"How did you find things?" Martha asked.

"Good. Rain has soaked into the ground. If it gets harder, it could do some washing, but nothing to worry about. As long as the wind doesn't blow too hard, we'll be fine."

"I'll put on some coffee and start breakfast," Martha said. "I think Channel Six gives an early weather report. They said last night it would likely be clearing before noon. Perhaps we can get an update."

Fifteen minutes later Joseph took a chair in the breakfast room and Martha brought over two cups of coffee. "The weather man says it could rain for the next forty-eight hours. Really don't need that much but we'll be fine if it stops by Monday morning. He said there was a 'low' hung up over south Georgia and north Florida and he saw nothing to move it either way immediately. But that's God's work. He can move a 'low' if He wants to. Rain seems to be harder than yesterday. I'll need to watch closely."

Joseph and Martha heard the alarm clock go off a little after four. "I hear it raining right on," Joseph said. "I'll put on a rain coat and some boots. I wanta check my shades. I think everything's fine but I'll feel better after I look."

In forty-five minutes Joseph was back. "So far, so good. We have a few spots where it hasn't soaked in but that will clear up in an hour if it stops raining. I can catch up on some things I need to do inside."

On Wednesday morning it was still raining. They looked up into the sky. The clouds were thick and dark. Lightning was in the distance and the roll of thunder could be heard. Joseph again examined the fields. They seemed better than he anticipated.

When he returned to the house a special announcement on television reported that a high was moving in and that by midmorning on Thursday they would see the sun again. Joseph smiled. He moved from one member of his family to another and embraced them. "I just felt the Lord was on our side. We can make plans to start on Monday. We'll be ready." He called three farmer friends; they had already heard the news.

It was nine o'clock the next morning that they looked into the heavens and smiled. The rain had stopped. An hour later the sun broke through the clouds and again they smiled and offered a silent prayer.

At eleven it seemed that most of the clouds had vanished and the sun seemed even brighter than an hour ago. "Everyone has a job so we can get ready," Joseph said. "I think we have rested enough the last six days." Joseph's face seemed to beam and glow and the spark returned to his eyes. He placed his arm around Martha's shoulders and they understood without saying a word.

Martha went in and prepared an early lunch. "By the time we eat, some of the water will have drained off or entered the earth. I know you want to be off and running."

At a quarter after twelve they noticed that the sun was less bright. Joseph rushed out in the yard and saw some dark clouds in the southwest, an area all the farmers called 'Peter's mud hole'. Ten minutes later they heard the rain in the trees and on the roof of the house. In moments they saw the last of the sun disappear. Everyone gathered on the front porch except Joseph. He remained in the yard, his clothing soaked. He looked in every direction and could see the clouds getting darker. He walked to another part of the yard and looked up. It seemed even darker than before. He saw that the sun made no effort to return. He walked up the steps of the porch in total silence and never spoke a word. His gloom seemed to spread among the whole family.

The telephone rang constantly for the next two hours as the farmers once again discussed the weather. It was a case of everyone talks about it but no one changes it.

No longer did the rain fall gently, but in torrents. Martha announced that food and drink were on the table, but no one seemed to have an appetite or thirst. Martha walked to the windows facing the porch. She saw her husband pace unceasingly from one end of the porch to the other. His face was red and his clothes were dripping water. She saw the anger and wrath in his face and eyes. She moved toward the front door but she was unsure what she would say or do. As she quietly opened the door she noticed Joseph had stopped less than two steps away. He was unaware of her presence.

Martha heard him say, "You think You got me whipped, damn You. No one whips Joseph Randolph. I have worked for too long and too hard to be stopped now." He shook his large clenched fist toward the Heavens and said, "How can You do this to me at this time?" He shook his closed fist again and raised it upward once more. "By God I ain't gonna be stopped now, not by You, not by anyone."

He turned and once again walked to each end of the porch, then returned once more to his original spot by the post near the steps. "Don't try and treat me like Your Moses. It ain't gonna work! I'm going to make it to the Promised Land. I'm too close to stop now. I won't be denied. I have given my whole life and I damn sure won't be stopped. Delayed? Perhaps! Stopped? Never!" He walked down the steps, took a long look into the sky and said no more.

Martha, without a coat, went out into the yard and put her arm around her husband, then led him back into the house.

"Let's get some dry clothes," Martha said. "One day we will look back on this as a short, bad dream. You are the light of my life and together we will succeed."

Slowly Martha led Joseph toward their room. Water squished in his shoes and he left a trail behind him, but didn't seem to notice. He spoke to no one but they saw his eyes filled with despair, anger and defeat.

CHAPTER 50

On the fifteenth day the rain stopped as abruptly as it had started. The low moved out and there was not a cloud in the sky. The weather man reported a high would be stationary for a week or more.

The *Atlanta Constitution* stated that the governor of Georgia expected some emergency aid in grants and loans with low interest. They were told that Congress was meeting in Washington. They appointed a committee to appoint another committee to investigate and report back to the original committee, who would report to Congress and the President.

Joseph and his sons inspected each area. The tobacco had turned a light rust color and mold had formed on the stalks and leaves. It was in a final state of decay. The plants had been totally destroyed.

They looked at the corn. A line of brown spread along the edge of each bayonet. The stalks were no longer stiff and erect, but formed a curve because there was no strength left. The beginning ears that had started developing were ready to fall to the earth. The Randolphs shook their heads and went toward the peanut fields.

They examined the peanut plants closely. There was some hope, as the peanuts had been planted in sandy soil, which soaked up most of the moisture. The manner in which they were planted also provided a drainage. They would have to wait. It was too early to tell and too late to plant again.

They moved on and examined the irrigation ponds and the lakes used for swimming. Because of good construction and proper spillways, they could be repaired. They looked at April's two ponds. The large spillway had held. It would require less work than any.

They examined their pastures. Some work would be required, but they were pleased to find them in fair condition. They needed something to feel good about.

The telephone rang unceasingly but it was not his tobacco friends calling. It was all the people that needed road and bridge repair. A large number demanded that the commissioners go to Atlanta and Washington to demand some immediate help and relief.

For three or four days Joseph remained calm. He attempted to tell each that help was on the way but they would have to be patient because they had only so many men and pieces of equipment. Several demanded more from the prisoners that were helping. He told them they had some liberal lawyers looking over their shoulders, insisting that minimum hours apply or they would lodge cases for cruel and unusual punishment.

After five days Joseph began to lose the little patience he had. Martha heard Joseph speaking to someone on the telephone. "Do you think you are the only one with problems? We are moving as rapidly as we can. Everyone is hurting. No, the damn idiots in Washington have done nothing."

The next day he had even less patience. "Hell, man, we all got problems. Yes, we'll get there when we can."

The next day all of Joseph's patience was gone. "Damn it, we are moving as fast as we can. We can double your taxes and get some more equipment. Hell, man, talk to God. He did it, I didn't! What do you want me to do? Call the Chairman."

Finally, the next day she heard him say, "You have the wrong number."

CHAPTER 51

In October Coach Daniels had his basketball teams ready to play. This was the season, the year all was to come together.

It was April who provided the leadership for the girls and Robert White for the boys. These would be remembered as good days, the best of days.

None of their first six games really tested the girls or the boys. First it was Midway to feel the sting. Then Whigham, Apex and Midway were to become victims. The fans filled the gymnasiums to capacity. Some became rather silly, with their bobwhite calls when Robert excelled and a chorus formed to sing "April Showers" as April put on a show. Coach Daniels smiled and seemed more relaxed than anyone could remember.

Before the second half of one of the girls' games started April came over to the bench and lightly touched Coach Daniel's cheek with her hand. The nearby fans heard her say, "Just relax. We have everything under control. Just sit back and enjoy yourself." Both smiled and the fans enjoyed every second of what they saw and heard.

In the month of December the Attapulgus Boys' Basketball team was invited to the Albany Invitational Tournament. Here Robert led his team to four straight victories against teams whose high school enrollment exceeded a thousand students. Robert was selected Most Valuable Player and April was his greatest supporter. No other team had come closer than ten points in the four victories.

Some other things occurred in December that seemed significant. On the Saturday nights that April had individuals gather at Somewhere Else she made several interesting observations as they ate, danced, played cards and socialized. Jerome had found reasons not to attend. April was concerned.

The other observation, a most pleasing one, was the change occurring in Michael John. He felt secure among the group. He talked much more than he once had. He became quite a gifted player in several card games they played and this added to his secure feeling. Where once he was accepted as a partner, he was now pursued. More than once he played as a partner with Robin; they seemed to play well together as a team.

Meggie helped Charles to complete and chart the figures he had accumulated from his pilot study on transportation. When he looked at the results he quickly exclaimed, "We have made an error. We must have. There is no way this could possibly be true." He and Meggie reviewed each calculation and detail for the third time.

"You are shocked, aren't you?" Meggie asked. "You were certain there would be a large, significant difference."

"And you were not? I still can't believe our findings, nor can I understand why you felt there would be little difference between the two."

"I had suspected little difference, certainly less than the five percent you had considered significant. The difference was that in this school the teachers made up for any differences with their superior teaching. Had the faculty been weak, the differences would have been greater. I also believe the differences would be greater in larger schools. I have no proof or way of knowing with certainty.

"Now let me go a step further, as did some of the other people in earlier studies. Though you were searching for significant differences in achievement, had you expanded your study to include roles of leadership, class officers, extracurricular activities and participation, I believe some differences would have prevailed. You have limitless opportunities to discover so much in studies of this nature. It could greatly influence many aspects of school life for students and teachers as well. There are so many doors to open and so many areas to explore."

"You seem to like research," Charles said, as if it was both a statement and a question.

"Yes, very much. I find nothing in all my learning experiences quite so exciting. Why, a few years of extensive research could change many practices now believed good or outstanding and this may not be true."

Then Meggie's facial expression changed from elation to anxiety. "If you do a large study, it will help educators and students but you will be looked upon unfavorably.

"How so? If we gather facts and act accordingly, we will move into a better situation. Everyone wins."

"No. Everyone wins except you, and I do not feel I can stand for this to happen. A discovery of this nature should be praised and rewarded; however, this will not be the case.

"Let me explain. If in a major study you find a significant difference, it will require more buses, drivers and fuel. It all adds up to more money. For this you will be damned for higher taxes.

"If there is no significance, busing will be used as a tool or vehicle for mass integration. The proponents will say there is not an adverse effect, as proven by you in the study. So, again, you are damned." She laughed. "Damned if you do, damned if you don't. Everyone is waiting to find someone to blame, be it integration or taxes. You will have the donkey's tail pinned on you. I don't wish this. It will be grossly unfair! I don't' think I can let you do it."

"I'll have to go ahead, Meggie. I'll do it not for the sake of a unique dissertation, but for a study to learn the truth. It is truth that will free us!"

"Truth may get you hung, Charles," Meggie said.

CHAPTER 52

Following a good Christmas Martha was certain that 1964 would be a good year for the Randolphs, for the farmers, and hopefully, for everyone. She had many reasons to feel as she did. Not once had she witnessed unkindness among her children or Joseph and it had been a season of good tidings, exchanged gifts and new promises.

During the two-week holiday, after helping her mother as much as possible, April spent many hours with some of her favorite people at Somewhere Else. The regulars included Robin, Eric, Robert, Charles and Michael John. Jerome had even come once to dinner but he seemed a little strange, which puzzled her.

Everyone expressed their surprise as to the facilities. Eventually it all added up to, "I don't believe this. It is truly Somewhere Else."

Even Joseph was exceptionally jubilant during this time. The seed bed for tobacco had been started and he talked about the prospects of a good tobacco year with prices unbelievably high because of the shortage from the previous year. He had said, "I would have preferred Kennedy live because of his strong feelings about Cuba. I don't believe Johnson can give everything we have away in such a short time but with his 'Great Society,' he will try."

When the students returned to their classes the first week in January, an epidemic that seemed to be a strain of flu appeared. Some doctors said it was a virus. Whatever it was, it spread like wildfire. It seemed to be everywhere and bore no respect for age, sex or race. Charles missed some classes at college. Kathy was home in bed for several days. Stephen stayed in bed for four days with a high fever. At times it seemed there were not enough well folks to care for the sick.

The epidemic blasted the quarters in full fury. Mary helped Martha and April was in constant motion at the end of each school day. There was talk of the school closing. It seemed that someone was always cooking soup, taking someone to the doctor or going after medicine.

About the time they were on the verge of closing the schools throughout the county, everything started to improve. Both Charles and Stephen returned to school. Kathy was strong enough to give some much needed aid in the quarters. It was then that Mary became ill and Kathy doubled her efforts to provide the assistance needed and to accept the role that Mary had been forced to relinquish.

After another week the worst was over and most were well or becoming so. Then it happened! Kathy developed a high fever. She needed medical attention so David took her to the hospital in Midway. They were told, "She must have some strong medicine and complete bed rest!" The doctor also recommended she remain in the hospital. However, she insisted on returning home and assured them, "I'll be fine in a day or two."

Twenty-four hours later David rushed her back to the hospital. The doctors conferred and hinted that the hospital in Tallahassee could serve her better. As plans were being made for the transfer a doctor approached David and said, "We have done all we know to do. We can offer no hope unless God intervenes." In an hour she was dead. David was by her bedside. Many of the family were nearby but David, so lost in the moment, would not remember.

A few minutes before Kathy died, April stood near David as he held Kathy's hand and heard him say, "God is with you. He will save you. We must never doubt His power, my darling. This is our God of love, of understanding and compassion. Believe, my darling, believe in Him and He will fulfill His promises. You must not leave me, my darling, because I cannot go on without you."

David could not remember clearly the different members of his family coming to him. Nor did he remember the Lanes, Kathy's mother and father.

First he saw his mother approaching but she could not speak. Real sympathy does not require words. The full meaning was there and he saw it in her face and in her eyes.

Later he remembered Mary. Her eyes were great with suffering and he knew it was for him. Then her eyes filled with tears and she placed a hand on his shoulder. She then felt she could not remain and rushed from the room.

David turned and saw Mike Harper, then burst into deep anger, with fire in his eyes.

"Tell me, Mike Harper, tell me what my Kathy did to deserve her death? Tell me!" He struck his fist on the table top nearby with such violence that its contents scattered on the floor. "Tell me," David shouted. "Damn you, tell me! You know I have tried not to question your Bible but when it speaks of the wicked flourishing like a green bay tree and their children dancing with joy in the streets, it becomes obvious that something is wrong! Why are the trusting deceived, the faithful betrayed?

"Don't talk to me about your loving God! Satan, yes, the very Devil is the prince of this world and who in the hell do you think made the prince? Your God! Not mine! Your God! Yes, it was your God, your Lord. It was your God that made this evil world. Suppose you take your God and go. Damn your God, Mike Harper! What did my Kathy do to offend your God so deeply? Did her virtue outrage him? And the punishment for virtue is death?

"We had both made a promise to Him and He had promised He would not forsake us. Now don't tell me she is at peace, that she suffers no more, that she is among the angels and perhaps playing a harp and that is her reward for an unselfish and blameless life. I have no God. There is no God!"

Then Mike said, "If there is no God, there isn't anything for Kathy and she deserves a God. All that is left for us is to believe. That's all we have, David. To believe in God is all we have, even when we cry out in pain and hate and misunderstanding."

David said, "There are some that say He was invented by the priest and the preacher. Some say He was invented by the rich and powerful to keep the poor and needy in a state of obedience. Some say the poor invented Him because that is all they will ever have — a belief."

David continued, "Why should I not question? Even Christ, in his agony upon the cross questioned. To question is natural. And I find no acceptable answers."

In a quiet voice Mike said, "God is not the adversity of man. Man is. God is not to be understood by man, only trusted. You will know this some day, but not soon. Your hurt is too deep. Man will survive and endure. He always has. And the day will come, though not for a long time, that you will find joy again."

Michael John approached his brother, but the paralyzing impotence of childhood was still with him, heavy upon him. He had no words to express his true feelings and no means of communicating his pity, as well as his love. Tears filled his eyes as he held his brother in a firm embrace. He turned away quickly to hide the emotions some had once termed weakness. He prayed David would understand what he had wanted, but failed, to say.

Susan Lee made her way to David and embraced him. She spoke quietly, "I wish I could take this cup from your lips. I am old and it would not have been a real loss. A day, as Mike has said, will come when you will find joy again. The clouds, though you think not, will vanish and the sun will shine again. I speak as one who knows. In the meantime, let your family and friends sustain you. We want to because we loved Kathy too."

David looked at Susan and said, "Kathy wanted so little in life. She wanted only to serve and be happy and make others happy. She called it a small thing. I called it everything."

David looked at no one in particular and continued, "Once I looked at our world and I loved it, as well as the One who created it. I constantly expressed my thanks, my gratitude, for this beautiful creation. It was a creation that was made for Kathy and me. God, then, was everything one could need, everything one could want. He was Teacher, Father, Companion and Friend. I was so happy, so pleased. I felt so strongly. Then He raised His hand and let it fall. And now I have nothing, nothing at all!"

After David returned home Mike went to him and embraced him warmly. Yet David gave no sign of knowing his presence. He remained silent, with no expression in his face, no light in his eyes.

In a little while Mike went over to Martha's home. He said to her and a few family members, "We were taught in our preparation and training for the ministry that under normal conditions, there are usually six stages of grief. First, there is numbness. This is his current stage. Next there is emotion and pain. He is experiencing this also. Then comes a period of loneliness. This can last longer than one would like. Then follows resentment and guilt, in which one often blames God or self or both. Lastly comes reality. It means one can face life again. Most of the time we can. You are the ones to witness these periods. I will help, but at the moment he feels toward me as he feels toward God."

Martha went over to David's house, since he had refused to come to the family home. She was accompanied by April, Mary and Mike. The Lanes were there when they arrived.

When they entered Martha said, "David, we are here to assist you with some plans that must be made. First, we want to tell you how much we love you. We want to help bear your pain. Let us do this, please. The time has come to make some plans, some decisions. We must decide on times and the people you would like to assist you."

"Mother, Kathy is not dead. You must know this," David said.

"No. She is not dead. Her soul is now with our Lord," Martha said. "She cannot return here, however, in earthly form. This is the way of life."

David demanded,"What guilt can you find? She taught Sunday School. She sang in the choir. She made her gifts, far greater than suggested, to the church. She stayed in the shade, the shadows, and brought sunshine into the life of others. She fed the hungry, she nursed the sick. The color of one's skin did not deter her.

"Did you ever see her perform a selfish act? Did you ever know her to be boastful or self-centered? When we married she gave me the most one could give, an untouched and pure virgin body. She was always cheerful and friendly. What was her sin that was so great that God punished her so? Or, if it was not God, it must have been Satan. Thus, if God cannot control His fallen angel, why should we call him God?"

Martha said, "I cannot give you an answer, my Son. I am not sure you will ever completely understand, though I think the time will come when the pain will not be so great. I don't understand either. Why do the aged that have lived a life and can get nothing more of real value live while babies die, while young soldiers die, while people like Kathy die? Perhaps God will reveal these things to us if He wants us to know. Please forgive me for not helping you when you need me so."

April said, "She was all these things and more. She brought more sunshine to everyone she touched than anyone I have ever known. In time you will know, my brother. I suspect you would likely not accept the answers if you knew just now. No. None of us understand God. He wouldn't be God if we did."

Mike said, "Kathy no longer has a living earthly body. Her soul has departed. We don't even have to give a second guess as to where. She is in Heaven, a place that is everlasting, where one never grows old; where one is not sick; where there is no pain. One day you will join her. In the meantime, God has a purpose for your life. All of this is God's will."

This seemed to inflame David. "You speak of the will of God? Doesn't this mean a wish or desire or purpose to be carried out and ordained? I was taught that God was good. Isn't that the blessing we instruct and teach our little ones? Yet we talk about this as an act of love? God is good and He loves me so He takes my life away?

"You said in a recent sermon that God wanted the best and called His children home. Certainly after thousands of years He must have found a few good ones to keep Him company. Why, some were even given a title of saint. Isn't it important to leave a few saints here to help others find a path, a road, a way? Our God takes care of the drunks, the dishonest, and those that bring so much misery to others and He takes my Kathy away!"

David spoke again. "God, if we are to believe Him, gave his Son the power to make the blind to see, the deaf to hear and the lame to walk. If God has this special power, why would He wish to permit blindness and other such suffering in the first place? Why are some born with handicaps and others without? Why is your God so inconsistent?

"I have seen no vision of Heaven. Have any of you? How can we know? I have not seen God or His Son. I don't believe you have either. How is one to know above and beyond all doubt?"

April responded, "If God is forever, then all of us, His children, are forever, as we are created by the same One and we are created in His image."

Mary interrupted, "Is it possible that this is the only Heaven some will know and He has given their only gift to receive while down here? David, tell me how I can take some of the pain from you. I will gladly accept it."

April said, "We don't know everything about God. He hasn't returned to tell us, though it was alleged there was One. We can't prove there is a God but we can't prove there is not. The bad man hopes with all his heart there isn't and the good man fervently hopes there is. It is all according to what hope you prefer.

"We cannot reverse God's acts," April continued. "We have to go on, as the poet said, when there is no desire to go. Now we must plan a course of events. We have no choice."

Then David spoke once more and that was all. "Religion has failed. The church should move immediately. Man is told the positive but you no longer speak of the negative. We have forgotten the Commandments. Are they not negative?

"Man should be told he will suffer, that he will face death and lose all of those who matter. Shouldn't some teaching, some preparation be forthcoming to prepare for the agony and parting? In this one thing above all, man should not be ill prepared!

"I guess faith leaves us in one of many ways. For some, faith seems to sweep away as the gentle rain seeps into our earth. For others, it seems to slash and slap and stomp and it is all destroyed in a single moment. It disappears forever. For me, it was the latter."

Mike said, "There are a dozen of the kids you and Kathy taught waiting to tell you of their love and help you get through your darkest hour. Lean on them. Children never come as some adults come. In them there is no guile, no show. They bring only love. Let them help you."

However, there was no sign that David heard a word. Later he could not remember when told of the hundreds that came to pay their respects.

The following afternoon they buried Kathy in the Presbyterian Cemetery that was now used primarily by the Methodists. No one could remember when so many were present. There were more outside the church than inside. School had turned out early so that the students could come. All the county officials were present because of the position held by Joseph. A Negro delegation of more than fifty stood grouped together at one side of the entrance in silence. Many of them were from Randolph Place.

April wondered what Mike would say. He had asked her for suggestions. She had told him. "Her life spoke for her. That is all I can say."

After a prayer and the Scriptures, in which he used the 23rd Psalm, Mike said, "As a student in high school I was assigned a play written by William Shakespeare entitled Julius Caesar. We were required to learn some lines that Marc Anthony spoke at Caesar's funeral. Some of the words went like this: 'Friends, Romans, Countrymen, lend me you ears; I come to bury Caesar, not to praise him. The evil that men do live after them; the good is oft interred with their bones.'

"Today I come to speak differently. I have come to praise because in the time I knew Kathy I saw no evil — ever! There is no way to do justice in describing this beautiful lady — this Katherine Lane Randolph of whom I speak. There are no adequate words to describe her and her wonderful works.

"Actually many of her works were secret, hidden, as this was the way she insisted it be. I promised this would never be revealed as long as she lived. Today, however, you should know of some of her acts and deeds.

"Let's talk first about some things that you did know. She and David were the Sunday School teachers for our high school age group. She sang in the choir. She can be heard even now as we close our eyes and hear her beautiful voice in song. She usually was present for the mid-week services where our attendance was often less than we desired. She played the piano when the regular people were not present.

"Now there are some things you likely didn't know. She and David were our biggest contributors within our church as to the tithes and offerings. The beautiful piano you heard when you entered was a gift from them, but they wished it to remain a secret. The song books from which you sing were another gift. At Christmas, Thanksgiving and Easter they provided dozens of baskets for the needy. At school they bought several senior class rings which some poor students could not afford.

"They always worked in the shadows but their gifts brought light and sunshine into the lives of everyone around them.

"This was the Kathy I knew. David gave her full credit for the many changes in his life.

"We are here to pay our final respects. We need to remember the manner in which she gave her greatest gift, her life. In spite of the prevailing dangers, she went forth and gave herself. She gave the final measure. She laid down her life for her friends.

"I must speak of one last thing, to which I do not know an answer. Why Kathy? Why this beautiful, unselfish and talented girl at such an early age? I know a dozen people who wish God would take them, as they suffer hourly.

"Why does a young girl die of cancer at twelve and a soldier give up his life at twenty so that we may live in peace? Why does the thief live in luxury and another holds two full-time jobs to feed and cloth his family in a meager way?

"Why did the Lord turn Lot's wife into a pillar of salt when her only guilt, according to the Scriptures, was looking back? How can one prosper and send a man to his death so he may possess another's wife? Yet this man wrote the twenty-third Psalm, which we read moments ago. There is no evidence that God punished King David, unless it was the removal of the first born to Bathsheba.

"I cannot tell you the answers. But just as Kathy placed her faith in God, we, too, must do so."

At the cemetery Mike prayed, "Dear God, thank you for the life of this sainted one whom You gave to us that we might learn from her. She has departed to be with Thee. We know she is safe in Your loving arms. Now we ask strength in the days to come for those whom You have left to carry on Your work as Your good and faithful servants. Guide us in the paths You would wish us go. Amen."

After they returned home David came before his family and said, "I must spend some time alone to sort out many things. Do not fear that I will seek to join Kathy, though it has entered my mind more than once. You must be patient with me. There will be many times I will prefer to be alone and you may not understand.

"I know you love me, though I am not sure I am deserving. Likely there will be times you will fail to understand. I thank each of you. I must return now to the home that Kathy built. You may feel this unwise but this is the way it must be.

"Perhaps in time God will explain Himself more fully. At this time I do not understand." With these words David left the group and walked slowly to the house where there was once much joy.

April asked her mother, "Do you recall when Mike came here?"

"Yes," her mother said. "We could tell he was different. The ones before him were mostly involved in fund-raising and social justice. They had one project following another. The cause seemed unimportant; only another crusade that would surpass the last one.

"Mike, however, seemed to have time for the agonies that devour and destroy the human spirit and alienate man from God and from fellow man. Yes, Mike is different."

Mike Harper, after the service, returned to the sanctuary and thought about many things. He looked over at the organ and he remembered accepting the gift from Joseph Randolph with grace and appreciation. He knew why the gift was given. But after all, had not Mary Magdalene's gift been accepted by the Lord?

Then he remembered the quiet secret that he, Kathy and David had shared when they gave the piano. How different the purpose. But if the devil or an angel should come your way bearing gifts, why seek a different path?

He knew his thoughts were not all good, yet he seemed to feel better. He would go and prepare for another day.

CHAPTER 53

"Jerome, I must talk with you," April said. "I am disappointed. I never seem to make connection with you. Couldn't I make it a home visit and visit with your mother and brother? Why, I may be able to save a fee that way!"

Jerome laughed. "Maybe hasn't pulled another stunt, has he? I have missed you so much since those special days. Yes, do come to our house. Mother will monopolize you for a time but eventually I will get you to myself! As you are busy on ball nights and such, why not come this Thursday evening? By coming that night, I will not have to share you with my brother. It seems he has found a new interest in town. I'll tell you about it."

On Thursday evening April went to the small frame house occupied by Susan Lee and her two sons. "Oh, April, do come in," Mrs. Lee said as she greeted her at the door and kissed her on the cheek. Jerome was standing just behind his mother.

As April hugged Jerome's mother she said to Jerome, "See what you are missing! It's been a long time since you embraced me properly!"

Jerome blushed slightly, caught off balance for the moment. Then took her in his arms and kissed her on the lips, holding her quite closely. As he did April pressed against him so that he might remember once again that she had grown up.

After they had seated themselves Susan asked, "What can you tell me about David?"

"I don't know, Mrs. Lee. I wish I did. He doesn't look good. He speaks no more than yes or no to a question and sometimes he doesn't even respond at all. He is not eating properly. On occasion he will come over, but usually after everyone has finished the meal. Between Mary and Mother, they keep something in his refrigerator that they think he will like.

"He works all of the time. He starts before daylight and often it is after dark when he returns. They take his dirty clothes and wash them, as well as his linens. When his sink gets filled with dishes, we take the clean ones out of the dishwasher and fill it with those that are dirty.

"I have talked to Mike Harper more than once. He discussed the various stages one usually follows after an unexpected tragedy of this sort. I feel David is experiencing all three of the first stages at the moment.

"We were afraid at the beginning that he would not want to live, that he might even consider taking his own life.

"But in spite of all this he'll make it. He has strong support from everyone. We have the best mother in the world to give him the support he needs. Sometimes she insists, after letting him know we care, that he be left alone unless he asks for help. Mary has been unquestionably a major source of strength. I have learned a great deal about her, some things I didn't know, during this period. Joe has no idea how fortunate he is.

"Michael John, being a quiet person himself, has been with David when he felt David needed company. Charles has given his full support. Joseph, Joe and Stephen have done what they could but it would seem they fail to understand his needs.

"No one, in their special way, seems to care more than the Jenkins family. Meggie helps me with David's home.

"He can have no doubt as to how everyone feels. He knows that time will be his friend, but it will take a great deal of time to heal the wounds that occurred so quickly, so deeply and without warning.

"Tell me about Mr. Lee — Eric that is. Sometimes I nearly forget in the classroom. I believe you said he has a new friend that he is quite excited about."

"Jerome can tell you," Susan said. "She works in the courthouse and Jerome sees her quite often."

Jerome responded, "I know little of her background. Her name is Jane Dawson and she works with the records in the clerk's office. She probably has been working a year. She is a pretty girl and she gets along well with everyone. All of the lawyers seem to like her and she, in turn, seems to like them. She is friendly. She is very efficient. I guess this is really all I know. Eric seems very excited about her and feels that she will go far because she has, as he says, all the equipment to be successful."

"I'm so glad he has found a friend," Susan said. "He brought her home for me to meet and she has had dinner with us. She has also made a couple of short visits. I really think Eric is quite excited about her and she seems to be very fond of him."

"I'm glad," April said. She laughed and continued, "I had Eric and Jerome all staked out for myself. Looks like you are it, Jerome."

Jerome changed the subject. "April, has David returned to church?"

"No, and since the funeral he has refused to talk with Mr. Harper, Mike, if you like. I don't think Mike felt this unusual but I got a different interpretation. David has some strong beliefs, as strong as Kathy's. He cannot comprehend why God ordained or permitted this to happen. In short, I think he feels God let him down. I would guess that he will not return soon. I think it will be a long, long time before he does. What do you think, Jerome?"

"I don't know him as well as Joe or Charles because he is younger. He is not as outward in his feelings as some of your family. It is possible for David to have a much deeper and longer depression than someone like Joe. At least I think so. His closeness to Kathy, in so many ways, would make it even more difficult. His total life was integrated with her. He has, however, three things in his favor. Any or all three could be deciding factors. He is young. They can usually bounce back better than someone much older. He has time on his side. Perhaps later he can find someone else, though I am sure it would not be soon. Then, he has family and friends as constant supporters. This will not do it alone but it will help. I was about to say a fourth but I hesitate."

"Tell me. I would be interested," April said.

"I was about to say his love of God and his strong faith. Usually this would be so. I'm not sure in his case. You did not use the word blame as one of the steps but it is possible that his blame, his resentment, could be pointed in this direction. Let's hope not."

After they had talked about other events, ranging from public speaking to basketball, Susan said, "This is a school night. All of us must work tomorrow. Let me leave the two of you to the business you need to discuss. Please tell Martha I will see her shortly. Goodnight." She left the room.

"What possible legal needs do you have, April? You can't need a divorce!"

"I can't be married because I'm waiting on you. You sure are slow about some things. Seriously, Jerome, I simply need to know if I have a leg to stand upon."

"You have two beautiful legs to stand on and you always seem to know what to do, when and why. I thought I told you how beautiful you were. Certainly I have not made that mistake."

"Jerome, I wish I knew when you were serious and when you were not. For the moment suppose we leave my legs and talk about the G.H.S.A."

"The what?"

"The G.H.S.A. This stands for the Georgia High School Association, an organization within the state school system. They establish the rules, regulations and schedules of all of the extracurricular activities for all the public schools within the state."

"So, what does this have to do with you? I am sure you have met, are meeting and will continue to meet all the requirements."

"I'm not sure this is so," April said, looking Jerome directly in his eyes and smiling as she responded.

"Has Mr. Baggs slipped up in not listing you as an eligible participant? This doesn't sound like Mr. Baggs, or Willis Daniels either. I'm still lost and for your information, lawyers don't like to get lost and if they do, they must not remain in such a position very long."

April produced a handbook for the Georgia High School Association. "I borrowed a copy from Coach Daniels. Take a minute and glance through it. While you are doing that, I'll be looking you over as a possible prospect for a husband. Have to be careful, you know. One can never know enough!"

Jerome glanced at April's smiling face and dancing eyes. He then averted his gaze to the book and flipped through it hurriedly, pausing to look more carefully at the table of contents. After two or three minutes he looked back at April. Before he could speak April said, "That's a very good sign. You can't keep your eyes off me."

Jerome shook his head once again. "It would take some time to review this manual. Should I? Is there something wrong with it? I think you can save us some time."

She explained, "My question is really this. Would or could the Georgia High School Association be required to follow their manual, excluding, of course, something like an error in printing?"

"Yes, I would think so, but what are you really getting at?"

April took the manual. "Here is the section for girls' basketball." She flipped several pages and said, "Now here is the section for boys' basketball. Naturally the rules, number of players and the like are defined in each section." She waited until Jerome nodded.

"Now what do you see under track and field events?" April asked.

"About the same as to rules, tournament sites, dates and the like."

"And golf. What do you see here?"

"Again about the same. Here are the sites for the tournaments in the classes C through Triple A. Actually there is no difference in organization or format."

Suddenly, Jerome turned his face toward April and said, "I don't believe it. I simply don't believe it. You devil, you! I know what you have in mind and you think you can get away with it. And you know what? I believe you can too!"

"Jerome, I thought you would never catch on! Maybe you had better employ me as your assistant. I think it would be a lot of fun in more ways than one."

"Tell me why you want to run track? This is for boys!"

"While the courts work on integration of race, I propose to work on the integration of sex, male and female. I may not wish it to sound like it sounded." She laughed and shook her black hair, which reflected the light; her black eyes continued to twinkle. "Actually, you may be a master of said subject!"

"Someday," Jerome said, "someday, things will be different but for the moment, we will keep our attention focused on the G.H.S.A., as you call it.

"April, there is no way they can prevent you or any other girl from participating in spring sports. I'm sure it never entered their minds that there would be females who wished to participate. Thus, nothing, they felt, was needed to describe the sex angle."

Jerome looked at April as if to say 'go on' but she said nothing. "I believe you said that Mr. Baggs and Coach Daniels file a report each semester. You make sure your name is included on all spring sports sheets. Have them send me a copy. I'll keep this manual for a day or so and get such information as names and addresses that I will need. It would seem to me that you are going to be running around in circles and hitting a lot of golf balls. As I understand golf, however, you would prefer not to strike the ball any more often than necessary."

"You are a bright young man, Jerome. Susan Lee hasn't raised a foolish son, at least in some areas. Since I don't have a checkbook with me to put up a proper binder, I guess the best way to make it binding for the moment is in this manner." April let her arms encircle Jerome as she pulled his head toward her, pushed her body against his and closed her eyes. She waited and nothing happened. In a few seconds she opened her eyes and saw him looking directly into hers.

"Let me give you some advice," Jerome said, as she continued to hold him tight. "Keep your eyes open — always. You might miss something." He lowered his face and their lips touched for a second, then he withdrew. "The time has not come. If it is to come, we will both recognize it."

April turned away, a look of disappointment on her face and in her eyes. "Thank you for seeing me on such short notice. I am completely sure about one thing! You may know everything about law and courts but you don't know the first thing about courting. But, have hope. There is still much time and even the slow learners will catch on sooner or later if one keeps doing something over and over until getting it right. It just might be good that you will require a lot of practice before we can consider passing you on!" With that she was gone.

After she had gone Jerome found himself in a state with which he was not familiar. He seemed to tremble inside. He held out his hands, the G.H.S.A. manual in one of them, and noticed his hands trembling. He thought, I am the one acting like a school boy. Goodness, here I am nearly twenty-eight years old and this girl, definitely not a child, will not be eighteen for two or three months. He picked up the manual once more and thumbed the pages, then dropped it on the coffee table.

I must get some matters cleared up in my mind. April has a semester before she finishes high school. I have seven years of formal education beyond that point. She is really a person of means, I know. She has assets of nearly a half million. I couldn't earn that much in a lifetime. Again, nothing in common. She is a farm girl and I am a professional person. Again, so far apart.

What would her mother say if she knew of my feelings for this lovely lady? I can just hear Joseph demanding to know why an old man like me would be interested in his daughter. He would want her to find someone like Victor McPherson, who would add power, money and more importantly, prestige. Wake up, silly boy, he thought. You are an old man dreaming the dreams of the young.

April left the Lee home with some strange emotions. She had acted like a very silly school girl. Had not Jerome said as much by his actions when she had demanded that he kiss her? Had she not let him know once more that her body was not that of a child? Yet he had said she should keep her eyes open. What kind of remark was that? But in the end he had given her hope. "The time has not come," he had said. "And we will both know it if and when it does."

As April was a practical person, she began to ask some questions. Why was she interested in this man? He was handsome, but he wasn't as handsome as Victor McPherson. He wasn't as young and strong as Robert White. He would never be a wealthy person like Victor. Why was she attracted to this man in such a special way? She would just have to think on this more.

What are the important things in life? What are the things that really matter? It was then that she began to understand. He is good! Nothing can compare with goodness over a lifetime. And goodness included truthfulness, honesty and fair play. He has a compassion for the weak, the poor. Why was he here in Decatur County, except for his love and devotion to his mother? Yes, he had all these characteristics and more.

There was one thing, however, that April could not determine. He never let anyone get more than a glimpse of his inner self, his total self, his very soul. One always wondered about the real Jerome. She would give this more thought. If she observed carefully, asked the right questions and listened intently, she would someday discover the real Jerome. But, she asked herself, if I do this, will my interest and desire remain the same? This certainly would require much thought.

She did not remember her drive back. When she got out of the car, she found herself in front of David's house. She had no more of an answer for her actions in coming to David's home than she had memory of driving there in the first place. She knocked on the front door and heard a voice, "Come in. The door is not locked."

David was sitting in a chair facing the television but the television was not on. She saw a newspaper to the side of his chair but it did not appear to have been opened. She saw a Bible near the paper and noted slips in it marking some places, for whatever reason. She saw his blank eyes and noted his thin face, his uncombed hair.

"How are you, David? Mind if I visit with you a few minutes?"

"I'm all right, April. Yes, it is always good to see you. You are very special and have been so considerate, not only since . . . for as long as I can remember. You have always been special and sometimes I think you understand my feelings and beliefs more than anyone, unless it is our mother."

April smiled and took a seat slightly to his side, but positioning herself so that she could look at him. This, she realized, was the most he had said to anyone since . . . the event.

"Have you had your dinner? If not, let me fix you something. I'm learning to cook so I can catch me a man one of these days." The moment she said it, she had regrets. It could remind him of things that once had been.

David seemed lost in his thoughts, or in the lack of them; she wasn't sure which. Finally, he said, "I believe I ate something some time ago. As I recall, Mother . . . or was it Mary . . . brought over a plate."

April said, "I could tell you that you are not eating properly but I will not. I suspect you have heard that too many times already. I could also tell you that you are killing yourself with your work but again, I will not."

"Does it matter, April? Does it really matter?"

"It matters to me! It may matter more than you realize. You see, David, I understand so much about you. I know you and your values. I know how important certain things were to you that often seemed unimportant to others. You said a moment ago some things that pleased me more than you can know. You said I was very special and considerate. You have often said I was one of your favorite people. If this is so, and I believe it or you would not have said it, then you must do some things for me. You do things for people you love." April wondered again whether she had gained or lost with her last statement.

"David, you must talk to me. I want to help you start living once more. Life should go on, though there are times when you wonder if it is possible or necessary. You can't let me down! And there is our mother. Oh, God, how she loves and respects you for all you have been. You are her son. Then there is Mary. Poor dumb Joe doesn't know a valuable prize when he sees it. She is so concerned about you. And Michael John. How fortunate we are to have this beautiful brother. He is not real good with words but no one could love another more than he loves you. Why don't we just talk, about whatever you will talk about? I'm not sure you want to but do it for me."

"April, I'm not sure it will help. In fact, I think it may make matters worse if that is possible. I don't think you could possibly know what it is like. Kathy was my life. She was everything."

"Only you would know that better than me. I have often wished I could have some of her characteristics and how wonderful the world would be if everyone did. I could tell you what they are but you know them better than anyone." Again April wondered if she was wise in speaking this way.

"Today, I grew weary while working. For some reason, possibly because today was quite warm for February, I returned here and sat in the gazebo. I saw the peacocks strutting around, their feathers making a huge fan. I heard the tom turkey talking to the hens that were not very far away. I saw the squirrels playing as they chased each other up, down and around the tall pines. I heard and saw all of this and I felt that Kathy was with me once more as we enjoyed the simple acts of nature." He paused and April wondered if he would stop or continue.

"I was sure," David continued, "that I could hear Kathy's clear voice and see her big smile on a face as beautiful and open and undevious as in life. I could see her large blue eyes, direct and clear, with an expression of love and beauty and openness that was always there. When one saw her face, they could see many things, but kindness always reigned supreme.

"I could see her blond hair with its silken sheen, blowing loosely in the wind. Though she was an outdoors girl, her complexion was not dark and it blended with all her other features. She seemed small, as she was in life, but durable and strong and ready to offer a hand where needed. Yes, she was slender and small but with more energy than anyone I ever knew." He didn't stop. "I can see Kathy walking down the lane with our mother to offer some help where needed. I can see her in the choir singing her heart out, her voice blending with the others as they sang a joyful praise of thanks to our Maker. I can see her in the Sunday School room, explaining and discovering the blessings of our Lord and helping the young to understand the meaning of the Scriptures.

"I can see her in the kitchen with an apron wrapped around her, preparing my favorite meal just the way I liked it. You see, April, everywhere I go I find her, I see her, I hear her beautiful voice. She is in my every thought every second and it seems I can't make her go away. Nor do I want to.

"And finally," David said, "I cannot understand why this has happened. It is better that I not express some of my feelings because I find myself rather bitter. I know you care, or you wouldn't be here, and I am more than grateful for your concern and your love. I know my actions have been such that no one would really want to be near me and for this I ask for your forgiveness."

"There is nothing to forgive. I am sure I would have responded as you have. I would, however, like to ask you some questions. You need not respond, because I know your answers, but I hope you will think about them.

"If Kathy were sitting here with us tonight, what would she tell you to do for the rest of your life? Would she want you to grieve on and on for her? Would she wish you to be cross or indifferent to the ones that love you the most? Would she want you to be bitter toward others or bitter toward her God and your God? Would she want you to blame yourself or anyone? Would she want those who love you most to be ill at ease in your presence? Would she not want you, after a reasonable period of time, to go on with your life?

"I want you to think as you go through each hour of the day, 'What would Kathy have me do?' What would you have her do if you had died and left her? I think I know the answers but you must find them for yourself.

"You are, in a way, destroying the lady that loves you most — your mother. She sees you not eating, not sleeping and trying to destroy yourself through unnecessary physical labor. Would you do this to her?

"If Kathy could speak to you from above, I am sure she would say, 'David, please don't do this to me. I understand how you feel. I have never doubted your total love. But now you must put together another life. I want you to be with others, make new friends and, in time, find another to share a life with you. No, I know you won't forget me. No, I will not think you selfish, because you have never been so even once in your life. You must do this for me, David, in order to save yourself. Do this for me because I love you so.'

"You will not do these things immediately. The healing process requires time. Take one step at a time. Let others help to make you well again. They want to do this. They love you. It would be selfish and unfair if you did not allow them to do this. Thank you for letting me say this, David. Please think on these things."

David did not speak so April got up and left. As she passed by the house where Joe and Mary lived she saw a light on and movement in the den; she decided to stop a moment. She had not been in their home in weeks.

She rang the door bell, turned the knob, pushed the door open slightly and yelled, "Anyone home?"

Mary finished opening the door and said, "Oh, April, I'm so glad you stopped! If I had not known your schedule, I would have thought you unkind or unfair. I don't know how you do so much. You go to school, play basketball, study, prepare speeches, keep Somewhere Else going, help your mother and give as you have to David; I don't see how it can be done. Here I stand talking. Come on back to the den. Will you have something to drink?"

"No. I think not. I'll stay only a moment. This has been an interesting and eventful evening and I have school tomorrow."

April looked at Mary more closely, noticing that her eyes were red and perhaps she had been crying. "Are you all right? Is something wrong? Where is Joe?"

Tears flowed from Mary's eyes in a profound way. She turned to find a tissue and to compose herself. "I'm sorry you saw me like this.

I'm all right. Sometimes one reaches a point where their emotions show. Tell me, how did you find David? Oh, April, I am so concerned about him!"

"Let's talk about you first. Please tell me what is wrong. I know you are very upset, as I have never seen you this way before. Talk to me! Let me help you! You need to talk to someone and I can be a good listener."

"April, I'm fine. You know how girls are, especially at certain times of the month. I just lost my composure for a moment. Some days we all feel this way."

"Where is Joe?" April asked.

"He had to go out for a while. He has a lot of business and he has his mind on this new crop of tobacco they will plant this year. I think he went to Midway to see about something but I don't remember just what it was. You know women can't keep up with all the business men have. Now tell me about David. You did just come from his house?"

"Yes, I was there for a while. I got him to talk to me for the first time. Of course, the subject was Kathy but that's fine. He needed to talk, to have someone listen. Mother is so proud and so indebted to you, Mary. We all are. She said you have given of yourself in a most unselfish manner. I want to thank you as well. He is a very special person and what happens in the next few weeks can make all the difference."

"I do what I can. He doesn't talk to me. He just — well — looks into space as if he doesn't see or hear anyone. I would help more, without hesitation, if only I knew what to do. Can you tell me how I can help, other than with food, and keeping his house clean?"

"Continue to be kind. Talk to him. He hears more than you think and more than he himself realizes. He told me how kind you had been."

April changed the subject. "Now let's get back to you. "I'm not satisfied about you, Mary. Would you like to talk? You are very special to me."

"I'm fine now. You always make me feel better. I think you always make most people feel better. I am so happy to have a sister like you. You may be a sister-in-law but to me you are a real sister."

A short while later April left, then drove the short distance to her home. As she did she found her thoughts and concerns stronger about Mary than about David. She wondered if she should talk to her mother or Charles about Mary, then decided, No, not now. I'll wait but I'll watch. I will need to see her more often.

CHAPTER 54

Yes, soon Attapulgus School would be gone forever. Never again would this institution produce the many students who would continue their educational endeavors in preparation to serve themselves and others. Charles got up and paced around the room but the feeling of depression did not leave.

The door opened and his three girls entered. "Sorry," April said. "We can go elsewhere. We didn't know you were here."

"Sit down." He spoke in such a manner they did not know if it was an order or an invitation. "I'm trying to make some decisions and I have never been so unsure." The girls had never seen Charles this way before.

Meggie said, "Let us help you. Tell us your problem."

"I wish you could. I am at a complete loss. It involves so many people. It involves a way of life. Life in Attapulgus will never be the same again and I can do nothing to stop what is to take place."

"Tell us why you are so upset," April said. "Let us help you. You have done so much for the three of us."

Charles told them of the proposed consolidation plan. "The final bell will toll for Attapulgus. The community will die when the school leaves. The community is built around the school.

"When the people think they can have a new three-million-dollar facility for what they believe will be no cost to them, they can't wait to get to the polls and vote. There is no possible way to prevent this from happening."

Meggie said, "You are not seeing the trees for the forest. You have not projected the different options."

"There is no option. I don't understand what you are saying," Charles said.

"Have you thought of a way to save our school?" Gena asked.

"No, but you might not want to retain a school here," Meggie said.

April said, "I don't understand what you are saying. I'm still in the dark."

"Let us suppose one of two things occurs. It has to be one or the other. First, Charles, you say the referendum will pass. This means the four white high schools will be housed together in some new facilities.

It will certainly be in Midway, as this is the center of the county. As the students go, so will our fine faculty. This will help.

"Now for a means of comparison, let's suppose it doesn't pass. In three years, perhaps four, the government — that is, the courts — will demand the schools be integrated. This would mean the consolidation of the school I attended earlier and this school. However they arrange it, the ratio would be four to one at the beginning. In one year, it would be eight or ten to one because the whites will flee. This would even be more accelerated when the students and parents learn of the deficiencies of the black faculty members. I am sure since they hold a degree, be it bought or earned, that the government would require they be retained. The concerned white race will not accept this type organization. Anyone with children, not forced to stay for some reason, will leave. Now I ask you to compare."

"Won't the schools still be required to integrate?" April asked.

"Yes, but the ratio may be one you can live with in time. Education would require some form of evaluation, in a manner similar to that of lawyers, who are required to pass a bar examination before they are permitted to practice. There will be several changes of this sort, I would guess."

Charles asked, "You are saying that consolidation will serve Attapulgus best?"

Meggie said, "I will say this and no more. Take it from one that has been there. Let them vote for consolidation. I would vote for a referendum; the people have a right to speak. I'd vote against it so I could tell my people I opposed it. All the votes in Attapulgus will not change anything. It will pass. They have the votes."

"I think you are very wise, Meggie. You were right; I couldn't see the forest for the trees. How stupid of me not to have projected it to a conclusion. Thank you for your insight."

"This may fit into Eric's plans," April said.

"Why do you say that?" Charles asked. "Eric will surely stay here until the consolidation."

"I don't know. Yes, I guess he would, but he is quite excited about a little girl in Midway. There are those who believe he is quite serious," April said.

"I had wished it might be me," Gena said. "I had my eye on that young man."

April laughed. "Five years ago I staked him out for my very own. I guess we both missed the boat."

"Tell me about the girl! Why is it that no one told me about this?" Charles asked.

"You have your mind on other things. I suspect you have a girl or so staked out. There are still rumors! Many rumors!" April said.

"Who is the girl? Do I know her?" Charles continued.

"I believe her name is Jane Dawson," Meggie said. "I don't know her but I have been told she is very pretty and has a great body!" Meggie blushed as she spoke.

"Do you know a Jane Dawson?" April looked at Charles.

"I believe I recall someone saying she worked at the courthouse. Was it the office of the Tax Commissioner? Perhaps it was the Clerk of the Court's office. Anyway, yes I have heard of a Jane Dawson."

"I heard the same thing that Meggie heard," Gena said. "I understand she really has a beautiful face and body! Surely you know a pretty face and body when you see one, Charles? Around here, when one speaks of a ladies man, you are at the top of the list!"

Charles laughed. "I'm not sure you girls are being nice to me today." Then he said, "I've got to run. I've got an important errand that shouldn't wait. Let's leave what we have discussed between us. Some things will become obvious in the near future." Charles left the room in a hurried manner.

Charles went directly to the packing house and his office, then dialed the telephone. "Jerome, this is Charles. If you can possibly make it, I wish to see you immediately. Why not come to the office rather than the house. You will remember, it is in the packing house. We have something important to discuss."

As Jerome walked in ten minutes later he said, "You seemed quite excited and felt it was urgent. I didn't take time to dress properly. But, as you said so little, I didn't know how to dress."

"You are fine, Jerome."

"Is something wrong? This is not like you, Charles."

"Maybe in time you can tell me," Charles said. "You are supposed to know the answers. I trust you are free for a time?"

"Yes. I told Mother I wasn't sure as to when I would return. What is so urgent? Are you in trouble with some lady friend? Is an irate husband looking for you? You are not about to become a father! I've been expecting something for some time. Sooner or later it will catch up with you!"

"Oh no, Jerome, you have it all wrong. You are suggesting and accusing me unjustly." Charles laughed. "Get into my car. We can talk as we ride."

"It *is* urgent! You have been caught. I don't want to get shot because of some of your wild escapades." Jerome laughed. "It may not be a lawyer you need!"

"The matter is not one of my making," Charles said. "Let's talk a moment about Eric."

"Eric? That timid, innocent brother of mine cannot have a problem! Innocent is a synonym for Eric!"

"Do you know Jane Dawson? I'm sure you do, since you are often in the courthouse."

"Sure, everyone who goes to the courthouse knows Jane. Everyone likes her. She is very pretty. I don't know much about figures but I would say she has one. Eric has been dating her for some months. She has been in our home. My mother was quite impressed. Mothers always see the best in their own children but can usually look more objectively at others. Most of the time mothers can be a good judge.

He continued, "I believe that Jane and Eric are very serious. I had thought perhaps he would take another look at Robin Wells. She isn't as pretty but they have a lot in common, as Robin is a teacher, a professional person. They seem the best of friends, but nothing more. Jane is an extrovert. She never meets a stranger. She makes people feel comfortable. Sometimes, opposites attract; Eric is a bit timid and shy."

"Eric does not need Jane Dawson." There was no smile on Charles' face.

Jerome sat up straighter in the car seat and looked at Charles. "It is strange that you would say something like that. This is not like you. I have never known you to get involved with the affairs of others except perhaps in relation to Meggie. You know more than you have said."

Charles did not respond. He drove through Midway, crossed the river on Highway 84, then pulled up at a small motel. He parked in the shadows where they could not be seen. "Now we can talk as we wait and watch."

"I don't understand, Charles. I need an explanation!"

"I want the best for Eric. No, I don't wish to select a girl for him but he deserves a very special lady to share a life with. Jane Dawson may not be the girl for him. Let's watch and wait."

"I would think Eric is smart enough to select a very special lady," Jerome said. "I know he has had few experiences but he is not a dumb person. We don't all like the same person, the same kind of person. I think this is good."

"She is not being honest with Eric. She is not the girl Eric believes."

"How do you know?" Jerome asked.

"It's not important how I know, but what I know."

"Have you been involved with her? Are you involved now? How can you be so sure?"

"I just told you that how I know is insignificant. Suppose we look for a few minutes. You may see someone you know. It is quite possible that you will not need to wait a long time."

They did not speak again for ten minutes as Charles continued to survey the parking area. They soon saw two cars turn in, one a short distance behind the other. They moved to an area that was nearly in darkness, beside the first room. "Watch closely," Charles said.

For a minute no one got out of either car. "Watch closely," Charles said for a second time.

They heard a car door open after another minute, then saw a man emerge from the dark area, unlock the door, enter and close it immediately. Jerome whispered, "My God, that was Joe Randolph. That was your brother!"

"Quiet," Charles instructed. "Look closely now, as the next occupant will likely move quickly."

Immediately, another car door was heard and they saw a woman emerge into the light. She was there for only a second or two. She quickly opened the door Joe had unlocked and dashed into the room.

Charles and Jerome remained silent, each with his own thoughts. Each seemed to be waiting for the other to speak.

Finally, Jerome said, "Poor Eric!"

Charles nodded in agreement. "I did not know that it would be Joe but I had an idea it would be somebody. Poor Mary."

Again, for a minute, they did not speak. Then Charles said, "Eric isn't committed, but this is not true where Mary is concerned."

"Are you saying that you didn't know about Joe?" Jerome asked.

"I did not know about Joe. This was a surprise, not that Joe hasn't been running around. The surprise was Jane. I didn't even know they knew each other."

"Let's go home, Charles. I have a great deal to think about."

As they moved in the direction of Attapulgus Charles said. "Some women are like Jane; it's a game with them. Just as some men move from one conquest or triumph to another, there are some women that do the same. Sex, for them, is as essential as air to breathe. I am told that some are born that way, that the genes can cause this. As they make one conquest, they have two or three more already lined up. They do not seem to be satisfied. I am reminded of the explorer. He can never remain in one place. He must see what is around the curve and over the next mountain.

"I do not understand, Jerome, why she would play this game with Eric. Usually they want some experienced person, as they don't wish to take time to train one."

Jerome said, "Someone like you? You know a great deal more about this girl than you have told. If you knew all of this, why didn't you tell me sooner?"

"I didn't know who Eric was dating until today. I spend all my time on the farm, at F.S.U. or going and coming. My three girls told me."

"Do they know about her?" Jerome asked.

"No, and it is best they don't."

"Thank you, Charles. I needed to know. I am not sure just what I should do."

"You know, Jerome, there seems so little sense in throwing your life away for a toss in the hay. There are young foolish men that do not see the whole picture. There isn't a woman alive that is worth a man destroying his whole life for. Oh, it would be exciting for a while, I suppose, but you can't stay in the hay all the time. Even that might become boring. The morning always comes and when it does, it won't be as you first saw it. Sometimes such as this can even become uncontrollable, even nasty."

"You don't sound like the romantic man so many believe you are, Charles. You haven't told me yet how you were led to this exact spot. Do you care to say more?"

"Conversation and words are usually a product of lawyers and preachers. I do not profess to be either nor do I plan to be. It is always best, if you are not in one of these two professions, to leave a little to one's imagination." He continued, "I had to let you see for yourself. A picture is worth more than a thousand words. I am not sure I could have found the right words. This way was best."

"Do you have some suggestions, Charles? Once the problem is identified, it requires a solution."

"It may be best for everyone if she just left the area," Charles said. They did not speak again until Charles let him out to get his car.

"I know what I will do," Jerome said. "I shall always be obligated to you. Eric and Mother must never know what we know." He added, "One other question before I go. What is to happen to Joe and Mary?"

"I have no idea. I am not sure I want to know."

Three days later Jane gave notice to her employers that circumstances required her to leave immediately. "I know you deserve more notice," she said, "but an unexpected emergency has come up." They wrote her a letter of recommendation and gave her the final check, then she was gone. No one ever knew her new destination.

Some days later Eric said, "I can't understand this. I was about to give her a ring and ask her to marry me. Nothing makes sense."

"God works in mysterious ways, our Bible tells us," Jerome said. "I'm sure you are stunned at the moment but it will pass."

Their mother said, "I believe it involves more than the work of God but suppose we leave it at that." She never brought the subject up again.

CHAPTER 55

For the first time ever, both the girls' and boys' basketball teams were to go to the state tournament in the same year.

The boys were to go a week ahead of the girls so they would not be delayed for the spring sports. They played well and won their first three games by significant margins. In the finals they were unable to compete and lost by thirteen points. They had won thirty straight games before they were defeated. Coach Daniels was disappointed, as were the boys, but they would always remember this as a time of elation.

The following week the girls went to Macon. They won their first game by ten and the second by only one. In the third game everything was near perfect, as they won by fifteen points against a good team.

As in the boys' tournament, the girls lost the final game. It was close, the difference only four points. The same emotions were present once again for the coach and the players alike.

On the following Sunday April had several calls about the basketball tournament. She was a little surprised. Often one had to win it all to be remembered. Then she reminded herself that Attapulgus was not like some of the other places.

She went to Somewhere Else for a dual purpose. She needed to check the place, since she had been away. Secondly, she wanted to think about such matters as David, her father and Mary. She remained concerned about each.

She would be going to college in September. Where would she go? Where should she go? Perhaps she should stay at home because of the many problems and go to F.S.U. Why did one have to make so many decisions?

She heard a car drive up. She looked out to see Jerome moving toward the house. She smiled and felt a warm feeling inside.

Jerome smiled as he entered. He took both her hands; for a moment April thought he would pull her into his arms but he held her at arm's length. "Shall I tell you that you are the most beautiful lady in the world?"

"We wanted so much to win, Jerome. This could be the last opportunity, as it will all end shortly. Robert felt the same way. It would have been so nice."

In less than ten minutes Jerome said, "I have some work to do. It is essential that it be completed. Welcome home." He pulled her closer and kissed her lightly. He turned and in a moment was gone.

Though April had planned to remain longer, she closed her house and returned to her family's home.

The next hour was one of joy. She saw her father in the best mood ever. "Tomorrow we get our plants in the ground and under the shade. Ain't it nice to see things fall into place once again?" This was the first time in months that Joseph resembled his old self.

She next went to David's home. She knocked, turned the knob, as it was unlocked, and yelled, "Anyone home?"

David met her as she entered the room. "Congratulations," he said, a smile on his face. "You represented your school and community so well." April was stunned at the change. She saw Mary sitting in a chair across the room. She, too, greeted April with a big hug.

"David is in good spirits," Mary said. "We have been talking. He has told me how dedicated some people have been in recent weeks. He placed you at the top of the list." She beamed with delight.

"No, Mary. It has been you and Mother that have been responsible. I am so pleased with my dear brother. Is Joe around?"

"He is in Midway playing golf. He and his father will be off and running in the morning. He may be unable to play, with the season upon us," Mary said.

As April returned home her mother asked, "How did you find David?"

April beamed. "He has changed. He is going to be all right, but he still has some doubts. I am pleased. Mary was with him. She has made a big difference. However, I am concerned about Mary and Joe. All is not as it should be."

"He has had too much time on his hands because of inactivity. He will be better now. So will your father. I can sense a change as the season starts."

"Yes, I do think Joseph will be a different person now," April said. "I could tell that a few hours ago. But I am still concerned about Joe."

"He will be fine. Now that David is better I want you to slow down a bit."

Chapter 56

The usually calm Michael John paced back and forth in his room like a caged lion. He picked up the telephone and dialed a number. "This is Michael John, Eric. Are you busy?"

"Grading papers as usual. I haven't learned as yet another way, another method, to evaluate students." Eric knew that he would never change. Students had to learn to express themselves and a true-false test offered little to improve communication skills.

"If you can spare a few moments, I'd like to run over and talk with you. Perhaps you need a break?"

"Come on. Indeed I do. It would be nice to see you. Mother is at a church meeting. I have no idea where Jerome is. I need some company."

Michael John got into his car and drove down the lane. He had not felt so unsure of himself since he was in grade school. He held the steering wheel tighter because his hands were moist and shaking.

"Come in," Eric said as he opened the door. "I'm happy to see you." He rubbed his eyes. "I guess the next thing will be glasses.

"How are your folks? Tell me about David."

"Some in the family feel that he is better. I think there is still room for a lot of healing yet. Few couples were as close as Kathy and David. I had wondered earlier if he would make it but now I believe he will. Most of the credit goes to Mother, April and Mary. No three could have been more patient. They have made the difference. And your family?"

"There are two items that concern me more than a little. Mother seems a little depressed, as she feels that we are here because of her. She feels that Jerome remains because of her and she even has similar thoughts about me.

"Naturally my thoughts return periodically to Jane Dawson. She was special. She was a happy person and I was happy when I was with her. Oh, how she loved life and she just seemed to like everybody. You know the story. She just left suddenly and no one seemed to know why. But that's history, as they say.

Then he asked Michael John, "What's on your mind? I'm not sure I liked the way you sounded over the telephone."

"I've got to talk with you and I really am at a loss as to where I should start. I'm not even sure I should be talking to you!"

"The Lee and Randolph families have always been close enough to talk about anything. Please go ahead."

"I need to know about you and Robin, Robin Wells. You two even seem closer since Jane went away. I have to know."

Eric was about to ask why; then it was obvious the question was not necessary. "I doubt that two people closely associated for six months could be closer — closer friends, that is." He smiled and saw an expression of relief appear on Michael John's face, then he continued.

"We have a great deal in common. Actually we are similar in many ways. We are both teachers. We have little experience. We both come from families with limited resources and we like many of the same things. But that is all. There will not be a different type relationship. We don't love each other in that way. It's that simple. Did I answer your question? Is this what you needed to know?" He looked at Michael John, whose expression provided an answer.

He then asked, "You are quite fond of her, aren't you? I don't blame you. She is a precious and special lady. She is a good teacher. In time she will be used as a model by which to evaluate others. I just hope the people of Attapulgus know what a prize they have!"

Michael John asked, "Then you are not in love with her?" Eric wasn't sure if it was a question or an expression of relief.

"No, but I think you are. If I had been smart, I'd have known. Stupid me. It was there before my eyes several times at Somewhere Else."

"How do you think she might feel about me? Has she said anything? Has she given you a clue? Don't try and make me feel good. I want the truth. I am learning to live with it."

"She likes you very much. I don't think she understood you for a time. You are quiet. You don't let people see you until you feel very secure. But yes, I am sure she likes you very much. She has made some remarks. She has asked me many questions. She likes you a great deal."

"Eric, please don't just try and make me feel good. This is too important. If she didn't like me, I could understand. I am not tall and handsome, like so many. My formal education is limited. She is a teacher, and as you say, will be a great one. It was not easy for me to finish high school. You see, I don't have much to offer a girl. Besides, I've never been out with girls. I wouldn't even know how to court one!"

"You are not being fair to yourself, Michael John. First, you have character, the most important thing. Then there's your skill. If I could only build and fix things like you! You have — you are all the real things that count."

"I just don't know," Michael John said. He continued to feel uncertain and insecure.

"Look. You have a special family. Your father is the best of farmers. There is a huge plantation. There is a County Commissioner in your family. Who could ask for more?"

"What you said may be true but these are not the things that matter the most. Some day I'll explain. I've kept you from your work long enough. I remember a teacher saying something once about having 'miles to go before you sleep.'

"I want you to do me one favor. The next time Robin is at Somewhere Else and we are both there, I want you to find a reason, an honest reason, I hasten to say, to leave early so I can take her home." Then he quickly said, "Goodnight, Eric. Thank you for seeing me," and was out the door without another word. Eric noted a special spring in his walk.

April said, "I will expect you Friday night, Michael John. I need you. I need a cook, among other things. School is nearly out and tobacco season about to start. I have an unusual guest list. Mother, David, Mary and Charles have accepted invitations. Joseph, Joe and Stephen seem to have conflicts. School is almost out so I will have Miss Wells and Mr. Lee coming. Also, I want to get David away from the house. He is better and we must do all we can to keep him on track. I'll have some of the others next time."

Friday night was cool, but clear. The dinner was near perfect and nearly everyone ate too much. David talked and smiled; April could not have been more pleased.

"I have to finish a payroll," Charles said an hour after dinner.

"I'll go with you," Martha said. "The others do not have to leave." Yet Mary and David decided to depart with Charles and Martha.

Thirty minutes later Eric stood quickly and said, "It's just like me! Can't remember anything. I've let something slip. Michael John, could you see Miss Wells home?" Without further conversation Eric left, as soon as he saw Michael John nod. In a moment he was in his car and gone.

April said, "Charles said the referendum will pass about school consolidation. He also said our community would change drastically. I'm sure you are concerned." She directed her statement to Robin.

"What will you do?" Michael John asked.

Robin replied, "I'll teach here again next year. Then I'll take a look once again. We live a day and a year at the time. That's all we are given." She smiled.

"Help me get things back in place," April said. "I'm going to send you two straight home!" Both blushed noticeably.

As they drove away Michael John said, "Our community has been so fortunate. I don't think many, perhaps most, have figured out what will happen. Or, perhaps they have and do not talk about it."

"Sometimes there are those that refuse to think about reality," Robin said. "This is nearly always true of all negative issues."

"I don't want to talk about such things," Michael John said. "I'd rather talk about you. There are so many things I would like to know."

"There is little to tell. You see, I don't know my early history. I was adopted by two wonderful people. They were good people, so very good. They were quite poor, but there was a great deal of love.

"After I finished high school I applied for a scholarship. I was lucky and received a full scholarship. Now I am a teacher and have a chance to help others to prepare for life.

"During my senior year at college a tornado struck our home, our little farm house. My adoptive parents were killed instantly and the house destroyed. There was a little insurance, but it took all of it to bury them. By the time adequate graveyard markers were in place, there was nothing left. But I was all right. I still had my scholarship.

"I finished college, applied for a place in Attapulgus and received the position. It worked as if God had guided me here. I asked my college advisor how he knew of a position open here. He simply said it was his job to know such things.

"Before I left I attempted to secure some information, as I wished to express my appreciation to some civic group, corporation, company or individual for my assistance but I was unable to determine such. They gave some reasons, some good reasons, why they did not disclose this information. It was a disappointment.

"Say, we're nearly home, but this is Friday night and I can sleep late tomorrow. Why don't we ride some more and you tell me about you," Robin said.

"I wasn't ready to go home either," Michael John replied. He was glad it was dark because he felt himself blush.

"There is little to tell about me. What you see is it. My role is quite different from many but I enjoy what I do. Hopefully, I do something to earn my keep."

"I like what I see," Robin said. "You never let me, and perhaps not others, see the real you. I would guess April knows the most about you!"

"April knows a lot about a lot of things. Guess that is bragging but I believe it correct."

"I want to really know you, Michael John. Am I being too forward? I want to know what you will do with your life. I not only wish to know what you think, but know of your dreams and ambitions as well. Tell me what you see two, five or ten years from now. Oh, I'm sure no one can be certain but we all have our dreams."

"As you say, we all have our dreams and I suspect for me they are and will always be just that — dreams.

"I enjoy building. In a way I may get some of the same pleasure you get when you see a student learn. I like machines as well. I do a lot of fixing. This gives me satisfaction, knowing I have done something worthwhile. And a year or two or five or more from now? Would you really like to know?"

"Oh yes, Michael John. I would be very interested in hearing. Do you suppose they would fire a teacher if they found her parked with a very special gentleman?"

"I am told that some parking is done out near the Crescent Lake but I cannot say." He did not care to tell her he had never parked before with a girl.

"Is this all right?" Michael John asked as he pulled in under some trees.

"Oh yes. I feel very safe with you. I think I would always feel that way. You know, I have often wondered as to your thoughts during the occasions we have spent at Somewhere Else. A dozen times I wondered how I could get you interested in a little country girl that doesn't even know who she is." She reached over, took his large hand and placed hers in it. Then she moved their hands so that his touched her warm cheek.

At this moment Michael John knew he was no longer a child. He knew this girl had set him afire. It was a desire, and a tenderness as well, a combination he had not previously experienced. It was a mysterious urgency. He desired to touch her, to smooth her blowing hair, to kiss those red lips and her face and her pale throat, and to hold those little hands in his large strong ones. He did not know how to accomplish these desires he had. He longed to have her arms around his neck.

This girl was different from all others he had known. Suddenly, it struck him that she might not know how he felt or know his inner thoughts. Her actions could be based on compassion, on sympathy. It frightened him.

She looked at him and gave him a blissful smile. Her eyes gleamed and sparkled. She reached to pull him toward her; it was their first encounter. Her touch ran up his arm like a bolt of lightning and struck violently at his heart. Then she was even closer, smoothing his shirt as she looked up into his face. It was then that he knew. He pulled her toward him and she moved even closer toward him at the same moment. He held her and gave her his first kiss on those beautiful, moist, red lips. It was sweeter and more fragrant than he had dreamed during his days and weeks of anxiety. Again, he looked into her eyes; they were beaming and joyous.

"I've never before kissed a girl in my whole life," Michael John said. Quite by accident, his hand rubbed against her ample breast and he hurried to say, "Sorry. I meant no harm. This is all so new to me."

In response Robin pulled him against her once more, as her lips sought his and they kissed long and deeply. Both seemed in a dream world all of their own. "I have never felt this way," she said.

Moments later Michael John released her. He looked at her pretty face in the moonlight. "You asked me what I wanted to do with the rest of my life. I can tell you but you would likely think it foolish."

"Tell me. I want to know this very second. Let me judge for myself."

"I want to build a house with my own hands that would become more than a house. It would become a home. I want to find a very special girl that could and would love me in spite of all my shortcomings. In return she would let me give her all my love, everything I have to give. In time, I would want a family so that I could love them and in turn, be loved. I guess all of this sounds silly to you. As I said, it is a dream and perhaps that is all it can ever be."

"Would you want this person to be a part of the church and school and community life? Would you wish this person to be uncomplicated and just enjoy the beautiful simple life, to enjoy nature and all that God has offered? Would you wish to find one so foolish that she believes even just two people can make a life better for others as well as themselves?"

"Are you saying what I believe you are saying?" Michael John asked.

Suddenly, Robin reached over once again and pulled him to her, seeking his lips and holding him tight. Then she pulled away. "I have no words that can tell you what I feel, what I hope you feel. This is the best moment of my life. Please take me home now and let me think about all we have said in these moments. I think we need some time, both of us. There will be a tomorrow and another tomorrow. Yes, I think it is time for me to go home. I cannot take this all in at once. Thank you for a lovely evening. It all seems like a dream."

CHAPTER 57

"You are the best. This is a proven fact," Gena said. "You have no choice."

"Our school needs you," Meggie said. "I have never known you to be indifferent about our school."

"I cannot take on more," April said. "Such a speech would require time for research and writing. Then it must be memorized. I must say no."

"Who will represent us?" Gena asked. "Robert is as busy as you. Also, he is not experienced."

"Meggie can do it," April said. "She is just the person. She has been in the shadows long enough. I'll give her a hand but she doesn't need it."

"You are elected, Meggie," Gena said, smiling. "I don't believe you have told me how you feel about the topic. Just where do you stand on capital punishment?"

"My personal feelings should not be a concern. The issue is really based on what the law may say. Our highest law is the Constitution of the United States," Meggie responded.

"Then you'll do it?" Gena asked. "I knew we could count on you."

"I'll try. Even if I fail, I will have learned about things that are important," Meggie said. "I'll try but don't expect very much."

Three weeks later, after hours and hours of work, Meggie was declared one of the three finalists in the county. Two days later she was selected as the winner.

April asked Gena, "Have you seen the change in Meggie? How wonderful it is. This has given her the confidence, that last little boost she needed."

Yet it was Uncle Edd who was beside himself. "This tells me so many things," he said. "Many of my apprehensions have melted away."

A week later Meggie received an invitation to give her address before the Rotary Club in Midway. "I can't do that," Meggie said. "I don't know the first person. Also, they are all adults. I would not feel comfortable. In addition to that, they are all men. They don't have women in their club."

April smiled. "I'll go with you. Mr. Lee will be with you. They were nice to me when I delivered my speech. As you told me, you owe it to the Attapulgus School. I also think Uncle Edd would like for you to accept."

The day arrived. April and Eric Lee sat at the head table with Meggie. The program chairman introduced April and indicated she would introduce the speaker.

April said, "It is my pleasure to be with you again. I commend your organization for your support of our educational system and of our youth." She smiled and her eyes sparkled.

"Three years ago Meggie Winter was both the least known and best known student in Decatur County. Now this is behind us. Meggie is my schoolmate, my classmate, my housemate and my best friend. Equally important, she is a lady, a scholar, a thinker and a speaker. I present to you Meggie Winter!"

The group applauded generously as Meggie made her way to the microphone. She smiled at April, then at her many hosts. The audience seemed friendly but unsure as to what they might expect.

"I am here to make a presentation on a major issue of today, capital punishment." She began her address.

"On a Monday at high noon, in the very near future, we may expect nine robed officials, led by Chief Justice Warren E. Burger and followed by eight associates, to step forward in order of seniority and announce the decision reached relating to capital punishment. We all eagerly await their decision.

"Upon what must these nine men base their decision? Personal feelings? Religious beliefs? Customs of the past civilizations? These nine judges have taken an oath to uphold the Constitution of the United States, the highest law of our land. It is their responsibility to interpret the Constitution as written.

"What, then, does the Constitution have to say about capital punishment? Certainly it must tell us something! Would you believe it reveals nothing, absolutely nothing? Not once does it refer to this matter. In fact, it defines only one crime and that is treason.

"Then let us look at the amendments. Certainly something is to be found here. Yes, this is the place we find some answers. The Fifth Amendment, adopted in 1791, states that 'no person shall be deprived of life, liberty, or property without due process of law.' It would seem, therefore, that with due process of law this act may be permitted. Certainly this becomes obvious. So when the Eighth Amendment, describing cruel and unusual punishment, was adopted on the very same date, it could not have been interpreted to exclude capital punishment. I repeat, Amendments Five and Eight were proposed by the same Congress at the same time and adopted by the States, and thus, the people.

"The only other reference to this subject is found in the Fourteenth Amendment. It states '. . . nor shall any State deprive any person of life, liberty, or property without due process of law. . . .' So, in 1868, some seventy-seven years after Amendments Five and Eight were added, our Constitution reflected the same as in the previous century. Nothing else is to be found with reference to capital punishment in our highest law of the land.

"I do not propose to hazard a guess as to what these learned and gifted men will announce. On the last occasion the Supreme Court rendered an opinion on this subject, they delivered a five to four split decision. Their beliefs differed so greatly that there were nine different opinions as to why they voted as they did.

"Today those who oppose capital punishment usually cite such reasons as that it is morally wrong to take the life of another and that the poor and minorities make up the greatest number who have been executed. Those who support capital punishment suggest very strongly that such punishment is a major deterrent to crime.

"I am not here today to take a position, but to tell you what our Constitution stipulates. Until and unless another amendment is added through one of the four methods that we may amend our Constitution, I could only interpret capital punishment as legal.

"In conclusion, I leave you with these questions: What causes an individual to become involved in such conduct that would result in a capital crime? Would it have been different if Mother and Father had taken time to be a real mother and father? Could the math teacher, so intent on explaining how one is to find two unknowns, have recognized the real needs and taken a personal interest? Could the minister, so busy with his paperwork, his reports and his next crusade, have found some time and means to satisfy a basic need? Could the employer, more interested in the bottom line of a balance sheet or profit and loss statement, have made a difference? Could the best friend have taken a few moments to explain that popularity and materialistic needs were of less value than were thought? Shall all of us not share in this tragedy? Let us think on these things."

When Meggie finished the group rose as one and applauded generously. Meggie had been letter perfect. The president of the club presented Meggie with a Savings Bond. "Perhaps this is one small step in an effort to help one who will certainly help others. May God bless you."

Following lunch Coach Daniels assembled those in the gym that had indicated an interest in spring sports. He began, "We have two problems that I will identify immediately. First, I see a girl among us. Perhaps she is really a boy or she is completely lost." Everyone laughed and looked toward April, but she did not speak. She only smiled.

"No, just kidding," Coach Daniels said.

"She has never been lost nor has anyone ever failed to identify her sex." He blushed as he spoke, then continued. "She has been approved by the Georgia High School Association. We will need to amend our training facilities."

"We have three spring sports, which, as you know are track, baseball and golf. You select the two you prefer. There are not enough hours to get involved in three. We have eight baseball games scheduled, three track meets and three golf matches before the tournaments. You have some decisions to make.

"Obviously, I cannot be everywhere with everyone. I must have a commitment from you to work at times without supervision and little assistance. If you feel you cannot operate this way, you should not be here. You will also maintain your grades."

April selected the mile relay and the four-forty relay. "It's very demanding," Coach Daniels said.

"I can do it," she said. "My difficulty will be in the exchange."

The days passed and the weather got hotter but the team worked and worked. They perfected the passing of the baton and improved their speed and durability.

As they participated in the local meets which preceded the District Meet April received many stares and many shakes of the head. At one meet a lad from Apex commented, "Your school will do anything to win. You think we are going to stay behind that girl just to watch and, no doubt, she is a sight to see, but your trick won't work. We're too smart for that." It brought a lot of laughter.

At the District Meet the relay team of Robert, Kenneth, Glenn and April ran off from the competition. A newspaper article reported: "A track relay team that includes a girl wins the tournament. There are many, however, that believe this girl, who has invaded a man's world, cannot measure up against the best in the state."

The day of the State Meet arrived. News that a girl was participating had reached the track long before the participants. For the first time there seemed to be a greater interest in the relays than in such popular events as the hundred-yard dash.

The gun sounded and the Attapulgus team ran like never before. When they finished they had run themselves into the victory circle. The spectators could not believe their eyes.

When April was singled out after the race she said, "When you run for the best school and for the best coach and with the best teammates, a number of good things will happen."

Only five Class C schools had golf teams in the second district. This was not difficult to understand, as a Class C school meant a high school enrollment of under a hundred and fifty. In places this small there were few public or private golf courses. Again, Attapulgus was blessed, because of the course at the Crescent Lake Country Club.

The four person team was made up of Robert White, who had been selected captain, Carl Lynch, Travis Cross and April. They played extremely well in the district and won by a whopping thirty-one strokes.

They went to the State Tournament, which was held at Valdosta. It was only a two-hour trip so they were well rested and relaxed when they arrived.

"If we can play well out of the traps," Coach Daniels said, "we have a chance." There had been no traps at the Crescent Lake Country Club and the four had worked several hours on several occasions in the traps at April's home.

The media were there in greater numbers than ever. April's name, because she was a girl, seemed to be a household name. When she was asked to make a statement she said, "I have the good fortune of being here with three fine young men and golfers. I have a fine coach. We will certainly try to do our very best."

April played extremely well. Her iron shots were accurate. Her putting on the greens was superior. When the day was over she had shot a one under par seventy-one and the total score for her team was three hundred and five. The team that finished second had a score of three hundred and twenty-two. Attapulgus had won by seventeen strokes. April also received a trophy as the low medalist, having won by two strokes over a nice young man from north Georgia.

When approached after the ceremony, April again praised her coach and teammates. How did she feel about being the best golfer of the day? "The men were kind," she said. "Women, as a group, will never be able to compete with men. Our team wishes to express our thanks for your hospitality. It is not important that anyone know

April Randolph but it is significant that we represented Attapulgus High. Our school and our coach made the difference!"

CHAPTER 58

"You are sure some kind of brother! Our track team wins. Our golf teams wins and you don't even say a word! After all, it isn't everyday that a girl competes in a boy's world!" She had brought a folder with her.

"I'm sorry. For a few days I have seemed to move backward. This is the time of the year that Kathy enjoyed so much." As April embraced her brother she realized that he could not leave Kathy yet.

"If we could have had a child," David said. "We both wanted one so much. I think that would have helped. In a way, Kathy would still be with me."

April was about to speak but she could see that David wanted to say more.

"I keep asking myself as to my belief in God. Some days I think so, then I think of the awful things and I say no. I am not sure. I've been reading some. There are those who believe God was invented by the rich to keep the poor 'in their place.' Other writers point out the inconsistencies in our Bible. April, I don't know what to believe! I thought I was at a new level and was on my way, but now I find myself slipping back into an area of uncertainty."

"David, there are many people, smart and important people, that believe many things. As we have talked over the weeks I did some research. I wanted to know what the beliefs were of some that we have all known through their discoveries, their inventions and their accomplishments. When I discovered some of their beliefs, I made some notes. I did not follow much of a pattern. I simply read about some of our greats and some I had felt strongly about because of their contributions. Perhaps you will be surprised about some of these. Would you care to know what some of these thought and said?"

David nodded. "I think it would certainly be of interest. Perhaps it may give me something that I need."

"I shall not attempt to rationalize why they said or why they felt as they did. I have not probed that deeply yet. It is simply a summary of their feelings about life and death. I have sought people in literature, science, politics and other areas."

"I understand," David said. "I'm listening."

"George Washington said, 'The liberty enjoyed by the people for these States of worshiping Almighty God, agreeable to their consciences, is not only among the choicest of their blessings, but also of their rights.'

"Thomas Jefferson said, 'It does no injury for my neighbors to say there are twenty gods or no God. The question before the human race is whether the God of Nature shall govern the world by His own laws or whether priest and kings shall rule it by fictitious miracles.'

"Calvin Coolidge said, 'It is only when men begin to worship that they begin to grow.'

"Now we will go to some scientists.

"Charles Darwin, whom man loves or hates, said this. 'The mystery of the beginning of all things is insolvable by us; and I for one must be content to remain an agnostic.'

"Thomas Huxley said, 'I neither deny or affirm the immortality of man. I see no reason for believing in it, but, on the other hand, I have no means of disproving it.'

"Albert Einstein said, 'I do not believe in the God of theology who rewards good and punishes evil. I cannot imagine a God who rewards and punishes the objects of His creation, whose purposes are modeled after our own — a God, in short, who is but a reflection of human frailty. Neither can I believe that the individual survives the death of his body, although feeble souls harbor such thoughts through fear or ridiculous egotism.'

"Thomas A. Edison had this to say. 'So far as religion is concerned, it is a damned fake — Religion is all bunk.'

"I have listed some writers. William Shakespeare said, 'In the matter of religion, the choice lay between Christianity and nothing. I choose nothing.'

"William Faulkner, a Nobel prize winner in 1950, said, 'I believe that man will not merely endure; he will prevail. He is immortal, not because he alone among creatures has an inexhaustible voice, but because he has a soul, a spirit capable of compassion and sacrifice and endurance.'

"Thomas Payne, who gave us the name of our country, said this. 'I believe in one God and no more; and I hope for happiness beyond this life.'

"Then there was the great statesman and Prime Minister of England, Benjamin Disraeli. 'Religion should be the rule of life, not a casual incident in it.'

"David, I have selected these few from a hundred that have strong feelings. I have attempted to give a number that are quite divided as to how they feel or believe. I must confess, I was disappointed to know how some of these men felt. I will spend some time reviewing these, as well as doing other research."

"How do you feel, April? You and Charles are the thinkers in this family."

"How can you say that? Charles and I are very limited in such matters, most matters.

"I am not ready to discuss this at the moment. I think I know how I feel, but I want some time yet before I can really express myself as I wish. The matter is much too important to take lightly. The entire future of an individual is at stake. You, of all people, would know that. But in the near future, be it right or wrong, good or bad, I will express myself.

"I am two houses down." April smiled. "I have a heavy load for a few weeks. But if you need me, I'll be there."

In a week, April returned to David's home. He remarked, "I had not expected you so soon."

"I'm on schedule now. I've had some time to think about what we have discussed. But first, I am interested as to your feelings about the people I had listed for you to review. Do you wish to express yourself?"

"There were some surprises, some major surprises. I suppose I would say that I am disappointed in some of them."

"Such as?"

"Perhaps William Shakespeare. How could a man of such thought, a great thinker, feel this way? He chose nothing!

"I had guessed Faulkner would have felt the same. I don't know why I say this. I'm glad he spoke of man with a soul, man as immortal.

"I suppose we both may be disappointed in Einstein and Edison. I would never have thought they felt so. I guess it is because I admire their achievements to such a degree.

"Let me say two things at this moment. I guess I have a strong belief that you feel very strongly about our God.

"Secondly, thank you for your work, your assistance. It has been most useful in some hours of darkness. You didn't tell me how I should feel. But you knew, didn't you? You never once had a doubt. You let me work it out for myself. I believe I can sum up my feelings by saying I believe but I don't understand," David said. "Now why don't you tell me how you feel and why."

"I believe in God. I believe that God was the Father of Jesus. I cannot believe that a creation could be so perfect without God. I do not believe that man, as complex as he is, has evolved from lower animals. I do not require scientific proof of creation. I cannot prove some things but neither can others disprove the same.

"There are thousands and thousands of things I do not understand nor can I explain. Why is one born blind? Why is one born deformed? Furthermore, some are born where every opportunity is there for them. For others this is not so. My point is made.

"I have chosen Christianity in preference to some other religions for one specific reason. As I review all the founders of the many religions, I have found only One that lives. It is a major reason why I accepted Christianity over the others, though there are other reasons as well.

"I have so much more thinking and learning and growing to do yet. I felt it was important, however, that you know my beliefs. As you said earlier, you believed but you did not understand. I suspect we can know more but we will never fully understand. Perhaps we call this faith."

David said, "You cannot know the sleepless nights when I sigh and toss and turn and stretch out my hand, only to find an empty pillow, an empty place beside me."

"It will not always remain so. Time and belief and faith and a dozen other things will change this feeling," April said.

"Perhaps you are right. I owe you and others so much. I had so far to return, April. I didn't, for a time, believe there was a God and if there was, I didn't feel that I could accept Him. I didn't want to ever see another preacher, another church or another Sunday School room. You have no idea of the rage that was within me. I thought often of taking my own life but you helped me to see differently. Mother and Mary were always present or nearby. Some way I found something to keep me going. My work helped, but at the same time it nearly destroyed me — or perhaps I should say, I nearly destroyed myself. Now I am ready to move back into life. I will ask not to be rushed because I still have some things yet to sort out, to accept."

"You will succeed," April said. "I know this now. I know some other things but we will not talk about them at this time.

"I have one last thing to say and I have debated this many hours. We talk about the will of God. There are some that interpret this to mean He wants it, He desires it, He demands it and so it will be.

"I feel it means He will permit it, He will accept it, He will follow the laws of nature He has created which, in a sense, are His own laws.

"A man can stand on a railroad track in front of a moving train and say that God will not let the train strike him. Not so. He has made man in his own image. Man is God's creation. And man must use the tools he has been given."

David said, "I have often thought about what Heaven is like. Where would such a place be? In what form? And where is Hell? And what is it like? Are there degrees of Hell?

"If one goes to Heaven, will he know people as he did in this life? What meaning will time have? What will we do twenty-four hours a day, if we have days? Will there be night and day? There are a thousand questions I cannot answer. I don't believe that any of us can know."

"David, suppose the two of us live a day at a time and do the best we can. Oh, we'll make errors and that is the reason we have a forgiving God. As so many things get more and more complicated, I have sought a more simple solution and perhaps I have found it. Mr. Abe Lincoln said he too wished something simple and he suggested we simply follow the first two commandments. If we love God with all our hearts and if we love our neighbor as we love ourselves, everything will work out. Think about this, David.

"I'll go. You have a life to live. Let's start all over again. I know you can and I am sure you will."

As April was returning to her home she thought about what Mike Harper had told some family members. "David has removed himself from the church but he will return. His deep moral teachings that you and others provided in early life remain deeply hidden at the moment but as soon as some of the pain is removed, as something replaces the anger, you will find him returning. It will take more time for David than some others because of the great loss."

Chapter 59

The Wednesday edition of the county newspaper told of the deaths of the three small white high schools in Decatur County. Attapulgus had voted fourteen to one against consolidation. Apex had voted twelve to one against and West Midway had voted three to two against but Midway, with the largest turnout ever, had voted twelve to one for consolidation. With a vast majority of the voters in Midway, the efforts of the smaller communities had been meaningless; the final passage had been five to one. In 1966 they would have one all-white high school unless the courts said something different.

Charles hoped the healing process would begin. For the last several weeks much had been said and written about the referendum. Feelings had run rampant and the antagonism between Midway and the rural areas had increased.

Attapulgus had expressed openly they did not wish to join an inferior school and had supplied statistics to support their claim.

Midway in turn had said Attapulgus had no feeling, no compassion for the hundreds of students housed in buildings constructed in 1912 and 1922.

Charles had never once doubted the outcome. Now he was glad it was over. He only hoped that the exchanges had not left a bitterness that would continue when they consolidated in 1966.

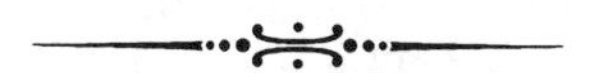

After the banquet three other closing events were to follow. There was the Honor's Day Program. Over four hundred guests braved the hot gymnasium, where all the honors and awards for the year were presented. Certificates for Honor Roll and Perfect Attendance were presented. Trophies and plaques were given. Athletic letters were presented.

Near the conclusion Coach Daniels stepped forward and Robert White presented him with a beautiful Browning automatic shotgun. On the stock of the gun were the statistics for each sport. It was a very good day for the school, the community and the hundreds of students.

Baccalaureate services were conducted in the auditorium on the Sunday before graduation. The students were responsible for the entire program, except the guest speaker. Again, the people gathered together. This time, however, the program seemed to reflect the beginning of an end, as the people knew that in two years all of this would be gone and it would never be the same again. After the program they did not speak of the future and seemed to move away to their homes more rapidly than in the past.

On Thursday evening the people gathered once again at 8:15 p.m., as they had done for a quarter century, to see and honor the graduates.

The graduates once more assumed all of the responsibilities, except the presentation of the awards made to the Honor Graduates by the Kiwanis Club and the presentation of the diplomas by Principal Baggs. April had been asked to give the main address.

She rose and spoke, "Members of the graduating class, Mr. Baggs and faculty members, parents, members of the student body and friends." She then paused for three or four seconds to look at all the people present, giving each the feeling she was speaking directly to that individual.

"Is it possible to paint a portrait of an entire graduating class? We have as many faces and as many voices as we have members. We do not all think or believe the same. This is as it should be. Often our motives and desires remain hidden. It is likely a medley of good and evil, promise and threat, hope and desire. We are likely different from our previous generations and we should leave a distinct picture of ourselves.

"Robert Frost, our respected American poet said: 'Two roads diverged in a wood, and I . . . took the one less traveled by, and that has made all the difference.' These words are as significant now as when written. We, too, must select a road. Some roads will lead to Viet Nam, while others will lead to Canada. Some roads will lead to a secular panacea; others will seek God. There will be a road representing right as opposed to wrong. There will be one of evil and another that is good. There will be a road for leaders, another for leaners.

"And as we travel these many roads we will falter and fail, sometimes falling on our faces. As this occurs, and surely it will happen, we ask our parents and our good friends not to rush to pick us up and make excuses for us, but to let us pick ourselves out of the dust and dirt and mud and stand once again on our own. It will provide us with a feeling of pride. Let us learn that special efforts are required to be successful and grow. Many times it is through our failures that we learn the most. We must learn that life is not always easy and that only through persistence and effort, our own efforts, are we able to become strong and successful.

"You know by now that we can be rebellious against convention or instruction, against state or fate, even against family and friends. We know we need more discipline than we get and we will need your patience and guidance to help us find the less traveled road.

"Now we have reached a point in our lives that it has become our right to select the road of our choice because God has made us this way. The two roads are before us and I believe we will choose the one less traveled and it will make all the difference.

"So now it is time for us to go. As we do so, we ask that you continue to remember us in your prayers and we, in turn, shall love you as we always have.

"Our class bids you an affectionate farewell."

Mr. Baggs rose after the applause and said, "This is our finest hour. It is likely that this class, in time, could become the most honored and successful ever."

The diplomas were presented, the tassels shifted and the benediction delivered. It was over.

This event was different from the event the previous Sunday. Few people were to leave immediately. They shook the hands of the graduates and told everyone how great the exercise had been. Everyone sought April to express how well she had performed.

Twenty minutes later Robert approached April. "I need to talk with you. I have something important to say and it cannot wait."

"I'll go directly home. Come anytime you wish. I'll change into something more comfortable." April was not sure just what Robert wanted. As she drove home she remembered she had previously told Robert she had some family plans but would be free the following evening. It seemed something of a puzzle.

Robert arrived fifteen minutes later. He joined the Randolphs, who had gathered in the den. "Your April was perfect," he told them, "but you knew that. I cannot remember when she has failed to perform at the highest level."

Martha said, "And you, Robert, are the most delightful young man I know. You are a total person. You have so much concern for others. I'm sure you have some specific plans."

"I am in the process of making some decisions," he said. "In fact, that is my purpose in being here tonight. I need to take a few minutes with April. I would not keep her from her family, as this is a special night."

April led Robert to the library and closed the door. "Robert, you don't seem to be your usual self. This is a great occasion and you do not seem to savor the moment as I would have expected. Is there something wrong? We have always been able to discuss most things." They seated themselves in chairs facing each other.

"I am leaving in the morning for a period of time. I have joined the Marines. I have taken some tests. If my basic training is acceptable, I can go directly to officer's school. I did very well on my tests."

Robert could see that April was most upset and was about to speak when he continued, "I had given much thought to this matter. It seemed to be the thing to do. I have not discussed this other than at home. I wanted you to be the first to know."

"Why, Robert, why? I am not sure this is where you need to be! I am not sure this is the kind of war our country should be involved in. Oh, I don't want you to run off to Canada but I am not sure about this. You don't have to go now. Your new life is just beginning.

"What will I do? What will I do without you? You have been a special part of my life for twelve years. The last two years have been very special, very meaningful."

"They have for me, too," Robert said. "I suspect you can never know, never guess, how special it has been.

"I must go now. This is your night with your family. I need to be with my family also. It will be quite early when I leave.

"This is the way I have to do it, April. I love my country. I can make a little money if I finish officer's school successfully. I can earn some college time. For each month I serve, I can get some college help. I can help Father and the twins if I am needed. I have to do this my way.

"Our lives must go on. Let us not have any of that 'I'll wait for you' and such. We must live our lives as best we can. In turn, we will see. It's best this way. It must be this way.

"Perhaps I will be back a short time after one or both training periods. We will have no tears and no goodbyes. I am going to kiss the only girl I have really ever known goodbye." He kissed April and for a moment held her close, then released her. He turned, opened the door and quickly left the room.

"Are you all right?" her mother asked as she returned to the den a minute later. "Robert walked through the room, said goodnight, and was gone. Has something happened?"

"Robert is gone, Mother. He has gone to war. He gave many reasons for his going. No one can guess how much I will miss him or how much he meant to me. It is likely that I will never know anyone like him. He was the best person I have ever known. You were so right when you described him earlier." She sighed. "Graduation had a different meaning than I had expected."

CHAPTER 60

"A week from today we will begin our tobacco harvest, about a week later than we usually start. This is our year. Everything looks good," Joseph said.

"Our crews are organized," Joe said. "At least school is out so some official won't be raising hell about school absences."

"We need one more rain," Joseph said, "but when I consider everything, I believe it is just as well we irrigate. The word rain scares me to death!"

"The stringing tables, sticks and twine are in place," Stephen said. "Happy days are here again." He could not hide his enthusiasm, nor did he try.

"It pleases me to see so many of you in a good mood," Martha said. "Perhaps it will slow our youngest son down a little. I don't see him very much."

"Let up a little on the boy," Joseph said, smiling. "Perhaps we have now reached a time when we can no longer remember the youthful energy and the restlessness of one his age." Joseph winked at his youngest son.

Joe said, "You may not realize it but only the big pond has a lot of water. We will need to move a lot of pipe to give the tobacco one last drink before next week. It will take about three or four days to get all the pipes in place."

"I'll take a night shift," Stephen said. "We can get it done."

David said, "Take the men I have been using. I'm fine for a week, maybe two." He turned and left. He did not enjoy the tobacco planning sessions.

"I could have used Robert this summer," Joseph said. "He could have helped us and he probably needed a job. It beats me why a young man wishes to go to war. We ain't got no business over there anyway."

"Better watch that Johnson," Joe said. "He wants to outdo the Kennedys. Yes sir, better watch that boy!"

Stephen said, "I believe April is really in love with Robert. I have never understood. He is big and strong, and a handsome boy as well, but they are so poor and I see little chance of things getting better. I'd wait for Victor McPherson. Now there is an ideal prospect. He has everything."

April moved quietly to the door and left the group. It was not a time to make an issue of it.

Joseph moved from his chair. "Gotta go, folks. Tobacco needs one more good drink. Stephen, don't you be running off. You can frolic later."

April said to Michael John, "I need to see you."

Her brother smiled. "Is it car repair, bird houses or lawn chairs?"

"No car repair. There are some other things. Meet me in the gazebo in fifteen minutes."

As April waited on her brother she thought about how much he had advanced in so many ways. She also was reminded that she had seen little of him recently.

She heard a voice, "What is it you want? You do know that Papa expects me 'Johnny on the spot' from now on."

"Sit down," April said. "I haven't said I wanted anything."

"You don't fool me a minute. Women always want something." He then asked, "You hear from Robert?"

"Yes. He writes but he is quite busy. I don't think he has too much spare time. The training program is quite comprehensive."

"Some bad things could happen to Robert. Have you thought about that?" Michael John asked. "Are you prepared for the worst?"

"Let's talk about something else," April said. "Actually, I want to talk about you. What of you and your future? It is time for things to happen! You have grown up. I want to know what you plan to do with your life?"

"You don't need to be concerned about me. You have Mother to help during this season. You have to get ready to go to college. David may need some attention yet for a spell, though he seems better. Don't concern yourself with me."

"You are twenty-two. I think it is time you found a lady friend. I know three or four you should consider."

"Now you didn't call me out to tell me I should find a girl?"

"Yes. That is exactly what I did. Do you want some names? I know one who has just graduated and one that will finish next year. It's time you moved along! I need a new sister. There is a lot next to David waiting for a house."

"What would you say if I told you I had a girl friend? What if I told you I am excited about a certain lady?"

"Are you telling me you have a girl friend? A close girl friend? Are you saying something has been going on behind my back? Something I didn't know?"

"I said suppose! And who are you to be looking over my shoulder? Who are you to get involved in my affairs?"

"I thought you were seeing a movie or perhaps bowling. You have a girl?"

"I have a girl. I have a very special girl. I believe you know her quite well. You seem to like her. I . . ."

"I don't believe it! You devil! You didn't say the first word."

"Robin Wells and I love each other very much. We have been in love for some time."

"I had thought perhaps Eric was interested."

"Oh, they are friends. Robin and I will marry before long. We wanted to be sure. Her school situation was not clear for a time, but now everything has fallen in place. I am the most fortunate ever," Michael John laughed. "Don't you hear me using better English? Even that is rubbing off."

"Next to you and Robin, I am the happiest person in the world. This is perfect, just perfect! You're still a devil for keeping me in the dark. It's obvious I must watch you more closely!"

"We wanted to be sure before we said anything to anyone. We have gone over our differences, and there are some, but we have much in common. We've talked about many things. We like simple things. Both of us want an uncomplicated life. She likes the outdoors. She loves a home. She wants children. Everything is just so perfect I am afraid it's too good to be true. I feel like I'll wake up and it isn't so."

"I'm so excited, so pleased. Have you thought about a time to marry? When are you going to tell the others? Our mother will be thrilled beyond belief!"

"We talked about Christmas. It seems practical. She will be off for two weeks or so. I want to get some plans. We are working on this. We are together on the type and style of home. I'll need to start as soon as tobacco season is over. Don't say anything to anyone. I want to be the one to tell my family."

It was Sunday. The Randolphs had gathered for Martha's lunch. It was a happy time. Joseph and Joe were busy again. Stephen was no longer in the classroom. David was on his way to recovery. It was the best of times. They smiled and spoke kindly of others. Martha felt a great sense of relief.

Suddenly, there was a knock on the back door and they looked at each other. "Now who can that be?" Joe asked. "Probably one of the hands needing something. They always need something!"

As Martha opened the door she looked into Jack's face and knew something was seriously wrong. "Come in and have some lunch. We were about to finish but there is always something left at our house!"

"Thank you, but no, I've had dinner. I've got to see Mr. Joseph. There is something wrong," Jack Jenkins said.

Everyone became alert when they heard those words. Joseph was on his way to the door. "Tell me, man," Joseph asked, "has something happened to your family? Tell me!"

"It isn't my family. It's the tobacco. Something awful is happening. All the leaves are turning brown. I have never seen such before!"

Joseph, Joe and Stephen rushed through the door and raced toward the nearest shade, only a short distance from the house. April moved quickly but she did not follow the men. She rushed to the telephone, found a number and dialed the local Coastal Plains Experiment Station.

"This is J. E. Lipton," she heard a voice say.

"Mr. Lipton, this is April Randolph. I am Joseph's daughter. Please forgive me for calling on Sunday and at the lunch hour. Something is happening or has happened to our tobacco. I'm sure my father would consider it a personal favor if you could drive out. It apparently is something new and could be quite serious."

"I've finished my lunch and I'm on my way. Tell your father I will be there in ten minutes," Mr. Lipton said.

It took April less than two minutes to get to the nearest shade. As she entered she heard Joseph say, "I've never seen anything like this. It certainly ain't no rain problem."

April said, "I called Mr. Lipton. He is on his way. He did say that no one earlier had let him know of a problem. I hope I have done the right thing."

"You did right, exactly right. I guess all we can do is wait." Then abruptly he exclaimed, "Boys, let's check the other shades. Certainly this is an isolated problem!"

April heard a voice behind her. She turned and saw that Mr. Lipton had arrived. "Thank you for coming. The men have gone to another shade to check and will be right back."

Mr. Lipton examined some leaves and the stalk, then probed around where the stalk entered the ground. Suddenly, he turned to April. "Tell your father I'll be back in a few moments. I need to use his telephone. Your mother or someone is in the house?"

"Yes." She did not have time to say more.

In three minutes Mr. Lipton had returned and was again looking at the plants. April heard voices, then saw her father; she did not have to ask or even guess. Joseph reported, "It's all the same everywhere. Can you help us? What is happening? It's not a water problem!"

Mr. Lipton shook his head. "I've never seen this before. I have called the field representatives in Tifton. They will leave immediately but it will take about two hours. At the moment, I wish to do two things. I'll return home and review the various diseases to see if I can identify the problem. Then I must know if this is an isolated case or if it is everywhere. I have some calling to do, but before I go, review with me all the chemicals you have used. Go through the entire process."

When Joseph had finished Mr. Lipton said, "I find nothing wrong. All the farmers are doing basically the same." He turned and rushed toward his truck.

In a few moments Michael John heard April say, "Come with me. We have something to do."

As April and her brother drove toward the big pond she said, "Joseph said it isn't water, but it certainly isn't too much rain, as last year; it has to be the water."

They looked at the pond. It was lower than they ever remembered seeing it. The water was not clear. "Take the containers, Michael John, and dip up some water."

As they returned they stopped to look at two other shades. The color of the leaves was somewhat darker than an hour earlier.

"You think the worst, don't you?" Michael John asked. It seemed that he had answered his question.

"Yes. I believe the tobacco has been destroyed completely. This is going to nearly destroy Joseph. As I think about it, I want to ask a favor of you."

"Certainly."

"Why don't you hold off on announcing your plans to marry? It would be best. Joseph has enough on his mind at the moment. He might even associate the cost of a house with your announcement. We want this event to be one to bring happiness to everyone, as it should." Michael John nodded in agreement.

Michael John said, "I'm worried about another thing. This will not do Joe any good. I've not liked what I've seen in recent months."

"This one event will change our lives here more than one can guess," April said. "I can just feel it, sense it." Again her brother nodded.

Two hours and fifteen minutes after the call the people from Tifton arrived. They looked at the tobacco and shook their heads. A moment later Mr. Lipton returned. "I found nothing in my materials to give a hint. I also learned this is an isolated case. The farmers have looked at their shades and called back."

April moved toward the men. She held two containers in her hands. "These are samples of water from the big pond, which is nearly dry. I would guess that it is a water problem. By the process of elimination, this must be the problem." The men looked at her, but did not respond.

An hour later a call from the Coastal Plains Station told them the answer. "It is a fungus, a rare fungus, in your pond water. It has happened a time or two before when ponds got too low. There is nothing that can be done. You will need to get your insurance people over. They will need to review this matter so you can file a claim."

Joseph remained silent. He did not move. He looked into space but saw nothing. He never even bothered to thank the man who had identified his problem. For the first time since he was a boy he felt he had no one and no place to turn to. He felt overcome, subdued.

He seemed clothed in pain, defeat and hate. He looked about him at the world, yet saw nothing. There were moments to follow when it seemed he would fight himself out of his prison; however, the bars of despair were too strong. The cloud over him remained. All of the attempts made by others did nothing to fill the void or ease the pain. Never again would he be the same.

Chapter 61

No one could have described Randolph Place. Few words were spoken and even those only in a low voice or a whisper. Joseph said nothing. After several unsuccessful efforts the family members did not attempt to say more. A stranger would have guessed a tragedy had occurred, that several family members had died.

On the third day Joseph said, "April, I want to talk with you. We will do so now and alone." April looked at Joseph. She could never recall him looking so dreadful.

"Anytime you wish," April said. "I have been trying to give Mother as much help as possible. She is very depressed. But you know this. Only when Kathy died did I see her look and act so."

Joseph did not respond about the welfare of his wife. April wondered if he even heard. "Let's go out to the gazebo where we can be alone." It was in the middle of the day and the temperature had soared to nearly a hundred degrees, yet Joseph seemed totally unaware of the heat.

"I had a call from Bruce McPherson today," Joseph said, taking a seat.

"Oh? I suppose bankers always have to think of money sooner or later and apparently he preferred sooner."

"No, this is not what he called about. I talked money with him yesterday. He had something else on his mind. He said that Victor was home from college and would like very much to see you while he was home for a few days."

April said nothing but continued to look into her father's face, waiting for him to continue. Then she said, "Do you not think Victor is old enough to speak for himself?"

He either ignored, or didn't hear, her question. "I think it would be nice if you could go out with this fine young man. He will be returning to Harvard soon."

April continued her silence.

"He is a very special person," Joseph continued. "He is a handsome young man and quite intelligent. He comes from a good family, an old Attapulgus father. His family is very wealthy and in time he will be also. I think you would enjoy the company of this exciting man. I am sure you should be pleased with his interest in you because he can have most anyone he wishes, as is plain to see. Bruce also seemed to be pleased that his son would have such an interest in you. I believe he is as pleased as I am. I hope that you might find a special interest in him. He will truly be a 'catch' for the lucky one that gets him."

Not once had April interrupted or even attempted to interrupt her father. It was not her desire at the moment to bring any additional anxious moments to his burdened life. She decided she must choose her words carefully, very carefully.

"Joseph, he seems to be many of the things you have described. He is a handsome man. I am sure he is intelligent. Even without the family money he would have been accepted at Harvard because of his great mind. Yes, he is or will be a very rich man some day. I suppose he will work with his father with the understanding that he will assume the father's responsibilities in time, perhaps as soon as he can learn something of the people with whom the bank deals. Yes, Joseph, all of these things are true. But I must tell you, I do not care for this man, nor do I trust him."

"Now, April, you are seeing a brash young lad you met some years ago before either of you knew much about this world or about each other."

"Joseph, certain things are obvious about Victor McPherson. His interest is in a world completely different from the world I know, for a world I would not seek. After our unfortunate beginning I really tried to be fair. I didn't care for his company then. Nothing has happened to make me feel differently."

"There are two things I must say," Joseph said. "I don't know that you will like either, but the time has come for people to say what they think and what they feel and . . ."

"I just did. I told you how I feel. What more is there to say?"

Joseph's face turned red and April could see his anger. She knew that he was under great pressure and that it would not take much for him to lose control.

"I am your father, young lady. I think that recently you have been so involved with your own self and accomplishments and your little playhouse that you have forgotten you are a member of the household and that much has been done by me — and your mother and others who remember what is important."

"Joseph, I know life has not been easy or kind for you and for others. For more than a year I'm sure that you've felt that everything that can go wrong, has. Because of this I have doubled my efforts to accept the assignments for which I am responsible. I have watched my mother endure a painful period and I have made special efforts and done everything within my power to help the family. At the same time I have attempted to help David overcome his great depression. If I have failed, you have an obligation and responsibility to point out these failures. I don't always agree with your policies and your beliefs but I have never failed, to the best of my knowledge, to avoid doing anything that would create a problem for you or make life more difficult. Would you please explain to me where I have failed?"

"Have you lost sight of our family? The efforts to become someone? Our need to work together? Ain't you realized we have a crisis, a dilemma, a crunch to consider? I think our entire family has been considerate of you as you have gone from one event to another, while someone has been required to pick up the slack while you were making a name for April and having fun.

"Here you are all depressed because a young man has gone to a war. He didn't have to go. He is a young man with an unstable family background who may or may not become something. Oh, he will probably be able to run a filling station or even a service station perhaps, but this ain't the issue.

"Here is Victor, who is going somewhere. He has it all. I ask you to consider seeing him. I ain't demanding you become serious with this man. I just ask you, because he is special and because there are some needs at the moment."

"Let's go back to Robert White," April said. "We can't leave that subject yet. You know this young man. He has been in our home. He has worked for you. He has worked for Michael John. He has a scholastic average in school of over ninety-six. He helps his father, his sisters. Are you saying that because his father is poor, there is a problem? Have you ever heard of an unkind thing about Robert and his family? Are we talking about values and standards? I know of no better human being in the world! He has more character than most anyone I have ever known. He is good, honest, fair, thoughtful . . ."

"He is yesterday! This is a new day. Let's forget Robert. Let's talk about now. It's time to be realistic. Let's look at life as it really is. This may be difficult for you because I have always made sure you had everything. There are times when I wonder if you have forgotten this also!"

April took a moment in an attempt to compose herself. She thought, I must remain calm. This is not the time to say things that will hurt him.

"Joseph, I know you are upset and depressed. I understand. The family understands. Certainly we are all realistic enough to know of the time and money and satisfaction one needs as a part of one's life, but these things are gone. No one can change that, not even God."

"Let's leave God out of this. I don't think He knows us anymore. I don't think He has known us very much in recent years. You mentioned our losses. We are nearly a million dollars in debt. Part of this is from last year, part from this year and part from a balance we owe on my land.

"The fact is, I will need some liberal terms, some understanding, in dealing with this problem. There are those who can help us. We need this. Certainly it can only be beneficial to keep a good relationship with the bank — with the McPhersons. This is a time to be cooperative and considerate. I would think it proper, an honor, actually, to have Victor ask you out. I am sure dinner or a movie or an evening of dancing can be fun for the two of you.

"I trust you will think of your family, your brothers and your mother and for their sake make some practical and reasonable decisions." Before April could even respond Joseph had stood up and hurriedly retreated to the house without another word.

April was not even aware of the minutes that passed after her father had left. Then she heard a voice. "I didn't know where you were. Everything has been so hectic and we have all been so busy, I haven't seen you," Charles said as he sat in a chair next to her.

For a minute April said nothing, then abruptly she asked, "What did you say? I'm afraid I wasn't listening."

From what she had said and the look upon her face Charles knew that something was wrong. He said, "I have missed you but no one has had a spare minute. Perhaps I interrupted your thoughts. You have been so busy, and with Robert leaving, I'm sure this has not been a good time for you."

April said, "I must go in. I am not feeling too well. I'll be better tomorrow." She left and hoped that Charles would not know of the conversation with her father.

A few minutes later Charles walked into the breakfast room and saw his mother preparing for the next meal. He knew his mother was going through a difficult time.

He mentioned, "I saw April a few minutes ago. She didn't seem her usual self. I suppose it is a combination of the tobacco loss, Robert leaving and making some decisions about her future. She can't put off her college decision much longer. Many of the colleges, the good colleges, have a cut-off point, regardless of one's academic standing."

"Charles, I think it is all these things. Certainly Robert leaving and his leaving so abruptly without anyone knowing has been upsetting and disappointing. They were close. She has also helped me more than ever before, realizing that it was not a good time for me either. And yes, she has some doubts as to her future in relation to college. Her talents, as you said earlier, will make a decision difficult. I also think she is tired. Reviewing her last three months, I don't know how she did it. There are times when she has been with David that no one knew about. She loves David very much and understands his loss. But, knowing April as we do, she will be up and going tomorrow. It is her way."

At ten-thirty the next morning April was called to the telephone. Victor said, "There is a great show on in Tallahassee and I want to take the most beautiful girl out to dinner and then the show. Tell me you will accept my invitation, even on such short notice."

"I learned you were back home. You have finished your work at Harvard?"

"No, not exactly. My father has accused me of going to school as a profession, but there are two or three special courses I want to take. Only one more quarter. And you? How have you been?"

"It has been an unusual time for all of us, but we will make it. I guess you could say the Randolphs are survivors.

"Victor, if we could go early it would be helpful. I'm a tired girl and I don't care to be away too long from the family at this time. Perhaps you may wish to consider another time and if so, I can understand."

"Oh no. I can pick you up a five-thirty, dinner at six-thirty, a movie at seven-thirty and home by ten-thirty, no later than eleven."

"Bankers are always one step ahead of most everyone! I will be ready."

"I'm really looking forward to seeing you again. I will be the envy of everyone in Tallahassee! See you at five-thirty," Victor said.

Victor arrived at the exact time he had specified. He was dressed in a banker's blue suit, tailored to perfection. His blue and red tie blended well and his fresh white shirt was without a wrinkle.

Martha answered the door and said, "Please come in, Victor. Mr. Randolph is in the den. I'll tell April you are here."

Joseph rose as Victor entered. They shook hands warmly. "Welcome, Victor. I know that Bruce is delighted to see some help on the way. It seems he can never get away from the business world and a man should get away from time to time. Please sit down. You already have that banker's look."

"It seems that it would be appropriate for you to take some time off, Mr. Randolph. I think that you and my father have many things in common."

"It seems I will have a great deal of time to do other things. As you know, my tobacco was destroyed for a second time."

"So I have learned. I guess lightning does strike twice in the same place. But you are a tough one, a survivor. I also learned something else. It seems you are to be challenged for your commissioner's seat, but I'm sure it isn't to be a serious challenge."

Joseph felt his face turning red but he controlled his emotions. "Yes, I heard one of the men at the Clay Company may throw his hat into the ring."

"I think," Victor said, "that he is wasting his time and money. Sir, I don't believe I would lose any sleep over this one."

"Welcome home again, Victor," April said as she moved into the den. She held out her hand as a way of greeting. "And look at you. Had I known you were to dress so, I would have put on something less casual. Maybe I should change."

"Oh no. You look great. Everyone will be looking at your natural beauty. I only dressed this way to please my father."

"I'm sorry you can't take me on a tobacco tour once again. I will always remember that special day. It was the best of times," Victor said. He then looked at Joseph Randolph and realized he had said the wrong thing. He could see the painful expression on Joseph's face, his eyes indicating the tobacco situation was still fresh in his memory.

"Victor is taking me to dinner and then to a special movie he has recommended. He has promised that he would have me in early, perhaps ten-thirty."

"Early to go, early to return," Victor said with a big smile on his face. "We'll ask to be excused and be on our way."

The ride to Tallahassee was really an update on Victor. With some degree of modesty and with the assistance of April he related he had graduated at the University of Georgia with highest honors and was doing quite well with his work at Harvard, which would be completed in the near future. April encouraged him to talk for two reasons. First, she had no intention of talking about herself; plus, if she could keep him talking, she could learn something of the real Victor.

Victor became aware the conversation had been a one-way street. "Tell me about yourself. I have been selfish in talking only of myself."

"I found it very interesting," April said. "I feel that I know you better."

He continued, "You graduated from high school with honors, I understand."

"I have a certificate of attendance that represents twelve years."

"You won the State Oratorical Contest." April was not sure if this was a statement or a question.

"I was lucky," she said after several moments.

"And a member of the boys' golf team! Father said you won the state in your division."

"I was a member of the golf team. Again, we were lucky. I had some fine golfers that were able to carry me. It was the 'golf team,' not 'the boys' golf team'."

"How were you able to participate?" Victor asked. "It seems this was a first."

"The manual for the high schools simply stated golf. Perhaps I was the only girl interested."

"And you were on the boys', I mean, the track team? How and why?" Victor asked.

"Oh, country girls like to run. We don't sit around waiting for something to happen. Again, the manual said track, not boys' track. I suppose they understood." She had no intention of speaking of the role Jerome had played.

At this moment, she decided that the conversation needed to be shifted once again to Victor. "Since you dress like a banker, look like a banker and perhaps even act like one, I gather you will return soon to work with your father."

Victor asked, "Does this surprise you?"

"Yes and no. That's always a safe response; a fence rider, if you please."

"Want to explain?" Victor asked.

"I can picture you more easily in a larger setting. I would guess that all of the things you find important and meaningful in your life cannot be obtained in Midway and Decatur County. After all, the word Victor means winner.

"I can also picture you as an able student and assistant to your father here in this setting. I am afraid I do not see you beyond this,"

April said. "I think, if you remained here, you would always know and remember this was your father's creation. I suspect you want to create something that is yours and yours alone. Inherited wealth is a big handicap for personal satisfaction."

"Your perception is uncanny. I still see you at times, until I take a second look, as the young lady just finishing high school in a rural setting. You have the ability to see a great deal more. Forgive me for not recognizing your maturity and your keen insight. I think your youthfulness, your beauty, your charm has caused me to under evaluate you in other ways.

"I intend to have the best of all worlds. I need the knowledge my father can provide for me. His success has proven certain things. You would accept this. After all, he is an old Attapulgus boy. I think I can master the art of banking on a level he would consider satisfactory in two, three or four years.

"After that, I'm not sure. I probably would consider something different in a much larger setting. I need a challenge. I need to prove to myself and others some things that I believe important. Perhaps that is the reason I was named Victor."

They reached the restaurant, one of the better ones, where Victor had already made reservations. During the course of the meal he said, "In light of the last two years, what do you think your father, or perhaps I should say, the corporation, will do?"

"We have not reviewed that matter but I'm sure we will soon. I think we can overcome the adversities that have been experienced. It is possible that we may wish to consider some new adventures. Our world and the markets are changing rapidly and constantly. The government, so it seems, would like to intrude further into the lives of the people." She had no intention of pursuing the matter beyond this point.

The outstanding movie that had been advertised as "one of the best" was some more of the same. April found it to be far from entertaining or educational. A well known actor's name appeared to assure a box office success.

Several times during the movie April was tempted to suggest they leave, because the production was second rate. She was also annoyed at Victor's hand as it touched her leg from time to time. She believed it not accidental, but by design. However, she was not absolutely sure. His arm also encircled her shoulder and his hand seemed to be drawn toward her breast. Suddenly, she sat up straight and at the same time drew his arm away. She sat in a rigid manner but she did not look toward him. It was clear that this man was not acceptable.

On their return home April referred to several current subjects, such as the Viet Nam conflict and the "Great Society" movements of the president, including his declarations relating to poverty and civil rights. She made a special effort to keep any conversation away from her or directly on him.

"You have made a decision as to college?" Victor asked.

"No, but I must very soon."

As they drove up into her yard Victor cut the lights and the motor. "I'd like to talk with you about us."

"Us? I don't think I understand."

"April, you must know that from the time I saw you years ago at your father's birthday party I have felt very strongly about you. In recent years we have been busy growing up and preparing for life. You must know you are one of the most beautiful and talented girls ever. We have reached a new plateau, so to speak. As we have matured, we are now more able to recognize our goals in life. There are so many things we can have and do together. There are parties we can attend. We can go out dancing. We can cultivate new friends, those whose interests are similar to ours."

"We hardly know each other, Victor. I have years to go before I can or wish to become serious about anyone. I, at this time, do not know with a great deal of certainty what I wish to do. We can be friends but I am not ready to encourage or become serious with anyone. I have just finished high school."

"Your family is facing a difficult time. A close relationship can help to make these times easier. I am and will be in a position to give a helping hand. That's what good friends can do for each other. I hope we can have the right kind of alliance and that we may start soon. Actually, there is no time like the present. I suggest we start now."

Victor, at that moment, pulled her toward him, then his arm went around her and he cupped her breast. He pulled her head toward him and crushed his warm lips upon hers, his tongue seeking an entrance into her mouth. She felt his other hand move upward under her skirt, along her leg toward her thigh. The entire movement had occurred so quickly that April was not prepared. For a moment she did not move; she was stunned by his actions. Victor, finding little resistance, interpreted a stillness and lack of resistance as an acceptance of his advances.

She heard him say, "I can do so much for you and your family. I know you understand. We can have a great time together and I think we should start now." He roughly pulled her toward him and at the same time a hand slipped into her blouse.

"I want you, April, and I think you want me as much as I want you. We can and will make a great team together."

Suddenly, Victor was stunned, both by her actions and by her great strength. She jerked herself free from him and yanked open the door with her free hand.

"The Randolphs are not for sale. You don't know the first thing about me and little about most of my family! Goodnight. Please never attempt to contact me again." She rushed to the front porch of her home and quickly went into the house. As she entered the hall she saw that two buttons were missing from her blouse. She made her way directly to her room. She was shaking all over. As she had passed the open door to the den she thought she heard someone turning a newspaper but she didn't look in, nor did she stop. After she closed the door to her room she quickly dressed for bed, then lay awake, reviewing the events. It was a long time before she closed her eyes and slept.

April was up early the next morning. Sleep had eluded her for the most part, but she felt the need to busy herself, having learned that this therapy had given her the greatest relief over the years.

As she entered the kitchen she heard her mother say, "It is not necessary for you to get up so early. You needed some sleep, some rest. I can look at you and tell you are not resting properly. Without a tobacco crop, our whole schedule has changed, except for your father. He was in the truck before daylight. He would not let me get up when he did. He said he could get a bite on his own. I heard his truck crank a few minutes later. Sometimes he returns in an hour and just paces around. At other times he doesn't come in until around lunchtime. He says little to anyone. I have tried to fit into his mood. Seldom do I say anything unless he asks a question or unless it is necessary. He is going through a troubled time. When he learned a day or two ago that he would be challenged for his seat on the commission, he seemed to lapse into further silence. April, we must help him but I don't know how. I have never been so concerned.

"On one occasion when we were alone I attempted to talk of our blessings. 'All is not lost,' I told him. We have so much more than most and we can make some adjustments. I spoke of our health and the blessing of a close and loving family. He exploded as I had never heard him in our years together. He cursed God and nature and all the forces that he feels have joined together to bring about his downfall. He spoke of being so near to his goal of becoming someone and now he has lost all of his dreams. He would not listen. He said that I had failed in not realizing his dream. I am alarmed. April, somehow we must help him. He needs us more than at any time before."

"Mother, I don't know what to do or what to say. He has never felt the same toward me since I said what I did about our people here in the quarters. Someday, when we can sit and talk, I have some things to say. At the moment, I believe I can serve everyone best by not saying anything. I have a feeling this will not go away soon.

She then asked, "Do you need me for a few hours? I have some thinking to do, some decisions I must make. I believe I can do this best alone and that Somewhere Else may be the place I need to be."

"Nothing is pushing. Sandra is available but I'm not sure I need her. I believe Gena and Meggie got up early and went to F.S.U. with Charles. I think they feel better about going to school as day students for a while but they may decide on an apartment. Their schedules will differ so Charles feels it best for them to establish residence in Tallahassee. This, after one year, would eliminate their out-of-state fee."

"Is Charles all right?" April asked. "I have seen so little of him."

"Should we have had a successful tobacco season, Charles might have considered withdrawing from the corporation. I think he feels his goals have been accomplished. I'm sure he will tell you more than he will me. The two of you can talk. Now run. Do your thinking and make your plans."

April sat on her deck. There was a shade and a nice cool breeze. Suddenly, she said out loud, "I don't know. I just don't know!" She was as unsure of her future as she had been five years ago. Then she spoke out loud once again, "But I don't have to know now or for a year, even two years!" With this a smile came on her face. She knew what she would do. She could not remember being so relieved.

Chapter 62

"Are you back so soon? You have made some decisions? Your mind seemed so cluttered that I felt you would need a much longer period of time," her mother said.

April smiled. "It occurred to me soon after I arrived that certain decisions were not essential at this time. I am going to Auburn University. It is a good school. It has high academic standards. I will take my basic courses the first year. I suspect this will provide some insight, as other decisions are required. I feel better now.

"Let me hasten to say I do not feel good about being away from home at this time. David is improving but is not fully recovered. Joseph has not come to terms with what has happened. You will need more help than ever since Meggie and Gena will not be around. It makes me feel like a coward or a traitor making such a decision. I suspect there will be those that will not feel kindly."

"Please don't feel that way. Perhaps you have forgotten, as you have not been among our people a great deal lately, but your father brought Big John Jackson and his wife and daughter in some weeks ago. He had felt more discipline and supervision were needed. Well, he promised Big John there would be some work for his wife and daughter. I insisted, at that time, that I wanted to continue with you three girls and Sandra. As I will need some help, and to see a promise fulfilled, I will call on Ella and Pearl. They can never take the places of 'my girls' but I will not need as much help."

April and her mother continued to peck at their food after the men had moved out. At that moment the door bell rang. Martha moved to the door.

"Have some flowers for Miss April Randolph, ma'am." Martha noticed his uniform identified him as an employee for the leading florist in Midway. "Man said they are to go directly to her and no one else. You are Miss April Randolph?"

"No. She is my daughter. I'll get her. Just a moment, please."

She returned to the breakfast room where April was sitting. "Someone has sent you some flowers with instructions to deliver them only to you. Better go to the door."

She told the delivery man, "I am April Randolph."

"Good. Was supposed to deliver them to you personally." He smiled as he handed her the beautiful roses.

"Just a minute, please," April said. She took the attached note, opened it and read it. "Would you hold these a moment, please? I'll be right back."

In a minute she returned. She attached the note back to the flowers. "Do you deliver flowers both ways?" She held a ten dollar bill in her hand as she asked.

"Oh yes, miss. I sure do. Do you have something to send?"

"Yes. Please return these flowers to the original sender. I have written a response. The sender will understand." She handed him the ten dollar bill and closed the door.

The messenger stopped before he entered the highway to return to Midway. He took the card from the envelope and saw she had written one word, "Sorry!"

April returned to her mother. "What did you do with your flowers? I guess they were sent by Victor. It must have been, because they were so large and obviously quite expensive."

"I sent them back," April said in a quiet voice.

Her mother looked alarmed for several seconds but remained silent. "Mother, I'm going to my room for a few minutes unless you need me to help you." She gave no further explanations.

April sat in her chair with her hands back of her head. She wanted to close out everything from her mind. Shortly, she heard a knock on the door and thought it must be Joseph or Mother. Then she thought, I don't think it would be Mother because she would know I wish to be alone. She rose and went to open the door.

"Hi." There was a big smile on Michael John's face. "Can I come in? Are you sick or something? Not like you to be sitting around like this in the middle of the day!"

"Come in." She closed the door behind him and they took seats.

"I need to chat with you, April. Got a minute?"

"From the look on your face it is obvious that you are excited about something. Tell me what's on your mind."

"Robin and I want to get married in August. We don't wish to wait. We feel very strongly about it. December seems so far away. Why should the two of us wait when we feel so strongly about each other? We could get away a few days in late August. Since the tobacco is gone, I could go all out to build my — that is, our — house. We have our plan ready. Don't you like the idea? Your face tells me you are not pleased and I thought you, of all people, would be most happy for us." There was a strange expression on his face. He seemed startled.

"Michael John, no one could be happier than I am for you. You are the greatest of brothers. I could not wish more. Robin is the perfect mate for you. I am equally sure of that. But I wish you would wait until Christmas time."

"But Christmas should be for Christmas, April. We don't need a marriage all mixed up with Christmas time. I hope you understand."

"Let me finish, Michael John, and I think you will understand why I said what I did. Joseph is in a bad way. Not only am I concerned about his health, but I am concerned that he is so distressed about money problems. Your house, really, is a small item. I know this was promised to all the children, but Joseph is so upset that anything that relates to money just now can set him off and make matters worse. Do you understand what I am saying?"

Michael John's face seemed puzzled for a moment, then he smiled. "Sis, we don't have to take a dime from the Corporation at this time. I have more than enough money saved to build a house. Later, when we are back on an even keel again, I can accept a reimbursement." His face again turned into one huge smile. "I'll tell him that."

"I don't know, Michael John. For some reason, I feel this is not the best timing. But if you decide to move forward, please explain your position for the cost of the house. Oh, Michael John, I do want you to be happy! I know Robin is the best thing that has or could happen to you."

"I have to do it now, April. It is the right thing to do. I think of David and how little time he and Kathy had together. I am selfish enough to want every day, every hour, that I can have with Robin. Yes, I must plan for August. I'm going to announce it at supper tonight." He walked quickly to the door and was gone.

The family gathered around the dining table for dinner. Joseph had not returned for lunch so Martha had prepared a special meal of the food that Joseph enjoyed most.

In the middle of the meal Joseph said, "Perhaps my daughter is gonna tell us about her new boy friend. I am sure she is pleased to be dating a young man so fine and handsome and so rich. She may give us a clue as to how it is going. I'm sure Victor did everything to make it a special evening!"

"Joseph, I think it best to talk of other things. For example, what directions are to be recommended when our family meets again? I'm sure it has taken some time to get over the initial shock. I suspect that it will be well to review our future."

"My daughter is trying to change the subject. In three or four years Victor could well be one of the most respected and powerful figures in Decatur County. It all depends on how fast he can travel and how much Bruce will turn him loose. If April is as smart as a lot of others give her credit, she ain't gonna lose sight."

"If I was April, I'd go after that man," Stephen said. "You'd never have to worry after that."

"April, a few minutes ago you showed so little enthusiasm. Why, four-fifths of the girls would be on cloud nine if they had been with Victor last evening," Joseph said.

Michael John spoke as if to sidetrack his father from his continued efforts to promote Victor. "I haven't had much to say recently. Our housing projects seem to have disappeared but maybe we should start again!"

"Who needs more housing? David is all alone in his big house. Charles stays gone half the time and has made it plain that he has no plans to be a permanent part of Randolph Place. What do we need with more housing? I hope April hasn't got things stirred up and is gonna put all our quarters people in new homes! Heaven forbid!" Michael John and April looked at each other. April's eyes shot toward the ceiling but she said nothing.

"Looks as if I am forgotten again," Michael John said. "I had some great news to share with my family, with everyone. Robin Wells and I are going to get married. We had planned to do so at Christmas, but we believe the last of August would be better."

For a half minute you could have heard a pin drop. Everyone seemed to look at another member of the family. Michael John looked at his family with alarm. The first to speak was his mother. "I think all of us are in shock. We had no clue about a relationship with Robin. I knew she visited with Eric and the others at April's place but I never dreamed of such. Oh, I am so delighted. She is so sweet, so good, and so talented. I just can't believe the good news!"

"Best news I've heard in months," Charles said. "He did it right under our noses and we didn't even know, didn't even guess!"

In a quiet voice they heard David say, "Don't wait. We don't know how many days we are given. Enjoy each precious moment. I congratulate you."

"I guess I'm stupid," Stephen said, "but I can't see someone like Michael John marrying one with all that college. Also, I don't think she is as pretty as some other girls I know."

The room became totally silent once more. Every person except Joseph looked at Stephen as if he had shot and killed his own brother.

In an attempt to save the day and bring some of the lost joy back for Michael John April hastened to say, "For some reason, my dear baby brother has placed a dark cloud over an area where sunshine was everywhere a moment ago."

"I've never been more disappointed," David said looking at Stephen. "There is no excuse, none whatsoever, for such remarks. I'll see you a little later, Michael John. I'll ask to be excused." He looked at Stephen and started to rise from his chair.

"Wait!" Joseph spoke much louder than he intended and in the total silence it sounded even more pronounced. "I don't think some of you understand what Stephen was gonna say. I believe he is speaking of a point worthy of looking at. Here we have a boy, my own son, who had to work and work to get through high school, and a young girl, not dry behind the ears, so to speak, that has years and years of college. What can they have in common? What is gonna hold two people together in marriage with such differences? Ain't it possible that she is simply seeking security? Lastly, what do we know of this woman's background? We ain't got no knowledge about her family. I'm not much of one for the Bible but doesn't God speak of people being unequally yoked?"

Again there was silence. The look on Michael John's face told a story that one would prefer to forget. What had been a highlight of his life had suddenly become a nightmare. Martha saw this and spoke in a quiet but strong manner.

"I knew a girl once who married a man eleven years her senior. She was not a very pretty girl and did not have a family background that would have impressed anyone. Twenty-eight years and six children later this lady thinks she was the most fortunate person in all the world. Surely, there were differences. They belonged to different churches, they had different friends and on and on. I think that today it is a stronger union with shared love. Two can adjust if there is love and understanding."

Joseph seemed determined. "There is a difference, Martha. I was older than you. This ain't true about Michael John and this Wells girl. And I did know your family — good people, honest people. Can we say this is true of the family of this girl? Can we know? How can one be sure?

"It goes beyond that. Here we are with greater losses than ever before. We don't even know how much we owe and certainly have no idea how we can pay our debts. Then to make things even more difficult, he wants to add to our woes! I don't think he is thinking of his family in the least. In fact, I am disappointed."

Charles spoke. "I suspect Michael John has ample funds. If not, I know he can find some among his family if our corporation cannot manage. As I recall, this was part of the arrangement. No one has worked harder or served more unselfishly."

David spoke once again. "It is your life. You have only one. You are a grown man now. You make your decisions as you feel you want. You have no written promise as to tomorrow, as to the future. As far as I can see and know, I see many things that remind me of Kathy and she had few faults. She was pure and lovely. I believe Robin to be the same."

Everyone looked at Joseph. The expression on his face was drastically different from the one they had seen before. They could not decipher it. All the other sentiments, aside from Stephen's, had been in Michael John's favor. Michael John got up and was about to leave the room when his father spoke sharply. "I want to see you privately in a few minutes but I want to see April first. Don't go away until I can talk with you. Since everyone seems to have finished eating, we will go. April, come to the library with me — now!"

April sat facing her father in the small library. He seemed so dominant and so stern. "I was in the den when you returned home last night. I guessed something was wrong. I trust you were smart enough to keep a good relationship going, keep all doors open. It is most important." He did not smile.

April said without emotion, "Just as a ship can't come in if one has not been sent out, neither can a door remain open that has been closed from the beginning. I told you earlier that I did not like this man, that I don't trust this man. I preferred not to go but did because you insisted. He is not an honorable person. He is not trustworthy. He is an evil man, one that will use any means to get what he wants. He is a selfish person. I cannot accept someone of this sort."

"You ain't very smart. Doors should have remained open during this crisis. We are in a dilemma, you know! I can't understand. He has all the things that are important — to me, to you, to everyone. Surely you can see this."

"Joseph, I hope you are not saying what I may have reason to believe you may be saying. He is good business? We need him?

She continued, "Aren't you more concerned about your daughter's feelings, her wishes, her standards, her beliefs? I have never seen you compromise on certain things, even though I have not always agreed with you, as we both well know. Please don't tell me you wish me to compromise my standards and values to promote a favorable business arrangement!"

"Victor ain't gonna ever do that, April. He is interested in you. It is much more than a passing fancy. He ain't gonna place you or let you to be placed in a compromising position!"

"Joseph, I had wished that you not pursue this matter but you continue to insist. Please excuse me for half a minute. I find it necessary to be excused." She rose. His expression remained the same.

When April returned she was carrying a small package. "I think some things must be said now, so let me tell you a story." April opened the package and produced the blouse she had been wearing the previous evening. She held it up so he could see it was torn and two buttons were missing.

"Take a good look, Joseph. This is the blouse I was wearing last evening. Last night he attempted to force his affections upon me. Without warning and catching me off guard, he tore my blouse as he thrust his hand inside and felt of my breast. At the same moment his hand went up my skirt and I felt his fingers clawing at my panties. He held me so tight and he did this so suddenly that I was unprepared. I was caught completely off guard. As he was doing this I was stunned to hear him utter the statement that he was in a position to make life better for the Randolphs and all I needed to do was submit to his passion and desires, suggesting that I needed him as much as he needed me." Joseph let his eyes drop to the floor.

"I am not finished. He continued to hold me and attempted to feel me in the places I described. Finally I was able to break free. I thought my skirt was ripped. I felt the buttons go on my blouse. I rushed from the car and made a wild dash to the house. As you know, I went directly to my room.

"I had hoped that the matter, as frightening and dreadful as it was, could remain a secret. But no, you continued to encourage me. I can hear his voice now as he said, 'I am in a position to make sure that nothing drastic happens to Randolph Place.' Joseph, would you have me make compromises? He spoke of financial favors! You know, Joseph, there was a time in my life when I would have guessed you would have been moved to say, 'The son-of-a-bitch! I'll blow his damn head off!' I think if our positions had been reversed, I'd probably be in jail because I think I would have rid this world of this person, who you feel is so special!

"This morning I received some flowers, some beautiful roses, from this man. There was a note that suggested he had possibly made a mistake and acted in haste. I returned them. I wanted to say a great deal but for your sake and others, I simply said, 'Sorry.'

"I hope we never have to discuss this again for the sake of us both. I hope other members of the family can be spared this knowledge because I suspect that some of my brothers might feel too strongly about the matter. If it can't stop at this point, I have no choice but to leave and go elsewhere.

"Now I am going to walk out of here as if nothing has happened and go to my room. I'll tell Michael John we have finished. I hope you will reconsider your position with him but I'll leave that up to you. Again, I am sorry it had to come to this. Goodnight." She left the room and knocked on Michael John's door.

She then went to her room and cried as she had never cried before. She sat in the rocking chair staring into space. She sought some peace of mind but her tears continued; she found herself more tormented than at any other time in her life.

An hour later April head a knock on her door. No, she thought, I cannot say or listen to another word this night. I'll just have to tell Joseph I cannot talk with him. Slowly she went to the door and opened it. It was Michael John. His face was distorted beyond description.

He pushed into the room, closed the door and locked it. He had not uttered a word. He stood for some seconds, then slumped into the chair and held his face in his hands. He was shaking uncontrollably.

"Are you all right?" April asked. "Michael John, are you all right? I've never seen you look this way! Talk to me! Tell me what has happened."

Michael John remained silent. His body moved as if with a convulsion. Then he said, "No! No! It isn't so!"

"What could Joseph have said to you to get you this way?" April asked. "Didn't you tell him it wouldn't cost him a dime — and only one acre? I had hoped you could wait a little longer, until he got over his shock of a lost crop and the challenge for his commissioner's seat. But you have a life to live and this was the most important thing that could ever happen to you. I understand — truly I do."

"April," Michael John said quietly, raising his head so that they could see each other, "I am going to leave Randolph Place. I have no choice. I must leave immediately. I have to go."

"Let's talk about it," April said. "It is not like you to be like this. Let's not do something that you will regret later. Don't you want to discuss it with me?"

"I have to get you to do something for me, April. You are the only one I can trust completely. I can't speak, I dare not speak, with Mama or Robin."

Again April said nothing for some time. Finally she got up from her chair and went over to her brother, taking his big strong hands in hers and saying, "When you feel that you can, suppose we talk. I think you have a load you cannot carry. Let me help you. Please tell me what occurred. Start at the beginning."

"You heard what Papa said earlier. Well, he went over the same things again. He said you can't hitch a horse and mule to a wagon and expect very much of anything good to happen. He spoke again of the lack of knowledge of her background. He spoke of hard times and how people needed to be aware of his needs and the family's needs. He made me feel little, made me feel cheap, made me feel like I was stealing, like I had no feeling for my family. He reminded me that children should honor and obey their parents. Not once did he ever say anything nice about Robin or me. It was always what *he* wanted, what was good for the family and how much he had done to make his family into somebody."

"Try to understand Joseph," April said. "I have failed to understand many things. I do not know why he causes others to suffer so. At times I felt he had no compassion for anyone, yet from time to time, I see something that makes me feel differently. For example, he relented and permitted Meggie to stay with us. Perhaps our mother forced this issue but in the end he did the right thing."

"He is not a good man, April, though he is our father!"

"Should you say and think that, Michael John? He has worked and saved and done without so that his family could be secure. No one works harder. There is something to say for this."

Michael John said, "Sis, how many basketball games did he ever see you play? Not the first one. How many speeches did he ever hear you make? Only the last one at graduation and I heard Mama say then that if he didn't attend, she would do some things. I never heard him say the first thing to any of his children to make them feel good. He never said a kind word about my gazebo when it was so important to me to find something that I could do successfully. He never told Charles he was happy to see a member of his family graduate from college. I heard him brag on Joe and Stephen a few times as to their long hours and successful work in tobacco.

"If he had just said, just one time, that he was proud of you, of me, it would have made all the difference. He is not a good man!"

"Some people are like that," April said. "I think he thinks good and means good but he doesn't feel it necessary to put it into words. I have seen a couple of others like him. It's like telling a husband or wife that love abounds. He feels, I am sure, that it is not necessary to express the obvious. But what else did he say? What happened? Obviously there is more, much more."

Michael John said, "I told him I was not the least bit concerned as to the differences he had mentioned; the important thing was that we love each other. So, finally, I said that while I would hope it would be with his approval and blessings, we were going to marry with or without them. You have never seen, Sis, such a look on a man's face!"

"What did he say?" April asked.

"He said he would not permit it."

"And what did you say then?" April asked.

"I told him I would leave immediately, as much as I would miss the family and Randolph Place. I told him that Robin and I would get married immediately.

"He arose from his chair and said that he didn't want to tell me, he did not want anyone to know, but that I would not marry my sister, my half sister!"

April was stunned, so stunned that she could not speak for a minute or more. "What did you say? I'm sure I didn't hear you correctly! Did he say that you couldn't marry your sister?"

"Yes. And he said that if I ever told anyone it would destroy all the Randolphs."

"What did you say, Michael John? What did you do?"

"The best I remember I stood up and looked at him and I said, 'You are not a good man, you are not a good father. You are an evil man!' When I said this he slapped me across the face. He did not utter a word. It was at that time, without saying anything else or doing anything, I left the room. I was too upset to remain!"

"What will you do, Michael John? I can't even think at the moment," April said. She had never once found herself in such a dilemma.

"Well, Sis, there are some things that I must do and some that I must not. I must have your help."

"What can you do? What do you plan to do?" April asked, still too stunned to think.

"I am going to leave. Now. This night. I cannot spend another night here. I am going to pack up my clothes and slip quietly away. Now there are some things you must do for me, though I hate to ask you. But first let me say that no one, I mean no one, must ever know this but you and me and the man we call Father. It would completely destroy Mama. It would kill her. She must never, never know!

"Now you must tell her that Papa and me had a disagreement and that I felt I could not feel comfortable here any longer. Tell her anything, but never the truth.

"This may even be more difficult but you must tell Robin something for me. You think about what you should say but she, too, must never know the real reason. I can't think at the moment and I'm too much of a coward to see her again.

"Sis, surely you see that I must leave. I've simply got to depend on you. I've got money and I'll make out. I'll find some way to let you know where I am so we can contact each other in time to come. It may not be soon."

"Where will you go, Michael John? What will you do?" April asked.

"Sis, I don't know. I'm much too upset at the moment to think. But I'll be all right. I'll go to a vocational school and learn the building trade. I can get a job with a construction company. Don't worry. I'll be all right. The important thing is for you to find a way with Robin and my family. Try to do it in such a way, if you can, that I will not become too bad in the eyes of Robin and my family.

"I've got to go now. There is much to do. If you don't mind, let me have a bag or two of yours. I don't have that many clothes but I had better take enough. Tell Robin and my folks I love them. I am not sure at the moment how I feel about Papa. I'd rather not think of it. Goodnight and goodbye."

This was the second night in a row that April did not sleep. She sat in her chair and tried to think of some way she could go about the tasks that had been thrust upon her.

CHAPTER 63

The hand of the clock pointed to 3:00 a.m. April could not sleep. It seemed that calamity had been with them constantly for more than a year. She compared it with a river, always running, rushing to the sea, seemingly without effort.

She turned everything over in her mind. What do I tell my mother? Not only will she be upset but when she discovers I have no idea how to reach him, she will panic. What will our brothers think? Will this not cause further division in the family? Will Joseph suspect that I know? How will he respond to what has occurred?

April wondered how would she be able to talk with Robin Wells. What would she say? For a moment she wondered who was Robin's mother, then decided she would think about that later. She wondered if Joseph had played a role in putting Robin in the school system, in Attapulgus. She suspected he was the one who had provided Robin's scholarship.

At 5:00 a.m. April managed to fall into a light sleep. She had never dressed for bed and still sat in her chair. She was awakened at 5:30 a.m. by the sound of voice; they indicated excitement. Had they discovered Michael John had left? Had David regressed to the point he had been months ago? Had Joe been in an accident? His drinking was no longer a secret. Had Stephen been in an accident? She thought, Oh, God, please don't let anything else happen!

April rushed from her room, her clothes wrinkled, her hair uncombed. She practically shouted, "What's wrong?" She saw Charles embracing their mother. "What's happened?" She repeated.

Martha turned from Charles to respond and would have fallen had not Charles moved swiftly to catch her. She sat in a chair nearby and looked at April. "Your father is dead. Jack found him in his truck."

"How did Joseph die? Has there been foul play?" She wanted to ask if he had taken his own life but decided this question should not be asked, at least not at this time.

"Jack guessed a heart attack. There was no heart beat or pulse when Jack found him; no sign of foul play. The sheriff, the coroner, the funeral home and Mike Harper have been called."

No one seemed able to speak. Martha continued, "I heard a noise twice during the night. I have not been sleeping well recently. I don't know about the first noise but it sounded as if some vehicle was driving away. The second noise was Joseph getting up. It was just after four. I heard him in the kitchen and then I heard a door open and close. I guessed he was unable to sleep and wanted to be up and doing. I know the feeling.

"I stayed in bed a time, as I felt I needed some sleep and rest. But I never went back to sleep. Shortly after I went to the kitchen Jack arrived and told me of Joseph. I still cannot comprehend the fact that he is dead, that he is gone. It seems that he should be coming in any moment for coffee."

April responded, "I can't believe Joseph is gone either!" After a moment she asked, "What can I do? I can't just sit here."

Martha spoke quietly. "Go tell your brothers and the others that should know. I want five minutes alone. Then we will need breakfast. Some of us must think about breakfast."

"No one will be interested in food," Charles said. "I'm not sure we should leave you."

"Go. Do it now. I'm fine," Martha said.

After Joseph's body had been taken to Midway the family gathered in the den. No one spoke. Martha looked about her. Abruptly she asked, "Where is Michael John?"

"He is not here," April said. "He told me last night he would need to be away for a few days. He did not tell me where he was going. He said he didn't wish anyone to bother him for a time. I have no idea where he is so I do not know how to reach him." The others added that they knew nothing of his whereabouts either. "He had a great deal on his mind," April continued. "I am sure he expects us to do what is necessary in his absence."

It was decision making time. "Let us plan together what we feel Joseph would have wished. We need to do this now, as there will be people coming and others calling," Martha said.

An hour later all the details had been worked out with the assistance of Mike Harper. No one was to remember how Mike had learned of Joseph's death but he was among the first to arrive, along with Susan Lee. When they had finished Martha said she would like to be alone with her family for a few minutes. Mike, Susan and Mary started to leave. When Martha saw Mary leaving she motioned for her to stay.

All were silent, the pain of death upon them. Finally Martha said, "Let us remember some things that I would have you know and I think your father would want you to know. Joseph Randolph was a good man, a good husband and a good father. He loved each of us. He loved his family. Most often his decisions were based on what he believed best for all of us. This was evident when he formed the corporation some five years ago. His dream was for his family to become someone special. He worked night and day to make this possible, make this dream come true.

"Sometimes I thought he loved things too much. No, let me rephrase that. Sometimes I think he loved land too much. He could not separate land from living. It was a big part of his life. But you know that.

"How would he have us react on this occasion? He would choose to be remembered and loved. He was not one to weep a great deal nor would he have wanted such when he left us. He knew there is a time to plant, a time to grow and a time to harvest. He also knew there is a time to live and a time to die. His legacy would be: 'Work hard and be somebody. Do something special with your lives.'

"Finally, we must remember that he was human. He made mistakes and he was not one to easily admit them. He sometimes spoke before he thought. So do we all. Most of the time his pride refused to let him admit he was wrong; however, you knew he had a way of admitting his mistakes.

"Let us, the living, bury the dead. We will miss him. Oh, I can see a thousand ways I'll miss him each day. Let all of us try and be brave. Now let us turn our minds and our hearts toward the earthly man who did so much for all of us and upon our God who made our lives possible on this earth.

"In a few days, after we have had time for the healing process to begin, I will get the proper officials to read his will and others to do what must be done."

After they had finished Susan and Mike returned. Mike said, "There was a call. It was a massive heart attack. They said he died instantly without suffering. It is so much better that way."

For the next thirty-six hours Susan Lee remained with the family, except for a few hours of sleep. No one had guessed so many would come, so many would care and so many would bring food or send flowers. There were his church members, members from the other two churches, the county commissioners, the members of the Board of Education and all the others that made up the courthouse crowd.

Gena and Meggie were responsible for the food. Others brought enough to feed fifty people for a week. Then it was time for the funeral. A strange selection of citizens tiptoed by the open casket. They knew an institution was gone from Randolph Place.

Martha insisted the services by Mike Harper be short. "Do not make it hard on the family. This is not the time to save a thousand souls, but to put my beloved husband to rest. He would not have liked a long, drawn out service. 'Let's get to it and finish the job,' he would have said."

There were more people standing outside the church than could be seated inside. "Joseph," Charles said later, "would have liked this immensely. This was proof that his lifetime dream was not a dream, but a reality."

In time to come people would speak in many ways about the service and Joseph's death. Some said he died of a broken heart because of the consecutive crop losses. Others believed that he had driven himself so that he had literally worked himself to death.

The family returned home after the services. It was not unusual that many others felt an obligation to the family and also returned to the house. A short time later Susan Lee stood and said in a clear voice, "I must go and I think all of you should do the same. Let the family get some rest." As the day ended a feeling of emptiness arose. The family was alone to reflect on the past and present, and to wonder about the future.

Charles and April walked out to the gazebo after Martha had told everyone she wished to be alone for a time. Charles spoke first. "It has all happened so suddenly. I think it has not hit us yet. If there had been a long illness, it would have been different. We would have been better prepared."

"I think you are wrong in one case. I'm not sure that Mother was as totally surprised as you may think. For some reason I feel she was pre-warned, that it was not altogether unexpected. I think she had seen Joseph give up, so to speak. Naturally, this is just a guess. However, if she had not had some premonition, she could not have been so calm. I really think she had thought through this in advance."

Charles asked, "Do you know the whereabouts of Michael John? I think this was the second most dreaded thing for Mother."

"No." April did not respond beyond the one word.

"Do you know why he left?" Charles asked.

"I think all of us know. The most exciting thing to ever occur in Michael John's life was his relationship with Robin Wells. He was devastated. Certainly this played a role in his departure. I think you would agree with this analysis. Do you not think there was a relationship between the feelings of Joseph, for whatever reasons, and Michael John leaving?"

"April, you answer questions by asking questions. You would make a great lawyer. I will not probe any further. I think you have said all you want or intend to say. But it doesn't sound like you." He switched subjects. "Do you want to tell me what Father wanted to see you about when the two of you talked earlier? I guess it was related to Victor McPherson."

"No. Joseph is gone. Let it be," April said.

"No, you don't care to talk about it or no, it wasn't about Victor?"

"What does it matter, Charles? I am not trying to be difficult. I simply do not care to discuss the matter."

"Have you thought about Father's will?" Charles asked. "Have you given some thought as to the future?"

"I suppose it has crossed everyone's mind. No one would admit it, as they would have a feeling of guilt thinking of such matters so soon. Yes, I've thought about it. I think all our lives will be greatly influenced and changed. However, I want to change the subject a moment. Do you think Joseph getting upset like he did was a cause or partial cause of his death? Don't lie to me!"

"What killed our father was the huge loss of two consecutive tobacco crops. The first one did a great deal of damage. The second one was just too much. Until now hard work and good planning had moved him toward his goals. He didn't know how to deal with this. Strangely, we could have absorbed the losses and still been wealthy, by the standards of most.

"I think in the end the burning desire to have more land, more wealth, more of everything did it. His heart was not in it after the crop losses. I also feel that he felt very unsure about the upcoming election. There were many who felt he did little to serve Decatur County. I am not sure he would not have been defeated. I think he knew this. He was not a fool."

"Charles, I saw one thing today that made me feel a little better. This was the first time David has entered a church since Kathy died. Perhaps this could be a new beginning for him. Yet, he could react in the opposite manner. The last two times he entered the church were to bury his wife and father. What do you think?"

"I don't know. Back to Joseph. He did not have to spend all of his life determining what he wanted to do. He seemed to know from the beginning. Starting early seemed an advantage."

April said, "He spoke repeatedly of the Promised Land. Should he not have asked himself if Moses failed, as God's man, how could he expect to reach such a place? I believe only Caleb and Joshua made it."

She continued, "Joseph did not own Randolph Place. Randolph Place owned him. Land can be either a slave or a master. Riches either serve or govern the possessor. The love of land grows as land itself grows."

Charles asked, "What will it do to those of us who remain?"

"I don't know but I am sure it should not require a lifetime of preparation." She smiled and continued, "From the time the corporation was formed the stockholders voted only once, and that was to secure a slate of officers. I do not cry for Joseph because he just died. I cry for him because he never really lived. To have failed, even so short of his goal, is the same as if he never began."

"No," Charles said. "This is not so. He lived as he wanted. I believe God spared him by taking him. I believe he would have been more disappointed if he had completed what he set out to do. When he discovered the Promised Land was not the Promised Land, he would have died of grief and disappointment. He would have died of a broken heart."

After a moment Charles continued, "I once said to him that if a man works every waking hour, his life is worth nothing. Uncle Edd said he suggested the same only recently. Work should be done in a period of reasonable hours, then we should have time to savor the amazing wonders and joys that have been provided to us. Our father could not understand.

"I told him that by the standards of integrity, honor, intelligence, charity, goodness, dedication and decency should all people be judged. But he told me it didn't work like that. He said, 'It's what you are worth. It's land and money. These things bring power and power brings respectability. That's how it works. That is how it has always worked, since the beginning.'"

April thought for a few moments and said, "Joseph was a rare personality and he selected the goals of security, attainment and acceptance as his objectives. When you think of it, it can be deadly. It can destroy all other parts of life. Someone once described it as a rut. When it becomes deep enough it can become your grave."

"Let us hope, April. You spoke once so strongly about that word. Without hope, we are lost.

"Now I suggest we try and get some sleep. There will be many things to occur in days to come and I believe we will need all the strength we can muster."

CHAPTER 64

Three days later the Randolph family gathered to hear the words of the Will and Testament of Joseph Therin Randolph, Sr.

"It seems a bit early," Martha Randolph said, "but I believe your father would have expected us to be up and doing. That was his way.

"I have asked that our friend, Jerome Lee, read the document so we may learn of your father's wishes. As an attorney, Jerome will be able to explain all legal terms so that we can clearly understand."

They all sat in silence and looked at Jerome. He opened the document and read:

"Last Will and Testament
of
Joseph Therin Randolph, Sr.

Georgia, Decatur County

I, Joseph Therin Randolph, Senior, of said State and County, being of sound and disposing mind and memory, do hereby make, publish and declare this instrument to be my Last Will and Testament, hereby expressly revoking all others heretofore by me made.

ITEM ONE

I desire that my body be disposed of in a Christian like manner in accordance with my circumstances in life.

ITEM TWO

I desire and direct that my Executrix, hereinafter named, pay all my just debts and funeral expenses as soon after my demise as is practical.

ITEM THREE

I do give, devise and bequest all of my stock in Randolph Place as follows:

Martha Whigham Randolph: Ten (10) shares of Randolph Place stock.

Joseph T. Randolph, Jr.: Five (5) shares of Randolph Place stock.
Charles Randolph: One (1) share of Randolph Place stock.
David Randolph: One (1) share of Randolph Place stock.
Michael John Randolph: One (1) share of Randolph Place stock.
April Randolph: One (1) share of Randolph Place stock.
Stephen Randolph: One (1) share of Randolph Place stock.

ITEM FOUR

Other than the Randolph Place stock above mentioned, I do give, devise and bequest all other of my property, real, personal or mixed, of whatever kind or nature, and wherever situated, to my beloved wife, Martha Whigham Randolph, absolute and in fee simple.

ITEM FIVE

In the event that my wife, the said Martha Whigham Randolph, should predecease me, then do I amend this document in accordance to my wishes.

ITEM SIX

In the event that my wife, the said Martha Whigham Randolph, and I, of some cause, should demise simultaneously, I appoint Joseph T. Randolph, Jr. as Executor of this my Last Will and Testament and with his brothers and sister make such determination as required and/or desired.

ITEM SEVEN

I hereby empower Martha Whigham Randolph to sell any and all property except the Randolph Place stock, at public or private sale, with or without advertisement, for any consideration which her judgement may dictate.

ITEM EIGHT

The power has been given the stockholders of Randolph Place to proceed as provided in the laws of the Corporation of Randolph Place. You would know that in your resolve, that you retain as much land as possible. If this should not be desirable, you may, however, proceed in such ways as you find essential and necessary under the laws of Decatur County and the State of Georgia.

ITEM NINE

In life as well as in death you know of my love for all of you, my beloved family. Because this is so, I leave to each of you my love. It is my wishes that your goals be a continuation of the goals we established long ago. Let Randolph Place be my legacy to each of you.

Joseph Therin Randolph, Sr. (seal)

Published, declared and executed by Joseph Therin Randolph, Sr. as his Last Will and Testament, on this 5th day of July, 1964, he signing in our presence and we signing in his presence and in the presence of each other and at his special instance and request.

Ralph E. Chase address Midway, Georgia.

Bruce McPherson address Midway, Georgia."

Jerome looked up from the document. "Do you have questions? I believe it to be spelled out in a manner that is clear and precise." Several seconds passed and no one spoke.

Martha spoke, "I wish to call a meeting of the stockholders a week from today after our evening meal." She added, "Jerome will please remain so that I may confer with him."

When all of her family departed Martha said to Jerome, "I have some information I wish you to obtain. I will sign such authorizations as needed."

Jerome took out a note pad and pen, then waited for Martha Randolph to continue.

Martha said, "We will need the amounts and balance of all accounts. We will need to know the amounts, interest and dates of all monies owed to The People's Bank or whether there are others elsewhere. We also will need the balances of the operational fund and the emergency fund. Verify that all lands owned by Randolph Place are on record.

"Next, please determine if the Decatur County Bank would be interested in the Randolph Place accounts. It is possible that a change in banking institutions may be in order. I am sure a great deal of money is owed to The People's Bank. Determine if funds can be made available to close all accounts there. I trust this could be done. I hope that all of this can be done with the least possible attention."

"Mrs. Randolph, I will move on this immediately. I will need the authorization forms signed. May I say I am pleased, perhaps a bit surprised, at the manner in which you are moving. I must confess, I have always admired you but had envisioned you as a home body, like my mother. I still believe you are that in your heart." He continued, "Thank you for permitting me to represent you. There are many experienced and qualified attorneys that likely could have served you better."

"Jerome, you are my attorney. I would have it no other way. It is not simply because of the relationship between your mother and myself. I have complete confidence in you."

"Thank you. I trust I will not disappoint you. Again, my family is thinking of you and your family. My mother is very concerned about you and is available to assist in any way."

"She can continue to be my friend, my very best friend. I know her many prayers will assist us during this period of adversity and change. Thank you again."

A little later the telephone rang. "This is Henry Adkins, Mrs. Randolph. I do not know if you knew it or not but your husband took out a policy with my company for a significant sum. It was a term insurance policy. I was left with an impression that he did not wish for anyone to know about it. More than once he cautioned me to remain silent.

"I have waited this long to determine a number of items. I had to know if his death was natural or otherwise. I had to determine if a sufficient time had elapsed to make the policy valid. Lastly, this was not a time in your life to interfere. I am sure there is a policy among his papers, but we can deal with the matter later if you are unable to locate your copy.

"I now have all the necessary information that I need. The policy is valid in all aspects. I would like to meet with you five days from now to give you our check and let you sign some papers."

"Was the policy made out to Randolph Place or to one or more individuals? I speak of the beneficiary or beneficiaries," Martha asked.

"You are the sole beneficiary. By the way, the policy is not a small one. Would you prefer that I come to your house or would you like to come by the office? I will be happy to do as you wish."

Martha said, "If it is all the same, I will come to your office."

"Suppose we say at three o'clock on Thursday if this meets with your approval."

"Thank you, Mr. Adkins, I will be there."

When Martha finished talking she went directly to April. "There is a box that Joseph kept locked in the warehouse office safe. I want you to look through it. There is an insurance policy Joseph kept someplace. Perhaps it is there. I can deal with such matters should we not find it but the policy would be helpful to the agent and insurance company. On second thought, I'll go with you."

After they found seats and secured the box Martha said, "Look through the papers, April. I suspect he held on to many things for tax purposes and such. You know, in a way it is strange that Joseph never discussed this box with me. Perhaps there is something for us to see, to know."

April took the box over to a table some distance from her mother. "Here are some papers relating to his father and grandfather. I'll set them aside so they can be reviewed later. Yes, here are some old deeds and his father's birth certificate. Why, there are his report cards for the first two grades."

She came upon a paper that seemed different. She read a few words, placed it aside and continued, "Perhaps this is what you are looking for. It appears to be an insurance policy and it seems new and fresh as if it had been here a short time." She passed it to her mother.

As her mother settled back to review the policy April slipped the other papers into her blouse. She saw that her mother continued to study the policy closely.

"This is it, April. I'll get it to the agency tomorrow. Your father was very thoughtful about his family." She smiled. "This is all I need now. I'll just take the box to the house and review it all later."

When April returned to her room she withdrew the package of papers from her blouse. This was the first time she could ever remember stealing but she did not feel guilty or unclean. Later she would remember it as a noble act. It would make all the difference in her mother's life. As far as April knew, only she and Michael John shared the secret of Robin Wells. She thought of a quotation, 'You shall know the truth and it will make you free.' Not so. In time to come, Martha Randolph would sleep in peace.

Five days later Martha went to the office as instructed. A nice secretary informed Mrs. Randolph that Mr. Adkins was expecting her. After she was seated Mr. Adkins said, "I have everything prepared. You will need to sign some documents."

"Here is the policy. It was among his papers, as you suggested." She handed it to him.

"Your husband was more thoughtful than most." He handed her the check.

She saw it was for one million dollars. "I had no idea. This was never discussed. I will wonder now about several things and be assured about others. Is it possible that he had a premonition that he was going to die?" After Martha spoke she wondered why she had asked such a question of this man she knew only by face and name.

"I cannot say, Mrs. Randolph. However, if we associate the amount in direct relation to his feelings about you, it is obvious that one could reach some probable conclusions." He went on, "Now please, if you will, sign these documents which mean, in simple lay terms, that we have fulfilled our contract in full."

As Martha signed them she said, "I trust that this transaction is not to be discussed with anyone, that it is confidential. I would prefer it that way."

"The most that I or my company will say is that Mr. Randolph was a policy holder. All other details remain private. Oh, I nearly forgot. We are required to report this to the National Government." Mr. Adkins saw Mrs. Randolph turn a bit pallid and he asked, "Are you all right? You seem a bit pale and unsteady."

"I'm fine, thank you. This has been an unusual day. It is beginning to sink in. Yes, I'm fine, thank you."

Martha found herself outside his office, yet never remembered leaving.

Jerome called on the day of their planned meeting. "I am ready with the information you requested."

At the time of her appointment Martha entered the small building where Jerome had his office. In a matter of moments she was seated comfortably. His desk top was covered with several folders.

Jerome looked at Martha and thought she must be as brave as anyone he had ever encountered. "I have attempted to secure the information you requested. Every effort was made to keep it a private matter. Sometimes our best efforts are less than sufficient when a number of people are involved. I suspect there are those who have guessed and come to certain conclusions."

She reassured him. "I'm sure no one could have done better. I am sure you operated discreetly. I may understand people more than some have guessed over the years. The world would be awfully dull without people, Jerome. I've learned long ago that most are different from Susan Lee and a few other such special people."

"Shall we get started?" Jerome asked. "There is a great deal to discuss." He picked up a folder and opened it as she nodded.

"There are three mortgages held by The People's Bank. We will look at each separately for a clearer understanding. The first and oldest is for $300,000 at seven percent interest payable on the anniversary date of the loan, which is November of this year. This seems to be the third and remaining payment of the last tract of land purchased."

She said, "He was a rascal. He left his family believing he owed two payments of this size for the land. Sorry to interrupt you." She smiled.

He continued, "Last November he paid the interest on the loan and renewed it for one year. I would guess this was due to the first crop he lost. Thus, in November there is a note due for $300,000, plus the interest of $21,000. Do you have questions?" Martha shook her head, indicating she understood.

"The second mortgage is for $200,000 and was made in March, a year ago. I assume this was to finance the first crop that failed. Last March he paid the interest and extended the note for another year. Thus, this note will be due in March, 1965. There will be interest of $14,000. So the total here is $214,000." He looked again at Martha, then continued. "The third mortgage was made in March of this year. This time he borrowed $300,000. I suppose his needs were greater or he had increased the acreage. This loan carried an increased rate of interest. It is eight percent. So, once again, this note will come due next March for $324,000, principal and interest." A third time Martha nodded she understood and for Jerome to continue.

"Now let us do a little arithmetic, Mrs. Randolph, so we can see the total picture. The three mortgages total $800,000. If you wait until the mortgages mature, you will owe $59,000 interest or a grand total of $859,000."

"I had guessed more," Martha said. "He seldom discussed any details relating to money matters. To an extent, it continued to remain Joseph Randolph's Place. My husband, in a sense, was the Corporation. Shall we move on?"

"I suspect you will be surprised as well as pleased at the next figures. There is $300,000 left in the emergency fund. This was invested so he could get his hands on it immediately but if it remains as it is, the five percent interest will give you another $15,000. It matures at the end of this calendar year.

"Now your operating account, as of the end of May, has a balance of $225,000. I suspect he had planned to use this for current expenses and to harvest the last crop that was lost. I do not know the extent of indebtedness, if any, on such items as cheesecloth, twine and the like. Such information should be available wherever he keeps his papers.

"There is, perhaps, another surprise. It is possible that you or others did not know of a Certificate of Deposit of $200,000, drawing interest at the rate of six percent at the Savings and Loan Bank. This certificate matures on December 31, 1964. Should it remain, you will have a $212,000 value at the end of the year.

"He also had a personal checking account in his name with a balance of $11,000. If I understand the provisions of his will, these personal accounts not in the name of Randolph Place belong to you as an individual.

"I have checked all the sources where I believed it possible he may have conducted business. I believe this gives you the whole picture. You may be assured any further debts will surface immediately. Where money is a concern, people react quickly." Martha nodded once more.

"Now you ask for some information as to the size of Randolph Place. Based on his recent survey, Randolph Place encompasses 18,600 acres, which includes the last purchase, of 3,000 acres. Some of the old deeds indicate 'more or less' but I base this figure on the recent survey.

"I did some additional reviews that will likely help you see the total picture. Checks to the eight persons in the corporation were $15,000 monthly. This includes all changes, such as April's increase, as she has finished high school.

"Your taxes will be about fifteen percent more with the purchase of the 3,000 acres recently added. You will need to see your tax auditor for income taxes and such. But with the recent losses, I would guess they would decrease considerably.

"Now about a change in banks. Following a private conference with the bank's president, they would be delighted to have an opportunity to serve you and your family. Based on the conference, you could expect the transaction to be about the same as The People's Bank.

"There are many decisions for you and the Corporation to make. For example, some like to always operate on borrowed money, where others do not. Women and older people often wish to keep debts to a minimum."

"Jerome, I am going to put you on the spot, so to speak. I would be interested in your suggestions on a course for the future. We think very much alike. Is this asking more than I should? Tell me. This is between the two of us. I just think we need to plan ahead."

Jerome remained silent for more than a few moments, then said, "I know so little about farming activities that I could only suggest or guess at best. I believe the first two things you will need to decide are how you will pay such debts as we reviewed. The second decision one must make is whether you continue in the tobacco operation. This would determine so many areas, such as personnel needed."

"Place yourself in my place or the Corporation's place and assume you have the power to make any and all decisions," Martha said.

"I do not believe this wise because I know so little about farming, about agriculture."

"Jerome, I have more confidence in you about all matters than anyone I know. I feel you can help me, help all of us. I feel I must know your thoughts. If, for some reason, the directions you recommend are not followed, I do not wish you to feel unkindly toward me. We are a corporation and henceforth we will vote on such business as needed."

Jerome paused for several seconds as if to determine if he should respond and if so, how much to say. "Let us review the money matters first, since we are talking about large sums of money. In a nutshell, your corporation owes or will owe $859,000. As we speak, I will keep your own personal accounts separate. Your corporation assets in the emergency and operating funds total about $540,000. Based on these figures you would need more than $300,000 to pay off the debts. This would also reflect balances of zero in those two accounts. I suspect you would need to keep such an amount in these two funds so you really need new revenues of about $900,000. Thus, the question is, where do you find nearly a million dollars? I have some suggestions but I do not feel comfortable with such figures."

"First, Jerome," Martha said, "should we continue in tobacco? I trust you. You must help me."

"I would not grow a single stalk of tobacco ever again for a dozen reasons; but I am not you and you are not me."

"Jerome, I have a secret." She paused and Jerome felt sure he had expressed himself too strongly. "This is not about tobacco, because you may be assured we will never grow another golden leaf, but something else. There is a great deposit of fuller's earth under a thousand acres of the three thousand my husband last purchased. Do not ask me how he knew because I don't know but he had no doubts whatsoever. Now in light of this, perhaps our task can be less depressing." There was a warm smile on Martha's face.

"How much did your husband feel he could realize out of this thousand acres?" Jerome asked.

"He guessed fifteen hundred dollars per acre. This acreage is the one that has virgin pine growing on it."

"I would sell the land after I cut the forest. I would not keep land that has little use," Jerome said.

"My husband said the same."

"I would clear cut the thousand acres," Jerome said. "Then I would sell the land. I would guess the total from this would be about two million. I would then thin the other thousand acres he last purchased. While I was doing this, I would thin the other acres needed. I believe a realistic figure would be about two and a half million. I would pay off all debts, leaving the amounts that are currently in the two funds. This would give you more than a million and a half, likely more, to invest. This is the best time for tax purposes, considering the two lost crops.

"You would still have over seventeen thousand acres. Joseph Randolph would be smiling at you when land was the subject. Let me go a step beyond. David wishes to increase the cattle and peanut operation. He wants to increase the pastures and increase the corn acreage as well. This operation seems safe and profitable, as well as honorable.

"You may wish to look at catfish production, as suggested by April. Vegetable growing will soon be big here because of climate, land and water. I have some other ideas I will save for later.

"One other thing. Take some time off. Travel. Buy a new car. I'll wait and let my mother tell you what you ought to do." They both laughed.

"How quickly can all this happen that you have mentioned, Jerome?"

"If you move immediately, it could be completed by the first of the year."

"Jerome, I hope that you will send me a generous bill for your services. I know what has been said and done will remain our business alone." She left with a smile on her face.

No one seemed to know what to expect when the family shareholders met as planned.

Martha said, "A few days ago we paid our respects to your father and my husband, who made all of this possible. I think he would want and expect, if he were here, for us to get on with the business at hand. I think the first order of business is the selecting of a new slate of officers. I believe this is required. Is there a suggested slate to amend the previous one?"

David rose. "I would recommend the slate as follows: Martha Randolph, president; Joe Randolph, vice president and operational officer, operating under the direction of the shareholders; and Charles Randolph as our secretary-treasurer."

Charles stood. "Before we take action, I must ask you to withdraw my name. I do not know of my future at this time. I am not prepared to discuss such but I would ask my name be withdrawn. I would like to substitute David's name in my place. He is quite capable." Charles sat down once again.

April stood. "I believe some things are obvious. Mother is the major stockholder. Joe has the next largest amount. Charles is really saying that a residency is required for him to complete his degree at school. No one is certain about Michael John at the moment. I will be away at school full time. Stephen will be a full time senior in high school. I believe the slate proposed and amended by Charles will serve Randolph Place best. I move we vote on the slate as amended."

"As president, I will preside at the regular and/or called meetings," their mother said after the slate had been approved.

"Now I have a sheet of figures for each of you to read and study. It is important that all of us know exactly where we stand on our operation." She passed out the first sheet, providing the information concerning the mortgages, the reserve and operating accounts and the interest.

After some time had passed and each had looked carefully at the figures Martha said, "I do not wish that we begin with debts of this sort hanging over us. I do not believe you wish to operate in this manner as a group.

"After securing some facts and figures I present to you some possibilities, recommendations if you like, to consider as a means to place this organization in a position that will free us of debt and provide ample security as we begin anew. Perhaps you will offer different or better suggestions. Study these for a few minutes and we will open the floor for discussion."

For several minutes no one spoke. Finally Joe raised his head and asked, "Where did you secure all these figures? All this information?"

"I don't believe that is important unless we find it to be incorrect. I have consulted with such officials as I consider necessary. This information is based on bank balances and other such information I could secure."

"Is this the work of Jerome Lee? I think we have a right to know," Joe said. It was obvious he was not pleased.

"Jerome did some of the work for me. I am quite pleased that he has assisted in providing the essential information needed, much of which only your father knew."

"I see there is a firm recommendation to eliminate tobacco. This has been our bread and butter. This has been the backbone of Randolph Place. I am sure we would not have a third bad year in a row!"

"In a few minutes we will let the shareholders decide. The information I have provided for you is correct and up to date. The recommendations are just that, recommendations."

For several minutes questions were asked and explanations provided concerning the information sheets.

"Shall we vote on the recommendations as a whole or individually?" Martha asked. Then she answered her own question. "We must do so individually."

Joe spoke, "Stephen and I can't win. The cards are stacked. I think Joseph Randolph would consider this the worst day of his life. I am glad he did not have to witness this decision. If you heard a noise it was my father turning over in his grave." He quietly got up and moved toward the door.

"I wish you would remain, Joe. I thought we were a family."

Joe turned once to look back at the assembled group, then left the room without another word.

"I'll go too," Stephen said as he jumped from his seat. "It would have been different if Father was alive."

"You will remain here," Martha said. "You are still a minor. We need you to assist in making important decisions." Stephen sat back down but did not utter a sound.

"There will be a review of what has been done at our meeting next month. We should be able to know a great deal more at that time. The meeting is adjourned," their mother said.

Charles and April sat in the library and looked at each other as if each was waiting for the other to speak.

"I'll go first," April said. "This was the best thing to happen to us in a long time. I would not think of Joseph in a manner that is disrespectful but tonight we finally got on the right track. The thing that more than amazes me is what Mother has done. I had no idea this was in her. All of my life I saw her as a domestic person, leaving everything to Joseph. I can't believe what I heard and saw. No experienced business executive could have prepared or performed better!"

"I agree. I had no idea. I'm still not sure I saw what I saw. She had every necessary fact needed, with the possible exception of some projected taxes."

"I believe she is more concerned about Joe leaving than we know. This was a bitter disappointment. You can also tell she is most concerned with the absence of Michael John," April said.

CHAPTER 65

How many weeks had passed since he had left home? Ten? Fifteen? Longer? It must have been about June first, since he remembered April's graduation. Yes, and the tobacco harvest, had it not been destroyed, would have started. But why be concerned? What did it matter?

When Michael John had left home, no one could have been more unsure. He had never been away from home for two consecutive nights. He had never been more than three hundred miles from the place he once called home.

After riding westward for nearly a day he had stopped at a truck stop. Never before had he realized the number of trucks on the road and how many traveled at night.

As he was eating a person at the next table had asked, "Going far?"

"I'm not sure," Michael John said. "I would like to find a vocational school where I could learn more about woodworking."

The stranger said, "The best school in the entire area is about two hundred miles from here." Michael John asked a number of questions and was impressed with the answers he received.

Michael John arrived there at noon the next day. He drove around and looked. He asked questions at a café and at the gas station. He was impressed. He liked the size of the town. It was too large to be called a town, but nothing like the two or three cities he had seen. He asked himself aloud, "Why not? I've got to go someplace." Before three o'clock he had found a place to get a room and meals and had paid his fee to enroll in a study of carpentry.

Days passed slowly at the beginning. He flung himself into his work, more to relieve his thoughts than to improve his skills. During the first week not ten minutes passed without him thinking of Robin, April, his mother or someone at Randolph Place. More than once he was about to return, regardless of everything. However, as the days passed into weeks he became more reconciled and it was not as painful as in the beginning.

After several weeks he became concerned because he had not let April know where he was, despite his promise. He tried to think why he had continued to remain in isolation and confessed that had he contacted April, he might have learned of something to add to his problems. He decided to wait longer before contacting anyone.

It was in his leisure hours that he felt the most pain. It was then that the lonely feelings seemed unbearable.

One Saturday, as he walked through the city park, he saw some men and children feeding the squirrels and birds. He watched for a few minutes, then learned what kind of food to purchase and where. Each Saturday morning following he found himself anxious to secure some food, get to the park bench and start his feeding. Before long he had some squirrels that would take a peanut from his hand and two or three birds that would fly in and sit on the back of the bench a few feet from him. After a while he found himself talking to them; they seemed to understand.

Another Saturday morning, after he had dispensed the food, he looked about him and at the bench on which he sat. It had been worn slick by the many people who had come here over the years. Naturally, he looked to see how it was constructed and in moments he knew that he could duplicate the structure.

Suddenly, and unexpectedly a girl appeared, seemingly from nowhere, and sat on the far end of the bench. He had not observed her before she sat down and he had no idea as to the direction from which she had come.

A quick glance at her revealed colorful, flamboyant wearing apparel. He could see that it was cheap and worn. The wrinkles revealed that it had not been ironed recently. He looked at her hair. It was a washed-out blond. It did not look very clean. It had not been combed recently and the edges were uneven, as if she had attempted to trim it herself.

Her face had more than a shade too much of powder and paint. He looked at her eyes. They were a pale blue, different from any he could remember seeing. As he looked more closely he could tell they were hard and knowing.

How old would she be? Twenty? Twenty-five? Fifteen going on forty? He could not tell. She could be any age.

He realized he was staring at her. He knew this was rude but it didn't seem to matter. Then she gave him a big smile and as her lips parted, he could see the discolored teeth. As she smiled some lines formed across her forehead that were much too pronounced. The eyebrows and lashes had been darkened.

She smiled again and asked, "You got a name? Ain't seen you before. Reckon this is not your home." Michael John did not respond. He realized he was blushing.

She continued, "Pretty day, ain't it? Ain't no clouds around. Won't be no rain. All our days ain't like this." Michael John remained silent.

The girl stared at him. "Yep, I can see you ain't from around here. Bet you're a school boy away from home for the first time. Bet you are lonesome." She gave another half smile and Michael John felt his face darken even more.

As she rearranged her position on the smooth bench she let her skirt rise well above her knees. She inched closer toward him. He let his eyes drop toward her legs and noticed they were thin and somewhat emaciated.

As she saw him look down she gave a lavish smile and he realized she knew where he had been looking. She saw his face grow darker. Again she lifted her body and her skirt inched a little higher; she moved even closer.

"Ain't got no one with you I see. No one. Not a soul. I can see you are quite lonely, maybe homesick. Yep, you look a little withdrawn. Ain't right for one to be lonely except now and then. Just not good for a mortal being. Reckon that's why God created Eve. I'd guess you needed company but I'd guess you'd know that." She looked him over with painstaking scrutiny, then continued, "You look about as timid and downcast and mournful and inexperienced as any I've ever seen."

For several seconds neither spoke but continued to look at each other. Michael John thought, Why am I here? What am I doing here with this person? He looked to see if any other students from his school were nearby. Then he remembered the story about the old lady in the nursing home. The visiting preacher, with an audience greater than in his home church, had asked, "Why are we here? Why are we here?" The old lady in the back had raised her fragile hand above her head and said, "Preacher, I don't know why you are here but I'm here 'cause I ain't all there!"

Michael John smiled at his thoughts. The girl interpreted the smile for her and moved an inch closer; her skirt rose somewhat higher than before. As she moved closer he felt the edge of the smooth seat and knew he could retreat no further. A slight part of him already extended beyond the smooth edge. He wanted to get up and leave but his sense of curiosity seemed too great.

Michael John asked, "What do you want of me? I have no more food to give the birds and squirrels!"

"Why you ask me that? I ain't said I wanted nothing, have I? Why, I don't even know you, not even your name. No, I ain't asked the first thing about you." She looked directly into his eyes.

For a moment she was silent. She looked him over again from head to toe. Then she smiled, "I can tell about you. I've seen a lot of 'em from time to time and looked 'em over good. Yes sir, I can tell about you. You ain't been around a whole heap of girls; you ain't used to girls. Bet you ain't never had a sho-nuff real girl. Bet you ain't never knowed one as you oughta in all your born days!"

Michael John flushed even more deeply. He looked at her and felt genuine sorrow. He suspected she had known every form of misery. Yes, there would be hunger. Sorrow? Alienation? Abuse? He could guess all these and a dozen more. He felt a touch of kindness and asked, "When have you had your last meal? I'll buy you a dinner if you are hungry."

"How old are you?" she asked, ignoring his question.

"Old enough." This was the first response that came to mind. "How old are you?"

"Just short of twenty. Bet you thought I was thirteen or fourteen, maybe even sixteen or seventeen. I ain't no child. Been a whole heap of time passed since I've been a child."

Michael John surveyed her again rapidly. He knew beyond all doubt that her experiences and maturity were far beyond her actual age. He wondered if she could even remember her childhood days.

"You asked me if I need to eat, if I was hungry. Do I look like one to ask for something? Something for nothing? Would you think I'd take charity from you? No, not you, not nobody. Ain't my way. My mama warned me about many things. She said, of all things, to sho-nuff watch out for such forward men who would offer such without a just cause and I ain't seen no just cause. You don't fool me none, not for a minute. Fact is, mama gave me a whole list to watch out for but she said none was as dangerous as men who offer without a reason."

"You mentioned your mother. Where is she? What kind of family do you have? Why are you not with them?"

"She warned me about that too. Ain't right you asking all them personal things. That ain't your business to know. Not you or no one else. But I'll tell you what. I'd be happy to work for a meal. You ain't had no girl and a little taste of experience would be helpful, would go a long, long way toward your manhood. I'd say, after looking you over good, you need it more'n most.

She continued, "Yep, I could do that very thing. I'll show you some things to carry over with you. Ain't no other way you gonna learn. Ain't no words or pictures gonna give you the help you need. It would take some of that timid feeling right out of you. If you think you can take a little or a lot of this kind of learning, I'd be glad to earn that dinner! All you need to decide is if we need to be friendly or not. Like I told you, you need experience, I need a meal, and I ain't gonna have no charity. No sir, no charity."

"But wouldn't you feel this would be wrong?" Michael John asked.

"Ain't important! Wouldn't take long. Yep, like I said, no charity!"

"Let me buy you a meal. I really believe you are hungry. Yes, you even look hungry." He surveyed her once again. He noted the skirt another two inches higher. He didn't know why but he had never felt so much sorrow and pain for anyone, including their own people in the quarters. She was so thin. "You must eat something. I insist."

She gave her biggest and brightest smile. Once again he saw her dark teeth as she turned toward him. "Bet I could have made you happier than you've ever been, happier than you have ever known. I know how to do a lot of things, how to get the most out of anything, how to deal with those who ain't been there before. Yep, could have removed that timid feeling that's always there for beginners. You've got a chance to lose a thing or two you don't wanna keep. That shyness, boy, will cause you all kind of trouble and pain down the road. The longer you wait, the harder it's gonna be. And you know, only the two of us would ever know about the things said and done. You could put that dread, that horrible feeling, behind you and I could earn a good meal. I'd bet you'd think I'd earned a fine meal, maybe two or three meals!"

Michael John could not speak and it was obvious that there was only one way she would eat. Suddenly, she looked him over one last time, got up, pulled her skirt down and tossed her uncombed hair to the side. She then moved in front of him and placed a hand on each shoulder. She looked into his eyes and he could not turn away; her eyes bore into him. She gave a half smile, shook her head and slowly moved away. She did not look back even once until she reached the sidewalk. She turned, shook her head once again and slowly crossed the street. When she reached the sidewalk on the other side, she turned one last time and raised her hand in a gesture of nonchalance. She then proceeded down the sidewalk and turned the corner.

A sadness filled Michael John's heart. When had she lost her innocence? Was it at age ten? Twelve? Probably no later. How had it occurred? Had it been some older person who had abused a youthful child? But more importantly, when had she lost hope? He suspected all hope had been abandoned. He remembered April discussing the meaning of hope.

Michael John looked in the direction she had gone. He had a strong feeling, a powerful urge to do something. He rushed across the street to where he had last seen her. He had no idea what he would say. As he turned the corner she was nowhere to be seen. He walked hurriedly down the street, looking into each store, but she was nowhere to be found. She had simply disappeared.

In a few minutes he returned to the park to the same smooth bench, hoping she would return, but he knew deep down that she would not.

Michael John did not fully understand why he returned to the same park and that same smooth park bench every day for the next two weeks. As the days passed he felt that she would not return. On the last day, as he waited, he suddenly realized that perhaps there was some hope for her, that all had not been completely lost. Yes, where would you find another that would go hungry, perhaps starve, before they would take charity or welfare. No, this girl was not all bad. There was more than a flicker of hope.

Michael John did not see this strange nameless girl again; however, few days would pass that he did not think of her. He closed his eyes in an effort to remove the memory but continued to see her, see those eyes that had seemed so harsh and knowing.

Within days he seemed to know it was about time to go home. The feeling increased daily. Soon he must make plans. He felt it was time to end his self-imposed exile.

Chapter 66

"It is time for you to go," Martha said as April climbed into her Chevy, on her way to enroll at Auburn. Martha forced a big smile as she saw her only daughter about to begin a new adventure. It was a practiced and forced smile. Her heart was breaking but she could not let April know. There comes a time in life when those who are ready to fly must leave the nest.

"You will not drive fast. You will call and write often. Now go, before I make a total fool of myself." With that Martha watched as April drove down the lane where, in time past, they had planted the flowers and trees together.

As Martha turned to reenter the house she could not help thinking of a remark April had made as she was packing. "I shall cut away a part of my life. It is time to put away, as Paul told us, some childish things. I have closed one chapter and started another. My childhood has ended. It must remain only as a memory. When change occurs, it should be so that few messy details and frayed edges will remind me of the days of yesterday." Martha was again reminded that life must be lived for the moment.

A day later Charles stood before his mother, Jack and Sandra Jenkins and Uncle Edd. Gena and Meggie were to depart for Tallahassee and F.S.U. "These girls are no longer children. You must allow them to grow up, to become independent, to make a life for themselves. I know that for you, as well as for them, life will never be the same. I know that you would not have them stay. Much of your work and plans were centered around this very moment. I'll keep an eye on them but I insist we let them grow up."

"Could they not commute as you have done?" Sandra asked. "Would it not be better to take one step at a time?"

"You are telling me that Gena is your baby and this is all you have. However, college is not the same if one doesn't live there and become a part of the school. It is difficult, nearly impossible, if you do not live there, to understand the true meaning. I want them to have and know the thrill of college life. No, the right decision has been made. You can get there or they here in less than an hour. It's not like Eric Lee coming home once a year from Oklahoma.

"I have an apartment in the same complex where they will be staying. I need to be there because of my work. I'll let you know of their progress, as I am still involved here and will return regularly."

Meggie said, "We will not become a burden. Charles has many responsibilities. He has his own graduate program. Now why don't we go before someone gets emotional." She saw that Uncle Edd was making a major effort to keep his tender emotions under control.

As they moved along the road to Tallahassee Charles said, "You are not children any longer. I hope, however, you will always let a little childhood remain in your heart. For you, a new life has commenced. I will not be your nursemaid. You don't need one. I have supreme confidence in the two of you. You must learn many things for yourself. Think before you act. If you have to ponder for hours as to something being right or wrong, step back and take another look. Usually right doesn't require a close examination. You will make mistakes. Some mistakes one can erase, can overcome. Some leave scars forever. You don't need a lecture. I shall say no more."

When Charles returned home on Friday evening and went to the store he was greeted by Jack and Uncle Edd. "Where are our girls?"

"They are involved in some wholesome and decent school activities. This is a part of college life. Trust them. I do. I don't believe we will ever be disappointed.

"I'll finish some work and I have promised to help David learn some of the book work here. I'll tell you later of some things that will make you proud." He smiled, turned and left for the office.

An hour later Charles said to David, "Let's stop until tomorrow." They locked the safe and the door, then left. Never had Charles seen David improve so much. For the first time he seemed his old self.

After they parted company David passed his mother's house but did not stop. He knew Charles would be with her and the conversation would center around his three girls. He passed Joe's house and could not help thinking about his oldest brother. How tragic, how sad. With no duties, no tobacco, no Joseph, he was no longer the same. David thought about how he might help but quickly acknowledged that any suggestion he made would be both rejected and resented.

He felt hungry and hurried his steps toward his own home. The pain that had been so severe and had lasted so long had finally dissipated. No longer did he dread to enter as he had for so many months. He could never repay his mother, Mary and April, who had helped so much to make him whole again.

He entered the bedroom and found some clean clothing that had been prepared by his mother or Mary. He kicked off his shoes, shed his clothing and stepped into the shower. The water was so refreshing that he made no immediate attempt to hurry and for the moment forgot the earlier pangs of hunger. Tomorrow was Saturday and he decided he might sleep late. He let the water trickle over his body. He realized his recovery was nearly complete. He remembered Kathy saying, "You must find a new life." Now for the first time it seemed to take on the meaning he knew she had in mind.

David continued to linger though he knew his body was clean. Then he heard a voice say, "Are you going to stay in there all evening? Your cook is preparing your dinner and cooks do not take pleasure in serving cold food." He heard the door close and knew Mary had retreated to his kitchen. For a brief moment he had, for some reason, hoped she had remained in his bedroom. He wondered why such a thought had entered his mind. It was the first time this had ever happened.

Ten minutes later David approached his combination kitchen, den and dining area. He asked, "Did you clean and iron my clothes?" He looked down at the clothes he was wearing.

She smiled, ignored his question and said, "I thought you would never finish and I am famished."

David looked about him. He could see a red light on the stove marked "broil." He could smell the wonderful aroma of the beef cooking. He heard the percolator make a final gurgling sound, its duties completed. On the table he saw two plates with silver, napkins, cups and saucers, and two glasses filled with ice cubes and water. There were two bottles, Heinz 57 Sauce and Heinz Tomato Ketchup.

"I can see there is much to do to train you properly. Perhaps, though, too much value is placed on such things. Oh, I suppose we would always wish to be correct but there are other things more important. This would take time away from other pleasures." She looked at David and he smiled and nodded. She turned back to her cooking duties. "Stay away. You would only get in my way. So sit in the chair over there and relax. You work much too hard." She carried him a small glass of wine.

David looked at her, as if he was seeing the real Mary for the first time. She seemed to be slightly taller than he remembered. Perhaps she had on heels. He looked. She didn't. She seemed even more slender than before but she had always been slender. He wondered if she had lost some weight. He looked upward and saw her profile. Her ample breasts remained high and she wore a blouse that seemed a little tight; he noted that not one but two buttons had remained unfastened at the top. He could easily see the swells of her breasts as they pushed outward against the cotton blouse.

The rather long, oval face was smooth, pretty and pleasant, all in a rather strange Gypsy sort of way. Her hair flowed slightly over her shoulders. The whiteness of her forehead did not tell of the hours she spent outdoors. Her hair was the color of dark rust, like an oak leaf in the winter before it was to fall.

He looked at her eyes. Eyes usually told more about another than any other feature. They seemed to be the same color as her hair. In them glowed kindness, tenderness and compassion but as he looked more closely, they seemed to display a form of sadness as well. Then in a matter of moments they seemed to change, to sparkle and brighten. They seemed to dance with a mood of merriment as well as devilment, an imperishable beauty not easily described.

Mary took two steps toward him, turned back to pick up a cloth and wipe her hands, then again made her way toward him. When she reached where he was sitting she placed her hands on his shoulders and said, "Thank God you are a real human being again. There were times when I wasn't sure. Now I know that you are well and I always knew you were worth saving." She dropped her hands and turned quickly. She moved into the den area and turned on a switch, then he heard the soft sounds of the slow and romantic music of some decades ago. She moved back into the kitchen area and said, "I like the music of our last generation best. It seems to say some things I cannot hear in our music of today. I hope you don't mind a little music with your meal."

"You seem to always know so many things," David said. "Would you know that is my favorite record? How would you guess or know such things? What other surprises may I expect?" He smiled as he had two years before.

"Well, I have a pie and more wine in the refrigerator. Perhaps we will both need to sweeten up a bit. On the other hand, however, I have always been sweet and it seems this is the first time you noticed." He looked at her and smiled, but did not speak.

"I hope I am your favorite sister-in-law." She placed an emphasis on in-law. "In fact, I am your only one. I had thought some months ago that Robin would be one as well but something happened. I would guess April knows but she has not spoken about it. Charles said I knew as much as he did."

"I was quite excited about it. I probably disturbed my father when I suggested Michael John not wait. I thought Robin and Michael John would make the perfect couple. You know, I doubt if the reason or reasons are ever known. Perhaps it is best."

"Get to the table, David. Just move out of my way. Men do not understand about kitchens and cooks. While we are eating, I want to talk about you." David looked at her but still did not speak. She added, "Take your wine glass."

Mary was about to say the blessing when David stopped her. "I haven't blessed anything in a long time. Suppose I start now." She knew that he was well.

As they began their meal he asked, "How does one truly thank another for saving his life? It was not only the hundreds of meals or the clothes you washed and ironed or the clean house where everything was always in place, but also the way you did it.

"You never sought a reward. You have never received one. I would guess for weeks I didn't say thank you or even acknowledge your presence or the contributions. But I received something in addition to the items I mentioned. I had a chance to really know you for the first time. One can see a person daily for years but may never really know them. I have been attempting to think of something or some way to repay you. I must. I could not live with myself if I didn't. You must help me once again." He looked at Mary and could tell she was pleased with his thoughts.

She responded, "Someday I will likely need you as I believed you needed me. I have no doubt but you would do the same for me, even more. Just to know that is all the payment I need. You are kind. You are special. You are worth saving."

He explained, "Let me refer to Kathy once more. She was my great love, my life. I don't have to tell you about her. Now I accept that she is gone. Before she left me she suggested, actually insisted, that I, in time, should seek another. She spoke of the meaning of love and she also spoke of growing old alone. As the days pass I am able to see more clearly what she meant. This is not to suggest that she will not always remain dear to me. Now let me leave Kathy. I felt I had to say this once more. Now I feel it is time, as she said, to move on with my life."

"David, you need to review something else. Your mother, April and I did what we did because we love you. It was not done for payment in return. People that love each other do not act except in a spirit of love. We love you. It's as simple as that. Now, as you said, it is time to put Kathy to rest. It is also time to put the idea of repayment to rest."

"I should have seen the real Mary in the time you have been here. I never saw the real you."

"There were few opportunities and fewer reasons. I am happy that you feel kindly about me." She went to the turntable and turned the record.

She returned to the table and looked again at David. "This is my favorite time of the day. The last fading light casts a shadow over the panes. It is twilight time and it says to me that day is done — as the song says, a time when shadows fall."

They ate Mary's pie and remained silent. Each seemed to reflect on the twilight and the music, each seeming to say that silence can be golden, a thing of beauty.

Mary went to the refrigerator and returned with the bottle of chilled wine. "Even our Lord participated. Was not His first miracle the changing of water to wine? And did not Paul say that a little was good for one? We can always finds ways and means to justify our desires." They drank in silence. Mary refilled the glasses again, then said, "Let's sit on the sofa. We will clean the table later. I have some things I want to say to you, some things I have thought about for a long time."

When they were seated she said, "You said earlier this evening that you wanted to do something to show your appreciation for my concern for you in recent months. Perhaps you can. First, I wish you to start by being a good listener." He nodded but seemed unsure as to how she would proceed.

"When there is a story to tell, it is only logical that one should start at the beginning. You will recall when I came to the Randolph plantation as Joe's wife, we stayed at the Randolph home until a house could be constructed. I loved your brother and I believe he loved me at that time. A short time after I arrived I heard a conversation between Joe and his father. They were unaware of my presence, though I had made no effort to be an eavesdropper. I never let anyone, until tonight, know what I heard.

"Your father was very upset that Joe had married me. In the course of the conversation I was referred to as a whore. I was stunned. I wanted to scream out and to race away from that place. For a time I thought I wanted to die. Later I was to discover that your father had picked out a wife for his son and that any person other than Mr. Randolph's choice would have been a whore. Knowing the things that mattered most to your father, you would guess that property and money were major issues. Perhaps there was some consolation knowing the label given to me was more or less a figure of speech. Yet no one could ever guess the hours that I relived those awful moments.

"I am not exactly sure what occurred when the place was incorporated but after that time life was never the same. I can only guess that Joe had envisioned himself in a different capacity, a different role. Though I was not a part of the decision process or anything else in the corporation, it seemed that he took his disappointments out on me. Perhaps he looked at me as the woman who destroyed the dream world which Joseph had envisioned for him. I do not know. It really doesn't matter now.

"It was not very long before changes occurred. With the loss of the first crop of tobacco, he ceased to have any interest in me. Oh, he would greet me at times with a form of congeniality but this seemed to result from early habits, or perhaps a weary or guilty conscience, or both. Long before the second crop was lost even this ceased.

"A moment ago we sat in silence and it was good. This, too, can be a beautiful form of communication. But the silence at my home is different. It is not a silence of nature and harmony and love. It is a silence of unconcern and indifference. I find myself alone in thought as well as in bed. For two years this has been true. I cannot continue this form of silence. One is created for other things, not for this loneliness which is above all others.

"For two years Joe has followed a rather specific pattern. He has evaded all responsibility because there has been no tobacco. He leaves about noon. I suppose he goes to the club to play golf, to drink and to gamble. Most week nights he gets home between twelve and three. On Friday and Saturday it is closer to four or five. It is not uncommon for him to be quite drunk. I have no idea how he drives under such conditions. It is not difficult for one woman to detect the tell-tale signs of another woman. He usually says little. If he does speak, it is something unpleasant. I can never remember a kind word or compliment since this farm became Randolph Place.

"I guess your first question would be why haven't I left him? Why have I continued to stay here under such conditions? Oh, a woman can find reason after reason. I felt he would change in time. Perhaps he would awaken to discover he had a wife who cared. Then, too, most women do not care for divorces. They are usually ugly.

"Perhaps it has dawned on you that I am happy with many who live here. Many members of your family are special. And yes, there is another reason. Where would I go and what would I do?

"Several times I have actually packed some bags to leave but I never did, for good reasons and no reason at all. It isn't that easy.

"The last time I was packing to go, an event, a dreadful event occurred in your life and I found a new reason for staying. I was needed. I didn't know exactly what I should do but there were some things I knew I could perform. For a time this need filled a void where love had once existed. Just as some people live daily to see certain things happen to them, I found a deep satisfaction as I saw you become well and whole again.

"In some ways the relationship between Joe and myself has deteriorated even further. There are calls about debts, gambling debts, I suppose. I have been asked to tell him of some threats being made. Women call. Yes, more than one. A man called recently and asked if I knew my husband was with his wife at that very moment. He offered an address, a telephone number. Why, he would even come and get me so I would go and see for myself. Naturally, I refused his information and invitation. I had reached a point that it no longer mattered.

"You have been patient, David, I believe more than I could have been if you were telling me such a story."

She emptied the wine bottle into their glasses. As she did David looked upon the sad face before him. Then she said, "You, David, have lived and loved and, in turn, were loved with a love beyond description. I live with someone that ceased to love me years ago. It is like living with someone who died long ago. Need I say more?

"Where would he be tonight? In a game? Drunk? With a woman? It doesn't matter anymore. Perhaps I loved him once. I believe I thought so. Now you are well and my reason for staying is over. In a short time I must make some decisions. As April said about the quarters people, there is no hope!

"I have finished now. There is nothing more to say."

David had been a good and patient listener. "I had guessed but had not believed it had reached this point. I don't see how you have managed, have lived under such conditions. You are an amazing person with strength and courage and faith. You are full of common sense that seems to evade so many. I do not know what to say, what to do. I was the lucky one. I feel so utterly helpless."

Mary got up. "Don't feel too helpless. We have to clean up this mess." They carried the dishes to the sink and returned some items to the refrigerator.

"Too few for the dishwasher," Mary said. She opened a drawer and removed two aprons. She tied one around herself and one around David. As she finished tying the string she slapped him on his seat and remarked, "Now get to work and prove you are worthy of my keep." She washed and he dried until they had finished. Then she went over to the far side of the table with a cloth to wipe the surface. As she worked David saw a person who was sweet and tender, honest and humble, beautifully simple and gentle. She was not an avaricious flirt or schemer, not one of falseness or lies. She was, simply, Mary.

As she cleaned the table David could see much of her breasts where she had left her blouse unbuttoned. He looked at her figure with all the fertile curves; he did not think of Joe or Kathy, but only of Mary. As he gazed at her, he was unsure of himself.

She saw him staring at her and smiled. She approached him and removed the apron. As she did she put her arms on his shoulders, lightly at first, then more firmly. As she rested her head on his chest and let her arms drop about his body, he heard her say, "Let me cry on your shoulder. You think you are lonely. You don't know the word or what it really means. God recognized the agony of loneliness and created Eve for Adam. Man and woman were not made to be lonely."

David looked into the rust colored eyes and saw the tears that had formed. This was the first time he had ever seen her cry. In a moment the eyes seemed to brighten and even twinkled slightly. In those eyes he seemed to see first a note of sadness, then one of exuberant hope, a sparkle of wonder and anticipation.

He looked down to see her beautiful mouth slightly open and a flush on her face. His arms encircled her body. He noticed once more the inviting breasts pressed against her half-open blouse. He pulled her toward him and she responded in like manner.

It seemed very natural and right to do what they desired so ardently. In their natural embrace they found comfort and tenderness, as well as intense pleasure. They clutched each other and neither expressed betrayal, only joy.

At first his lips touched hers only lightly, then he realized her moist lips were waiting for him.

Mary felt beautiful inside as she had never been before. It was as if she was in the heavens, floating away into the soft white clouds. She felt a warm swelling in her breasts, a richness in her thighs and an urgency throughout her body. It seemed as if she had no control, nor did she wish to.

It was at this point that David made a slight and feeble attempt to withdraw; yet he knew he had only acted half-heartedly and decided against it. Mary seemed to sense this and pulled him closer, her warm body pressed against his. She shuddered and clung ever closer, as if he might escape.

Then she released him, took his hand, led him into the bedroom and closed the door. The light from the bathroom was more than ample.

They removed their clothes and shoes and when they were naked, they pressed against each other and seemed to become one. They moved toward the bed and eased in beside each other. They kissed, touched and explored. Then David heard a soft but urgent voice say, "Now, David. It's time." In moments they engulfed each other.

The second time they moved with less urgency and seemed to savor each second, each moment. For a long period they seemed content to hold each other and there was a silence of peace, harmony and satisfaction.

A few minutes later David kissed her again and again and for a third time they made love. For Mary the past two years had seemed like a long time of emptiness. She now realized that the man she thought she had once loved did not seem to matter anymore, yet she had no commitment that David wished to take his place.

A few minutes later, as they continued to hold each other close, she said, "I must go, dear David. We both have a great deal of thinking to do."

He responded, "I can now understand the words of a wise one: 'Where there is marriage without love, there will be love without marriage.'" Mary thought of this many times before the night was over.

As she placed her hand on the door to leave she said, "Dearest David, I guess what we did could only be defined and described as adultery. But real adultery, my dear one, is living with someone who does not love you. If you really think about it, it is adultery of the soul. I have no guilty feelings. I have no regrets. None! And yes, I'd do it again and again — and again!"

CHAPTER 67

David had insisted on walking Mary to her home but she refused. "Wait until you see my lights come on and you will know I am inside and safe." She switched on lights in two rooms and saw David cut off his porch light.

She went to her bedroom and took off her clothes. In the bathroom she looked at her naked body in the full length mirror. She adjusted the shower and let the spray spill over her. She was in no hurry. She knew she could not sleep. She knew that Joe would not return until after three o'clock on Saturday morning. As she soaped her shapely body, her breasts and thighs, she felt a sudden urge, as if David's hands were upon her. She smiled with excitement as she remembered.

Later she sat in the den and drank a glass of water. She thought about her life here at Randolph Place. She had been so unprepared. She thought about Joseph. What had he received in life? He worked all the time. He never took a vacation. Had he used his life unwisely? Suddenly, she saw a picture in her mind that had never occurred to her. He nearly accomplished everything he had established as goals. There was a lovely and beautiful wife. He had fathered six children that she knew about. He had put together one of the largest plantations ever. He was the largest independent tobacco man. He had become a county commissioner. And yes, he probably had convinced himself and others he had become somebody. He had accomplished all of these goals. She suspected in light of what so many now felt was important, his peers would label him a success. Perhaps that is what is important. Yet, in her own mind, he had never really lived. Who was right?

As she considered the last few hours and thought once more of Joseph she suspected that, wherever he was, he had an 'I told you so' smile on his face. She could still hear his words as he had asked, "Where did you get this whore?" Was that what she was? She decided to attempt to read some and go to bed.

In a few moments she dropped her book as her mind raced in another direction. Did I plan this? Did David plan this? Did he *believe* I planned it? How will he act and what will he say when we see each other again? Will he wish me to come again soon? Did he not enjoy the evening as well as I did? Will he want me enough to marry me? Will I continue as tonight if answers are not found?

She could not help wondering if he would leave Randolph Place. Was David truly as passionate as he had demonstrated? Could they really separate or transform their physical attraction for each other into a love deep enough to last? She had a thousand questions. She was not sure of the first answer.

She went to bed and somehow managed to sleep. She slept deeply. Sometime later she felt an arm reached around her and for a moment thought David had come to her. Then she heard a drunken voice. "It's love making time!" She felt Joe's hands on her body, took off her gown and gave herself to him. In moments he was asleep. She wasn't even sure he would remember.

David lay on his bed, wide awake, his hands folded under his head, a habit he had developed early in life when he felt he needed to plan or review something important. An aroma still lingered that was not unusual after such an evening.

As he reviewed the events he pondered how all of this had come about. It had all happened so suddenly. He could not be sure if he or Mary had been the party to initiate the ensuing events. Did it matter really? He believed not. It had happened and the only question that really mattered now was how to proceed in the future.

For a moment a feeling of guilt engulfed him and he thought, I was raised and taught to be my brother's keeper and I now have become the keeper of his wife. He knew right from wrong. He knew that one of the ten great laws had been broken. He remembered Mary's words. "But real adultery is living with someone who doesn't love you. That is adultery of the soul."

His thoughts turned to Joe. If even a third of the reports he heard were true, he knew that the time was near for unpleasant things to happen. But even so, this did not give him an excuse for his behavior.

Mary had said she felt no sense of guilt, that she would do the same again and again. A smile slowly appeared on his face as he reviewed the evening. She had given herself so freely and so completely. She was so beautiful, so delightful.

His mind returned again to the many unanswered questions. Had she felt sorry for him? Was this an act of pity? If so, she did not understand men. A man, if a real man, deplored pity.

When he saw her tomorrow or the next day or the next, how would she react? Would there be remorse? Would one or both feel guilty? Would she wish to repeat the occasion?

What of the long run implications? He could not even guess. He arched up and turned out the light and as the room was engulfed in darkness he asked a question that he had deliberately blocked from his thoughts. Was this just a night in which two people gave to meet the demands of the body or was this more than that? Could it be that love had played a role?

He turned over and fell asleep, a smile on his face.

On the afternoon before Mary and David were to complicate their lives Martha said to her son, "Stephen, I'll have to call on you to take Pearl home, as I will need Ella for another two hours. I want to finish the loose ends before the weekend. She is ready when you are."

Pearl climbed into the seat of Stephen's new car. "Nice," she smiled. "I'm going to have a car like this some day."

"Cost a lot of money, Pearl. You'll have to marry a wealthy man because your present job will not get it done." He looked at her for a reaction. She had a smile on her nearly white face. He took one glance at her profile, then noticed that her skirt was halfway between her knees and hips.

Pearl had not missed his observation and said, "You know, I'm not like all these other girls on this place. I don't look like them, I don't talk like them and I won't be having one or two or more babies. No, I'm just not like them. You understand? I know you do because I've watched you."

"You are different, Pearl. I've noticed that. You have a lot of things going for you." Once again he looked at her furtively, allowing his eyes to linger. "I don't exactly know why you dropped out of school as soon as you were sixteen. I think this would be important but I won't say more. I've hated school all my life and in a few months I'll be as free as a bird."

"Stephen, everything a person is to learn is not in a textbook." Again she gazed sidelong at him and smiled. "There is not a great deal to learn where I was going to school. Can't get much out of walking classes or in classes of fifty, sixty, seventy or more.

"I'm not going to be here a lot longer. I suppose you can understand why. I don't fool with these people any more than is necessary. I find myself a little like Uncle Edd. Someday I may find myself a young Uncle Edd. I find him very special.

"You know, Stephen, I suppose I've been thinking about you more than I should, a big, strong handsome man with a new car. You have a lot of spare time now, as tobacco was your thing. I bet you have girls running after you and you don't really know what to do. You may know about tobacco and cars but I would guess you need some other training, some other skills." She looked at Stephen, let her skirt move upward another two inches and saw him look once again, then quickly turn his eyes toward the road.

Stephen's face turned a slight pink and he asked, "You could teach me?"

"Perhaps. It would depend on many things. You've thought of this? Life is not always a free ride. Then there are those who learn rather quickly but in your case, I would suspect you would need a full course. And no, I wouldn't charge you a cent. This would be wrong. I would feel like a call girl. Not me. Usually when one receives something special he usually wants to do something for the other party. Makes both parties feel better. You understand?"

Stephen looked once more at the skirt that had managed to move another inch or so. He saw her profile and could tell she had received many blessings. "Just when," Stephen asked, "could such a course begin?" He looked into her face. He did not have the courage to look down again.

"Never put off until tomorrow what one can do today! I'm going to be home for two hours or more before anyone comes. I think I could adjust any previous plans I had. I must repeat that generosity is a trait that enriches one to another."

An hour later Stephen left with a big smile on his face. It had not bothered him when he had taken his billfold from his pocket and pulled out a ten and she had reached over and plucked a twenty to go with it. He remembered her words, "Don't forget to pick up what I mentioned. My father would become suspicious if his belongings were missing. I won't be running around with a knee child, a lap child and another on the way. Wouldn't be good for us to do that!"

Stephen was to get a very special education. Not only did he enjoy every minute of his instruction but he also knew he was gaining some valuable experiences. Yes, it would not be long before he would wish to determine if he was ready for graduation and new conquests.

CHAPTER 68

Christmas of 1964 was special for Martha. As the season approached she felt a slight depression. Joseph was not to be among them. Kathy could not be forgotten. Then suddenly Michael John returned and she was filled with joy. "You're home! Oh, you're home again. Thank God. This is the best Christmas present ever!"

"I'm back and I'm here to stay," Michael John said. "I should have written and let you know. I didn't think. I'll not do that again."

He gave few details of where he had been or what he had been doing. He had asked about his father but his questions were few and he never asked a second time. He learned about the family members and the changes that had occurred. In a matter of days it was as if he had never been away.

April arrived from Auburn and Charles and "his girls" were home from F.S.U. for the holidays. Martha felt better than she had in months.

"I'm so happy you asked me out to dinner," April told Jerome as they dined at a restaurant in Tallahassee. "It seems ages since we were 'courting.' We learned so much about ourselves over lunch. As I recall, you were not as observant as I had believed." April discovered that Jerome could still blush.

"Yes, and you insisted on getting a full report. 'Oh, would some power the gift to give us to see ourselves as others see us!' Didn't Burns say something like that?" They both laughed.

They talked of many things. Jerome said, "I never suspected your mother to be the special person she is in business or farming. She is quite a leader. I had looked upon her as a mother and a homemaker."

"She has surprised everyone," April said. "She has put some things behind her in recent weeks. She seems happier than some would have guessed."

The dinner was delightful. They ate slowly and talked about families and current events. Both worked hard to keep things light. They were even silly from time to time.

As they started home April noted that Jerome had grown quiet, as if he had something on his mind but was hesitant to broach the subject. Sensing this, April decided she would probe. "You haven't told me of your future plans. Does your practice continue to grow? Are you happy with what you are doing? Are you happy about where you are doing it? What kind of social life are you having? I've got the questions! I move where angels dare not!"

"My business continues to grow. In the process I've learned a great deal about law and about people.

"My mother feels that I remained here because of her. This is not true. I returned here in the beginning because of her but I would prefer she not know this.

"I find myself more selective as to clients. I find it difficult to accept assignments to help or defend those where respect and values are missing. I am reminded by others that all deserve representation and I should give my best effort.

"I suspect my business has grown for two reasons. You gave me my start. No one had ever heard of Jerome Lee prior to the Maybe case. Secondly, I have smaller fees than most. I guess I was brought up to live and let live. Recently another lawyer described me, because of these strange standards, as 'crazy as hell'."

"And your social life? I may be more interested in this question!" April smiled. "A handsome young attorney on his way up must be pursued by many on a regular basis! You do know I am concerned!"

"No one has knocked down my doors. In fact, I'm afraid there have been few knocks. I suppose, however, it's like a man and his ship. You can't be waiting for one to return if you have not sent one out. I'll just wait."

"Do you have someone in mind? Have you just sat there and not let the lucky girl know?"

"Perhaps. It is possible that someone will show up, that perhaps she does know. A man can feel as strongly as a woman about being rejected. There is the unknown, the fear."

"You are afraid to let her know?"

"I am a coward at heart."

April said, "I've been thinking of adding my name to your growing list but I may be a coward also."

"With the Victors and Roberts and yes, even my baby brother Eric, I do not feel I could compete successfully. But I may decide in time to think about it." April did not respond.

Upon arriving at her home Jerome spoke, "This has been a delightful occasion for me. Will you let me do this again?"

April put her arms around him and kissed him in a passionate manner. "Yes, please ask me again. It was special for me also. Perhaps you can come and go fishing. I hear you enjoy the sport. I could cook dinner for us at Somewhere Else."

"I'd like that. I'd like that very much." He walked her to the door, she pecked him on the cheek, then he turned and was gone.

As Jerome returned to his car he remembered she had not made a comment about the three men in her life.

Three days later the family met. Each was encouraged to speak. David spoke of his area of work and they agreed to expand.

April told of the many things she had learned about the catfish industry. She discussed pond size, water depth, types of food and other things she had learned. "The demand is already greater than the supply. Fish seem to be a health food. Perhaps we should make some plans soon. I want to visit a processing plant. Then I will be ready for some recommendations."

Michael John said, "I think this may be something we can get into, as there will be amble labor. We have the water and the climate. Let's think seriously of such things."

Finally their mother said, "I have some other recommendations for all of us to think about, to consider. I want us to get away from the quarters settlement as we have known it. I have some steps for us to consider. We need to know our labor needs. Once this is determined, it is obvious that some will be leaving. I suggest we cancel all previous debts and give the people who remain here or who leave a fresh start. Since some will not get immediate employment, give them a generous time, if needed, before leaving. They have to live somewhere. We may wish to give them a termination bonus.

"I would recommend we build some new homes with ample facilities for cooking, washing and bathing. We can and must be very selective about those we wish to employ."

Charles said, "I don't know how much thought has been given but one aspect will be grossly misunderstood. If it is not understood, it will cause some heartaches."

"I don't understand," his mother said.

"All you have suggested is good, fair, honorable and desirable, but have you considered that few feel so generous and others are reluctant to change, be it selfishness or ignorance?

"You are changing course during a time when others feel unsure, insecure. They are not receptive to change. When our neighbors and fellow farmers learn of canceled debts, increased salaries and new homes, they will become more than alarmed. The old practice has lasted over a hundred years and for such a change as has been described, they will panic. *When* they do, not *if* they do, their frustrations and anger will be directed toward the Randolphs. I hope we all know this and prepare ourselves. When people we have known and befriended turn against us, this is a price we must be prepared to pay. Many will not understand such a new program. Most will not try to understand."

The family members looked at each other. It was not something to take lightly. Even after discussion, however, they decided not to alter their plans.

"No man can pull himself up by his bootstraps and only a very few of the rich are capable of true charity. Why not let the Randolphs be different?" Martha asked.

"Who can say that a mere precedent is either right or honorable. Precedent is man's work, not that of God."

Martha continued, "I have some other recommendations. We should do it all at one time and get it behind us. I have talked with different individuals and I know the wishes of some.

"David does not care for inside work. Charles is leaving. I want Uncle Edd to take over the bookkeeping. A lotman will not be needed again because the mules go with the tobacco. These are David's wishes. Uncle Edd will accept the new responsibilities.

"Next, it is time for Big Jack Jackson and his family to depart. They were needed because of unrest and tobacco. Hopefully this need has disappeared or will disappear." No one saw Stephen swallow deeply and drop his head.

"I do not wish any more salesmen and peddlers here. They have fleeced our people too long as it is.

"I want to promote Jack Jenkins to a position of additional responsibility. His pay would be increased in proportion."

After discussion and approval Martha said, "I have one more item. I want to give you a Christmas present from your father. I believe he would be pleased." Martha reached into a folder and produced some envelopes. She looked into her children's faces and at Mary. "A month before your father died he purchased a large term insurance policy. I was made the sole beneficiary. I can't tell you why he did it. Perhaps he knew something we did not know. I believe it was a gesture of love for his family.

"In each envelope is a Certificate of Deposit for one hundred thousand dollars. There are no strings attached. You can let it remain and draw interest. You can cash it immediately. In all cases, except one, you may do as you wish. The exception, at the moment, will be Stephen. On June first, after a successful graduation, it will be waiting for him.

"Now let us join hands and attempt to reunite the circle that was broken.

"Dear God, let us remember Your birthday in a very special way. Please be with my family and help us to become whole once again. Amen."

Chapter 69

"Oh, April, what a delight! You did not have to take the few days you have off to come and see us." April could see that Clint did not look as he did six months ago, but she knew there would not be a day that Clint White would not think about his son. She suspected he had offered many prayers as well.

April accepted Clint's hand. "You are kind to think of me and the twins. Been a bit lonely this time of the year." She could see a slight mist form in his eyes.

"Mr. White, unless you have objections I am going to call you Clint. You will recall I referred to my father as Joseph."

"Please do. We would both feel more comfortable. My boy tells me he hears from you twice each week and on some occasions even more."

"Clint, I must ask you a question. There are those who like to talk about their children under certain circumstances. How do you feel?"

"I would be hurt if you didn't talk about Robert. Robert thought you were the most special person ever. I guess he still feels that way."

April talked of the many virtues of Robert and she could see that Clint White hung on each word.

Mimi and Michelle entered. "It's so nice to see you," Michelle said. "It's next to having Robert home."

"Let me look at you young ladies," April said. "You have become adults. Your father does not have small children anymore but I expect he is reluctant to turn loose. It is the same everywhere. You are both pretty as a picture though you are different."

The girls talked about their senior year and they asked about Auburn.

"Does Auburn specialize in medicine? In the training of doctors?" Mimi asked.

"It has an excellent pre-med program but it is best known as an engineering school. I believe some of the engineers at the Clay Company finished there."

"Mimi thinks she wants to be a doctor," Clint said. "I think her grades are high enough to be considered.

"And Michelle will major in boys!" Clint laughed.

"Not all bad, Clint. No, it's not a bad major at all. I would know."

They talked for another hour. Clint did not let the subject stray very far from his son.

As April was about to leave Clint said, as he looked into April's sparkling black eyes, "I can understand why my son feels as he does about you. I think you have influenced his life more than you can know. Thank you for writing him so often. I know how much it means to him.

"One last thing, April. Hopefully God will take care of my boy; but if he should fail to return, I'll have to lean on you. I couldn't do it alone." His voice quivered and tears filled his eyes. "I have just received word. He is on his way to Viet Nam."

"Clint, Robert will do fine. He will be back before you know it. I would be there for you. You know that. But Robert will be back." She smiled, embraced the three, and moved quickly to her car.

She drove home in a depressed mental state. Why had Clint spoken so? Then she knew. This was the deep love Clint had for his son. It was the most natural thing in the world.

CHAPTER 70

With everyone back in school it was a lonely time for Martha.

David approached. "Guess you are lonely. It is really quiet here. In fact, too quiet."

"I'm fine. As long as I know everyone is all right, I can get by. It is so nice to see the old or should I say the new David again."

He smiled. "You ladies make the difference. I'm fine."

"I'm surprised there is any work left to do. There were weeks you worked eighteen hours a day."

"Tell me about Joe," David said. "I had thought he would have come to terms with himself and found some area of interest. Any suggestions?"

"No. Well one, I suppose. I think he must take the initiative in this matter. If another makes a suggestion, the wrong suggestion, it could cause even more damage. You agree?"

"Yes."

"Have you talked at length with Michael John since his return?"

"I opened the door. He did not say much as to where he was or even why he left. Best to leave it that way. He did mention some courses in woodworking at some school. I believe he is thinking about the future. He needs something more to do than what he was doing."

"I agree. I will move on such things soon."

David started toward his home when he heard a voice. "Wait. I'm going your way." He saw that it was Mary.

"I've missed you," Mary said.

"I've been busy, Mary."

"That busy? Can we talk? We should."

"Come on to my house," David said. "Joe has left?" He didn't wait for a response. "He comes and goes at some unusual times." She said nothing.

David poured them a glass of ice tea and they sat facing each other. Mary asked, "How do you feel about everything? I've been nearly crazy!"

"I believe both of us have discovered a new beginning but we don't know what to do about it or how," David said. "There is Joe. He is your husband! He is my brother!"

"Do you have regrets? About that night, I mean?" Mary asked.

"No. I don't believe so except to say that in time some decisions must be made."

"Do we love each other, David? Love each other enough to share a life together? It was not a one night stand? If there is love, we have decisions to make. If not, I have a decision to make."

"As much as I want you, Mary, as much as I want you now, let us wait a few days. It will involve a number of people. Let's give it a few more days. Now why don't you leave before I find myself in another room."

As she walked back to her home she knew she had been wise not to tell David she had missed a period. She had no desire to have him make decisions because of that.

Suddenly, she remembered Joe coming home that night and making love. If she was pregnant, who was the father? This could even complicate matters beyond the present stage.

The next day Joe charged around like a caged lion. She knew he was waiting for a time in which he could leave. "Joe, how would you feel about us having a child?"

He turned quickly. "What do you mean?"

"Well, we made love some weeks ago and there was no effort made as to safety."

"You pregnant?"

"You said you wanted children when we married. I suppose you could say it's possible."

Joe looked at her with an expression different from any she had ever seen. Was it happiness? Joy? Disbelief? She couldn't guess.

He started laughing and she had never seen him laugh so. Then he shouted, "I don't believe it. I don't believe it. You're going to have a baby!"

"It's possible. It's more than possible that you will be a father. And I feel this could make all the difference."

Joe broke out again in another siege of laughter. Mary could not understand. "Are you sure?" Joe asked. "I just can't believe what you are saying."

Mary looked at Joe to see if she could determine if he had been drinking this early in the day. Suddenly, his laughter ceased. "You little bitch! You little slut! Father tried to warn me. He said you were a whore. I can hear him now. 'Where did you get that whore?' When I protested his prediction, his words were, 'Just give her time.' You know, until this day I really never believed him. I suppose I should ask who!"

"Joe, have you lost your mind? What are you saying? How can you speak this way about me? About your son or daughter?"

"Wonder who the little bastard belongs to? I ought to beat it out of you but I'll wait. I want my little whore to think about what she has done.

"You see, two years ago I had a little surgery, a vasectomy. It can't be my child.

"Yep, when you're young you don't always believe your elders. But my old man was a hell of a sight smarter than I believed. Yep. Told me I had missed the big boat and got me a little whore.

"Well, I want you to have that little bastard because he doesn't belong to me. I would think by the end of the week you'd be gone. Seems the right thing to do. I'm not sure I owe you anything but I'll keep quiet. There are those who know of my operation. Wouldn't take long for such news to travel fast. Lots of folks will feast on this kind of doings and they will talk. Better leave before they know."

Joe was still laughing in a manner of contempt as he slammed his car door and hurriedly made his way down the lane.

Mary burst into tears. She had rolled the dice and lost. Oh God, oh God. For the next hour Mary walked from one room to another. She found no answer.

She walked over to the store but she had no need. She just had to do something. "Are you all right, Miss Mary? You seem pale," Uncle Edd said.

"I'm fine. One gets lonely from time to time." She turned and retraced her step back to her house.

At nine-thirty she took two sleeping tablets. Thirty minutes later she took another two. She felt she had to sleep so she could be ready to make some decisions tomorrow. Just before she dozed off she wondered what Joe would say when he returned home some time before daylight.

Suddenly, she was awakened from her drugged sleep. Was it the telephone? Had someone called? Was there a knock on the door? Then she heard a loud knock and a voice, "Mrs. Randolph, please come to the door."

She slipped on her robe and staggered to the door, heavy with sleep. She snapped on the porch light and looked through the narrow window. She saw two uniformed men. "Who are you? Why are you here? What's wrong?"

"Are you Mrs. Joe Randolph? May we come in, please."

She opened the door and said, "Yes. Why are you gentlemen here?"

"Please sit down, ma'am. I'm afraid we have some bad news. Your husband has been in a wreck a short while ago. It was a one car accident. Apparently he lost control of his car. I will not go into any details. He was dead when they got him to the hospital. We're sorry ma'am. Suppose you tell us what you would have us do. I'm sure you need some help. We can call or go get others."

"A one car accident? He's dead?"

"Yes ma'am. I think he died instantly."

"And his body?"

"At the hospital, ma'am. They will need to learn some information."

"I'll have to go to the hospital immediately."

"Tell us who to get or call, ma'am."

Mary gave them David's number as well as the number to call Joe's mother. Moments later they were there. She seemed unable to speak and the officers repeated the information they had given Mary. Michael John came in as the officers spoke.

In fifteen minutes a large number had gathered. There was Sandra and Jack, Uncle Edd, Susan, Jerome and Eric Lee as well as Mike Harper.

"I think I want to go to the hospital where they said Joe was. After that we can start some planning. You will have to help me. I don't know what I should do, or do first."

David spoke to Mary. "We don't know how Joe will be physically."

"I have to go," Mary said.

The funeral was at three on Sunday afternoon. The church was full but not overflowing. Charles noted the absence of the many political officials. He also noticed many local farmers missing. Many things had changed in a very short period. He hoped his mother did not realize about some of the old faces that were missing.

Mike's services were short as requested. When it was over they returned to Martha's house. "I'll stay with you tonight but tomorrow I must be about the things I need to do," Mary said.

"I will call Jerome for you," Martha said. "He will know what to do. Would this be what you would wish?"

Mary nodded but she did not speak.

CHAPTER 71

The depot agent took his pencil and wrote the message that had been delivered in Morse Code. When he had finished he asked that the message be repeated. The words were the same. He went over and typed the message on the official yellow sheet. He could never remember a telegram that was not on yellow paper.

When he had finished he picked it up as if it weighed a ton. He could deliver it in twenty minutes after he closed the depot. He dropped it back on the table and shook his head. He walked out on the ramp where freight was loaded and unloaded. He saw Dwight Clark, a twelve year old youngster, who usually hung around a lot. He had his fishing pole and a can of worms as the Little Attapulgus Creek flowed less than a hundred yards beyond the railroad tracks. He motioned for him to come.

"Got a telegram that needs to be delivered. Can't go myself at the moment as I am expecting a train. Trains sometime run late. You know about these things. Wouldn't be right not to wait for the train or deliver this telegram. I can't do both. You want to make a quarter? Lots of money just to ride up the hill. Wouldn't take but a few minutes. It's down hill all the way back. You'd have time to fish. What do you say? I must be here for the train." He hoped Dwight didn't know the train schedules as the next freight wasn't due for another eleven hours.

"I'll go. Gimme a minute to get my worms in the shade." He was back in a moment. "Where do I take it?"

"Name and address right there on the telegram."

"Don't reckon they would wanta answer?"

"No. I would guess not. Get it to him and come on back. I'll keep your fishing pole and bait."

When Dwight handed the yellow envelope to Clint White he looked at it closely and cautiously. He turned it over as if he expected something to be written on the back. He tuned it so he could see the name and address again, as if a mistake had been made. He weighed it in his hand, as if he was mailing a letter and did not know if one or two stamps would be appropriate. He looked again at the transparent front. He could not remember when he had last received a telegram.

"Ain't you gonna open it?" Dwight asked. "May need to answer it. Got a quarter for bringing it up. Guess I'd charge fifteen cents if you wanted to answer it. It would be down hill all the way." He gave a half smile.

Clint looked once again. He remembered as a young boy that they always seemed to bring bad news, usually in ten words or less.

But maybe this wasn't bad news. It could be that his boy had some time off and needed to be picked up in Quincy or Tallahassee or Midway. Just maybe his boy was coming home.

With this thought he carefully opened the envelope and read silently. The color seemed to leave his face as he returned the message to the envelope. After some moments he removed the sheet from the envelope a second time and once again read the contents. All this time he had not spoken.

Suddenly he looked up and saw Dwight waiting, shifting his weight from one foot to the other.

It was at this moment that Dwight spoke. "Wanna send something back? I'd charge only fifteen cents as it's down hill all the way." Clint White did not respond.

"Bet something is wrong. It's bad news, ain't it? These things always seem to bring bad news. I ain't ever seen a good one."

Slowly Clint White removed the message from the envelope for a third time and read these words. "Robert White, your son, has been killed in action. Stop. Body will be returned to your home in three days from receipt of this official notice. Stop. Military officials will accompany the body. Stop."

A sadness seemed to fill Clint White's face as he spoke once again. "Now I know how God felt." His eyes moved once again over the words on the yellow sheet as he spoke one last time. "Seems the government spends the life of boys as well as our money. Each word after ten costs more. Guess lives are like words. Don't mean much to our Washington bunch anymore. My only son. Yes, I know how God felt."

"Took it hard, sir," Dwight reported to the depot agent. "Took it real hard! Never said another word. Took it mighty hard. But he is usually a quiet man. Don't talk much unless he's got something to say.

"You sure you had a train coming? Ain't heard no whistle. Ain't heard no whistle at all. Believe I'll take my pole and worms now but I don't believe I can get my mind on fishing for a time. He turned once more and repeated the words of Mr. White, 'Now I know how God felt.'"

There was a rap on the dormitory door. "Come in," April said. "The door is not locked."

Ann Murphy, a nice girl who worked at the desk, stuck her head inside and asked, "Can you come to the telephone? Long distance I believe. Someday they will have telephones in all our rooms. We freshmen get the old dorms."

"Coming," April said as she moved from a study table, cluttered with papers and books. They walked toward the lobby together. "Not many boys in my little town of Attapulgus. It's likely my brother or mother. Now a girl like you from a place like Montgomery could create a great deal of interest."

"Tell the boys in Montgomery the first chance you get. Suppose you go over to the telephone across the room. I'll connect you. You'll have more privacy."

"Hello," April said. She did not hear anyone but it seemed the circuit was open. She looked at Ann and pointed to the telephone. Perhaps she had failed to connect them. But she saw Ann nod that the call had been transferred.

April repeated herself, "Hello. Anyone there?" She waited.

"Is that you, April?" She heard her mother's voice.

"Yes, it's me. Perhaps we have a bad connection. You don't sound like yourself. Can you hear me?"

Several seconds elapsed and April asked, "Is there something wrong? There is, isn't it? What is it, Mother? Is someone sick or has something happened? Please tell me!"

"I have some bad news, some awful news, for all of us." April realized her mother was struggling and having difficulty speaking.

"I wish I didn't have to tell you. Clint White just called. Robert has been killed in action in Viet Nam. He said . . ." There was total silence.

In a moment Martha spoke again. "The body will be here Thursday. The funeral will be Friday afternoon."

Again there was silence. Then a voice again, "Are you still there? Are you all right? Of course you are not all right. I wish I could have found another way to tell you."

"This can't be," April said. "Perhaps it's all a mistake!"

"No, April, I wish I could tell you there was some doubt."

"Oh, no! Not Robert. This can't be!" April thought about David when Kathy died.

"Clint wants you to come home and be with him during this time; be with the twins. He said something about a promise but I did not understand. He is completely destroyed. He has refused to talk or see anyone. He needs you."

"Oh, God, Mother, what can I say? Of course I will leave as soon as I can. Tell Clint I'll be there tomorrow.

"What will I do, Mother? We were so close. He was so perfect. I am sure the world has also been turned upside down for Clint and the twins. Tell him I'll be there."

"Now you drive carefully."

"Should I call Clint now?" April asked.

"I believe not. He needs to see you. I'm going now with the boys. Susan and her two boys will be there.

"You trust yourself to drive home? I can send for you."

"I can get home. That's not my problem. I don't know what to say when I get there. You go this minute to see him. You and Mrs. Lee must take over. Mike can help, but Mike is not his preacher. I'll get there. You run."

Minutes later April heard a voice. "You've been sitting there for minutes. At first I thought you were still talking," Ann said. "You don't look right!"

"Yes — no. I don't know."

"What is it, April?" Ann took her hand and placed an arm around her.

"My dearest friend has been killed in the war. He was so good, so perfect. We had been so close for so long. I'm all confused at the moment. I'm not sure what I should do or what I should do first."

Ann called to a girl nearby. "Stand in for me for a few minutes." She took April and led her to her room.

For ten minutes April cried as never before. Ann held her hand but felt it best she remain silent and let her cry.

Minutes later April asked, "How long have we been here?"

"For a few minutes. Go ahead and cry. It will make you feel better. I'll stay with you."

Suddenly April seemed to hear a quiet voice. "You must be strong because others will be weak. They must lean on you. I will give you strength."

April talked with Ann about Robert for several minutes, then she said, "I'll be all right now. Thank you for being so kind and thoughtful. I'll need to do several things before I leave. I'll get started now."

April left the campus immediately after lunch the next day. She had discussed her needed absence with her teachers and they had understood.

As she approached Midway and moved around the by-pass that had been constructed by their own Decatur County Governor, Marvin Griffin, her thoughts began to center on what was ahead. What do you say to a man who has lost his only son? What do you tell the twins who had lost their mother earlier and now their only brother? She asked another question. What has happened that the God of love has delivered so much wrath on the Randolphs? She was reminded of Job and she knew she did not possess the same goodness or patience.

As she passed by the Baptist Church she saw a grave being dug and some people getting ready to erect a tent. Her eyes filled with tears. Then she thought, I must be calm, at least on the outside. I have to do this.

Her mother met her at the door. "I'm glad you are safe. I have worried. It is well that you decided to come now. Clint needs you."

April embraced her mother as if she was seeking to sap some strength from her. "I am so ill prepared."

"You must be strong, April. I see some of the signs with Clint that I saw with David except David lashed out. Clint says nothing."

April embraced David, then Michael John. Tears filled his eyes and he could not speak. She understood. David said, "You were my keeper and my salvation. Now you must let me try and help you."

"Mimi seems to be the one holding them together. She keeps her emotions inside but I suspect she has her limits. Michelle shows her feelings. Clint has let it all close in on him. He sits there and doesn't say anything," her mother said.

"Do you have a suggestion as to a time I should go?" April asked.

"No. I can't say. I wish I could. But you may be the person to bring him out of this," Martha said.

After a few seconds April said, "I find myself in a difficult position. I've never found myself in such a no win situation."

"I don't understand," her mother said. "You can relate to his needs because of our own lives."

"This is not exactly what I was speaking about. If I am emotional, I can only add to their dilemma and this would create more problems. If I am without emotion, it could be interpreted as a lack of concern."

"Clint knows how you feel. He would never doubt. I think strength would serve their needs best. He needs a pillow, a crutch, an outstretched hand, a safety net. He is in a sea that is turbulent and unrelenting. I suppose I would really suggest you be yourself. This is why they love you so," her mother said.

"A little later I will go. You asked about going with me. I prefer at this time to go alone. You have had too much rain to fall in your life recently," April said.

She drove to the small frame house. As she approached she noticed a wreath of white flowers by the side of the door. She did not knock but twisted the knob and the door opened into a small modest living room. She saw Clint but did not recognize him instantly. He looked twenty years older. When their eyes met she saw a brief spark appear, then it was gone. He got to his feet, approached April, and they placed their arms around each other, holding each other tight. They patted each other's back and shoulder. Not a word was uttered during this time.

Suddenly April heard him say in a quiet but emotional voice, "He's gone. He's gone, April. We have lost him forever. He loved you so much. He loved his family. He loved everyone. He must have loved his country." Few knew that these were the only words Clint had spoken in several hours.

"Let me see the twins a moment, then perhaps we two can slip away for a few moments where we can be alone."

April walked over to the area where the twins sat and each stood to receive her. She embraced Michelle first. She saw red eyes and felt her body quiver when she held her.

As she placed her arms around Mimi she heard a low whisper, "Please help our father. He just sits there and says nothing. This will surely kill him unless you can help. I can't stand to see him in so much pain."

April released Mimi and said, "Why don't you girls move over near the door as people come. I'll not keep your father long." She took Clint by the hand and led him to the windowed back porch which originally had been screened. She pulled two chairs close together and they sat where they could touch each other. She reached over, took his hand and pressed it against her cheek.

"I want you to listen to me, Clint White. I have some things I must say. I have some things that Robert would want and expect me to say." The dull look continued in his eyes.

Suddenly Clint spoke out with a rather strong voice. "There is nothing that anyone can say or do to give me back my boy, my only son. My wife, the joy of my life, was taken away. Now my first child and only son has been taken. Have I not a right to ask why? But I won't ask because there is no explanation. Besides, it wouldn't bring him back. No one can. So why bother to ask."

April spoke quietly. "It may have little or no meaning, but we know of a beautiful and wonderful lady who lost her husband when she was thirty-four. He left her with five small children. In less than a year her car was struck by a man taking drugs and three of her children died. She was unconscious for eighteen days. The other two children were severely injured."

"What has this to do with me?" Clint asked.

"I am sure the mother felt as strongly as you, perhaps more so, if possible. She had lost three instantly. But this mother, this brave mother, said, 'He has left two for me and has sent three Home to be with my husband!' Perhaps God has left Mimi and Michelle for you to love and has sent Robert Home to be with his mother."

"You have helped me, dear April, but all is not clear yet. I may be selfish. I am human also."

"Clint, no one can guess how I felt about your son. No one. Not even you. I could not know him as a father. No, not even as a sister. But in some ways I knew him like no one else. I'm not sure he ever told you but he wanted to be a doctor, wanted to help others. I think he kept this a secret because he knew it would hurt you when the money was not there for seven to ten years preparation. I offered some assistance but knew he would not take it. At times he would become disheartened, then he would say, 'I can do it! I can do it!' And I knew he would find a way. He had a way of making dreams come true."

A spark returned to Clint's eyes. "You must do it. You must do it for me and my girls."

"What are you saying, Clint? I don't understand."

"I want you to deliver the eulogy at his funeral. You once made me some promises. You are the one who really knew him. You are the only one truly qualified. I've heard you speak. You are the best. Tell me you will do it for me, for him, for my girls."

April thought for a full minute before speaking. "I'll make a deal with you, Clint. It will come close to killing me, but I'll do this for you and for the twins. In return I want a promise from you. I want you, starting this minute, to put away some things — for Robert, for me. I want you to go back inside, talk with your many friends and let them comfort you. They have come to pay their respects; a respect for you and the twins, a respect for Robert.

"I will come back before Friday. We must talk again. There are many things that we both should say to each other."

"When you return I'll give you some details," Clint said. "The military will send some representatives. We'll talk about this. I'm going to make it, April. You have told me how. You have lighted a candle for the darkness."

April drove home slowly. She knew that a great deal of preparation would be needed. Not only must she organize what she wanted to say but she had to get herself emotionally prepared.

CHAPTER 72

April spent the next two days with Clint and the twins. She was trying to make preparation to fulfill a promise as well.

Hundreds were to come to the little frame house. There were Baptist and Methodist and those that didn't belong. There were the old as well as the young. All of the athletes that had been associated with Robert came. The girls who were close to Mimi and Michelle filled the house. There was enough food brought to feed fifty for a week. And yes, there were dozens of plants inside, on the porches and elsewhere.

April could not have been more pleased as she witnessed Clint, in his quiet way, meet and talk with those who came. Indeed he was living up to his end of the bargain.

At mid-morning on Thursday April saw her mother return. "I know you get tired of seeing me, Clint," Martha said, "but I could not remain away. You look better. I see you are talking with your many friends."

"We thank you for all you've done. You and Susan Lee have brought enough food to supply Attapulgus. I must also apologize for my earlier behavior. I couldn't think or talk. April has helped me. How fortunate Robert had her for a close friend for so many years."

"Don't worry about yesterday, Clint. My family has known the same recently. Before I go, what can I do? I suppose your church and transportation plans are complete? There must be something I can do. I feel so helpless."

"Only one thing, Martha. Let April stay with me as much as possible. She is my source of strength. I know you have seen little of her but I may need her more at this time than anyone else."

"Clint, I couldn't drag her away. Lean on her. She has that special strength that even I do not understand."

April spent some time in the twins' bedroom with them. "Be with him in days to come when routine begins again," April said. "The people will keep him occupied for now."

"How can we best fill this void?" Mimi asked. "Should we talk about our brother? Perhaps we should do nothing to bring back memories."

"If he cares to talk, listen. This is a part of the healing process. When he is not working perhaps one, maybe both of you, should be around. No one can tell his needs at this time.

"I guess he would be interested in talking about you two. You will soon graduate. Get him involved in your closing programs and your future plans," April said.

Mimi said, "You have the ability, the gift to place yourself in another's place. Few can do this with fairness or success."

"Tell me your plans," April said.

Michelle saw that Mimi preferred her to respond first. "Mimi and I are oceans apart. She is a straight A girl. I work to make a B. I do not try to compete with Mimi. Socrates said, 'Know thyself.' I do. I want to be a housewife and a mother. Someday I want to find a nice farm boy that believes and thinks as I do. I'll find him. He must just be himself — nothing complicated. Mimi is different. She is much too innocent. She never looks at a boy. She never flirts or laughs around them as I do. She doesn't know what fun is. Perhaps some day she will discover the world of men!"

Mimi said, "Oh, my sister. She wants a life filled with fun and laughter. I guess I am more serious and likely unrealistic. I wish I really knew the extent of my ability, my few talents. I want to be a doctor. Perhaps I can be the doctor Robert would have been. I've studied about the preparations. It is long and hard and expensive. At the moment I cannot tell Father about my dreams. He would kill himself attempting to make it possible."

April looked again at Michelle and asked, "You have found this farm boy? This husband to be?"

"Have my eye on one." She laughed. "I haven't told him yet that he is it. But I will in time." April smiled and knew that the girls had forgotten, but for a minute, what was yet before them.

"Let's go out and relieve you father. He may like to rest, but I hope it won't be lengthy. It is best for him not to be alone yet."

April looked at Clint's girls. No one would have guessed twins. Mimi was tall. She had perfect posture. Her brown hair came down on her shoulders and her face was clear skinned and well formed. Her soft gray eyes reflected superior intelligence. She at times seemed much too serious.

Michelle would have to stretch to make five-two. Her eyes were bright and large. Her face was more oval. When looking at her, one saw fun, delight and good times. She seemed totally unconscious of her beauty and well proportioned body. The young full breasts were much more pronounced than those of her sister. She flirted constantly with all the boys, but didn't seem to know the meaning of flirting.

April approached Clint. "Can you eat something now? Will you try?"

"No. I can't eat but I would enjoy your company. I have some things to tell you. I want to know what you learned from the girls."

When they had settled in a bedroom April said, "They are special, each in her own way. They are both a delight and as different as night and day.

"What would you like to see them do in time to come?"

"Be happy. I see so many that are not. Some would say Mimi is too serious. Some would say Michelle is not serious enough."

"You said you wanted to talk."

"When their mother died years ago, I called my three children before me. I told them it was now up to me to be both Mother and Father and to do right as I know to do right. I told them I would always explain what I did and why so they would understand. We seem to have been a proper family. As you look from afar, a distance, do you think I've done adequately or poorly? You will be truthful."

"No one could have done better. I have never heard a negative remark. You can be most proud."

"When Robert was about to decide to go into service he wanted to talk. I told him that life is given to each of us. It will be the only one you will ever have here. No one should live it for you.

"I told him to live in accordance with his own nature, urges and beliefs, not those of someone else — in such a way that there will be no regrets when it comes to an end. Some believe they will remain and live on this earth forever. They are fools.

"I told him to get all the facts he needed or could find before making a decision, then to move as he felt wise, so that when the end came he could say he lived a good life and did it his way.

"Now April, was I right to tell him this?"

"Yes. This would apply to all of us. It is what I will do. You did the right thing."

Suddenly Clint's eyes misted; April was about to speak when Mimi entered. She saw her father. "Why do you cry, my father? Robert would not want you to do it. We all know that nothing can bring him back."

Clint did not answer immediately but finally he spoke. "That is why I weep, my Mimi. I weep because he is gone. He is gone forever. Nothing, not even our God of love, can bring him back."

Then Mimi said, "There are some military people here that need to talk with you. They want to discuss your wishes and their procedures."

"I will go home now, dear Clint. I need a little time to prepare and be with my family," April said.

Friday morning arrived. It was a beautiful day. People, especially those most closely involved, needed sunshine.

Martha greeted her daughter. "Good morning. You must eat a good breakfast. I do not disagree with my dear mother who thought it the most important meal of the day."

Charles said, "I have gone over every detail I can think of. It seems everything is in place. I will drive the car that takes Clint and his girls as well as yourself."

"I hope you got some sleep," Michael John said. "I don't like such days as this will be."

"What will happen later, after the people leave?" April asked. "This will be a crucial time."

"Susan and I have thought of this. We have some ideas. We will be there to provide support," her mother said.

April drove by the school. Mr. Baggs told her of his plans to dismiss school early. She drove once again to see Clint and the girls. "You go get some rest," Clint told her. "I am glad the day has arrived."

When April returned home she remembered she must select the proper clothing. She selected a black dress and put it on. She shook her head. Then she saw a dress that she had worn just before Robert had left. "This is it," she said aloud. "Robert told me how much he liked it."

Charles and April arrived to pick up Clint and his girls. "Today I give up my son forever. Pray for me that I will find strength," Clint said.

"You will be strong. You will be strong for Robert and for Mimi and Michelle," April said.

Charles said, "It is time."

The pastor entered followed by Clint, Mimi, Michelle and April. Hundreds filled the seats and chairs that had been placed about. April noted that some looked upward while others looked downward, as if in prayer. Still others shifted slightly, to catch a glimpse of the family. It was always the same.

The casket had been placed in the center. A beautiful flag of our country covered it. Two large wreaths stood at each end. April knew the two families that had been responsible. The pastor said in a quiet voice, "Please be seated." It took a few moments as the people sought a comfortable seating position.

A Marine captain and two enlisted men who had stood by the casket at attention took their seats.

Jim Smith, the pastor, read verses from the Old and New Testaments. He prayed a brief but touching prayer. They listened as they heard the organist play softly.

At the conclusion, Jim rose and said, "The family has asked that a close and devoted family friend give the eulogy. It is well to have such devout, affectionate and caring friends." He returned to his seat. Some had learned of the role April would play. Others had not. The church became even more silent as they waited.

April moved from her seat beside Clint. She patted him softly on the shoulder and gave a slight smile. She moved to the pulpit with dignity and reserve.

April paused for two or three seconds and looked at the congregation. She knew they were waiting to hear what she would say.

"Nineteen years ago a child, a first born son, was born to Clint and Mary White and they named him Robert." She paused. She knew the people were listening.

"From the moment he arrived he brought a joy to the household. He was wanted. He was loved. He brought great happiness to his parents.

"He grew as all normal children grow. In what seemed like moments, six years had passed. He was ready to enter the first grade as thousands had done before him. He would miss his two sisters a year younger who remained at home but he knew they would be together again in a year.

"It was at this moment that he became a part of my life as we began this new adventure together in a world of mystery. As all beginners, we felt a degree of uncertainty. But this did not last as we became involved with new faces, loving teachers and many books. It was an exciting time as it should be.

"Thus in 1952, our twelve wonderful years of togetherness began. Robert was large for a six year old. He could have dominated the class from the beginning but this was never to occur during the next twelve years. Not once did I ever witness his use of size and strength to get an unfair advantage.

"What kind of student was this young man? The best. The very best. His report card never reflected a letter beyond the first letter of the alphabet. But one would never know of this superiority as he was the most modest ever. With these characteristics he became our respected leader.

"He was likely the best athlete the school has ever known or will ever know. He brought recognition and glory to our school but he worked diligently always to keep himself in the background. The older adults who have watched athletes come and go say he was the best ever and would be a model for all others to follow.

"He was a great family person and member. He probably worked as much or more to assist his family as all the others in his class. In the summers he helped his father or worked in the community.

"On Sunday and Wednesday evening he would be found in this very building. He was not a vain person. His strongest slang was 'gosh.' He did not drink. He did not smoke. Sometimes he offered good advice to others, but he never condemned. He made it clear this was not to be his life style. He never sat in judgement of others. Not one classmate, not one person, can say they were influenced by a bad example. I never heard him say an unkind word of another.

"First and foremost, he was always a gentleman, a gentle person. He respected every individual. He respected womanhood. He respected authority. I'm not sure I remember a teacher correcting him.

"He wanted to be a doctor. He would have made a great one. This was part of his plan when he entered service. He could save some money and earn some college time. He was too independent to accept charity, or gifts or even a loan from others.

"I have told you only a little of how this man, this great person, lived. Now I must go a step beyond. I must tell you how he died.

"'The sooner I start, the sooner I finish,' he informed me and joined the Marines immediately after graduation. It was not just for personal gain, but for love of country that he was influenced. He never spoke unkindly of those who rush to Canada for one obvious reason, but he said this was contrary to all he stood for. He also remained silent when many of us wondered about the war in which we were involved. 'I must go,' he had said. 'My country needs me. I must follow the dictates of my conscience!'

"After a period of training he became an officer, a leader. And this is the way he died. He attempted to rescue a wounded man under his command. In doing so he gave his own life to save another. No man can give more."

April pointed to the flag that graced the casket. "Look at the flag that covers this near-perfect man. There are bars with colors of red and white and white stars on a blue sky. What does it mean? To you? To me? It means freedom, safety, integrity, opportunity, kindness and perhaps most of all, hope. The very blood of Robert colors these stripes. The white represents the love and faith he had for all of us. Robert gave so we might live and be free.

"And so today we gather to pay a final tribute to the memory of this great young man. I suspect if he were here, he would have very mixed emotions about this service. He would have said, 'I did my job. I did nothing special.' Yes, those would have been his words.

"Listen, dear friends, and see if you do not hear his soft, quiet voice as he tells us to love our neighbor, think good thoughts and be kind to each other. It is in this spirit we should live and die.

"As Abraham Lincoln said in his Gettysburg Address, 'The world will little note or long remember what we say here.' But the deeds of this great young man will be remembered as long as we shall live."

April returned to her seat by Clint and took his hand in both of hers and whispered, "Smile. Robert is watching. He would insist."

Jim Smith stood before the hundreds assembled. He saw in the eyes of those present that all that could and should be said had been spoken. "Let us go to God in prayer. Thank You for the life of this young man whom You have given us to love. Give strength to his family and loved ones as only You can provide. Amen."

Eight former teammates propelled the casket to the doors. In moments they were at the grave site. They sat under the small tent that had been erected. Jim Smith read only one verse of scripture. His prayer was equally brief. "May all of us seek to be more in the image of Robert White. From him we have learned how to live as well as how to die. Amen."

The enlisted men took the flag from the casket, folded it and handed it to their captain who in turn presented it to Clint White.

In the distance they heard a three shot volley, a salute to the fallen warrior. Then they heard the bugle as "Taps" was played.

Clint turned to April and saw she was weeping uncontrollably. Clint turned to her with a smile on his face and said, "Let me do something for you as a small payment for all you have done for me."

As April arrived home she knew that Clint would survive though there would be hours of despair. She realized that Robert and Clint were so very much alike.

CHAPTER 73

"When will you return?" Martha asked April.

"Sunday. I may leave early. I am behind in my work.

"You and Susan Lee must be there for the White family for a time. It is likely he will lose himself in his work as David did."

"How did you do that?" Charles asked. "I have never heard anything so appropriate. I was afraid you would not be able to control your emotions. I have never heard so many speak of what you said. They shook their heads in disbelief."

"Be sincere and be yourself. Mother has given me this advice all her life, by example."

"When will the group meet again?" Charles asked. He looked at his mother.

"At Spring break. All of you will be out at the same time."

April looked at Charles. "Think about a room or apartment for me."

Martha looked up quickly. "You are leaving Auburn?"

"Yes. Auburn is a fine school and I have learned some valuable things there, but it's time that I head back nearer home." The look on their faces told April they were both surprised and pleased.

"I'll go get some of my things together. I want Michael John to look over my car. Come by my room for the keys."

Fifteen minutes later April heard a knock on the door. "Come in."

"Michael John, I am about to do another first that I do not recall doing. I think it is time you look around a bit. I will need another sister in time."

Michael John's face grew red. "I haven't been interested since . . ."

"I'm going to give you a name. I know a very special and beautiful and delightful girl who . . ."

"Just give me your car keys. I know more about cars than girls."

"Michelle White is a very special young lady. Have you noticed? Now here are my keys. Please check my car."

A week later Mary received a telephone call. "This is Bruce McPherson. Perhaps you can drop by and review some business matters?"

"I had planned to come by earlier," Mary said, "but the unexpected death of Robert White has delayed some matters."

"It was an untimely death," Bruce said. "I'll expect you at two o'clock tomorrow if that time is satisfactory."

Mary was uncertain if Mr. McPherson was speaking of the death of Robert or Joe. It didn't matter. She did not remember any of the McPhersons being at either funeral.

Mary went over and discussed what she had learned from Mr. McPherson with Martha. "May I suggest you pick up such information and papers required. I would make few comments. Jerome can look into the matters."

"I knew nothing of Joe's business," Mary said. "He gave me some money the first of each month for food and other expenses."

"I suspect there will be surprises," Martha said. "We will talk when you return."

Mary was ushered into Bruce McPherson's office and he directed her to a seat. He gave a half smile. "It is sad to lose a husband so early in life." There was little detection of sympathy in his voice. Mary said nothing.

"I have no idea how much you knew about your husband's business." Mary continued to remain silent.

"Your husband has a note that he consolidated recently from several smaller ones. He owes the bank one hundred and sixty thousand dollars plus interest. It is all here in a file I prepared for you."

"The due date? The maturity date, I suppose it would be called?" Mary asked.

"It's all here in the folder."

"Everything is here I need to know?" Mary held up the folder. "Were there other accounts? Perhaps a savings or checking account?"

"It's all in the folder. I believe the savings account was closed about two years ago. There is a small checking account but as it was not a joint account, some legal work will be required." He got up from his seat to indicate the conference had been completed.

As he walked over to open the office door he said, "Perhaps there are other accounts elsewhere. I believe a number of accounts with the Randolphs were changed some months ago. Good day, Mrs. Randolph."

"I see you are back," Martha said. "It didn't seem to take long." She handed the file to Martha and told her what happened.

"Permit me to deal with this, Mary. I'd like to do so."

"Would you? I know so little."

"I'll get Jerome to help us. He would know about such matters. It will be my pleasure to get this matter settled."

Two days later Martha saw David. "I am concerned about you. I am concerned about Mary also."

"Me? I don't understand."

"At the next meeting I had planned to discuss a change in our by-laws. Under the present code it left Mary in a unique position. You will remember that only Randolphs by blood could be stockholders.

She abruptly stated, "David, Mary is pregnant."

"She told you she was pregnant?"

"Yes. She said she was pregnant and was thrilled to have a Randolph on the way. You and I know which Randolph was the father. Joe could not have children. I hope no one knows. It seems you have some options." David's face had changed from one color to another.

"I believe the two of you are very much in love. If I am correct, this leaves one of two options. Do you wish to have your child born as a premature baby or do you wish to announce you are adopting your nephew? Your baby is a child of passion and neither of you can afford to acknowledge it."

David could say little for some moments, then he spoke. "You get right to the heart of the matter, don't you? And yes, Mary and I love each other very much. I want to think as well as talk with Mary."

"We will not discuss background matters again, Son. You will need to chart a course for the future," his mother said.

"Now, back to other things. I will get Joe's financial woes corrected. I also believe that a marriage would eliminate changes in the corporation. You and Mary will let me know your plans." It was not a question.

At spring break two weeks later the family met. Martha said, "David and Mary would like to make an announcement."

David said, "Please welcome my new wife. Mary and I were married a week ago. I am so lucky and so happy. We have another surprise. I will adopt my new nephew or niece when he or she arrives."

Mary said, "David and I are very happy. He is a wonderful husband. Perhaps we did not give ample time following Joe's death but we are the ones to know how precious time can be!"

Martha said, "I will be a grandmother. I could not be more pleased." Everyone expressed their pleasure except Stephen. He said nothing.

During the meeting Martha explained about the payment of Joe's debts. "He was my son. Mary did not need this hanging over her." She gave other such information as to his financial affairs.

Stephen jumped up. "My father wouldn't like this. She is no Randolph."

Martha said quickly, "Let's discuss our other business." Stephen quickly left the room and no effort was made this time to stop him.

Martha gave a summary. "We now have seventeen thousand, six hundred acres. We have more than three million in the reserve and operating funds. There is a report here for you to review."

In the course of the next hour plans were made to double the operation for which David had been responsible. Four houses for their people were to be constructed. A criteria for occupancy would be studied.

Charles said, "Let me remind you once again that our relationship in the community is not the same. It can only grow worse. I hope we are prepared."

"We must do what we believe to be right," Martha said. "It is even more difficult to live with yourself than with your neighbors when wrongs are committed. We have crossed the Rubicon."

Mary stood. "Thank you for accepting me as you have and for the business matters you have concluded." They smiled and nodded.

Chapter 74

Every change that had occurred in the previous months had seemed negative in nature to Stephen. There had been the loss of the two consecutive tobacco crops. Then the loss, the devastating loss of his father, who had seen him differently from all other family members. Then his last fortress seemed to disappear with the death of his older brother. Finally, the only thing that had meaning and remained had been removed. Big Jack had gone and Pearl, who had been such a part of his learning experiences, had gone as well. Not only had they moved but they had left the State. However, Pearl had assured him before she left that he had successfully completed his apprenticeship and had made a great deal of progress beyond. This had boosted his confidence but he could not be sure as he had no way to know except by her evaluation. But with her gone he felt he needed a little excitement in his life.

"Hello," Stephen said, "I hope you will let me take you home in my new car." School had dismissed for the day.

Helen Hurt looked at Stephen. For years she had watched him in class. He was handsome. He was talented but he seldom used those talents in a positive way. She looked at his new shiny car.

"Certainly it would be all right. You know me. We've been in school together for years."

She climbed into his car and they raced down the road to her home. He stopped in front of the house. She got out and thanked him and smiled. He smiled in returned and waved out the window as he moved away from her house.

Three times in the next week he maneuvered in a similar manner. Each day they seemed to draw nearer. Soon they were laughing often and learning more about each other.

The next week Stephen said, "I'll take you home again. We don't grow tobacco anymore and I have time. I really need to talk with you. You are a very pretty girl."

"All right. I have a little extra time. My father is on the afternoon shift at the Clay Company and Mother said she would not be home before six."

"Beats riding that rough school bus," Stephen said. "I do want to talk with you. I think you know my thoughts about you." He put his right arm out and she moved close to him.

"Who could keep from loving you! Bet you got boy friends galore." She blushed slightly. "I wish I could call you my girl. You're pretty and smart. I think I'm in love with you. You know, we have a lot in common. We are in the same grade and we both live on farms."

"You're very nice," Helen said and inched even closer. As she did he let his hand touch her breast. For a second she looked slightly apprehensive but moved an inch closer. This time he let his hand close firmly on her breast and she did nothing to stop him.

A few moments later he removed his arm and let it touch her legs. As he did he seemed to feel her body tremble against him. They both gave a half smile. Then he moved his hand under her skirt and he could feel the warm smooth skin. Again she trembled but did nothing to stop him.

Again his hand reached higher and her skirt moved up half way her legs. Then she took his hand and stopped him. "I am not sure this is wise."

Then Stephen used the oldest ploy in human relations between girl and boy. "If we love each other as I believe we do, you could not think this wrong. People that love each other want to do something for the other; something to prove their real love."

Helen smiled and he knew that some of the doubts of a conquest had been removed. His hand again moved slowly upward as he touched her. Again she trembled more than she had earlier. "Your legs are as beautiful as your face. I'll bet no one has ever really told you how beautiful you are. I cannot understand why I had not seen all of your beauty earlier."

Helen removed his hand from her leg and pulled her skirt down slightly. She was not sure why she did. Perhaps it had been an impulse. Then something seemed to speak inside that said, "He loves you. It's all right." Suddenly there was an intensity that told her she was no longer a child and a sudden passion rose in her nubile breasts when she thought of Stephen. She was seized with a sudden urge as never before. She felt as if she were flying, that she was rushing into the ebb and flow of the sea tides. She suddenly wished to grab Stephen and hold him so tight he could not breathe, and prove to him that she loved him. She wanted them to feel as one. This desire was beyond all she had ever known. She had no description of it. It was shapeless and without form, even without a name. She knew that she was closing in on a point and time that there would be no return. Whatever the feeling, it seemed to eat at her very soul.

Stephen pulled the car off into a wooded lane that seemed to go nowhere except into a grove of trees. She heard him say, "There seems to be a nice shady place ahead under the oaks. No one would ever know we are here."

Helen looked at Stephen with a built in alarm, but when she looked a second time at this handsome lad her fears took wing. He took the keys, opened the door and walked to the trunk. He lifted out a folded quilt that was made of butterfly squares. She knew her mother had an old quilt at home with the same pattern. For a moment she thought of home, of Mother. Then she looked at Stephen and all thoughts of her family disappeared.

Stephen spread the butterfly quilt upon the ground under the massive oak and pointed to Helen that she sit and join him. She hesitated for a long moment, then took his outstretched hand. She dropped beside him on the worn butterfly quilt. "This is much nicer," he said, "than a cramped car and no one can see us." She gave a slight apprehensive smile.

She turned toward him with a more than slight uncertainty. Her mouth was slightly open and she could feel her heart beat more rapidly than ever before. She looked at Stephen and all doubt that may have been in her subconscious mind disappeared.

Stephen looked at Helen. He knew that she felt she loved him. He knew she was already aroused and he decided that he would try and remember some of Pearl's advice. He did not wish to move rapidly and miss the joy of anticipation.

"You are beautiful, so beautiful, my wonderful Helen." He lay back on the worn butterfly quilt as he said it and indicated for her to lie beside him, patting the quilt. For one moment, one last moment she hesitated because she knew in her heart and soul that this would be the last moment to escape but she found herself on her side and facing him.

His mouth found hers, moist, ready and in full anticipation and at the same moment she felt a hand slip into her blouse and under her bra and his fingers moved slowly about her breast. At that moment she felt a heat rising and a desire for a more intimate contact. She took her hands and reached back to the point the bra was fastened. He now unbuttoned her blouse and he could clearly see where his hand had been. He remembered once again the demands Pearl had insisted upon and his mouth touched her breast and his tongue slowly moved around the nipple.

As he did this his hand moved to her leg above the knee and he slowly moved upward and he could feel her entire body tremble. It was at this moment that his last doubt disappeared for now she was his for the taking.

"Oh, Stephen, oh Stephen" she cried out and her body arched as she felt his fingers slip inside her panties. He touched lightly and ever so slowly. It was only later that she remembered assisting him with the removal of all her clothes.

Stephen removed all of his clothes quickly. Then he remembered that he had all the time in the world. "Make her really want you more than life itself," Pearl had told him.

She waited for Stephen to continue but he insisted that she remove her shoes as well. In a moment she could feel the weight of Stephen's body upon her and she closed her eyes with the thousand sensations she had never experienced. Her arms moved to enclose his chest and she felt the heat of his body.

Without warning she experienced a pain in her loins, intense and piercing. For a moment she struggled to rise but could not. Her legs seemed to thrash and her hands pushed against him but he held her with his weight and she could not rise. Then almost immediately the pain was gone. She joined with him in a rhythm that seemed more natural than breathing.

She did not feel deflowered, feeling instead only the explosion of ecstasy, an unbearable feeling beyond her imagination, her dreams.

Then Stephen kissed her deeply, seeming to devour her. He cried, "My love, my love, I'll never let you go!" His chest pressed harder against her breasts and his naked body seemed to press so deeply that they could merge no more.

In minutes they seemed to be unconscious of everything. She did not seem to be timid about her naked body, nor did she feel unclean.

She had discovered a new joy superior to all others. She had reached a state of complete womanhood. She suspected he had been served as he wished though she had no way to know. At the thought she again flung her arms and legs around his body. She didn't want him to go, not now, not ever. She could not think of being without him.

The second time, with the fears removed, she gave of herself even more fully and again she knew no way to describe the moments. The butterflies on the quilt seemed to lift her in a suspended state and she had never had such an experience.

Stephen then rolled off her body and for a second remained on his knees. She wished he wouldn't go but he got to his feet, searching for his clothes.

Helen was not ready to go. Her father was working. It would be more than an hour before her mother would be at home. She was ready for more kisses, more caressing, more touching and exploring. She began to tremble again thinking about it. But she saw Stephen get up and in moments he was dressed and again sat on the butterfly quilt to put on his shoes.

As Helen replaced her shoes she looked at Stephen and said, "I love you. I gave all I had to give to prove it to you. Could you possibly love me as much as I love you?"

"More! How could you ask? This, in time to come, will be the day I'll remember above all days."

"Me, too, Stephen. Oh, I hope we can marry soon. We wouldn't have to slip around. Oh, Stephen, I do love you so!"

After Stephen had taken Helen home he took a different road to return home. It wasn't good for others to know too much about one's whereabouts.

Suddenly he laughed. It had cost him more than he would ever reveal but now he knew that Pearl was special. Perhaps it had been worth her demands.

The days passed. Helen made school life much more enjoyable. He had believed no one could be so passionate. Once she started, there was no inhibitions, no restraint, no restrictions. And she told him over and over again of her deep love.

Then one day she told him that perhaps something had happened. Her period was late. "But it doesn't matter," she said, "we'll graduate in a few weeks and we can belong to each other as we should."

The next time they made love Helen could sense something wrong. He put his arms around her but he did not press close as before. Was there an atmosphere of coolness or was it her imagination?

She pulled him nearer, closer. But she could tell it was not the same. She had offered her honor and he had honored her offer. For Helen, life would never be the same. Now she was telling him of the possible fruit from their experience and she seemed to find a rejection on his part.

The next time she was left without any doubt. He had accepted her gifts with even less enthusiasm and the fruit seemed to leave a different taste.

As Stephen left her this last time, he thought about offering money. After all, he had learned from his father that money could buy anything. There was nothing like the feel of money in the whole world and he knew there was little to be found in the Hurt family.

Yes, this would be the way. She would take it since her choices would be limited. Was he sure she would take money? Yes. No one could resist. He didn't know much about the Bible, but had not one of the chosen twelve proven this? Corruption had always been with the world.

Then he thought of something different. Why spend my money? Another type of corruption would be much less expensive. It was like Joseph said about land. You didn't sell land, you kept it.

CHAPTER 75

Spring was here again. The girls had adjusted to school and were doing well. Charles seemed tired but could see the end in sight. Michael John seemed happier than at any time since he had returned. David and Mary were in a world all of their own.

"Yes ma'am, Mrs. Randolph, I think we are going to have some good times. It will not ever be the same but times will be better. I can just feel it," Sandra said. "Made a lot of changes and I see more coming. In the long run it will be much better for all."

"Sandra, you have helped me to see the blessings. Thank you. It is time to be happy."

There was a knock on the door. "Must be Mrs. Susan. Be nice to see her again. I'll get it," Sandra said.

In a moment she returned to the kitchen and said, "There is a man out there who wants to see you. I asked him if I could help him but he insisted on seeing you. I don't know that man, Miss Martha. He doesn't look just right to me. Let me go with you."

"I'll be all right, Sandra. He probably wants to see someone on the place for some reason. I expect he is here to collect from one of our people."

"Don't look like a salesman to me. He isn't dressed like a salesman. I don't like the way he looks," Sandra said.

Martha reached the front door. "I'm Martha Randolph. Perhaps I can help you."

"My name is Steve Hurt. I live out in the country a piece. I know you but you probably don't know me. Have no reason to know me 'till now. I'm Helen Hurt's father. She is a senior here at this school, the same place your son goes."

"Come in, Mr. Hurt. I seem to have forgotten my manners this morning. It is nice to meet Helen's father. I think I heard Stephen or April mention your daughter's name. As I recall you live out some five miles north of town. Is it a farm or do you work at the Clay Company? Goodness me, I don't seem to remember. I guess it's my age!"

Steve Hurt took the seat Martha pointed to and sat down. "Ma'am, I'm both I guess. I work at the clay mine and I have a few acres to tend. But my reason for coming ain't got nothing to do with my jobs, my work.

"It seems that I've got a problem or that Helen has a problem. Or, it could be that we all got a problem."

"I don't understand, Mr. Hurt. Is there a school problem or some need or whatever? Tell me about it. Has Stephen created a problem for her? Has he spoken unkindly? All too often he talks before he thinks."

"Ain't what he has said, ma'am. It's what he's done done. My Helen is pregnant, ma'am. Don't mean to talk rude, but she is with child. It's your boy's child!"

"Oh my God! Surely you are mistaken. I hope this is a joke of some sort."

"Ain't no joke, ma'am. Not at my house. She said it was your boy. What you reckon we gonna do about it? My ole lady is 'bout to have a fit. I thought about beating Helen but it ain't gonna help none now. What you think, Mrs. Randolph? Think yor boy oughta marry up with my Helen? Seems right to me and would give the baby a name."

"Mr. Hurt, please let me get myself together. I am in a state of shock. I . . ."

"Yes'm, I been that way myself. Her ma and me don't hold with nothing like this, ma'am. Your boy gotta do the right thing."

"Can you give me a clue, Mr. Hurt? Some details? You see, I was unaware Stephen was seeing your daughter. Sometimes he brings a girl home but I don't remember Helen."

"'Bout two months or so ago, he brought her home from school. Said the bus left her. Can't say where it did or didn't. But he brought her home in that fine new car of his'n. Ma said Helen was all smiles when they drove up. Your boy didn't get out. She got out and he drove off. A few days later my ole lady said the same thing happened again but this time it was a little later than the bus runs.

"We keep a close check on Helen and her friends. Don't seem right him not coming in and meeting Helen's folks.

"Then 'bout three weeks ago she comes in and tells us she is gonna marry yor boy. Said he done up and ask her to marry up wid him. Promised her a big new house, good furniture, some fine clothes and a trip wherever she might like. She was all excited. Never seen a girl so happy in all my life. Since my Helen is pretty and right smart and real good, I thought she was right about it. Seemed sorta right both being country folks and living on farms. You can see how I saw it.

"Then a day or so later she said they oughta marry as soon as school got out as they were gonna have a baby. I took her right to the doctor and sho' 'nuff, he says she's in a family way.

"Then it all happened. The next day or so my Helen comes in all in tears and shaking all over like she done had a chill. Can't talk fur cryin, poor little thing. Says yor boy done backed outta his promise.

"That's why I'm here, ma'am. Things don't seem right to me."

"You are sure Stephen is the father? The only boy she has been with?"

"Yes'm. I made sure. Told her I'd beat her half to death or get the truth. She ain't lying none, ma'am.

"Me and my ole lady is at row's end. Thought about talking to my preacher but decided a'gin it. Ain't no reason to talk to him if they ain't gonna be no marryin. What you say 'bout all this?"

"Mr. Hurt, would you give me three days to do some things? You have caught me by surprise as you can well see. Do you have a telephone?"

"No ma'am. They ain't run no line out on my road yet. I live way back in the country. Ain't enough houses out my way to get a line, a phone that is, according to the phone people. Don't seem right 'cause my wife could get sick while I'm on shift work. But that ain't the reason why I'm here. You understand?"

"Yes, Mr. Hurt, I wish it was a telephone problem. Where can I see you on Thursday?"

"I can come back, ma'am. I'll be back. But you know, we ain't got a lotta time on our side. You can see what I mean."

"Yes, Mr. Hurt, I do. Indeed I do. Please come back on Thursday unless I can meet you somewhere. I could possibly come to your home?"

"No ma'am. I don't think well of that. My ole lady is upset some and I'd rather handle this myself.

"I'll be going now, Mrs. Randolph. I just hope you can come up with something." He reached down and picked up his hat off the floor by the chair and left without saying any more.

As Martha walked back into the kitchen, Sandra said, "Forgive me. The door was open. I wish I knew how to help you, Miss Martha. I got a girl. You got a girl. Would be a lie to say we never thought of such about our own. What you going to do, Miss Martha?"

"I don't know, Sandra. I just don't know. But we will leave it between us. You have any good ideas?"

"I wish I did, Miss Martha. I wish I could take this from your heart but I don't know what to say."

Martha was not sure how she got through the day as she did not remember doing many of her tasks.

At nine that evening she went to Stephen's room and knocked on the door. She could hear the T.V. going so she knocked again. In a few seconds the door opened slowly and Stephen stuck his head out. "Why are you here? Is something wrong? I was looking at a good program."

Martha pushed the door open and entered. She saw clothes had been thrown around on the bed and on a chair as well as on the floor. She walked over and turned off the television. She returned to the door and locked it. Then she turned and took a chair. She had not uttered the first word.

Finally she said, "Yes, Stephen, there is something wrong." She motioned Stephen to sit in the other chair. "We have some talking to do."

"Talking? At this hour? What about? I was watching one of my favorite programs."

"You asked a moment ago if everything was all right. The answer is no. I am sick, Stephen. I am hurt and disappointed as well as embarrassed. I'm sick because my son is not a responsible person. It is obvious that you have not grown up as I had hoped. I blame myself more than you. I held back when your father was alive for his sake. You were the apple of his eye. He could not see you as you really were. I kept thinking he would see the real you. I had anticipated you would grow up on your own that you would change as you became a man. I called it patience but it was really to avoid a clash with your father.

"Then I looked for other excuses for you and myself. I convinced myself you were a little child much too young to know. And yes, I told myself all of us had spoiled our baby boy.

"As a result of my distorted evaluation I have failed. I have failed you as well as myself and my family. I saw you close to your father and Joe. When I spoke to your father he would laugh and say, 'Let him grow up. He will learn along the way.' When they were no longer here I became even more reluctant, since they were your role models. So, I kept hoping and believing and praying. Now I know I failed. You had so much, so many opportunities. You were handsome and strong. You had a mind but did not develop it. You took the easy way out. There was too much time and money, too many automobiles. You had more clothes than you could ever wear." She looked about the room and noticed the strewn clothes again.

"I had a visit from a Steve Hurt." Stephen pretended he didn't understand what she was saying. She repeated, "I had a visit from Steve Hurt. He came about his daughter, Helen. Do you want to talk about it? I want to hear from you — now!"

"Mother, in the state of mind you are in it wouldn't be fair. You have already made up your mind before I even have a chance to tell you my side. There are two sides but I don't think you would believe me. So, why don't you just go ahead and believe him. Go ahead and believe as you want to.

"You see, Mother, in your view I'm not much of anything. You didn't agree with my father. You didn't agree with Joe. Now they are gone and I am alone.

"Now I have no one on my side. I think you have forgotten that tobacco and hard work gave you all you have. Now you want to change it all. I feel it is time for me to leave. I wouldn't wanta stay where I am not wanted, where I am not loved. You can say what you like but that's the way it is."

"Stephen, I can't believe you are saying this. I suggest we not continue. I will come to you later and we will talk. I'm most disappointed. When you come in Thursday, don't leave to go anywhere. If I have to wait, you will walk until school is out; there will be no more car! I hope you understand what I am saying."

On Thursday morning Martha had arranged everything so that she was alone. She wanted it that way.

At exactly the same time, he arrived for his second visit. When she opened the door she saw a very beautiful girl with Mr. Hurt. She looked into the girl's eyes and saw a sadness, a far away look.

"This is my daughter, Helen. Helen, this is Mrs. Randolph. This is Stephen's mother. I thought it would be better to have her tell you her story and such details as you might wanna know."

"Please come in." She pointed to two chairs in the den. "Can I get you something to drink?"

"No'am. We didn't come to drink. Thank you just the same. We just come to talk."

Martha looked at Helen. She could see she was shy and timid. It was obvious she was frightened as well. Her dress was plain but clean. Her hair was clean and combed, a ribbon holding it in place. Her shoes were old but had been shined. She sat very straight in her chair. No one could doubt she was ill at ease.

"I had not expected Helen but I am glad she is here. I'm afraid I still don't know where to start. Perhaps we should hear Helen's story."

Helen's face turned red and she remained silent. "Tell her, girl. Tell her exactly what happened and how it happened. Tell us what was said and done," Mr. Hurt said.

In a moment Helen began. "Stephen took me home once and asked to do so again. He was nice. He told me how nice and how pretty I was. He told me how much we had in common in that we both lived on farms. Of course I knew we had nothing to compare with your place but he made me feel good and important.

"As time passed we saw each other more and more at school and we talked about many things. Finally he told me he wanted to marry me and that he loved me and believed I loved him as well. I saw a handsome man who had everything. He said he wanted us to share a life together. He made a great number of promises.

"A few days later he said if I really loved him, I would make love with him. He said as we were to get married soon, we were missing out on the things most important." She paused and tears filled her eyes.

"I don't need to tell you what happened. If we loved each other, that was all that mattered. Then some time later when I missed a period I didn't worry too much because he had promised to marry me as soon as school was out.

"When I told him I was expecting our baby, he changed. He said he wasn't sure he still loved me. He said that maybe we had made a mistake.

"I told him how much I loved him and wanted his baby. I reminded him we could marry and be in a new home long before the baby was to come.

"Then he said he wasn't in love with me and wouldn't marry me. I was frightened to death. I didn't know which way to turn. Finally I went and told my daddy. That's all I knew to do.

"I loved your son, Mrs. Randolph. If I hadn't, we wouldn't have done what we did. I wasn't brought up that way. I have never done anything like that in my entire life. Naturally I haven't since.

"I don't know what else to say. The baby belongs to Stephen. Now that things are as they are, I just don't know which way to turn."

No one had spoken as she told her story. When she finished her face had tears streaming down, her eyes red and filled with tears. Her father handed her his handkerchief.

"You now know the story, ma'am. Thought it would be best to hear it first hand. You said you wanted some time. Some time has passed. What do we do, ma'am? I ain't seen too many ways out of this matter. You talked with your boy? What did he have to say? Me and my girl need to know."

"I talked briefly with Stephen the night after you came to see me. He . . ."

"Briefly, ma'am? Don't seem no brief subject to me! Sorry, ma'am, I stepped in while you were talking. Another bad fault of mine."

"I wanted to talk with you in more detail before we had our real talk. I must confess he was not cooperative.

"Please listen as I suggest some possible solutions. Then both of you tell me what you think. First, hopefully the two of you really do love each other. This would solve the problem and give the child a name." She continued, "If they once felt they were in love, perhaps it is still true. Perhaps a successful marriage is possible."

Helen said, "He doesn't love me. He said he didn't. I now have doubts about his intentions from the beginning."

Martha responded, "But maybe a second effort would have a different meaning. After marriage, the child would have a name. Then if you couldn't live together, the child could be cared for."

"Neither me or Helen feel this possible," Mr. Hurt said.

"Suppose we look at some other options, though I must say I do not feel good about them. You could go elsewhere as soon as you graduate and have the child. If the child wasn't wanted, you could put it up for adoption."

"I don't like that, ma'am. Just don't seem right to have a child and give it to another," Helen replied.

Martha continued, "A last resort could be an abortion. There . . ."

Mr. Hurt interjected, "No ma'am. That's killing. Ain't gonna be no killing. Once a baby comes together, it's a baby before and after. Ain't gonna be no killing!"

"I am sure that Stephen would offer support of his child," Martha said.

"There ain't but one solution, Mrs. Randolph. I feel he oughta do the right thing, the honorable thing, if there is anything to this boy of yours. You can tell him that for me so there won't be no misunderstanding.

"There is an old saying, ma'am. Beware a patient man when he comes to the end of his patience. I done got to this point. I hope he knew this.

"We'll go now. All that can be said has been said. Again I thank you. I have all reason to believe you are a good woman. Never heard anything different. Can't say that for everyone in your family. We'll be going. Tell your boy I want to see him in a week or so. Like to see him even before then. Don't want no trouble with him, ma'am. I ain't one to look for trouble but the right thing should come out of this."

They moved quickly to the door, walked rapidly to his old truck and were gone.

The moment they left Martha picked up the telephone and called Jerome. "I'll see you in an hour," she said. Moments later she wondered if she had done the right thing.

"What shall I do?" Martha asked after all the aspects had been reviewed.

"It seems that anything you do will be wrong," Jerome said. "I believe you have considered all the options."

"In a small community like Attapulgus the people will feast on something like this. It will be devastating," Martha said. "At the moment I am equally or more concerned about Helen and her family than the Randolphs. What am I to do with Stephen?"

"Let's not discuss Stephen at the moment, Mrs. Randolph. I have observed, in some misunderstandings, that if the principal parties can sit down and talk without anger and emotion, it can be helpful."

Martha said, as mist filled her eyes, "Since his father and brother have died, he has felt he is no longer a real part of the family. The view of the three were nearly the same. He is like a little boy lost."

"I can see that this loss has been devastating but at the same time I feel he is using this to serve and protect himself. But let us not dwell on this.

"Would you have me attempt to set up a meeting with the four of you? Perhaps Mrs. Hurt should participate. If we did this, caution must be considered. The fewer people who know of this, the better. Let me think about this a day or so. I want to review the options, if there *are* options. I'll not linger, since time is a major factor."

"Do you think you could talk with Stephen? Sometimes an outsider can accomplish more than a family member. I know he feels I would be unfair regardless of what I said," Martha said.

Jerome gave it a few seconds thought, then responded, "At the moment I would prefer not to do so. I think Stephen would feel that

I was a tool to serve you. You think about it. I believe you will see the implications.

"I'll be in touch in a few days. In the meantime should any change occur, please let me know."

Jerome watched Martha leave his office. What a brave woman. Why has so much happened to her in such a short span of time? His thoughts turned to Stephen. This may be only the beginning. I don't believe that Stephen will do much changing.

For Martha, time stood still in that nothing changed. She was no nearer a solution. She had not heard from the Hurts. Apparently Jerome had not reached a conclusion or he would have called.

Stephen dashed into the house. "Three days from now I'll be out of that prison called Attapulgus School," Stephen said. "All these finishing programs are about to drive me nuts."

"I wish you had gone to the banquet," his mother said. "Someday you will look back with some regrets. I do not understand why you did not accept a part in the graduation or the Baccalaureate Services. Mr. Lee offered several parts in an effort to get you involved."

"It's all silly children's stuff! It's sorta like playing dolls or play house. It is all a make-believe type thing.

"I want you to get our business lined up. I may wish to leave the moment I get that diploma. I can't stay here. I would have quit school if you had not withheld my money on the Certificate of Deposit. You do remember your promise? I also hope you won't take long to get my share together. As I recall, it's two hundred thousand plus an additional hundred thousand plus ten dollars an acre for land owned. Not counting Father's gift of a hundred thousand, it would add up to four hundred and seventy-five thousand. I hope you will live up to Father's promise."

"You may be assured your father's wishes on this matter will be followed. But I do wonder if he would approve of you acting in this manner? I loved your father very much. I believe you know that. There were few things we did not agree upon."

"If my father was living, he would be on my side. But that's not to be, now or ever."

"Stephen, you are my son, my baby boy. I love you though I sometimes do not understand you. I must ask, what do you want to do with your life? You have so many fine qualities. You could do so much for yourself and others."

"I hope you are not talking about that poor little Helen Hurt! That backwoods no-good has caused all my problems. She didn't even have sense enough to keep from getting pregnant. I hate her. After graduation I hope I never have to see her again!"

"But Stephen, she is carrying your child! Don't you feel some responsibility for what you have done? She is pregnant because of you."

Stephen laughed. "I got it all worked out. I ain't so dumb as some think. You just watch and see." With that remark, he got up and left.

On the Thursday morning before graduation Steve Hurt and Helen appeared once again at her door.

"Come in, please," Martha said. "I hope you have reached some conclusions. Please have seats." Again she pointed to the seats where they had sat before. "I'll get you a glass of tea."

"Don't need no tea, ma'am. Come to talk one more time. I think you need to hear my Helen again. Matters are getting out of hand."

They turned and looked toward Helen. She was constantly opening and closing her hands. She looked even worse than she had the first time she came. Suddenly she burst into tears. Again her father produced his handkerchief from his overall pocket. He patted her shoulder and said, "Now, now, Helen, just be calm. We'll tell Mrs. Randolph and then be gone. I don't think we need to stay here any longer than we got to and I'll not bring you here again."

Some two minutes later Helen seemed to get her emotions under control to a degree she could talk. "I went back to Stephen, Mrs. Randolph, and asked him didn't he want his son whether he wanted me or not. It doesn't matter much about me anymore."

"What did he say, Helen? I hope he was thoughtful and willing to accept his responsibility," Mrs. Randolph said.

Again Helen broke into tears and again they waited until she was calm enough to continue.

"He said he didn't love me. He said it was all a trick to get my dress up and my panties down. He laughed so hard I thought he was ill. I asked him if he wanted his child, his baby. I asked him what I was to do. I told him I could take care of myself someway but I wouldn't know what to do about the baby, his baby.

"He laughed again and told me he wasn't sure it was his baby. He said he had two or three boys who would swear they had made love with me." Again she broke into sobs and again her father pulled her to him and held her tight.

"Mrs. Randolph, I have never had a relationship with anyone else. I let Stephen do what he did because of the love he expressed for me. I was child like. I guess I saw myself as Cinderella. I guess all poor country girls feel that way at one time or another.

"But ma'am, the child belongs to Stephen. I think when he told me this I nearly died. Not only does he not love me but he gets pleasure out of using people. When he lied and got others to lie to cover up, I felt like my life was at an end. Now I know your son for what he is. I didn't believe anyone could stoop so low."

Steve Hurt said, "Mrs. Randolph, ma'am, I saw your son up town as he was getting out of his car. I was mad. I was more than mad. You ain't got no decent son, ma'am. I hope you know that. I'd rather take Helen out and shoot her before I would let her ever marry your boy! I told him we would make out. Poor folks always find a way. You know, he still seemed to think everything was funny. After he made another smart remark, I told him that after he graduated tonight, I never wanted to see him again. I told him if I found him on Monday or later, I'd kill him on the spot and feel I had done my best day's work.

"Now I think all has been said that needs to be said. I thought I had problems, ma'am. But you are the one with problems. I hope he gets gone 'cause I don't wanna have to kill 'im."

Steve Hurt got his hat by the chair, got up and helped Helen to her feet. He walked out with his arm around her shoulders and moved to the door. He helped Helen into the old truck. Martha watched as they moved slowly down the lane. Her eyes filled with tears.

On Friday afternoon following graduation Stephen walked in and confronted his mother, who was talking with Mary, now large with child.

He demanded, "Where is my Certificate of Deposit? I hope you remember your promise. You said I could have it after I graduated."

Martha went to her room and returned with an envelope. "Here is your certificate, Stephen. Remember, it was a gift of love from your father, through your mother. I hope you will use it wisely."

"Don't guess I will have much time for a while. I joined the army this afternoon. Nothing to do here anymore. I'll be leaving in the morning bright and early. I'll say goodbye now, since I have some things to do and places to go.

"By the way, tell Michael John I'll leave my car at the bus station in Midway, with the keys under the floor mat. I want him to keep it in good condition for me."

He turned and said no more. They heard tires screech as he rounded the driveway in front of the house.

On Thursday morning of the following week Jerome called Martha. "I need you for a few hours. I want you to make a short trip with me. You need not dress up. I'll be at your home in fifteen minutes."

When Jerome arrived Martha asked, "Where are we going, Jerome? You are acting so strange. This is so unlike you!"

Jerome said, "I was not in a place when I called that I could speak freely. We are going to the hospital in Tallahassee. Helen Hurt has apparently had a miscarriage from what I can learn from a private source. I thought it would be meaningful for you to be there, since I am sure you are concerned."

Martha said nothing for several minutes, then asked, "Could this be a blessing for everyone? I hope I am not selfish. May God forgive me." She seemed to be in deep thought and said nothing more for several miles.

Suddenly Martha turned toward Jerome. "Listen to me. I know this is a sensitive matter. It is my wish to do two things and I want to know how you think the Hurts will react. First, I wish to assume all medical and hospital bills. Secondly, I want to provide an education, a college education for Helen. I have learned from Eric that she is quite capable. I will do so through the Robert White Scholarship Fund. What do you think? Can I do it in such a way that they will accept it?"

Jerome thought for a few seconds, then said, "I think that is generous and so much like you. I expected you to say something like that. But you must be careful; they are a proud family. I went over the graduation list with Eric. She can easily do college work. She made nearly twelve hundred on the S.A.T., an excellent score."

"I will do it then. You must help me to plan so as not to make them resentful."

They arrived at the hospital and went to the emergency waiting room. Mr. Hurt saw them and moved toward them. "Helen started to hemorrhage and we rushed her down here. They said she would be all right, would be fine. How did you know?"

"That's not important, Mr. Hurt. Is this Helen's mother?" She looked at a frail, thin lady beside Mr. Hurt.

"Yes'm. This is Lucile, ma'am. Lucile, this is Mrs. Randolph and Mr. Lee. He is a brother to Eric Lee, Helen's teacher."

Jerome held out his hand. "Yes, I am Jerome Lee. I'm glad Helen will be fine. I gather that she has lost her baby?"

"She has. Little thing been so upset recently I'm not surprised. Could well be the Lord's work. Lucile said the Lord musta stepped in and took over. Now maybe we can get ourselves back together. I decided on Tallahassee. People in Midway know everyone's business. How did you know?"

"Let's talk about that later," Martha said. "The important thing is Helen will be all right. Yes, it could well be the Lord's work. Who is to say?"

"Girl ain't had no peace now in weeks and weeks," Lucile said. "Been real hard on our girl.

"Bet this place is high in its prices. But if they will give us a little time, we will pay ever cent. Reckon they'll give us some time, Mrs. Randolph? You and Mr. Lee oughta know about such things."

Martha spoke. "They will do the right thing, but let's consider the welfare of Helen first. Do you suppose they will let me see her soon?"

"Said it would be a while, ma'am. We ain't got nothing pushing this morning but it's shore hard to sit down through some'in like this."

"What does Helen plan to do, Mr. Hurt?" Jerome asked. "What I am saying is, what does she want to do?"

"Wants to go on to school and get some more learning but nothing like that ain't ever happened in mine or Lucile's family and we don't even know enough to ask about it. Bet it cost a heap of money. Couldn't help but cost a lot. That's the reason us poor people stay that way. Ain't no way to do better. Just ain't no escape."

Martha said, "Jerome and I want to inquire about a patient we know. Mr. Lee and I will go now and perhaps we can see Helen when we return. I certainly hope to see her before we go home."

"Right kind of you, ma'am, to be concerned. Lot of people ain't thoughtful when it comes to others. I'm sure Helen would like to know of your concern 'bout her," Mr. Hurt said.

As Jerome and Martha went around the corner, she said, "I need to find the business office. I hope the Lord understands what patient I was seeking."

After being referred to three people, one nice lady said, "May I help you?"

"I think so. I am Martha Randolph. This is my friend, Mr. Lee. We are here in relation to a patient named Helen Hurt, who was admitted some hours ago."

The clerk looked through a file of folders. "Yes, there is a Helen Hurt here. How can I help you?"

Martha said, "I want to take the necessary steps to assume all financial costs relating to this patient."

After looking in the folder again the clerk answered, "She doesn't seem to have any insurance. There are still so many uninsured."

Martha asked, "Would you wish to bill me? Shall I pay now? No, I don't suppose we would know the costs yet. How would you suggest we deal with the matter?"

"It will be some time before we can arrive at a figure. Why not have the hospital bill you when we have finished? You can leave us your correct mailing address. We have a form. We have a form for everything." She smiled.

"Oh, yes," Martha said. "Please give me the necessary form."

"Are you a relative, Mrs. Randolph? Your request is somewhat unusual. We don't have many like this." Again she smiled.

"We are friends. That is what friends are for. I am sure you will handle this in a professional and confidential manner," Martha said.

"You may be assured." Martha filled out the form and left. When they returned to the waiting room they found the Hurts. Lucile had a slight smile on her face. "She is going to be fine. Said she'd go home tomorrow. I'm gonna stay and let Steve get back and see about things. Left in such a hurry I don't remember locking the house. Don't guess I should worry though. Ain't much worth stealing. He'll come get us tomorrow."

"Can Mr. Lee and I see her? I am sure she is weak but we would only stay a minute. We would really like to see her alone if we may."

"Works out just right," Steve Hurt said. "Ain't but two at the time can see her. She's in room seven forty-seven. She'll be proud you all have come."

Martha and Jerome entered the room and saw Helen on the bed. She had a needle inserted in her arm and the fluid dripped steadily from the tube above. She was quite pale but there was a slight sparkle in her eyes as they entered.

"Hello, Helen. You remember me. I am Martha Randolph. You were in our home."

Helen nodded and smiled. "Thank you for coming."

"This is Jerome Lee. His brother, Eric, was your teacher this year."

"Mr. Eric Lee is a nice man. I'll bet you are too. Are you a teacher in some school?"

"No. I am a lawyer. I am also a close friend of the Randolphs. My mother and Mrs. Randolph are very close friends and have been for many years."

"Are you as nice as Mr. Eric Lee? He is the most special person ever!"

Jerome blushed, "I expect he is a much nicer person. Teachers have better reputations than lawyers." He smiled and Helen returned his smile.

"Are you feeling all right, Helen?" Martha asked. "I guess that is really a foolish question! How could you?"

"I'm hurting some, ma'am, but it will be better. I'm sorry I have caused so many so much trouble. I haven't been very nice or thoughtful."

"Helen, you are very special. I have two requests to make of you and one of them will not be easy. It also may take some time."

"I expect I can do it, Mrs. Randolph. I have discovered you are a very special person. What would you have me do?"

"First, I want you to forgive Stephen Randolph and not hate him as you have a right to do. This is a big request. He has been most unfair and inconsiderate. I have been deeply hurt. I know you have as well. If you did not forgive, I could understand. It wouldn't be easy for me. But think about it. As unfair and unkind and selfish as he has been, he is still my son and I love him. I have hopes he will grow and mature. Perhaps a change, in time, may occur."

"I have thought of nothing else for days, actually weeks, and, as you said, I believe he has been unkind and . . . Anyway you know him better than most, perhaps anyone. It is possible that mothers do not always see the faults in their own children. I believe this is true in my home," Helen said.

"I'll forgive him but I can't promise to forget. At this moment, though it may be difficult for you to understand, I would not care to see him again. It would be better for both of us, for everyone. I will forgive him, but he will need to ask God to do so as well. I'll do my part. You can count on it. There was a second item?"

"Yes, I have learned you are a fine girl and a scholar as well. You have both mind and character. It is my understanding that you want to go to college and . . ."

"We have no money for such things, Mrs. Randolph."

"I want you to go see Mr. Baggs about a scholarship when you get home. He is the chief trustee for the Robert White Scholarship Fund. Perhaps he will have an idea. Please make an application."

"Do you think I have a chance? Especially after this has happened?"

"I do. I bet he can help you. Will you promise me you will do that?"

"I promise, Mrs. Randolph. Thank you for being here and giving your support to me and my parents. Please tell your son he is forgiven and ask him to pursue it one step beyond. I think I had better rest now. Goodbye."

As Martha and Jerome were returning to the waiting room, Martha said, "How foolish Stephen has been. If only he had loved her!"

When they reached the waiting room Martha said, "I have only a minute before I must go. Would you allow me to come get Mrs. Hurt and Helen tomorrow? I am sure I will have ample time."

"My truck will be fine, ma'am. I'll go slow and we'll be all right. Charity is for others but it ain't for me. You are kind and thoughtful."

As Martha and Jerome neared Attapulgus, Martha said, "Please get in touch with Mr. Baggs. I will drop by and leave him a check. I want Helen to go to college."

Jerome didn't answer immediately and Martha looked to see if he had heard her. Then Jerome said, "Give me your check and instructions. This will help you, since the Hurts will give you credit. This way you can tell a little white lie." He laughed. "After all, Jesus forgave Simon Peter!"

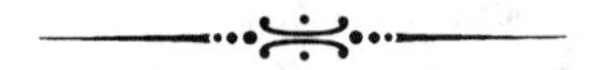

"Come in, Jerome," Mr. Baggs said. "I've been waiting to talk with you."

"Mr. Baggs, here is a check for the Robert White Scholarship Fund."

Mr. Baggs looked surprised. "This person has already contributed, most generously."

"Mr. Baggs, there are some strings attached."

"Strings? I don't usually like strings!"

Jerome said, "Sixteen thousand of this is for a four-year scholarship for Helen Hurt. You may use the other nine as you believe best. Remember, if you are approached about this, Mrs. Randolph has not even seen or visited you recently."

Mr. Baggs replied, "What shall I tell Helen and her family? They are poor but proud folks!"

"I'm sure you will think of something. After all, they pay you all of eight thousand dollars a year! Earn your money!" Jerome smiled.

Mr. Baggs laughed and said, "Get gone. I've work to do!"

Chapter 76

"It's nice to have you home again," Martha said. "What do you have planned this summer?"

April stretched in the platform rocker, extending her arms and legs as far as possible. "After a full twelve hours of sleep I'll be off and running. It's so nice to be home with the family again."

"You seem different, April," her mother said. "I can't explain but you are different."

"One does not stay the same always. I am a bit restless for some reason but I have no explanation. I still have some puzzles to sort out."

"Have you seen Jerome? He is always asking about you."

"No. But I plan to see him soon. I saw David and Mary. They are excited about a new baby coming. Are you prepared to become a grandmother?"

"Oh yes, I'm excited! I worry a great deal though. Grandmothers see dangers young people never see. I'll just be glad when the baby arrives and we know that the baby and mother are unimpaired. Yes, I suppose I am excited as the parents to be are."

"I'm going to Somewhere Else," April said. "I'll be home before dark. If Charles comes in, tell him to drop by. We haven't had our regular chat in a long time."

April had not been gone five minutes when Martha heard a knock at the front door. When she opened it she saw Steve Hurt and Helen. "Come in. Have a seat. Helen, I hear you are doing fine." In moments Martha had glasses of ice tea in their hands. "Weather is getting hot. This will cool you off a tad. I can't get over how well Helen looks."

Helen smiled and said, "I'm fine, Mrs. Randolph. We have only a few minutes. I think my father has some things he wishes to discuss with you."

"Ma'am, I think there are some things we need to talk about, like Helen said. First, when I went to the cashier to get Helen out of the hospital, I was told I didn't owe nothing. Gotta be a mistake, I told them. Places like that don't operate free or come cheap. The lady said there was no mistake and that we didn't owe nothing. Now ma'am, I just . . ."

"Please call me Martha or Mrs. Randolph, whichever you feel most comfortable with."

"Well, ma—, Mrs. Randolph, I ain't so educated and calling you as I did weren't meant to make you feel bad. I'll try and remember. Now, about the hospital bill. You paid it, didn't you?" He had a strange look about him.

"I did, Mr. Hurt. I did just that. There were a number of reasons but I see no purpose in reviewing them."

"I 'spect we better, Mrs. Randolph. I shore need to talk about this. I ain't got much but I am honest and I pay my debts. There are times I have to do a little at the time but I do it. Can't say I like you running off and doing this with no talk. Just don't seem to be right."

"Mr. Hurt, Helen was not treated right by my son. I was hurt that he acted as he did and more than hurt by some of the things he said. Your daughter would not have been pregnant except for his false and inappropriate behavior. You acted more kindly than I would had the situation been reversed."

"But Mrs. Randolph, I ain't been nice at the end. I had no business talking to a child thata way. Guess I just lost control. Our children do this to us at times. I ain't been kind one bit."

"Mr. Hurt, this is behind us. Helen would not have had a problem except for Stephen. This is a way I can say I'm sorry but I can never make up to Helen or her family what has been done. Just as you say, it was important to pay your debts; it is equally important for me. You cannot deprive me of this moral responsibility. Now let us be done with that for all times."

Helen looked closely at Martha. "You set up that scholarship with Mr. Baggs. I know you did. I hardly had my application in when he informed me I had been selected."

"I'm delighted. I am not surprised that you were selected. Eric Lee and I talked about all the members of the senior class months ago. He spoke highly of you and several others. I am delighted you have been selected."

"But Mrs. Randolph, I suspect you insisted to Mr. Baggs as to my selection. There are several students equally or better qualified. I guess they need assistance in some cases. I am not sure I can accept the scholarship."

"Let me tell you a little story, Helen. That scholarship fund is in honor of Robert White. My daughter respected him more than all others. Because our family is able to contribute, I send a check each year to help deserving students. For your information, I have not talked with Mr. Baggs. You were deserving or you would not be one of those selected. I am delighted at his decision."

"You didn't tell Mr. Baggs to select me?"

"No. I have not seen or talked with Mr. Baggs since graduation and at that time you were not a part of our conversation. I did receive a thank you note through the mail for the small gift I made for my family. Now let us put this behind us after I once again congratulate you. I know you will do something very special with your life."

"Mrs. Randolph, I need to get you to talk to your boy for me," Mr. Hurt said. "Tell him I ain't gonna do nothing bad to him. I was told he went away. Tell your boy to come on home. We can all live in peace."

"I thank you for those sentiments. I will relay the message immediately. He cannot come home soon, however. He is serving our country as a soldier."

"We'll be going ma — Mrs. Randolph. Helen ain't gonna let no one down with her scholarship. Nobody will use it better than her. We'll be going now." As he walked out he turned and said, "The ice tea was good and we thank you again."

When they were gone Martha spoke out loud, "Lord, forgive the white lie and let it be our secret. She will use the scholarship wisely. Amen."

April heard a car coming. She had not expected Charles so soon. As the car drew nearer she saw it wasn't Charles. She recognized it was Jerome and her heart beat a little faster. He got out and quickly approached her on the deck.

"Jerome, what a delight." She rushed forward and pecked him on the cheek. "Best I can do at the moment." She smiled and her black eyes twinkled.

"You are even more beautiful than I remembered."

"Can you stay a while?"

"No. At the moment I just had to see you! But I can come back in an hour or so from now with some steaks and goodies. I will even do the cooking. I also wanted to fish an hour. I believe you gave me an invitation."

"Indeed I did. I'll get things ready. Would you stop by and tell Mother you are with me? She will worry when dark comes and I haven't returned."

"I will. I'll be back in an hour or so."

April continued to stare in the distance. She looked out across the lake but she saw nothing. Her thoughts continued to dwell on Jerome. She asked herself a dozen questions but found few answers.

I wonder what goes on in his mind?

April heard another car. This time it was Charles. As he got out of his car she could see he looked tired and weary. He didn't look relaxed as usual. She wondered if it was one or several things he was concerned about.

"April! you are just the person I need. You look so good." He pecked her on the cheek and she returned the peck.

"Charles, you look tired or troubled. You look as if the burdens you seem to carry are more than you can bear. Want to tell me? You can't lie to me. I know you as well as you know me. I'm here to listen."

"Let's talk about you first," Charles said. "Let's start with Auburn."

"Auburn is great. But I need to be nearer home. There are many reasons. I have been accepted at F.S.U. but I am going to rest this summer. Please get me an apartment at the complex where you and your girls stay."

"What reasons?"

"We will discuss this later. They are sufficient. Let us not dwell on this. As I said, I've been accepted. After all, someone must keep an eye on you!"

"You still think of Robert." April was not sure if it was a question or a statement.

"Yes. It is not easy to believe he is dead. You may not understand, but he still helps me over some rough spots. I learned a great deal from him. I suppose no one will ever be as perfect as Robert. Now I can understand better why David had so many questions, why he felt so unsure.

"How are Mr. White and his family? I must see them soon."

"Outwardly they seem to manage. No one can see the inside where it hurts. The twins are growing up in a hurry."

"Tell me about Susan Lee."

"She is the same wonderful Susan. Now I want to talk about you, Charles. You are not hiding your problems too well."

"I will be on campus in September. The end is in sight."

"What about your dissertation? Has it been accepted? I understand the professors demand something special."

"It is nearly completed. Once it is accepted I will be required to go before a select group of professors and defend it. There are also a few other courses they have suggested. Finally, there are the oral and written examinations. I can see no unusual problems. I've been somewhat involved in another study. Later in the summer I will give you some details. It's quite unique."

"Meggie? Gena? I know they have been academically successful. Have they adjusted to college life?"

"Indeed they have. I am so pleased. In their spare time they help me with my research. Meggie is especially interested in research. For her it is like Daniel Boone going over the next mountain wondering what will be on the other side."

"I wish you would refer to another explorer, Charles. That rascal left a wife and a house full of children home alone without ample resources and the neighbors had to care for them. Why is this not in a history book?"

Charles laughed, then said, "If history recorded all the details, we would kill all of our heroes. You would not wish this."

"You have a problem, Charles, and as dumb as you are you haven't recognized it."

"I have no idea as to what you are referring?"

"Meggie and Gena. Both have been in love with you forever. You have not noticed? You have believed it is a sister-brother type thing? Not so. You are not as bright as I thought. You don't understand women and you are supposed to be at the top of your class in such matters! By the way, did you ever hear from Sara Knight?"

"No."

"Did you try to find her?"

"No."

"Do you want to tell me why?"

"No."

"You sure are stuck on the word no."

"Yes." Charles smiled. "I had thought some day I might tell you about her, but no, you wouldn't understand.

"Did you find special people at Auburn? Men?"

"I met a number of people I liked. Some were girls, some boys and yes, some professors. But I found no special man for my life. I wanted to discover many things I had not looked at before. I was burned out when I got there.

"Let's go back to you. If Meggie and Gena are fine, your paper is in good shape and Uncle Edd is proficient in his new role, what is your trouble?"

"Uncle Edd is most efficient. But you knew that. He still has many stories. He is a smart man and very loyal. Don't ever underestimate this man."

"Then it has to be the family," April said. "Is it Mother? It couldn't be David and Mary. I would guess the problem is Stephen. I don't believe he is so patriotic that he left to serve his nation. There had to be other reasons. There is something I am not seeing. I can just sense it. Why haven't you written or called? I think I would have called you, if our positions were reversed."

"There is nothing you could have done about that. As to the family problems, some of it started months, maybe years ago. Part can be placed at my doorstep. First, my transportation study was not understood. Many believed it was in support of integration. They needed to blame someone. Next, I moved to get Meggie in her current position. I was the one who brought a black into our school, our church and our home. Next, I supported a referendum so the people could express themselves. This was not understood.

"Now, let's go in another direction. We gave up tobacco. Others didn't and they lost their shirts. For some reason, we were the villains. It was a poorly kept secret that many of us did not support tobacco. This did not create good will. Next we changed the wage scale. There were no secrets. In twenty-four hours the workers at other places were unhappy and insisting on a higher wage. Next, our project for better housing was tossed about among the people. It had an impact in many areas all through the county.

"Next, our father, before he departed, angered many when demands were made after the fifteen-day rain. He lost his patience. He said some things that were not forgotten.

"In our community there was also much speculation about Michael John and Robin Wells and their departures. There are few secrets in a small community.

"The Maybe Jones situation never was completely put to rest either. Then, since no one has heard a word from Posey's boys, many feel this was perhaps Maybe's work.

When April started to speak Charles said, "Just hold on. I'm not through. With our reorganization and our father's entry into politics, our economic status was not as many had believed. When a family's assets are likely greater than anyone else's, the 'have-nots' wonder why. The fact that it was a combined effort of hard work over nearly a hundred years was not readily seen.

"Besides all this, there has also been talk about the union of David and Mary because Joe had not long been dead when they got married. The fact she is pregnant gave them other reasons to wonder.

"I have said enough. Everything seems to have changed. We, as individuals as well as a family, are looked upon in a different manner than in the past.

"People do not forget easily, April. This is their nature. They see what they wish to see.

"To sum it up, we don't seem to have many friends left. Perhaps it could be said that this doesn't bother us but it does. It bothers Mother more than anyone but she doesn't discuss it. She attempts to go on as if it was not different but it is eating her up inside. Actually, it doesn't bother me too much except that it bothers other family members.

"Let me go one step beyond. I feel that some of the negative attitudes relating to the Randolphs have carried over to some of our friends; for example, the Lee and White families. It seems people are saying you can't be a friend to the Randolphs, and still be their friends. You can't hold the Randolphs' hands and theirs too.

"I believe Mother feels and sees this but pretends things are as always. Neither of us how to turn things around. For years we were considered backwoods people. They associated all of us with our father in early years and those of his family that came before. Then all these changes occurred. There was land, wealth, achievements, political positions and so on. It was too much, too quick."

April responded, "Charles, we have done nothing illegal. The family did what they felt was best. We have cheated no one. We have given back through the church, the scholarship fund and in other ways. We have tried to make up for some possible errors by establishing new policies for our people. These are the people who helped us get where we are. Is it not right to share with those who made it all possible? No one has said that life was fair. What do we do, Charles?"

"I wish I knew," Charles said. "Perhaps you can think about this and come up with something. You may be surprised who sees the problem best."

"Oh, I could make a good guess. Without hesitation I would say Meggie and Uncle Edd. Perhaps they have some suggestions."

"Perhaps. They are wise. I must go now. I'm sorry; I have spoiled your day."

"No, don't feel that way. You don't solve many problems by pretending they do not exist. Some would likely go away but I am not sure about our dilemma. Now you see one reason why I need to be nearer home. There are others."

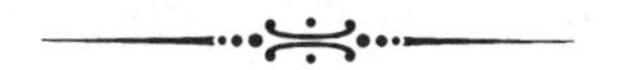

"Want to help me?" Jerome yelled to April as he got out of his car. Between the two of them, they brought all of the bags and packages into the house, placed some in the refrigerator and others on the table. Then they turned toward one another and Jerome placed a hand on each of her shoulders. He looked into her eyes, but was unable to read her thoughts. She saw his half smile, a bit mischievous. He held her at arms' length and looked at her feet. Then his eyes moved upward, taking in her beautiful legs, her narrow waist, and her full and shapely breasts straining against the soft blouse. For three or four seconds he let his eyes linger. Then his eyes made contact with her face, the raven black eyes, lashes, brows and hair.

He could see she wore no cosmetics. He thought, how can you improve on perfection? During all of these moments he had not spoken a word. He pulled her into his arms and she offered no resistance. His arms moved around her and pulled her closer, his lips seeking her moist red lips. For a moment there was little response, but then she flung her arms around him and pulled him even closer as they kissed, deeply and passionately. Seconds later he raised his head and spoke. "Welcome home. I don't think I can let you continue to roam. You are so very special."

"You didn't close your eyes when you kissed me. I am told there are advantages both ways," April said. She pecked him on the cheek and continued, "It is good to be home. I could find myself spoiling you if I am not careful!"

"This is the most delightful place I have ever seen. I seem to see a part of you everywhere I look."

"You have never seen or known the real me, Jerome. If you had, you might be running for your life!" She laughed, then said, "Now I am going to show you how to catch a fish. First, you must learn to think like one. In a way they are like people."

They moved around the water wheel and he saw she had readied a boat for them. There were two rods with reels, with plugs on each, a tackle box, one paddle and two small anchors.

"I will sit in the back of the boat," April said. "You get in first and we will shove off." The boat moved without a sound as she sculled the boat in an expert manner.

In the next fifteen minutes April had caught four bass, weighing up to three pounds or more. She had also untangled two back lashes of his reel and pulled his plug out of the branches of a tree. During this time she had not spoken. Then suddenly she said, "Why do you like Somewhere Else? There must be a reason. What do you like most?"

"You. You are my first, second and third reasons. Beyond that I must give some thought."

"Now, now, you know that isn't what I mean."

"Yes. I understand." He smiled and continued, "You feel you are away from most of the problems about you. It leaves you free to think, to dream and to plan. You have the exact name you needed. Yes, one is Somewhere Else. Perhaps you want to tell me your thoughts."

April said, "It is a place of contrasts. It can be light and gay and friendly or it can be quiet and peaceful and yes, even solemn. It has a mystical sense about it. But I suppose the thing I like the best is that it is unfinished. It is like the life of a person. We never cease to grow, learn and even change. I suppose we could say it is unfinished and I wish it to remain so. It is a song, a sunrise, a sunset, a beautiful poem or a love story. It is what you want it to be. Does that make sense?"

"Oh yes. I agree completely."

April said, "This tells me something about you. You are a mystery to many, perhaps most. You never let anyone see the real you. Is it so important to keep the real Jerome a secret?"

"I am not sure anyone should be an open book. Certainly you are not. I learn something new, something different, each time I am with you," Jerome said.

"Some way and some day I am going to see the real you, Jerome. I don't think I will see it all today so let's catch the big fish."

They remained silent for a minute. Then April said, "Cast near the point on your right."

On the second cast Jerome caught a bass of four or five pounds which he released. "How did you know?"

"Know what?"

"That a fish was there?"

"I told you to think like a fish. Now we are approaching the spot where Temptation stays." She eased an anchor into the water. "Cast off the point near the low hanging trees. She is smart. You will have to cast several times. You must make her mad or tempt her. She is a female. You know how girls are!"

After five minutes Jerome said, "She isn't home today. She is likely teaching others bad habits!"

"Not so. She is home. Cast nearer the point where you see some overhanging bushes."

On the third cast it sounded like a gun as the fish exploded out of the water. Jerome hung on for dear life. Ten minutes later he brought her up to the boat. April picked her up, removed the plug and returned her to the water.

"Jerome, there are several lessons to be learned from this experience. I trust you were alert. I know already that you know little about females. But you are intelligent and I have high hopes for you! Now it is time for you to have another lesson. This time it is cooking."

As Jerome broiled the steaks he said, "You have had an unusual life. It will be interesting to see what you do with the rest of it. You have a way of attracting people, especially men. Victor was in love with you when you were thirteen. Robert discovered you at fifteen. My brother never doubted you hung the moon since he was a junior in college. I suspect half the men at Auburn were bowing at your feet. Now you are nineteen and I have no idea where I fit into the puzzle. I trust you do not think of me as you would a brother or a father."

April looked closely at Jerome, as if she was about to speak, then changed her mind.

"Would you like to tell me how you feel?" Jerome asked.

Again April did not speak, only looking and saying nothing. Finally she spoke. "Tonight I will say the blessing. I can only hope there is another opportunity soon so you may say one too." The blessing was in the form of a prayer and again Jerome continued to be amazed at this unusual lady.

When they had finished their steaks, Jerome got up and approached the refrigerator. "Let's see what my mother prepared to sweeten us up a bit."

Moments later Jerome said, "It is a pecan pie. Suppose I cut the pie and get some ice cream. How does that sound?"

"We both have very special mothers, Jerome. If we don't make something out of our lives, we can't blame anyone except ourselves."

Jerome said, "I continue to be amazed at your mother. I never saw these traits earlier."

"I didn't see it either," April said. "We are both fortunate."

When they had finished with the dishes and cleaned the kitchen Jerome said, "This has been a perfect evening." He pulled her to him and kissed her tenderly. He stood for a few seconds and looked into her eyes. She smiled.

"Let me drive ahead, please. Mothers are concerned about their children and their safety."

As they walked to their cars Jerome asked, "Did you tell me why you named your fish Temptation?"

"You know of such things, Jerome. Please tell your mother I enjoyed her pie. Goodnight." She closed the car door and moved down the lane.

CHAPTER 77

Susan Lee looked at Jerome as they sat at the breakfast table. "Your body is with me but your mind is far away. I've noticed this more than once lately. And another thing, I haven't heard about your fishing adventure."

"What do you think of April? Have you ever really told me how you felt about her?" He knew that he had not responded to his mother's question.

"Why would you ask? Is it important you know how I feel?"

"Yes," Jerome said. "You seem reluctant to talk about her."

"My answer is not to be evasive but I don't know how. You see her and then you don't. She is full of surprises. I'm not sure that April is one person. She seems to be many. Who can say who the real April is? She has some characteristics of one that is six as well as forty years old. She is a deep thinker but she often will not let you know her thoughts. She is good. She is kind and thoughtful. We don't have to talk about her physical characteristics. They are self explanatory. What do you two talk about? Did you catch any fish?"

"She discussed the three important things in her life. Actually it should be so with everyone. First, her relationship with God. Second, the selection of a spouse and thirdly, a vocational choice. Few nineteen-year-olds think of such matters as she does.

"As to our fishing, you wouldn't believe it! She sculled the boat, caught fish after fish, untangled my reel repeatedly and taught me how to think like a fish. Then she told me where and how to deal with Temptation. I . . ."

"Temptation? What has that to do with fishing?"

"She has named this large female bass Temptation. She has reasons for everything. We released her, naturally. It was some experience."

"How do you feel about April, Jerome? You couldn't keep your eyes off her when she was thirteen, six years ago."

"I want to say I don't know but perhaps it is best to say I am afraid to say."

Susan smiled as only a devoted mother can do. "I would not have my son hurt, possibly destroyed, but if I saw something beautiful and good and decent and intelligent, I might just go after it. I think the time is near when you must make some decisions. You are a patient man, a patient son, but I believe there is a point when such patience may leave one."

"Suppose we leave April at this point and talk about some other Randolphs. How have they managed with the deaths and the changes?"

"Martha?"

"Yes. I never knew of her talents and her inner strengths. But now she has Stephen. That is enough to try one's soul!"

Jerome did not smile.

"There are things you know about Stephen? You have some answers?"

"Yes and no. Always a good response. Yes, I know some things. No, I can't talk about it, not even with you."

"Does Martha see the many changes as it relates to community life?" Susan asked.

"I don't know. She must see many attitude changes among the people. We know what and we know why but let's leave it at that."

"But we can't leave it, Jerome. I believe this is eating her alive. If she has a problem, I have a problem. She is my dearest friend. Mercy me, what can I do?"

"Oh, God, Mother, where does one start? Joseph did not make a good commissioner. It was not a good time to be a commissioner. Joe's behavior complicated matters. The union of David and Mary was not understood. The transportation study Charles made was equally misunderstood. Then there was the referendum to consolidate and some misunderstood Charles once again. Then, the attitudes about tobacco did not endear them to the tobacco farmers.

"There were different opinions about Maybe's escapade. The salary increases for the underpaid workers were misunderstood, or perhaps understood, but resented. When Meggie popped up in school and church she was resented. People change slowly. The debt cancellation for the quarters people added more fuel to the fire. Now the housing project has them upset once more.

"The Randolphs also lost some goodwill in the county, especially in Midway, by changing to another bank. Bruce McPherson has considerable influence.

"One last thing. Money! The people did not know of the Randolphs' financial situation until Mr. Randolph ran for commissioner. They lived in such a way that no one knew or could have guessed. Those who have little, the have-nots, most often resent those who have money. Then those who did have money and property found they were not in the same ballpark. Joseph had surpassed them all. The old settlers, the blue-bloods, were no longer looked upon with reverence. They felt someone was taking their place. It is quite amazing to observe people!"

"Jerome, this is so unfair. One is to be punished for trying to help people and alleviate suffering? A little more income, a decent place to stay and better working conditions should merit applause."

"Doesn't work like that. From a personal viewpoint I feel this is great. But watch. They will pay a big price. The workers will say, 'Look what is happening over there." Then trouble will start and profits will fall. As I said, it goes back to money."

"Do you believe the Randolphs are aware of these things?"

"I think there is some awareness on the part of all of them. Some likely see a great deal more than others. I doubt anyone has seen the whole picture."

"Why don't you tell them, as you have told me?"

"I don't know how to tell them. Sometimes the messenger who brings news of such nature is not viewed with kindness. It is also possible that I could be wrong about some of this."

"This is all so unfair! Young people are going to school on scholarships provided by them and some of these very parents may be major critics. They have served in the church, the school, and yes, the community. If you look closely, you see some evidence of the Randolph's concern everywhere. Jerome, there must be some way to help. I can't let Martha down if I can help it."

CHAPTER 78

"My baby is coming home! It's been so long. Michael John, you can meet him at the bus station in Midway at two o'clock. Oh, it will be so nice to see my boy again."

Michael John said, "Wouldn't it be best for you to meet him? Perhaps he would be disappointed if you didn't."

"I can't go. David has taken Mary to the hospital. I must remain here until I hear from them. I could send Jack but I don't think Stephen would feel good unless some family member was there."

"I'll go."

An hour later Martha heard the door open and heard Stephen shout, "Where is everyone? This is not much of a welcome!"

"I'm here for you, Son! Your mother will always be here for you." She rushed into his arms.

Stephen gave a brief embrace and drew back. "I can't believe this. I had felt my sister and brothers would be here."

Trying to hide her disappointment, Martha explained, "Charles had to go before his committee at F.S.U. David has taken Mary to the hospital so I can become a grandmother and Mary asked April to go with her. Seems as if everything is happening at once."

"Well, I hope Michael John at least has my car ready like I told him. It will be nice to drive again. Where I have been you walk, you trot, you run and you wait."

"You look so good, Stephen. Oh, I'm so happy to have you home again! The uniform is just perfect!"

"Bet I can attract some girls with it. They like uniforms. I could see that where I've been."

"I'll bet you can too!" His mother smiled and went over and hugged him again.

"I sorta like the military in some ways. Perhaps it's just as well. I don't fit into anyone's plans around here, not since Father and Joe left. I don't really need to be here."

Michael John stepped forward and handed Stephen the keys to his car. "Your car is ready. I've checked it closely."

Without a word of thanks Stephen said, "Well, I hope so. That's the least you and my family could have done!"

"How long will you be with us?" Martha said. "I hope they have given you a long vacation after all that training."

"Fourteen days plus travel time. Then I'll go back for assignment. It's just possible I'll go to officer's school. My record was probably the best in my outfit."

"Stephen, go over and stand by the window. I just want to see how handsome my son is." Stephen moved over. "You are the best looking soldier ever. You stand so straight. Your posture is perfect!"

"Like I say, it's not all bad. I'm thinking of making it a career. I know the pay isn't good but I have another source of income." He smiled.

"I've got to run," Michael John said. "I've got David's duties as well as mine."

Martha turned to Stephen. "I'm planning your favorite meal. We'll eat about eight. Why don't you go over and see Jack and Sandra? Uncle Edd will want to see you."

"They are not concerned with me. Can't say as I've got any special interest in them. I'll just ride around for a while." He turned and left without saying more. He had left his bags in the middle of the room.

At ten minutes after nine they heard a motor racing down the lane. Stephen rushed in and said in a shout, "Hope supper is ready. I'm as hungry as a wolf."

Charles and April approached ready to embrace him but he held out his hand to shake in an unconcerned manner.

Charles said, "Sorry we were not here. Looks like the two of us got caught up in the events of the day." Charles could smell alcohol strongly on his breath.

"I'm disappointed but not surprised. Things are not the same. Never will be again." As he spoke he moved toward the table filled with food.

When they were seated April reported, "Guess what? I'm an aunt, the boys are uncles and our mother is a grandmother! You should see that beautiful girl. She is a darling and has hair, lots of hair, like her mother! She weighted in at an even seven pounds. The mother and baby are doing well. As to David, I'm not sure!"

"Time to eat," Stephen said. "Nice to get some home cooked food again. I trust Mother hasn't forgotten how I like my steak cooked!" In moments he had cut his steak.

"Suppose we ask the blessing. Perhaps it's not a custom in our military," Martha said. She watched as hands were extended.

"Thank you, dear God, for the lives of all my children. Thank You for letting Stephen return safely to us. Remember our newborn and her parents. Bless this food. Amen."

"I hope all of you have worked hard this summer. I trust another bonus, a big bonus, is waiting. Of course it will not be like the one Mother gave to us from Father but I suppose we'll see."

Charles turned red. "Everyone has worked hard in your absence. We missed your contribution but we all knew you were serving our country. As I recall, I sent your checks from the corporation each month as if you were here. This included the increase that was automatic after finishing school. I didn't hear from you but I could tell you received them as the canceled checks were in the bank statements." Charles looked to see a reaction but Stephen was wolfing down his food.

"Could have been more for us if wages hadn't been increased and new houses going up. Joe tried to tell you those nigs would just wreck them and they will. No one listened to Joe. Could have been more for us," Stephen repeated as he continued to eat rapidly.

After a few seconds Martha said, "In time to come we can have a better group. We can help them and they help us in return. It should prove a better life for everyone. They have had so few opportunities."

Stephen, displeased with the conversation, said, "I'm sure of one thing. There is no place here for me. I hope the funds for leaving will be ready because I know I can't stay. No farming, real farming, goes on here anymore!"

"What your Father established for each of our children is available but I hope you will return here. We're going to try several new approaches. We want you to be a part."

"No place for me!" Stephen snapped.

"Mothers live in hope, dear Stephen. Your father always said no one could do as much as you on a farm."

As the meal was about to end, his mother said, "We have had all your clothes cleaned and ready for you on your vacation. I hope, however, that you would let others see you in your uniform. You do a great deal for it!" She smiled. "But relax, and have a good time. You've earned it!"

Stephen practically jumped up from the table and said, "You can depend on that!" He left the room and did not speak of enjoying the special meal his mother had worked so hard to prepare and waited so long to serve.

"I'll call the hospital once more," April said. "We will all rest better knowing my niece and her family are doing well."

As the clock struck eight the following night, the telephone rang. Martha had gone to see her grandchild since David, Mary and the baby had returned home that evening. Charles was at the office and Michael John in the shop. April answered the telephone. "Randolph residence, April Randolph speaking," she said.

She heard a voice. "Is this the home of a Stephen Randolph?"

"Yes. He is not here. Would you like to leave a message or . . ."

"Miss, there has been an accident, an accident between Midway and Attapulgus. He has just been taken to the hospital in Midway. I expect the family or someone to come immediately."

"Is the accident serious? Of course we will come immediately. Do you have any details?"

"It's serious. Can't say more at this time." She heard the telephone go dead. She did not remember if the voice had identified himself.

As April hung up the telephone her mother entered, saying, "My granddaughter is precious." Then she looked closely at April. "What is it? What's wrong, April?"

"Stephen has been in an accident! Get what you need and we'll get Charles and Michael John. Stephen is in the hospital in Midway." In three minutes the four were en route.

April told Charles, "You drive and Michael John can sit with you. I'll look after Mother."

"Is he hurt badly?" her mother asked. "Who called? What did they say?" Martha had never been so upset. "Don't keep something from me! Who called?"

"I can't tell you who called. He hung up before I could ask. I was upset. He wanted to know if this was the residence of a Stephen Randolph. He said Stephen had been in an accident between Midway and Attapulgus. He said it was serious."

"They must have said something else! Try and remember. Were others involved? Surely they said more!"

"No, Mother, that was his message." She held her mother's hand and looked at the dashboard ahead. Charles was driving much too fast.

"Oh, April, I'm so nervous! Oh God, don't let anything else happen to my family! I don't think I can handle any more!" Tears streamed down her cheeks. April had never felt more helpless. She knew that Charles had increased his speed but she decided not to look.

As Charles topped a hill rounded a curve they could see lights flashing up ahead. It was obvious that several law officials were on the scene. As they moved closer they could see a wrecker moving into position, lights flashing. April could see two State Patrol cars and two cars from the sheriff's department as Charles slowed down.

April peered into the darkness but with all the lights, the people and the vehicles, she could see little. The little she did see did not raise her hopes. She attempted to keep her body in front of her mother so Martha could not see outside.

"Move on out but move slowly," a deputy said as Charles rolled down his window. "Watch out for the wrecker. We will need to get some lanes cleared as soon as the officials complete their inspection."

As they drew parallel April got a glimpse of the two cars. They seemed totally demolished. "Move on Charles, she said. "You heard the man." She hoped her mother had not seen.

"Oh, God, be merciful," she heard her mother say. "Please don't let my baby die!" She repeated it over and over, then became silent.

Charles drove to the emergency room parking lot. As he turned in April could see an ambulance backed up to the loading ramp. They were not removing someone but were placing someone inside. She knew without being told someone was being transferred to Thomasville or Tallahassee. The ambulance driver had already turned on whirling lights. He seemed to be waiting for a signal to move.

"Look after Mother," April yelled as she rushed to the door. As she moved inside she saw a man's face which looked familiar but she could not be sure. Then she recognized him. "Why, Mr. McPherson, what are you doing here?" She saw an expression of horror on his face. He stared a moment, as if in a trance, then spoke loudly, his voice filled with scorn, anger and hate.

"Your brother just killed my children, both of them. He'll pay for this! He'll pay if it's the last thing I ever do." He turned away as Martha and her two sons rushed in.

As he ran toward his Buick Martha thought she recognized him and was about to speak, then decided he was a stranger after all.

April rushed up to a lady dressed in a white uniform who occupied a small enclosure. She sat behind a desk with some papers in front of her. "Please tell me about Stephen, Stephen Randolph, that is. Is he all right? Is he alive?"

"Who are you?" the woman asked without expression.

"I am his sister." April pointed behind her. "This is his mother, my mother, and these are my two brothers."

The woman answered, "He is in the emergency room. Doctors are with him. I am not permitted to give out information. Do you know if he had any insurance? Perhaps his mother would know."

"Lady," April said, "you ask about insurance at a time like this? I can't believe this!"

"Don't get sassy with me, Miss. I'm just doing my job. If the system doesn't please you, then you should direct your questions to those who make the policies." She looked down at her desk, picked up a paper and placed it in one of the files.

April turned to her family. "Remain here until I get back. Someone must know something."

The woman pointed to a sign. "No admittance!"

April pushed two double doors open and moved in quickly. She rushed down the hall until it bisected another, then turned to the right. She saw a door that said, "Emergency Room One." She was about to push on the door when she felt a hand on her shoulder. "Sorry. You can't go in there. It's against regulations."

April was about to tell him what to do with his regulations when he continued in a soft warm voice, "Lady, tell me what you need to know. Perhaps I can tell you or find out for you."

"My brother," she said, "is Stephen Randolph. I must know something about him. He's been in a wreck. My mother back there is nearly crazy."

"Please wait here a moment." He entered the room and in moments returned.

"Stephen Randolph has some problems. We do not believe they are life threatening but they are quite serious. His face and head are cut badly. They will require some special care. There may be some broken bones also. At the moment we are not sure. I do not believe it would be wise to see him at this time. The important thing is that he is alive. I'm sure the doctors will talk with the family a little later. I guess they will transfer him to Tallahassee. Suppose you update your family."

She turned to leave, then turned back. "There were two or more cars involved. I saw them on the way. Can you tell me about the occupant, or occupants, of the other car, or cars?"

"It's not good." He looked at his feet. "I am not allowed to discuss the others. I'm sorry. Now, go tell your family and wait with them." He turned and left.

She returned and told the family what she had learned but did not speak of the others involved. They sat down in some chairs against the wall, in silence.

The lady behind the desk consulted some folders before her. "I must have some information and some forms completed." She spoke in the direction of the four of them.

April was about to move forward. She had an impulse to go and slap the woman. She had never felt this way before. Then she felt a hand on her shoulder and a soft voice. "I'll look after this, April. Please say no more." Her mother seemed calm, at least on the outside.

Martha stepped to the office window. "I am Stephen Randolph's mother."

"Some questions, ma'am. You say he is Stephen Randolph?"

"Yes."

"Age?"

"Eighteen."

"Married, single or divorced?"

"Single." Martha added, "He is insured by our corporation. He is likely covered by the U.S. Army also. I will accept full responsibility for all obligations. Now, if you will be kind enough to supply me with a form that I can sign, indicating I will accept full responsibility, we'll go from there." The two women stared at each other. "I am becoming more inclined to agree with my daughter's original evaluation. When you have the form completed I will sign." She returned to her seat. As Martha sat down she wondered why she had conducted herself in such a manner.

They heard a voice as the double doors opened. "Are you the Randolphs?" He did not wait for an answer. "Come this way, please."

When they were seated in a small conference room he said, "I am Doctor Bell. Stephen will live. He was lucky, very lucky. I am sending him to Tallahassee. Over a period of time some special care must be given him. He has been severely damaged in the face and head. We are rather certain that his eyes are not seriously damaged. We do not believe there has been brain damage but we can't be sure.

"As I said, we're in the process of transferring him to Tallahassee. I must warn you, it will be disturbing until some work can be done on his face.

"I think it best you not see him. I believe you live in Attapulgus. I suggest you go home and get some rest. You couldn't see him tonight even if you went to Tallahassee."

As he turned to go, Martha said, "I must know about the others." There was fear written on her face. "Can you tell me about them?"

"Are they relatives? No, I suppose not. I'm not supposed to say but if circumstances were reversed, I'd have to know also. They were not so lucky."

"They?"

"Yes. There were two in the other vehicle. I believe they were brother and sister. The girl was D.O.A., dead on arrival. She was killed instantly. The man is alive. He has many problems, many serious injuries, and we are not sure of his condition. They were the children of Bruce McPherson. You may know of them. He is a local banker. Please forget I have told you this." He turned and was gone.

When they returned home they found David waiting with Jack and Sandra. Susan Lee, Eric, Jerome, Uncle Edd and Meggie were also there.

"I'll stay in the room with your mother," Sandra said. "I'm sure she will want to go to Tallahassee early." As Sandra led Martha to her room Charles and April gave the details they knew.

"The McPhersons?" Susan asked. "Does Martha know?"

"She was told but she was in shock," April said. "I hope she didn't hear Bruce McPherson as he left. I'm not sure she even recognized him. I wasn't sure myself. He did not look like I remembered him. Thirty thousand people in Decatur County and it had to be the McPhersons!"

Jerome asked, "Was Stephen drinking? Perhaps this isn't a good time to ask."

"No one said so in my presence," Charles said. "Perhaps someone said something to April when she went inside."

"No. I was not told," April said. "But he has been drinking since he returned. I know no details."

"Suppose we get some rest," Susan said. "I'll be there in the morning. Martha is going to need some support. She has not healed from all the other problems. Let us all be prayerful."

CHAPTER 79

April approached the kitchen at five o'clock the following morning only to find her mother and Sandra preparing breakfast. As soon as Martha saw April she turned her head abruptly so that April would not see her crying.

Charles entered immediately after April. "You don't need to do this," he said shaking his head.

"I am better when I am occupied, Charles. It doesn't allow me to think so much. I should have gone to Tallahassee last night. My baby boy was all alone. I am sure I could have helped him in some way."

April said, "They explained that, Mother. There is nothing anyone could have done."

"No one was allowed with him," Charles said.

Michael John entered. His appearance suggested he had slept little. "Will we go to Tallahassee soon?"

"Yes," Martha responded. "I must go quickly and check on my boy. We will go as soon as you eat a bite and get ready."

Everything suddenly became very quiet, as if no one knew what to say, when their mother asked, "Who did they say was in the other car? I am sure they mentioned it."

April and Charles looked at each other as if to ask who should respond.

Martha saw them and demanded, "You know, don't you? I hope they were not hurt badly! Was it one? Two? Several? Tell me. I've got to know if they are seriously hurt."

Charles, in an effort to soften the blow, said, "I saw the car. It was destroyed." He knew he must tell her. "It was Bruce McPherson's children, Victor and Lesa."

"Oh my God," Martha nearly shouted. "They are not hurt? Not hurt seriously?"

Everyone looked at April as if she had been chosen as the messenger. "Lesa was killed instantly."

"Oh God. Don't tell me Victor is not alive!"

April continued, attempting to choose her words carefully. "He was hurt seriously but they were not sure as to what degree. It was impossible to know last night, but they thought he would live. That was Mr. Bruce McPherson leaving as we arrived." Martha looked as if she might faint, and Charles moved over to sustain her.

"Why did you not tell me last evening?" She looked first at April, then Charles.

April continued, "It would have been too much at one time. It was because we love you so. I did what I believed best at the moment."

"Oh, poor Bruce and Agnes," Martha said. "I must see them. I must talk with them immediately, tell them how sorry I am."

April continued, "I think you must know something immediately. It was Mr. McPherson I met leaving as I rushed into the hospital. He spoke most harshly about Stephen. He said Stephen had caused the accident. It was not a good time for him. He was very bitter. Please wait until you know more, I beg you!"

A few minutes later Charles drove his family toward Tallahassee. Upon arriving they went as a group to the hospital station and learned, to the surprise of no one, that Stephen was in intensive care. The receptionist pointed out an intensive care waiting room. "Someone will see you soon," she said.

As they entered they saw many who seemed to have arrived moments before and others with wrinkled clothes, uncombed hair and haggard faces, who apparently had been there throughout the night. After they had all found seats, Charles spoke, "Suppose all of you wait here as the receptionist suggested. Let me see what I can learn."

Ten minutes later Charles returned. "He has been in the operating room but has now been returned to ICU. They believe it will be possible to see him later. He is in no danger. He is stable. They are sure he will live. They have concluded there is no brain damage in spite of the fact his face has been damaged severely."

"My boy will live!" their mother said. "I think God must have known the limit one can stand." She bent her head in a gesture of thankfulness and prayer.

"Suppose you continue to wait here. I'm sure the military authorities will need to be notified. Some papers will need to be signed when they get them prepared." Again he was gone.

Twenty minutes later Charles returned once more. He looked about, but did not see his mother.

"Mama is with him," Michael John said. "They did not want more than one to go in at this time." Charles found a seat.

When Martha returned there was a hint of a half smile on her face. "They said he would regain his health, but it would require time. They talked about weeks. His face is completely covered but he was conscious. He did not speak clearly. But the important thing is that he will live and, in time, regain his health."

Charles spoke, "The hospital believes they will transfer him to a military facility as soon as he can be moved."

Martha seemed to ponder what Charles had said. Then she said, "I'll need to go home shortly and get some things. They will let me see him every six hours so I'll need to stay here."

As they rose and were about to move toward the door, they saw Bruce McPherson enter. He glared at them and his face turned a deep crimson. He trembled as he managed to balance himself in the doorway. For a moment it seemed he would have a stroke.

Then he spoke, first looking at Martha, then the others. "My daughter, my beautiful Lesa, is dead. My son's condition is uncertain. I can only hope. If he lives, he will never be the same again. They know he has lost his sight. They are afraid it will be permanent. My boy, if he lives, must go in darkness the rest of his life. He has an arm that has been amputated, the lower part so damaged it could not be reattached. He will likely never look the same as parts of his face are missing!"

They all listened and remained in stone silence. No one moved. Finally Martha took a step forward and said, "I'm so sorry. I'm . . ."

Bruce McPherson interrupted, "Nothing you can say or do will give me back my daughter or make my son whole again. It is the same as if I had lost everything.

"That son of yours, that drunken fool, has destroyed everything that was meaningful in my life. All my dreams have vanished. In one second my life was left without meaning. There is nothing you can say. I hate this boy, I'll hate him until I die! I will destroy you as he has destroyed my family, if it takes the rest of my life and all my resources! I want to see you suffer as I have suffered. Only then will you truly understand."

No one spoke. No one moved.

Then Bruce McPherson spoke once more. "May all the Randolphs be damned forever from this moment on! I want you to awake each morning and think what he has done. I hope it will be stamped in your mind forever." He turned and was suddenly gone.

Charles and Michael John helped their mother back into her seat before she fell. She was as white as snow and shaking all over. The people about them looked on in awe, then with an expression of sympathy. A sadness seemed to fill every face.

Ten minutes later, with Michael John on one side and Charles on the other, they led their mother down the hall. As they moved down the corridor Martha said, "We can find a room nearby where I can go see him, then rest. I feel so tired. The boys can run the place but I may need April with me. Let's go home and get the things I need, then I can sign any papers required when I return."

Two hours later Jerome went with Martha, his own mother and April to find a room near the hospital.

After they were settled Jerome said, "I'm not sure this is a good time but there may not be one real soon. Thus, I feel you should know a number of things. You said on the way down that Bruce McPherson is angry. That is not an adequate description. He is bitter, very bitter.

"First, it seems that nearly all of Midway is up in arms. I am not sure I've ever witnessed such strong feelings in a community. They are furious, even wrathful. I did not wish to tell you this but, in the long run, it is better that you know and that you learn such from me.

"This is not all. I'm afraid," Jerome continued, "he is in the process of filing a civil suit against Stephen and Randolph Place. He will seek damages. Since Stephen was under the influence of alcohol and was driving at a high rate of speed on the wrong side of the road, Mr. McPherson obviously will prevail. Not only will he win, but his suit will be so great that Stephen can expect to lose all of his personal and corporate assets. The only good news I can associate with this legal procedure is that it will not affect the corporation or the other members.

"Mr. McPherson is already in the process of having a special grand jury called to indict Stephen on criminal charges as well. He is powerful and influential enough to get this done. They will find several true bills of indictment including murder. If not murder, they will indict him on manslaughter charges or charges of vehicular homicide. I have no doubt but such a group would find a number of true bills.

"Why do they want him back here?" Jerome continued. "We might ask why not let the military be responsible for his conduct. I think the answer is obvious. They want to get him back here so they can get revenge. I guess they believe the Army would not deal with the matter properly. They want him punished severely.

"My only suggestion at this time is to notify the military authorities of what has occurred and ask that they retain jurisdiction of Stephen following his treatment and recovery. The pressures here would be so great that he would likely be punished much more severely, perhaps unduly and beyond reason.

"I know you do not need added anxieties but it is best you know. An informed person is in a better position to deal with matters."

A day later Charles visited his mother, Susan and April.

"He is better!" Martha said smiling. "I can understand him much better when he speaks. His mind seems clear." Martha's appearance indicated that she felt much better as well.

Charles said, "I have been in contact with the military authorities. They are in the process of sending some of their people to evaluate. They will move him to a military facility as soon as it is practical."

"I would like Stephen to remain here where I can look after him," his mother said. "I would feel better."

"Stephen will get the best care in their facilities. All of his needs can be met. They will make him whole again," Charles said.

The county newspaper's latest issue detailed the accident, including pictures of both cars and the accident site. This article reported that they had learned, from unofficial sources, that alcohol had been the root cause. It also mentioned that a civil suit was being filed against Stephen Randolph and the Randolph Corporation.

There were strong hints that a grand jury would be assembled to make criminal charges and that it was believed that Stephen would be returned and placed under the jurisdiction of local authorities.

In a week Stephen was transferred to a hospital in the area of Washington, D.C., and Martha was home again. In a matter of days, actually hours, one could look at Martha and tell all was not well. She ate little, slept less and became very quiet.

Martha called Jerome. "Come tell us what to expect."

Jerome arrived and Martha assembled her family. Jerome said. "We will look at the civil suit first. Stephen will be sued for an amount much greater than his assets. The suit will be successful and will cost him all his personal and corporate assets. He would lose all his equity in the corporation. Since this is a closed corporation, they will demand his full portion. We can only hope it will be limited to the amount stipulated in the Charter, between four hundred and five hundred thousand dollars.

"I believe the corporation is set up so this would be all they could get. If they considered the stock in relation to the total value of Randolph Place, it could cost that percentage of the total value, or about three times as much as the figure I gave you. Do you understand?" They nodded.

"Now as to the criminal charges, I would . . ."

"Before we go further," Martha said, "Let me say my son could have been careless and made a mistake but I do not see him as a criminal!"

"Mrs. Randolph, it is true he has not robbed a bank, shot someone in anger or raped some helpless individual. Yet he is responsible for his conduct. Should the military or local authorities gain jurisdiction, he will be found guilty of some very serious charges.

"If he is retained by the military, a judicial tribunal will try him in what is known as a court martial. A panel would be selected of commissioned and non-commissioned military personnel to hear the case. He would have a well qualified attorney from the military to represent him. The panel assembled would perform as would a jury.

"I believe he would be found guilty of several charges, one of which is most serious. He would be sentenced and serve his sentence under military personnel.

"Now if the local authorities are successful in securing jurisdiction, he would be returned to Decatur County and charged as a civilian. He would have an opportunity to plead guilty to the charges and be sentenced by the judge. If he pleads not guilty, he would be tried here in Midway. A change of venue could be requested but they will keep him here. Public opinion here will not be in his favor. Quite the contrary. I feel they would deal with him harshly.

"My recommendation to you is to request the military retain full jurisdiction."

April interrupted. "Stephen had no ill will toward the McPhersons. It was an accident. He did not intentionally try to harm anyone."

"I understand what you are saying, April," Jerome said, "but the act he committed will be classified as a criminal act. A death occurred. A serious injury occurred. Stephen was responsible for both, though not intentionally. He has a debt to pay to society under the laws of Georgia."

"You are recommending," Martha said, "that the military retain jurisdiction?"

"Strongly, Mrs. Randolph. I suspect you have no idea of the hostility that exists here in Decatur County and especially in Midway."

"If the Army discharged him, would you defend him," April asked. "All of us have confidence in you."

"April, Mrs. Randolph, and all of you, I would recommend you secure an experienced trial lawyer. He would serve you better than I could. I would not want, in time to come, for Stephen to be penalized because of my inexperience and inability. It would not be fair to any of you."

Martha asked, "The civil suit is a foregone conclusion?"

"Yes."

"What kind of sentence could my boy expect?" Martha asked.

Jerome was not ready for this question. "I cannot say, Mrs. Randolph, I can only say he would be dealt with more severely here, perhaps double that of a military decision."

"Thank you, Jerome. You have been helpful."

CHAPTER 80

September marked a lonely time for Martha Randolph. Everything had changed. Charles was required to stay in Tallahassee as never before. April, Meggie and Gena were now in college. David and Michael John never seemed to have a spare minute.

Martha looked about her. Never again would Joseph run in and get a cup of coffee and smile as he described the golden leaves that had been such a big part of his life. Joe and Kathy remained only in her memories. Now she must direct her attention toward Stephen. She was certain that once his health was restored, he would be faced with severe charges.

Unexpectedly, Charles walked into the room. She anxiously asked, "Is everything all right? You have come home at an unusual time. Has something happened to one of my girls? So much has happened and it seems to be all bad."

"Everyone is fine. I just needed to visit with you. I'm glad I came. I can see that your thoughts are about Stephen. I must confess, I have had many negative thoughts recently as well. Some of my instructors' demands seem quite petty. For example, I turned in a paper with a split infinitive. For twenty minutes I was lectured as to the proper uses of prepositions. I am of the opinion that the mole hills have replaced the mountains. But I didn't come to talk about that."

"I worry about you, Charles. Last year you had Gena and Meggie. Now there are April, Mimi and Helen."

"They are all fine. You could not guess the hours they have given me. They do most of the calculations in my research. By the way, you should know that Mimi and Helen suspect you are the one responsible for their college scholarships."

"But they must *never* know! I must think of some appropriate responses should they approach me."

"What reports of Stephen? Is he making progress?" Charles asked.

"Yes. His physical condition continues to improve. I talk on the telephone with him each day."

"His mental attitude? Is it better?" Charles asked.

"I can't say. He must have a great deal on his mind."

"You have seen David and Mary? How is my niece and your beautiful grandchild?"

"Yes. They fill a part of each day. My granddaughter is truly a gift from God. I could not make it without her. She reminds me of all of my children when you were babies."

"Michael John?"

"Oh, Charles, I am so happy with Michael John. This the best of the best! He and David work together so well. Now he has found a new interest, a new world so to speak!"

"Michelle? April suggested such."

"Oh yes. I had wondered if he would ever get beyond Robin. He is so much in love. I believe Michelle feels equally so."

"How does Clint feel about this? Sometimes fathers feel no one is ever good enough for their daughter," Charles stated.

"I believe he is as pleased as I am. You know I have an idea that an announcement will be made soon." Martha smiled and Charles knew his mother was delighted.

"Back to Stephen for a moment," Charles said. "Has Stephen ever asked or made any remarks about the others? The victims?"

Martha did not answer immediately. She seemed to look out into space. Finally she spoke. "Stephen has so much on his mind and I think his pain, his physical pain, has not gone away."

Charles did not pursue the matter. She had already answered his question. He could see the pain on her face and in her eyes.

"Mother," Charles said, "we need to talk of another matter. At this time we will keep it between the two of us."

"Another problem? I have used up my quota!"

"No. I hope you will not classify it as a problem."

Suddenly Martha gave a big smile. "I know what you want to discuss. Sara told me something years ago. Yes, I know."

"This is not possible. I am the only one that knows."

"Yes. I know. Mothers have a way of knowing. It is Meggie, isn't it? You are in love with her. You have been for a long time. She has always been in love with you. Oh, I know others have as well. Sara Knight loved you. Gena Jenkins has loved you for years. But after Sara left, I knew it would be Meggie. A mother has a way of knowing."

"I am ready to ask her to marry me. I love her very much. As you say, I have loved her for a long time. She is so special in every way!"

"I am not surprised nor could I be more pleased. She will be all a wife could and should be. You will make a fine husband. There will always be excitement where Meggie is found. Sara said as much."

"I am so happy you are pleased."

"Love is all there is in the world that is truly worthwhile. Without a deep love the physical and mental aspects are meaningless. Yes, I think you have a deep love for Meggie.

"Now you are going to talk about another matter. There is Uncle Edd that she will always love as a grandfather. There is Craig, who is a young black man, her half-brother. I hope you have enough love for her to understand these relationships. You will destroy this beautiful and talented lady and her love for you if you are not understanding.

"Now I will say this and no more. If both of you are sure, don't wait. I had wished a longer life with your father. Think of David and beautiful Kathy. You may wish to remember Robert White who never knew the full meaning of life. If you are sure, don't wait!

"Some eyebrows will be raised. There is and always will be such. I am not blind. I know of these things. Do it soon, Charles!"

Susan Lee sat drinking coffee with her two sons. There were times when conversation filled their room and other times they seemed to enjoy the beauty of silence.

Suddenly Jerome said to his mother, "I want you to quit sewing; that is, sewing for others. With your little investments plus what Eric and I can contribute, there is no longer a need." His statement as well as the tone of his voice seemed to leave little room for compromise.

Susan looked at Eric. "I didn't hear you say anything. Do you have an opinion? The two of you have apparently discussed this matter in recent times. It seems that my way of life is not acceptable to everyone!"

"Jerome and I have not discussed this since back in college days. Yes, I do have an opinion."

"Just what is your position?" Their mother did not have a smile on her face.

"I no longer feel it has the same meaning as it did years ago. Many years ago it was a matter of support, of making ends meet as some express it. No longer is this so.

"But I see another side to this. I cannot imagine you sitting here reading and watching television all day. Idleness would destroy you in a short time. It would also deprive you of many associations that are rich and long lasting. Unless you found something meaningful to do, I believe you would be miserable.

"Then, when we do those things we enjoy, we do not look upon this as work. I find many of my teaching responsibilities as pleasure more than work."

Their mother said, "I'm going to ask one question. It will likely offend you. Are either of you concerned that my work will be a reflection on either of you? If so, as much as I would hate to, I'd give it up. But unless this is a reason, I will not change anything. I believe I know your answers.

"Now, let's talk about my dearest friend. The last time I saw her she had aged ten years. This is tearing her apart, destroying her. A mother can understand. Stephen is her baby. He always will be regardless of his actions. Nothing can change this.

"She cannot be blind as to the changing attitudes in the community. Combine these and it is not difficult to understand her despondency. Mercy me, I would have been destroyed months ago."

Jerome said, "She is very special. I would go to great lengths to help her if I only knew what to do."

"I would do the same," Eric said. "It is a sad day for a lady to be treated as many have. She has done so much for others."

"Let's go back to Stephen," Jerome said. "He is a very selfish person. He is a living embodiment of selfishness. He has little or no compassion for anyone. Some would classify him as evil. I know much more about this young man than perhaps you realize. The only thing he was consistent in doing was being foolish and selfish."

Susan said, "Martha did not contribute to his wayward conduct and irresponsible behavior except to remain silent because of the relationship between Stephen and his father. At such time this relationship ceased, the habits had become so deeply ingrained that change was next to impossible. You seem unsympathetic with our dearest friend.

"Perhaps you are a little harsh in your evaluations, Jerome. He is young. In a way he continues to be a child. He is the baby."

Jerome said, "He is about as stable as a man with both feet in the air at the same time."

Eric said, "It is true that he is only about eighteen. Perhaps all of us did not see some things clearly at that age."

Again Jerome forced himself to remain silent.

"They will bring Stephen back here to face charges?" his mother asked. "Surely he would be treated more fairly here among friends, among his own people."

Eric said, "As I understand our Constitution he has the right to be judged by his own peers."

"Let's hope not," Jerome said. "With the attitudes that exist, they would want to hang him! It is preferred that the military have jurisdiction as to Stephen's fate."

"I cannot see or understand why the people here would feel so strongly," Susan said. "Surely they can see and know it was an accident. It was not intentional." Susan saw a truculent resentment in Jerome.

"Mother, Stephen was drunk, twice drunk, so to speak. He killed an innocent girl. He maimed a young man for life. He destroyed the dreams of a mother and father. This boy or man must pay his debts to society. That is the way it works.

"Stephen must be responsible for himself. He has never done this before but he will never have a moment of true peace until he does."

Eric asked, "Would you take the case if he were discharged from the Army? They would likely ask you."

"No! No! Indeed not!"

"The Randolphs have been our close friends, our best friends. Should not a tape measure work both ways?" Susan asked, feeling an affectionate tenderness for an old friendship.

"Mother, when I decided to go to law school, I decided upon the principles and standards I would follow. No. I could not do it. But there is no purpose in talking about something that will not occur. The army will retain jurisdiction."

Susan decided to change the subject. "Are you happy that April is closer to home?"

"The Randolphs are having some difficult times," Jerome said. "She will be a source of strength. Martha can rely on April. She may need her even more in the weeks to come." Jerome knew this was not what his mother really wanted to know.

Susan turned to Eric. "When will you bring me a daughter home?" She knew that Eric had not expected such a question.

"Got my eye on one, Mother. Be patient. Can't rush these things. After all, Jerome is the one you need to be concerned about. He is getting close to completing a third decade." Eric smiled at both of them.

Jerome said, "Let's change the subject. Lawyers do not have a favorable reputation. In fact, I heard one man say recently that he had never seen the first lawyer but that he would surely go to hell."

Suddenly Jerome laughed and did so profusely. Susan and Eric were sure he was laughing about all the lawyers going to hell.

"What's so funny? I see nothing funny about my son going to hell! I had hoped differently!"

Jerome said, "Years ago, in fact, many years ago when I was but a child, I vaguely remember a case similar to Stephen's case. As I recall, an unusual thing occurred. The person being tried was found not guilty and got off without a penalty of any sort. I am not sure I remember what occurred but I remember questioning the conclusion. I don't know why I thought about it. But if Stephen gets out of this one, it will be based on mercy, not justice!"

"Where are you girls going?" Charles asked.

"To dine and dance, Charles. Can't stay here and study all the time. You know bout Jack becoming a dull boy? Get ready and go with us," April said. She smiled and the black eyes sparkled.

"Can't go. I have a great deal of paperwork to finish."

"We will help," Gena said. "We five girls can do anything, well, most anything!"

An hour later Charles said, "I can see where I am going now. Get out of here. Go on! Stay together. I'd feel better."

"I'll stay and help Charles finish," Meggie said. "If we get through, we will join you."

Two hours later Charles said, "Thankfully that part is finished." He looked at his watch. "It's later than I realized. I'm sure our girls will not expect us."

"I'll fix us a bite," Meggie said. "If you are real hungry, you are in trouble." She smiled. She could see Charles was exhausted.

"I'll just sit here a few moments. I want to relax."

When they had finished eating, Meggie said, "If you are not too tired, I want to talk to you. I've wanted to for some time."

"Oh?"

"Yes. I've been doing a great deal of thinking recently. I may withdraw after the end of this semester."

"I didn't hear you," Charles said. "It sounded like you said something about withdrawing from school. I am sure I did not hear you correctly."

"You heard correctly. It is not a hearing problem. I've given a great deal of though to the matter. In fact, for weeks this is all I have thought about. I need to make a change."

Charles stood for a moment, then sat back in the chair. "You have to be joking and I do not care for this kind of joke."

"Calm yourself, Charles. You have been on edge lately. I do not think it is good for your blood pressure. You are usually the calm and collected one. Guess all the paperwork is getting to you."

"Don't play games with me, Meggie!" He spoke louder than he had intended.

"Charles, I want your undivided attention for ten minutes. I do not wish or expect the first interruption. If you do, I'll walk out that second." Charles did not speak.

"Many years ago you gave me a life, a new life. So many things happened. You know all the details so I will not review them. In the process of these changes I nearly destroyed you, your family, your church and the Attapulgus School. I created some deep divisions in your own family. In a number of ways the storm has never subsided. Some of the effects are obvious today. Some will likely continue as long as we live.

"Years ago I fell in love with you. Like all little girls, I was a dreamer. I believe my first serious endeavor to express my feelings occurred the night you graduated from college. As I look back I can see how you must have reacted to this childish gesture. It was not long before I realized how foolish I had been. But you remained always in my mind and heart, in all my thoughts." She looked on his arm. Yes, he was wearing the watch she had given him.

"Then it dawned on me the things I refused to allow myself to think about earlier. First, there was a significant age difference. Then, the enormous economic differences. I knew I could never totally remove Uncle Edd and Craig from my life. A half-brother as a Negro could not be accepted in the world in which we live.

"I have watched you continue to grow in every way. Then another reason surfaced. I could never fit into your life, the lifestyle in which you and others would expect me to live.

"It was then that I knew I could not remain and continue in a fantasy world, a dream world I had created as a child. I knew that if I stayed, I would die a little more each day.

"Now I have finally mustered the courage to tell you my thoughts, my feelings. It was not easy but I knew the longer I waited, the more difficult it would become. I had really planned to do it weeks ago but I was selfish; I was a coward. So now I have said it. It was best for both of us.

"I'll go now. Please don't say anything. I am not strong enough to listen. Thank you for listening to my story." Her eyes filled with tears and she ran from the room.

Charles did not move for an hour. He reviewed every single word she had spoken. He had never seen a person so brave and so honest. Then he smiled. He now knew, beyond doubt, that he loved this girl as he had never loved anyone.

His mother, apparently, had seen all of this for years. She had known but she had said nothing. He had to learn it for himself. Until an hour ago she had never let him get a complete look at her very soul.

Suddenly Charles jumped up and rushed to her door and knocked loudly. "Open the door. Now! You must hear me!"

Meggie opened her door very slowly, as if she was undecided. Charles saw her beautiful face and he saw the tears had continued to run down her cheeks. "I've come to ask you to be my wife. I love you as I have never loved another, as I have never loved before. I want to spend the rest of my life with you. I want to marry you — tomorrow — the next day — next week. I love you, Meggie! I should have told you a long time ago."

She looked at Charles but did not move as he extended his arms for her. "You are saying this to be kind. You are trying to keep from hurting me!"

"I love you, Meggie. It is not sympathy, it's love. I guess I have loved you for a long time." His arms remained extended.

One look told Meggie all she needed to know. She rushed into his arms and kissed him again and again. "I will spend each minute of each day loving you and making you happy. I'll never let you go."

Suddenly she drew back with a startled look on her face. "You are sorry for me!"

"No. No, my darling. I love you. It is so strange, so very strange I had not admitted this to myself earlier. It is strange that others knew before I did!"

"April?"

"Possibly, but it was my mother. When I told her of my feelings for you she already knew. No one could be more pleased!"

He pulled her to him as he kissed all the tears away. "If I stay, I might want to spoil things for us. You are too precious, too sacred.

"Tell me when Meggie. Mother explained to me the meaning of time. Make it soon, Meggie." He kissed her on the forehead and left the room immediately.

Jerome drove up to Somewhere Else. Again he had a package in his hand. April was sitting on the deck. She got up and moved toward him as he climbed the steps.

"A penny for your thoughts," Jerome said as he pecked her on the cheek.

"I may need two pennies because I have two secrets. Can you believe I am to have two sisters soon?"

"Two?" Jerome asked. "I had guessed Michael John. My mother was delighted when your mother told her. Both mothers were so pleased. But another?"

"Yes. I had guessed so for a year. A girl has a way of knowing these things."

"Charles? After Sara left I had guessed he might remain single."

"Meggie and Charles will be married soon. She had been in love with him for years and that blind brother couldn't see it or refused to see it. I think all of you men are the same!" Jerome smiled but said nothing.

"Hey, you're in a new suit! Looks great. I can see that things are getting better. Bet old Slick Cannington insisted you raise your fees!"

"No. Actually your mother is most responsible. She provided a great deal of work. She has been more than generous. But actually, it was you and Maybe that got me going."

"I had no idea how smart my mother was until she insisted on your services! You know, she had more knowledge about the operation of Randolph Place than I would have ever guessed."

As the food was cooking they reviewed every detail and aspect of Stephen's impending cases, both civil and criminal. When they had finished eating, April asked, "What is going to happen to my mother? She can't continue to take the pounding. Deaths, court cases and community attitudes have taken a great toll. Where will it all end?" There was a film of moisture in her eyes.

"It seems so unfair," Jerome said. "I wish I knew how to help her. Can you suggest some way? If she could get Stephen's problems behind her, I believe things would change. Now that she has a granddaughter and will soon have more daughters, life would be different, will be better."

April said, "If Stephen goes to prison, there she will be also. She has heaped much of the blame about Stephen upon herself. Is it not possible that you could save the two of them? The only way to save Mother is to save Stephen."

"Are you saying, April, that the guilty should be spared to save the innocent? It happens often, perhaps more than you think."

"You couldn't or wouldn't do this?" April asked.

"April, forgive me in advance for what I am about to say. Stephen has taken the life of one, maimed another for life and destroyed a family in the process because he didn't think. Though it was not intentional, it was because of his behavior that it happened. I do not believe he should be excused for his actions. Let me continue a moment. No longer will anyone hear the soft voice of Lesa around the house. No longer will Victor see a sunrise or sunset or a pretty lady unless a miracle occurs. Stephen was responsible. If you were killed and Charles blinded and maimed through the fault of another, how would your mother feel? How would your brothers feel?"

"There is another side, Jerome. There was a fine lady that married in 1936. From that moment she has given and given and given some more. She asked only for one thing after she married and she didn't get that. She has always been a giver but never a receiver. She probably has done more for people than any other in Decatur County. You know this to be true.

"If Susan Lee had the same problem that Martha Randolph has, she would cry, 'Help me, help me, somebody.' If Eric, her baby, was facing what Stephen is facing, she would cry out for help. Martha Randolph is doing the same thing, that very thing!

"Our mothers have few secrets. You know that. In days past you mentioned remembering a case that had some similarities. Is that not possible again? Were you concerned about the moral values involved? Has not an attorney the right to defend his client as long as it is legal? I know we both respect standards and values. But try to remember what I said, what I asked. What would Susan Lee expect? Would it be different from those of Martha Randolph?"

"Your mother deserves the best legal counsel possible. A young, inexperienced country boy cannot provide what she needs."

"You can win the case, Jerome. You know it and I know it."

"This old case was so long ago. Everything has likely changed. I have, unfortunately, given others false hope."

"Substitute Susan Lee for Martha Randolph. Then you make a decision. Perhaps everyone deserves a second chance. The Lord gave hope to those who did more than Stephen did. Did our Lord place a limit on forgiveness?"

Jerome went over and kissed April on the forehead where she sat. "You have reminded me that mothers, good mothers, are concerned about their sons and daughters."

CHAPTER 81

"Mrs. Randolph, you have some company. Can't say as I know the car." Sandra continued to look through the window. "Why, it's Clint White. I know it is him but he usually drives an old truck."

"I'll see to the door, Sandra. If you will iron the three or four pieces left, we will call it a day."

Just before Clint could ring the door bell Martha opened the door. "What a surprise. I'm so glad to see you. Seems like ages since you have visited us. Come in. Sandra didn't know you with that new car. Come on in and let me get you some coffee or iced tea."

"I drank a Coca-Cola some minutes ago. I'll pass this time. I need to talk with you about two matters. I hate to create problems in taking your valuable time but I feel we need to talk."

"Of course we can talk. I have missed your company. We have so much in common but I am sure it is not about that. Tell me what you have on your mind."

"Well, Mrs. Randolph, I . . ."

"No more of that," Martha interrupted. "Please don't refer to me as Mrs. Randolph. Martha will do. After all, you are some older than me!" She smiled.

"If you insist. As I was saying, two things have been weighing heavily on my mind. I want us to talk about these matters real plain as this is the way friends should always talk.

"The first thing is Mimi. I . . ."

"Is Mimi all right? There is nothing wrong with her?"

"No. No. Mimi is just fine. She is very happy and doing well in school thanks to so many. Actually that is what I wanted us to talk about."

Martha said, "I don't understand!"

"Mr. Baggs has informed me that the fund started in my son's name is doing quite well and that funds have been set aside for my Mimi for her first four years of college. I had not expected this. There are many deserving graduates. I don't think we can accept such a gift. Now, I've said all that in order to say this. I suspect you are responsible."

"What did Mr. Baggs say?" Martha asked.

"He said a lot of people gave to the fund. That's about all he would say."

"Clint, I have given to the Robert White Scholarship Fund each year. I could not do anything less. It is wonderful to see these talented young people get a little help. Perhaps, if the systems works right, they in turn will help some others some day in a similar way.

"Hundreds of people have contributed. Your Robert was so special. But, you must remember, it is Mr. Baggs and his committee that make selections for those they feel deserving. I have not given Mr. Baggs instructions." She hoped he would not ask if Jerome had done so in her behalf.

"Some day Mimi will become a great doctor. I think she will go into medicine because of her interest. I believe Robert would have done so. Attapulgus is well known for the many doctors that finished here. Two are in Midway; one is a fine surgeon. Another is the Chief of Staff at Emory. I could go on. Your Mimi will become a great doctor as well. She will dedicate her life to helping others. Surely you cannot oppose such an idea. Now you said there were two things."

"Yes," Clint said. "The second is quite different and I do not know how or where to begin. I want to talk about my other girl."

"I knew that, Clint. You didn't have to tell me."

"You know my Michelle is different from Mimi. She is my happy one. Some are born to be intelligent, some selfish and some to grieve. Michelle was born to be happy, to smile, to laugh."

Martha said, "Michelle is so precious. She laughs often and finds happiness in life. We all need more of this. Girls who laugh a great deal never arouse envy or hatred among others unless one is totally void of happiness. I only wish I was one of these girls!"

"I don't know how to say it but Michelle says that Michael John has asked her to marry him — to be his wife. You know about this?"

"I am so pleased," Martha said, "if you are equally pleased. I had guessed what was happening."

"My Michelle is not very mature. She is not smart like Mimi. As you know, she is not a person with wealth. I suspect she can only offer herself."

"Michelle is a beautiful girl. She is a fine girl, a good girl. She has character. She would be very good for Michael John. I would be most pleased if you consented for your daughter to marry my son.

"There are some things I want to say about my son. He was never outstanding in school. In fact, he had to struggle in some areas.

"He was rather strange in his early years. He felt insecure. At this time he found that obedience brought inattention. He preferred it this way.

"A year or so later he seemed to change. He was like a season of storms and lightning, weariness, pain and despair. This again made him wish to be alone. For a year or so, perhaps longer, he seemed to accept loneliness as a major part of his life.

"Then some changes occurred again in his life. With the help of Charles and April, he began to feel more secure. He had some success and recognition as a builder. He had a special talent in mechanics. Farming became more meaningful to him.

"He will tell you he is not like some of his brothers. He is not very handsome but he is good, kind and always thoughtful of others. Naturally all sons are very special to their mothers.

"Why don't we just leave everything to Michelle and Michael John? I think the two of us know and understand our children. Perhaps it would be well to touch on one other area, but I suspect they have discussed it. Michael John would prefer to remain here in his farm work. But again, suppose we let them work out those things." She smiled at Clint and he nodded.

As Clint said goodbye, he thought about Martha Randolph. She was the one who had instilled her children with those things needed in life. He could never remember seeing a person like her. He wondered why he had never thought about her in this manner before. As he walked across the yard toward his car he reached down and scooped up a handful of soil, looked at it and let it trickle through his fingers.

Martha watched Clint as he picked up the soil, then returned it to the ground. For a moment she did not understand this gesture, until she remembered that April told her that Robert had said his father had started out as a farmer.

Martha, through their meeting, became aware of the goodness of Clint White. She was astonished that she had seen and known this for a score of years and only now did this strange and excellent thing strike full force. How wonderful it was to see such a man. It was like sunshine following a storm. She now realized why Robert had been such an outstanding young man. He had been like his father.

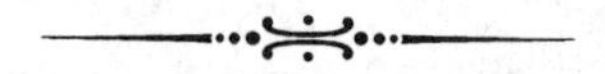

An hour later Martha had another visitor. "Susan Lee, you look so good. Come in and we will have that cup of coffee."

"I know you have Stephen on your mind. Please bring me up to date," Susan said.

"I am told the authorities will now let me see him. I want to go to Washington as soon as possible. The last time I talked with him, he seemed a little down."

"This will be good for both you and Stephen. I am so happy for you."

"If my son could only have one more fresh start in life," Martha said. "I guess when one's own is involved, mercy exceeds justice. Our Lord said we can be forgiven over and over again. If I could only get him one more chance, I think I could then accept whatever the future holds. I still feel I am responsible for so many things."

An hour later Susan left. The following day Martha and April landed at the National Airport in Washington, D.C.

"Stephen, you are looking so much better than we had expected," Martha said. "It seems the doctors are very good."

"I guess they are all right," Stephen said. "I'll never look the same again but I'm sure no one will care. What are they saying back home about me?"

Martha and April looked at each other. It was his mother who responded. "Some people are still talking about it but you would expect that. A Decatur County Grand Jury was convened and has indicted you but this has no meaning since you are in service. I am sure they are reviewing your case. It is likely you will find yourself being evaluated by the military personnel. There are some who feel it best to let the military deal with this matter."

"It doesn't make any difference either way. They are going to blame me anyway. If Victor had been looking after his business, this would not have happened. He could have avoided the accident. He was not alert, and now I must shoulder all the blame.

Stephen continued, "My legal counsel has said I cannot win; the evidence is much too strong. I had thought the military would see differently since I was a good soldier, one of their very best."

"Did he suggest what kind of penalty?" April asked.

"He talked about five to eight years, but he could not be sure. He made it clear he was not one of those to judge. Besides, it doesn't make any difference any more. Since my father and Joe died, my world has never been the same. Nothing matters any more."

As Martha and April returned to Tallahassee, by way of Atlanta, Martha said, "Stephen has not changed as I had hoped."

April answered, "Stephen continues to blame everyone except himself. Not once has he spoken of the death of Lesa or the condition of Victor. He didn't even ask about the McPhersons."

Tears filled Martha's eyes. "I am not positive he will ever change or that it will be different, yet still I find myself asking and praying for one more chance for my boy."

"We need to talk," April told Jerome. "Perhaps you can come to Somewhere Else this evening? I'm not going to feed you this time, so it would not have to be early," April said.

"I have some work to finish," Jerome said, "but I'll be there at eight."

After April and Jerome had talked for an hour, there was a moment of silence. Then she said, "You haven't asked what Mother and I learned when we went to Washington."

"No."

"Is it of no interest to you? You have no idea what this thing has done to my mother."

"I saw your brother, April. I have just returned from Washington. I had to learn some things for myself; from him and from others. I suspect we all encountered the same with Stephen."

"Jerome, I believe that if you represented my brother, you could get him off. I believe you know a way. Why don't you agree to do it? You are a fine attorney. You remember I have watched you work first hand."

Jerome laughed and looked at April. "Stop and ask why a person consults a lawyer. Do you believe it is always to adjust the legal affairs relating to the existing laws? Nonsense! A person wants a lawyer to show them how to get around the law." He looked at April for a reaction.

"You haven't answered me," April said. Her eyes flashed and her usual smile was missing.

"Stephen needs to pay his dues, April. I've watched him most of his life. I may even know some things you do not. Again, I recommend the military deal with the matter. Sometimes they seem to understand accidents better than those of us in civilian life, especially where alcohol is involved.

"I have told you and I have told your mother to get another attorney, one who is experienced. Your mother deserves the best representation she can get." He hoped April did not note he referred to her mother rather than Stephen.

Jerome rose from his chair and as April walked toward him she asked, "Do you know how I feel about you?"

"Why don't you tell me!"

"I love you, Jerome. I've loved you since the time you thought me a child, since I was thirteen. I've never stopped loving you. Oh, there was Robert and Victor and yes, even your brother, but we will not discuss them now."

She placed her arms around his neck and pulled him closer to her. Jerome could see the black eyes sparkle and twinkle as he looked into her face. "If you love me as I love you, I am sure you will help my mother and Stephen."

April pressed forward and pressed more strongly against him. Her lips pressed against him, but she felt no response and she drew back. "You don't love me as I love you."

Jerome put his hands on April's shoulders. "I have loved you from the day I saw you as a thirteen year old. There has never been a day I felt differently. But I had believed all of the gods of the world were against me."

Jerome pulled her to him and saw the tears in her eyes and on her face and he kissed them away. He kissed her deeply.

As the kiss ended April said, "You are the only man I have ever truly loved as one should love and be loved."

"What can I say, April? I can't believe this is happening."

"Tell me you want me, need me and love me as I do you. You . . ."

"April, do you mean what you say?"

"You think I'm using you, don't you? You think I have . . ."

"No. Don't say that. I didn't say that," Jerome said.

"Kiss me goodnight, Jerome, and follow me back home. I still have a mother that feels as you do, that I am just a child!" She did not smile.

When Jerome returned, Susan was waiting, as if she had a great deal on her mind. "How was your evening?"

"Fine. April is always special. I enjoy her company." They sat at the breakfast table.

"Are you hungry?" his mother asked. "I gather you did not eat?"

"No. We only talked."

Jerome looked at his mother for a long time. They stared into each other's eyes. It was a moment without end. They both seemed to search into the deepest part of the other's soul. Never had they looked so deeply, searched so longingly, be it a time of joy or sorrow.

Jerome looked away for a few moments and he continued to feel his mother's presence as they remained at the table. Jerome looked once again and this time saw a tender and gentle presence as in no one else. He saw her eyes filled with tears. No longer was there a question or a doubt. He knew what he must do, though it would cost him everything he had said he believed. Yes, he must do it. He had no choice. He wondered if everyone had such a moment as this to face in life. For some it had been thirty pieces of silver but for him it was the love and trust of three women.

Jerome felt a strong urge to express his feelings. "Humanity is not to be understood, not even by other humans. We do abominable things in the name of love. We do disastrous things to protect ourselves and others. We allow evil to grow more powerful each day, each year, yet do so little to prevent it. We refuse to see the truth. We do it through lies, through compromise. We commit ourselves to something less than good or ideal. Fear always seems to be a part of our lives, in that we may wish to be something other than what we are. Sometimes we do things to excuse ourselves for our own weaknesses. And all too often we do it for a woman!" He looked more deeply into his mother's eyes.

"Sometimes we lie and condemn and destroy by speaking when silence is golden. Sometimes we become cowards and do not speak at all. For this I hope we can be forgiven. I am guilty of all these things and more, much more!

"I can think of a dozen occasions in my lifetime in which the guilty escaped so that a precious soul might be spared."

"My dear son, do you know that a mother can forgive almost anything or anyone except the one that does not love her baby? I would be no different."

"Mother, when I went to Washington I was not sure what to ask or to say to Stephen. I had hoped to find a feeling of concern and some remorse for the destruction he had caused. I said to him, 'Stephen, say what you wish to me. It is totally confidential, as much as a confession that is made to a priest.' And he said, 'I have no confession to make.' Then I questioned myself as to why I had approached him in such a manner. Nothing has ever been sacred to Stephen."

"No man can possibly feel as a mother, my son. The day will come when this will become more meaningful."

Two nights later Jerome and Susan arrived at the Randolph home. "Bring your mother," Martha had told Jerome. "Only mothers understand mothers. The four went into the small library with instructions not to be disturbed. They all looked at each other as if each was waiting for the other to speak.

"How did you find Stephen?" Jerome asked, looking at Martha and April.

Martha felt a color come to her face that she could not hide. "He looked better than I had expected. Naturally his mental attitude, because of all that has happened, left something to be desired. But the doctors did a remarkable job. He is still my handsome son."

"I am not sure my question is a good one," Jerome said, "but it would be helpful to know. Did you see strong evidence of remorse? Did he discuss the McPhersons with you?"

"I was disappointed," Martha responded honestly. "Actually he exhibited more of a persecution complex. He felt he was without friends and had been rejected, that there were those out to get him. He still misses his father and Joe more than one can know."

Jerome looked at April. "I would agree with the description Mother gave," she said.

"Before I go beyond this point, there are some things I have discussed with my mother," Jerome said. "Where lawyers are committed to keep all information confidential, I must tell you that my mother knows of my thoughts, my feelings."

"Susan is my dearest friend. I would have been disappointed if she had not expressed interest and concern," Martha said.

"I have told you earlier that I feel strongly about certain things. I repeat once more that Stephen would be better off to remain in the service, if the choice is his. If he should be released, you should get the best legal minds, with the most experience, that you can obtain.

"I saw Stephen and must confess my deep disappointment. I am sorry to say this. I wanted to talk with him. I felt I had to talk with some military officials. After doing so, I still refer again to my earlier recommendations."

Martha said, "I love my baby with all my heart. All real mothers do. But I am so afraid. I look at him and see a stranger, so lost, so terribly afraid. I can only hope a little and pray a lot. Beyond that I am helpless. I believe a Hindu suggested it is a dangerous thing to love a child too much. Thus, I cannot be a Hindu.

"I believe that, deep down under the surface, Stephen is filled with fear but he wishes no one to know this. I am afraid of his fear, but I believe it unwise to let him know that I know.

"At times I now find myself impatient. I was awake the other night and got up and read some in the Bible, about Job. Our Lord asked Satan, 'Have you considered my servant Job?' Abruptly I felt that I had no resemblance to Job. My patience and confidence seem to have dwindled to nothing.

"Jerome, you must save my son. I think you have the ability to do it. I am relying on our mutual respect and love and understanding. Yes, I go a step beyond. I must include sympathy."

"Martha, there are some things that I must say now. It could make some decisions easier," Jerome said. "I would guess there is one chance in ten he could escape punishment, that is, punishment by the State. This has nothing to do with his innocence or guilt. Now if a decision was made to gamble, to take the one chance in ten, and it proves unsuccessful, I am sure the punishment here could easily be twice as great. It really doesn't sound very practical. Having said this, how do you react?"

"You give me hope," Martha said. "April once discussed the term hope and the lack of it with our family. A person without hope is doomed."

April said, "If I follow what is being said, it would seem to me that he would have to be tried as a civilian. You are saying he must be tried here. It could not be otherwise, could it?"

"That's correct," Jerome said.

Martha said, "I don't understand. I was sure you said the army should retain control."

"I did say that. I still recommend that."

April asked, "Are you planning on using insanity as a justifiable excuse? Are drunkenness and insanity the same? I didn't think so."

"No. They are different. I did not, nor would I, suggest a plan to use insanity as a defense. I will not attempt to save him based on the fact he was insane, though it is more a legal than a medical term. If we did this, we would be in a crimeless world. We would all be excused because we were crazy."

"Do you think that the army would release him or that the civilian authorities can get him out?" Martha asked.

"I don't know. They will try. They have already started. Perhaps we could influence the decision. I am counting on it."

April raised her eyes slightly and said, "This hasn't all come into focus yet. You recommend he be disciplined by the army. He will be found guilty. But his only chance to be released must come through the efforts in a court here. The odds are ten to one against Stephen. If he is released from service and we are not successful, his punishment is likely to be twice as great, thus we must work to influence his release?"

"You have it exactly right. You haven't missed the first thing," Jerome said.

"You further state that we would not be in a friendly environment. The people of Midway and even Decatur County would not be sympathetic. Many seem to look upon the Randolphs differently now than they did some years ago," April said.

"How will the people look upon you, Jerome?" Martha asked. "I have been so self-centered that I didn't think. If you lost, it would not enhance your reputation. If you were to win, they may wish to destroy you. People can be vicious."

April said, "I have been selfish also, I suppose. I had given little thought to what Mother has said. Perhaps we should not let Jerome do this."

"A lawyer has an obligation to his client," Jerome said. "But we must talk about some other things yet. We must not have any misunderstandings."

"What else is there, Jerome?" April asked. "It seems perfectly clear, based on what has been said."

"No, I have not finished. It is important that you hear and remember. If we are successful, Stephen will be damned forever. As Thomas Wolfe said, 'He can't come home again!' People would never let him forget. He would not be treated or accepted as you would like by most people, some of whom you had previously felt were your close friends.

"I must go one step further but I can't explain at this time. He will be destroyed even more within himself. There is no other safe way. Again, for the last time, I prefer the military way."

Martha questioned Jerome as if she had not heard his previous information. "What will be your fee? I feel I must know."

"That is a strange question, Mrs. Randolph, coming from you. Are you fearful I will not be fair? Do you feel I have been excessive in previous transactions? I think we would approach it based on hours worked and a few extra expenses that would be involved. In the past, you have always sent more than I have billed you. It was not fair that you did this. Why do you ask this question?"

"You must let me determine the fee, Jerome. I will be most unhappy if this cannot be so," Martha said.

"I detect I have given you false hope. That was not my intention. The odds are greatly against us."

"I understand."

Martha continued, "Jerome, if you lose, your contemporaries will call you a fool. But if you win, you will lose everything. They will join together to destroy the country lawyer from Attapulgus."

"You think you have it all figured out?" Jerome asked, smiling. "It may surprise you if we should have the good or bad fortune to win. The world loves a winner. How many losers do you recall? It's always the winners. Now take our presidential elections. You probably can remember all the candidates that won, but I doubt the average citizen could identify five losers since 1789.

"Two other quick items. I must ask that April assist me again as in the Maybe Jones case.

"Secondly, you will need some money available to deal with the civil suit against Stephen. In this you cannot win. It will cost him all of his equity in the corporation. It will cost him all he possesses. I don't think the judge will deal with this before his trial; but one cannot be sure.

"I think it is time we left and let you and your family determine what you wish me to do, if anything. Let's act within forty-eight hours. Time, at this point, is precious."

Twenty-four hours later Martha told Jerome, "We have decided to ask you to do what you can, based on what you have said. After I have done all I can, perhaps peace will come to me. I trust you completely with the life of my son."

"If that is your wish, I will do my best. Now suppose we get started. I want you to let it be known in many circles that you will do everything to keep him in the Army and let them court martial him. In some instances, pretend it is a secret and that you would not wish for this feeling to get in circulation. This will ensure us that it will."

"But you said . . ."

Jerome laughed. "That was a first request and already you doubt me."

Martha said, "Yes, I guess we are about as faithful as the Lord's Disciples who could not stay awake an hour."

As Jerome sat at his office desk the next morning, he thought about what he had done. He realized again that he had destroyed everything he held dear and sacred.

Miss Adamson, his secretary, entered, yet he did not see her as he sat staring into space.

"Mr. Lee, are you well?" she asked. "You don't look as you normally do! Is there something I can do? It would seem as if the world rests on your shoulders. Perhaps it has fallen upon you!"

"It is entirely possible that you have identified my problem correctly. Could you please get me a glass of water?"

Chapter 82

"I would prefer my part of the estate to stay as it is for a time," Charles said as he was about to enter his final year at F.S.U. "I have no current needs."

"As you wish, Charles. I can see my son is nearly ready to abandon his nest and fly away."

"I will more likely leave with a whimper as I crawl away. I wish I could be with you every moment but if I am to finish the program, I am required to be in residence. I will be here often for you. I am only twenty-seven miles away.

"I have another purpose in being here at this hour, this day. In a few moments Meggie will join us. We have some things to tell you."

"Hello, Mrs. Randolph." She embraced Martha in a very special way. "It's nice for me to be home again."

"Mother, Meggie and I are going to be married this week-end. We wanted you to be the first to know. In a moment we will tell Uncle Edd. I don't believe any two people can love more deeply. I believe I recall you suggesting that we not wait, that a little time is all we have at best."

"We would like to marry here, Mrs. Randolph. We want to marry in your home, our home. It would be best that only the family be present. You will not be disappointed?"

"No. Certainly not. I want what you want. I want what you and Charles prefer." Without a word spoken the three knew that a church wedding would not be understood.

"It would be helpful as to the number. I'll need to get the house in order."

Charles said, "We will invite my brothers and sister. Then there will be Mary. I think Michelle would want to be present with Michael John. Then there are my other four girls. Susan Lee and her two sons I hope can come. I would also ask Clint White.

"Here on the place we will invite Uncle Edd. Craig may be here. And certainly Jack and Sandra. Are there others?" He looked at Meggie.

"I believe this covers it. If we go beyond, there is no beginning or ending." She smiled as only a bride to be can smile.

"Mike will perform the ceremony. We have the documents we need."

"You haven't seen my ring!" Meggie said smiling. "I wouldn't have had Charles be so generous but I'm not going to let him take it back."

They went over to the office where Uncle Edd was working. Meggie said, "This is the man I love above all others." They told him of their plans. They could see Uncle Edd could not have been more pleased.

"I once told Charles that there were only three people I would trust you with and Charles was on the list. You lived with one, you go to school with one and you are marrying the other!" He embraced her as a father.

"I leave you with only this thought. Don't put too much value in things. That is not what is important. We are only permitted to use a few things in our journey here. Some seem to get so little, like Kathy. Some seem to get more than their share. However, these are material things and they are only on a loan program.

"Time, of which we fortunately do not know the length, is all we will ever have in this world. When this is gone, we have nothing left; we return to the clay and dust from which we came. Think, dear ones, on these things."

Uncle Edd watched as they took each other's hands and squeezed tightly. They smiled as only two in love can smile. He said, "Love is the only enduring part of one's life. This is a special love that will bind you together. We have a God of love and to God, one of less love would be an insult to both God and man."

On Friday evening the group assembled. It was a beautiful and simple ceremony. When it was concluded no one doubted that love reigned supreme.

In a matter of moments they left. No one except April knew of their first night's destination. In minutes they were at Somewhere Else.

Charles carried Meggie into the room and placed her down. He pulled her into his arms. "I have loved you so long," Charles said. "I shall always love you." He kissed her hard upon her red, moist lips and repeated the process in a slow, gentle manner.

"Let me get out of these wedding clothes," Meggie said. "I'll join you in a moment." She moved into the bedroom where she had placed some other clothing earlier.

Charles entered the other bedroom and as he did she heard him say, "This is the last time we will ever use separate bedrooms again."

In moments Meggie reappeared. She had on a housecoat and slippers. She had let her hair down. There was a smile on her face, a gleam in her eye.

"It all started for me the night you graduated," Meggie said. "I believe at the moment we kissed that I knew."

Charles beamed as he looked at Meggie. "A lot has happened since that moment."

As they went into the nearly darkened bedroom Meggie said, "You didn't tell me how to dress or what to do!"

Charles smiled, "I don't know that dressing is important. Nature tells everyone in time what to do. You are not afraid?"

"No, Charles. I'll never be afraid as long as I have you. But at the beginning you must be patient until I can learn of some things. I feel so warm inside."

Some minutes later she thought, as she lay in his arms, of how she had delighted in his body, the touch of his hands, his mouth. In some early moments he had seemed to be a shade rough but for the most part, he had been tender. In return she gave all she had to give in a wholehearted abandon, a feeling of joy, and in total surrender. Shortly afterwards he rested in her arms with his head on her breasts and he kissed them in a very gentle manner.

In moments he let his hand move across her body and she felt a tremble inside. Suddenly she asked, "I know so little. It is not desirable to do this all over again?"

However, Charles did not move as rapidly as earlier. He continued with his hands and placed his mouth over hers, then moved to her neck. Then his tongue touched her nipples and again she shuddered. She anticipated that the time had come and snuggled against him. The glow inside seemed unbearable. "We have the rest of our lives, my darling," Charles said. "I want you to really want me."

His movements continued until she said, "You must, Charles. Now! Now!" She pulled him down upon her with an excitement she had not believed possible. Her legs encircled his body and once again she gave all she had to give. She knew then, beyond all doubt, that she had taken the first step toward becoming the wife she wanted to be, the wife he deserved.

"Was I what I should be?" she asked a short time later. "My desire, above all desires, will be to make you happy, to be the wife you deserve. Answer me, my darling. I must know."

He answered her by holding her tight once again, then said, "I may never wish to go back to school. I'll just stay here with you!"

Two hours later they were still talking and holding hands on the deck. There was a slight ripple on the water and the water wheel made a slight sound as it dumped its water below in its never ceasing motion. They did not speak but enjoyed the silence of the night and the thought that never again would they be separated from each other.

Charles was awakened by a noise at the break of day. He felt quickly and realized she was not beside him. Then he smiled, as he smelled the coffee.

"You are about to spoil me," Charles said so that she might hear.

"I'm going to spoil you for the rest of my life."

In a few days Jerome returned to confer with Martha once again. "I have returned from Washington, where I filed a request that he be disciplined by the military. I wanted it as part of the record. I cannot explain more at this time. Please trust me.

"There is great pressure being applied for Stephen's release from several sources. I may need to make one more quick trip to complete the initial stage of my plan."

"Did you see Stephen?" she hurriedly asked, apprehension in her face, her voice.

"Yes. I would say his health continues to improve." He said no more and this gave Martha all of his unsaid answers.

"You believe with certainty they will discharge him?"

"Yes."

"And he can come home?"

"Yes. But I must tell you that I think he will have to remain in jail. I do not believe you will be able to post bond. This is part of their plan."

"You spoke of April helping you again. She has no legal experience. I don't understand."

"She will be helpful. She is a thinker, a good observer and she can detect things I may miss."

Four days later Jerome called. "He has been discharged. He will be here in two or three days or as soon as they can make the transfer."

For the next week the papers were filled with facts as well as editorials of untruths and half truths. It was not a good time for Martha.

Bond was denied as Jerome had predicted. The papers speculated he might disappear and no chances would be taken.

Jerome visited Stephen as did the Randolph family. On Martha's second visit Stephen said, "These people, damn them, do not understand. I have not tried to hurt anyone. It's like my father said to me once in that they would never let the Randolphs be more than backwoods clowns. They are jealous. They envy us. We proved ourselves better than the others and this is the way they have of getting even and putting us back in our place. To hell with them." Martha left not knowing how to respond to one so bitter. Now she was beginning to guess why Jerome had preferred her to get someone else.

He had told Jerome that he did not understand why his mother had not secured the services of a real lawyer. For a moment Jerome was about to tell him that he had suggested it a dozen times, then realized this would make him only more antagonistic toward his mother.

A week later Martha tried a new approach. "Jerome has a chance, a slight chance to have you set free and you could start your life over again. I think it is about time you thought of someone other than yourself. It's your life," she said. She left hurriedly before Stephen could see the tears in her eyes.

A week later Michael John and Michelle told Martha of their plans to marry immediately. "We had thought about waiting until Christmas or until after the trial. We have decided to marry now. We want exactly the same deal as Charles and Meggie."

Perhaps it was a blessing in disguise because Martha found herself busy doing the things she needed to do and her thoughts were to leave Stephen for a few hours.

"Will you build a home immediately?" his mother asked.

"No. Not immediately. Joe's house is available. I think we should wait until later in the year, perhaps after the first of the year."

With the same guests present Michelle became the bride of Michael John. When the ceremony was over Michelle had a moment with Martha alone. She whispered, "I'll look after your son and make him happy. No one, unless it is you, can love him half as much as I do!"

Michelle lived up to her laughing reputation as she said, "My dear husband, you can carry me right over that threshold like a good husband should. Somewhere Else has lived up to its name."

"Michael John," she said, as he put her down, "life is made for laughter and fun. There are too many people who worry and fret over so many things that are not important." She looked closely and it appeared that her husband was at a loss for words and he was unsure as to what was expected of him next.

"I don't think either of us know exactly what to do next," she said laughingly. "But whatever it is, we should get started." She put her arms around him and kissed him with all the passion she could muster. At first he seemed to remain uncertain, then he began to respond. She continued, "I'm going to take it all off, my dear husband, and you can see if I am something you can live with the rest of your life." As she started to unbutton her blouse Michael John remembered the offer that had been made on the smooth bench in the park. For a moment he questioned his decision on that occasion.

Meggie told him, "I wish you to go into one of the bedrooms and remove your clothes and your shoes. Put on your robe. I'll do the same. After we have done this I want you to make love to your wife. It will be new for me but new things can be exciting." She had never once ceased to smile since she had entered the house.

They both arrived in the den at the same moment. She rushed into his arms and flung her arms around him. He kissed her with such passion that for a moment she was caught off guard.

Then Michelle took his hand and led him to the bedroom where she had changed. She had left a light on in the bathroom, with the door slightly open, which gave them a feeling of security.

Michelle took off her dressing gown and lay on her side. "Hurry. I want to know what so many have been so excited about for so long."

Suddenly, and again unexpectedly, he was beside her kissing and touching and exploring. She guided his hands to the places that gave her the most excitement.

In moments she felt herself tremble and a feeling of delight abounded. She knew that never again would Michael John, whom she loved so deeply, be timid and shy.

Two hours later Michael John whispered to Michelle, "I'll love you as no man can love a woman. Promise me that you will let me do the things that will make you happy. You are right. Happiness and joy should abound. I have lived where some felt other things more important. We must not do that. Do I make any sense?"

"Michael John, I understand. This will be our new world. We will be free to laugh, to tell our secrets to each other, to be silly and carefree. Our love for each other, be it good times or bad, will only grow deeper and stronger. Our mutual love and adoration will bring color and light and brightness. We will know that we will always be there for each other."

Michael John knew that after all his insecure years, he now had someone who had freed him at last from all the uncertainties and self-consciousness. Forever he would be free to know and understand as others did.

He pulled her to him once again and this time he knew that he was safe and sure. She recognized this change, feeling his hands touch her as their lips met once again.

CHAPTER 83

The large trees released their leaves, which then made their way earthward. The colors of brown and gold told Martha that September was giving way and the days of October were upon them. As the leaves drifted downward, in their erratic pattern of twisting and turning, Martha was reminded that life was much the same.

Strangely, for some unknown reason, Martha felt less depressed than in previous weeks. For the first time her mind focused on the good, the living, the many blessings.

For days all she had been able to think about was the past, of Joseph, Joe and Kathy. Robert could not be forgotten either. She had been anxious to visit her son in jail but after each visit she departed with a confused mind and a heavy heart.

Today seemed different, however. The good things, for a moment, seemed to take precedence over the bad. She thought of David and Mary without first seeing Joe and Kathy. David seemed his old self again and there were no words to describe the joy in Mary's face. Naturally, there was no other grandchild in the world like Kathy Lee.

Martha had been elated with the happiness displayed with Charles and Meggie as well as Michelle and Michael John. She knew of the good fortune of her two recently married sons. Again she smiled. Once she had felt sure that Sara Knight and Robin Wells would have been a significant part of her life but God had decided differently and God had made things good.

Then there was April. No one really knew how to describe her. She remembered the words of Charles some six or seven years ago when he told her of the gifts she possessed and suggested that in time to come it would be much more of a problem than a blessing. She seemed to have changed many of her old habits, her old loves, but had not established new goals or a new road to travel.

Seldom did she involve herself with the sports she had dearly loved. She had watched the girls practice one afternoon and hit a few golf balls but it was not the same anymore. She even fished less than she once had done.

Sometimes she spoke of Robert, of wonderful Kathy, and of Joseph. She mentioned the McPhersons more than once but it was of a different nature altogether. She spoke with a sadness as she pondered how the lives of all of them had been changed.

What would April do with her life? Perhaps this was what Charles had been saying when April had days of agony years ago in an attempt to place her life into some meaningful mold. Victor really had never been one to consider though Joseph had not understood. Robert was gone. She had reason to believe that April and Eric had arrived at a point of deep friendship but nothing more.

There were times when she believed most strongly that Jerome would be the man in her life but she had not seen sufficient evidence to believe this with any degree of conviction or assurance.

The next day seemed to be the opposite of the previous day. The first thing she did was visit Stephen. "You are back among your people," Martha said. "A number of friends have asked about you. Susan and Eric are always concerned. Uncle Edd has asked if there is something he can do. Clint White has called. Jack and Sandra extend their best wishes. It may surprise you but Helen Hurt is concerned. These are your people and they want to help you!"

"My people?" Stephen asked. "My people? I have no people! You should know; you should be the first to know. I feel as if a group of buzzards were flying over, with smiles on their faces and with twinkling eyes, as they wait to finish off the little that remains. My people are gone. With the departure of my father and brother, my people no longer remain. They loved me. They understood me."

"I love you," Martha said. "I believe your brothers and sister care. I am not sure you are being fair."

"You know, Mother, I do believe you love me. Sometimes I felt you loved some of the other children more. You seemed to show your love to some more than others."

Martha was speechless. She had not been prepared. "There were two or three years Michael John had some special needs. He was not secure like you. Yes, there was a time that I spent hours with David after his loss. He needed me. I have tried to be there for all of you always and to go the extra mile when one needs special care. This is why I am here today. I'll always be there when you need me, doing all I can."

"I make a simple mistake, not meaning to hurt anyone, and the world comes crashing down around me. I didn't take a gun out and rob and shoot someone.

"They will not let me go home. They will not accept any size bond. They treat me as if I was a black field hand. Why don't you just go on home. There is nothing you can do." Martha left with a feeling of hopelessness and melancholy.

Upon returning home she found herself in a state of despondency. When Michael John had approached about the construction of the houses she said, "Let's wait and talk about this another time. I don't feel that I can get my thoughts together or really get into it." He seemed to understand.

Jerome appeared. "I haven't seen April recently. Is she around?"

"No. I'll get a message to her if you like," Martha said.

"Oh, there is nothing special. There is nothing that cannot wait. No. I'm sure she is busy and has a lot on her mind."

"Have you seen Stephen again?"

"Yes."

Martha immediately interpreted the one word response to mean that nothing had changed.

"How did you find him?" Jerome asked.

"I'm not sure. Not good. I had thought we had seen a slight movement in a positive direction. Now I am less sure.

"It isn't a good situation, is it? Mothers always hope. I suspect they see something from time to time that they wish to see and it is likely an incorrect assessment."

"Mrs. Randolph, I have something that eats on me more than I wish. I saw no remorse as to Helen Hurt. I see none here. This isn't normal. Now if we should be successful in getting a favorable verdict, what next?"

"Jerome, I wish I knew."

"One last question. I can ask for a delay. I could find some justifiable reasons."

"Are you ready? Would it serve to an advantage to delay?"

"No. I think it best to go to court now. I suspect he will grow more resentful the longer he remains incarcerated. I am as ready as I will be. Again, the odds are not good."

"Then let's get it over."

CHAPTER 84

Jerome could not sleep. He got up, turned on the light and looked at the small clock. It read twenty minutes to five. He knew he could not go back to sleep so he put on his robe and began his morning ritual. When he had finished shaving he stepped into the shower and felt the warm water trickle down his body. His thoughts raced from one subject to another and he could not remember how long he had been there. He reduced the warm water and increased the cold in an effort to awaken his full senses for what he must face this day.

He put on fresh underwear, then put on his robe again. He laid out his best blue suit, his white shirt, his tie and a pair of shoes. Then he opened the door and walked down the hall to the small kitchen. Before he got there he saw a light and heard the sound of footsteps. He heard the scrape of a cooking utensil and knew that his mother was already up.

"What are you doing up, Mother? It's much too early. You should be sleeping."

"We understand each other's problems, my son. I didn't sleep very well last night either. I would wake up and think of Martha and the task before you. If Eric was in Stephen's place, I think I would just die."

"But Eric and I would not do this to you. But let us not talk of such things. I hope you haven't cooked a big breakfast. I get a little nervous and a great deal of food will serve no good purpose."

Susan placed a cup of steaming coffee before her son, "Drink this. I'll have breakfast finished in a moment. My father always said that breakfast was the most important meal of the day. You have a hard day before you. You must try to force yourself to eat something. You must have your strength. We both know this could be the biggest day of your life." She placed eggs, bacon and toast on a plate before him. There were two jars of jelly on the table and a large glass of orange juice.

"You're not going to eat now?"

"No. I'll wait a bit and eat with Eric. You must sit and relax. There are few things like a good hot cup of coffee." She refilled his cup.

"Do you still insist on going to court? I had hoped you would reconsider. There will be much said, a great deal described in vivid detail that will be difficult."

"I have to go."

"Why?"

"We have talked about this earlier. Do you think Martha would not be there for me? She will need all the support that we can muster. I might consider staying away if you said it would hinder your performance; but you will not tell me this."

"You, dear Mother, will not understand some of the things I must do or must not do but as I told Martha, please trust me."

"You really don't care for Stephen do you?"

"No."

"Is he that bad, that detestable?"

"Yes. You would not know everything. Even I don't know everything, thank God!"

"Jerome, tell me you haven't led Martha to believe there is some small hope where there is none?"

"She knows the odds, the chances. A court-martial would have been better. You recall I insisted."

"I am to blame. I told her when she was so devastated that you might know a way to help. She felt that another chance was only fair."

"Don't blame yourself. I didn't have to take the case. You did what you believed best. But as far as one more chance, I have many doubts about that!

"You know, if Stephen should be acquitted, I think I am going to hate myself. If I lose, the Randolphs cannot be happy. If I win, I think all of them will hate me even more."

"I don't understand. I thought that winning would please them and what friends we have left."

"They don't understand either and I can't tell them, not now anyway."

"How long will the trial last?" his mother asked.

"I would be afraid to guess. The State will go into great detail. It is to their advantage."

"You know, Jerome, it all sounds like a riddle! If you lose, you lose, and if you win, the losses are even greater."

"Let me get another half cup of coffee. I have a feeling I will need it," Jerome said.

"About seats, Jerome, won't the place be crowded?"

"I have seats reserved for the Randolphs and a few close friends. But yes, I suspect the group will be larger than anyone can remember.

"Your breakfast was wonderful. But everything you do has always been that way!"

"Get out of here now! Hurry! I have things to do."

Three miles away the Randolph family arose from a sleepless night to face the morning. Martha said to her family, "I am so glad the time has finally arrived. I do not believe I could endure many more days. Let us hope that life will continue after this week."

Just after eight o'clock Jerome moved in the direction of the courthouse, noticing that cars were already everywhere. People rushed toward the courthouse from every direction. As he got closer he saw two boys holding signs. One said, "We will get even!" Another said, "Randolphs beware!" He attempted to pretend he did not see them but he could feel the color rising above his collar.

When Jerome arrived Martha had already taken her place. She sat straight and rigid. She was pale, quiet and very frightened. She looked so thin, so tired, so weary. He wondered how she had survived the last two years.

In moments he saw his mother come in and take her place beside Martha. She sat down with all her natural, unhurried grace which was so regal, so quietly elegant. He saw the affectionate tenderness of their long friendship.

In a matter of moments April took her seat beside him. As beautiful as she was, Jerome could detect her weariness and insecurity. She smiled at him and patted him gently on the shoulder as she took her seat.

"I have never seen so many people," April whispered. "From where have they come?"

"From everywhere. This may not be the only show in town, but it seems to be the most exciting." April could see that Jerome was not fully relaxed.

"Why don't you dress as you are now when you come to see me? I'm disappointed." She wanted to say something to get him to relax.

It was then that Jerome met the combined assault of his two opponents. He did so without fear or embarrassment. He returned their look calmly. He could see the case was tempered to their liking. Then he imagined hearing a voice say, "Get ready. Here we come!" They acted in a pompous and pretentious manner.

However, he kept his face expressionless. These two great warriors, these skilled and experienced attorneys, looked at him once again, then at each other, exchanging poorly disguised smiles.

Suddenly Stephen appeared between two fully armed deputies. You could hear the hundreds of people whisper to each other and see two dozen pointing their fingers in Stephen's direction.

At nine o'clock the same Deputy Smith, Deputy Harman Smith, whom April remembered from Maybe's case, shouted above the noise. "All rise. The Superior Court of Decatur County is now in session, Judge Hollis C. Whitehead presiding."

Judge Whitehead appeared, dressed in a flowing and freshly cleaned robe. He stood before his court, then took his seat. He waited until the courtroom noise ceased, then heard a group outside chant, "Hang him! Hang Him! Hang him from the highest tree!"

Judge Whitehead motioned for Deputy Smith to approach the bench. In a matter of moments Deputy Smith hurried from the room. In less than a minute there was a dead silence.

Judge Whitehead said, "Those who can find seats, please take them. We will deal with those standing in a few moments.

"I will ask our clerk to call the first seventy-two names on the jury list. As your name is called, answer and take a seat to your right, my left, which has been reserved. Speak loudly so we may determine your presence.

As the clerk, Travis Johnson, called a name, it was repeated a second time, much more loudly, by Deputy Smith.

When the seventy-two had been seated, the judge spoke. "We will begin with the State of Georgia versus Stephen Randolph. Since this is a capital case I must ask each of you how you feel about the death penalty. Those opposed may rise. We will take your name and you may return to the other side, from which you came."

Eight people stood. They gave their names as instructed and returned to their former positions.

"Please call the next eight names on your list, Mr. Johnson."

When seventy-two had been seated Judge Whitehead said, "I am going to release all of the jurors whose names were not called and those excused from this case until Thursday morning at nine o'clock. You may remain in the courtroom or you may leave. Those standing may be able to find a seat when these leave." Fewer than a score left.

When the room had again become quiet Judge Whitehead said, "Let me tell you I will have order here today. Any evidence otherwise and you will be immediately excused. I will clear the entire room if I find it necessary.

"Now Mr. Wilson, suppose you introduce your associate."

Herman Wilson rose and smiled. "If it pleases the Court, this is Mr. Willis Cannington, who has been engaged to assist the State." Mr. Cannington rose, smiled and sat back down.

"Mr. Lee, please present the person seated next to you."

Jerome stood and motioned for April to do the same. "If it pleases the Court, this is Miss April Randolph, who will assist me. You may remember her, Your Honor, as the person who provided assistance some three years ago." They sat back down and Judge Whitehead nodded as he recognized her.

"Is the State ready to proceed, Mr. Wilson?"

"We are, Your Honor."

"Is the Defense ready to proceed, Mr. Lee?"

Jerome rose and said, "We are, Your Honor."

"The defendant will rise," Judge Whitehead said. Stephen stood by Jerome and April.

Judge Whitehead read out a half dozen charges against Stephen, which included the death of one person. "How do you wish to plead?"

"Not guilty, Your Honor, on all charges." There were voices to be heard all over the courtroom.

"Once again is all it will take," Judge Whitehead said. "I gave my instructions less than five minutes ago. We do have some with short memories. I am not thrilled to have so many standing but we will try once more."

"Now, let us begin," he continued. "In order to expedite matters, I will ask the following questions: If any of you are related by blood or marriage to Mr. Wilson, Mr. Cannington, the McPherson family, the Randolph family or Mr. Lee, please stand." Three stood, gave their names and the manner in which they were related; they were excused until Thursday.

The judge continued, "For the last several months the case we are about to hear has been spread over all the news media, from newspapers to television. It has been discussed, I'm sure, by many. My question is not whether you have heard this case mentioned or discussed in some form but whether you can listen to the evidence you hear and make a decision solely on the evidence. If you feel you would have difficulty, please rise and give your name to the clerk; you will be excused." Seven more stood, then departed.

"There may be many questions that will be asked of you but I will leave such to the State and the Defense," the judge said. "I will recess this court for fifteen minutes at this time. If you wish to leave, do so. I will allow no one to leave and return again until we recess for lunch." He quickly moved to the rear. Only a half dozen left the room. Others would take no chances of losing their seats.

When everyone was in place fifteen minutes later, Judge Whitehead said, "Mr. Johnson, you will call the individuals on your list. We will ask each to give his or her name, address, occupation, or if retired or disabled, their last occupation."

The clerk called, "William L. Jackson." A middle aged man stood. He wore a coat but no tie.

"I am William Larson Jackson. My mailing address is Route 2, Box 136, Apex, Georgia. I am a self-employed farmer."

Mr. Wilson asked, "Are you married? If so, how long? Tell us if you have children and if so, their sex and ages."

"Yes, I am married and have been for twenty-two years. My wife and I have three children, ages eighteen, fourteen and eleven."

"Is this your first marriage? Had your wife been married before?"

"A first marriage for each of us."

"Are your children boys or girls or both?"

"The two oldest are boys. The youngest a girl."

"Have any of your children even been in trouble, sir?"

"I guess all children get into something. I suppose all have stayed in at recess at school."

There was some laughter in the court but before the judge could pound his gavel it became silent.

"Have you or your wife ever been in trouble? Perhaps jail?"

"No."

"Have you or your wife had close relatives that have been in trouble?"

"No."

"How well do you know Stephen Randolph and the immediate members of his family?"

"I knew Mr. Randolph, his father, before he died when he was a commissioner. I knew his son Joe before his death but only on a speaking level. I know there is a Charles Randolph but we are only close enough to speak. We have no business with them. Everyone nearby knows the girl sitting with Mr. Lee if they kept up in sports or other school activities. How could we forget her?"

Again some laughter was heard but quieted immediately. "I understand there are other kids in the family but I have no knowledge of them."

"Do you know the McPhersons?"

"I know Mr. McPherson, Mr. Bruce McPherson." He looked in his direction directly back of Mr. Wilson, sitting with a lady.

"Do you bank with him?"

"No. I use the other bank."

"Is there a reason?"

"A reason?"

"Yes," Mr. Wilson asked, "is there some reason why you use a particular bank?"

"No special reason. The bank is where my father and his father did business. Sorta like belonging to a particular church I guess. Washington will probably instruct us before long on such matters." Again a reaction and heads nodded.

Mr. Wilson paused, walked over to Mr. Cannington and they whispered to each other.

"Mr. Wilson?" Judge Whitehead said.

"Yes, Your Honor, we ask that Mr. Jackson be excused."

April whispered to Jerome, "It will take a month to pick a jury!"

April turned to Stephen and whispered, "How do you feel?"

"Why go to so much trouble? They will railroad me anyway. I don't have a chance. I can look into their eyes and tell. There is nothing but hate."

Jerome whispered, "Look toward the front, the judge, the Clerk. You must not appear nervous. Do not look back."

"Why is Mr. Wilson going into such detail?" April whispered.

"There are probably two reasons, both important to him. He has a great audience and he is very confident. Part of this is for show. He is at the height of his glory!"

"And secondly?"

"Many times a lawyer will study the prospective jurors more than a case. It is important."

"Why do you think he excused Mr. Jackson?"

"Because he had sons and because he is a rural person. It's hard for one farmer to condemn another."

The second person called was Henry L. Torn.

"My name is Henry L. Torn. I live at Route 1, Midway. I work at the box factory across the river. I am married. We have three girls. There ain't no boys."

After ten or more questions and another conference with Mr. Cannington, Mr. Wilson said, "Juror on the Defendant."

Jerome rose and asked, "Do you bank at the People's Bank?"

"Don't have no account anywhere. Get my check cashed there about half the time," Mr. Torn said.

Jerome then asked, "What was the highest grade you attained in school? Perhaps a high school diploma?"

Mr. Torn's face turned red as he responded in a less than pleasant voice, "I quit in the seventh grade. I was already sixteen and they weren't learning me nothing."

"Where did you last go to school?"

"Midway. Right here in Midway."

After two more meaningless questions, Jerome said, "Excuse the juror."

April whispered, "Want to tell me why?"

"We need intelligent people regardless of where they live."

The procedure continued until five minutes to twelve. Four person had been selected to serve.

Judge Whitehead said, "We will adjourn until one-thirty. This case will not be discussed by selected jurors or those waiting to be considered." Two deputies came and took Stephen away.

As April and Jerome were leaving they noticed about half of the spectators remained in their seats. "A seat is more meaningful than a meal," Jerome said.

As they walked out Jerome asked April, "How many strikes were used by the State?"

"Five."

"And we have used three?"

"Correct.

"Have you ever seen so many people, Jerome? This is unbelievable!"

"Schools would be much better if such support was given. I understand that the Midway P.T.A. had a big crowd of forty-five people present recently including thirty of the teachers. Attapulgus has two hundred and fifty with only 325 students."

"Where are we going to eat, Jerome? Can we eat in the same café as three years ago?"

"Yes. But I have reserved a different booth."

"Smart bunch, Jerome. We could have learned. I can't believe you did this! They tried to tell you something." Jerome's face colored slightly.

This time they found themselves two booths away from where they last ate. They pulled the curtain and sat down. They placed their orders and looked at each other without a smile.

Suddenly they heard voices and April smiled. "They are the same crowd in the booth we had before. Listen now and let's see what we can learn," she whispered softly.

"Got that same girl with him, Don."

"Yep and those tits ain't changed a bit. Stick out even better I believe. Maybe a bit larger."

"I thought you were here to hear a court case."

"Looking don't hurt none. Helps to pass the time away."

"You know, Nathan, ole Herman ain't gonna let Lee get away this time. Gonna blow his ass right out of the courtroom."

"Wonder what old Bruce is paying Slick Cannington? That greedy bastard doesn't work cheap!"

"That boy's a damn outlaw. I hear all kind of things about him. Heard he was sticking half the blacks on their place. Man, there'll be more high yellows than the welfare rolls can feed."

"What kind of defense you reckon young Lee will use? Ain't no knife involved this time."

"Oughta hang that young wild boy. Let him out and none of us will be safe."

"Wilson has been waiting on this one, to even the score with Lee."

"Why did Lee take the case? Is he after the Randolph girl? Don't blame him too much!"

"You ask why, Harry? Two reasons. The first is money."

"And the second?"

"Money. Hell, there ain't no other reason."

"That girl was a hell of an athlete. She use to play with the boys."

"Yep and I bet the boys wanted to play with her. That, my dear Nathan, and a good glass of cold water would kill you dead as hell."

"Back to the case, boys. You have lost sight of why we are here. Don't sell this young Lee short! He knows something we don't know and I bet ole Slick and Herman don't know either."

"I hope to hell we get a jury. Old Wilson just wants to strut around and be seen. Ambitious son of a bitch he is. Better watch him. He wants to be governor."

"You fellows just sit back and watch, be it the case or the tits. Lee and that girl are gonna pull one out."

"Bull shit, Harry. When they describe the death of that girl and the jury sees that blind boy with no arm, you can know it is all over."

Jerome nearly laughed out. "April, I am told you once used some of this language. Perhaps you can tell me what it means!"

April turned many colors. "How did you know that? I haven't expressed myself like that in seven years. One can't get away from her past!"

"I can hardly wait for our next installment," Jerome said.

"But I don't understand. You wanted to leave last time."

"I've grown some since then. You were already grown! I know more about where I am going this time. I am speaking of the court case!"

"You still want a jury of good minds and reasonable character?" April asked.

"Exactly. Nothing has changed."

As Jerome and April walked back toward the courthouse, April said, "I still see you as a loser. You lose — you lose. If you win, the big boys will drive your fanny right out of Decatur County."

Jerome smiled, "People love a winner. It still, unfortunately, isn't how you play the game. I think it will always be that way."

At one-thirty they took up where they left off. When they had finished selecting the jury there were nine men and three women.

"Would we have been much better off with more women, Jerome?"

"I have some fears. They will describe Lesa in great detail. Women can get upset and emotional about such matters. It really doesn't matter though if they are honest and intelligent."

"I am lost, Jerome. I have no idea where you are taking me."

"Where do you think I would want to take you?" Jerome turned a pink color as he thought about what he had said. "I'll withdraw the question!"

In the late afternoon the judge said, "We have spent the day getting a jury. We are behind schedule. We will be here on time tomorrow. I will warn the jury not to speak to each other or to anyone about the case.

"I want everyone to remain seated until these twelve jurors and the two alternates have cleared the building. I will set the rules and guidelines the first thing in the morning."

As the hundreds left the building you could hear the voices. "Better be here early. Will be twice this many tomorrow. I'll bet you could sell your seat for fifty bucks!"

CHAPTER 85

April approached the courthouse on the second day of court. She saw a large group that she estimated at three or four hundred. Two deputies were busy keeping the group in check and a lane open in which one could make their way inside. She saw a large group of young people holding cards that were negative about Stephen. Many pointed at her and jeered, sneers on their faces. She looked ahead, head high, pretending as best she could that it was not so. One could sense an atmosphere of contempt and hostility.

Once inside, April saw a courtroom so crowded that no one could move. As she moved toward the front she saw her family with Mrs. Lee and Eric. She saw Mr. Wilson and Mr. Cannington in place as well as Jerome.

As April took a seat she said to Jerome, "It must have been like this two thousand years go when the Romans went to the arenas to see the Christians thrown to the wild animals. Nothing much has changed in twenty centuries! What is in a person to make one think and feel as he does?"

Jerome said, "I don't know, but apparently it has always been so."

"It is rather ironic," April said, "that one can look into the eyes of another and tell so much. I suppose you could divide them into three groups. There are those opposed, those neutral and those supportive. I can see there are few that fall into the last two groups."

"Let us forget these people. Let us hope the jury will be fair," Jerome said.

"How will things get started today?" April asked.

"Judge Whitehead will get himself firmly in charge from the beginning. He will set the rules for the spectators as well as the attorneys. With this number of people present, he has no choice."

At that moment, Deputy Smith, dressed in his best uniform and armed with his big pistol, led Stephen to his seat. He seemed reluctant to leave for a moment as he continued to stand back of the chair where Stephen sat.

April turned and looked him in the eyes. "You can leave now, Deputy Harmon Smith. Everyone has seen you and no one is in danger!" His face turned red. Jerome looked back and nodded to the deputy. Reluctantly he moved away.

"I couldn't help it, Jerome," speaking before he had time to ask why. "I don't like the mockingbird!"

"Mockingbird? I don't understand."

"I'll tell you sometime when you are old enough to understand." She smiled but Jerome continued to stare.

Jerome turned toward Stephen. "How do you feel?"

"It doesn't matter. Nothing matters. After all, what difference does it make?"

"It is important, Stephen, that you remain quiet and calm. Keep your eyes forward. Everyone will be watching you closely, especially the jury."

Jerome went over and said something to the clerk, Travis Johnson, who nodded his head in agreement. As he returned toward his seat, he saw his mother sitting next to Martha Randolph. Neither looked relaxed. There seemed to be a degree of both tension and sadness in the faces of each. He could see an expression of deluded hope. He tried to smile but could not. He wished he had not looked.

"All rise," The voice of Deputy Smith could be heard above the hundred conversations. "The Superior Court of Decatur County, State of Georgia, is now in session. The Honorable Hollis C. Whitehead presiding."

April whispered to Jerome, "Why Smith rather than the sheriff?"

Jerome whispered back, "The sheriff is a witness called by the State."

Before Judge Whitehead could pound his gavel the courtroom had become deadly quiet, as if an execution was about to take place.

After Judge Whitehead looked over his court to see that everyone was in place he said, "My first remarks are to the hundreds of spectators who are present, whatever the reasons. It is your right to be here, but only under certain conditions. It is my right and responsibility to see that you do not interfere with the proceedings under any circumstances. You will remain silent at all times except when the court is in recess. There will be no moving around. There will be no crying babies. This is a courtroom and not a nursery. If an emergency occurs, you may leave quietly but you will not be permitted to return until there is a recess. Under no circumstances will I tolerate an emotional display such as applause or disapproval.

"Now this trial is likely to involve vivid and graphic descriptions. This is essential. If you are not prepared or if you have doubts as to your emotions, this is the time for you to excuse yourself." No one moved and the deadly silence continued. One could feel the tension throughout the large room.

Judge Whitehead looked at the jury. "You have been selected in a manner prescribed by law. It is the responsibility of each of you to remain alert and attentive at all times. You will listen carefully to all of the evidence that you hear from each witness. Later it will be your responsibility to evaluate and weigh such evidence that is provided and make a decision. I will give you detailed instructions from time to time as we proceed."

He turned to the front once more and said, "I am gong to ask the people representing the State and the Defense to rise. I have some rules and instructions for you."

Herman Wilson, Willis Cannington, Jerome Lee and April Randolph stood before him. "Gentlemen and lady, this is a case that has drawn a great deal of attention. I will expect each of you to perform in a manner that is ethical and proper. Where I am going to allow a great deal of latitude, I will not tolerate any behavior I consider objectionable or unethical in my court. Do you have questions?"

In unison they spoke, "No, Your Honor."

"You may be seated.

"Deputy Smith, give me a status of the witnesses."

"Your Honor, all witnesses are present and are currently in the witness room. They have all been sworn in. If, however, other witnesses should be called to testify, they would need to be placed under oath."

"I am perfectly aware of the status required of witnesses, Deputy Smith." The face of the deputy turned a dark red.

Judge Whitehead pounded his gavel. "You who are present will remember what I have said. Do not expect me to be very flexible."

"I will recess this court for five minutes. I do not expect anyone to get up or leave unless they do not plan to return."

April smiled and whispered to Jerome, "Do all men his age have trouble with their bladder? I am told that some men have difficulty commencing the process and others difficulty ending it."

Jerome smiled, "You are inquisitive! You will have to ask another. I do not admit to the age and maturity of our Judge."

When the judge returned he said, "It is customary but not required that the State and the Defense provide an opening statement as we call it. The jury will remember that this is not a sworn statement and is not considered as evidence. It usually provides an outline of what the two sides plan to follow. Does the State wish to make an opening statement?"

"We do, Your Honor," Herman Wilson said as he rose and moved to within several feet of the jury box. One could readily see the D.A. was ready for battle. He turned for a second toward the spectators, turned back toward the judge in a deliberate and calculated manner and said, "If it pleases the Court."

Then he turned once again to the jury and said, "Ladies and gentlemen, I am Herman Wilson, the District Attorney for this district of which Decatur County is a part. Sitting at the table to your left is Mr. Willis Cannington. He will be assisting me throughout the trial." He turned toward Mr. Cannington and saw Mr. Cannington nod in acknowledging the introduction.

"You have, a few minutes ago, heard the charges made against the defendant, Stephen Randolph, who is sitting at the table with Mr. Lee and Miss Randolph. The State is prepared to present to you such evidence, such unquestionable evidence, that it will be impossible for you to doubt that he is guilty on all counts. We will prove, above and beyond all reasonable doubt, that this man did take the life of a beautiful young lady who had just started her life, that . . ."

"That's him! That's the very outlaw that murdered my beautiful daughter and destroyed my son and . . ." Her finger pointed at Stephen.

All heads turned to the source of the voice as Judge Whitehead pounded his gavel and the courtroom became silent. Agnes McPherson stood at the rail where she and her husband had been sitting, just behind Mr. Wilson and Mr. Cannington. Bruce McPherson rose and placed his hands strongly upon her shoulders, forcing her back into her seat and demanding at the same moment that she remain silent.

Judge Whitehead glared at Agnes McPherson, whose face and neck had turned a stained, russet color. "You have disregarded my instructions! Bailiff, please come forward."

Jerome stood and asked, "Your Honor, may I approach the bench?"

Judge Whitehead nodded and said, "Mr. Wilson you will approach the bench as well." When they stood before him he said to Jerome, "Mr. Lee, as you know, you have the perfect and legitimate right to demand a mistrial. I do not need to explain further."

Jerome looked back at Agnes and Bruce McPherson, then turned once again to the judge. "Your Honor, I am sure you will tell the jury to disregard the outburst made by Mrs. McPherson. I am sure she is going through a dreadful period with her losses. I believe I can understand though I am not a parent.

"Your Honor," Jerome continued. "I would like to make a proposal if it is in order."

"You may do so," Judge Whitehead responded.

"I would ask the court to continue. The jury has been selected. I believe they are very qualified to make decisions. I believe they will let the evidence and evidence alone determine their decision.

"I would prefer we not add to the time and expense of Decatur County. I would also request Mrs. McPherson be permitted to remain upon a promise from her that such an outburst will not occur again."

Judge Whitehead said, "You are a very fair and understanding person. I will do all within my power to prevent another such outburst or escapade such as this. You two remain here a moment." He turned to the large group assembled before him. "This will not be tolerated again by this lady or any other. I speak to all of you."

He turned back to the two attorneys before him. "I hope this will not occur again. Again I express my appreciation to the broad mindedness of Mr. Lee."

Herman Wilson said, "I appreciate the gesture exhibited by Mr. Lee and the Defense. I trust, however, that he will not expect special treatment and favors later because of his apparent generosity."

"Your Honor," Jerome said, "I can't believe our District Attorney made the last remark."

Judge Whitehead looked at Mr. Wilson, "Are you suggesting by any chance that I have been or will be unfair?" His face was crimson.

"No, Your Honor. I am not sure of Mr. Lee's intentions." He turned and hurried back to his seat.

Jerome turned slowly and as he did he saw Mr. McPherson, face distorted, telling his wife something. He did not know that upon hearing of the accident, Agnes asked only about Lesa. She never once asked about Victor. The strong feelings that Bruce had because of this did not go away. It would remain with him always. He had felt an anger and a surge of hatred. In time the last warm feelings that he had for Agnes would disappear and not return.

Herman Wilson looked at some notes at his table for a few seconds, stood and once again made his way before the jury. "Now, as I was saying, the young man seated before you, while intoxicated, no let me rephrase that, while completely drunk, did maneuver his automobile in such a way as to strike the vehicle driven by Victor McPherson, accompanied by his sister, Lesa, and destroyed, in a sense, the life of four people. Two, Victor and Lesa, through no fault of their own, were mutilated and destroyed. The remaining two victims are their parents whose lives will never again resemble its original state.

"We have witnesses, we have concrete evidence beyond all doubt, that stipulates that this defendant is guilty.

"After you have heard the testimony, you will be asked to make a decision based on the evidence you have heard, heard from those who will swear that what they say is truth.

"This case is different from many, perhaps most. You will not have to ponder who did it. He did!" Again he pointed to Stephen. "You will not have to ponder what he did! The evidence will be conclusive."

Mr. Wilson made a half turn, then looked at the jury once more. "Mr. Lee here is likely to tell you that the defendant is young, which he is. He will tell you he is a hard worker, which he was. He will tell you he was a soldier serving his country. He was. Not so anymore. He was discharged dishonorably. Yes, he will tell you it was an accident, a run of the mill accident. But this was no run of the mill accident when a drunk kills one and maims another for life. All the aspirations, hopes and dreams of the three remaining McPhersons are gone forever!

"I know you will base your decision on evidence and truth and fair play. We cannot, we must not, let this person remain where he will kill and destroy again.

"Yes, death, murder, blindness, limblessness are some of the things you will learn about. Our society should not be exposed to someone who is so dangerous. He has killed once. Certainly you will not let him kill again. I leave it in your hands; I know you will do your duty." Mr. Wilson returned to his seat, shaking his head as if he could not believe something of this magnitude had occurred.

"Mr. Lee, do you wish to make an opening statement at this time?"

"I do. Thank you, Your Honor." He moved in the direction of the jury box. As he stood before them he made quick eye contact with each. As he waited, the courtroom became more quiet, as he expected.

"Ladies and gentlemen, I am Jerome Lee. I am the attorney for Stephen Randolph, the defendant who is seated at the table." He turned to look back. "Also at the table is my assistant, April Randolph, a co-worker who has assisted me on another occasion.

"I am here of my own free will, so selected by the defendant and his family. I am not an appointed member of the court.

"Stephen Randolph, who lives near Attapulgus, is a young lad of eighteen. While he was at home on furlough from the United Sates

Army, he made a mistake, a miscalculation, and was involved in an automobile accident. We all, no exceptions, make mistakes and use poor judgement from time to time. Yes, all of us. He was in the Army as I said, serving his country while at war at the same time some of our youth were fleeing to Canada and elsewhere to dodge their responsibilities. Our nation called and this young man responded. He enlisted.

"It is obvious that Stephen Randolph did not willfully and intentionally cause an accident because he or no one in his right mind would put their own life in such jeopardy. No, at best or worst, he made a mistake. It was an accident. It was nothing more. It was an act of poor judgement.

"Now I am not going to tell you what our District Attorney, Mr. Wilson, is going to say. I do not profess to have any supernatural powers. We will leave such things to him because he has great insight that I do not profess to have.

"I believe you should be warned that you will likely hear some vivid and graphic descriptions as we proceed. I hope you will remember that all major accidents can bring about some results that are not always pleasant. I know you will understand that this is the process of seeking the truth. This young former solder's life is in your hands. I know you will do what you think fair. That is all we have a right to expect of another." Jerome returned to his seat. He looked neither left nor right.

Judge Whitehead said, "If the State is ready, we will proceed. Call your first witness."

"I call Lieutenant Henry Watson."

When he had been seated in the witness box Herman Wilson said, "Please give your name, address and occupation."

"I am Henry B. Watson. My address is Donalsonville, Georgia. I am a Lieutenant in the Georgia State Patrol where I have served for twenty-two years."

"Tell us, Lieutenant Watson, where you were on the evening of August 30 of this year and what you did."

"Corporal Brown, my assistant, and I were on patrol some two or three miles from Midway, shortly after eight o'clock, when we received a radio message that an accident had occurred some four and a half miles south of Midway on U.S. Highway 27, which is the same as Georgia Highway 1."

"Did you report to the scene of the accident and if so, tell us in your own words what you found."

"When we arrived at the scene we found two deputies of the sheriff's office on the scene, directing traffic. I quickly learned that two ambulances had been called. There were some twenty or more cars parked along the highway."

"What did you do first?"

"Corporal Brown and I went to the two vehicles, which looked as if they were totally destroyed. First we looked into the car which remained partly on the road. I could determine that a female was crushed in the wreckage. There was absolutely no doubt about her condition. She was dead. Parts of her face and head were missing. It was not a pleasant sight. It required some skilled technicians to remove her from the vehicle because the car was crushed in on her.

"I next noticed the man under the steering wheel or where the steering wheel was once located. I could tell he was living. His face was a mass of blood and flesh. He had an arm severed and was bleeding profusely."

"What did you do?"

"With the help of Corporal Brown and a deputy, we managed to remove him. We knew of the dangers in doing this but circumstanced demanded it."

"Please explain."

"We knew we had to stop the bleeding. He would bleed to death if we didn't. Secondly, there was the fear of fire. You could smell the gasoline very strongly."

"Then what happened?"

"We got him out and stopped most of the bleeding. An ambulance was there to get him to the hospital, about a five-minute trip."

"Then what did you do?"

"We went over to the vehicle that was shattered, which was off the road, over near the ditch. We found a young man, who was unconscious, lying on the ground about six or seven feet from the car. His face was covered with blood. We gathered that he had gone through the windshield upon contact with the other vehicle. I felt of his pulse and it seemed quite strong.

"By this time the second ambulance, with medical technicians, had arrived. They placed him in the ambulance and rushed him to the hospital. I believe this young man was the defendant but it would be difficult to say with certainty because of the condition of his face.

"It was some time before we could get the girl out. She, too, was transferred to the hospital but we knew she was dead already. She never knew what struck her."

Jerome stood. "Your Honor, the defense recognizes and accepts the testimony of Lieutenant Watson. Would it not be well to leave it at this point? I am sure there are several here today that find this an unpleasant reminder."

Before Judge Whitehead could react Mr. Wilson spoke. "It is essential that the members of the jury get a clear and precise picture of what occurred and what was found. It was stipulated earlier, Your Honor, that this information was necessary to get all the facts."

"You may continue, Mr. Wilson, but let us not get too carried away. There are limits in all things."

"Thank you, Your Honor.

"Now let us see if we have this correct? In the one car were two occupants. The girl was killed upon impact, her body mutilated and pinned within the vehicle, from which experts were able to pull the body later. The other occupant in the car was a male. He was alive but bleeding profusely as an arm had been severed completely and there was additional damage to his face and other parts of his body."

"That is correct."

"The occupant in the other car, or from the other car, was alive. He had a strong pulse but was bleeding severely. He was found about seven feet from his car in an unconscious condition."

"Again, that is correct."

"After these three people were transported to the Midway Hospital, what did you do next, Lieutenant Watson?"

"There were a number of things we did. We reexamined the cars carefully and took some measurements. We questioned some people who had witnessed the accident."

"Lets go back to the cars. Did you find anything significant?" Mr. Watson asked.

"Strange things happen which are unexplainable. Usually in this type of accident nothing remains in tact. This was an exception. In the car driven by the defendant, we found a bottle of whiskey that had somehow managed to survive without breaking. It was on the floor board. It was what we usually refer to as a fifth. Some may not be familiar with this term. This is a bottle that, when full, usually contains about four-fifths of a quart. The bottle was a little less than half full."

"What else did you determine?"

"We took pictures. We made measurements. We reviewed every detail that we considered important. I have turned the pictures over to the State, along with diagrams and measurements.

"What conclusions, sir, did you and Corporal Brown determine?"

"First, it was obvious from the tire marks that the defendant's car was completely on the left side of the road.

"Secondly, a great deal of speed likely contributed to the accident. A number of factors make this obvious."

"Other observations?"

"Yes, you could smell alcohol very strongly on the defendant. Tests later proved this to be so. According to the alcohol tests the defendant was more than legally drunk. In fact, he was more than twice over the limit that defines drunkenness. I believe you have this evidence as a part of your records."

"Please step over here, Lieutenant Watson, and look at the diagram on the tripod. Please show a sketch of what you saw."

When he had finished it seemed very clear that Stephen had made a number of gross errors to cause the crash.

"One last question," Mr. Wilson said. "How can you be sure of such excessive speed? How did you arrive at this conclusion?"

"After twenty-two years you can look at all the evidence and make a determination. The condition of the girl was one thing. The condition of the automobiles told a story. Then there was a witness we talked with that substantiated our observations. I believe you have his name."

"You mentioned the condition of Lesa McPherson. Can you go into more detail?"

"Her body was severed in several places. The skin of the neck was all that held her head attached to the body. I can go into more detail but I believe that is sufficient."

"How did you determine the victim was a woman?"

Lieutenant Watson's face turned red. "Most of her clothing on the upper part of her body was missing. There was one breast remaining!"

There was some talk immediately and the judge pounded his gavel several times before order was restored.

"Where are the cars now? The cars that were involved?"

"They have been impounded as evidence. They are under lock and key at the moment."

Herman Wilson turned to Judge Whitehead. "Your Honor, I have no further questions of this witness. I wish to enter as evidence the diagram he drew as well as the pictures that were taken. Later I will wish to add the alcohol tests that were made."

"Very well. Mr. Lee you may now cross-examine the witness," Judge Whitehead stated.

"Thank you, Your Honor. I will not take long. Lieutenant Watson seems very efficient, very thorough."

Jerome turned to the witness. "How can you be sure the defendant crossed over into the left lane? You said you were several miles away when you got your first report of the accident. I don't believe you witnessed it when it occurred."

"No sir. But the evidence is there. It is obvious. I am certain. There is also a witness I questioned who did see it."

Mr. Wilson jumped up. "Your Honor, we have witnesses that we will call later to substantiate this evidence, this report." He sat down.

"Only one other question, sir. This bottle, this bottle of whiskey? How can you be certain it belonged to the defendant? Where is the bottle? It doesn't seem to be exhibited."

"It has been turned over to the State. The bottle was found in the defendant's car. I believe it can be traced to its origin. I would guess Mr. Wilson will give further details. As we said, the tests on the defendant proved he was twice the legal limit."

"No further questions." Jerome returned to his seat.

"Your next witness, Mr. Wilson," the judge said.

"Your Honor, Corporal Brown is present but I feel it unnecessary to call him. He could only testify to the facts just presented. I believe I will delay his presence at this time."

Jerome stood up. "Your Honor, I have no objections as to whom he calls and when. I hope we can move on at this time!"

Mr. Wilson glowered at Jerome, then said, "I call Sheriff Ralph Henderson."

When Sheriff Henderson had taken his seat Mr. Wilson said, "I believe all present know you, Sheriff Henderson, but for the record please give us your name, address and occupation."

"I am Ralph Henderson. I live here in Midway. I am the Sheriff of Decatur County where I have held this position for three full terms of four years each. My fourth term will expire in December, 1968."

"Were you on the scene of the accident that occurred on U.S. 27 on August 30, 1965?"

"I was. I arrived some minutes after the deputies arrived at the scene of the crime, as the bodies were . . ."

"Your Honor, I object," Jerome said rather loudly. "I was of the opinion that it had not been determined that a crime had been committed. For some reason, I thought that was the purpose of our being here!"

"Sustained," Judge Whitehead said. "I will not permit this. Please rephrase your response. You know better than to try this in my court! Strike that from the record."

"What did you see and do once you arrived at the scene of the — accident?" Mr. Wilson asked.

"I first assisted in getting the traffic moving. We did not need a lot of people present to interfere with the investigation."

"Did you go then to the scene of the — accident? Did you examine the cars? Did you talk with witnesses? I would hope, for the benefit of the jury and court that you would describe in detail what you saw and did, as painful as it might be. Tell us exactly what you saw."

"I went to the vehicle on the right of way, but away from the paved surface. This was the vehicle of the defendant traveling north as determined by the State Patrol. There was a young man near the vehicle. He was unconscious. There was a great deal of blood and torn flesh about his head. He was moved very carefully to an area because of the danger of a fire. We took every precaution in moving him.

"Then I went to the second vehicle that had been traveling south. There were two occupants. The male was removed because of the danger of fire and because he was bleeding. His arm had been severed. His face was a mass of flesh and blood.

"I recognized the second person in the car as that of a female. There could be no doubt as to her condition. She was dead. She probably died upon impact." The sheriff paused, as if looking to see who might be offended, before continuing. "Much of her head was missing. The upper portion of her body above the waist was mutilated, a section missing. Parts of her body had been severed. It was a deathly scene, a most unpleasant sight. We requested by radio for some assistance. Some cutting torches were needed before the body could be extracted."

"Did you see Lieutenant Watson during this time?" The D.A. asked.

"Yes. We worked together as a team."

"Do you know for certain that a bottle of alcohol, a bottle of whiskey, was found?"

"Yes, there was a bottle of whiskey about half full of liquid. The bottle was four-fifths of a quart. Someway it had managed to survive. Rather difficult to understand when you look at the passengers and the vehicles."

"Where was the bottle found?" Mr. Wilson asked.

"On the floor board of the vehicle traveling north. It was the defendant's car."

"Do you see that person in this room?"

"I do." Sheriff Henderson looked at Stephen as he pointed.

"Now Sheriff Henderson, I ask you this question based on your years of experience. Do you have any doubt that the vehicle traveling north, the vehicle of the defendant, was some eight to ten feet over the center line on the wrong side of the road?"

"No. I have no doubt."

"Could the automobile have been traveling at an excessive speed?"

"I cannot say how fast he was traveling but the results indicate excessive, very excessive speed. We have a statement from an eye witness. I believe he can tell you in his own words what he saw."

"One last question, Sheriff Henderson. Did you take tests as the amount of alcohol found in the blood streams of each?"

"Yes. The two in the car traveling south had no measurable amount in their blood streams. The defendant did. The figure was twice the amount needed to call one legally drunk!"

"There is no doubt as to the accuracy of the tests?" Mr. Wilson asked.

"No."

"Thank you. I have no further questions." The D.A. returned to his seat with a pleased expression on his face. Mr. Cannington nodded his approval as Mr. Wilson took his seat.

Jerome stood and walked several steps toward the witness stand. As he did he recalled the Maybe Jones case. Perhaps he had been careless in this investigation. Then he realized that he and Lieutenant Watson were in complete agreement. "Your Honor, I have no questions of this witness at this time but I would like to reserve the right to recall him later." He returned to his seat beside April.

April said, "I thought you might question him. He is certainly subject to error. We both know that."

"I'll tell you why later," Jerome said.

"Your next witness, Mr. Wilson."

"I call Sherman Joiner, Your Honor."

A middle aged man who was of average height, and also rather stout, appeared. He moved slowly to the witness stand.

"Please give your name, address and occupation, sir."

"I am Sherman Joiner. I live at Oak Hill, some six miles or so north of Midway. I am a clerk in a local furniture store."

"Please tell the court, Mr. Joiner, where you were on the evening of the thirtieth of August of this year. Tell us what you saw."

"I was returning home and I was about five miles south of Midway on U.S. 27. I looked in my rear view mirror and saw a car coming up so fast it nearly scared me to death. I knew he couldn't stop in time without hitting me if he remained in the right lane. I was on a very sharp curve. I thought I was a goner. Then the car went around me as if I was standing still. Had another car been approaching from the north it would have likely killed all of us. As I rounded the curve, I saw the same car go out of control and cross over the center line into the left lane. I saw it strike an approaching car head on. You have never heard such a noise upon impact! The front of each car seemed to bury itself into the front of the other. As the north bound car struck, it seemed to go to the left, into the right of way."

"What did you do?" Mr. Wilson asked.

"Well sir, I drove on down and got out and took a quick look. A truck with a radio stopped about that time. He made some calls and in a matter of minutes the law officials were on the scene. A short time later two or three ambulances appeared. The Georgia State Patrol was there. In two or three minutes several other cars came by and stopped. I told a Lieutenant Watson what I saw. He got my name and address and told me I could leave."

"How fast were you going when he passed you, Mr. Joiner?"

"I would guess fifty. I try not to hold people up but I am not a fast driver. Yes, I would say fifty."

"After you rounded the curve, how far ahead of you was he when you could first see him?"

"Three, maybe four hundred yards. Didn't seem like he was too bright of a fellow."

Jerome got half out of his seat to protest, then decided not to do so. He didn't believe Stephen was very bright either.

"Mr. Joiner, without too much detail, just what did you see when you stopped?"

"Awful. Just awful. Blood everywhere. There were people with their bodies torn apart and . . ."

"That's enough, sir. I believe you have made your point." Herman Wilson took a side glance toward the jury box and was assured that what he saw was ample. "No more questions."

"Mr. Lee?"

"No questions, Your Honor."

Judge Whitehead took out his watch and looked at it slowly. He looked at the clock at the rear of the courtroom on the wall. "It is a little early for lunch but we will recess until one o'clock. One o'clock, not one-thirty. Now there are two things I will call to your attention. First, the jury will not discuss the case with anyone. Secondly, when you return, be prepared to stay late, quite late. You may need to call at lunch if you feel it necessary. We want to move this case along." As he moved toward his chambers the crowd rushed for the back door. The deputy was there to escort Stephen to the rear.

Jerome returned again with April to the same café, to the same seat. Already their four old friends were in their customary booth, partially curtained, situated next to April and Jerome. April smiled and whispered, "We will now get an update on the most recent happenings."

"Old Wilson is in high gear. He wants the jury to get a complete picture of the McPhersons."

"I still don't see why Randolph didn't plead guilty, fellows. I think it would have been better for everyone."

"Yep, you're right, Howell. Did you see the faces of the members of the jury?"

"Harry, it was nothing to compare with the expressions of Mr. and Mrs. McPherson."

"Why you suppose he doesn't have that boy on display? With eyes that can no longer see and with an empty coat sleeve hanging down, that would finish the Randolph boy off."

"They will see it. Hell, Wilson is too smart not to place him on display. He is just waiting for the right time."

"Don't guess there is much young Lee can say to defend this boy. Seems like he oughta be doing something but I don't know what it would be."

"Is the loss of sight temporary or will he be blind for the rest of his life, Nathan?"

"I hear they fear the worst but some say there is a very slight chance. I doubt it. Still being evaluated by some doctors in the North, I understand."

"They should give that son of a bitch the chair! A damn drunk destroying the whole family."

"Fine family, too. Powerful people. Money people. Old Bruce will stick it to that fellow. You know, he is paying old 'Slick' to help Wilson. I heard he told several that he wants justice, not mercy!"

"I hear that McPherson boy used to court that Randolph girl. That Victor had a hell of a reputation with the women. Suppose he was sticking her?"

Jerome was rising from his seat when April caught his arm. "No. No, Jerome. Just remain quiet. It doesn't bother me."

Jerome, his face red, said, "I should have never suggested this place again."

"We need to know the thinking of others. It can be helpful."

"Well, tomorrow it will end," Jerome said.

"Things do not look good, do they?" April asked. "You really don't have a case. You took it to please our mothers. I can also see you do not care for Stephen."

Jerome said, "This will be the last chance Stephen will have to grow up. It will all be up to him. I hope he can succeed but I have many doubts. As to why I took the case, I stay awake at night wondering about that myself. When we finish I feel I will be as discouraged as Stephen will be. However, you know why I took the case.

Then he changed the subject abruptly. "Now let's eat a bite. It's going to be a long afternoon. It could easily go into the evening hours."

CHAPTER 86

"Mr. Wilson, Mr. Lee, please approach the bench," Judge Whitehead said. When they arrived he continued, "I need each of you to provide some information so I can plan to use our time and the county's money wisely. Starting with you Mr. Wilson, can you give the Court some idea as to the time needed to call your remaining witnesses?"

"Your Honor," Mr. Wilson said, "I plan to call no less than three and no more than five witnesses. As to the time, I cannot be sure, as I have no idea how long the Defense will take to cross-examine. I believe a safe guess would be about two hours."

Both Mr. Wilson and Judge Whitehead looked at Mr. Lee. "What can you tell the Court, Mr. Lee?"

Jerome responded, "No less than three and no more than five witnesses, Your Honor. As Mr. Wilson has said, one can never be sure as to the time required for cross-examination. Perhaps two hours or just a little longer would be a reasonable estimate. As you say, time is money and money seems to be a factor."

"You may return to your seats. I can plan more efficiently with these assessments," Judge Whitehead said.

"Call your next witness, Mr. Wilson."

"I call Dr. Hugh Bacon," Mr. Wilson said.

A person small in stature appeared and took his place. "Your name, address and profession, sir," Mr. Wilson said.

"I am Doctor Hugh Bacon, Doctor of Medicine. I live here in Midway where I have practiced twelve years."

Mr. Wilson surveyed him for some moments, then said, "I believe nearly everyone in the courtroom knows you so I shall not ask specific qualifications.

"Now tell us, Dr. Bacon, where you were and what you were doing on the evening of August 30th of this year."

"I was in the Emergency Room of the Midway Hospital. Most all of our doctors are asked to serve in this capacity periodically."

"Who did you see and treat on the evening of this day and at what time? Give us such details as you remember."

"About eight-thirty two ambulances arrived. Each brought a male patient that was injured in what I discovered later was a car wreck about five miles south of town, on Highway 27. If you need an exact time, I can secure it from the hospital log."

"Your estimate is most adequate," Mr. Wilson said. "Tell us in your own words who these people were and the condition in which you found them."

"The first person brought in was a young white male. I later learned he was Victor McPherson."

"Describe his condition, please," Mr. Wilson said.

"He had an arm severed from his body. We moved quickly to stop the bleeding. Unfortunately, we had no personnel on duty that could reattach an arm. Next I examined the head and neck area. There were some portions of his face missing. As I looked at his eyes I knew that there was a great deal of damage. After completing a quick examination, it was obvious that he needed some help, some attention, that we could not provide. Thus, we dispatched him rather quickly to Tallahassee. A transfusion was given at the hospital. Another was given in the ambulance, en route to Tallahassee.

"Since that time I have learned that the arm could not be reattached. We also have learned that he cannot see. We are not certain of permanent blindness but it appears that the chances of seeing again are poor, very poor. We hope this evaluation is incorrect. What a tragedy for one so young, so talented, to be handicapped in this matter. A terrible thing!"

"And the second person, Doctor Bacon?"

"The next patient was Stephen Randolph. I would guess his head and body may have gone through the windshield, because his head and face were cut badly. We sewed and clamped but recognized that again we were not equipped or staffed to meet his needs. Thus, he was dispatched to Tallahassee."

"There was a third person?"

"Yes. It could have been thirty or forty minutes later that a third person was brought in to the hospital."

"Why do you suppose that she was not brought in immediately?" Mr. Wilson asked.

"I was told that she had to be cut out with torches before she could be removed. I am also told that it was determined she was dead at the time they arrived. I was not present at the site of the accident. It was obvious she was DOA, that is, dead on arrival."

"Do you recall her physical disabilities? Did she die because she bled to death?"

"I would say she died instantly upon impact but again I cannot be a hundred percent sure. There was a great amount of blood and her body was mutilated. I trust this description will be ample. I see no purpose in going beyond what has been said." He was looking at the McPhersons.

"I agree," Mr. Wilson said. "I know it is painful for many. I have no other questions."

Doctor Bacon stood up to go when Judge Whitehead said, "One second, Doctor Bacon. The Defense may wish to ask some questions." Dr. Bacon sat down.

Jerome stood, "I have no questions. I am sure he is a busy man and I have no need to recall him later."

"I call Victor McPherson," Mr. Wilson said. All eyes in the courtroom seemed to center on the door from which the witnesses entered. There was total silence as all waited in anticipation. The door opened, then a deputy sheriff led a young man toward the witness stand. They moved very slowly, the deputy giving instructions as they moved forward. Victor wore a pair of dark glasses. One of his sleeves dangled at his side. The noise increased as he moved toward the witness stand. The deputy said, "Now turn slowly, sir, and move a step backward." The deputy held open the small swinging door. Victor moved backward until he felt the chair with his hand. He sat slowly, facing the jammed courtroom he could not see.

An eerie stillness filled the courtroom. Victor moved his hands around, becoming familiar with his surroundings.

"Sir, would you please tell us your name, address and occupation," Mr. Wilson said in a very soft voice.

"I am Victor McPherson. I live here in Midway. I have just returned from graduate school at Harvard, where I received my MBA degree. I was just beginning a career with my father in banking at the People's Bank."

"You have just received a Master's Degree in Business Administration at Harvard?"

"That is correct. I did my undergraduate work at the University of Georgia in Athens," Victor said.

"Please tell us what occurred, as painful as it will be, on the thirtieth of August of this year."

Victor paused, then said, "My sister, Lesa, and I were on the way to Tallahassee to have dinner and see a movie. This was her birthday and I had promised her an outing. Some five miles or so after leaving Midway we were struck by a car racing northward on U.S. 27. It appeared to be traveling at a high rate of speed. Just seconds before the vehicle got to us it veered across the center line into our path. I did not have ample time to dodge, to leave the highway. There was no warning. That was the last I remember for a time."

"Who was driving?"

"I was the driver."

"Were you speeding?"

"No. I am not a fast driver."

"Were you sober? Had you had any alcohol to drink?"

"No. My sister and I were sober."

"After the crash, what occurred?"

"I vaguely remember being removed from the vehicle and given some medical attention. I could not see. Their voices were not too clear as it seemed that many voices were in the background. I remember feeling for my arm but it was missing." He gestured, touching the empty sleeve. "I remember an ambulance taking me to the Midway Hospital and then to Tallahassee."

"Do you have any sight at all in either eye?"

"No. I am hopeful but not encouraged based on the medical report."

"They could not reattach your arm?" Mr. Wilson asked.

"I was told later that it was so severely damaged it could not be reattached."

"Back to the accident, Mr. McPherson. Would you care to guess your speed?"

"Fifty to fifty-five. The weather conditions were such that this seemed a practical speed."

"And the other vehicle as to speed?"

"It appeared he was speeding but it all happened so fast I cannot be certain."

"I have no further questions," Mr. Wilson said.

"Mr. Lee, would you wish to cross-examine?" Judge Whitehead asked.

"No questions, Your Honor."

The deputy returned, opened the gate and led Victor. "One step down," he said as they left the witness stand. "Hold my hand and I will guide you." Slowly in silence they returned to the door from which they came.

"I call Bryon B. Boyd," Mr. Wilson said.

A middle aged man appeared. He was groomed in a flamboyant sport coat and tie. His hair was thick and black and combed back on his head. He moved swiftly toward the witness stand. It was not difficult to determine the high regard he had for himself. He took his seat, looked at the mammoth crowd and smiled and turned toward the jury in the same manner.

"Mr. Boyd, please give your name, address and occupation," Mr. Wilson said.

"I am Bryon B. Boyd. Sometimes I am called Byron Boy Boyd or three B's. I live in Midway. I am a merchant. I sell merchandise. I have three stores. There is one in Midway, one in West Midway and one in Attapulgus which I opened just recently. Currently, in order to get my last store functioning as I wish, I spend most of my time in Attapulgus."

"What kind of business do you operate?"

"I sell liquor and wine. I have a license from the state, county and each city where I operate. I have been in this business about ten years."

Herman Wilson walked over to the table where Mr. Cannington sat, picked up a paper bag and walked back toward Mr. Boyd. He pulled a bottle from the paper bag. It was less than half full of some reddish liquid.

"Mr. Boyd, did you sell this bottle of whiskey to the defendant, Stephen Randolph, who is sitting at the table?" He pointed to the table where Jerome, April and Stephen sat. "Did you sell him this bottle on August thirtieth of this year?"

"I don't know, sir. I cannot say."

"Are you refusing to answer, Mr. Boyd?" Mr. Wilson asked.

"It's not like that, sir. It is not possible for me to know if that is the bottle that I sold Stephen Randolph on that occasion."

"Let me rephrase the question. Did you sell a bottle of whiskey to the young man at the table on such a date?"

"I did sell him a bottle. I can't be sure if that is the very bottle. In fact, that is certainly the brand I sold him in a container that size."

"How can you be sure? How can you remember so clearly?" Mr. Wilson asked.

"For a number of reasons. I know the boy. I know the boy's car. I also knew he was in service and he was in uniform when I sold it to him. He is the man. I sold him a fifth of whiskey of that brand. I suppose I should define it more clearly when I speak of a fifth. Actually it contains about four-fifths of a quart."

"You are positive?"

Mr. Boyd gave a big smile and said, "I have no doubt whatsoever."

"I have no further questions, Your Honor." He saw that Mr. Cannington gave a nod of approval as he returned to his seat.

"Cross examination, Mr. Lee?"

"Yes, Your Honor," He moved toward the witness stand, picked up the bottle and looked at it carefully for a full two minutes. There was total silence in the courtroom.

"Mr. Boyd, how long have you been selling this, er . . . merchandise, as you call it?"

"I believe I have already said ten years or so." He smiled as if he had caught someone with a hand in his cookie jar.

"Mr. Boyd, how do you feel about selling this . . . this merchandise, as you called it? This is a bottle of whiskey, is it not?" Mr. Lee asked.

"I object, Your Honor!" Mr. Wilson shouted. "Mr. Boyd is not on trial and I believe an opinion is not required! He has done nothing illegal!"

Before Judge Whitehead could respond Mr. Boyd said, "I don't mind answering the question. It does not bother me in the least. I sell legally and only to those who qualify. No. It doesn't bother me at all. Give the people what they want."

"Are you certain, Mr. Boyd, beyond a doubt, that you sold this bottle or one like it to the defendant? To the man sitting there at the table with the young lady?"

"Yes sir. I recognize him, though his face looks a little different since he had his accident."

"You sold it to him? He didn't take it? He didn't steal it? You didn't give it to him?"

"I sold it to him. I am sure. You don't give away liquor. For that matter, I don't even sell it on credit." He looked out as if to say, 'I know what to do, how to be successful.'

"Now Mr. B. B. Boyd, when Stephen Randolph purchased the bottle of whiskey, what did you say?"

"I don't understand, unless you mean how much it cost. He paid me in the same manner as all customers."

"You didn't say anything else?"

"I may have asked him where he was stationed or how long he would be at home. He was in for only a minute or so."

"I see," Jerome said. "Now you don't recall discussing with him the dangers of the contents of that bottle or one like it?" Jerome picked up the bottle for a second and returned it to the table.

"No sir. A man knows about whiskey. There is not a drinking man alive that doesn't know that one should stay within limits!"

"Limits? Limits? What limits, Mr. Boyd?"

"Everyone with any sense at all knows too much whiskey will do you in. Everyone knows that!"

"Did you tell him a certain amount, more than whatever the limit is, would do him in as you described it?"

"Your Honor. I again repeat that Mr. Boyd is not on trial and there is no purpose in this line of questioning," Mr. Wilson said loudly.

"Your objection is overruled. Please continue, Mr. Lee." Judge Whitehead looked sternly at Mr. Wilson.

"Let's go back, Mr. Bryon Boy Boyd. Did you tell him that a certain amount would do him in? Please answer yes or no."

"No." Mr. Boyd's face was quite red.

"Now, Mr. Boyd," Jerome said as he picked up the bottle again, "take this and read it carefully. Read everything on the label. You may do so out loud or silently."

Mr. Boyd did not take the bottle. He attempted to withdraw his hand. Jerome quickly pushed it toward him and he took the bottle. Jerome turned his back for two minutes, then looked back at Mr. Boyd.

Jerome asked, "Did you see any form of warning on the bottle as to limits or dangers? Does it say take one ounce, or two ounces? Does it say don't take more than 4 ounces in a given period? Did you find any instructions?"

Mr. Boyd, his face now a crimson red, said, "Like I said before . . ."

"Just answer yes or no, Mr. Boyd. That kind of response is all my questions calls for."

"No."

"Now, if you didn't warn Stephen Randolph and there was no warning of any sort on the label, perhaps he was totally unaware and acted as he did from lack of information."

"Your Honor," Mr. Wilson practically shouted, "this kind of questioning has no meaning. Mr. Boyd isn't on trial. The company that produces this drink is not on trial. Mr. Lee is using this ploy to justify the defendant's unlawful acts when everyone knows he or she must be responsible for himself or herself."

"Your Honor," Jerome said, "this young boy has been sold a substance that can be life threatening, that is extremely dangerous. He was not warned or instructed by the manufacturer or producer. He was not warned by the sales person as Mr. Boyd has admitted. I am not sure that he can be held totally responsible, perhaps responsible at all, for his conduct. Perhaps many must share in the outcome of this accident.

"Suppose we leave that line of questioning for the time being. I wish to review another area that all of us would be greatly concerned about.

"Mr. Boyd, you did say you sold this bottle or one like it to this young man?"

"Your Honor, this question has already been asked more than once and answered in such a manner as required. He has testified to that fact. What else can he say?" Mr. Wilson demanded angrily.

"Answer the question once again, Mr. Boyd. Perhaps Mr. Lee missed it earlier," Judge Whitehead said, a slight smile on his face.

"Yes, I sold that bottle or one like it to the defendant. I have absolutely no doubt. He is the one that bought it. That's the man there with the girl." He pointed directly at Stephen and smiled.

"I will keep you only a short time. Do you know how old Stephen Randolph is? Please answer yes or no."

"No."

"Then how can you be sure he meets the minimum age requirements to make such a purchase? It is my understanding that whiskey cannot be sold to a minor. Did you ask for his driver's license or other acceptable proof? You did ask him?" Jerome asked.

"Well, if a man . . ."

"No, Mr. Boyd, just answer my question. Again I believe it can be answered yes or no."

"No."

"Why not?"

"As I was about to say a moment ago. A man old enough to be a soldier, to fight for his country, is old enough to buy alcohol and drink it as well!"

"Is that what the law states, Mr. Boyd? Would you show us that in the regulations, as to whom you may and may not sell the . . . merchandise, as you call it? We are waiting on your answer, Mr. Boyd."

"Everyone knows a soldier can drink!"

Jerome turned to the judge. "Sir, are there reasons why this merchant of merchandise cannot answer the question asked?"

"Mr. Boyd, I will require you to respond," Judge Whitehead said. "Just answer yes or no."

"No! I cannot show you."

"Am I correct that the legal age is twenty-one or older?" Jerome asked.

"Yes."

"Therefore, if a person is born in 1946, is it not true that he cannot be twenty-one?"

"That's correct."

"Do you know, Mr. Boyd, what happens to those who do not follow the age requirement?"

"Your Honor, again I must remind the Court that Mr. Boyd is not on trial," Mr. Wilson shouted.

"Mr. Wilson, I am perfectly aware who is on trial. Are you suggesting I do not? I believe you are intelligent enough to know what I am saying!"

"Yes sir, Your Honor. I do understand." He sat down quickly.

"I have no further questions, Your Honor," Jerome said.

"I would like to redirect, Your Honor," Mr. Wilson said rising.

"Proceed."

"Mr. Boyd," Mr. Wilson asked, "did you force Mr. Randolph to buy this merchandise?"

"No."

"Did you encourage him to buy it?"

"No sir."

"So he purchased this of his own free will?"

"Yes sir. Of his own free will."

"It was not you that struck the vehicle Mr. and Miss McPherson were in?"

"No sir."

"No more questions."

Suddenly and unexpectedly they heard Judge Whitehead. "The plans of the Court are changed. We will ask Mr. Lee to be ready to call his witnesses the first thing in the morning. Then we will have the closing arguments. Again, I warn the members of the jury to not discuss this case with anyone. Court is adjourned until nine in the morning."

As they moved out of the courtroom April asked, "Why did Judge Whitehead change his plans?"

"I don't know. He seemed upset. It is possible he was sick."

"Will the whiskey deal make any real difference in the trial? A lot of people drink, Jerome. Actually you could have upset some members of the jury, perhaps most of them."

"That's possible. I could have. Actually the testimony of Mr. Boyd will not influence the outcome. I do believe he will close his store in Attapulgus. If not, someone may insist he close all of his stores. I don't like the man, April. Perhaps I was a little harsh on him."

"Jerome, can this case be won? I see no hope. I don't believe anyone can help Stephen. Mother has gone about as far as she can go. At one time she believed there was a chance. Can you truly give us hope?"

"Suppose Stephen was found not guilty as charged, can you and your mother believe he would be different? Sometimes, as I said before, when you win, you lose. Trust me. One more day will tell the story."

"You talk and have for weeks about no one will win if you win. I fail to follow your thinking."

"Trust me, April. I have to do certain things my way. In the end it could totally destroy Stephen. I said all this a dozen times before. I said this when I agreed to represent him. You will understand more before another day ends. I hope I will not be hated too much at the end."

"You are very complex. I can see more and more about your standards, your values."

"I hope you can understand how I feel. It is very important to me about how you feel. Tell your mother to hold on another day. I have an idea this will be the beginning and ending for what is to come. She may wish to make a civil and/or criminal case against Mr. Boyd. She can sleep over it for a few days." He added, "I'll see you tomorrow. Trust me."

CHAPTER 87

April was up early the next morning. A dim crown of crimson fire was brightening the east but the sun would not rise for several minutes. For April, this was one of the best times because in this quietness she was able to think more clearly. As she reviewed all that had occurred the last two days the case seemed crushing and conclusive. There was no chance for Stephen.

April took her chair much earlier than usual. The courthouse clock had just struck the half hour. As April looked to her left she saw Herman Wilson and Willis Cannington completing their strategy for the conclusion. The expressions on their faces showed complete confidence. She could understand why.

April looked behind her. Mrs. Lee and her mother were in place. She saw the haggard look on their faces.

She looked and saw Bruce and Agnes McPherson. There was a look of bitterness and unyielding hostility. April suspected there would be an undying hatred forever.

Little did she know that at that very moment Bruce McPherson was thinking about Lesa. She had great style, marvelous taste, both in dress and speech. If she had lived, she would have inherited a huge fortune, to which he knew several young gentlemen had given considerable thought. Yes, the fortune would have covered many little malicious sins of commission as well as omission. It would have disguised and blinded the eyes of her suitors as to her intellectual deficiencies. But with her death it had all become meaningless. He had come early to get himself mentally prepared for the day.

At eight forty-five April looked at Jerome as he entered the courthouse and could tell he had not slept well. His eyes seemed to sink deeper in his face. His hand was shaking as he picked up some notes he had made on a yellow legal pad. He seemed less cheerful than usual. His smile was less friendly. It appeared that he was attempting to muster enough strength for the day.

At nine o'clock as promised, Judge Whitehead once again rapped his gavel and called the Court to order. He could never remember seeing so many people in the courtroom. He hoped the fire marshal was not present. He looked below him and saw Herman Wilson and Willis Cannington, ready and eager. There was a poorly concealed smile on the face of each. Why not? He could never recall a case so completely dominated by the State. He could readily understand their elation as things now stood. The verdict seemed foreordained.

The judge then glanced toward the table for the Defense. He could see that Jerome was nervous; yet the look in the lawyer's eyes did not portray defeat, but sadness. The judge also noticed that Stephen sat motionless, showing almost no emotion, as he had throughout the two previous days. The judge wondered if Stephen had been coached in such a manner or whether this was Stephen's normal behavior. He suspected the latter. He thought Stephen was probably spoiled; yes, Stephen had possessed a car, a pocket full of money and more freedom than he had merited, as well as too much time and too little responsibility.

The judge's gaze moved to April Randolph. Her black eyes sparkled but this was nothing new. He had learned years before of her talents as a non-conforming individual. He nearly laughed as he remembered the stories Bruce McPherson and Sheriff Henderson had told. He remembered that she was the first to play on what had previously been a boy's only golf team and track team. She would not be easily tamed.

He looked into the eyes of the many observers. It was the same as it had been twenty years ago, or even two thousand years ago, when the Christians had been tossed into an arena with the wild lions and tigers. No, the nature and hearts of men were little different now than from the time of Nero.

He studied the twelve members of the jury and the two alternates. They would be happy to have this case reach a conclusion. On several occasions he had seen them close their eyes and swallow deeply as Herman Wilson had dragged the visual scenes of agony and death before them. Wilson had milked the udder dry.

Judge Whitehead knew that the sooner he started, the sooner he would have it behind him, so he had placed this case first on the calendar. With this case behind him, he would feel more relaxed. Suddenly a strange feeling came over him as he realized Jerome Lee had been too calm, too unemotional, too cool from the beginning. Did Lee know something that no one else knew? No, the case was cut and dried. He began the day's proceedings. "Mr. Lee, the Court is ready for your first witness."

"Thank you, Your Honor. But before I do so I wish to make some motions previously made as a part of the court record."

"This seems highly unusual, Mr. Lee. I can see little or no value in doing so. What exactly are you speaking of?" There was no smile on his stern face.

"Your Honor, I think two motions that were denied would serve a purpose."

Mr. Wilson stood. "Your Honor, I have no objections to his denied motions being a part of the court records."

"Very well, Mr. Lee, proceed," the judge said.

"The first motion was made requesting that the United States Army retain jurisdiction of the defendant as he was, at that time, a member of the United States Army when the accident occurred. I made such a request and sent copies to you, Judge Whitehead, to the District Attorney, Mr. Wilson and the foreman of the Grand Jury that was called and assembled to review this accident. I also sent a copy to the United States Army requesting they retain jurisdiction.

"After this was denied I moved to have the venue changed as I felt so much had been said and written that it would be difficult to assemble a proper jury. Again this was denied. I would simply ask this be a part of the court record."

"No objections, Your Honor," Mr. Wilson stated.

"Very well, Mr. Lee, I order this to be a part of the official record," Judge Whitehead said. "Now let us get on with your witnesses."

"Thank you, Your Honor." He moved forward slowly and said, "I call Jack Jenkins."

Jack Jenkins made his way to the witness stand. His clothing was sparkling clean and neatly pressed though this style suite had disappeared several years earlier. You could easily tell he was unsure and ill at ease as he sat down.

"Mr. Jenkins, please state your name, address and occupation."

"I am Jack Jenkins. I live on Randolph Place in Attapulgus. My address is Route One. I am a farmer, that is, I am foreman on the Randolph's farm."

"How long have you been there, Mr. Jenkins?"

"More than twenty-five years."

"Then you would know all the members of the Randolph family?"

"Yes sir, you can say that. I've been around all the children from the beginning."

"How would you describe the Randolph family as a whole? How would you evaluate them?"

Mr. Jenkins said, "Some things come to mind quickly. They are a close family. They stay at home most of the time unless they have business elsewhere. They work hard. All of them. Guess you might say there is not a lazy bone in the whole crowd. They help people who need help, go to church and support the school. But they are home people. They don't mess with the business of others."

"How have they treated you and your family?" Jerome asked.

Mr. Wilson jumped up hurriedly. "Your Honor, I can't see where this has anything to do with the defendant. Where is this kind of questioning going to lead us? I am not sure the Court needs a history of the Randolph family!"

Judge Whitehead glared at Mr. Wilson. "Why don't you let the Court decide what it needs! I have given you great latitude as I promised. The Court will continue the same practice. I trust we can avoid non-essential interruptions. Continue, Mr. Jenkins."

"As I said, they have been very good to me and my family. No one could have treated a family better. Because of this I can send my girl to college.

"They own a big place. They once raised a lot of tobacco. They don't ask anyone, black or white, to do anything they don't do."

"So they have paid you and your family well? They have treated your family with kindness?"

Yes sir. I understand their pay scale is far above average. Caused some hard feelings, I understand, but they do the fair and right thing."

"Let's get to Stephen. Is he a hard worker?"

"Works as hard as his daddy did and no one ever worked harder than Mr. Joseph!"

"Have you known Stephen to be in trouble with the law in any way before this?"

"No sir. Never!"

"Now Mr. Jenkins, you don't know of any violation where he has been apprehended, fined or carried to jail?"

"Not to my knowledge and in a small town everyone knows everything!"

"Based on your personal knowledge, then, he is a good boy?" After asking such a question he wondered about the Hurt affair.

"Yes sir. I did hear he did not always study as he should but I guess most of us did some of this when we were in school."

"No more questions, Your Honor."

Mr. Wilson rose slowly from his chair. He knew he had irritated the judge and he needed to be careful. "Now Mr. Jenkins, how long did you say you had known the defendant?"

"All his life."

"But you are not with him every day, are you?"

"Well, I see him most . . ."

"Wait, Mr. Jenkins. You really don't know first hand what he does all the time, do you? You are not at school with him. You do not ride around with him. You don't know what he does at night. You don't know anything about his life while in the United States Army, do you?"

"No sir, but . . ."

"Do you know what he did on August 30th of this year? This was when he was home on furlough."

"I know he had an accident."

"Did you see him that day before the — the accident or the day of the accident?"

"I don't know. He was on vacation and not working. I saw him while he was home but I can't say just when."

"But you can't really tell the Court that you saw him on these dates?"

"No sir."

"You can't really say you knew what he was doing on many, many occasions?"

"No sir."

"I have no further questions," Herman Wilson said attempting to look less elated than he felt at the moment.

"Call your next witness," Judge Whitehead said.

"I call Sergeant Conners."

When the tall, weathered solder had taken his place on the stand, Jerome said, "Please identify yourself, your station and your duties."

"I am Sergeant Michael Conners. I am stationed at Camp Stewart, Georgia, near Savannah. I am a member of the United States Army. I have been in service eighteen years. My present assignment is working with the recruits. Some refer to our role as basic training for those entering service for the first time."

"Did you know a former soldier, Private Stephen Randolph? If so, how did you happen to know him?"

"Private Stephen Randolph was in my company. A company usually runs from ninety to a hundred and twenty men. I try to learn all my trainees by name. Yes, I knew Private Randolph. Most everyone in our company knew him."

"Why would you say that, Sergeant Conners? Is there some special reason?"

"Yes sir. The former Private Randolph was selected by his superior officers and his peers as the top recruit in his company."

"What criteria must one meet to qualify for such a prestigious honor?" Jerome asked.

"Well, we look at a lot of things, a lot of characteristics. We look at the physical aspects as well as the mental aspects. We look at the leadership potential. We look at the manner of performing as a soldier, which often differs greatly from that of a civilian. We look at how his peers accept him. We look at the individual as a part of a vital team. In all aspects, he was graded superior. I believe his chances of being selected for officer's school were very good. Yes, I believe he would have been selected. He was most impressive."

"You are saying, as I understand it, that he was made up of what one calls the right stuff? Am I correct?"

"Yes sir."

"How long have you worked with recruits, Sergeant Conners?"

"Three years."

"How would you compare him with the others that showed great potential?"

"I saw no one with greater potential!"

"Thank you. I have no further questions," Jerome said.

Again Mr. Wilson moved forward in a very deliberate manner. Then he seemed to pause, seeking the exact words he needed. He had sized up this man as one of high standards. "Actually, Sergeant Conners, just how long did you know the former Private Randolph? He is the one I am sure you recognize as the defendant at the table." He turned and pointed to Stephen.

"Three months, give or take a day or so. Recruit training, if successful, lasts three months."

"Had you known the defendant prior to the three months of training?"

"No sir."

"Did you associate with the former Private Randolph on a social basis?"

"No sir. Our superiors do not believe it wise to get too close on a social basis. Actually, for a recruit, there are no social events."

"Have you been associated with him since he returned home?"

"No sir."

"So what you are saying is that you have known the former Private Randolph in a military manner for only three months?"

"Yes sir. That is correct. I knew him only as a soldier in basic training."

"So you are also saying that on the thirtieth of August, you would not know firsthand if he was drunk or sober, or if he was driving thirty or eighty miles an hour?"

"I would not know."

"One last question, Sergeant Conners. Do you know if he is still connected with the United States Army? Would you know if he has received a discharge and if so, what kind of discharge?"

"It is reported that he is no longer associated with the United States Army. I cannot say with absolute certainty about his discharge as I have not seen the records."

"Those are all my questions, Your Honor, of Sergeant Conners," Mr. Wilson said.

"Redirect?" Judge Whitehead asked Mr. Lee.

"No, Your Honor."

"Then call your next witness."

"I wish to call Colonel Buckley Haley."

A man of medium height in what one may call middle years of age moved into the witness chair. He looked much like what one would expect a professional soldier and officer would look like because of his posture, his wrinkle free uniform and his close haircut.

"Colonel Haley, please give us your full name and your current assignment. Tell us what you do as to your assignment."

"I am Colonel Buckley Ace Haley. I hold the permanent rank of Colonel after a tour of duty in Korea. I serve in the Pentagon in Washington, D.C. I am associated with the legal department and do such legal duties as assigned. Most of my work deals with military personnel relating to conduct and military regulations and Codes of Law."

"Were you assigned, sir, to deal with a case associated with the former Private Randolph?" Jerome asked.

"Yes sir."

"Colonel Haley, please tell us of your role relating to the defendant."

"My commanding officer assigned me the responsibility of reviewing in detail the actions of one Private Stephen Randolph following an incident that occurred while he was on furlough."

"Please give us such details as you recall," Jerome said.

"We learned, through his brother, Charles Randolph, that Stephen Randolph had been in an automobile accident on 30 August, 1965.

Mr. Charles Randolph called on the morning of the following day, according to my records, reporting that then Private Randolph was in a Tallahassee hospital. The records show he was transferred the night of the accident from the Midway Hospital.

"I dispatched two groups to your area. The first went to Tallahassee to see Private Randolph and learn of his condition and needs. The records show this group did recommend he be transferred to our hospital near Washington for treatment and rehabilitation as soon as we were assured he could be transported safely. We felt we were better equipped to deal with his problems which required a number of specialists."

"Was this done?" Jerome asked.

"Yes sir. We moved him when we were told he could travel safely."

"You mentioned a second group assigned."

"Yes sir. We sent an investigation team to determine all the details relating to the accident on 30 August, 1965. They met with all officials they believed essential to get all details. This included, according to my records, the Georgia State Patrol, the Office of the Decatur County Sheriff, the doctors at the hospital and all other personnel that would provide a realistic picture of what occurred.

"The details of this report were of such a nature that the said subject, Private Randolph, was arraigned on criminal charges resulting from what was learned."

"Then what happened?" Jerome asked.

"I was instructed to make formal charges based on the facts we had learned and set up a time and site for a court martial."

"Did you do this?"

"I did. I had most of the details concluded which included a military tribunal, a prosecuting and defense team and other such details. There were charges ranging from the death of a victim to a half dozen lesser charges. We had set a tentative date in November. The United States Army prefers to always deal with our people who are a part of our service."

"Do you recall my visits with you in Washington, Colonel Haley?" Jerome asked.

"I do."

"Do you recall our conversation as to what was said or done or both?"

"I do."

"Tell us about it." Jerome went over to the table and picked up the communications that he had made a part of the court record.

"First, you wished to learn of the charges made against Private Randolph. We reviewed these in detail. They seemed basically the same as have been made in this court."

Jerome handed him a sheet of paper. "Do you recognize this, sir?"

"I do. This is a copy of the recommendation you made to me and to the United States Army."

"Tell us briefly what the request was or the essence of this communication."

"As an attorney for Stephen Randolph and his family, you requested, as strongly as it could be worded, that the military deal with the charges against the defendant, one Private Stephen Randolph. This paper also stipulates a request was made or a copy of this request sent to other such parties concerned such as Judge Whitehead, District Attorney Herman Wilson, and to the foreman of the Grand Jury. It also indicated copies sent to all concerned including the defendant, the defendant's mother and I believe the father of the other two parties involved in the accident. You stated that you believed justice could best be served by leaving matters in the hands of the United States Army."

"What were your feelings, your recommendation to me, Colonel Haley?"

"I expressed this in the same manner as you did. I, too, felt the military could serve best in this manner. As I said, I did not ever once suggest it be otherwise."

"Then why, Colonel Haley, did not the military deal with this matter? It seems it was recommended strongly by the two of us. It would seem that the Army, as well as the Randolph family, had made it well known as to their wishes."

"First, there was a request by your legal system here in this Decatur County to deal with the matter as they considered the charges most serious. My records show that the first request was denied. I thought that would be the end of the matter. It wasn't. Later I received instructions to muster this Private Randolph out of the Army and make him available to your judicial officials here."

"And did you do this?"

"I did though I was unsure of the wisdom of the decision."

"What was the basis that was used to get him back in Decatur County?" Jerome asked.

"Two points seem to be the reason for the change. The first point dealt with the death of another thus classifying it as a capital crime."

"And the second?" Jerome asked.

"The legal papers stipulated it was based on the Sixth Amendment to our Constitution in the Bill of Rights. I'm sure, as an attorney, that you know of the major points. It guarantees the right to a speedy and public trial. It guarantees one the right to be tried by an impartial jury of the state and district and county wherein the crime has allegedly occurred or had been committed. One is guaranteed the right to be informed of the nature and cause of the accusation, a right to be confronted with the witnesses against him and to have a compulsory process for obtaining witnesses in his favor. This is why I am here. It permits and requires me to be here. Lastly, the defendant cannot be denied legal counsel for his defense. I have been told you are his legal counsel and not an attorney appointed for that purpose by the State."

"Do you notice anything unusual about this event that differs from other such similar situations?" Jerome asked.

"Yes. One thing stands out very strongly. Usually if a request is made to have one tried back home, shall we say, the request is made by the defendant rather than the State."

"Please explain."

Sometimes it can be an advantage to the defendant to have it moved to his home area, moved back among friends. We call this 'home cooking.' But this is the opposite. The State made the request. I have given you the reasons earlier."

"What else can you tell us about this matter?" Jerome asked.

"Nothing more than I received instructions as you see. These were my orders from above."

"Did you wonder about this?" Jerome asked.

Colonel Haley smiled, "We wonder about many things from time to time, but not too much. In the Army you follow orders, not question them. A good soldier always follows orders. One who expects to make a career of the military learns this quite early!"

"So you don't really know what took place, Colonel Haley?" Jerome asked.

"I received a directive, an order, to move as I have done. Again the only explanation that was made to me I have testified to."

"You do not wish to speculate?" Jerome asked.

Mr. Wilson jumped up and said, "Your Honor, he has answered that question three times already. We have plowed this ground over and over."

"You," Jerome said, "would not wish to speculate on some home cooking?"

Mr. Wilson shot up again as the Court heard Mr. Lee say, "I withdraw the question.

"Now, Colonel Haley, one last item." Jerome moved back to the table occupied by Stephen and April and picked up a document and moved once again before the witness stand.

"Sir, do you recognize this document?"

"It appears to be the Document of Release relating to the defendant."

Jerome handed him the document. "Please examine it. Is this the Document of Release?"

Colonel Haley looked carefully for more than two minutes, then responded, "This is the Document of Release for one Stephen Randolph. I am sure."

"How can you be sure?" Jerome asked.

"I wrote it as instructed by my superiors. It is all properly signed on the last page."

Jerome turned toward Judge Whitehead. "I wish to place this as evidence for the Defense. I believe you and Mr. Wilson have a copy."

Mr. Wilson said, "I have no objections, Your Honor."

Judge Whitehead said, "Let the record show that the Document of Release is a part of the record."

"No more questions, Colonel Haley," Jerome said.

Herman Wilson moved in close to the witness stand. "Colonel Haley, isn't it true that the Army releases, at times, when a death is involved? Are these not serious accusations?"

Colonel Haley gave it a few seconds' thought, then responded. "It does occur occasionally in peace time but very seldom in time of conflict. I believe this is the only way I can respond. We are at war!"

"Colonel Haley, would it not seem fitting and fair that this case be returned to our county as the Sixth Amendment suggests?"

"I believe this relates to civilians as far as I can determine. Perhaps this proves there are exceptions. I am in no position to question the process beyond what I have said."

"Did you say, Colonel, the nature of the discharge for the defendant? I would think you know."

"It was not an honorable discharge."

"Then it must have been dishonorable?" Mr. Wilson stated.

"Yes. That is so," Colonel Haley said.

"No more questions, Your Honor," Mr. Wilson said.

"Redirect, Mr. Lee?"

Mr. Lee stood, "I repeat a question asked earlier. Were not the recommendations of the two of us to let the military deal with the matter?"

Mr. Wilson started to rise but sat back down as Colonel Haley spoke. "That was the recommendation of the two of us."

"Your next witness, Mr. Lee," the judge spoke.

"The Defense rests," Jerome said.

Judge Whitehead called Mr. Wilson and Mr. Lee to approach the bench. "How long do you gentlemen anticipate your closing statements to last?"

Mr. Wilson spoke. "I had thought an hour but as things now stand, I would say something less than an hour."

"Mr. Lee?"

"Less than an hour, Your Honor."

Judge Whitehead said, "Today we will return at one o'clock. Again the case will not be discussed by the jury. The jury will leave the building first." He moved toward his chambers.

CHAPTER 88

As April and Jerome approached the restaurant, April said, "I am going to miss Don, Nathan, Harry and Howell. They have, from time to time, made many interesting observations. This will be our last time. Will not the case end this afternoon?"

"Yes. I'm sure this is so. It will end today. The jury will not be long in their deliberations."

"No, I guess not. All the evidence seems very clear. Jerome, you saw this from the beginning?"

"Yes. Let's go on in and get a bite as I will need to return to my office before I return to court." They took their seats once again in the semi-closed booth and listened.

"Harry, there is no way in hell that young Lee and the girl can pull this one out. They haven't had a case to work with from the beginning."

"Fellows, why do you suppose Lee called only three witnesses? Two of the three were military people. They can't help him. The boy is no longer in service. Besides this brought out the fact he got a dishonorable discharge. Wilson pounced on this like a chicken on a June bug."

They heard a laugh as one spoke, "Who could they call? No witness could help!"

"The jury won't be out an hour. Randolph will be found guilty on all charges!"

"Yep. I agree. Wilson will get that jury so worked up that it will not take much time."

"You know, Nathan, it is so sad to see a young drunk fool do this to anybody and especially a respected family like the McPhersons. I'll bet that young McPherson has wished a thousand times he could have died as his sister. What's he got to live for?"

No one spoke for several seconds, then they heard, "Remember last time three years ago? I told you that Lee and the girl would get ole Maybe off. They did. Wilson said it was like saving a person in the movies. Well, they might just do it again! There is something here that hasn't met the eye. We have missed something. Yes sir, there is something we have missed completely. That Lee doesn't say much but he is no fool. I've watched his face as well as the girl's face from the beginning. The girl seems to be afraid. Her folks back of 'em are too.

The face of Lee, however, has a touch of sadness. Yep, more sadness than fear. There may be another rabbit pulled from his hat again. I'd suspect he has known where he was going from the beginning. Hell, man, lawyers always know where they are going from the start."

"Bull shit, man. Lee will be going but only to the bank. Bet he charges a whole heap for a murder case. They are going to burn that kid a new ass hole!"

"Only right that he pay. With the old man of his gone and no power in the right places you can add this one to Wilson's victory column."

"Well," another voice said, "I am going to miss that pretty little thing. Just like she was last time, same pretty face and a figure to go with it. Seems a little more mature than last time but if there has been a change, it was only for the better!"

"Yep, some got it all and some ain't got none. You hear some say all people born equal. She's living proof that it ain't so!"

Jerome felt April's leg touch his under the booth and they both smiled.

"How you reckon the girl feels about the blind boy? Someone said they once went out with each other."

They heard another voice. "Blood is thicker than water but deep down I suspect she has a soft place in her heart for him. I'll bet she is that kind of girl."

"Hurry, fellows. Harry can't wait to see that pretty young thing one more time. We don't wanna miss the finish. Be like missing the last reel of a movie or the last chapter of a book."

Jerome and April heard a shuffle of feet, then a voice, "Well, at least they didn't hear what we said this time. Glad we changed to another booth."

After a few seconds of quietness, April took Jerome's hand and held it to hers. "It doesn't look good, Jerome. There has been no chance from the beginning. You were trying to give our mothers some hope. I can see more clearly now why you recommended the military be responsible. We were so wrong to insist you do this against your wishes." She looked into his eyes but could not guess his thoughts.

Finally Jerome spoke, his facial expression stern and serious. "This afternoon will be difficult, most difficult. I don't believe you understand the significance of what will take place. Yes, it will be a difficult afternoon for so many."

"I wish Mother was not present. This is going to kill her. If he is found guilty, and certainly he will be, when will Judge Whitehead pronounce sentence?"

"I can assure you he will not be sentenced today. Now why don't you go on back to the courtroom and make an effort to comfort our mothers. I'll be on in a few minutes. I will be delayed only a short time."

Five minutes later April was moving down a crowded aisle in the courtroom when she saw her four restaurant friends. They seemed quite excited about something. She reached the row of seats they occupied and touched one on the shoulder. "If it isn't my good friends, Howell, Nathan, Don and Harry. It's nice to see you again! Three years have passed and you don't look a day older." They smiled.

One said, "Well, at least you didn't hear us this time. We switched to another booth." He beamed in a more than generous manner.

April smiled lavishly and responded, "So did we. I just hope Jerome can pull another rabbit out of the hat. I believe that is the way one of you expressed it." She winked at them and they turned more than a modest pink. She moved in the direction of the two mothers with a half-forced smile on her face.

"Jerome said to tell you it would all end this afternoon," April said, the forced smile still remaining.

Martha attempted to smile. "I am so afraid. I see so little to be cheerful about. It would have been better the other way but I couldn't let myself think about my baby being a prisoner for such a long time. I had to do what I believed best at the time a decision was made. You know, I wonder if my children, when they are parents, will think the same way.

"I have thought about what you said in your graduation address. 'Let us fall on our faces and give us time to pick ourselves up.' Yes, I believe you saw the true picture that I failed to see as well as many other mothers. Now it becomes clearer."

"Don't give up was the word Jerome asked me to deliver to the two of you."

"There is no hope, April." Martha's eyes filled with tears. "I guess I really knew that from the beginning. Sometimes we see only what we wish to see. I hope Jerome will not think of me too unkindly because I insisted. He has done all he can do. Please tell him that for me," Martha said.

April turned to Susan Lee. "Please look after my mother." She turned and moved to her place beside Jerome and Stephen.

Judge Whitehead, after seating himself, looked over his court. The room had never been so crowded. It was not unexpected. The attorneys below seemed calm but he had seen too many before. He knew that stomachs were churning. He looked at the jury. They were all in place. They seemed weary after hearing so much in two and a half days. He looked again at the crowd. It seemed that they too were here for a smell and taste of blood.

Judge Whitehead turned and faced the jury. "Ladies and gentlemen, you are about to hear what we refer to as closing arguments. The State and Defense, that is, Mr. Wilson and Mr. Lee, are given time to review and summarize the case. They will review, in part, some of the evidence you have heard. What they may say will not be considered as evidence in itself. Once you have heard the closing arguments I will give you some instructions as to what you are to do, what your duties will require.

"At this time we will hear from Mr. Wilson."

Herman Wilson rose from his seat in a slow and deliberate manner and approached the area before the jury box. His dark blue suit was tailored to perfection. As he approached one could easily recognize that he was filled with confidence. This would be another great moment before the hundreds that had gathered. All eyes, he knew, were upon him.

"Ladies and gentlemen, the State as well as myself thank you for the attentive hours that have been spent hearing this case. Your patience has been an object of beauty. No one could ask for more. You are to be commended.

"Earlier I had stipulated to the Court that I would take an hour or more but I believe this unnecessary. It is obvious to everyone that there has never been a more cut and dried case. Actually I am disappointed that you were required to give your valuable time in such a manner. We could have saved time and a great deal of Decatur County money had it been different.

"I will take a few minutes to review and summarize some of the main points, some of the meaningful evidence. It is really very simple. There is not the first thing that would require any form of speculation.

"This is the defendant, Stephen Randolph, sitting before you." Mr. Wilson turned slowly and deliberately toward Stephen, pointing a finger for more seconds than necessary.

"A few weeks ago Stephen Randolph did return here to Decatur County following a three months course of basic training in the United States Army. Shortly after he returned he proceeded to destroy the lives of an entire family. Let us look at the highlights of how this occurred.

"First he goes to a store, a whiskey store, and purchases a large bottle of whiskey. The bottle contained four-fifths of a quart. He then proceeds to drink large quantities and consumed more than half of this bottle, enough to make him drunk, twice drunk. We had two reports to verify this fact. He wasn't just drinking. He was drunk, very drunk.

"The second thing we know is that he gets into his fancy sport's car and drives like a mad man, drunk as he was, and proceeds toward Midway. We have evidence from individuals that he was driving at speeds far above the speed limit. Actually we heard the evidence that he nearly caused an accident earlier by driving at speeds estimated at eighty or more miles per hour.

"Seconds later, traveling at this ungodly speed, he crosses the center line and strikes a car head on, in which the occupants were Lesa and Victor McPherson. This beautiful young girl, just entering the flower of life, was struck and killed by this young man seated at the table before you. She never knew what hit her. Her body was so mutilated that it required blow torches to cut away the metal to get her out of the vehicle." Mr. Wilson turned once more and pointed his finger at Stephen. "This is the man that did it! She died at the hands of this drunken man we call Stephen Randolph.

"Also in the car was her brother, Victor McPherson. He is seated by his father and mother behind Mr. Cannington." Again he turns and points. "You will recognize him because of his dark glasses that cover eyes that likely will never see again. You will also recognize him because of an empty sleeve dropping by the side of his seat. His arm was severed beyond replacement. He will always be as you see him.

"Think of this young man a moment. He was a college graduate from the University of Georgia. He had completed graduate work at Harvard University in preparation to work with his father at the People's Bank.

"When you and I look at a beautiful sunrise, Victor McPherson will not see it. When you and I look at a gorgeous sunset, Victor McPherson will not see it. For him there will be no sunrises or sunsets, only darkness.

"You who are parents can envision the years and years of effort to prepare for a profession. In the twinkling of an eye all the dreams and aspirations we all have for our children disappear. For these parents nearly all the things meaningful for them have been destroyed. It is all gone, shattered for all time.

"You have all been presented with conclusive evidence of what happened and how it happened. We don't have to ask if Stephen Randolph was drunk, we know! We don't have to ask or wonder if he was speeding, we know! We don't have to ask who was on the wrong side of the road, we know! No, we don't need to ask who maimed and killed, we know! You know! I know! He did it!" Again he pointed at Stephen Randolph. "This is the person responsible."

"I suspect that if I could know your thoughts, ladies and gentlemen of the jury, as you have listened carefully for three days you have wondered and asked, 'Why do the innocent have to suffer and die while the guilty escape such physical harm and death?' I have no answer.

"What else is there to say? As I said, you don't have to speculate about anything. You know!

"In a few moments Mr. Lee will come before you. What is he going to discuss with you? I can only speculate. It is possible that he will tell you that all the blame should be placed on the whiskey dealer or the company that manufactured the whiskey. He should know better than this. No one asked Stephen Randolph to come into the store. No one made him buy the whiskey. No one made him drink the whiskey — not one drop. He did all of this on his own and he did so, so excessively, that a family was destroyed.

"I would more than speculate that Mr. Lee, my worthy opponent, will tell you that he was a soldier and was serving his country. This is commendable but it has nothing to do with what occurred.

"Mr. Lee recommended that this defendant remain in the jurisdiction of the United States Army. I fail to understand. It was here he committed these awful crimes! It was here he took the life of another! It was here he murdered a girl and left another in the state that has been described. Therefore, it is here he should be tried and judged in accordance to the Constitution of the United States, the highest law of our land and by the statutes of the State of Georgia.

"I really cannot imagine what Mr. Lee will tell you. I believe he may ask you to be merciful to this defendant. Yes, he may suggest mercy rather than justice." Again he points to Stephen.

"I could guess at another area or so. He may tell you he didn't know what he was doing. He may tell you he is a hard worker. He will likely tell you he was a good soldier. He may tell you that he was a wayward country boy, living out in a rural community where he had to attend a small inferior school and did not receive the opportunities of our urban youth. He may prey on your sympathy because of the recent loss of his father and brother.

"Lastly he may use insanity as a reason for his conduct, his behavior. You have not heard the first word of evidence relating to insanity.

"I know you will not be affected by this kind of talk. You heard the evidence. You will make your decision based on the evidence you heard. There can be no doubt but what you will find Stephen Randolph guilty on all charges!

"It is your responsibility to put this drunken creature, this foolish lad away before he goes out on another drunken venture to maim and kill again. He is a menace to society. You must do your duty!"

Mr. Wilson turned from the jury and looked at the three McPhersons. "I must offer an apology as I have opened the unhealed wounds caused by the defendant. There was no other way. I believe you will understand."

Herman Wilson walked back to his chair. His eyes, his expression told the story. He wanted this man destroyed as he had destroyed so many others.

Judge Whitehead let the noise remain for a few moments before demanding order. He understood people more than he admitted at times. Then he rapped his gavel and silence prevailed.

"Mr. Lee your closing statement," Judge Whitehead said. He wondered what Mr. Lee would say. Yes, as Mr. Wilson suggested, the boy didn't need justice, he needed mercy.

"Thank you, Your Honor," Jerome said as he moved forward toward the jury. He could see the seriousness on April's face. He caught a glimpse of Martha Randolph. She was as white as a freshly washed sheet.

"Before beginning, Your Honor, I wish to make a special and unusual request. I believe you would understand. Much, in fact, most of what Mr. Wilson said is true. I had not anticipated, however, nor did I understand nor do I see a reason why a very fine community came under such scrutiny and condemnation. I feel it only fair to have a few short minutes to respond and address such an unfair and unjust and uncomplimentary pronouncement of its people, its institutions and their way of life." He looked directly into the eyes of Judge Whitehead.

"In all fairness to a community and its people you may respond as requested. I must say I, too, failed to understand his reason or motive. I do not recall you ever making such a statement about his community or any other community. As a native of Attapulgus I would believe you are capable and qualified to respond. You may proceed."

Jerome moved forward toward the jury. He looked relaxed but serious. He made some eye contact with the members of the jury and gave a slight smile. They did not respond but he could see they were attentive.

"Ladies and gentlemen, you have been most attentive and patient for nearly three days. As I see you as individuals and as a group, I know you will be fair. That is all the defendant or myself have a right to expect. I join with Mr. Wilson in expressing my appreciation.

"It is with some apprehension that I add to your time of service, but as our Judge Whitehead has said, it would only seem fair that some response be made concerning Mr. Wilson's remarks as it relates to a community, its institutions and its people. Let me see if I remember what he said. 'A backward rural community where the defendant had to attend a small, inferior school.' I find this most objectionable as well as unfair. I do not believe this statement to be accurate.

"At the beginning I wish to say that the city where Mr. Wilson lives and in the city in which I work is a very fine and special place. If I did not believe so, I would not be working here. People speak very highly of Midway. The community is composed of fine people who have established fine schools and churches.

"Attapulgus is an old town. It is rich in history. There was a church there in 1830. A school academy was functioning in 1837.

"But let us talk about the present. Too many have lived off the past. How should a community be judged? First and foremost by its people. Secondly, by the institutions. They cannot be separated.

"Attapulgus is incorporated with a city government functioning. They have departments of safety, water and sanitation. Most of the residents are members of the local churches. There are few who do not participate.

"They have recreation programs for the youth as well as the adults. There is a nice swimming pool with added facilities. There is a golf course in the community.

"Mr. Wilson seemed to give special attention to our school. He described it as 'a small, rural, inferior school.' It is small and it is rural. I agree with this part of his description but I do not believe these two items make it inferior. Smallness may make it superior as all individuals get a great deal of assistance, attention and encouragement.

"The proof, however, is in the pudding. We send fifty percent to college. The State of Georgia average is thirty. Midway is thirty-seven. It is commendable that it is above the state average. Two students were returned home from college in ten years for inadequate grades. One returned later and graduated.

"Let's look at the curriculum. Attapulgus is accredited and offers all courses that Midway offers except four. We do not have football, band, driver education and sex education." This brought some laughs and the judge pounded his gavel.

"Our athletic program is successful in basketball, baseball, track and golf. The Attapulgus Senior Classes have the highest grades in the county for the last twelve years. They have recently had first and second place winners for the state in public speaking.

"Two of your fine doctors in Midway are graduates of Attapulgus in 1932. The Chief of Staff at Emory Hospital in Atlanta is a graduate of the school. I could go on and on.

"Our graduates have had one divorce in the last twelve years. A mental problem was the cause of the one divorce.

"Up until this week no one from the school was involved in anything more than a speeding fine or parking ticket."

Suddenly Jerome stepped back three steps, turned and faced Judge Whitehead. "Thank you, Your Honor, for the opportunity to talk about Attapulgus, a small, rural community." He turned slowly toward Mr. Wilson but could not catch his eye. He surveyed him with undisguised distaste.

"Now let us put this aside and return to the purpose of our being here. Let me see if I remember some of the things I may use, according to Mr. Wilson, to defend my client. Insanity? No, this young man is sometimes foolish but not crazy. He is young but I will not use youth or insanity as an excuse. Hard working? Yes, indeed, but this will not be used as a defense. Death of family members? The Randolph family has seemingly had more than their share but, again, this is not a defense for his actions. A member of the United States Army? He was. No, he didn't flee to Canada and I commend him for this because so many do not seem patriotic. The merchandise dealer, that is, the whiskey dealer and the product? No one, as Mr. Wilson said, made him make the purchase or consume the alcohol. I do not feel kindly, however, toward anyone who sells whiskey to minors. No, none of this will be used for a defense." Many present looked at each other, wondering what defense he would use or what he would say next.

Jerome moved a step closer to the jury and said, "This day, ladies and gentlemen, will go down as the darkest day ever in the history of jurisprudence in Decatur County. I wish . . ."

There was a shout from the rear of the courtroom. "Hang the son of a bitch! An eye for an eye!" Everyone looked in the direction from which the voice was heard.

Judge Whitehead rose quickly from his seat, pounding his gavel. "Sheriff, remove this person from my court. Take him to jail and I will make contempt charges." He pounded his gavel again and again. The man rushed from the rear of the courtroom with the sheriff in hot pursuit.

When order was restored, Judge Whitehead said, "I'm sorry, Mr. Lee. But you may be assured one further outburst will bring about contempt charges and an empty courtroom. Please continue."

"Thank you, Your Honor. I believe the gentlemen who spoke misunderstood the meaning of my words." He turned to the jury once again.

"I will review the events from the point that Victor McPherson and Stephen Randolph were transferred to the Tallahassee Hospital from the Midway Hospital. I do not disagree with any evidence presented before this time.

"Victor and Stephen were transported to the Tallahassee Hospital on the same evening, the day this tragic affair occurred. In time Victor was returned to Midway in the condition Mr. Wilson has described. Stephen Randolph was transferred to a hospital near Washington, D.C., for rehabilitation. At this time the defendant was considering the military service as a career. I believe this commendable that one would offer his services and his life, if necessary, to protect his country in which all of us are a part.

"Meanwhile, here in Decatur County, a Grand Jury was assembled to review the alleged crimes committed by the defendant. They found several true bills of indictment against him that varied from drunk driving, speeding, driving on the wrong side of the road and vehicular homicide.

"From this point it seemed that a tug of war began between the military and the legal system of Decatur County as to who would get or retain jurisdiction. You will recall that Colonel Haley explained this to us. He said as part of his evidence that I was present in Washington more than once representing Stephen Randolph and the Randolph family and that I made every attempt within my power to have the military retain jurisdiction. For a period of time the Army refused to release Stephen Randolph. It was explained that it was the custom of the military to be responsible for their own. I had believed the matter concluded. Then I learned later that an agreement had been finalized and Stephen Randolph was to return as a civilian for a hearing and trial here in Decatur County. I believe Mr. Wilson expressed himself in support of such action. I felt then as I do today that this was a tragic mistake. True justice could have prevailed in the military. But, as you know, this was not to be." Jerome moved slowly back to the table for a drink of water. He moved unhurriedly. Everything had become quiet and still as everyone was waiting for him to continue.

This time Jerome got a little closer to the jury box and continued, "I cannot tell you how the transfer was accomplished. I suspect only a few know and most of us will never know. Should we not ask if it was done because there were those who didn't trust the military? Was it done to get this unfortunate man back in front of his home folks so he could be humiliated? Was it done because there were those who sought vengeance rather than justice? I am not sure the reason is important now but I will say a great pressure was applied, some very strong influence used, to cause the United States Army to reverse itself and get Stephen Randolph returned. This must have been a great pressure and greater influence to have the defendant released in time of war.

"Those who demanded he be brought back, that he be returned, made a serious error. Yes, I think these people did not have justice in mind. They were greedy. They demanded a pound of flesh. They were vengeful. Yes, this was a tragic mistake.

"Before proceeding, however, I want to say I agree with everything your fine District Attorney said in his closing arguments with two exceptions. I have addressed one with Judge Whitehead's permission. The other will have no significance as to the case. But those who choose to be merchants of whiskey, that sell to minors, have little concern for people, only themselves.

"Yes, our District Attorney, the Honorable Herman Wilson, has described the accounts of the evidence clearly, precisely and correct. The defendant did get intoxicated, drunk, if you please. He did drive his car on the wrong side of the road with excessive speed and did strike the car driven by Victor McPherson and occupied by his sister Lesa McPherson. It did result in one death and another maimed for life. I also agree that it had a profound effect or impact upon the lives of Mr. and Mrs. McPherson. Life can never be the same for either. Their dreams are shattered forever."

Once again Jerome returned to the table and drank some water. Then he whispered to April, "The next ten minutes will decide everything." He returned to his position in front of the jury. The courtroom seemed so quiet that it was eery. In his hand now he had a legal size folder.

"Listen to me carefully, ladies and gentlemen. The entire case will center around what I am about to say. In the process of this special group getting Stephen Randolph released and discharged from the United States Army, it would appear they did not read of the conditions upon which he was released.

"Here is the document or a copy of the document relating to his release, all sixty-seven pages. It is signed by the proper officials of the military as well as the proper officials of Decatur County. As you know our government can't say good morning in less than fifty pages of fine print.

"The conditions of his release are stated on page forty-seven. They are irrefutable and incontestable. It states very clearly that a release for the prosecution of a military person cannot be permitted in time of war unless the offense is a capital crime of the first or second degrees. It's all there for you to see. I have asked that this document be a part of the court record and be placed as a part of the evidence in these proceedings. I cannot tell you why he was returned unless the officials did not read the details or perhaps they felt they could do as they wished once he was returned.

"So, it comes down to this. Stephen Randolph must be charged with murder in the first degree or murder in the second degree. He cannot, I repeat, cannot be charged with a lesser crime because the United States Army refuses to release one except on one of those two charges in time of war.

"Suppose we look at murder in the first degree. In simple lay terms it means that a person has taken the life of another deliberately, pre-planned in advance. Certainly that is not the case here.

"A review of murder in the second degree means exactly the same as murder in the first degree except it was not pre-planned but was deliberate and intentional. Again, this is not the case!

"Stephen Randolph must be charged as prescribed and stipulated in this release document to which both parties have agreed. There isn't a jury anywhere that could believe Stephen Randolph deliberately attempted to kill Lesa McPherson. You know that! I know that! Why, he didn't even know Lesa McPherson.

"Later Judge Whitehead will explain the charges agreed upon between the United States Army and the local officials."

Once again Jerome moved back to the table. He saw the naked terror in the eyes of Mr. Wilson as he thumbed through the document of agreement. He noted that Willis Cannington's face was red as a beet as he stared in disbelief. He could see the anger and hate in the eyes of Bruce and Agnes McPherson. He saw a half smile on the faces of April and their mothers.

Suddenly everyone in the courtroom seemed to talk at once. Again Judge Whitehead pounded his gavel but he knew it would last for a minute or so. He could understand. In a matter of a few minutes there was quietness again as everyone wanted to hear Jerome Lee.

In a calm voice Jerome continued. "Someone wanted this boy returned here in order to seek revenge. Someone wanted and demanded that pound of flesh. Now, because of this, justice cannot prevail according to our Code of Laws. Why, he cannot be charged with any crime other than the two in the document that I have presented to you. He can't even be tried for drunk driving, speeding or driving on the left side of the road. Someone has stepped up and smashed justice in the face. The scales of justice can no longer remain in balance.

"If I could hear your thoughts, you would be saying that this young man, who has committed several offenses, is about to get away scot free. At the moment I would guess that you feel that someone should be blamed. I would feel the same way.

"It is possible that you may wish to blame me but I have done only what was required of me. It is my responsibility, according to my oath that I took upon being admitted to the bar, to provide the best defense that I am capable of providing. I have not misrepresented anything to anyone. Yes, you will remember my repeated request to let the United States Army be the one to bring charges.

"If someone is to blame, perhaps you should consider the unknowns. Who was responsible for the return of Stephen Randolph? But justice, in a sense, will prevail much more than one has likely envisioned. Though Stephen Randolph will be legally pronounced not guilty as charged by the Court, he will never be free a minute or an hour or a day as long as he lives. Every time he closes his eyes he will see this beautiful girl whose life he has taken. Every time he opens his eyes he will see a young man who cannot see again, if the evaluations are correct. Yes, he will see a disfigured face and an empty sleeve hanging down. Dark glasses will cover the eyes that will miss all the beauty of our world. Every time Stephen Randolph sees his parent or other parents he will be reminded of a man and wife from whom he has taken all that is important to them and there will always be an empty seat at the table. All the joy and sunshine has been removed from them forever. He will always remember that he was totally responsible.

"Stephen Randolph cannot find any excuse for his actions. He cannot say that his father whipped him, that his teacher disciplined him unfairly, that the policeman chased him or that the preacher lectured to him to cause this drastic error. He can find no excuse. He did it all alone.

"As Stephen Randolph was growing up he always found excuses or reasons to place the blame elsewhere. If he succeeded at something, he accepted all the credit. If he failed, there was someone else to blame.

"At night when he attempts to sleep he will find many nights in which sleep will not come. When he rises, he will know he has another day to face. He will be subjected to external and internal damnation! How long will it last? Perhaps for the rest of his life. He may be able to get away from his family, his old friends, if he has one or more left, and his neighbors. But he can never escape himself. He will never be free again.

"There is more punishment. A civil case is pending. He will lose all of his material possessions. All his interest in Randolph Place will be taken. For one who has never been denied anything, this will add to his pain.

"He must, in time, consider his life beyond this life. This will take on a deeper dimension as he grows older. Yes, he has a long road ahead.

"How much better it would have been if he could have paid his debts in a different way. Colonel Haley recommended this. I recommended this many times during the period prior to his discharge.

"I do not feel good about my role in this matter. Many of you may doubt this, as winning seems most important to nearly everyone. For some it is everything, the only thing. Not so! I repeat, not so! This is an empty victory. I am sure I, too, will be reminded of today for the rest of my life. Yes, I will wrestle with my conscience for a long, long time.

"Then you would ask, why did you do it? Why? Why? I know the answer. I have thought of nothing else for days.

"Esau was a traitor to himself. Judas Iscariot was a traitor to Jesus. Benedict Arnold was a traitor to his country. I am a traitor to justice.

"Esau sold his birthright for a mess of pottage. Judas Iscariot sold his Savior for thirty pieces of silver. Benedict Arnold sold his country for a British commission. I sold myself for the love of three women!

"There are no winners here today. The McPhersons lost their only daughter and a part of their son. The jury has lost because the law will require them to find the defendant not guilty in a decision in which they have no choice. Judge Whitehead has lost because he has seen the scale of justice unbalanced. Mr. Wilson has lost because he prepared a near perfect case, which is his responsibility, only to see jurisprudence tossed aside. The people present have lost because they know, in their hearts, that justice has not prevailed. Yes, we are all losers. It could have been different, so different.

"Ladies and gentlemen, again I thank you for your service as members of the jury. It has not been a good day for you or me or justice."

Jerome walked back toward his seat, paused and said to Judge Whitehead, "Thank you for permitting me to defend a fine community and its people. I assure you I found more pleasure in this defense than the latter."

Jerome returned to his seat. As he did, the courtroom was alive with a hundred conversations. It was five minutes before Judge Whitehead could restore order.

The jury was instructed by the judge as to their responsibilities and defined very clearly and fully the meanings of murder in the first and second degrees. He then moved slowly to his chambers, as if the world had collapsed upon him. He seemed to have aged five years in three days.

Jerome looked at April and saw a face without any expression or emotion. For a moment he was stunned, then he knew the reason. He said quietly, "Let us remain. It is likely it will take only a few minutes."

April did not respond to his statement. She turned away and looked back at their mothers. Then she turned back slowly and asked, "Why? Why did you do this? My mother looks so sad."

Jerome paused to select his words carefully. "Did I not tell you and your mother a dozen times? Were you not warned? Was she not warned? Let us not pursue the matter beyond this point." He turned and looked down at his notes.

In twenty-two minutes the jury returned. Judge Whitehead took his place on the bench once again. "Has the jury reached a verdict?" he asked.

"We have, Your Honor," the foreman responded. "He handed the paper to Sheriff Henderson who in turn delivered it to Judge Whitehead. Judge Whitehead looked at the paper and read the contents silently and folded the paper. A moment later he looked once again at the papers that told of the verdict, as if he had not already looked. Again he refolded it. Then he said, "In a moment the verdict will be read. Before this happens I wish to thank the jury for their services. I will also demand that no one leave this courtroom until the jury has cleared the building. I will ask the sheriff and bailiffs to see that this order is followed. At this time the foreman will read the verdict."

The foreman stood and read, "We, the jury, find the defendant not guilty as charged." He placed a great deal of emphasis on the words "as charged."

Judge Whitehead looked down as Jerome and April and Stephen stood to hear the verdict. "May God have mercy upon you, Stephen Randolph!" He moved slowly once more to his chambers.

Stephen turned to Jerome and asked, "Why would I lose my civil suit if I am not guilty?" Jerome turned and looked away. With a hard look of mirth in his cold eyes Stephen moved into the crowd.

April said, "My God, Jerome, he didn't even thank you!"

"Why should he, April? I have just damned him for the rest of his days! It will be the greatest injustice bestowed on him in his lifetime. Both of us will find a great deal of difficulty in time to come."

April patted Jerome on the shoulder. "Let me see my mother for a minute." She moved in their direction. When she returned Jerome had gone. She looked about but Jerome was no where to be seen. She saw an envelope on the table with her name on it. She pulled out the single sheet and read the two lines: "Once again the guilty escapes so that the innocent may be spared."

CHAPTER 89

As soon as Susan Lee turned the key in the front door lock and opened it she heard the telephone ringing. She moved quickly and picked up the receiver. "Lee residence." She listened, then said, "No, he isn't here. I am sure he will be home soon. Do you care to leave a name or number?" There was a pause of several seconds, then she said, "Call again if you like." She heard the line go dead.

Suddenly she heard a noise in the back of the house. For a moment she was startled. Then she heard a voice say, "Tell them I am not at home," Jerome yelled impatiently to his mother. "I will not talk with anyone."

Susan, with some apprehension, approached Jerome's bedroom. She knocked.

"Come in," Jerome said.

"I just told a lie. I didn't know you were home."

"You did not know," Jerome said.

"I suspect there will be many calls. You do not want to talk with anyone? With your dearest friends?" She looked at his bed and noticed a bag half packed. "Jerome, I can't tell them you are not home. Talk with your friends. They want to congratulate you. Martha was disappointed she did not have a minute with you."

Jerome laughed, filled with bitterness and sarcasm. "Friends? I would be surprised if I have one true friend left!"

"You won, my dear son. You don't sound like yourself. Wasn't that what you wanted?"

"Call it winning, if you like, but I feel it was the greatest loss I will ever experience. I have destroyed everything that has real meaning. No one won. As I said in court, everyone lost. Like Lucifer, I chose to do what God alone can do, can control. I also fell, as did Lucifer. It is now a hell I have created for myself."

"Is this your way of saying that you should not have been a lawyer? Now please tell me where you are going. I had not heard you had planned a trip."

For a minute Jerome and his mother were silent. Then Jerome spoke. "I have been unable to forgive myself. How can I expect others to do so? How can I hope for divine forgiveness? Thomas Jefferson said an honest heart is our first blessing and a knowing head the second. I once believed I had obtained these blessings but now I have many doubts.

He continued. "I saw the whole picture. I was not naive. I cannot use ignorance as an excuse. As I have said before, I tried to justify my decisions by saying the innocent should not suffer but God has never hinted that they would not.

"I have seen many men who believe they are not as other men. They believe themselves stronger, wiser and superior to all others.

"I blame no one except myself. After all, an individual must be the last supreme judge of what is right or wrong. One must live and die on this basis. God made us but I do not believe I have listened to Him."

Susan had listened patiently to her son, knowing a battle raged within him. When he finished she said, "Jerome, I have been giving a great deal of thought in recent days about you."

"In what way? Please tell me."

"I think the only thing missing in your life is a family of your own. Certainly there is sufficient maturity. You have completed the training for your profession. Your available income has reached a point that is adequate to support a family. I believe that is the one thing that would make your life complete."

Jerome looked at his mother. It was obvious she was both sincere and serious. "Mother, I must confess this has entered my mind from time to time. However, I do not believe most women are capable of love, real love, as the two of us would define it. I believe, at best, only a few have this capacity. I suspect for most it would border on frivolity. As I look about me I find they want pretentious houses, enough clothes to fill a dozen closets and big prestigious cars filling a garage. They would want bridge, tea and cocktail parties so they could show off their materialistic world.

"Some would want children, then would spoil them so much that they would only torment others. On the other hand there are those who would not desire any children. They would not want their time cluttered with something that important. They still prefer acting like children themselves.

"Men should watch carefully and wait. They cannot be too careful. For me, I could only hope or fear, pray or curse, love or hate. Why take such chances when the odds are not in one's favor?"

"My son, my son, the only two real loves in life are for a mate and family. Do not seek the perfect one because she is not to be found.

Yet, there are a few left who could love with the type of love that even words cannot describe.

"Perhaps a few days away will help you. Yes, I believe it would. But mothers always like to know where their sons are and perhaps have some idea of the duration of their stay." She smiled as only Susan Lee could smile.

Jerome said, "Please call my secretary, Barbie Adamson, and tell her I will be away a few days. I will leave a note under my pillow as to where I can be located. If you don't look, you will not know when you receive calls for me. I will be back Sunday afternoon."

"I think Martha will be disappointed," Susan said. "What shall I tell her?"

"Tell her the truth. Tell her I needed to get away. Martha, of all people, will understand." The telephone rang.

"Give me ten seconds and you can tell them I am not at home." He smiled, kissed his mother, grabbed his bag and rushed to the door.

Two hours later Jerome checked into a motel at Mexico Beach. Only a few from Canada visited this little Florida town in the winter. He decided to go walking on the beach. He could smell the salt in the water, as well as a faint smell of the paper mill at Port St. Joe located a few miles to the east. This was what he felt he wanted and needed. He felt this solitude would heal some of his wounds.

For four days and nights Jerome walked and rested. He had been much more tense than he realized. Yet his problems did not go away. When he walked his mind focused on one courtroom scene after another. He could see the faces of the jury and know they were ready to put this boy away. He could see Judge Whitehead pounding his gravel in an effort to restore order. He could see Herman Wilson and Willis Cannington nodding their heads in agreement as they planned their strategy. He could see his mother with Mrs. Randolph as they attempted to comfort each other but their expressions told him that all was lost.

From a restless sleep Jerome would awake and he seemed to hear the words of April once more. "Why? I cannot understand. It seemed so unnecessary. Why did you do this to my mother? She looks so sad." Jerome could see the dark, darting eyes and the serious look upon her face. Then he remembered his response. "Did I not tell you in advance? Let us not proceed beyond this point." All of this filled his mind.

Jerome returned home at five o'clock on Sunday afternoon. "Welcome home, Jerome," his mother said. "You needed to get away for a few days and rest." The look on his face told her he had not resolved his burdens he had taken with him.

His mother continued, "You cannot believe the many, many telephone calls. There would have been no rest for you here. Why don't you come with Eric and we can see and hear a special musical program at our church tonight? I am told it will be the best ever. You always have liked music and song."

"No. I'll get my thoughts together and finish some legal work that is past due." Jerome said.

His mother said, "You can't continue like this. The war is over. The battle is won. Nothing anyone can do will change the outcome." His mother hesitated, then said, "Why don't you go ahead and say I caused this? Why don't you go ahead and say I told Martha you might be able to save her boy, her baby? If one is to blame, I am most responsible."

"No. Please don't feel like this. You are not to blame. I took the case. I did it on my own. No one made me. I have no blame for others, only myself."

"You are sure you do not wish to go with us?" his mother asked.

"I want to catch up with my work. I promised my client it would be ready Monday afternoon."

After his mother and brother left Jerome spread his material out on the breakfast table. As he picked up his pen, he returned it to the table and moved toward the telephone and took it off the hook. Then he started on his work. He had just separated his material when he heard a knock on the door. "For God's sake," he said in a whisper as he pushed his chair back. Again there was a knock. As he moved toward the front door he said in a voice all too high, "I'm coming. I'm coming. I'll be there in a second."

He opened the door swiftly in a half measure of anger and looked into the face of Stephen Randolph. Jerome made no effort to disguise his surprise or uncontrollable anger. This was the last person he expected to see. He could not remember later how long he had remained at the open door in a speechless state.

"Will you invite me in?" Stephen asked. There seemed something different about his voice, his face. Jerome could never remember seeing him look as he did at this moment.

"Come in, Stephen. Sorry to keep you waiting. I must admit you are the very last person I expected to see. In fact, I had expected no one."

"I am likely the last person you wanted to see. If the situation was reversed, I would not care to see you either. In fact, should that be, I'd refuse to see you. But I hope you will forgive the unexpected intrusion and see me for a few moments."

They walked to the breakfast room table where many sheets of paper filled the surface. Jerome picked these up and placed them in one pile. "Please sit down. Mother left some coffee. Perhaps you would drink a cup?"

"That would be nice," Stephen said. "Without cream or sugar."

When Jerome returned with the steaming cups he noticed for the first time that Stephen was holding a rather large envelope. "It's piping hot, as my mother describes it. This is the way she likes it. Never saw a cup too hot for her." He knew he was simply making conversation for the sake of conversation, waiting for Stephen to tell him the purpose of his visit.

Stephen got right to the point. "First, I apologize for my behavior or lack of it. I have been awful, actually worse than awful. I didn't even bother to thank you. But I confess, this was nothing new. I doubt that I have ever really given concern or serious thought to anyone but myself. No one, and I mean just that, no one has ever had a poorer attitude, been more selfish or behaved as I have. So, at this point, what does one say? If I said I had changed or wanted to change, no one would believe it. I could readily understand.

"Four people, of which you are one, have given me a chance to do and be different. You have given me an opportunity to make my life meaningful and from this moment, so help me God, I will make a start or an attempt to begin to repay for my selfish, foolish and evil ways. I know this all sounds like empty words because you know me for what I am and have been. I will not make a further attempt to get you to believe me because, if it were reversed, I would not believe you, not the first word." Stephen paused.

"Stephen, I do know you. I have known you all my life. I must confess, therefore, that it will take a long time before I am willing to accept you or believe you. Your actions, for as long as I have known you, have spoken so loudly that I find it more than difficult to accept what you are saying, what I am hearing. I have seen some have a little remorse for a short time, then old habits returned. Forgive me if I am wrong but it will require more than a little time and effort before I can really believe. It will require a major change over a period of time, a long period of time."

"I understand. Again, if the situation were reversed, I would not believe the first word you spoke. There are few bad things I haven't done. I have been such a major disappointment to those who have loved me the most."

There was a pause and finally Jerome said, "I hope I haven't been unfair. It is not for me to judge others but we are told that by the fruits we shall know them. I will admit that you look different, your thoughts are different and you seem to see some things, perhaps, for the first time."

"I didn't come here tonight just to tell you I am different. I must prove that. It will take some time, not just a day, a week, a month or a year. Again I understand. But, I am here to ask another favor. I know you are one I can trust," Stephen said.

"I will listen," Jerome said. He hoped Stephen could not read all of his thoughts.

Stephen put a large brown envelope on the table. Jerome could see it was firmly sealed. He also noted that a smaller white envelope had been attached to the larger one. "I am going to stay around here through Christmas. Were it not for my mother, I would leave now but a family together is special at the Christmas season. Between Christmas and the New Year I will be leaving. At the moment I am not sure where I will go but go I must. In time, likely a long time, I will return but I have many things to do before this happens, things I must do first. To stay here would only remind many people of unpleasant events.

"Now, I have two envelopes as you can see, the smaller one attached to the larger. If, for some reason, something should happen to me before or after I leave home, I want you to open the smaller envelope immediately, at the very moment you learn of my death. I know there are those who feel so strongly that this is a possibility, a good possibility. I have caused a great deal of anger and hate.

"In the smaller envelope you will find some instructions. After these instructions have been completed, I want you to open the second or larger envelope. Again you will find some instructions. I know I can count on you to carry out my wishes. And . . ."

"Wait. Let me see if I understand what you are saying, what you are instructing. I should . . ."

"If I should die, Jerome, be it at the hands of others or by accident, this time I wish to be more prepared."

"Then you are saying, that should death occur, regardless of reason, I am to open the small envelope. Here I will find some instructions to follow. After these instructions are completed, I am to open the second envelope." He hesitated, then asked, "Stephen, this is not a way of saying that you have decided to take your own life?"

"No. I will not do that. There are two reasons why I would not do that. First, I am much too much a coward. Secondly, I hope for many years so I can make an effort to undo some of the things I have done. I know I can't give a life back but there are many things I can do. Again, thank you for seeing me. I had attempted to call more than once. I guessed you had the telephone off the hook.

"It would have been so much better had the military had their way. I think I would have felt I had paid for some of my crimes. But my mother felt differently. She placed undue blame upon herself. Few have mothers as the two of us.

"Now, I have two messages from the ladies. My mother would like to see you. I think she understands more than you might expect.

"The second is from my sister. April would like to see you. She will be at Somewhere Else for a time. She did not say more.

"Thank you for the coffee. You never really know another until they are tested under fire as the United States Army people say. In time I hope to have an opportunity to repay you. I want to show you what I can become. Goodbye, my friend." He rose, shook Jerome's hand firmly and said, "I'll let myself out." Quickly he disappeared into the night.

An hour later Eric and his mother returned. "Did you get your work completed?" his mother asked. "You have had company?" She saw the two coffee cups.

"No, I didn't finish my work. I had a visitor while the two of you were away, an unexpected visitor."

"Who?" his mother asked. "I thought you did not care to see anyone."

"I didn't. It was a surprise. It was Stephen Randolph!"

"What did he want?" Eric asked. "Let me guess. He finally got around to thanking you!"

"Yes, he did thank me. He seemed different."

"How?" his mother asked.

"It is really difficult to describe him. He seemed to understand himself for what I would guess is the first time."

"Then you believe there is hope?" Susan asked.

"Perhaps. But let's not get too hasty or excited yet. Let us wait and watch. He has or had a great deal of changing to do. By the way, how was your program?"

"You missed something very special, Jerome. You would have enjoyed the music and song."

Eric said, "There is talk of a second performance. Everyone should hear them."

Susan saw the envelope on the table as well as some of the papers. "Is this a part of your work? Did you leave it here for some reason?"

"That was given to me by Stephen. I am to keep it for him. I'll put it in my office safe tomorrow."

"What is it?" Eric asked. "It seems there are two envelopes."

"I don't know, Eric. He didn't say. I am to keep it until a given time."

"A given time?" his mother asked. "What you have said isn't very clear."

"It isn't clear to me either. It's all rather strange. In fact, everything about Stephen was very strange.

"I am going out for a little fresh air. I think I will ride around a while. I need to clear my head. Please don't wait up for me but I do not anticipate being out very late." He closed the front door behind him and felt the cool air of the December evening.

CHAPTER 90

Jerome could see the lights ahead. He could not understand April being here after dark by herself. There were two lights on the deck and the front of the house was well lighted. As he got out of his car he could see the water wheel as it made its continuous circle. He moved up the steps to the deck but he heard no sound from inside. It all seemed more than a little strange.

As he knocked on the front door he heard April's voice. "Come in. The door is not locked." As he pushed the door open he saw April sitting on the sofa. She had on a housecoat and bedroom slippers. The black hair fell about her neck. It seemed that she had been in deep thought as he saw no evidence of her reading. Except for her the room seemed empty. There was no television and the music was absent as well.

"Are you all right?" Jerome asked with some urgency. "Certainly you are not here alone? Why are you groomed this way? Are you ill?"

She looked at Jerome but did not speak. She remained on the sofa and nodded for him to take the seat nearby facing her.

After he had seated himself she asked in a soft quiet voice, "Why did you leave so suddenly? You rushed out of the courthouse before anyone knew. Why are you avoiding me? Why have you avoided my mother? You acted as if you were upset — angry!"

"It was all over. I was tired. I wanted to get home," Jerome said.

"There are those in our families that wanted to thank you, to congratulate you. Everyone seemed in such a state of shock that most had not let all sink in. Nothing seemed normal or natural." Again Jerome did not respond.

"Did you talk with Stephen tonight? I guess this is the reason you are here now."

"Yes. He spoke of you and your mother wishing to see me. But I don't think either of you really needed to see me. You have Stephen. That is what you and our mothers wanted."

"I trust he thanked you? I have never been so embarrassed and disappointed as he asked about the civil case, then rushed out."

Jerome did not respond to her question. Then he asked, "Why did you want to see me?"

"I needed you!"

"April, you have never needed anyone at any time."

"You are upset with me. Why are you so upset? I did not know why you did as you did. Is this not a fair question?"

"No, I believe not. The case is over. Let it be. Everyone was a loser. It is time to drop the matter — for now and for all times." He did not smile.

"Why was my question so unfair?" April asked.

"I can't believe you are asking this question," Jerome said. "Not now, not then. I asked both you and your mother to trust me. It is obvious that you did not. But there was a time you said you did. I believe all has been said that we need to say. I made it clear from the beginning what the outcome would be if we won. I must have said a dozen times that the price of winning would be destructive. It was necessary. I said as much at the beginning. It is equally true today. Did you call me to come for the reasons I have seen and heard?"

"No. I didn't. I asked you to come so I could pay a debt. I told you I would give you my heart and soul if you would save Stephen. It was not for Stephen but for my mother."

"Are you saying that the reason you are groomed as you are is because of a promise I did not ask you to make?" There was a slight quiver in his voice and the tone of his voice expressed a deep hurt.

"I always keep my promises and pay my debts."

"April, I'm not sure that there is ever a time one should give their soul to another. It is the one object that should not be given. It is the one object one should never accept. It is really all that one has. Do you not understand?

"I don't believe you know me at all," he continued. "I'm not sure you have ever known me. I am not sure you could ever know the real me!" He started to get up from the chair.

"Jerome," she cried out. "You must not leave me. For six years you said from time to time that the time has not come. I believe it has. I can see you are deeply hurt and that was not my intention — ever. I love you, Jerome. I've loved you every minute since I was thirteen. And don't you dare tell me that is my misfortune." Her eyes filled with tears.

Jerome looked away for several seconds. He did not feel he could look into her face, her eyes. As he turned he saw one of the bedrooms through a half open door. He could see her clothing on a chair. He saw the spread and sheet turned down. He looked back at her and knew the housecoat was all she was wearing.

Jerome turned and faced April once more. He looked into her beautiful sparkling black eyes as they glistened from the tears. "April,

I remember a little poem from years ago. I can't remember where I saw it. But it said something like this. 'Let love come last, after the lesson is learned.' Love, like anything of real value, must be earned. Love can never be bought at any price.

"Two people cannot survive successfully without trust because one can never know everything about another. Without trust as a prerequisite, there is nothing upon which to build. Trust is to people as the foundation is to a house. It is likely that two intelligent people may never understand each other and it is the trust that keeps them steadfast, that allows the differences to be resolved."

"But I do trust you, Jerome. I have always trusted you, perhaps more than any other. I want to live my life with you! Can't you understand that? This is not a point of trust, but understanding. Please believe me."

Jerome's expression did not change. He continued to look into her eyes. "There were four reasons, three important ones, why I pursued the case as I did."

"Then why don't you tell me?" April asked. "If you don't, I will feel you don't trust me. Doesn't it work both ways? You call it trust. I call it understanding. Two people, to be happy, should not only trust, but also help each other to understand."

Jerome continued. "There were four reasons, as I said. Let me review them with you because one or more you would not have known. First, I must compare Stephen with an alcoholic though I do not suggest he has reached such a point. An alcoholic can never really recover until he reaches the bottom. Oh, he will make his promises, all based on good intentions, but nearly everyone will find themselves breaking their promises because they believe there will be someone to catch them.

"There is no difference with Stephen. There was always someone there to bail him out, to catch him, to look the other way, to find and make excuses for him. First there was your father, as well as Joe. Then your mother continued the practice because of a feeling of guilt.

"He had to be stunned and shocked. He had to see himself as others saw him. He had to reach a point that he wanted to change. It all had to start with him.

"Perhaps a change has occurred. I thought I got a brief glimpse of that earlier tonight. Let us hope so."

"Could you not have told me this earlier?" April asked.

"I thought I did, though in different words. But it doesn't matter at the moment. Let me continue.

"We are in a war. Should one doubt it, ask Clint White. Since World War II we have been involved in many wars or clashes. Each time we have functioned as an individual nation or as a member of NATO or the United Nations. But, as well as you know your history, we have not been involved in a declared war. There is a difference. The United States Army, in this instance, acted on the basis of a declared war as to their policies and the release of Stephen."

"Why is this important," April asked. "You have lost me. Why are you telling me this?"

"The legal functions of releasing Stephen were based on the policies of a declared war. Some Washington officials, including Colonel Haley, had many doubts of their action and expected it to be challenged. He said an appeal could be forthcoming and the verdict could be voided or repealed. Should this happen, one of two things would have occurred. They could appeal to try on a charge of manslaughter or he could be returned to the military to face a court martial.

"Now, if the powers that be here in Decatur County had not believed that Stephen would be punished in the manner I described in the closing arguments, they would likely discover the actual status. He . . ."

"They could try him again? Would this not be double jeopardy?"

"I believe the proper grounds for an appeal would have permitted a second trial. If these forces feel Stephen will be or has been punished as I described, they may let it pass."

"There are other reasons?" April asked.

"Yes. I was told by some county officials that there were those who would take revenge on a personal basis. He was not safe. What has occurred should reduce such a threat or danger."

"There is still another reason?"

"This I am reluctant to talk about."

"Why?" April asked.

"Because I was wrong."

"I don't understand," April said.

"I decided to take it upon myself to play God. This was wrong, so very wrong. I could not believe that one who committed such acts should be excused from some recourse. I could not feel one should walk away free as a bird. Later I realized I had no right to judge but I could not see one escape after causing so much suffering and pain.

"For this I will seek forgiveness because this was wrong. I will seek forgiveness from those here on earth as well as the One above. I will never, knowingly, ever do such again.

"I told everyone in court why I took this case. It was for the love of three women. You knew that long before the trial started. I could blame them but that would be unfair. I do not blame them, only myself. But I would hope and expect such a request from these three would never be forthcoming again.

"Now you know the reasons, all the reasons. You may judge for yourself.

"I have a few more things to discuss, then I must go. April, I am not sure you know me, know the real me. I don't let many see inside. Let me tell you about the real Jerome.

"I am old fashioned. I want to be in a world where individuals speak the truth, even when it may produce pain.

"I want to see honest people, even when it means doing without.

"I want to see people that have a chance to improve their way of life, not by welfare but by opportunity.

"I would like to see people honored, not for acquiring great wealth, but for the use of it to make life better for the deserving.

"April, I hope you are not disappointed in that I do not choose to be rich. I have noted far too many are dissatisfied. Feed a man rich food, fill his closet to overflowing with too many clothes, put him in a big house, give him two or three automobiles and let him know his bank account is more than sufficient and he will die of despair.

"Richness, real richness, comes from other sources and fills the void in one's life. One must seek it, as it will likely not come of its own accord.

"I like to see people work. I deplore idleness and one who is lazy. I want to see callused hands and dirty fingernails. I want to smell the human sweat so that I may know he has done something.

"I want to see the Bible read by people as I find it the most interesting book ever. I believe Abraham Lincoln said that 'we have forgotten the gracious hand that preserved us in peace, multiplied and enriched and strengthened us; and we have vainly imagined in the deceitfulness of our hearts, that all these blessings were produced by some superior wisdom and virtue of our own. . . . We have become too proud to pray to the God that made us!'

"I am old enough to drink but I have no desire to go beyond a small glass of wine. I feel much too good to need stimulants.

"I am so glad that I was educated in a school of traditional values. Our three R's are about to disappear; students do not study and many teachers do not teach. We can't build a life, a country, a world this way. And along that line, I want a preacher who can stand up and say this is right and that is wrong; this is good and that is bad. As a great French writer said, 'Who knows how easily ambition disguises itself under the name of a calling, possibly in good faith, and deceiving itself, saint that it is.'

"I want to live in a place and with a person who understands the value of silence, sometimes total silence, so that one may ponder the million elements of our world, our universe.

"I want to live my life with a person who can accept the ways of life I have attempted to describe, that will not ask me to compromise my beliefs, my standards, and yes, even my soul.

"I am going home now. I do not wish either of us to say more at this time. Now, go dress and close up. I will wait in my car and follow you home. You must not stay here alone." In moments Jerome sat in his car and waited.

On Thursday of the following week Barbie Adamson approached Jerome. "Why don't you take a week off and get your head straight on your shoulders. I cannot recall you completing more than the one document you worked on at home. There is work up to your ears. Take a week off and get squared away. Your body is here but the real you is elsewhere."

"Where would I go? What would I do? Who would I do it with?" He finally gave a slight smile.

"I don't know, Mr. Lee, but it is becoming more difficult each day to tell two dozen friends and well-wishers that you are not available or cannot be disturbed. I am not sure I understand you. You won the battle of the year, perhaps the battle of the decade and you will not let anyone tell you how pleased they were or what a great job you did."

"I'll promise to be better next week. I need to get a different and better outlook. I am sure I have not been pleasant. My mother reminds me twice each day. I am, however, a bit curious as to what is being said but I have been afraid to ask."

"You name it, Mr. Lee and someone has said it." Miss Adamson blushed more than a little.

"You want to tell me?" Jerome asked with a slight smile.

"Yes and no."

"What does that mean? Now you are talking like an attorney."

"Some have said some kind things and others have been less kind. Everyone has an opinion. No one can seem to talk about anything else."

"Are you going to tell me? I am quite sure that many have spoken unkindly."

"The good news or the bad news first?"

"Perhaps the bad. If there should be some good news, let it come last."

Once again she blushed. "I am not sure you are being fair but . . ."

"No one said life was fair. Life is real."

"Well, here goes. You are a rascal, a scoundrel, a rogue, a villain, a scalawag, a trickster, a fiend, a snake-in-the grass, a deceiver, a scribe, a damned Pharisee, a sorry bastard and a first class son of a bitch. There were others." Her face was now a deep red.

"And someone said something good after all that? I can't believe there is anything left."

"Oh, yes. The descriptions seemed about equally divided. That should make you happy because ninety-five percent in the courtroom were not your supporters. Let's see. You are smart, well educated, brilliant, clever, bright, quick witted, alert, caring, spirited, competent, ingenious, perceptive, shrewd, a good looking son of a bitch and now probably the richest damn lawyer in Decatur County!

"I believe the second list more appropriate. Now I have no idea what kind of man I am working for." They laughed heartily for the first time in days.

"Do you have an opinion? What do you believe?" Jerome asked, still laughing.

"Oh, I think you hung the moon but you haven't seen me except as a secretary since the fourth month of the calendar year arrived in your life. So, if you don't get to work and get your mind off her, we are both going to starve to death. If April wasn't so perfect in every way, I would be jealous!" She returned to her office.

A few minutes later she called out, "Can or will you see Mr. Cannington? He said you would know why he needed to see you."

"Ask him to come in thirty minutes if he can fit it into his schedule."

"You are definitely the talk of the town," Mr. Cannington said when he arrived thirty minutes later. "You hold first place as the center of conversation around the courthouse and all the coffee shops."

Jerome said, "That is behind us, be it good or bad. I hope we can get the civil suit settled without another court battle."

"That would be nice. You are aware I set up the corporation for the Randolphs. I hope the Randolphs and McPhersons can settle out of court. Do you know of changes since the beginning?"

"Only as to the stock divisions. The two deaths changed the original division of the stock. I am sure you have reviewed the matter."

"Yes."

"Three thousand acres were added after you set up the corporation. They have retained two of the three thousand," Jerome said. "Currently there are seventeen thousand and six hundred acres."

Mr. Cannington smiled. "As I recall it was a two hundred thousand investment, an additional hundred thousand plus ten dollars an acre. We are talking about four hundred and seventy-six thousand dollars I believe."

"Yes," Jerome said.

"Mr. McPherson is not going to negotiate this figure. We both know he can prevail if we go to court."

"I have given it much thought," Jerome said. "I would recommend a settlement of that sum. I believe Mrs. Randolph and Stephen would accept this figure upon my recommendation."

"Then it is all settled?" Mr. Cannington asked.

"If both parties agree. I can let you know in a few days," Jerome said.

Mr. Cannington stood and held out his hand. "Again, congratulations on your victory. You have established yourself firmly."

"No one can compare with you, sir," Jerome said. "Everyone knows you are king. You have been for many years. You will continue to be."

Twenty-four hours later Jerome had set up a conference with the Randolphs at their home. He reviewed in detail his conference with Mr. Cannington.

"I'm sorry that April and Mary were not available. I'll consult with them individually," Mrs. Randolph said. "What is your recommendation?"

"I would accept the settlement Mr. Cannington and I have discussed. I would act immediately. There is a reason why time is meaningful."

"I don't understand," Martha said.

"If the court should evaluate the estate and base it on stock held, Stephen may be required to pay three to five times this sum. Just ten percent of the total assets would be more than three times this sum of which we have spoken. I hope I can have some final word immediately."

Martha said, "We will move immediately. Now, there are two other items. I have not received a bill for your services. Let us move on this very soon. Secondly, over the holidays, I want you to meet with us relating to several matters."

"Very good. I do not plan on being away. Please give me a few hours notice. I'll have the papers ready immediately on the civil suit. You need to be in a position to make this settlement and conclude this matter. It is nice to see all of you. I'll say goodnight and be on my way."

CHAPTER 91

Shortly after Stephen returned home Martha came to him and said, "I want you to know you are not alone. You may think so because of the weeks and months of confinement. Now that is behind you. You will want to make a new beginning. You must accept some help from others as you embark, then you will be able to move forward on your own. We will be available to assist, to encourage, to support.

"You are young. Your life is before you. It is not too late, though you will likely deny this consciously or unconsciously at the present." His mother looked into his face and, for the first time, saw a genuine expression of concern. She smiled and he returned the smile.

Martha continued to look at her son. His face seemed to express a feeling of trust. She could never remember seeing him as she saw him now. The empty feeling in Martha vanished and she could feel warmth, happiness and joy she could not remember feeling before.

Stephen looked into his mother's eyes and he waited for her to continue but she only looked and smiled in silence. Suddenly he felt a deep calm, the impatience and restlessness seemed to move from him completely. He could never remember feeling this way. There was a peace and rapture he had never experienced. There was a lightness that he could only describe as a type of tranquility. Was it joy? No. Joy was something one could know after success, after attainment. No. This was an awareness that the mean and selfish and shameful things of his life could be put behind him.

A week later Stephen said, "Mother, I need some time with you. It is warm outside today. Let us put on our coats and go out to the gazebo."

As they left the house arm in arm, Martha knew that something had occurred in her son's life. They made their way to Michael John's gazebo. The autumn flowers in the yard were rapidly disappearing. The leaves of the trees had turned a violent color of both scarlet and bronze and seemed to deny that winter was upon them and they would die so others could spring forth in a few months.

As they sat down Stephen said, "I hardly know where to begin but I must try. Since my entrance into this world, I seem to have been a millstone around your neck, not placed there by anyone other than myself."

Martha was about to interrupt and Stephen held up his hand to ask that she remain silent and listen. He continued, "I am sure you must have wondered what awful sin you had committed to deserve such punishment. But it was not you that sinned, but me. Now, someway, I want to start and spend the rest of my life attempting to right some of the many wrongs. I must start now, this day. Unfortunately, there are some that I can never right.

"I know now and can appreciate everything you have done for me. You have done too much for all of us and I am the only one that never showed any appreciation. Now I will start that long journey that will prove my sincerity.

"I suppose my greatest terror as a young child was a fear of rejection. It is a story, as Mike Harper says, of Cain and Abel. I especially felt rejected after the death of Father and Joe, though I had no reason to do so. Then following rejection comes anger and this is followed by a desire to do things differently from others, which often relates to sinfulness. That is the story of your foolish son. Yes, I suppose fear results when you don't care, when you hate and don't trust. You even get to a point you don't trust yourself.

"I have asked, in retrospect, why Father did not demand more of me. But it is not good for a son to speak unkindly of his father who loved him so much, likely too much. My father was a noble man. He worked harder than anyone I knew. I believe he was a good husband and I know he always meant to place his family first, sometimes, so it seemed, in a strange way. It is much sadness I feel for him.

"Years ago, Mother, you were the one I dodged. I feared you would change my world where a boy named Stephen was to be the first considered. Now I must prove to myself and then to others that I am truly concerned."

Stephen looked at his mother. He could see a sparkle in her eyes that had been absent for so long. It was as if sunshine pressed forth after a long period of gray and darkness.

"Mother, you gave all your children too much. Yes, too much love, too much devotion and too much of your time. You gave so much that there was nothing left for yourself. You even gave too much to my father. I was the only one that always received but never gave in return. After you had done this for so long it seemed too late for you to change. Actually, I never gave you a chance to change. When Father was living you looked the other way or remained silent to keep peace. There seemed to be no way to escape. Then, after Father died, you were to accept all the blame for my foolish ways. More importantly, I let you do it. It was so unfair to you. Now, if you still have this feeling, you must discard it. You must free yourself from this false feeling of guilt. Never again must you use this as a reason or excuse for my failure."

Martha looked at Stephen and knew, for the first time, that Stephen cared. She felt the weight of the world had been lifted from her shoulders. "You do not have any idea how good you have made me feel. I have clung to the umbilical cord until this moment. Now, my dear son, I believe it will not be necessary again.

"I believe it was Robert Louis Stephenson who said that 'an aim in life is the only fortune worth finding.' I believe you have this very aim and that it is not too late. It is a new beautiful beginning." She smiled and they walked arm in arm back to the house.

CHAPTER 92

Jerome and Willis Cannington concluded the legal papers relating to the civil suit of McPherson vs. Stephen Randolph. Martha had expressed that perhaps this would be an opportunity for her to see the McPhersons face to face. Not so. Mr. Cannington told Jerome, "I had hoped the McPhersons would come but there is still so much strong feeling, so much pain. I guess it will always remain the same. They have let anger, ill will and hurt crowd out the chance of feeling differently for the rest of their lives. It is sad."

Upon returning to his office Jerome was confronted by Barbie Adamson. "A call for you from your mother. She seemed quite excited. There was a depressed tone in her voice. I hope nothing is wrong. Shall I get her on the telephone?"

"Please. I will go to my office."

"Yes, Mother, this is Jerome. Is something wrong? You don't sound right. Are you all right?"

"I have the worst news ever. I can't believe it. I wish I could spare you," his mother said.

"What, Mother? What is wrong?"

"There has been a tragic accident about five miles out in the country. A house caught on fire. Stephen was passing by. He stopped and joined a dozen others who had gathered. The fire was completely out of control. As they stood there a cry was heard from within. Stephen dashed in against the advice of the others. He brought two young children out to safety, then he dashed in once more, even though his clothes were in flames, to save the third child. The roof crashed in on them and both were burned to death."

"Are you sure, Mother? This doesn't sound like something Stephen would do! Perhaps you are mistaken."

"No. I wish I was. There is no mistake. I am leaving to be with Martha. She seems much more calm than I expected. I am sorry I had to tell you this. Goodbye." The telephone went dead.

"Please open my safe," he said anxiously with a voice quite different. "Please hurry."

"Can you tell me what is wrong?" she asked as she turned the dial on the safe. "Your mother was definitely not herself."

"Stephen Randolph is dead!"

"You don't mean that someone in anger or spite has. . . ?"

"No. He was killed in an accident, a fire. He attempted to get some children out of a burning house. After he got two out, he rushed back in to get a third one. The flaming roof fell in. Neither got out of the house. I suspect the fire was not reported early enough for the volunteer fire departments to get there.

"When you get the safe open, please bring me the envelope with a smaller envelope attached that I gave you earlier. Then I will wish you to do a task for me. Call and cancel all appointments for the rest of the week."

Jerome opened the small envelope as he had been instructed. He read: "I want you to get the following persons together immediately: All of the Randolphs, as well as their spouses. Then get the Lee family, the Clint White family and the Jack Jenkins family. Add to this list Uncle Edd and Helen Hurt. Naturally Mike Harper will be there. He is always there when he is needed.

"When all of these are assembled, I want you to open the second, larger envelope and read to the group what I have written. Everything at this point will become clear." Stephen had signed and dated the communication.

An hour later each person had been summoned and had gathered in the den of the Randolph home. Everyone had become quiet as well as curious. Jerome said, "A few days ago I was handed two envelopes by Stephen Randolph. We had a short visit and I was amazed at what he said and how he said it. I had never seen Stephen before in this manner. He asked me to open the smaller envelope immediately if something happened to him. I have done so. You are the people he asked me to assemble and then open the second envelope. You are all here. I have no idea of the contents. He did say that everything would become quite clear."

Jerome opened the larger envelope and withdrew several sheets of paper, as well as another sealed envelope. He read, "I have left this communication in the hands of my good and trusted friend, Jerome Lee. I asked that he read this to you, as these are my wishes if I should die.

"But first I want you to know that something important has happened in my life. With the able assistance of Mike Harper and my mother I have turned over my life to the Lord. At such time as I am called, I am ready to meet my God. He has assured me I have been forgiven for my many and dreadful mistakes. I feel as assured as the thief did on the cross when our Lord was crucified. I am sure Mike can explain in more detail, should you wish.

"It is my plan to go away soon. I have found a special peace and now I must do something worthwhile with my life. I will return only when I believe I have proved to myself and others what I must prove.

"I do not have to describe my earlier life to any of you. It is all too obvious. Perhaps there are some things none of you knew about. It is best we leave it that way. I will do all I can to never create or cause another hurt knowingly.

"Now before you open the last envelope, let me tell you, all of you, that I love you very much and ask your forgiveness.

"I want to be buried near my father, who gave so much to me and my family. I insist on a graveside service only. I want it both brief and as simple as possible.

"Now, Jerome, it is time to open the last envelope. When he has completed this last responsibility I want all of you to rejoice with me because I am with the Lord. Do not weep unduly and let not your hearts be troubled. Again, I love all of you." It was signed Stephen Randolph.

Jerome looked about the quiet and sober group he had assembled. All had been deeply touched and tears could be seen in the eyes of everyone. His mother sat by Martha with her arm around her. There was a calm that prevailed and he was sure this would have been the way Stephen would have wanted it.

Jerome opened the last envelope and withdrew some papers and something that looked like an insurance policy. Jerome began reading: "I have taken out a life insurance policy, a term policy, and I wish the funds distributed as follows: I want to replace the $476,000 in the Randolph account which will qualify me to distribute the stock given me. I want a check for $100,000 sent to the Methodist Church here. I wish it to be used to set up an endowment and the interest used annually as the Board of Stewards believe wise. I wish $100,000 be given Jerome Lee in payment for services rendered. He is the best, the very best. I wish $100,000 be given to Victor McPherson. Perhaps he would wish to use it to hopefully regain his sight. I want April to use $100,000 to build housing for our quarters people. She is right. They must not be deprived of all hope. This leaves $124,000. I want $20,000 given to each of the following: Mimi White (she will be a great doctor), Gena Jenkins, Helen Hurt, Jack Jenkins and Edd Winter. Now this should leave $24,000. Use what is needed for burial expenses and give the remaining to Mike Harper (not to be confused with the church).

"If my death is an accident, I believe the amount of the policy will double. If so, I want my mother to use it as she wishes, for herself or others. I have little doubt that a significant sum will go to the Robert White Scholarship Fund. Please use it for the good of deserving people.

"Again, do not grieve for me. I am truly a happy person for the first time in my life. Be happy for me!

"Oh, I nearly forgot. There is forty thousand dollars remaining from a special gift. You will find it in my chest of drawers. Give this to Helen Hurt, as I want her to become the best she can be. She will understand.

"The premiums have been paid in advance on the policy. As far as I know, I have no other debts.

"And one last request. I want April to have my stock in Randolph Place. Through this she can start a new venture that will, in the end, save mankind and provide hope.

"Again, may God bless all of you. Signed: Stephen Randolph. Witnessed by Edd Winter and Jack Jenkins."

Jerome said, "This seems to fulfill my instructions. I will see, if it is your wish, that the details of his policy are rendered as requested.

"I have one further word to say. I believe that Stephen Randolph surprised everyone and I now have no doubt that he had his life in order. By the way, you should know that the two he saved were Negroes.

"I now suggest we follow the wishes of Martha Randolph and her family. They will need to make some plans. I thank each of you for your presence. You had so little notice. But you would have been here on your own to support Mrs. Randolph and her family." One could see that Jerome's eyes had filled with tears as he hugged Martha Randolph and left the room immediately.

Two days later there was a short memorial service for Stephen Randolph as he was buried on one side of his father. The grounds were filled with people.

When Jerome returned home with his mother and Eric they sat in their small living room in total silence. Finally Susan Lee said, "For the sake of Martha and her family I am happy that so many came to pay their respects. I am sure this meant a great deal to everyone.

"Now I want to ask the two of you a question. You may not wish to respond. Why do you suppose so many were present? I had not expected half the number because of so many unfortunate events in recent years."

Eric nodded for Jerome to respond. "Attapulgus and its people are different. This was a way of the community saying you are forgiven and we have forgotten."

"It goes beyond that," Eric said. "Jerome did a great deal to heal some wounds in recent weeks."

"Me? You have that all wrong. I'm the one who upset the scales of justice. There are many who cannot feel kindly toward me."

"Not so," Eric said. "You were fair and honest with everyone. You will never be better as long as you practice. You made us all feel guilty in a way. There are still a large number of good and honest people."

Susan said, "Whatever the reason, it worked. I believe the people know that Martha Randolph is the most tender and gentle soul that one can ever know. She is so good she is almost sinless. The only sin of which she may be accused is putting her family always before herself. I do not believe the Lord will hold that against her. If so, I am equally guilty."

A week before Christmas Jerome was asked to meet with the Randolphs in relation to their corporation.

"I had planned to meet after Christmas," Martha said as they assembled, "but I think we need to get some things behind us. I have requested Jerome to meet with us. He can help us all to see the whole picture." She smiled and nodded toward Jerome.

In a quiet voice he said, "I believe all of you know that the civil case was completed before Stephen's death. It is nice to have this behind you. Your mother and I suspected some dangers earlier and we felt time was of the essence. She can discuss the reasons with you if she wishes. I'll leave that up to her.

"I have received the funds from Stephen's insurance. It was a double indemnity policy. In a week or ten days I will be prepared to disburse such funds in accordance with Stephen's wishes. If it can be arranged, it may be nice to have the entire group together again before the first of the year.

"I will be ready to complete the agreements with the old and new tenants as soon as you conclude such details as you wish. I don't believe you have finished the criteria needed for occupancy or ownership. I'll be ready when you are.

"I have your final financial status up to date. I'll have it concluded completely for the year shortly after the first of January. I will require a CPA to assist on some matters, as before.

"I believe that covers what I have to report. Perhaps there are questions?" Jerome looked from one to another. As he did he saw the intense look in April's eyes but he could not tell her thoughts. He excused himself and left immediately.

Martha looked about her and everyone seemed to be waiting for her to continue. "I have a list of recommendations." She passed slips of paper to each. "Naturally, I have talked to all of you but seldom were we all together. It is not a case of divide and conquer. In fact, I hope our differences, certainly the larger and important ones, will never surface again." She read her list:

1. Double the livestock operation. (We have ample land.)
2. Buy or rent peanut allotments so this may be doubled, if possible.
3. Purchase the needed equipment.
4. Double the corn operation.
5. Double the pastures. (Again, ample land.)
6. Start a small catfish operation. (We will learn by doing.)
7. Experiment on a small scale with vineyards (grapes).
8. Experiment with truck farming (especially tomatoes).
9. Plant a thousand acres of pines (under the government program).
10. Determine if the tobacco barns can be used for something worthwhile (including the packing house).

"I am not ready to make firm recommendations as to the people who will live and work here but I have some ideas I will present soon. This will include housing that would lead to ownership, a percentage of the net profits, tutors to help children and more. We can make a better life for many, including ourselves. Think about this.

"Now I have three or so additional recommendations that are different. They may surprise you.

"I want to deed Joe's house to Jack and Sandra Jenkins. I would, in turn, deed the house they currently occupy to Edd Winter. Then, in time, I may wish to build a medium-size house for myself. We can keep the present house for when all the children and grandchildren come home."

"You have never mentioned a house in years. When did you decide on this? I am not in opposition; in fact, quite the contrary. It has apparently caught us all by surprise," April said.

Martha blushed deeply. For a time she could not speak. Then she smiled and said, "I may not wish to grow old alone, nor do I intend to create problems for others. There is a very special man that may become even more special.

"On December 30th I want to have some people in for dinner, as Jerome suggested. Please keep this date open."

When April left the meeting she called Jerome. "It seems we have been occupied by many events recently. Now, with this behind us, do we have reason to see each other? I have spent many hours in thought since we last talked at Somewhere Else."

"There has been little time before now," Jerome said. "I, too, have had many thoughts since we last met. I am ready to see you. I have thought of little else. What kind of schedule do you have?"

"Christmas Eve and Christmas Day belong to the family. I do have an obligation on December 30th but I hope we can meet sooner."

"Shall I cook or take you to Tallahassee for dinner?" Jerome asked.

"Do I have a choice?"

"You do, indeed."

"Let me suggest December 23rd at Somewhere Else. It gets dark early. Come at four?" April asked.

"I'll be there," Jerome said. "Goodnight."

CHAPTER 93

April was an hour early when she arrived at Somewhere Else. The winter day seemed reluctant to let go its bite. The winters of south Georgia usually made their appearance in the first three months of the new year but it had come early this year. She laughed, thinking of the man near the courthouse she once heard tell another, "It's those damned rockets they fire to take man into space. It's spoiling the weather. That belongs to God. Man ain't got no business up there till he is dead."

As April stood on the deck she could see the sweet gum trees. Most of the leaves had fallen and now they seemed slender, solemn and naked. A white light in the background highlighted the aisles of the trees like a misty light in a gentle fog. She could see the sky through the branches, pale and shadowy, silent and serene.

April looked in all directions and felt all alone, as if she were in a giant forest. She unlocked the door and looked about her. She went over and set the thermostat to heat. As she looked about she knew that this was the most special place ever for her. She could come, tired or weary or sad, and it seemed to immediately disappear. Here she could muse and think, give reign to her fancy and find herself renewed in every way. Here she could let her thoughts and dreams soar and in minutes she could find a peace, her strength and courage renewed. All the burdens seemed to disappear. In moments she was revitalized and felt whole again.

She seemed to feel as did Uncle Edgar in the quarters. He had told her, "I see the wonders of the world. I see the wonders of industry and work in the colony of ants. I see the honey bees as they delight in garnering from each flower. I see the hummingbird and find joy as he seeks food for life. I find a feeling of ecstasy in the flight of the wild geese as they fly over each spring and autumn. I talk to the red robins as they bob along, enjoying the coming of spring. I see the black birds filling themselves beyond capacity because of their greedy nature. Yes, and the cowardly crow speaks louder than most but dominates few, none his size. Life is like nature and nature reminds one of God."

April's thoughts once again returned to Jerome. She must have done this a thousand times since he was here. Suddenly she saw Jerome in a different manner than before. He was much more self-confident than she realized earlier. Often this characteristic had been hidden because he spoke less often than most. Did he know what he wanted in life? It was apparent that he had rejected her when they were last alone. He usually seemed so sure. Her doubts increased.

April had learned that his values and goals were different from most. The external did not mean to him the same as others. Money was only a means to survive. She had never once heard him speak of wanting a great sum. Fame had been at his doorstep, yet he removed himself and looked in another direction. Yes, it was the internal that had meaning. Character, loyalty and uprightness was what he sought. She had not realized how deeply these characteristics mattered until he had told her that night how he felt. Had she destroyed it all by offering herself?

Does he want me as I want him? Will he think I am too young?

He had spoken more than once that the time had not come. Was she too immature? Too bold? Too possessive? What would he say tonight?

How should I be tonight? I want this man more than anything else in life. Oh, God, help me to know.

April heard a noise outside and could not believe, until she looked at the clock, that an hour has passed. She opened the door and looked out. Jerome took two bags from his old car. She held the door as he entered. He deposited the bags on the cabinet top near the refrigerator. She sensed a peace within him; it showed on his handsome face and even more so in his eyes. Carefully he removed all the items from the bags, placed some in the refrigerator and left the others on top of the cabinet.

April watched him in silence, amazed at his manner. The thought of not seeing him again brought more than a feeling of sadness and melancholy. Suddenly she felt differently. There seemed to be a hotness in her virginal loins. She felt a slight shame, yet at the same moment was deeply excited.

Her eyes continued to follow him; he seemed to feel as much at home as if in his own house. Suddenly all the longing and nameless urges seemed to gather in her with such force that it was a new experience. She wanted Jerome's arms about her. She wanted his lips pressed against hers. She was not sure what she wanted but her instincts urged her to a new level she had never experienced before. She wanted to lie in his arms and crush him to her.

Then she experienced a new feeling as she felt a surge of love. Love took on a different meaning. It was deep and full. She wanted to spend all of her life with him.

Again she felt a warmness, perhaps a wetness in her loins. She had a vehement desire to take off her clothing. Better still, a desire for him to do it. This moment she felt no shame, no remorse, no guilt and no regret. If he rejected her, she felt there would be nothing in life ever again.

Suddenly Jerome turned toward her and he seemed to read her every thought. "You are so beautiful, so desirable," he said. As he approached her he extended his hands to her shoulders, pulling her ever so gently toward him. When he took her hand and placed it on his cheek, it was like the touch of a rose petal.

The feeling grew stronger in April. She yearned for his hands to be upon her, his mouth on her lips and on her neck and on her breasts, touching, seeking. She had never been so excited. Lust she had not known, but she was ready for total surrender.

He pulled her closer and kissed her forehead, his hand touching her long black hair as it streamed over her neck and shoulders. Her brown arms were bare and firm as he felt them encircle his body. He looked down at her red lips; she smiled. Her cheeks had now changed to a different color, more like that of a light-colored rose.

As she moved closer Jerome could feel a sensation like a tongue of flame. He bent forward and his lips met hers; a fire ran through his body in a sheet of joy, extending beyond him; he felt as he had never felt before.

As she withdrew her lips, he looked into her face, her black eyes seeming to sparkle in a mist. He saw a beauty and a light he had never before witnessed.

She looked into his face and he was smiling. He pulled her closer once more and kissed her eyes, then she closed them. His mouth found her urgent lips once again. First there was tenderness and rapture and fulfillment. They became so intense that there seemed to be no movement, not even breathing. Each seemed to be waiting for some expression from the other. Then suddenly, without a word being spoken, they both knew beyond any and all doubts.

Jerome moved a step backward and took both of her hands. "I would like to share the rest of my life with you. Will you marry me?"

"Oh, Jerome, I have wished this since I was thirteen. I have wished a million times to hear those words. There is no possible way I can express myself, my feeling, my love!" She pulled him to her once more and kissed him deeply.

"You know I am one without patience," she said. "Can we marry soon?"

He placed his arms on her shoulders once again and gazed longingly at her. It was the most beautiful face he had ever seen. The black eyes under the black brows and lashes truly sparkled. He could smell the scent of her flesh, warm, clean and fragrant. He looked at her full breasts, her shapely body. Again he felt a tension within. They smiled at each other. Words would have been useless.

"You haven't answered," April said. "I don't think I can wait much longer."

"Why don't we marry on the first day of the New Year. This would be the first day of 1966 and the first day of the rest of our lives. If we hurry, we can meet all legal requirements. We do need a contract, a license!"

"Could we marry at my home? Could we announce it on the night Mother has her guest for dinner? Those people will likely be the same ones we would wish to be present. Are you listening, Jerome Lee?" She looked at him with a devilish smile. "I've wished this to happen for so long that I have already become aware of my new name."

He pulled her toward him once again. They could feel the each other's heartbeat. Then he said, "You are the wonderful one who will burst into life each spring and with April comes all the wonders of God's creation. You will always be the real and true April I find between March and May."

April said, "Let us witness as many springs as God wills but let us witness the autumn season as well. Many have not known its full meaning. Most associate it with a time of sadness and death but this is not so." She got up and opened the front door. "What do you hear and see and feel?"

"I hear the waterwheel in what seems to be an endless circle. This reminds me of our earth. I hear a slight wind in the trees with a strong hint of winter. I hear a crow in the distance but I do not know his language. This reminds me how little knowledge one can acquire in a lifetime. There are so many areas to explore."

She said, "Some call this the season of death but it is really the season of life. Seeds drop from the fragile cases and pods and enter the soil. They nestle there waiting — waiting for the moment in which they can renew life. The earth becomes busy seeding and planting and garnering. It is a time of quiet, of silence.

"In the spring they will rise and bring gifts to us and all of those about us. No, spring is not the beginning. It is only the flowering of what has been seeded in the autumn, the real beginning of the season of life. And you, Jerome, will always be my autumn, the foundation of our lives. You will be my rock, my fortress. You will be the one to establish our standards, our guidelines; to help me determine good from bad, right from wrong. Sometimes our choices are not always clear. Because I trust you, I will go where you go and do what you do. I have this kind of confidence in you, this kind of love for you. Perhaps together we can make a better world in which to live."

"April, I don't know what I could have done to deserve you. You have the beauty and the talent to be whatever you would be. You are a picture of perfection," Jerome said.

"Not so," April said. "We know that perfection is impossible. Actually it would be unbearably dull. I think both of us would prefer more than a touch of imperfection. I don't feel we should ever be totally predictable."

Jerome stood up. "I think I could live on love but since I have brought food and committed myself to the role of cook, I suggest we move in that direction. We can make some plans as we do."

"Could we spend our first night here at Somewhere Else?" April asked. "It seems right that we should do so!"

Chapter 94

It was a wonderful dinner Martha served on December 30, 1965. The same guests had assembled as on the recent occasion.

Following dinner Martha spoke. "It is a delight to see and be with you again. I wish to make a few remarks that reflect on yesterday and tomorrow. Some of these are with sadness and others with joy.

"For a period of time it seemed that tragedy lived on our doorstep. Many of our dear ones departed. At times I wondered if we would survive. There were so many events that were not understood by so many of us. God promises that He will not place more upon us than we can bear, than we can endure.

"First it was our young Kathy. She died in the service of others. There was the young and wonderful Robert White. He gave his life for our country and for each of us. Next was my beloved husband and the father of our children. All of his life he gave as he understood for all of us. Then my oldest son and the brother of my other five children departed. He died so unexpectedly and once again I had a heavy heart.

"Then my baby boy, Stephen, lost his life so others, children, might live. Few things can be more noble than laying down your life for children. I had promised God and myself that, should Stephen have a chance to overcome his adversities, I would accept the future, whatever it held. I believe he was saved and found our Lord before he departed. One cannot ask for more.

"There were some economic losses but God, as I understand, was sending to me and mankind a message. These losses are materialistic and in time become meaningless.

"Now let us think of the many occurrences that have brought joy to all of us. Again they are many.

"First there was the union of Mary and David and the gift of a precious granddaughter. I am pleased, so pleased.

"Then there was the union of my second son to one of my three girls. Meggie is so precious and Charles is so fortunate.

"Next was the union of Michael John and the beautiful and delightful Michelle. Again, I am so pleased.

"Now I understand that I may expect other wonderful news and announcements. I believe it appropriate that further news should reach our ears. Who wishes to speak first?"

April and Jerome stood, broad smiles on their faces. Jerome said, "April, please tell all our friends the good news."

April said, "I've been after this man since I was thirteen and I can't wait any longer. Two days from now, on New Year's Day, we will be married here at this home and all of you will be our special guests." She held Jerome as if he might escape.

Gena and Eric bounced up. Gena said, "This summer Eric and I will be married. I do not believe anyone else could love so deeply."

Mary and David stood. "Our secret is not a secret anymore." She looked at her waist. "We will present our dear mother with a second grandchild soon. We are so happy."

Charles and Meggie stood. Meggie said, "Charles has received news that he will be asked to serve in the Educational Department at F.S.U. in an area of research. We can remain near and I will continue my education as planned. We are most gratified."

Martha rose again and said, "To live the life of old age is not an easy task. In time I may not wish to grow old alone. Enough said on this subject at this time.

"Now let us turn to Jerome for some presentations and information he wishes to discuss."

Jerome stood and said, "I am about to conclude most of my assignments, but not all. First, here is a check for Mrs. Randolph to replace the loss of the civil suit, as Stephen requested. In time I will place his stock in April's hands, as he also instructed.

"Next I present Stephen's request to Mike Harper for the Church Endowment Fund.

"Here is a check, again as Stephen requested, to be presented to April to use to improve the life of the people you select for the future. I believe he suggested housing.

"I have sent, by registered mail, a check to Victor McPherson. The good news is that they now believe he will see again.

"Now I have checks for our doctor to be, Mimi, and for Gena, Helen, Uncle Edd and Mr. Jenkins.

"I have paid all expenses, as Stephen requested. The balance is found in this check for Mike Harper.

"Here is another check for Helen Hunt. I deposited the currency and used a check so we might have a record." He could not help wondering how much others knew about Helen and Stephen.

"I believe that concludes my present responsibilities," Jerome said and sat down once again.

"Indeed it does not, Jerome Lee!" Martha stated. "I will need evidence that you have been compensated as Stephen instructed."

Jerome stood once again, his face a shade darker. "We'll get together later, Mrs. Randolph. I cannot accept a fee of this sum."

"Do you live up to your promises, Mr. Lee?"

"I try to do so."

"Well, you will remember that I said the Randolphs would determine this. I'll see you in a few days. I insist Stephen's request be honored.

"I have one further announcement. I will send a check for one hundred thousand dollars to the Robert White Scholarship Fund," Martha said.

One by one, all of the individuals receiving a gift expressed their appreciation for Stephen's generosity.

April said, "I will be in touch with all of you concerning our wedding."

"Now," Martha said, "suppose we go outside and see if Jerome can find anything this key will fit!"

Together they moved toward several parked cars. There Jerome found a new shining Buick awaiting him. For a moment he was speechless, then said, "Mrs. Randolph has had many apprehensions about my means of transportation. Since her only daughter is now involved, I can understand her motive. Thank you, not only for the car, but for the trust you have placed in me. I hope I am worthy."

That night Martha Randolph lay in bed and thought about the events of the evening. She smiled as she fell into a merciful and dreamless sleep.

April and Jerome sat on the deck at Somewhere Else on the evening of the first day of January, 1966. They heard the waterwheel make its endless circle. They saw the stars twinkle and one fell across the night sky. They heard an owl give a hoot and another responded some distance away. The silence of the night embraced them as they held each other.

"What will we do with the rest of our lives?" Jerome asked April.

"As long as autumn comes and spring follows, we will love each other as few have loved. As each day passes, we will seek a way to serve and make a better world for ourselves and others.

"For many years, Jerome, you have repeatedly told me the time has not come. The time has come." She took his hand as they moved inside to begin a new beginning.